Leslie A Kent

SYMPHONY FOR G
A wildlife novel

The Scottish wildcat
painted in oils by the author.

SYMPHONY FOR G
A wildlife novel

Leslie A Kent

Leslie A Kent
2018

First Printing: 2018

ISBN 978-0-244-39720-3

Cailleach Publishing
Cellardyke
Fife, Scotland
www.leslieakentwildart.weebly.com

Ordering Information:
Special discounts are available on quantity purchases by corporations, associations, educators, and others. For details, contact the publisher at the above listed web address.

Dedication

To my wife Laura, whose patience is everlasting and often un-deserved, and to the wild things I am lucky enough to be inspired by.

Contents

Leslie A Kent

Author's Acknowledgements

I was told that I would and should never write a book when I was at senior school. Maybe they were right? But others have since disagreed, and following on from the encouragement of those others I have sat down long enough to write this book.

Of course, to do this has required the efforts of many people. Chris Haslam has been a continuous and consistent source of encouragement, literary criticism and humour, and I owe much to his friendship and his eternal enthusiasm for writing himself and engaging others with the written word. Sean Hamill has yet to finish his own work, but spent time reading mine and giving me the benefit of his well-informed thoughts and comradeship. Louis Dunn was the first man in a decade to read my first literary attempts and his kindness led me to completing the '*symphony*'. And Laura, my wife, has been patient enough to listen when I've tested ideas out on her and read aloud. She smiles when I feel desolate and points me to the great outdoors when I need a break from modern living, and understands me better than anyone ever could.

And of course, I have to acknowledge the wild things that we share our planet with too. Without them I would have no inspiration and I believe that we would all be much worse off.

Foreword

Each chapter of this book is accompanied by a suggested piece of music that crossed my mind at some point during its writing. Thinking in music, I often look at scenes and have my own accompaniment, like a film score, running through my mind, giving added texture and atmosphere to any experience or view. I only wish that I were skilled enough to write down my own mind's eye scores. However, we are lucky to be able to enjoy some of the most incredible classical and contemporary music and to access it electronically whenever we want. I hope that the suggested pieces help add another dimension to your enjoyment of this book.

Believe me, as one who has experience, you will find more among the woods than ever you will among books. Woods and stones will teach you more than you can ever hear from any master.

Bernard of Clairvaux

Prologue: The Bothan (an advertisement)

***Bothan Faobhar (Rural Dwelling and land for sale, NW Scotland).* Unique House & Adjoining Grounds and Surrounding Buildings for Sale**
We are delighted to offer this rarest opportunity to acquire a truly unique two bedroom, sea loch side cottage and its surrounding land and encompassed buildings benefitting from unrivalled views and offering an escape from the busyness of urban life with its own private drive. Other buildings provide excellent storage, there is a wealth of parking, and extensive grounds and gardens encompass a variety of natural assets and a planted area. Situated in splendid isolation, the property would suit that special person who is interested in wildlife and the peace of the countryside. Some modernisation may be necessary.

Conditions do apply to the management of this property and its land – further details available on request.

POA (Contact Details Below)

Prologue: The Bothan (an advertisement)

Chapter 1: The Civilised

*(Piano Concerto No.2 in F Major, Op.102: II. Andante,
Dmitri Shostakovich)*

Anger is never the best fuel for driving a fast car. It amplifies acceleration and reduces the sensitivity to brake, increasing the desire to move, whatever the cost, in reckless pursuit of a clear road ahead. The needle creeps further round the clock, the jaw straightens, and the abuse of those less fired up than yourself becomes increasingly vocal, then later physical as you swerve just to get past regardless of what approaches from the other side.

"Leave then!" were the only words he heard, cycling and recycling around his head and the pedal dropped further as he forced the roar of the engine to take yet another pole position from the wrong lane.

"Now, if it helps." She added those words to intensify effect, and effect they had had.

Now, then, later! What did it matter?

And so he had gone.

The things he needed, those items he considered essential, were rammed into an old sack holdall, thrown into the boot of the car, and he was gone.

"Leave then!"

Her words were cold, measured and controlled – and he had left.

From that first moment of shock until now, when two hundred miles of relentless tarmac later he reeled in an angry self-pitied world, those words had turned and turned around his mind, eating its sense up.

"Leave now!"

He was haunted.

The motorway services were adequate, but busy, and that was not what he needed. It was not what the therapist, that constant fee-charging inheritance of the highly paid, had suggested would help, and so he found himself calling the number, the one scribbled on the crinkled tobacco packet's inside, like some pencil written cliché. As everything now was texted or digitally produced, he had almost forgotten how to form the numbers and had had to concentrate in a way he was not used to. Now it needed fishing out of his receipt-filled wallet where it lay scrunched up, but not forgotten.

He slurped quickly produced takeaway coffee from a plasticized card cup and thumbed the number into his finger-greased mobile.

Cars droned by in anti-parallel lines on the motorway, each following the one in front on their relentless journeys from A to B and then probably back again in the interminable commute of daily British life, and he munched on the end of a drooping roll-up contemplating what he saw and heard. The view of the badly managed, litter-decorated hedgerow couldn't quite hide the orange-brown of fumes that hung about the highway. Fresh green buds threatened to break and fill in the gaps where a mechanised clipper had done its worst, and a lump-barked standard oak tree, one that had stood for centuries, juddered under the vibration of the traffic that shook its historic root stock. An unidentifiable brown striped bird hopped amongst the lowest branches and 'cheeped', whilst two large grey-winged gulls fought over tyre-marked chips on newly laid gum-dotted tarmac. It was black and smooth, emitting that human-linked aroma of bitumen synonymous with recent development.

'Just an attempt to spruce up a 1970s Moto?' he thought taking in the human-scarred scene.

However, it was still just a 1970s Moto, complete with peeling paint, garish Thunderbird tower design and a sea full of car-infested blacktop, however new it was. It stood as monument to progress, like an ill-placed runway control tower, set beside six lanes of droning vehicle that bisected directly through the monoculture landscape. A kestrel hovered motionless against a fume-stained sky watching the embankment rodent trails, on the hunt for its late brunch. It at least welcomed the motorway's intrusion.

The phone connected by microwave, probably via one of the curiously angled dishes secured on the service station behind, and it rang somewhere in a distant office. It could have been at a desk anywhere in the world.

People persistently flocked by with their attendant disposable plastic wrappings, cardboard cups and cellophane. It was as if they needed it, or gained comfort from it. Once emptied of their *edible* contents, some made it to the litterbins and yet more was dropped in the backs of cars or the foot wells, and the rest joined the gulls or the little brown birds hidden in the hedgerow.

This was civilisation.

The distant line clicked to answerphone and over-politely stated that a message should be left.

Waiting for the tone, he drew deeply and then tossed the roll-up aside, sacrificing the rest to the *'wildlife'* of the smoking area, where other hunched figures huddled against a hot wind to light up their dried leaf habits. He judged them, being blind to his own stooped smoker's figure.

The tone was then followed by electronic near-silence.

"Hi, yeah," he began with unusual difficulty, and then he re-started with more confidence.

"This is Solomon, Jake Solomon...   ...Sol. We spoke earlier this month about the House? Is it still available? I hope so as I'm travelling up north to see it now. I wonder? Can you give me a call on this number if it's still on the market? The funds are arranged, I just need the address...   ...I'll be in Scotland in the next few hours and then hope to be up to the house soon after. Today if possible...   ...or else? Or else...   ...I'm sleeping in the car." He laughed falsely, and then added, "I...   ...I look forward to hearing from you. Cheers."

He hung up, sweating.

This was Sol; city buyer and financial success.

This was Sol; arrogant and wayward, the secrets to his success.

This was Sol; large desk, large office and even larger and more conceited ego, results of his success.

This was Sol; forcibly between roles right now and without long-term girlfriend, not for the first time, but probably terminally on this occasion considering his last relational error.

This was Sol.

He continued to perspire, holding the phone in a clammy hand. *What was wrong with him?* He conducted business on the phone all the time. It was his job and he was very good at it; or at least had been until his recent run. Maybe the idea of the *retreat* was a good one after all. Before now he had remained cynical about it.

Leaving his cup to the wind on the fake-wood bench, that fooled all but the wildlife, Jake used the facilities, hardly daring to touch anything in the toilets. It was as if people thought that at services hygiene and good standards could be thrown to the wall, things could be left unclean and well... ...anything could go, and did. Still, it kept someone employed clearing up after the *more* civilised. He pitied the cleaner and barked rudely at the lady behind the coffee shop counter whilst scanning his card wirelessly to pay.

"My pleasure, enjoy your day." She thanked him politely, even though he knew full well he did not deserve it.

"You being funny?" he asked with an insincere smile. His internal anger and self-restricted thoughts were spilling out and he felt the need to express his feelings at the expense of others in that way parents hope their children won't, at least not in public.

She shook her head as she backed nervously away from the black imitation stone worktop. Nothing seemed quite as it naturally appeared.

He ignored her behaviour and grinned smugly to himself as he left, clipping another customer as he barged off, head in the air and chest puffed out. The barista attempted to judge the attitude of the next in the queue and remained edgy and anxious.

She continued to dream of the better life she had always imagined there would be once she left school. She would have her own flat one day, intended to get married and have children. At the weekends she cycled with a group of friends, but because she was quiet usually didn't speak much and felt that she wasn't as good as the rest. However, she was skilled in other ways and was actually an excellent chef, trained by her Italian grandfather to make sauces from scratch.

Sol didn't care, didn't stop to ask and certainly wasn't interested. The service girl needed a lucky break or a serendipitous conversation to be noticed and only fate would decide if she would fulfil these potentials.

Unlike Sol, she hadn't been so blessed yet.

Back in the car, he nestled down into the seat, revved up the engine and set the car to the road again. Where anger had subsided, over-priced cheap coffee had taken over, even if it wasn't the grade he normally purchased and had delivered to him in the city. And so, on his way again, Sol continued to play a cautious roulette with the traffic police and speed cameras and lotto with his life as he weaved between the cars of those who limited themselves to the law.

Heading north, the M6 fell below his wheels and except for a re-top of fuel Sol made good progress through the Lakes, bypassing Carlisle where the brown tourist signs indicated there was a historic city and other items of interest. The radio blaring, Sol missed a call from an un-known number and ignored several demands from work; it was holiday time he was taking and hadn't *they* suggested a move of office for him? *She* had also tried to contact him, but he was not ready to listen yet. He hurt too much and currently his thoughts were about him and not about her. There were seventeen texts, mostly from *the woman*, but one drew his eye as it was from the unknown caller starting with the words '*Dear Mr Solomon, I apologise for missing your earlier call…*'

Not good at waiting he wanted to read it immediately, finding his heart beating quicker than it would for an ordinary message, but he was aware of the presence of police cars about. There must have been one somewhere near as everyone was driving at the speed limit, which they rarely did. True to form just ahead he could see the waspish fluorescent yellows marking the back of a patrolling vehicle crawling along waiting for just one fool to speed by. This time, it wasn't him.

Sol licked his lips and abnormally indicated to show his intention to leave the motorway at the next junction and sped up the slip road to find somewhere to pull over. A few miles on and a gravelled gated entrance to a fresh-green spring-sprouted farmer's field provided a place to stop.

He never noticed the skylark limp along a planted row in pretend injury from its future nest site and then, its deception complete, its leap into the sky full of song. The soaring silhouette of the wandering buzzard was missed, wide-winged and with finger-feathers stretched out to grip the currents of the air and direct its glide. A chestnut furred stoat hugged a rocky hedgerow in pursuit of rabbit who timidly nibbled, watchful and alert, whilst the roe deer stood to attention at the woodland's edge. But Sol was office-blinded to these wild visions. No text notified him of their presence.

Window down, he lit up and unlocked the phone to check the text, ignoring those from the city and those from *her*. The message was unusual in that the author had taken the time to paragraph it properly and had not used any of the usual text speech words Sol was more accustomed to.

'Dear Mr Solomon,
I apologise for missing your earlier call.

I am pleased to report that Bothan Faobhar is still available and we can continue with the sale as discussed last month if you are still keen to proceed. I do recommend that you look at the house before you decide to purchase or move in though as it does require some work as stated in our original conversation.

Although the cottage was occupied until just last month it will not have all the home comforts you may have become accustomed to in the city.

I can advise you of a number of good hostelries to stay in whilst...'

The message ended abruptly, obviously cut off in mid-flow, but Sol could imagine that the text ended in the way a formal letter was finished, with a *'yours sincerely'* and a name. The text spoke of age-related politeness and was written in the way that only English teachers expected. It was a language unsuited to a mobile phone and to the pace of proper business.

He replied, quickly.

'GREAT. SEND POSTCODE 2 TXT AND WILL USE SAT-N. FUNDS ALREADY B TRANSFERRED. HOUSE IS MINE.

SOL"

He waited for a reply, expecting the instantaneous he was used to.

Nothing.

He arranged the transfer of money, wiring it magically through the ether without the need for a personal meeting, a signature nor any other convention of a historic deal. Times had changed.

Nothing.

Cars passed by and Sol became semi-aware of the build-up of cloud somewhere over the north. Shapes of moisture were boiling up from the hills to eclipse the sky and even he knew that somewhere it must have been raining hard. He laughed at the thought.

At least it wasn't him getting wet.

He checked the message had sent and after a windswept second fag threw the mobile into the passenger seat, turned the car in an over-revved traffic-stopping arc then headed north towards the border.

Here he was greeted by the large blue sign and white Saltire that indicated he was in a different country and he felt the anticipation of arriving at the front door of his new purchase. Buying was his job and for the first time he found himself on a busman's holiday actually getting something concrete for himself. This was a move up from the rental world he was used to and a move on from the buying of goods to help the firm only, a mentality he had been trained for. Gut reactions seldom failed him and so why now?

With no message from the unknown caller, he could do little wrong but head north for an hour or two and wait to hear from them.

Bothan Faobhar.

Sol wondered how it was pronounced and settled on a phonetic interpretation. *Bow-th-an Fay-ob-har,* and he turned it experimentally over in his head trying to guess its meaning, if it had one.

Miles passed by, unseen buzzards flashing behind in their lazy circling, valleys widening and hills climbing, with Sol furtively glancing down to the seat where that electronic parasite he carried everywhere with him remained dark and silent except for *work* and *her.*

He hit indecision at Glasgow, not knowing which way to pass it, and so headed north again being surprised that the country seemed to continue beyond his English- schoolboy's appreciation of the size of the nation.

The phone bleeped, that tone designed to spike the wits and irritate the sensitive – a message from the unknown author had finally arrived. He was off the motorway at the next services before which a second text from the stranger had also been received.

'Dear Mr Solomon,
I apologise for missing your call again and for my delay in replying.

Thank you for arranging for the funds to be available so rapidly which are now being wired to the appropriate account. I can confirm that Bothan Faobhar is now yours.
I suggest that you leave your car at the bottom of the drive unless it is a 'country vehicle' and you will find the property unlocked. There is a key and message from the previous occupant left on the kitchen table. Furnishings are simple.
I hope that you find all in order at the Bothan. She has been in the family for more than two hundred years and they are sad to see her go. Postcode in next message...'
Like the first text, the script was cut off.

The second text was a simple postcode and there was another mention that he should look at the place first before deciding to stay over, as it was likely to need cleaning up.
He needed something to do whilst away and what could be hard about '*cleaning the place up*'? After all, he employed a semi-literate to do the cleaning for him back in the city. He'd soon find another local to do the job for him on minimum wage.
He laughed to himself, unkindly. This was a characteristic feature of being Sol.
Postcode in the sat-nav, he was surprised to see the journey was still another five hours, but he always trusted in the power of the digital and followed the pink guidance line on the small screen suspended in the centre of his field of vision. As far as he was concerned, he was now going home – to his new home – and the time it took was incidental. Even the low cloud and incessant rainfall that had blotted out the view of the hills from the road did little to dampen his spirits as he travelled north; yet more north – more north than he had previously appreciated there was.

It was fading towards dusk when the nav clinically asked Sol to take the next road that left the main highway. He passed a town with the uninspiring name of 'New Town' and then later a cottage shop, now closed for the night. The upstairs windows were bright and attractive, spilling the light of a burning fire out into the approaching night air. There was a man digging a patch of garden in the front dressed in dishevelled garb with a straggled beard that enclosed a wind-wizened face. He smiled and waved as Sol sped past unnecessarily quickly.

'Scruffy bugger,' Sol muttered.

The electric pink route line still extended beyond the edge of the screen but it was now down to the last thirty minutes or so and Sol felt confident that he would make the *Bothan* by sundown. He followed a low-slung wall on the left beyond which he could see deep-blue waters extending from a rocky shoreline.

Ten minutes remaining on the clock and there was a hard left-hand turn off into a well-treed lane that appeared to end in a rising mud track signposted 'NO ACCESS TO UNAUTHORIZED VEHICLES'.

In the gloom Sol leant as far out of the driver's window as he could, not easy from the low position of a sports car's bucket seat, and wondered for the first time whether or not the navigator was right. He looked back to the sat-nav and tapped it thoughtfully.

The pink highlighter on the screen took a spindly path upwards and off the upper edge and a large pale blue stain indicated the track followed the edge of a lake.

He glanced back to the signpost.

It was richly lichened with green-blue growths and bright yellow encrusting. Condensed mist dripped quietly off their fronds, leafy extensions that competed with a dense mat of moist green mosses, and Sol felt the cold for the first time.

Lost?

Cursing out loud he found himself automatically reaching for the phone on the seat beside him.

No signal?

More cursing and he hit the well-padded CD rack between him and the passenger chair before banging off the wheel. At this mood stage in the office, staff normally rushed in to help their leader keep calm and focus on the job in hand. But not here, in a car, on a lane, in a wood, by a sign that translated as *'no entry'*. He was on his own to deal with it and his heart lurched at the thought.

The plaque remained unaffected, quietly dripping mist-dew to its base as cloud-dulled silence gripped the scene.

As a man of action he re-gripped himself and then looked around for a clue as to where he was in relation to where he should be.

Trees.

A roughshod lane.

Low clouds that hung close to hills not really seen.

A loch.

Then he saw it; that small flash of hope he needed.

There, down by the abounding bog grasses beside the track, was an unkempt wooden letterbox, once painted red, slung badly from a length of wire below the oh-so-welcoming *'no access'* sign. Despite the wear of age and the peel of paint, even though the light was fading and the colours draining from the woodland ahead, letters could be made out on the box.

Bothan Faobhar.

He *was* here, almost.

Excited and ready for the warmth of home, he put his foot to the floor spraying mud up from tyres designed more for the race and motorway speeding than a country track. The mud scattered up in artistic patterns onto his usually well-polished white car.

Eleven minutes and then the comfort of home, the new home.

The car slipped as it struggled for traction but held to the road as Sol reduced his pace and started to worry about the bottom of the vehicle as it scratched over rocks he hadn't seen on first inspection. He flicked the headlights to full beam and then inched up the road.

The sat-nav predicted a later time of arrival based on his safer speed of travel.

The lane took him up into thick haze that hung limpid amongst the trees and he struggled at times to keep the car on the road. It then levelled and the surface seemed to improve such that Sol felt secure enough to increase the throttle, being wary of a ditch of running water that had opened up to drain the thin track on either side.

A flag appeared at the top of the sat-nav screen marking the destination he aimed for and he made a mental note to look at getting the driveway re-metaled as soon as possible. All his friends drove cars like this. If they were to visit, they would need a good road.

20mph.

The lane dipped and turned to the right before he started to climb again with greater confidence.

30mph.

A sudden drop in the road found him faster than he wanted to be and the car's thin tyres struggled to grip in the wet red muds; Sol turned the wheel defensively and tried not to brake so as to avoid the skid. The lights caught the illuminated vision of a large, round-winged brown owl drifting low over the road and, distracted, Sol allowed his eyes to track it left.

45mph.

His attention back to the road and he could see the descending track drift waveringly off to the left where its outer edge met a well-rocked beach and then water, a sharp corner suddenly clear of cloud and clag. He knew the brakes would be too late but slammed them hard anyway and attempted the kind of manoeuvre really only successful in movies or in stunt shows and with better tyres; the car lurched as he pulled the wheel down hard to the passenger side. Although the underside complained at the touch of the rocks below and the mud-filled tyres only slowed his progress a little, Sol felt a form of exhilaration and relief, as if he was actually going to make it round the corner, and strangely he laughed to himself. But then he saw the bend coming up too quickly, the pebbles at the edge, the mud that gave, the ditch, the rocks, the beach, and he knew in that moment of quick time that he was going to end on or in one of them.

Spinning, be it slowly in the mind of a crash victim, the lights faithfully showed the way he had come already. Somehow the car ended facing back up the track, rear end in the ditch. But he was safe and it didn't feel that he had ended that badly.

However, the car was stuck and all revving simply churned the wheels in wet puddles that splayed mud into the drainage dyke. The car rocked slightly, but was too well secured by rocks and a rooted stump.

His first reflex was to shout, swear and hit the wheel with his palms.

No better.

His second reflex was to reach for the phone. His secretary and other staff could fix anything.

No signal.

And so he cursed and hit the wheel and sat swearing loudly out of the open window as water dripped without concern off of the roof and onto the leather upholstery.

Still no better.

Sol climbed up and out of the car - one of his prides and joys.

From the outside, in the dark, it didn't look so bad. Yes it would need some work on it and he wasn't sure how he was going to get it out of the ditch. But it was off the road and with a little pressure applied to the boot he could get his belongings out.

With driving not being an option, he slung his sack over his shoulder and grabbed his phone, which he set to '*torch*'.

There was a battered black case amongst the other things and curiously he felt it was one of those items he might need, if not tonight then soon, and besides he always liked to know where it was. Its contents and he had rarely been separated throughout that portion of life he could really claim to remember. It was his violin.

He considered the case for a while, its shape and scuffs, and then took it with him and set off by foot along the track.

It couldn't be much further and he would be able to phone from the cottage using any signal there. Somebody could pick the car up for him and get it sorted in the morning.

The air was damp and he felt the cold of the ground through his wetted shoes. Suede was fine for driving but not for walking wear. He had left his leather jacket thrown somewhere in the back of the car and soon regretted having nothing to keep the attention of the night air at bay. The strings of his bag started to rub through his soft lamb's wool jumper, the weight of the violin, although slight at first, was beginning to drag on his fingers, even though he swapped it from hand to hand, and a feeling of deep misery began to spread through his body. It seeped its way into his muscles and joints with the ease of the air's moisture.

It could not be far. *Could it?*

He cursed the *woman* for making him do this.

He cursed his *employers* for the forcible change of office, for driving him to the decision for time out.

He cursed the *therapist* who was obviously in league with the other two.

He cursed the *world*.

He cursed *life*!

But *he* was Sol and *he* would show them. This was *his* house and from its office he could still change the world and demonstrate what *he* was capable of. The world could never change him – they *all* knew that!

He trudged on, feeling water and mud creep up his trouser legs and wick down his socks; wool-cotton mix ideal for the workplace.

There were noises he failed to recognise.

Something barked and there was a reply. An owl hooted that call used for detective and horror films, and the wood came alive with the caterwauls of several answering cries. Too great an imagination and Sol was there in a scene when the murderer was stalking him somewhere just off the trackway. Water ran in excited trickles on one side of the lane and the loch waters lapped incessantly on the other, and he tried to think of the positive elements of the nightmare he was walking through.

He stopped when he heard brushed movements not far away, to the left, now above, then somewhere off behind.

Sol became aware of a dread that bothered him.

There were no streetlights, and for more than ten minutes he had been walking and he had seen no shop, no house, not even a window lit up on the hills that he could see; there was nothing signifying the presence of humans bar this track. Instead, he felt the aura of the needle-clad trees hemming the road.

And again he wondered, '*could it be far?*'

Suddenly concerned about the life of his phone's battery, Sol started to worry how he would find his way when the building first made itself known to him.

It surfaced from the gloom as a long light grey structure with hard edges cut out of the un-definition of the trees. A dark slate roof was a stain against the sky and there was an obvious chimneystack at one end and another not quite in the middle. As he approached closer windows appeared like eyes that ran along its width with a wooden door off centre that opened into a porch. Enclosed in a rough walled garden it stood by a flat expanse of close-cropped plant life that ended in a beach of rock and cobbles spilling and falling down to the loch side. There were sheds behind and a tumbled pile of chopped wood that seemed to melt into the forest; it nestled from the worst of the wind behind a pillar of rock face stretching out into the water.

But he was tired, and though he was touched by this first experience, he really just wanted to be in through the door, out of the cold with the heating on, and with something warm inside his belly.

A post in the wall was accompanied by a wooden house name now on the ground. Sol picked it up and turned it over with his mobile's light for guidance.

It was not clear but it was there. *Bothan Faobhar.* This was it.

Sol stepped through a hole in the wall where once a gate had hung and ventured up to the cottage door as the last of the light fell away. Leaning on the door, he twisted the metal handle and pushed.

He did not know what to expect, what magic the moment of owning his own property would bring with it, what sounds to imagine or what feelings. But here he was stepping over his own first threshold.

It was cold, as cold as outside, but it was still. The air had a mustiness about it, not really foreboding or dangerous, but old and comfortable, if also damp. He could hear dripping from somewhere, but otherwise he was struck by the quiet and the genuine darkness. He switched off his phone's light and automatically fumbled forward through the open doorway of the main house and ran his hand down the wall for the light switch. *Nothing.*

The wall was damp to touch and he felt plaster that left a layer of wet dust on his fingers and there was exposed stonework in other places. He reached further and further. *Nothing.*

'Just one of those odd houses where the switches are all in the wrong place.' It was nothing that a good electrician couldn't fix.

He continued to hug the wall on his right as he edged down a blackened corridor until he reached a door into a larger space, the first window from which enough light was cast for him to see a table in the middle of the room. Dropping his bag and carefully placing the violin case next to it he went over to inspect this heavy wooden structure on which was a hand-written letter, a large key, a paraffin lamp, a metal bottle and a slightly old, damp, cardboard box of matches.

With the light of his mobile phone he read the letter, noting that it addressed him less formally than the texts, by his nickname 'Sol'.

'*Dear Sol,*

Welcome to Bothan Faobhar and congratulations on the purchase of this very special cottage. I am very fond of her and hope that she brings you much happiness. You will find some notes on her history and wildlife on the reading desk.

I am afraid she is quite a basic house and may need some upgrading to suit your requirements. Your enquiries ask little about her services and so I feel it necessary to explain.

Water runs from the hillside. It can take a little getting used to its taste and colour, but it is clean so long as you keep the header clear of dead things and dirt. Do make sure that the lochan is kept full, otherwise you will dry up.

The water is heated behind the fireplace but I cannot remember when the chimney was last swept so do beware. I have left wood chopped in piles. They are arranged on the type of wood as the smell from different species has quite an effect. There is bottled gas but again I've not used that for so long I have no idea as to how much use it is.

I've left you the lamp for your first night and there is spare paraffin in the store shed out the back of the cottage. I am certain you won't need them but instructions for its use are on the reading desk.

You will have left your vehicle at the end of the drive and so will have had a long walk. I have left some provisions in the cold store in case you have gone without.

With very best wishes,'

Below this was an indecipherable letter as a signature.

The writing was black ink-written and scrawled, and Sol imagined it was produced by a person of age. The paper was thick and it smelt of something akin to tobacco, the scent of which hung about the place.

With the phone battery on eight percent, Sol quickly located the reading desk, placed under the third of three windows, this one located in the house's end wall from which any author of a letter could easily watch the loch. He had never seen, let alone lit, a paraffin lamp.
There was a pile of paper, mostly hand-written, and neatly to the side was a red and yellow lamp manual stating it was from 1932. Pausing for a moment and checking the phone battery's life, he scanned the instructions. His mobile warned him of low power and imminent switch off and so he rushed back to the table.

Seven percent.
Lamp off, loosen pump then retighten. Easy.

Six percent.
Check mantle. What is a mantle? No, move on.
Soak preheater in paraffin. Rushing with the metal bottle he presumed was paraffin, Sol spilt liquid everywhere. At least he knew this was flammable and so wisely moved the lamp away.

Five percent.
Clip in and light. One match. Damp. Start again.
Second match. Damp. Snapped. Start again.

Four percent and another warning.
Third match. Lit. Pre-heater lit.
Leave till spirits burn down, turn on, and then pump.
'Pop' and a slight yellow light emerged as if by charmed incantation from within the illuminated lantern mantle.

Wait thirty seconds and pump again until burning bright white.
The room was suddenly bright with white incandescence.

It was a moment of childhood enchantment.

A wooden floor extended from the pool of light out from the table to walls of rough stone and cracking plaster where a picture hung crooked and reflected back the light. A large bird in a glass cabinet sat on a chest of drawers topped with a dusty white lace runner and heavy curtains draped the windows. An open fireplace sat central to the rear internal wall and shadow-filled doorways passed off from either side of this end of the room. Two armchairs were angled to enjoy the heat of any fire.

The low ceiling was wood-beamed and spider web clad with the slate of tiles clearly visible above. There were books on the reading desk and the occupier of the wooden carver had left their pen where they had signed off, together with a pot of black ink.

Sol's phone died quietly and not keen to be without it he retrieved its charger from his bag. Still struggling to find a light switch, he realised that there were no lights hanging from the ceiling nor attached to the walls. There was just this old lamp that flickered every so often and spat.

He checked the walls to find no electric points either. He would have to find those in the morning.

Leaving with lamp in hand Sol found a kitchen off to one side at the back of the house where a large, iron, wood burning stove dominated the room. There was another lamp at the table that he lit so that he could have two rooms alight at a time. There was no fridge but pantries built into the walls, several cupboards and a cold store behind where he found cheese in a tin, butter under a cover and some delicious bread of a kind he had never tasted before in a wooden breadbin. It was crispy on the surface, mealy in texture and full of seed. He would need the bakery's email to get more.

Sol ran water from a tap in the side porch that was set over a large white porcelain sink with a big, brown-etched chip in its front. It trickled into a glass he found in a thick-dusted cupboard and after a frosty, dirt-textured gulp he held it up to the light to inspect more closely. The liquid was peaty-brown but mostly clear and so he ran the tap for a few more minutes. The second glass was dark too, the colour of strong tea. He tried three more times before he wondered if this *was* the colour of the water. Thirsty, he drank anyway and was surprised at the flavour. Ice-cold, it had a smoked taste about it and he just hoped that he was not going to regret anything he caught from drinking it. He would need to purchase bottled water in the morning.

Sol followed a draft to the back of the porch. There he found a door to the back, but wanted food and then sleep now deciding it was not the time for exploring. He found a knife and plate from a cupboard and under drawer, and sat at the patchwork-clothed oak table on a straight beech wood chair and ate cheese, with buttered bread and he was strangely happy. It was a long way from the city life and seemed very basic at first glance, but at least it would provide some home comforts. True, work was needed, but he wanted a focus.

He sat, arm hairs erect in the cold, and contemplated, listening to the steady drop of water from a tap or a roof, perhaps inside, maybe out. A tawny owl hooted from the wood beyond the house and was greeted by its mate.

The food was good and the water had the consistency of odd, but fine, ale. He could live with that for now.

Plate, glass and knife left on the table amongst a scattering of crumbs, he shut off the kitchen lamp and carried the first through to the living room where he finished his meal with a chocolate bar. Discarding the internally shiny wrapper on the table, he went on and back to the front hall where the corridor led to a bedroom filled with a large metal sprung bed. There was a door off the corridor too to a second bedroom with just a single in it, hemmed in by wooden cabinets, but for now the double would do. He collected his bag, threw it to the sagged mattress that awaited him, turning out its contents, and selected his electric toothbrush, paste, soap and a small towel.

Bathroom?

In the central room there was an interior walk-in store shelved from floor to ceiling and lined with papers, books and jars, but no bathroom. Eventually Sol turned to the kitchen sink and resorted to brushing his teeth in the brown water that the tap emitted in an air-bubbled spurt. Hot water would come once he had lit a fire in the morning or worked out the gas.

He knew he hadn't left enough time between eating and brushing his teeth, but he had every confidence that dentists were good these days and with the colour of the water it was difficult to see the chocolate as he spat out into the sink anyway.

Toilet?

Suddenly aware of an over-filled bladder, he urinated from a few paces out into the back garden accessing this from the side porch in the kitchen. Although it was dark and there was no evidence of anyone else being remotely near, he still worried about what the neighbours might think.

'You'd never do this in London,' he thought chuckling.

There was a cold wind now and he shivered.

It was awfully quiet.

No cars passing on the road, no sirens forcing them out of the way, and no background hum of computers. He could sense neither voices nor music, and there were not even the tinny rhythms of someone's radio intruding on everyone else's sound space. There was just the rush of wind journeying through the bristles of pines and the bud bursting branches of spring deciduous trees, the dull sounds of thick needle-forest floors and the serenity of water lapping on the shore where birds called and chattered.

Sol had always been around people and gained security from their presence.

His phone was dead, his car in a ditch, he had left the city and on a whim bought a house all in the space of twenty-four hours. If they all thought he needed a retreat, well retreat this seemed to be, but Sol made it his morning's intention to find the neighbours and to get some ideas as to how they had improved their pads.

He thought about the *woman* left behind and anger started to surface again.

He thought about work and the anger was replaced by resentment.

Then, probably worst of all, came self-pity and the temptation to blame everyone else for where he found himself.

No, that would not do.

He was known for his ambition and his unconquerable drive, and he would show them all, however hard it was going to be.

Sol went to bolt the outside doors but was surprised that there were no locks on any of them. He would have to look into security in the next few days too. For now he moved furniture to behind doors, noisily scraping chairs over the wooden floors, to stop any being opened by a potential intruder. This made him feel better and safer – you never knew who was out there – not these days.

Making his way back to the bedroom, he spread a thin sleeping bag out over the mattress, kicked off his wet shoes and socks, noisily got in, sinking deeply into its tobacco-smoke comfort and then silenced the lamp and was surprised by two things: first, a level of darkness he had not experienced before, one with no orange glow on the horizon and no neon, no streetlights and no windows; second, that he slept so well, rapidly falling away into the other world with that typical westernized thought of how he would 'never sleep in a place like...'

Chapter 2: Bird Song, an Awakening

(The Swan of Tuonela, Op 22, Jean Sibelius)

Sol became aware of the bright sounds of bird song.
It wasn't just one bird, like in the city where only the coo of the feral pigeon would accompany the fat grey squabs that seemed to breed on every non-proofed window ledge in monoculture. This was different in its diversity and breadth with whole octaves of sound creeping into his sleep in a strange avian symphony of sound that snatched him from his dreams and drew him back into the living; a world he would rather have avoided after recent experience.
There *was* a pigeon of a kind. It lulled rather than called.
Unlike its city cousins, its was quiet and melodious with a plea that echoed through cold woodland, egged on by mist that reduced sound's refraction and extended its reach. The drum of a woodpecker reverberated from a deadwood resonant chamber, with a quick metre first, which then turned slow, a stanza to be repeated time and again. Something flute-whistled from on high whilst varied finch '*chip-chip'd*' and blue tits scolded in whirring abuse. There was the unmistakable quack of a duck that cracked harshly across the loch's water and the constant '*there-there-there*' of a thousand geese by the beach that splashed as they bill-dabbled the shallows. What Sol would one day come to recognise as a grebe whinnied, and mixed gulls '*scrarch'd*' and brought a taste of the seaside to this vocalised scene. It was an orchestrated masterpiece of bird song written in notes he could not name and played on instruments of unknown species.
Sol was brought too by a tapping, as if an agitated fingernail pattered on glass was being used to penetrate his sleep. The noise dropped down through his subconscious and became part of his dream – an irritated manager mid-rant slapping the desk, a moment with *her* in discussion about *them* where she drummed long

perfect-painted nails on the surface between them, a charging therapist rapping out the bill on an old-fashioned type-faced calculator, the barista at the Moto awaiting apology thumbing the counter edge with aggression. Memories extended back; the office, then early work, study, school, home, childhood walks and a happiness that he found difficult to recall but which seemed linked to a family far off.

The tapping continued, not always regular but unremitting and with changes of pitch and roll. It dragged him up and out of sleep and into the awareness that he was re-entering the genuine world and leaving the pseudo-reality of his mind's fantasies, however authentic it had felt to live in them at the time.

His brain started to acknowledge the volume of that song-scape that marked the early dawn, but always with that constant '*tap-tap, tap*' interfering as a scratch does on recorded vinyl.

Tap-tap, tap.

Sol felt the suffocating enclosure of his sleeping bag and pulled his arms up and free to escape the closeness of its mummy hood. The comforting humid air inside slipped out easily and was replaced with a damp moistness from the room around him.

Tap-tap, tap.

He stretched, arching his back skyward, and touched the metal frame of an unfamiliar bed, feeling the sag of a slightly clammy mattress he was unaccustomed to.

Tap-tap, tap.

Gone were the trappings of warmth and luxury. There was no firm bed, well sprung, body contouring and expensive, below his sinking torso. The air was not the usual conditioned, dry and heated affair he knew so well.

Tap-tap, tap.

Instead his nostrils felt alert to the sensation of a different smell, a cooler temperature, a greater humidity and difference.

Tap-tap, tap.

He reached out to find no deep pillows, plumped up with feathered comfort. The bed beside him was empty.

Tap-tap, tap.

Sol opened his eyes in sudden awareness of the strangeness of his surroundings and, temporarily paralysed, he looked from side to side, sweeping the room in a single neck motion.

He lay sunken into a musty old mattress, stained in places, more likely by coffee than anything untoward, on a dull brass-ended bed. It had possibly been buffed in the past but now lacked lustre except where the bed knobs had been polished by the regular squeezed-by passage of the previous incumbent. A once-bright patterned rug ran from under the bed, ending in tatty knotted threads from where the floorboards extended to un-skirted walls of harsh grey stone, well cut and solid.

The ceiling was low and badly plastered, once having been white but now curdled cream. A loft hatch allowed access to a space above from which Sol was aware of the scurrying and scratching of clawed feet. He was unsure if it were rodent, bat or bird but made that westerner's mental note that he needed to '*sort that out!*' as if any wild thing living in any house needed attention and instant eradication. Wildlife started outside of the door and preferably beyond the garden wall. In his mind, aseptic cleanliness and straight lines were the rule of measure for the more civilized in any given society without there being much room for anything else.

There was a bulky dresser under one of two large windows. The first was hewn out of the end wall revealing a view into a long woodland ride that passed from the timber piles of the back yard up towards the cliff-lined darkness of the peak behind. The sun was sliding down the hillside as the dawn broke, banishing the shadows of morning before it. Light caught the ray-greened backs of goldcrests as they hooped from branch to branch in an avian display. To Sol they were simply coloured blurs that folded in wing-ripped passage from this side to that side. *They were just birds, not species and he failed to acknowledge them as anything more.*

Ill-matched tiebacks tethered curtains to the wall and a metal coat hook to the right side secured a large hoop-shaped black net on a cane pole and a fusty green shoulder bag of unknown age.

Leaving the foot of the bed the view extended from over a thin chest of drawers out across the front walled-garden beyond to flat green cradles of plant life, to the shore, to the loch and on to a far coast cast a shade of blue with distance. From here forested hills grew and greened mountains rose until they were eclipsed by bright white peaks of snow hugged by wisps of condensation that churned over their tops. Sol found himself drawn out through that small dirty window into the waters and beyond. Firstly taken by the scale of this vision he drew breath, then moments later he realised that the one thing he was used to that was missing from this idyllic scene were the houses.

Where did they all live?

From where was he to draw his security?

For now he assumed that human life was not far away and simply out of sight.

An old oil painting of a low white-painted cottage hung over the bed on the one plastered wall in the room, behind where he now sat upright. There was a wooden boat hitched up on the floral carpet of grass and flower that grew thinly cropped by goat-like sheep on the shoreline, and a large expanse of water expanded from the rocks and pebbles. A smocked man was seated on a grey wall and mended nets, whilst children played in the water between shaggy long-horned cattle, and a woman picked flower heads on lengthy stems in the garden. He had a long pipe in his mouth and a patterned hat sat askew his head, and she wore a clean white dress mud stained at its hem. Clouds hung in a boiling sky over a cliff-edged mount that elbowed out into the welcoming blue water, and birds drifted lazily above a forest that stretched as far as the eye could see. Only a cobbled track cut a way through the picture off to the left.

Sol got out of his morning air-moistened sleeping sack and climbed down off the bed, whose springs complained as he left it, and he scanned from the window up the track he had walked along the night before. He knew without looking again that the painted house in the picture was the *Bothan* in which he now lived but he went back to check anyway.

There on a post by the gate in the middle of the wall was a sign. Here the painter had added that one important detail, revealed as Sol ran his finger through the accumulated dust, removing it from the troughs left in the oil by the passage of the artist's brushes. *Bothan Faobhar.*

Tap-tap, tap.

Sol turned to the side window where a red-chested robin chipped at the dry cracked putty that held the age-bubbled glass in its small squares.

Tap-tap, tap.

He walked up close and the robin continued its search for whatever morsel it believed would be there.

Sol stopped dead, unaccustomed to this lack of fear from a wild thing, and looked closely. Only just the thickness of a warped glass pane away, the robin sustained its attack of the lining ignorant of the man behind the bubbled crystal flatness.

This was no postcard creature or Christmas illustration. It tail-flicked in counterbalance to its movement forward. A brown back rapidly became grey and a bright range of burning colour made it into a reddened chest of fine wind-licked feathers that fluttered with the breeze. The bird had more orange than Sol expected, and its front had a speckled appearance, mottled with white, cream, brown and yellow. An intelligent eye with a sparkle of its own glistened over wet blackness showing in convex an untrue reflection of the window and Sol motionless in observation behind it.

Sol watched as details rose into his perception, the scales of the skin, the wrinkle of a knee, the polish of a talon, the gold of an eyelid, and the fluffing of down. Textures became apparent as this avian clockwork toy worked its way along the ledge and into the solidified gum.

Tap-tap, tap.

Then it found it; a living emulsion-textured insect grub made of what looked like a series of miniature writhing concentric tyres pinioned by a sharp grey bird bill. It wriggled, impaled.
The robin fell from the window ledge and gliddered down to somewhere hidden in one of the dilapidated back sheds.
The sunlight was reaching down the woodland ride illuminating a path he knew he would need to explore later and, despite the air's chill, he felt a growing warmth-giving sense of excitement. A small carved chair could be seen a way up the path basking in a pool of sunshine. It was so obviously placed to enjoy the light of morning that Sol imagined himself there already with a cup of tea at hand.

He stretched again and wandered along the front hall to find the kitchen. Passing through the front living room he was surprised again by the vastness of the loch view framed so well by the length of the white-painted wood frames. Loose gloss flicked upwards from the external surfaces leaving a pallid greyness behind etched by the dense rain-proofed grain of old oak. A strange thought, he wondered if these were the same wood frames that were painted in the oil copy of the *Bothan* that hung in the bedroom.
He looked out again to where the mountains appeared to almost grow organically from the water in rolling mounds that struck the sky in ice-pinnacles each alight with the fire of an April morning's sun.
Sol shivered with the cold, his breath hanging in the coolness of the room's atmosphere.

He turned to address the fireplace, longing for it to be lit already and the room to be pre-warm. After all, if he wanted hot water he was going to have to light it somehow. He was surprised to see an unlit fire readymade in the hearth. Paper was neatly crumpled and folded into balls and shapes over which smaller pine kindling had been laid in a pyramid which was then completed with large splits of half logs. The whole was hemmed in with an entire tree section at the back to reflect the heat in return back to the room. There was cut wood in a basket to the left and an iron poker waited patiently to the right on a pile of paper ready to set the next fire.

For the first time Sol felt a watched sensation as if the previous occupant of the house still owned the place and would be back shortly, with Sol only visiting.

He looked around the room curiously.

The curtains were tatty but were neatly tied back to the walls, which although they were poorly plastered in places and cold stone in others were perfectly homely enough in their overall rustic appeal. A rug covered much of the floor and two wool-clothed armchairs were welcoming in their sagging overuse, the one to the right of the fireplace being especially worn, and probably the last owner's favourite. The poker by the fire waited at a good arm's stretch from this armchair.

The table was water-stained, yet solid, with only two chairs, and next to the letter and spirits were placemats and coasters for four. On the reading desk were books and documents, writing paper and envelopes, and there was a magnifier and knife, both constructed with real bone handles. The carver chair was comfortable but used, with its threadbare cover being mostly hidden by a feather-stuffed pillow that leaked breeze-tickled down.

On either side of the room were bookcases filled with only the finger-ripped spines of the tattered hard-backed titles showing. Sol ran his hands through dust to read their names aloud. Books on flowers all in one section, birds and insects; there was a theme coming out. Then there was local history, folklore and, out of place, suddenly geology and next Celtic art. Poetry completed the eclectic library of the recent resident who by all accounts seemed well read like some old-school polymath. Stones and fossils, bone and fragments littered the shelf edges with a skull here and a tooth there, each with its own carefully handwritten label.

A large picture hung on one wall, a dark oil of a deer stag resplendent on a heather smothered peak. Hunting dogs were upon it, but even though it must have known its end was near the artist had allowed it the satisfaction of holding its antlers erect in stern defiant display. At its feet a black grouse fled and clearly they would both fall at the foot of a solid Pictish carved stone half buried in the peaty ground.

The picture was really too large for the wall, more a continuation of the room into a scene beyond it. It was life-like and life-sized, probably painted for a great house somewhere else, not here. But in its strange way it worked.

Behind the reflection of a thin-walled glass cabinet, a short-legged water bird followed Sol's progress to the chest of drawers with a red glass-eyed backward glance. Its black beak pointed upwards from a pitch coloured head and its white front gave it a pied penguin appearance. Sol wasn't used to a taxidermy specimen and despite his city disgust at the dead animal he looked closely and appreciated that the stuffing was old. Dried grasses had been added to fulfil the creator's artistic purpose.

Held by its false eye, Sol looked away to the writing desk to where of all things the discarded ink pen bothered him the most as it waited for further use. *It was as if they had never expected to leave.*

He looked at the hand-written letter left for him to affirm that the house was his and then down to the indecipherable signature at the bottom that he decided was the letter 'G' finished with an artistic flourish. The pen nib had flicked at the end to give an extra element to the letter and what he had thought before was a punctuation dot was little more than an artefact.

He settled on 'G'.

His breath hung vapid in front of his face and so Sol headed to the kitchen to get some form of breakfast. He was hopeful that the cooking range's fire would be as easy to light as the living room's looked and that he could find more food left by the previous resident.

As he entered the room there was a scurry of motion from the table as small rodents span in dizzy direction from the bread he had left out the previous evening. They fell easily down the table legs and off the chairs before disappearing into the gaps under the cabinets.

The stone floor tiles were cold to his toes, rough and unwelcoming, but once he had heeded the complaint of his underfoot, he continued and approached the table in disgust.

Sol inspected the bread, gnawed and chewed for what looked like most of the evening. There were droppings interspersed amongst the crumbs he had left on the plate and table top and there was the intense smell of ammonia on the butter which was marked with mouse incisor scrapes and long-toed footprints. It was that same scent of chemical toilet that he could only stomach at field-based concerts where glamping represented the limit of his *roughing it.*

He swore at the mice which had sunk unseen into the shadows behind the furniture. The food was ruined and he just hoped that there was more. Sweeping the crumbs up on to the plate he flung them out of the back porch door noticing the cleared track ways of snails where they had been cut cleanly through the algae that grew thick green across the glass of the roof. Slugs had left glistened trails up the walls inside and over what appeared to be a vegetable rack and several lines of ready-planted pots on a shelving unit.

Sol stormed back into the kitchen and threw the plates heavily onto the porch surface by the sink before flinging the range door open in vermin-raged anger.

Mice needed control!

Inside was a fire ready made for the lighting and in need of a match, and Sol, now feeling the bitter chill of the morning's air was more than glad to collect matches from the front room to oblige it. The paper took quickly, burning with a blaze that undermined then fiercely flamed the pine kindling strips, allowing the half logs above to catch. Mesmerised by 'real' fire, Sol felt its warmth penetrate something primal inside of him and so it was with some reluctance that he eventually closed the glass fronted door on the flames to watch them glow orange through its soot-caked pane. He turned the brass handle, already beginning to warm, and the cooker was lit.

He needed food, but not until he had relieved himself for the morning. But where was the toilet? Where was a bathroom? *Surely the last occupant hadn't used the garden for everything?*

An image of the service station toilets flashed through his mind. Unsavoury and unclean, he wondered about the garden, where waste went and what happened to it. He knew the answers really. Somewhere in some school class he had learnt about run off and eutrophication, decomposition and recycling. *But not in the garden!* This was supposed to happen at some distance from anyone's house where our waste was transported by pipes and deposited by sewers to a place where it couldn't be seen and far enough away for it not to cause offence or even be remembered. It was all part of being a civilised race of people.

Sol left the kitchen, slowly heating in the glow of the range fire. Slipping through the loose door of the porch he crossed the yard to look back at the house.

The grass was damp cold, dew splashed and fresh. Each droplet held the light, which it then reflected in diamond sparkles that lit the verdant blades into bejewelled splendour, knitted together by the webbing night-attention of a million small spiders.

The line of the house was in shadow. The systematic pyramidal log piles, each as promised in the letter stacked according to its kind, broke the clean lines of the cottage. But no evidence of an outflow pipe interfered with their regularity.

Sol stepped backwards, following a streak of bare-worn earth that suggested a once commonly used path. It took him to a line of sheds that seem contiguous with the mixed larch, pine, oak and birch trees that encroached onto the plot. Their branches hung low and encouraged a rich growth of thickly cushioned moss in their dappled shade. Sinewy bearded lichens were strung like Christmas decorations spread on a tree in artistic draperies that would have been admired in a high street department store window. Small birds elevated and descended between the levels of branch spans with '*t-seeting*' calls and Sol fancied he spotted spirally ascending movement up the gnarled trunk of an ashen-barked oak tree. This was the treecreeper circling its corkscrew way from tree bottom to treetop. But that knowledge remained secret to Sol. To him it was a branch-slithering movement, possibly a mouse.

Used to the constant business of town life, Sol was surprised by the noise that emanated from within the apparent darkness of the forest. Quickly his musical ear was able to distinguish repetitive sequences of song. He had expected silence and was rewarded with a living opus of bird sound. It was a long time since he had played in an orchestra, but he was strangely reminded of those times with what he now heard.

There were four rooms of stone erected as a long ambling shed on the boundary between the wood and the yard. Each was topped in the same lichen'd slate tiles as the house and was punctuated by a small wooden door, mostly painted in an ancient form of red, and with a cross sectioned window split into four panes of dusty, well-webbed glass.

The first held tools with workbenches set around its outside, drawers and shelves under and more utensils hanging from wall pins and poles set from the ceiling beams. There was a dirty window looking out of the back wall onto a green-painted bird box nailed to an oak trunk. Large red gas canisters rusted to the rear and an old wooden clock lay in pieces on a surface next to a grinding stone that had been used at some time in history to sharpen a knife.

The second room was stacked with drying logs and timber and by its door was an axe left embedded into a large root stump with several more blades and saws inside. This was obviously the wood store. Another window at the back was half hidden by upright poles of trunk and branch.

On the floor below a workbench sat neatly stacked hessian and paper sacks of muesli textured birdseed, peanuts and black bacteria-shaped Niger seed. Mice had successfully chewed through one of the dry bags and kernels spilled onto the floor. Several handmade wire and plastic-tubed feeders sat on the worktop. *The last man obviously enjoyed his birds.*

Third on the shed was filled with what at first glance looked like junk but on closer inspection seemed to be scientific equipment. Dusty brass lenses and a microscope sat together on a work surface. There were wooden boxes and glass sheets piled flat with a large paraffin lamp and several dented metal cans that were labelled 'SPIRITS', 'ETHER' and 'PARAFIN'. In addition, a set of cane fishing rods and a number of reels, lines, hooks and fishing flies lay about. By a small vice was a pile of feather, fur and coloured threads with pots of glue, enamel and a large lens attached to the surface by a heavy-weighted base. Two pairs of binoculars and a telescope hung from a peg hammered into the wall's mortar next to which an old green jacket swung from a hook obscured by a checked-patterned scarf and a cloth flat cap. Wellington boots stood in a pair that faced out from the wall below.

For the first time since leaving the house, Sol became aware of his bare feet and so after brushing them down, he dropped his feet into the rubber of the boots, wriggled his toes inside and walked with a greater confidence.

There was a wicker seat at the window end of the room where the glass seemed cleaner than the others. On the chair lay a notebook and several pencils and another pair of binoculars. Sol picked up the paper document and leafed through a series of hand-written notes and drawings, mostly birds, deer and oddly one page dedicated to a cat. It was leaping after butterflies in a playful poise with a well-marked forehead and tiger stripes. Obviously large, the animal's tail seemed bushed up and short.

'Could do with one of those around here!' he thought, half-seriously, thinking of the mice on the kitchen table.

There were some old rubber pipes with metal hose clips around their ends and a series of bolts and machine parts cast over one side of the room. They looked like fragments of an old engine with pistons, a radiator and several other pieces that vaguely reminded Sol of classes in Physics as a boy. He fiddled with them awkwardly; not knowing how such a jigsaw could be put back together to make a whole. To him, *'what happened in the engine, stayed in the engine,'* which was why he paid mechanics to service his car.

He left the room with his feet already sweating up inside the boots and beginning to stick to the rubber where the lining had worn thin.

The final shed held an old bath, leaf-filled and musty with tea brown stain lines that ran around it in concentric circles. The holes at the head end for taps were left empty save for cobwebs and it sat on stones to keep it secure and upright. There was a single pipe that ran out of a black header tank above from which he could hear the cock-stoppered hissing of water being diverted to an overflow tube behind. Water obviously ran under gravity from somewhere up on the hill to fill this reservoir and when released by a rusty looking contraption on the copper pipe's end it would pour down into the bath through a wide, tin showerhead. Sol tested it and shivered as the large drops ran into each other in cascades of half frozen, brown runnels.

A black rubber plug lay hopeful on the end of a chain at the bottom end of the bath.

Sol struggled to shut the water off and wondered when and how he was going to get a plumber up to the cottage as soon as possible as the water gurgled away into the hole at the bottom end.

A plastic chair sat next to the bath on which a dry-cracked bar of soap lay welded. It smelt heavily medicated. There was also a sink bolted to the wall under the window, which was similar to that in the back of each room before. Next to it a silver metal-lined mirror was hung by a chain-link from a large nail secured deep into the wall's pointing. But there was still no toilet.

Really feeling the morning's urge coming on, Sol returned to the yard outside, bright with sunlight that shocked his eyes as he left the shade of the end bathroom shed. A path ran in a continuation to the left of this cabin-like room and passed a huge metal cylinder labelled 'oil' and off into the wood.

Sol followed.

As a comparison to London life this short journey could have been little more different. Buds on trees were fresh and green with catkins falling from birch in pendulous floral arrangements, the kind not recognised as flowers by the layman. Sound was unremitting and sonorous, constant and companionable. There was freshness to the air and each footfall in the deepening soil released that woodland smell of fungus and humus, the scent of rich nutrients and decay, recycling and productivity that every ecologist feels compelled to fight for. It was the perfume of good, sweet, airy soil.

Sol could sense the earth, the atmosphere and the life, and for a moment, even though he little recognised it for what it was, it was good.

A short way ahead was a stone shed with a half complete wooden door. It was shaded and damp with a roof that threatened to collapse under the weight of moss, lichen, liverwort and fern. One ash tree grew from its stonework and another was bonsai trained to the roof. The whole building was constructed integrally into a cliff face that ran quickly up to meet what he presumed would be a mountain behind.

The door, solid timbered and firm, swung easily outwards to reveal a white porcelain toilet with a black seat. With its cistern above from which plumbed a metal pull chain, it took Sol immediately back to cigar adverts from the '80s and to scenes of terraced streets and shared privies seen in sepia museum photographs of Victorian England. A roll of medicated paper hung from a metal wire bracket about which cobwebs were woven hiding all but the fingertips of their large inhabitants.

Sol was stunned. Partly he was hit by the rustic simplicity of this most essential of buildings, secondly by its isolation, and finally by how very different this was to the fragrant comforts he had become used to.

Where was the warmth to welcome him to sit?

Where was the ambient light in which to relax?

Where was the aseptic cleanliness he had come to expect, even though he knew full well that dust is not dirty, nor cobwebs harmful?

This, he felt, was brutally basic as a toilet, but with little choice, he had to use it.

Cold, dark and primitive it may have been, but, thought Sol, this was nothing to what it would be like in the winter, and another tradesman was added to the growing list of home-improvers he would need to call as soon as possible. The seat bit icily into his bare legs and he felt the urge to scream, being hesitant only because he was still convinced that there would be people within hearing distance and he didn't want to alarm them on first meeting. Oddly, as he sat he also had a sense of being watched with the impression of something lurking behind him even though his sensible mind knew that the small room was walled with stone and nothing could have been there.

Crestfallen at his house purchase's obvious limitations he returned to the cottage with resentment about the building, its services and its position. He was angry at it as he crossed the yard in a long-legged rubber-booted strut where he noticed buckets, planters and pots he had not yet investigated. *Even this yard was a mess and weedy!*

Smoke rose from the middle chimney as he rounded the rear of the building to the porch and he unexpectedly found himself strangely calmed by the appearance of the cottage, nestled here by the shore side under the protection of the cliff.

He peered round to the front of *Bothan Faobhar*, daring to give her a name and thus a personality, and the loch opened up to his view and eased his un-quieted spirit. There was hope that when he came to sell it the cottage would fetch a good market value with a vista like that. *After all, how wrong was he usually on any purchase and deal? And, how often were his gut feelings proven correct in the end?*

The rich black earth in the front garden had been turned recently and the shoots of vegetables had started to show in their straight military lines of planting. The wall was edged with shrubs on the garden-side and by the crumbled left was a small wooden boat, upturned to keep it dry for now, revealing the water-fast stern of a well-made, clinker-built craft. Oars were tied beside her.

Trying to remain annoyed enough to hate the scene, he imagined taking the craft out on the water, launching her with a picnic on board and maybe using the fishing rods in the shed to catch supper; and he was suddenly drawn a little closer by the location.

No, it would never do. He was a city man, and with the way things stood right now he had to hate the place!

No hot water and what there was ran brown in colour.

No heating except for open fires.

No inside toilet for god's sake!

No indoor bath.

From what he could see no electricity.

Had he seen a shaver point? No!

No decent lights even.

No proper road or drive.
Not even neighbours yet.
The question dangled within his mind, '*What was going for the place?*'
And then a second query crept in after the first. '*What was he, a pronounced and dedicated city dweller, doing here?*' This did not feel like his kind of world. Here he was alien.
He swept around in an irritated circle. There was *just* this incredible and extensive view, the birds gathered in, a few tumbledown sheds, a primitive toilet at the end of a woodland garden path, and a cottage that oozed a feeling of time-stuck age and the essence of its previous, obviously reclusive, owner.
He breathed deeply, unsure whether to laugh or cry.
"What have I bought then?" he questioned aloud and he swore to himself as he returned with a bizarre reluctance to re-enter the kitchen through the porch door to see what else needed sorting. First things first, he needed to fix some breakfast. After all, any other food that he had been carrying up from the south was safely stuck in the boot to his car several miles back up the track. And, *he* was Sol, and *he* could fix anything – with the right sort of help on hand.
This was the man who had taken on the bosses and worked himself up the ladder following lucky gamble with lucky gamble. This was the man who had come from almost nothing and made more than seemed credible. This was the man who had secured the business for *them*, even though now he was considered at the moment as something of a liability and a loose cannon too confident in his own ability. *He could sort this!*
He kicked the boots off at the porch door and with a sinking heart looked around at the dimly lit kitchen. Light tried to enter through the porch and made an attempt from the one small window on the back wall. Closing the door he became aware that the heat from the fire had spread about the place quickly and saw that the logs were now nicely glowing and the hob roasting a hot red. Something

primal once again tugged at his heart and he went to the larder to the side of the room to see if anything had been stowed away by the mysterious letter writer; something that he could cook and eat.

There were numerous tins on shelves, and Sol quickly worked out a system to the storage and located a tin of rolled oat. With it was a hand written instruction label for porridge using a cupful of oat with water and some salt to taste. Heavy copper-based pans hung from a rack on the ceiling and he rapidly set to making himself a bowl of something he had not tasted since time forgotten.

He stirred the pasty stew with a wooden spoon taken from a kiln-fired pot jar and whilst preventing it from burning on the very hot stove he found a substantial clay bowl to eat from, searching the cupboards between stirrings. As the colloidal liquid, stained a curious grey shade of that funny colour of the *Bothan's* water and oat, fizzed round the edges of the pan and threatened to bubble up and over in a rising mass of porridge, Sol lifted it from the heat and poured the lather he had concocted into the bowl. The remains caught on the over-heated base and scolded into a crisped burnt ring, deep russet and scabbed.

Sol plunged the pan under the porch tap, producing a plume of steam, and left it to soak, then returning to address the lumpy mix in his bowl in the kitchen. He drew a chair up close to the fire, flinging a new log in from the wicker basket beside to keep it burning, and picked up the clumpy conglomeration he was daring to consider as breakfast.

Of all the words he could think of '*attractive*' was not one of them.

He contemplated it for a while and his stomach both lurched in despair and gurgled in anticipation as it considered the need for sustenance but recognised the fear of the unknown. He chuckled at this irony and the turmoil he had initiated within his own body, and then took a large deep spoonful.

It was sticky, with all the tackiness of good children's glue. The lumps were soft on the palate and there was a subtly of taste akin to the peat in an island malt whisky with that hint of salt that suggested the sea and enhanced the flavour of well-rolled oats. It was plain, but in a way satisfying, and Sol ate it, enjoyed it, and if it wasn't for the well-burnt pan and the efforts required to produce more, he may have considered making another batch.

It was surprisingly good and he sat with a certain smugness as his cheeks reddened in the heat of the moist-aired kitchen with his foot souls beginning to burn where they rested upon the basket by the fiery window.

He needed a wash but thought that he would leave that pleasure until he had hot water and instead simply brushed his teeth, spitting out into the pots left for washing in the porch sink. *He needed a cleaner as quickly as possible too!*

Not having brought many clothes to the cottage, Sol decided to stay dressed as he was now that he was dry and warm. The weather outside had changed somewhat and clouds had drifted in over the loch from somewhere out at sea. They seemed not to menace the scene but Sol needed a coat to hold off the worst should it rain and so went out to the sheds to collect the green jacket and hat that hung there. With the checked scarf wrapped around his neck, he found knitted gloves in a deep, wool-lined pocket of the jacket.

He felt a little guilt at taking the items. But then he considered that he had purchased the place and everything in it and they were therefore his for the taking.

When he left *Bothan Faobhar* by the hole in the wall, the wind had picked up strength and was playfully kicking leaves along the track. It gaily flushed him along through the woodland over the undulations of pebbles and rocks and Sol wondered how he had ever considered driving his car all the way along to the house. *Why had it even occurred to him as an option the night before?*

Again he found himself laughing at the foolishness of his situation and his lack of foresight in listening to advice or even visiting the property first. It was not the first time that he could have been accused of not considering the consequences of his rash actions and it would not be the last.

His safety net mobile lay dead in his trouser pocket and more out of hope he carried his wallet too, just in case he passed a shop. At the very least he could organise for a supermarket to deliver supplies if he could charge his phone and gain a signal. He had so far failed to find any plug sockets back in the cottage and considering the lack of easy access to the property he was beginning to understand why. *What electrical contractor would travel this far? In fact where would the electricity come from? There were no overhead cables anywhere.*

He trudged on tugging the smell of roll up after roll up after him until he suddenly reached the end of his tobacco and the realisation that he had forcibly quit for the present. Although this would please his friends and doctor, he was not happy with this thought and growled miserably to himself. In the knowledge that at least there was a bag of pre-ground coffee in the car, and that one of his vices would be satisfied soon, he flicked the collar of the borrowed jacket higher and held its wool lining closer.

By the time he found his beloved white car, mud-specked and bruised in the ditch at the side of the road, the weather had continued to worsen with huge drops of moisture dropping then whipping upwards in a mad dance to re-meet the sky. He walked around the stranded vehicle, struggling in the wet dirt under his ill-fitted boots, and looked critically at the damage to the bodywork, the dent to the front and the way the car sat front wheel upright pitched in the dyke at the side of the track. Streaked marks in the muck of the road stretched in arced trenches away reliably showing the last spin of the vehicle as it lost traction. There was the forensic evidence of how he had ended the journey and he wondered how long the car would remain here by the road as testimony to his stupidity.

The boots slopped about over his sweaty sockless feet and he muttered about his misfortune for a bit before returning to the front of the car.

He opened the unlocked driver's door thankful that in his rush last night he had left the keys in the ignition. Dropping carefully down into the seat, he reached for the glove compartment and extracted an in-car mobile phone charger and plugged it hesitantly into the snugness of the cigarette lighter and its other end into that hallowed rectangle of plastic, glass and microchip. He couldn't remember being without its use for so long, even though he knew they didn't exist when he was young. It was strange that he had become so addicted and reliant, that it had become yet another of his listed vices, and he licked his lips in anticipation of power surging back into it.

Nothing.

Next he turned the keys in the ignition and started the engine up in his typically over-revved style and after a short delay the mobile phone screen acknowledged that the purring engine was diverting a small part of its under-bonnet horse power into the little piece of technology that sat on the seat beside him. It was a moment of sheer delight and excitement for Sol, which then extended to minutes as he waited for enough energy to be transferred from fuel to engine to wire to phone for him to use it; this taunting small black box that urged him to connect with it continuously and without hesitation.

In the meantime he crouched in the rain to raid the boot, looking intently for useful supplies, finding bagged coffee that made his heart jump, a few biscuits, clothes and a too small holdall to contain the lot. At least this time he knew the way back and it would be light enough to see, even if it were so wet that he had the potential of wading where the pools were forming, expanding and crawling across the lane like organic beings in search of the sea.

A crinkly wrapped chocolate bar finished his extended breakfast.

Back in the front, seated, he switched the radio on, but with little signal it only picked up a local station in Gaelic. Not to his taste, nor language, he switched the source to a shuffle of his i-pod and sang along loudly for the rest of an hour. The phone steadily charged, the rain lashed and fell drumming out rhythms over the steamed up windscreen, and the wind buffeted the bodywork.

A red light blinked into life on the dashboard to warn him that his fuel was running low and Sol cut the power, leaving the keys dangling their dollar-shaped fob from the ignition. He would need fuel in the near future and having no idea where the nearest supermarket or petrol station might be he knew that it was important to conserve what he had left.

Leaving the security of the car and re-entering the slightly calmed weather outside, he looked hopefully down at his mobile. The squall was all but passed and a bright blue clarity was quickly enveloping the cloud above. The puddles below appeared to draw away and down into the earth, losing their grip of the land as they leached away and down with gravity.

Nudging back from the low profile of the vehicle Sol fumbled with his phone, turned it in his hand, held the 'on' switch down and waited.

A delay.

All he wanted was power in it and surely it had had enough by now. He spontaneously cursed and kicked the ground in an angry outburst, muttering under his breath.

All that was displayed was a blank screen.

Sol fell into a typical string of expletives concerned with the illegitimacy of the phone and the network, edging blindly backwards along the track towards the cottage.

The phone woke from its trance with its simple symbolic tone and electronic branding sign.

Sol leapt for joy, threw the flat cap in the air and swore as if for Britain.

"Yes," he screamed with all his might as slowly the screen took him through burgeoning emotions until it reached the home display. "Thank you, thank you and thank you!"

He looked intently down at it, almost in a sweat. The mobile registered no network coverage, with no illuminated bar for signal, and Sol launched into another round of abuse whilst extracting the now damp cloth cap from the wet muddy ground next to him. He fumbled thoughtlessly with it, eyes-hooked on the mobile device held before him, and then he stood up abruptly, in a full rage and shouted himself hoarse until he could yell no more.

Silence.

"You're not from round these parts are you?" asked the stranger stood on the track in front of him with his bedraggled collie dog to heel, and Sol found himself looking straight into the eyes of the most haggard and care-worn face he thought he had ever seen.

He couldn't help himself but scream.

Chapter 3: Of a Cuckoo and a Cat

(Pictures at an Exhibition: The Gnome,
Modest Petrovich Mussorgsky)

The man's eyes were sharp and quick, animated with a sparkle of life to them that shone through small black pupils wetted by wind-tugged tears. They contrasted smooth with the rest of his fissured face that was wizened with exposure and looked rough to the touch. Care-lines scarred his creased temples and his thinning wired hair was outgrown by a spiked beard highlighted white over grey and extended well up each cheek to frame his straight-lipped mouth.

His coat was waxed and had once been viridian green all over, but this former life was now restricted to the middle of the jacket being beaten back by weathered bleaching at the top and gripped by mud at the bottom. He wore dark flannel trousers that flapped in the wind and his thick wool socks were turned over to broadly border the interface between his black rubber boots and his trouser legs.

Sol took in the disturbing intensity of the man's observation of him immediately, and decided to take control, trying with all his effort to sound measured and cool; the way he did in business.

"No," he replied, and then reaching forward with an extended hand he started again, "the name's...."

"....Sol," the man finished for him. "Yes, we all know who you are. The first newcomer in a while." His hands remained resolutely still where they were and there was no offer of friendship in return. And then he mused for a minute before adding, "Solomon the wise I suppose? Still, even parents make mistakes and every family has a runt."

He crumpled his face and swallowed thoughtfully, holding Sol in his fixed stare, who feeling nervous and embarrassed withdrew his outstretched hand and grinned that rearward smile of the uncomfortable.

Suddenly the man's eyes flashed back to the white sports car upended in the ditch beyond.

"We thought you were dying in there with the engine running," and he nodded at the vehicle. "After all, who else would sit in a car with the engine ticking over when it obviously isn't going anywhere? You got us really worried. Not me of course. But the dog was concerned. She thought you were in real pain with all that howling going on. Then we realised you were just singing. Took us a while though. Not quite sure whether to leave you to it or to put you out of your misery...   ...or, us out of ours."

Sol laughed.

The man didn't and so Sol stopped quickly. He didn't know how to read this man and his instant disdain for Sol. This was not how ordinary business was conducted and not how Sol was used to being addressed by others. He felt unusually powerless and lacked his ordinary control of the situation.

There was a pause with Sol still being watched intently and he wasn't quite sure what to do.

"I'll get it shifted in the morning," the watcher suddenly announced.

"Thank you." Sol's reply was one of surprise. "How?"

"With brute force I expect," and the old man laughed and leaned heavily back on a worn but solid looking walking stick that had a small hand-smoothed roe buck horn for a handle. "Pity it's made of plastic," and he launched himself into a further fit of poorly controlled laughter. "Still, we'll try not to snap it...   ...much."

Sol was at a loss. He loved his car.

"That's...," he began, but the pied dog at the man's heel became restless and whimpered a submissive yelp and interrupted him.

The man looked down and his face took on a more loving and caring expression, one of unexpected empathy and compassion. It was as if a facial glacier had melted and suddenly become fluid and wet. Sol sensed he was seeing something of the real man behind the unwelcoming façade currently being displayed towards him; it was as if he were witness to some part of this man's character he should not have been able to see. It was a voyeuristic moment but he could not help but take note of it.

"Okay," the man muttered in a deep accent that rumbled earthily, nodding his head, and the dog launched off into the heather by the roadside. "She'll meet me at home," he muttered in explanation.

"So," Sol tried again, with an awkward gesture, "are you one of my neighbours then?"

He had the feeling that he wasn't sure if either of the most obvious alternative answers would be that good. If yes, then he supposed he did have a neighbour, meaning that he wasn't totally alone. But conversation wasn't starting easily and he couldn't imagine things improving for a while. This man certainly wasn't welcoming him to the area. If no, then what a relief it would be to know that he, Sol, wouldn't be holding conversations like this too often. But his status was looking increasingly isolated and lonely and not the place for a city boy like himself who was used to neighbours above, below and to every side.

"Well," the man pondered looking at the sky, "if neighbour means the man next door, then yes I am one of them. But if it means I live right next door to you, then no. I am not." There was a malicious edge to his gruff voice, as if he were sneering internally and enjoying a wicked sense of fun that only he was appreciating.

Sol struggled to develop an answer or a question. This response did not help.

"What I mean is, do you live locally?"

"A couple of miles, that's all. Up that way." The man indicated behind and smiled what Sol could only presume was supposed to be a friendlier and more encouraging expression that revealed a yellow-toothed jaw with gaps in it. He pointed over the hill beyond to where all Sol could see was grass, moss, heather and rock. A raven gambolled noisily, far off but vocally close; a black spectre of a shape above the knolls that added much to Sol's feelings about the stranger.

"Miles?" he spluttered.

"Yes, it's how we measure distance up here. What do they use in the city these days?"

Sol tried to explain that he was used to the same measurements too but sensing the man's disinterest he then tried a different tact asking, "what about other neighbours in the area?"

"Well there's the sisters over the water - you can row better than you drive I presume?" He raised his eyebrows questioningly and so Sol lied to suggest that he could.

"There's the arty woman who lives a couple of valleys on. But then," he added with a sigh, "she's not really your type."

"You don't know my type," Sol defended.

"Oh, I think I do. Then there's the big House - that's quite a way if you like a walk. But they don't much like anyone who lives in *that* old place of yours. Can you walk?"

Sol nodded.

"You'd have passed the shop on the way. It's quicker down the loch than along the lane, and then that road would take you on to the town as well if you followed it."

Sol sparked up at that word, "town?"

"Yes," the man replied. "We have them too."

"How many live in the town?"

"The old town has two or three families and their extended relatives these days and sometimes more during the holidays. People come in from the hills to the inn there though...   ...just once a week when they can. Not so much during lambing of course or when the weather closes in."

"Of course," Sol agreed with little understanding but with concern at the weather '*closing in*'.

"Your type normally live in the new town but that's quite a way away. More shops and people out there compared to *this* area."

"So, there are shops?"

The man seemed to ignore Sol and it was obvious that he still wasn't keen to befriend him quickly. He looked back up the track towards *Bothan Faobhar*. "You really must like living on your own to come out here. I hope you like it."

Sol's heart sunk further than he thought it could. "Yes," he mused. "I like what I've seen so far. It's very…"

"…isolated?" The man finished Sol's thoughts for him.

"There are no others then?" Sol asked unable to hide a certain element of desperation in his voice, his mind reeling at the thought of being so alone.

"Oh, there are a few living round and about. But they are quite distant."

There was another awkward pause that Sol decided he had to fill.

"So," he started, "if you live so many miles away, what brought you down to the track today then?"

"Well, truth to say I saw smoke coming from the chimney at the cottage and thought that you were either foolish enough to have moved in and made a fire without sweeping the chimneys out or stupid enough to have burnt the place down already. Then, walking over the moor I found your car and realised you were even more stupid and irresponsible than I first thought you would be. What with you singing and such like in your car and it crashed there in the ditch. I didn't have high hopes for you when I heard you were taking the place on from the city in the first place. It's just not the sort of place someone like you lives. But G knew best and said he'd selected a good one to take over from him."

The man looked Sol coldly up and down. "Of course, it turns out I was wrong."

Sol was relieved at this last statement as it suggested some hope for him out here in the country.

"Now I've met you and your car, I think you are even *more* bloody stupid than I first imagined. I don't know what you were thinking coming up here. You 'aint from round here boy and I don't really see you fitting in."

Sol was hurt, but indignant.

"Well that's not quite the welcome I expected. I don't think you know who you are talking…"

The man was blunt, "Oh, I do know who I am talking to. City hotshot, well-moneyed, expect you can pay for everything? Am I close? But with no idea of how to live out here… …on his own."

Angered, Sol felt his cheeks redden and his confidence surge as he built up his defence ready to be voiced out loud. *No one* talked to him in this way.

He opened his mouth to speak, but once again was cut down by the man's interruption. "Oh, and I brought you a cake from the misses. She says we should have you up for dinner in a few days' time. She also warned me not to speak my mind and that I should definitely not say what I think about a city boy moving in to the house in the glen. Bit late for that… …sorry. Never been that good at doing as I was told. That'll be why I'm just a shepherd and not a city hotshot like you."

Disarmed, Sol stood dumb as the man handed over an orange plastic bag that had sat behind him on the track. It was welling over with food and jars, mostly looking homemade or rustically sourced. Such an offer of produce did not fit well with the unfriendliness of the man in front of him and Sol wondered at the contradiction.

"Thank you," Sol replied taking the heavy bag from him. Its stretched handles had whitened where they had started to reach their elastic limits.

The man smiled in a more gentle way, just for a moment, as if a mask had cracked to reveal the true face behind. Sol sensed care about something; the house, the land or even Sol. However, he was unsure and he was definitely not supposed to have noticed it.

"I say you won't survive or else you won't stay that long, especially when the winter comes. But she's the boss so you better had live or stay put. Otherwise we're both in trouble."

Sol was again stuck for words as a result of this verbal brutality and honesty. But there was a playful glint in the man's eyes that suggested communication of some message other than the words he spoke.

"So, I'll come and find if you're still with us a week on Tuesday about six?" He paused. "You do measure time the same way as we do when you're down south don't you?"

Sol caught the hint of a grin and saw that wicked eye-sparkle again. "Yes. Yes, we do," he answered, making a mixed judgement about the character in front of him and trying to read the nuance of his behaviour; closed gestures and yet open face, aggressive words coupled with a humoured gaze. He was not all he appeared to be. "Six o'clock, Tuesday. That would be good. I *will* try to stay and survive that long." And a smile passed his own lips.

"Don't mind if you don't really. I've laid a bet on you leaving within a day or dying within the year, and there'll be more food for me if you're gone."

The man grinned and Sol tried not to laugh, but instead mirrored the expression. He was not yet really sure he found anything the man said that funny. But he was aware that not all of it was the truth.

"Only open the jars if you think you'll live long enough to finish them. No need wasting stuff is there?"

Sol felt the growing urge to interrupt the man before he started to listen and take to heart what he had to say. "If you tell me where you live, I can come and find you. All I need is your postcode and the car will take me there."

The man looked at the white sports car stranded obliquely in the ditch.

"Safer if I come to you don't you think?" he suggested questioningly with a raised eyebrow.

Sol thought, then added, "yes, probably. Six then.... ....Tuesday." They both nodded and something crossed between them. Not just a smile, but an understanding that not everything said was meant.

"Well, I'll be off," said the man sternly and he turned to follow the route that the dog had taken up into the heather growing by the track and across the hillside.

"Okay, goodbye. And, thank you," called Sol holding on to the brimming plastic bag of groceries feeling somewhat abandoned in the conversation. He watched the man heading upwards and springing over rocks, pools and a burn that tumbled down and over moss-enriched mounds of glacial-flung boulder. He had more energy than his aged look had suggested he would have.

A grouse stumbled up out of the undergrowth and took noisily to the wing *'chuck-chuckling'* as it tried to fight gravity and nearly made it to the sky. Its wings whirred as it came to a noisy rest amongst blue-green blaeberry tufts that grew upwardly mobile along the edge of a plantation wood.

Sol was suddenly struck by a question he had failed to ask.

"Excuse me," he shouted in panic after the disappearing man.

The man twisted round and cupped a hand to his left ear. "What?" he demanded.

"I don't know your name!" he called. "What's your name?"

"Hamish will do," was the reply as the man turned to bounce off again.

"And?" Sol continued.

The man crooned around and cupped his ear a second time with a look of resignation on his face. "Yes?"

"I need your phone number!" and he shook his mobile in a gesture to Hamish.

"Why?" he enquired.

"In case I need to call you."

"Don't I need one those phones myself then?"

"What?"

"To be called on," and with that he turned, laughing, and streaked up the hillside sending plumes of insects up in clouds in his wake.

"I really am not from round here am I?" Sol muttered to himself as Hamish topped the nearest hill. "I really do hope they're not all like that."

He stood for minute, watching till Hamish had gone from view. If there was a house up there then it was well hidden amongst trees and cliff faces, or maybe it was higher up still somewhere beyond where the clouds allowed vision to go.

Sol returned to the car to pick up his holdall and looked through the plastic bag that Hamish had given to him a moment before. Inside was a large fruitcake, a rich looking grainy bread loaf, biscuits, marmalades and jams, and at the bottom a jar containing a large orange-dripping honeycomb. The bag was packed about with well-soiled potatoes, carrots and a huge round swede that Sol wasn't sure what he was supposed to do with. He knew it was edible, but how to render it palatable he was not yet aware.

With the thought of a good coffee now stowed away in his holdall and access to boiled water only a few miles away up the track he started to look forward to the journey back to the *Bothan*. The woods were less sinister than he remembered them the night before. The loch was growing ever bluer with an improvement in the weather and he was aware of the drifting motion of gulls who lazily meandered the skies. Bright sun-yellow daffodils looked alien against the jade backdrop of forest, but added welcome colours that seemed to draw in bees who danced in drunken dizziness into and out of their trumpet heads.

The handles of the plastic bag Hamish had given him slowly tightened into the creases of his fingers and the weight began to drag, but still he pressed on. There was something hypnotic about the natural noises he was becoming aware of and they drew his mind away from his aches to the point that he started to ignore the pain in his hand from the plastic and the twinge in his shoulder from his bag.

The whole walk back Sol was accompanied by the multi-layered sounds of water. It dripped from trees and tinkled in burns, it lapped at shorelines and rolled pebbles and stones along streambeds. He heard it dribble through sodden soils and gurgle up in springs, and yet still it had more life and sound in it than anything he could describe. It was as if water itself was alive and his spirit yearned for it, and so he stooped to drink from a bubbling river enjoying its freshness, coldness and peat taste.

Every few hundreds paces he would stop religiously and check his phone for a signal.

None.

Primroses clumped in patches of pale washed out buttery petals with large lush leaves, were now becoming squashed amongst the rising dog's mercury spears and foxglove tufts. Masses of dandelion shone as bright as lead paint, each of their heads an assemblage of poorly finished petals that ended in blunt ragged borders.

Where snowdrop flowers now faded to brown, shadows of their springtime glory, deep blue-purple one-sided fluoresces of bluebell floated in airy colour above the mats of grass and tall fluffy viridian and lime mosses. A fallen trunk had been overtaken by unfolding fern fronds and dripped with lichens that near touched the ground. They left caves of darkness where deep coloured cushions of plant life seemed to thrive and penny ferns threw out random arms of tiny florets.

White flowers had sprung out of the dark stems of blackthorn where a wren staccato-whirred and chipped, and a variety of warblers called in descending, ascending and diverse stanza, and a black cap uttered rapturous, guttural tunes.

The trackside was littered with boulders strewn aside through the ages to keep the way clear. As they had sunk into the mud and backfilled with mired silts their surfaces had become textured with overgrowth, their bases fringed with the rich purple of dog violets and the dainty wind-dangled flowers of the shamrock-leaved sorrels.

Sol felt as if he had never walked with his eyes open before even though little of what he saw could be given a name. He found that as he looked up from his mobile, that electronic intruder into his consciousness that constantly interrupted his line of thought and demanded his attention, he saw more. It was as if he had been blind and had suddenly been granted full sight if only partial knowledge.

He still checked it though, just in case he got a signal after all.

None.

From somewhere above the treeline he became aware of a gentle two-note call. It stood out as different to the brasher songs of the robin, the blackbird and the finches. Its subtly was a contrast to the cackle of the jay, the gambol of the corvid, the screech of the buzzard, and even the melody of abandonment that was emitted from the singing thrush. Yet, it still took him a while to gain full understanding of it.

It was a call from the past, one he had heard a long time ago.

It was a call that spoke the name of the bird itself.

It was a call which took him way back to a time walking with his grandfather, a man well connected with the natural and obsessed with all things living.

He heard it again and was certain, feeling a strange sense of exhilaration for one who had spent so long in the city ignoring his rural roots.

It *was* real and he felt its meaning deep down inside.

It is strange that someone so disengaged from nature can re-enter its presence so quickly on hearing a familiar song, catching a special scent or by experiencing the taste of something fresh. But it happens, and our senses can sometimes return us to places that we have long forgotten or hidden deep down in our organic memory banks.

Sol was taken there, to a wood in the south flickering in sunshine descending in dappled rays through the ecclesiastical roof of a leaf-filled forest. His small hand was held firmly in the grip of an older, wiser and larger one and together they walked to a place on the edge of the elder wood to where new trees sprouted and the view opened up to encompass the valley.

Then they heard that onomatopoeic call, soft as a flute yet travelling the distance to greet them who stood on the thicket's edge. Two simple syllables noted by poets, composers, authors and laymen.

Cuck-oo.

Sol was back to this moment in the present as the bird called and called again, and his heart raced.

Automatically he reached to a hawthorn bud, as he would have done with his grandfather, and picked out the new brown-green and scarlet leaflets that sprouted at the apex.

Cuck-oo.

"Nature's salad," he said to himself, as *they* would have done all those years ago, and he put the leaves into his mouth for the tasting and the chewing, relishing an old familiar taste.

Cuck-oo.

The leaves were bitter and tannic, but refreshing and nutritious, and as he walked, revelling in the present sound of a memory bird and with the feeling of a fond recollection on his tongue, he chewed and considered. Despite all odds being against him he *was* lucky to have that memory, something denied to so many others.

Cuck-oo.

Sol thought of his momentary meeting with the disconcerting Hamish and his bet set against him, real or unreal, and there and then he made up his mind. He would prove the old man wrong, as after all he was Sol and had shown plenty of people the error of their ways when they judged him incapable.

Cuck-oo.

Hamish had as good as lost his bet.

Sol checked his data-less phone and then set off in a determined manner back towards the cottage.

It didn't take long to return to *Bothan Faobhar*. It stood solid by the beach, a bright white edifice against the wood and the cliff behind.

Hamish was right in that the chimney was producing a lot of smoke. But Sol hoped that Hamish was also wrong and that he, Sol, would survive the next couple of days, be able to sit it out at the house, or at the very least stay until after Tuesday at six.

Out of desperation more than hope, Sol checked his phone one last time.

No signal.

As he passed through the hole in the garden wall he switched it off to save battery and decided that, as it was already mid-afternoon and he wanted to continue exploring the house for the rest of the day, he would go in search of a signal early on the next morning. He would make a walk of it, find a signal and start the long drawn out process of re-shaping the *Bothan* to create a home.

For the first time in a long while Sol had intentionally switched the machine off. It had felt a bit of a relief not receiving texts all of the time and feeling compelled to read them, reply to them and the rest. He dropped the phone into his side pocket and looked up as he approached the porch door.

On the step was a vase of surprisingly bright flowers, a large pitcher of milk and a handwritten envelope. As far as he could see, the only way in to the property and out was along the track he had just walked. Except for the sea loch there was nowhere else someone could have come from.

He fumbled with the thick-papered envelope, which was carefully addressed to him at *Bothan Faobhar,* and he removed the card inside.

It was hand-painted in water colour and showed a view across a loch which he presumed was the same as the one his new property stood by now; he could see the cliff edge behind his house that stretched out into the water. But it was pictured from a different, more distant view. In front was the impression of the little *Bothan,* but so far away that only some detail was given. The water was still, but the sky was angry, and a few wooden boats were anchored in the water with bright orange buoys to keep them company. A black-headed goose made the scene, stood on the shore amongst weed and pebbles.

Sol enjoyed good art and immediately looked to the bottom right to see who the artist was. The single letter 'S' was painted in black.

He opened the stiff folded card carefully and read the spidery blue-inked writing inside.

'Dear Sol,

Welcome to the district.

We do hope that you are enjoying the Bothan and wish you every success in her. If you need anything please do not hesitate to ask for it.

Come over some time, best usually at about 4pm, and we will have you for supper. Take note of the tides as they can be a bit of a hazard.

We are easy to find. Head out straight over the loch and we are located E-N-E. White house. Only house. The bàta-ràmh, Sireadh-thall (which means Seek Beyond) will know the way if you let her show you.

Looking forward to seeing you soon.

Yours,

Iona and Skye

PS. We do hope that we meet you before Hamish does. If not, please forgive him. He doesn't mean half of what he says and he is the person most likely to help any of us in a time of need. And, if you have met him already and he discussed his bet then please be reassured we bet the opposite to him. If G chose you then we know you're the right man for the Bothan, whatever Hamish thinks. He will just need time to get to know you.'

The 'S' of Skye was the same floral letter as the signature on the front of the card.

Sol stepped inside and dumped his bags with relief in the corridor, digging out his precious bag of coffee beans as he walked through to the living room. He stood the card in the middle of the wooden table on one of the mats and placed the flowers next to it. They gave an artistic splash of colour to an otherwise drab slab and the message, the flowers, the milk and the card gladdened him, making the room immediately more homely.

Grabbing the pitcher of creamy white from the porch step he took it carefully through to the kitchen as quickly as he could for fear of it turning to yoghurt or curdling in the growing heat outside. He had no idea how fast milk spoiled as he only ever bought it in half or full litres and only then in plastic bottles which stated a use by date on the side. A pitcher full was a completely new thing for him and he found himself worrying whether it was red, green or blue top milk before he caught himself mid thought and simply told himself to be more thankful that he had any milk at all. *What did the bottle top's colour really matter?*

The container was made of dented aluminium and had oxidised at pressure points where years of use had helped speed up its steady corrosive return back to bauxite.

Sol struggled through the kitchen door and lifted the dead weight of the can up on to the tablecloth at which point he noticed the two feathered forms of a brace of pheasant lying in front of him.

For someone used to getting meat from the supermarket, plucked, bright pink and cellophane wrapped, the sight of two bodies lying dead, fully feathered and quite possibly still warm was more than Sol could cope with and he near dropped the milk which sloshed dangerously. He sat down stunned on a chair he scraped away from the fireplace, before swearing uproariously as he looked at the two dead birds laid out before him.

There was a scribbled note left with them which he gingerly retrieved, unfolded and read.

'Dear Sol,

Sorry I missed you. Just wanted to say hello before Hamish did. If you have seen him already I want you to know that I voted against him. You will warm to him.

Hope you like the birds. They have been hung well already so just need plucking and then they should cook well. I have more rabbits if you want any.

Have stoked fire and put more wood on as it was going out. Help keep you toasty.

Gerry'

It certainly seemed that Hamish had a reputation; one that Sol could thoroughly understand.

'More rabbits?' Sol thought about that word *'more'* and then looked worriedly at the birds. Naturalist he wasn't but these certainly weren't rabbits.

The cock was glossy feathered with bold markings, a green blue iridescent head bedecked with a white necktie ring and a bald red wattle that encircled each eye and the nostrils on either side of a slightly hooked beak. He wore an eared cap and his chest was covered in red-brown and golden feathers that were creatively specked with black and white paintbrush strokes and dabbed marks. Long streamers of tail feathers extended from behind and his clawed feet looked well enough equipped for fighting with their talon'd toes and spurs.

The female, although drabber, was large and plump, coloured richly in grey-brown and dappled with spots as tawny in camouflaged finish as a brown owl.

Thankfully their eyes, encircled by naked skin, were closed, that thin cover of pinked-yellow eyelid protecting the citified Sol from the death stare of these once living creatures.

Sol was both fascinated and appalled.
He turned away.

In a life like Sol's coffee solved much. Coffee was drunk before meetings, during meetings and after them too. It was drunk socially and through necessity in the mornings or when he was hoping to stay up late. It was a drink that was needed both for pleasure and to satisfy cravings and an addiction that spanned even beyond his growing desire for tobacco.

He split open the bag to enjoy that bitter baked aroma that only intensified with it being stored in an airtight environment. Small-scale farmers, who by being paid a reasonable enough wage had allowed the company to have an official stamp of fair trade to be added to their slogan, grew it especially for him. He '*knew*' this as a fact as the packet informed him. The marketing promised that the beans had been picked and dried and then roasted all within a few miles of their field of growth. It did not mention the air miles accrued since as it was transported by plane from source to depot to packaging and then on to two other countries before it arrived in England. From here it was shipped to the warehouse before the supermarket from which Sol had purchased it just prior to his journey up to the north of Scotland. These beans were better travelled than he was.

Grinder?

In an instant, Sol's caffeine-expectant karma was shattered. In a house with no electricity where was the grinder? He had no idea if there was a grinder let alone what a manual one would look like if it existed.

The inventive Sol eventually turned to brute force and used a wooden rolling pin and an especially strong looking bowl to pestle the beans into a shattered mess of moist powder, fragments and sharp-faced lumps of coffee. Next, sweating over the stove, he boiled water on the hob using a large metal kettle that whistled when it was ready. The good feeling returned and all seemed well so long as he avoided eye contact with the pheasants and bustled around the kitchen with only an occasional guilty backward glance at them.

Cafetiere?

The karma escaped and was lost again, evaporating.

Thinking, Sol decided to wrap the bean mash up into a clean cloth he found under the sink and then he left it steeping in the already brown boiled water in a large earthenware jug. He frowned as he watched lumps falling out of the cloth and lint collecting on the surface.

Still, it smelt good.

He gave it two minutes, guessing the time rather than measuring it as he lacked a watch and the mobile was switched off. As the water was coffee brown to start with, he had no indication using colour when it would be ready.

Locating a mug from the cupboard he tried pouring the brew, watching lumps of bean falling out over the lip of the jug no matter how hard he tried to avoid it. Even sieving it through a second cloth didn't really help and so he resolved to filter it through his teeth instead, spitting out lumps, grouts and cloth threads whenever they built up.

For all its texture it didn't taste so very bad and he slurped it noisily and started to consider how to broach cooking his meal. Coffee was something that he had grown to take for granted and for the first time in many years he suddenly appreciated the materials from which it was made and even those who worked so hard all day long to produce it in the bistros he often frequented.

It was not quite *Americano* and so he called it *Bothanicano* just to amuse himself. He would need to work on the technique by which this original concoction was brewed but it was warm, wet and contained enough caffeine to make him expectantly happy again.

He munched through some of the bread given to him by Hamish and enjoyed the moist granary taste of seeds and dried fruit that had been uniformly mixed into its thick-floured dough. It was a good loaf and he quickly finished more than half of it before he started to consider what would happen when the produce he still had ran out or went off. He would have to start rationing what he used until he could get a supermarket to deliver, or get transport to the local shop, and both of these options had to wait until he had phone reception.

Mug, plate and knife discarded amongst a growing pile of crockery that had not yet washed itself, Sol approached the two carcases sprawled lifelessly on the table top. They looked for all intents as if they were still resting, be it eternally, and about to spring back to animated life.

"Thanks, Gerry," he muttered as he prodded the male bird. "Whoever you are?"

He wondered if Gerry was the mysterious 'G' who had last owned the property and maybe couldn't quite leave the place. He worried that they might have returned for the clothing he had borrowed, finding them missing.

He then put his mind to rights remembering that *Bothan Faobhar* was rightly his. He had bought it, he owned it and everything in it was now *officially* his, and he could take, lose or use them as he desired.

Sol looked back at the birds on the table. He had never seen a chicken with this amount of feathering and had to hope that they were similar in all respects bar their current presentation. He decided that food was food and it was probably good for him to consider where his fare was sourced from. In this case, this was no doubt from the hill behind his house.

But what should he do? He couldn't leave the birds there on the table to fester, but he also did not want to process them and cook them for himself. They looked too much like the animals they had once been, despite being devoid of life now.

Skirting them, he checked the nearest cupboards for anything else substantial enough to act as dinner.

There was nothing and his heart sank.

No, this would never do. He had to face up to life here at some point and someone, Gerry, had offered him these two birds as a gift. And so he wheeled around on the table, pushed back his internal revulsion, neatly tucking it away in his subconscious, and addressed the two avian corpses, labelling them '*dinner*'.

Sol experimentally pulled on the edge of one long primary feather of the cock bird. Using little force he extended the wing into a magnificent spreading arc of radially perfect others, lined underneath by belly fluff and white down. He tugged and the pinion feather fell free, all too easily. He picked at another and then a third, quickly removing these long red-brown quills until he had a pile beside him. The second wing and tail were quickly denuded of their longer feathers and so Sol continued with his work and started toiling along the back, rapidly realising that the smaller the feathers then the further they went and the more there seemed to be.

How many feathers could one bird hold? He was fascinated for a while in that open-minded child-like manner that any scientist must adopt if they are to investigate and discover, and for a moment he forgot what he was doing.

The bird's sleep-eyed head lolled back and forth and he tried to push it away from vision as he laboured his way through thick down and quilled feathers to reveal goose bumps of flesh on a bird's body that was far smaller than its living shape would have suggested. The skin was yellow with the smell of fowl, and where he caught the skin he could see rich redness of the meat below. This wasn't so bad, but the mass of feathers produced was, and so after washing his hands well he moved a kitchen chair, solid and heavy, out into the afternoon's sunshine by the cottage side, towards the back of the house, and plucked the bird there.

Feathers flew up and away in the light breeze that was powered upwards by thermals climbing the cliff edge beyond the wood. Sol was fascinated to watch their fluid movements as they were caught, whipped up and then allowed to spiral and frenzy along with the otherwise invisible current of the air. He found himself absorbed in trying to remove every last trace of feather in an over-zealous and focused study of the bird's plucked skin, until he had forcibly undressed the creature except for the plume garters he left around the tops of the legs and the blue-feathered head that extended from the neck upwards.

He returned to the kitchen for a sharp knife that brought him to his civilised senses. He knew he was about to cross a line, one which he expected someone else, the unseen butcher, to do for him. This was one of those moments usually arranged behind closed doors, the meeting of a knife with an animal still recognisable as once living and not yet ready for the salver or the plate. He paused in thought, then wielding the flashing blade like an executioner, he decapitated the bird low enough down the neck to make the body look more like a store-bought chicken and then removed its legs.

It was easier than he thought.

Having passed this threshold he used the knife to gut the creature thoroughly and placed the feather-stuck scraps in a metal tub he found in the yard that flies were surprisingly quick to discover.

He looked at the bird, now mounted in a pose as near to what he expected to find in a shop as he could make it. It was presented on a large blood-smeared plate that he held like a trophy's plinth, the pheasant in all its now *'ready-to-cook'* glory.

The bird was relatively scrawny, but together with the vegetables he had been given, it would be enough to feed him and he felt a primal sense of achievement that he had done something that he never thought someone like him could. He had prepared food from animal to oven without relying on someone else to do the worst bits for him.

'It had been dead,' he chuntered to himself trying to console the torrid mix of emotions inside his mind. *'It was going to be eaten anyway'.*

He scrubbed and re-scrubbed his hands to remove the blood and feathers that had welded themselves sticky-dry to his skin, especially in the cracks along his fingers' sides.

'I didn't kill it.'

He scrubbed and scrubbed.

'It was bred to die.'

Then he half-thought what seemed at that moment quite a reasonable question. *'Where do pheasants come from?'*

Somewhere in a recess of his mind he knew they weren't native to Britain. But other than having them for dinner he had no inkling about their origins and felt suddenly convinced that one of the books on the *Bothan's* shelves would tell him more.

After he had rinsed the carcass clean, he went to the front room to research information about this common and overlooked beast and found a large leather-bound tome on birds that outlined the British history of this most oriental of creatures. A bird sold to Anglo-Romans by Phoenician traders, this Asian indigenous had travelled a long way to join him at the table. There was more to this every day bird than there first appeared to be. True it seemed plump enough to be shot easily, colourful enough to be seen from a distance, loud enough to be heard wherever it bred and even stupid enough to try and run down a car or towards the guns. But in terms of numbers and global spread it was a huge success.

Sol placed the bird on a black-encrusted cooking tray he found in a cupboard full of tins, tools and candles. Then, guessing which shelf of the oven was about the right temperature and after basting the bird with butter from Hamish's bag, he slid it carefully in with a strange reverence. Like some ritualistic offering, he had laid it on a bed of varied chopped vegetables so that it now seemed to float over a pool of *Bothan*-brown tap water. He secured the door to the hot oven and offered a prayer to the god of cooking that he wouldn't die from raw meat poisoning or cremate this offering in the fire.

The female bird was safely hung from an S-shaped hook from the ceiling of the larder to keep it clear of the vermin where Sol found a rabbit already strung up there by Gerry. He thought back to Gerry's scribbled letter. There were *more* rabbits to look forward to.

He then passed through into the front room and shuffled the papers on the writing desk. Fascinated, he picked up the handwritten notes left by G and returned to the garden to sit amongst the blowing cock pheasant feathers that ambled round the yard and enjoy the steadily slipping rays of the sun. They slowly fell from grace in a now fully cleared sky, wind-blown free of cloud and mist.

Song birds dropped on feathered down as it blew to the edge of the wood and they carried it off in soft-filled bills to line their nests. A chiffchaff echoed its name from somewhere in the canopy in competition with other warblers and the incessant *'sweech-her, sweech-her'* of a great tit.

Sol sat to read the yellowed paper book. It was bound in A4 using a gummed thread that hardened to form a spine. It was a diary of continuous prose and lists. Some names Sol recognised, such as greenfinch and goldfinch, but others seemed too mystical for reality such as drinker and sundew. Dated seasons were acknowledged and weather reported together with outlandish types, their plantings, their behaviours and their presence. It was the only nature diary Sol had ever spent time with but even he could appreciate the hours and efforts that had been invested into their careful writing and illustration; sometimes just pen and ink, other times paint-coloured and tinted.

They were better produced than the rough notes he had found on the chair in the shed, and they were more thorough, revealing something of the character of the person that was 'G'. Meticulous and comprehensive, scientific names were underlined and the writing elegant and of an old-style. They brought with them a sense of worth, as if they were in some way precious to the writer even though they were never really intended for any reader and Sol appreciated that he was blessed to be able to look at them, handle them and read them.

His financial mind wondered at their commercial value at a sale.

He turned to the last written entry and was surprised to see that it finished only two weeks before he had arrived; exactly when he had first enquired about the *Bothan*.

'Geese have mostly left but Brants (Branta bernicla) may stay to breed. Greylag (Anser anser) 250+, but no pink feet left.

Buck roe (Capreolus capreolus) and two does on beach, male otter (Lutra lutra) seen on shoreline trying to hunt waders. Oystercatchers (Haematopus ostralegus) have lain and both redshank (Tringa totanus) and greenshank (Tringa nebularia) displaying.

Insects slow to emerge but fish jumping this morning.

Stag red (Cervus elaphus) on cliff top.'

The last line was less carefully written than the rest as if it had been rushed.

'Sol to carry on and look after the Bothan - she chooses well.

G'

He carefully put the book down and closed his eyes for a few minutes. *He* chose *it* of course, not the other way around. *How could a house choose its owner?* There was no way that he could have been influenced by the place and certainly not all the way down in London.

Then he looked beyond the top edge of the diary and saw that he wore a borrowed pair of boots, borrowed socks, had left a borrowed jacket, scarf, gloves and hat scattered around the yard about him and was reading borrowed notes from a borrowed chair. Smoke slowly rose from the chimney, agitated every so often by the breeze, and the cottage looked more or less exactly how it had done all those years ago when it had stood as model for the painting above the bed.

Sol had had little influence over it yet. But the time would come when he did.

He closed his eyes again and enjoyed the sun and the sounds of the wild, the wind that freshened his brow and the taste of the sea in the air that mixed with the smell of steadily roasting pheasant and wood smoke from the chimney.

There was no doubt that the Bothan was having an effect on him, wending the natural magic of relaxation into his conscious mind. This was just what the therapist had said he needed.

He didn't mean to sleep for long, but fatigue and worry, anger and tension all take their toll, and when blended with air from the sea and scents from the landscape you can be knocked backwards into restfulness. Somehow he had kicked off his boots and had his feet now de-socked and planted firmly to the ground, with that sensation of earthing himself to the planet that only the few who walk sockless and shoeless understand. He could feel the cold beneath his feet and knew that he was making a deep connection with the very source of the land below him, his toes tingling.

This was no comforting deep pile of plasticised carpet that insulated him from being at one with the world. This *was* the world and his toes were aware of it, its course touch and roughness, its heat and its humidity. Every bump and fissure could be explored by his under-foot's sensitivity.

Sol slowly opened his eyes on the last of the sun's strength where it was beginning to wane ready for its descent into evening. The temperature started to drop and the sea loch took on a darker more menacing blue with white horses that broke out on the main waters where the currents confused the ebb and flow, and rocks demanded its attention.

The near-bare branches of sycamore and ash rocked gently and a cautious wind explored the forest with the rush of a gentle river. Unseen birds called and Sol was once again struck by the symphony of the wild world and its inherent complexity and richness.

He almost moved.

It was what his pre-stretched body demanded as he consciously rose from his brief slumber. He also needed to do it to check on the state of his roasting pheasant dinner. But something held him back. Another force and will, one that wasn't his own, kept his body static, and, strange though it may be, his mind at bay, and he felt aware of a presence.

Sol considered himself sane of mind and a man whose thoughts were planted solidly in reality. He wasn't the type to think of ghosts and spirits, but dealt in facts and money and the global power of the Internet. But for the briefest of moments he felt watched, as if some creature was observing him from the shade of the woods that surrounded his little white cottage.

For whatever reason he knew he was not alone and wondered if the previous possessor had come back to reclaim his own.

Was this the ghost of the mysterious G?

Unmoving, Sol gazed intently ahead through slit eyes aware that any body twitch now might scare away the observer or else bring him out of this watchful dreamscape, where he, Sol, was being haunted by some former occupant of the property.

He saw nothing but felt something.

He tracked around the yard. Feathers lay in abandon or launched themselves into the sky on brief explorations of the air's tides. Branches swayed against the toughness of rock buildings, stonewalls and the edifice of *Bothan Faobhar*.

Still there was nothing, and yet something that pricked his sense and agitated his soul was out there.

Spine a tingle and hairs erect he felt the thrill of the ghost story, the possibility of being the hunted, and he was primed to fight or flee. His world slowed down and his alertness engaged to a level of focus he had rarely experienced, and he watched, and he listened and he waited.

A patch of blackness within the tessellating patterns of moving branches and grass stood still. It was indiscernible in shape as it stalked low with straight back, first fast forward and then down. Now he could see that there was a head at one end and it gave Sol all the impression that he was watching a lion in savannah grasses trailing its prey. It had no colour and no real form until the light from above struck its side and he clearly saw diffuse dark stripes that descended its flanks in grey camouflaged streaks.

It moved quickly yet cautiously to the straight edge of the rear buildings and slunk low, walling its way towards the exposure of the back yard cobbles where weeds forced their way between the round-headed stones.

Scale became more apparent as the shape stole closer and two yellow-green cat eyes were illuminated in the darkness, caught by sunrays that enlightened a well-marked tabby face with a black paint-brushed letter 'M' over its eyes. Its pink-tipped nose searched the air and belly to the earth it crawled on, with obvious alertness to its exposure, out into the light with its ears up attentive.

Sol had seen cats before, but knew this one was feral.

It was larger than he had met previously and was cloaked in a body of thick fur that ended in a short bushy black-tipped tail that seemed to finish early in a blunt brush. Concentric circles of black formed perfect hoop rings from end to rump and a further black strip ran lengthways along its spine to the beginning of the tail, dorsally encompassing its body's back. He could make out auburn in its tabby all-brown colouration and its under-flanks were lined with bright chocolate that ran up to become diffuse khaki brown under its chin and around its muzzle.

This was a muscular animal, heavy-framed, firm-bodied and thick set, cloaked in a bushed up depth of fur.

It turned to observe the 'sleeping' Sol and sniffed briefly to test his airs. White whiskers emphasised its nasal movements.

Even Sol's poor connection to nature allowed him to understand that this 'cat' was timid and conscious of its position out in the open as it shimmied towards him and stalked his location wary and alert. It was constantly checking and re-checking for signs of danger or threats from above. Then, half way across the yard, it pulled up and started to pad with greater confidence in Sol's direction, every inch of its oversized non-moggy exterior sending out the signals of an African big cat.

It was nothing like the slight animals he had experienced back in the city, the vermin hunters. Wilder, bigger and more of a presence it restarted its walk towards him.

This felt more of a tiger and not just a cat.

It stopped short of him and then quickly, after looking all around, pushed its head down into the metal tub full of feathers and entrails he had left after dressing the pheasant. Cock bird head drooping in mouth, it checked for danger again and then left the scene of its theft in a light-footed, bounding leap which took it silently into the shadows of the wood, under the cover of the brush, and out of Sol's sight.

It was as if a ghost had been and gone, a burglar that of all things had taken Sol's waste, and it made him quite glad although it left nothing but a few spots of blood and a light, large pad mark on the ground.

He smiled.

He had a cat for a companion after all and so all he needed to do now was to tame it and he would have a pet. Maybe life was not going to be that lonely out here at the *Bothan* after all.

Clearing up the yard, Sol returned to the kitchen to rescue the remains of his dinner, which, not burnt, tasted surprisingly better and more gamey than its slightly toasted exterior suggested it would do.

Life today was good.

Chapter 4: Rain, Showers and Connection

(Five Variants of "Dives and Lazarus", Ralph Vaughan Williams)

Sol became aware that the day's light was fading fast and the earth's temperature falling as a clear sky allowed it to dissipate heat away into space's welcoming vacuum. An early rising moon half-smiled its constantly joyous expression from an acute angle over the cliff top behind and the shadows lengthened visibly as time passed.

Ensuring he had everything ready for the evening's house lighting, Sol had that feeling of grubbiness that follows several days of not washing properly. It had been nearly forty-eight hours since his last shower and shave, and his usual hygiene-obsessed mentality re-surfaced from its few days of slumber and was beginning to clock the minutes since his last warm and soapy soaking or dousing.

He lit the fire in the living room, which rapidly took, its tongue-like flames instantly licking up the chimney in sky chasing daggers that flicked around the charcoal-dusted back boiler's iron. However, he knew that hot water would take time to produce. Instead he heated the largest pan he could find, filled to brimming on the constantly glowing stove, whilst he harvested the items that he needed to get washed.

Gathering shower gel and a towel he headed across the yard, drained of colour in the approaching dusk light, to the washroom shed. After quickly cleansing the bath as best he could, he placed the black rubber plug into its complementary-fitting hole and started to fill the bath's basin with cold water that fell without sympathy from the header above. An iced brown tea of water spilled in waterfall cascades from the old tin head and crashed, splashing, into the marked, stained bath, where historically once had all been white. When satisfied that it would get no warmer and the white porcelain was as bright a colour as it could be returned to,

Sol drained the basin and then allowed a few centimetres to work its murky way up the bath's side. Then shutting off the supply from above he returned to the humid kitchen where water now boiled avidly on the stovetop, bubbling and steaming like a Shakespearian witch's cauldron.

He stripped down to his underwear, still conscious of the sightlines of potential neighbours, even though he now knew full well there weren't any. He was desperately attentive to his townie recollections of the need for privacy and, when confident that no one was watching, he left a pile of reeking clothes in the hallway. How he was going to wash those was anyone's guess at present but for now he was more concerned at cleaning himself and removing two days' grime from his clammy flesh.

Danger and hazard aside, he carried the blistering pan full of off-boiled water, using a cloth over the handles and a loosely fitted lid in an attempt to avoid scolds. Water spilled, Sol simmered and his language became more decorative as he struggled under the load. Eventually, straining and with red legs where the water had burnt, he made it to the shed and poured the liquid into the bath, hoping for a reasonable temperature.

He stood there in contemplation in all but his underwear and decided that it was best to get straight on with the job rather than delay. Stripped, he tested the bath with a toe and then took the plunge easing down into the shallow but comfortable covering at the bottom of the bath.

It did not take him long to realise that the volume of water was not sufficient to either wash any soap off nor to keep him warm between his rigorous sloshings. He finally came to the conclusion that he would have to resort to either using the shower or running down to the loch where the fat-insulated geese happily bathed, both of which were probably similarly cold in temperature. This time the shower won and facing the fear of a rural ice bucket challenge he stood, rested on the tap and lined himself up for the onslaught. Turning the tap handle, the water fell and his senses immediately awoke, even though he expected it, and with a sudden in-gasp of air he clutched the hard, unsympathetic stones lining the wall of the room and almost cried out in pain.

He washed the suds of soap away as rapidly as he could, shut the water off and shivered within his own blue-tinged structure. Pinpricked skin took on the same texture as the plucked pheasant before its cooking and he struggled to regain steady breathing as he gripped the side of the bath. He watched the oily soap bubbles crowd the plughole in fight for their exit to the gurgling pipes that shook and air-choked below.

Refreshed as he was, as he passed back over the yard to the rear of the house, he had not yet come to appreciate the pleasures of cold showers, *l'eau naturelle*. Even the cooling breeze of evening felt glowing hot to his pimpled skin, and his toga'd towel gave little protection. Once back inside, he sat close by to the front room fire and felt for the radiation of its heat before finding the insulation of covering. Later he searched for suitable clothing in his bag and also found a thick-knitted, cream-coloured, woollen Arran sweater in one of the bedroom drawers that 'G' must have left, possibly with the intention of Sol coming to use it. There were heavy trousers and socks neatly folded in the drawers along with a number of cotton shirts with light checked patterns. Each garment seemed eminently more sensible than any of the few more fashionable clothes that Sol had thought to pack, and with some embarrassment he borrowed yet more from the previous occupant of the *Bothan*.

He bundled his dirty clothes of the last two days into the large porcelain sink in the porch and after locating washing powder, on a shelf underneath, he scrubbed them clean in steaming water now warmed from the fireplace. These were dutifully hung to dry on a line stretched taught across the yard with algae-greased wooden pegs from an *Aspergillus*-black peg bag, originally made of a tartan weave, which hung in a valley fold it had created in the string.

The clothes flicked in the congregation of several winds that came to meet in the back yard, filling his shirt so that it billowed like a ship's sail and flicked and whipped in its turning wake. Clouds rolled up on to the horizon turning the loch a different mood, to one of depth and chopped up anger, fresh with the potential for racing in a boat and drowning in an eddy. Sol was glad of the jumper and felt reassured by its deep interwoven texture and the smell of fresh sheep it emitted as it warmed in his body's heat. He couldn't see it catching on in London as a fashion statement, but it was practical and suited the elements.

Sol also found himself cleaning the pots he had started to accumulate. He had had to remove them from the sink to wash his clothes and for the first time in a long while he realised that he didn't have someone else there to launder dirty clothes or clean up the crockery for him. He would simply have to do them himself and so he busied himself in the bubble-complete newly heated water watching the evening descend on the *Bothan* and seeing the birdlife prepare itself for the evening's rest; the bubbles of course being the result of detergent he found left ready for him to use.

This would of course never do and to his mental list of items requiring attention he added dishwasher and washing machine, before underlining the need for a cleaner again and again in his mind's eye record.

With one room left unexplored, Sol threw more wood into the fire, watching the sparks sent heavenwards, and with paraffin lamp lit, in the dying light of the day's remains he entered the final room to see just what lay in there.

It was a chamber into which a bed had been forced, but it was mostly hemmed in by a series of well-polished cabinets about the height of his chest, with drawers in them so thin that Sol wondered what they were for. Each was fronted with a single fragile glass-paned door framed in varnished wood to match that of the cabinet. Handwritten labels were slipped into brass plaques on each shelf.

Curious, Sol opened one of the cabinets up using the small brass key left secured in its complementary lock, turning it with a satisfying crunch and then pulling the brittle-feeling door wide. It emitted a creak that would have graced any scary film to add a spine-lurching effect. He withdrew a close-fitted drawer to reveal a uniformly arranged neatly labelled array of insects pinned out in lines of obvious evolutionary assemblages. Hand-written pen-inked labels, each of exactly the same size and shape, each in the very same hand, each dated and each with the same location of *Bothan Faobhar* announced with exactness the name of the given specimen.

Sol bent low in macabre fascination and scanned across this immobile mass of entomology, placing the lamp securely on the cabinet top so that as his arm moved upwards the cast shadows of the insects moved from oblique giants to acute imitations. He looked into the bi-symmetrical diamond-reflecting compound eyes of a thousand faces all lifeless but telling a story of what lived here at the *Bothan* and when, each in their season, their gender and their niche. Each concave eye, cupping the face, made up of hundreds of interlocking crystalline tessellations that reflected the light to give blues, greens and at times pink polish that danced as the paraffin lamp flared and dulled. It was a highly ordered, scientific and systematic entomological graveyard.

A handwritten book on top of the cabinet listed everything in it, a page for each immaculately turned out drawer.

Here were mayflies caught up by the brook that ran torrentially from the mountain down to the estuary and which opened out into the loch back and beyond the yard. Dragons and damsels were taken at bogs, mires, marshes, 'the pool' and the river. Butterflies and moths dominated drawers of a cabinet of their own, but nothing exceeded the diversity of beetles. Here metallic and brightly coloured jewels rubbed shoulders with the dull or the blue-varnished, and the tiny with the large, the long-nosed and the horned, the round and straight, the gangly-legged and the short.

Stripes, spots and blotches, it seemed as if some divine creator had an especial interest in making this group as diverse as possible not being satisfied with the few simpler forms of others.

Still there were also gaps in the collection, holes presumably left for things not found, and Sol saw something of the obsessive collector in 'G' and understood a frustration at not finding what he had thought present. *Had he left those gaps for species expected, creatures that should have been there, or were they just hopeful spaces?*

Flies seemed prolific too; spanning the range from specks of an insect glued to a card mount right up to the large buzzer horseflies labelled *Tobanu bromius*, both male and female. Sol was equally surprised at the array of what was called bee and wasp.

He closed the last drawer unsure whether to be fascinated or appalled.

Partly he saw a garish display of past life, prematurely ended to add to a fanatic's exhibition of ordered departed nature. It appeared to serve no purpose, being privately hived away here in the secret room of the *Bothan*, miles from anywhere from which science could gain access to its knowledge and content. Artistic it may have been, showing a fluidly coloured account of the natural world as it was at that point of each of the carefully labelled historical moments, but macabre it was too. And, Sol could not help wondering if it was entirely necessary in a time of the camera and the images brought to almost every home by the Internet. That was *except for Bothan Faobhar, which seemed not even to have advanced to electricity yet.*

'Give it time,' he thought. *'Give it time.'*

Then, he also acknowledged that here was a historical record of the insectan life located within the *Bothan's* biome. It was something he could never have appreciated before, it only being just tangible to his poorly versed sense of ecology, and suddenly he had a physical, quantifiable measure of the biodiversity of life here in scanning these pinned out bodies. This was an educational tool, even though intended as a purely private collection, and it could inform, teach and extend, and adding to it would simply be enhancing a huge body of knowledge about life in this very small area.

He remembered once being told that you could only learn a lot about very little. Here, if anywhere, was a lot about *the* very little.

A cabinet further on was a herbarium of carefully flattened and dried, colour-faded flowers and pale green leaves tenderly pressed between layers of desiccated paper. Beautiful ink-drawn illustrations accompanied several specimens, some tinted in vibrant watercolour, and once Sol got himself past the thought that they might be worth money, he realised they too were a collection of value for different reasons; they were beautiful in their scientific accuracy.

Shelves within the walk-in cupboard in this cornucopian-room of past life were stacked with liquid filled jars, assorted nets and devices. All was permeated fully with the scent of naphthalene and that constant mulling of something akin to tobacco that Sol had already taken on as his own. It had started to take residence of his clothing on his arrival and had etched its way into his skin, the way that a smell of dampened tent cloth embeds itself into the after-scent of every camper over his or her first night out under canvass. His nose had lost sensitivity to it and he was now aroma-blind to its presence.

A light tapping on the angled roof light above indicated that the oncoming night brought with it rain. But Sol was otherwise preoccupied with his pathological search through the last few shelves in the little central room. Bound volumes of loose-leaf paper contained previous incarnations of the diaries he had found earlier in the front room. It appeared that he had unearthed a continuous chronological history of the *Bothan* since a year that quickly followed the end of the war with it beginning with the first entry G had made in that characteristically elegant handwritten black-inked font.

'She may be basic and lack the facilities I have become accustomed too, but I am glad that I have decided to leave the big house to the others to keep, and to now start my refuge here in Bothan Faobhar. She has missed having people in her for a long time, but I am pleased that the family kept her standing all this while.

I know that she has always chosen her previous occupiers well and I have been blessed already today by a visit from the cat that haunts the wood, which is a good omen. She was a like a woodland spirit the way she appeared. There are so few of them left now that to see one here on my first day bodes well for the rest of my stay.

If I die, this diary is my gift to the Bothan's next choice of owner. If I leave, likewise.'

And it was signed off at the bottom with that now familiar flourish, *'G'*, and dated, *'Bothan Faobhar, April 22nd 1946'*.

Below this was the first biological entry in the journal. It was of a mammal and read.

'22nd April 1946   Arrived later than intended last night. Luckily my hand brought candles with him before he left back to the big house. Sat in yard during brief spell of sunshine and fell asleep. Woke to female wildcat (Felis silvestris) walking from woodland behind and through yard.'

Below this was a list of birds also seen during that first afternoon's vigil, and Sol liked to think that they had both sat in the same chair in the same spot and seen the same cat. Sensibility meant that he knew that this was actually a different animal sixty years on, but sentimentality gave him a shiver down his spine that he too had been greeted to the site by the spiritual element of the wildcat. He also knew that he had happened upon the first in a continuous record of organic events that had taken place at the *Bothan* and then stepped back to take in the number of rough bounded volumes that it was contained in, stood wedged side to side on to the long shelf linking spine to spine. Each thick volume took in five years' worth of comments and recordings and he suddenly felt a compelling interest and a desire to ensure that they did not end now that G had gone. Strangely, he felt an unseen urge to become part of this legacy.

The image of the cat padded through his mind's eye; a striped shadow of large feline stealth that crept into his conscience and then left for the shadow-lands at the corner of his inward vision in long, elegant bounding steps. He shivered spontaneously. He agreed with G. The cat spirit had *blessed* Sol's stay.

The rain pattered harder and Sol left with the first book in his hand to read by the light of a radiant lantern hung from a hook by the glowing hearth. There the embers shimmered in still recognisable shapes of wood and flames licked upwards in indescribably timed patterns.

Birds' and beasts' names took on personalities as he read aloud as if to be his own audible companion about how they appeared, what they did and when, and he eventually left for the bedroom at what felt like a late hour. He was drained by the air's freshness and the vacancy of light in a cloud-filled thunder sky.

He stood by the window for a moment before putting the lamp out and noisily squeezing down into his sleeping bag. Somewhere out there, where the bats were slowly taking the role of the bird, was a cat, possibly well fed enough on pheasant remains, possibly not, and he wondered if he would ever see it again.

The end of April is marked by showers that can progress in days' worth of wet from the lightest rain to the heaviest downpour. Sol's ambition to walk to find a phone signal was dashed the next morning by a depth of water that hung solid in the air and smashed the *Bothan*'s windows with driving waves that sang the rhythms the sea gave it. After porridge by the newly lit stove, he washed in the sink in tepid water boiled behind the fireplace the night before, and then returned to the front window to see if the sky was any less angry from the front of the house than the porch. He was met by an aggressive, grey onslaught where cloud and lake became one and the loch appeared to have swelled in size and strayed closer to the little cottage than he'd seen the last few days.

After completion of the breakfast clear up, he re-found the first notebook and using the library available to him began to research the names of creatures to give them faces. Not used to any investigation, other than that which involved money, market value and commerce, Sol was at first lost in a swollen sea of new features and titles but quickly became aware of the common and familiar, picking up a new batch of terminology as he wound his way through the literature.

The table was soon awash with tomes opened and coffee mugs stained at the base with drying lumps of grout, ringed with peaty silt. Lunchtime drew on and Sol's phone now lay abandoned somewhere within the mass on the surface, when it finally came to that time when his stomach lurched in its call for food.

He drifted hopefully to the front window and could see across the water more easily through windows less buffeted by squalls and he felt enlivened by the approach of better weather.

Loneliness also visited him that morning as he was not used to being so isolated and he was affected by the lack of background hum that normally followed his electronic existence. No computer, no fridge, no whirring accompaniments. Just the repetitive tap of the raindrops on the window and the whistle of the storm down the chimney and over the solid-held slates on the roof. Its power rose and fell as it beat the house front, time and again.

Sol read on, slumped by the dead fireplace until he eventually attempted a re-light, building it up in the manner he found made there for him before. It took quickly but he then realised that at some point he would have to visit the sheds at the back for new dry wood.

Fighting the dousing drops and wind-whip, he collected split logs from the sheds, then returned out a second time to the yard to locate his washing, some drenched and dripping from the line and his shirt pinned to a shed wall where it had been blown and caught. Trees flinched in the aggression of the air and grasses bent double and back again. He went out a final time to visit the privy, resenting the need to walk through damp woodland where the rain pattered noisily on every leaf. The drips fell constantly in heavy neck-searching patterns, random and accurate, and the distance seemed to have grown longer than ever before.

Back at the house he hung up clothes to dry and felt the humidity of the air thicken and snatch his usually easy breath.

Silence.

He read.

He thought.

He worried.

He felt alone.

Silence.

His thoughts drifted between notes read in Victorian penned script which flowed continuous in a fluid well-controlled action along each invisible line it tracked from left to right.

He wondered what *she* was up to and was surprised how only now, two days later he was thinking back to what they had, what he had done, what *she* had said, and what he had left. Theirs was a relationship that had lasted but hadn't the depth to be eternal. It was born of money and the reckless enjoyment of spending it with abandon, and they had little in common to share beyond the immediate and the physical. And yet, now he found himself in a place and time where money seemed insignificant and its presence or absence superficial, without even a cash point to claim back what was his or a shop in which to spend it. Money was important, but he wondered if Hamish cared if Sol was wealthy or not, whether Sol could close a good deal in the city, or if he had the gift of the gab when it came to sales, deals or an occasional business corruption and break up. He doubted any of these things were of concern to a man who in the briefest of moments had demonstrated he had all the confidence and skill needed to live out here without the need for any of that; and sadly those were the things Sol had always thought made the world tick.

Silence.

Sol's mind crossed the city blocks of London to that other place a million miles from here; the land of commerce, where the bottom dollar counted, boardrooms buzzed and men shouted, sang, cried or sank on the returns of their gambling with the money of others. He knew he had done bad things, trusted though he had been, in the name of profits and shares. But crashes and market swells could not affect the little *Bothan Faobhar*. It stood timeless and nature continued on as the diaries before him revealed and reflected. Season after season passed immeasurable.

Silence.

He dragged his chair to the front window.

Black-necked geese with white cutthroat scars of feather to their faces bubbled and gurgled their bills through the shallows of the loch in spite of the conditions, sifting for something he could neither appreciate nor see. There were six of them. Pied, black and white, fat yet elegant.

He watched them waddle the water with ducks further out.

Between them smaller long-legged waders, some tall and some short, dabbled and skittered.

Gulls rode the wind, unaware that it was hazardous to other forms of life.

There was just silence, but with a growing awareness of the noises of the weather on the cottage.

And Sol still felt alone being so much used to the presence, if not the company, of others always around him, even if he was disdainful of them at times. Loneliness brought with it a sonata of its own. He became acutely mindful of the cadence of his own heart beat as blood pulsated through his temples in its tobacco starved pressure, the dull thud of a headache and desire to be free of it. The sniff of his nose added riffles of drum snare and the scratch of his roughened hand's skin across his bristled chin added further percussion.

Now there was not just silence, but an array of sound that his senses had started to gain awareness of, and that sensitivity that can only come from being alone.

The tick of a clock would have driven him insane at that moment, and yet still he desired to know the time. A steady *'drop-drop'* accompanied water from the tap in the porch, echoing through the kitchen as each drip's suicide was amplified as it plummeted under gravity to meet the solid white porcelain and was obliterated. Each turned from dewdrop water bag to flattened fluidity in the time it took for the next to form and billow at the tip of the tap. Runnels of water cascaded earthwards in the downpipes, bringing a tune to the water's motion, or fell in waterfalls where the roof's surface collected it too much for the guttering.

The easing rain jabbered in torrential themes against the windows facing out to the loch.

And still the gulls cried, the geese honked and whistled, and the ducks gabbled. The mournful peep of the redshank stretched to Sol's mind and he was instinctively reminded of the wetlands and broads.

Then, in one simple thought, he knew *'there's no such thing as silence.'*

Reading by the fire, Sol became aware that the rain had stopped.

It is so much easier to decide when you have seen or heard something for the first time than to resolve with any accuracy when it has gone. Like a migratory bird that can be spotted in the sky, it is definite if it is there; but you are always left wondering if you will see it again if it has gone. This is the feeling any ecologist has when they hope for one more sighting of what they presume is extinct.

The emotions start with the realisation of absence. *I haven't seen it for a while?*

As time passes, absence is replaced by fear. *Has it gone for good?*

It takes a while for the suspected truth to become observable fact. *Still none?*

Even then hope stays alive for a while. *Maybe there is just one more?*

That is, until hope is gone and you, and others, have exhausted the search. *Gone?*

Only then can you miss it, and even then there is that slightest optimistic thought lingering that maybe one will be found and possibly someone stumbles over a population as yet undiscovered. At least if a migrant, free of human politics and boundaries, the anticipation is still there that it will return, so long as, if a bird, it isn't lambasted with lead shot as it passes over the Mediterranean and has successfully found a safe wintering site in Africa.

Spotting its return is easy. Noticing its demise or absence is harder and less perceptible.

But, when it is gone for good it is missed forever.

A spider dropped plumb line from the ceiling on a fine many-fibred streak that glistened in a ray of light that had cut through the monotony of the grey clouds, lining the break it had created with gold and found the *Bothan* in its sanctuary bay.

The gulls rode the wind, the geese honked and bathed, the ducks dabbled, the waders bustled in-between and from somewhere the greenshank '*pee-yewed*'. There was a musical performance on the water, played by a natural orchestra for no audience in particular, illuminated by the gods of the sky themselves, who looked down from above the cumulus and showed their appreciation by sunshine itself.

Sol took one of the heavy kitchen chairs and sat out in his solitude, unexpectedly surrounded by life that he thought he would never fully appreciate as companionship. He was lonely, but not alone.

He was found in silence, but it was not quiet.

The air was settled, but it was neither still nor dry.

He breathed in deeply, the seaweed-tainted air striking his open nostrils in all its humidity. This was not the manufactured air of the office; it was real and unsullied by the hands of man.

Sol sat for a while and watched silhouette birds skim the water's surface and others dive bomb from their agitated flocks that tumbled and traced the movements of fish shoals across the loch. Here were the gannets and terns descending like aircraft in beak-led nosedives that yielded fish lunches and sandeel suppers. Puffins in their comic clown make-up, dressed as neatly as waiters, stood on the rocks of a small island amidst thronging flocks of bright white gulls and pied razorbill. Beaks were replete with silvery trawls of easily caught fish.

He made a pact with himself. One day he too would be out there on the water and catch fish and he nervously eyed the upside down boat knowing that more storms were brewing out beyond the loch and on the sea if he cared to look for them.

A melodious anthem of 'peeps' caught his attention as a host of water-hugging oystercatchers crossed his view, showing well their black and white variegated colours and bright chisel-like orange-dyed beaks.

Only once did he hear a pigeon 'coo', from somewhere behind, and only then did his mind drift back to the city.

He ate a heavy lunch of cold pheasant, bread and butter, and drank tea-brown water, consuming it as a picnic on the foreshore at the mouth to the burn that chuckled to itself behind the cottage. The river's waters rattled boisterously as its contents jostled their way around rocks and moss-clad obstacles in the race to be the first to the loch. The river became a brook and the brook became a burn before cascading inanely from the cliff edge beyond the wood and here the fat, round, white-chested body of the dipper lived up to its name as it splashed for invertebrates.

The black specks of insects rose off the stiller waters and early migrated trout leapt either for the simple joy of living or after them, falling in belly flops that left spreading concentric ripples that blew out from their point of re-entry as testament to their now hidden activity under the flat surface.

His eyes were drawn up the cliff edge to where martins wheeled and screamed chasing the flies that had been driven up by thermals rising alongside the scree and water-quarried rock. Lemon-flowered gorse sprouted from fissures and nests lined shelves that faced the loch where seabirds *'zithered'* and *'caw'd'*.

Above them all two buzzards circled lazily overhead measuring the wind with their wingtip finger feathers and making their glides look effortless despite the strength of the air currents that they must have been experiencing.

He left the picnic spot, clearing away the remains of food, and checked the weather across the water before making his mind up that he would try to find a way to the top of the cliff to get a signal if he could. Crossing the yard he saw where heavyweight raindrops had flattened the earth and left saturated muds in their wake. But placed in the middle, squarely and surely near to the bucket with the now flooded remains of pheasant in it, was a large fresh mammal print with four widespread toe pads.

The wood spirit had been back again and Sol's heart raced with anticipation and exhilaration. He searched around not really daring to move his feet much for fear of wiping away the trace of this animal's presence. By the trail it had left in the recent cleared silts of the yard, it had not passed long ago and had returned to the forest shadows via the right corner of the sheds.

He wished he could still feel its presence here, large yet elegantly feline. But all he had were the tracks that left evidence of a passage past in time.

The wildcat had gone.

Sol collected his phone from amongst the sea of books and papers on the living room table and packed his holdall with the borrowed coat and scarf, and a cloth cap. He wore the borrowed jumper and found borrowed trousers to go with the borrowed boots and socks. Then attired and ready, he made for the wood at the back of the sheds and took a bearing towards the privy by the cliff.

The forest was damp and still dripped with the aftermath of the earlier drear, but the birdsong had returned. It had taken on that echo only usually found in cathedrals and great halls where stonework and lofty vacuous oak-beamed ceilings reflected every sound back down on to the listener and prevented anything from being done in secret. Every footfall was amplified by the earthy smell of the rich humus that centuries of the fungal recycling of leaf litter had brought to the naturally acidic land. Sol bent down to touch the earth and was surprised at the forest in miniature that greeted him there; mosses made for vibrant greened turf, where liverwort hedges grew thick and trees of fine stemmed mushrooms reached upwards in their dew-glistened wetness amongst the jungle of micro-fern. He sniffed a handful of soil in his palms and was surprised at its sweetness and its crumbling dry texture that dropped through his fingers as he tested and sifted it.

The river's valley was adorned with the green finery of garlic whose potency took Sol back to every Italian and pizzeria he had ever visited. It was unusually a smell he knew so well, but which had an immediate and very different effect on his senses to the memory-induced aroma of the restaurant. As his boots crushed the leaves and its heady scent tinged the air the solid sulphurous scent of garlic, he gained the smell of wild garlic, ransoms proper. This was a special plant, dissimilar to any that he had tasted before and he foolishly bent low, dug up a bulb and bit into its single swollen white flesh ignoring the papery pink coat that contained it.

Beyond the taste of good soil he was shocked by an overload of olfaction, to the point that his eyes watered and his nose ran. But he enjoyed its kick and knew that with help he could cook with these and their leaves, those that he had paid so dearly for in the London markets – *if only he had realised how prolifically they grew along the damp banks of rivers like this.*

Wedged below him he could see the body of a large stag lying devoid of life, now jammed between the rocks as if it had been brought down here by fast moving water. Lifeless, it had lost much of its majesty. But a deep chest and sodden mane were still visible, even though a broken neck hung limply where its head had been dragged by the flow of the river and anchored by the weight of its branching antlers.

Sol shuddered at the sight of this once impressive beast now rested forever. Precious life could so easily be taken away and there was only a very thin line between the inanimate body that lay complete but dead below him and the beast that was probably still walking only a few hours or days before. Its eyes were still shined with moisture as if with tears, although he understood that it could no longer see. But he still imagined the Frankenstein experiment that could bring back what was really and so obviously gone.

Following the brook up through the trees he soon made the rock wall at the base of the cliff and here he searched the tussocks of grass and gathered flora for a suitable route upwards. A small crumbed path of well-trod earth revealed where some hoofed animal took regular passage and so he picked a way carefully up to find a slowly rising ledge that took him above the height of the trees.

In an act of hopefulness, he switched his phone on and waited for that moment of connection when the device would be ready for reception if only there was some.

Nothing.

Again, head towards the cliff, he picked up what he trusted would be a safe route to descend later. Soon, sweating, he had climbed to a vantage point that gave him a good view over the forest and back to the vaguely smoking chimney of the *Bothan*, little perturbed by the wind, and he checked his phone again.

Nothing.

He now climbed vertically, ascending slippery rocks that were slimed over with viridian algae where the splash of the waterfall met and nurtured them into great strings of intestine-like mucus. The roar and crash of the water half deafened him and he struggled to maintain a grip on stone that was not keen to be of help to his efforts.

He checked again.

Nothing.

It was curious how excited he was becoming, and headstrong he pushed on upwards and away from the falls until he made the top of the cliff where he was struck by the view ahead and the impact.

The first sense was of the freshness and strength of the wind that he had been protected from as it now hit him full on, and he came to know immediately why the *Bothan* had been built in the headland's shelter. Currents smashed him with anger that only the sea could instil in them. He stood with feet planted firmly amongst lemon-flowered whin, the greening leaves of blaeberry and crisp-dried heather stems.

He thought he had climbed a long way, looking back on the dwarfed trees and dollhouse cottage behind him. But beyond was the real mountain whose head was lost somewhere up in a broiling cloud through which no peak could be spied. Here was something of humbling magnificence that ambled then climbed on through moorland into a land of spires, grey-stained snow and black rock. All rose up from where his feet were rooted.

That unfamiliar feeling of being insignificant hit Sol and he stared up in awe, trying to bring this mountain down to a scale he could comprehend. His mind's search could only register *'big'* and he ended with a second competitive pact with himself. *One day he would conquer this mountain.*

He turned towards the sea loch and beat a pathway through the heathers to make the end of the headland where he found a strange stone, angled backwards but obviously put there by previous men. They had fought the elements to place it there and to dig deep enough into the stone-clad earth to make a hollow that would hold it firm. Moss at its base made it tantamount with the ground as it left its heather footrest and then ventured up obtusely to meet the sky some two feet above its base.

Sol reached out with a reverence he was unused to, forcing his hand through the rush of loch air. His left forefinger, cold-sensitised to the wind's ice bite, contacted with the sulphurous encrustations that hugged the stone's form and gave it a texture above that of its base layer. Moss heads wavered on fine red-orange filamentous stems erupting from deep, over-stuffed cushions. But below it all he could trace the interlacing patterns that humans had gouged into the rock's flattest surfaces.

This was a holy rock, a standing stone, a manmade icon on the headland, facing outward to the wind and that most productive sea, and he immediately knew and sensed its significance. This was the rock in the oil painting of the stag that dominated the wall in his living room.

Through his hand, he felt an electric connection between the air, the sea and the land. The wind circulated his physical form; an invisible yet powerful force, which commanded the waves, brought the rain and influenced the sail. Below was the sea that shaped the land in swells that vibrated through his feet; the provider of food and transport to the people who had stood here in the past. Then there was the apparent solidity of the land; constant and concrete yet strangely morphed by sea and wind; churning with volcanic heat below the thinness of the earth's crust that Sol sensed he could almost touch.

Over his shoulder *Bothan Faobhar* nestled safely in the lee of the peninsula and he felt a continued natural connectivity. He then knew that his presence there might have been recent, the *Bothan* itself might have had age, but that people had lived just there, and for good reason, for centuries before, stretching back to a time when this holy stone was erected to some god of creation; a period when records could not be written. By accident he had been drawn to and found the *Bothan*'s Mount Halcyon and he was conscious that he had coupled with a millennia old relic.

The sea lay before him, opening up from the loch through mountain gateways to an expanse over which pre-recorded history had travelled and settled in *his* glen. He could imagine the small boats of Vikings and nomadic settlers, the arrival of the invaders, both physical and religious, pagan and Christian, venturing inward as the sea penetrated the land through the loch and the rivers that bled down into it. Seeing in his mind's eye, Sol had visions of eons of fishing and a scene little changed generation upon generation with this stone stood constantly proud of it all.

In a strange reverential moment he removed his boots and socks and stood bare foot in the heathers and emerging blaeberry, *'earthing'* himself as he had done in the yard, and enjoying that sensation of connectivity. It was stony to the feet, but the fresh coldness of the air, the wind-tasted sea spray and the soiled texture of the stony ground sent tremors and sensations up and through his feet to his legs and aloft to end with a spiritual leap through his scalp and immediate relaxation of his ever-troubled mind.

Then he sat down to take in the view, soak in the land, the sea and the fast-rushing air. He found he was on a raised hummock laid in a strip of well-tended vegetation. Someone had been here before him, sat right where he was, and Sol liked to imagine it was the man called G who had owned that little *Bothan* that now patiently waited for him in the glen below.

It was a patch of grass and flower cut into the heather and blaeberry, lain as a straight line slightly more than the length of a man lying down, and it pointed direct from the standing stone behind which acted like a back rest out to the sea in front. The spot commanded a view that extended full circle; *Bothan Faobhar* to mountain, to sea and back home, and Sol knew it was a special location and one he would revisit time and again.

And for a moment, loneliness was gone and forgotten.

His phone buzzed into life in his pocket and with one reflex the instant was lost and he had the device grasped firmly in his sweaty hand and he cursed himself angrily for forgetting himself. Civilisation had returned to him through that little black container of technology and the electric of the atmosphere was gone; broken by a modern signal.

Instead of inner peace, in an instant there were 197 messages.

Chapter 5: The Song of the Northern Loon

(The Isle of the Dead, A Symphonic Poem, Op. 29,
Sergei Rachmaninoff)

The mobile phone is a wonderful invention. It gives connectivity almost the world over and allows everyone the chance to become part of this interconnected, shrinking universe we recognise as the modern globe. One person can communicate with others anywhere and at any time. Information can be retrieved so easily using the web and the action of a thumb or a finger, so that regardless of age, so long as you have a signal, you can enter where you want and extract what you desire. Suddenly we can all see well beyond the confines of our own imaginations, gaining from the collective narrative that we call *'human'*, which reveals to us both the good and the interesting, but also the dark and concerning aspects, to that yin and yang bipolarity we label *'person'*.

And yet, with this tool comes a cost and we have yet to see if it is outweighed by the huge benefits and instant gratification this palm-held marvel brings to us all.

Privacy has gone, with the intrusion of a text, a call or an email.

There it is again, that spine-shocking bleep that raises the hackles as if designed to remove any sentiment of peace. It shocks the listener into alertness and an immediacy of reading, acknowledgment and reply. Constant readiness has given rise to the phantom vibration of a leg or a hand as a result of the ever-watchfulness we have gained by the phone's presence in our pocket.

We look for it, expect it and demand it.

But, is it commanding us or are we in control of it?

It has become a contemporary addiction, an expected prerequisite on any job application, shop order or at the beginning of a new friendship or relationship.

For the first time in our evolution we can almost always be contacted, and, if unrestricted, then others may rarely think of the impact of a call or message, story or picture on time, nor emotion, alertness or sleep. We are in constant contact and *how do we switch off once connected?*

Meal time conversations and meetings with actual humanity can so easily degrade to a circle of phone watchers responding to other people, their virtual lives-in-snaps and often inane debates and opinions, and the nuance of face, spoken language and the art of discussion are lost. They sit with each other, but they do not relate and they lose something of themselves, their families and their friends.

But what is 'friend' if all you chase is 'likes', on-line networks and followers?

The numbers game is a marketing ploy that plays on popularity and the insecurity that makes us feel the need to find out what was previously undisclosed, to have our stories broadcast to those we do not know, our secrets unearthed and our every thought read, sent on and re-read, despite the regret it can later bring.

There is an expectation that once we have sent, it is immediately received, and once read, it is action'd or responded to. But our minds need time, our lives need space, and our souls need rest.

And so, what is the true cost of the phone?

Sol took the posts in greedily, sucking the marrow from the texts and messages, listening to voicemails with avid attention, taking in the information he needed and discarding what he did not. It was a realm of diverting, networking, communicating, and yet strangely never actually connecting with any real person.

She *wants his stuff out...   ...soon...   ...arranged removal...   ...courier will be there Tuesday...   ...why does he not answer?*

Office *now closed down...   ...what did he know about the Tokyo deal?   ...anything else they should know?   ...why does he not answer?*

Therapist asking if he needs another session...   ...concerned not heard...   ...has he really gone away?   ...should always talk to her first...   ...she could help...   ...why does he not answer?
Friends inviting him to a party this weekend...   ...let's celebrate the Tokyo deal...   ...heard about her...   ...celebrate?   ...sorry, insensitive, commiserate?   ...why does he not answer?
Family keen to see the new house...   ...is it comfortable? ...hope all well, not heard for a while...   ...just learnt about her, hoping all is okay...   ...plenty more fish...   ...why does he not answer?
Authorities asking questions about the Tokyo deal...   ...no documents, no records, no criminal case...   ...will need to answer questions...   ...why does he not answer?
Solicitor calling to say the deeds for the property are on their way...   ...please confirm receipt...   ...should arrive by Tuesday... ...why does he not answer?
To the phone addict the worst offense ever is a lack of immediate reply. *After all, what else could anyone be doing that is really so important that they do not reply straightaway?*
Sol cast off a few texts to friends and family. He was alive and well. That's all they needed to know.

He switched over to the Internet and nonchalantly ordered food and wine to be delivered by a supermarket in the next few days. This was what mobile technology was invented for, *convenience!*
Then he had a thought and scanned the list for what needed to be kept frozen. Lacking the capacity to freeze anything he changed the order and watched the basket shrink.
Now he was satisfied. Everything else could be stored safely in the house.
But he looked and thought again, and then removed those items that required refrigeration and considered a much smaller list.
Better?
He hoped he could store it all and considered his cupboard space.

After a moment he saw that some of what was left was short shelf life and he was not keen on sharing some of it with the mice either, and so he studied the list another time before submitting the final fraction of an order in what was now quite a small basket. He ended by ordering it for Tuesday.

Finished.

Finalising the order he began to search the Internet again, linking with that impossibly large network of commerce, advertising and blatant over exaggeration and statistical lies. He needed to sort some things out in the *Bothan*, and there was the unbidden and addictive compunction to buy that always needed satisfying. It was something of the urge to be a hunter-gatherer that the marketers of the web had taken full advantage of so easily. He found a few options and added them to his basket before checking their reviews.

'Brings power to the powerless,' Outdoor World, four stars.

'I couldn't leave home without it,' Livin' the Undergrowth, 4.5.

'Makes for home when you can't. Some issues with connectivity.' Trek Tech, 7 out of 10.

He made his choice and completed three purchases that he hoped would solve the first of his problems. Each would be delivered on Tuesday. Today was Sunday.

After a moment of thought he rattled off a short but simple text to a friend.

'Al,

House is rustic but fine. Will sell when updated but may take time. Good profit potential – see picture. Found books, specimens and plenty of science kit. Looks valuable. Will send photos but little signal so may take a while.

Tell Pete there's a wildcat in the garden.

Will send pictures of that too.

Chow,

Sol'

He attached a photograph of the *Bothan* as it nestled idyllically in the glen behind where he sat and pressed for send with an awkward moment of regret and a strange dichotomy of thought where two opposing mind-sets fought bravely to gain supremacy of his brain and actions. There was the city-bred urge to sell and gain monetary value and a jealousy of what others had and enjoyed that he felt was rightfully his; *what could he make?* There was even that bravado which meant he wanted to show off, where the primitive within proudly boasted of what he had seen, a wildcat; *what can I claim?* But there was also a feeling of shame and the need to preserve the *Bothan's* confidentiality, a trust that he felt he had just broken, and there was a slight possessiveness of its secret location and contents.

Too late now, it's out there. Besides, what difference could one text make?

The phone rang and before he knew it he had lifted it to his ear in one reflex action.

"Sol?" he muttered with no real emotion.

"Yes… …yes, that's the address. The drive?" He thought back to the length and state of the road up to the *Bothan*. "Yes, it is quite long… …no, it isn't a major thoroughfare… …quite rutted in places yes… …at the end of the drive? But that's miles away. Yes… ….really? Well, no that won't do. There is no way that I am going to walk all the way… ….yes, I do still want the order!" There was a pause before the other spoke again, calmly and directly.

"Oh…," said Sol despondently. "Yes, okay. I will meet the driver and sign for it… ….at 4.30pm… …yes. Tuesday as arranged."

He had quickly found himself agreeing to a long walk to collect his shopping and he cursed angrily when the conversation was cut short after he had offended the clerk who was only trying to service his needs.

Didn't the man know that he, Sol, needed food just like anyone else? After all it was he, Sol, who was paying for it!

But in the mind of the other, didn't that man, Sol, know that the receptionist on the end of the phone was simply trying to apply the company's policy on delivery to within a reasonable distance of someone's house (unless they lived in the back of beyond, which was after all the choice of the customer and not him)?

Sol fumed and thought little of the effect that his outburst had had on the phone operator who sat bewildered at his desk as he completed the delivery instructions on the screen to help Sol get his groceries. His body may have been in the office, surrounded by the clutter of transport logistics, the ringing of phones and the intoned discussions between a hundred other operatives and the virtual voices from their headsets, but his mind was elsewhere. Truth be known he was jealous of Sol's location and would have given everything up just to have been there right now in the freedom of the *Bothan* and the abandon of its air, instead of the sweat-scented, fan-circulated oppression that was this low-ceiling'd open plan office where he worked with false politeness. The hum of IT drilled into his head and his fingers ached as they punched the final details into the keyboard.

Maybe this weekend he would get lucky? And, he hoped for a better set of numbers on the lottery.

His headset bleeped an acknowledgment that the next client was being called and a notification of the setback he needed to discuss materialised in digital on the screen in front of him. He put the thoughts of his conversation with Sol behind him, pushed his mind's eye view of the mountains and sea to the periphery of his mental vision, breathed deeply and waited for the line to connect.

"Hello," he called with dishonest jollity. "How are you today?"

He did not really care what the answer was to this question and he knew they, the customer, would be aware of this. But it's what he did day-to-day. The rules of engagement were that the client should never really know how he felt.

Sol fumed inwardly and watched the horizon over which the burgeoning clouds blossomed grey in voluminous sea-drenched mountains that rose from the distant waters and cast deepening shadows of genuine drear. The wind was suddenly wet-warm, draining the energy from his limbs with its heaviness and density; its coolness dissipated and was replaced by a stifling heat. The wall of rain and hail that pattered and smacked the waters in its race to be landward was on the move with the reflection of the approaching storm distorting the air.

Sol sat oblivious, his thoughts drawn into that little black handheld device and the potential it had to sort out his housing *'situation'*.

What was required now were some basics for the house before he could accept visits from the guests who were inviting themselves via text and he started to list the problems he needed to overcome in order to make this a possibility. There were the obvious issues of power, mobile coverage and transport. But then there was water, sewerage and plumbing. All of this would cost money. But at least he had plenty of this hived away and he could even raid the company accounts if he needed to.

His phone whistled electronically to life as a coincidentally timed text arrived from the office. Liking patterns in life Sol distrusted coincidence and always suspected the interference of some other higher powers when things fell right or wrong. It was why he could be so superstitious at times and the reason for so many of his customs and religiously played acts prior to making deals.

'Sol, accounts closed in light of Tokyo. Can't find papers. U 'right? Not heard for days. Not like u.'

He stared disbelievingly at his mobile and wondered at the chance timing of the most recent of his thoughts and the message. Someone was changing his accounts at a distance of hundreds of miles away even as he sat here.

How dare they?

The deals were all legitimate even if the paperwork was scanty in places. They were *his* deals, not theirs. It was *his* account, and not theirs. *He* chose who opened or closed them and where the money went, even if ultimately the company owned it all.

Irritation and resentment surged upwards in a welling of hate for those '*others*' somewhere in a different far off country and an alternative universe to the land of *his Bothan.*

Who were they?

He was making *them* money!

He angrily threw the phone to the side where it bounced on the dry canopy of a heather bush before it dropped down into the undergrowth. An orange wing-tipped butterfly fluttered inadequately in the wind and was beaten sideways with the force.

The phone called to him again from the jungle of the shrubbery and Sol had to fight through the sharpness of brash and twig to relocate this precious item.

'*Sol,*

Sorry the deal's gone sour mate! Desk cleared according to the lads at your place – causing quite a stir. At least you aren't there to cause any criminal damage or grievous. Good job you are up in the back of beyond where they can't jail you. All hell's breaking lose!

Sure will get it back on line as soon as. Know you on holiday but call in when you can. Could be worse...   ...I could be offering you a job!

Just got your text about cottage and stuff for sale.

Al'

And then it started to rain.

An onslaught of the weather's front hit the headland with a near constant outpouring of recycled sea and loch water that fell from the sky in oscillating rushes. Sol looked up from his phone, utterly miserable, but about to face the wrath of something far worse and raw; the great British weather as witnessed from the northwest coast of Scotland. This is what the ancients called the '*grey wind of the west*' and the '*bringer of the wet*'.

Engulfed in a solid wall of water, suddenly cold, Sol sprung to life, retracting from his life in the phone and downing it into a cavernous pocket, strangely feeling a sense of relief as it went from his sight. His anger was dispelled in seconds as he drew himself into action and stood to face the drive after drive of water that overwhelmed the promontory and all but enveloped the choppy waters below. Even so, he could still hear the tidal crash of the sea as the waves flung themselves in fury at the base's rocks.

He fled from what remained of the seafront view towards the top of the crags, bounding through heathers and moorland to gain the slippery cliff face back home. He slithered and fell more than climbed down and afterwards wondered how he had not fallen on the greasy rocks, new-wet algae complete, to the path that passed down to the growing river.

She sang happily, in a mystic jingling voice, of her forthcoming weather-filled spate as she tumbled down to the loch in gay abandon, draining the life-fluid from the surrounding rocks and the mountains above. She, in the speech of the river, knew that she would fill and brim within the hour, crashing the rocks and grinding pebbles along her bed in the madness that would ensue, bringing death to some but delivering life to others, and she teased the stag carcass as she rose. Desperate to re-join her mother loch and the eventual sea, she cried for joy, leapt over descending outcrops and bubbled as a cauldron in whirlpools where silvery fish leapt to beat her current.

Each minute was checked with the increasing roar of rain drops falling through the canopy onto a billion hatching leaves and Sol was glad to make the wood and to run past that dead stag with its great antlered head lolling in the climbing water of the brook. Face down, soaked cold to the bone, with clothes that stuck and stung to his pallid skin, and a temperature that now bit deep, he sped for the *Bothan*, and for home.

Home is an interesting if variable and flexible concept. It is at times so difficult to define and yet is something that each of us takes for granted if we are lucky enough to claim we have one. It can be our place of birth, a location that offers lifelong sanctuary, which in itself can span from a single room, to a house, a county or country depending on the scales we prefer to use and the breadth of humanity we wish to extend our communality to. It can change with time and state of migration, even age and desire, and for some it will never be a static condition, but will always be constantly developed depending on our mind's view. A change of relationship with a person, a place or a land can take home away or bring us a new place to give that name, and if we lose hope or depression creeps up on us unbidden, dangerous and insidious, we may lose sight of what home was or that we had it all of the time. Some, falsely gulled by those they call friends, or some whom they entrust wrongly as such, mistake home for another place and are entrapped and forever snared, and their lives can never be happy again.

Home can be where we simply rest each night. *But, is this is all home is?* Only the very shallow would really think they had got there truly if home were just a place to eat and sleep.

Home, the great indescribable; without it we are lost and left searching the seas of life and wanting for something just beyond what we can achieve. We each spend our lives on our own *Odysseys,* making for a place we can really name *home,* either physically as a place in which we live, emotionally as a place in which we can invest, or spiritually as a place in which we can find completeness.

As Sol rushed in to *Bothan Faobhar* that night, entering through the banging porch door that creaked already with a familiarity recognised by all his senses, as he dripped on the mat leaving pools of water-stain that oozed away from him like blood from a recently murdered cadaver, and as he stripped down hurling abuse at the weather, the house, the lack of electricity and the need to stoke a fire in order to create heat, he breathed a sigh and exclaimed something that stopped him in his tracks.

"I'm glad to be home."

He didn't remember the last place he naturally called home, except to say that it was a long time ago, and he didn't really understand why he thought it now. After all, the *Bothan* was simply a shell and lacked many of the features that made it a decent home. But already he was growing *au fait* with it and had taken on something from the place, and not just its smell of tobacco'd must.

Suddenly happy to be back, he bundled the driest of his wet clothes to the side and spread the rest where they would dry over chair backs, and he went through to find yet more borrowed, but dry clothes before he stoked the fire. He *was* glad to be back and not just pleased that he could shelter from the elements. All he wanted now was a supper on, a fire glowing, a drink brewing and a moment with G's notes. For now, trapped by sky-launched water, this would suffice as home.

It didn't take him long to pluck the second pheasant, casting feathers into the wet wind through the open porch door that he held back with his foot and then secured shut. The head and guts were placed in the metal bucket and kept inside for now, from which they would be later sacrificed to the yard dwelling cat-spirit once the rains ended, if they ever would.

Washed, basted and sat on a bed of vegetables, the body was placed reverently into the stoked and pre-warmed oven, and Sol left with a mug of hot *Bothan*-brew for the front room in the diminishing light of the day to prime a lantern for the evening's read. There on the table, half-hidden by the flotilla of notes and papers was a battered elongated case that in the melee of setting up house he had almost forgotten about. It's bruised and scarred form spoke of years of attention and at times abuse. It's fraying strap revealed threads, bared by constant carriage.

It had a feminine form that was attractive to the eye but only loosely moulding the shape of the instrument lying coffin-like within. Without its performer it was but a corpse, and he felt ashamed that he had left it here for the last few days when ordinarily he would have taken it out, aired it, tuned and played it at least once per day and whatever the season, the emotion or the stress. At times it was his muse, at others it was his counsellor, and yet again it could be the outpouring of so much of what he wanted to express but being just a man could not.

Flicking the clips that held this cist closed, he lifted the lid and looked down at the vibrancy of wood, gut and hair it held captive, smelling that richness of aged varnish and polish, rustic glue and chord. For days it had laid patient, locked in with its own scent, which had as usual amplified as it did if left. It was like a good coffee brewed and infused in a tight sealed pot or a well-left red, tilted at an angle off the sediment and left to mature with only its own company, the inertness of a glass bottle and a natural, hand-cut cork to interact with.

As an old friend greets another, Sol lifted the violin in an embrace that had that naturalness that only comes with ease in another's company. Left arm raised in a graceful effortless movement, he tucked the light body of tawny wood tenderly under his chin and took his podium by the window where he tuned the strings ready for his concert.

Eyes closed, he gave himself that moment required to distil a musical thought such that he could play how he felt; something known combined with other melodies spontaneous in their instant composition and resultant of his internal feelings, and the outward world, and even the contorted route and experience that had brought him uniquely to this place, here and now. There was an element of the arpeggio and scale, then a liquidity of expression, and finally a tune burnt through the haze of his thoughts and he gently rested the tightened bow on the now-tuned strings and striking the horsehair across it, he played from the heart.

In the music there was the loneliness of the *Bothan* and its location, but the grandeur of the waters, the woods, the loch and the mountains. It flowed as the burn from the hills to the sea, and then angled like the cliff that broke through them all. There were the birds that paddled and dabbled or soared and flew, and there was an emotional sonnet to the flowers, the trees that sapped the light and the openness of the moorland. Spiritually he found a melody to take him up to the standing stone that visited a prehistoric past, and then drew forward into the present, and finally he found that wild spirit cat that prowled the shadow-lands and hunted game by dusk.

This was his concerto to the land ending on that melancholic but pastoral tune that he felt best described the little cottage nestling in the glen on the loch shore side in the protection of the cliff by the woods; *Bothan Faobhar*.

Time became of little consequence and when he finished his performance and took a bow to an invisible audience beyond the glass, out in the darkness of a reflected window lit by the limelight glow of a spluttering paraffin lantern, he was surprised to see that night was upon the *Bothan*.

He replaced the violin with a deserved veneration back into its case and now tired, sticky-bead sweated, with a wetted shirt that clung to his arms, he returned hungrily to the kitchen to enjoy a pheasant supper.

The rain ended that night as April turned to May without the wild things or even the sleeping Sol noticing. The constant patter of the drops on the roof tiles had died away to leave behind a silent air sensitised by the high-pitched shrieks of the bats that, more felt in the temple than actually heard, flitted backwards and forwards to scoop hapless insects up from the sky. They worked unseen against a sky clear of cloud illuminated by the punctuated pinpricks of a vast firmament of stars that completed constellation maps over the heavens.

The northern lights were alive tonight, bringing an enchanted glowing edge to the world.

Sol woke from a deep slumber but did not know why.

It was dark and he was stiff, having taken the shape of the comfortable armchair he had moulded himself into to read the night before. The fire was blushing weakly, volcanic red embers enlightening the blackened charcoal of unrecognisable timber logs that had cracked almost back to nothing but grey dust and white wood ash. The night air had taken a chill from the outside beyond the thin-glassed windowpanes.

It took him moments to realise where he was and how silent the world could be. Then the owl called again, a haunting shriek that bounced round the valley from deep within the forest. He threw more wood into the fire and poked it in a way he hoped would invigorate it, and then he walked to the front window where the loch was in full nocturnal view.

The light was better than he had expected for this time of morning but seemed to be constantly changing colour and direction. Green and red folds of dust danced eerily in silence in the sky, sometimes receding to the north and then at others extending blanket arms. They were tumbling gestures that whipped across the sky as if some great beast were scooping up the stars in wild swings only to leave them behind moments later having missed every single one of them.

Sol was confused by what he saw; a night sky full of stars and strange mystical lights that reached out and retreated, snuffing out the visible suns one by one and then reigniting them as it withdrew back to the horizon. But the eeriest sensation of all was absence of a sense and a lack of sound. And yet, the aerial sky-wide display of colour and beauty that he was overtaken by was silent, and in some way this gave the impression that its huge scale of heavenly movement was impossible, or dreamlike, and not real. He almost felt the need to check that he was truly awake.

He walked out into the yard and round to the front of the *Bothan*, his path illuminated by a cascade of hues descending from the firmament above. On his way, he placed the metal bucket containing the pheasant's supper remains and castoff entrails in the middle of the yard and then he stood there looking and observing the sky with the loch waters lapping peacefully at his feet. To say surreal would not suffice, and where words failed to describe his emotions and the visions he saw, he allowed his heart to take over and beat.

Each noiseless wash of alien dust that extended from some place over the horizon brought its own feeling, with the scene ever-changing as the waters obediently reflected back in a near-perfection of what happened above. The hills were alight, as if they were some form of ancient cinema screen where the projector had struggled to focus. Seals, hoisted clumsily up and out of the water, cried as they carolled their moaning refrains, and some way off the loon called its winnowing ghost song that both raised the hackles in dread fear of its haunted potential and yet also sent the mind off in spirals to another, more gentle and saner place under the magic of its echo. Sol could see its black silhouette shape riding low in the water and knew it was a bird that called it, even though his spine still sang its own medley of vibration as he watched and heard; a creature with a song that distilled the very essence of an ever-changing northern-lit sky.

It was loneliness in a voice; a tearful well-whittled yelping that sparked the imagination to look into strange places and unearth sinister thoughts from parts of the mind sometimes better left in shadow. The voice of a ghost, it sang its strange lunar tune sending shivers of excitement and fear up and down Sol's vertebrae. And yet it was also the call of wilderness, a wolf on the water with little recognisably avian in its resonance.

A lone chorister, its voice resonated and continued as a reiteration of a call when it returned once collided through the rarefied air to meet cliff edges and trees in the coldness of night. A Viking call to the spirit of *Odin*, with his eyes closed Sol could have placed the distance between him and any one of the headlands that reached out to embrace the loch's dark waters by the delay in return of this lingering call.

It was a voice of beauty, clear and pure, rising and falling, warbled and confident. It struck the water and skimmed its surface, ringing from the cliff and filling the glen, harmonious with its own reflection.

It was a voice of strange hope; somehow it did not just call out to the sky, the moon, the mountains or the water. But Sol knew it was a message to a sought loved one and a potential mate.

It was also a voice tinged with sadness and sorrow, lonely and stoical, and Sol little knew the Gaelic rhyme that onomatopoeically described its call thus:

Mo chreach, mo creach,	My sorrow, my sorrow
M' uliadh!	My treasures!
M' eislean!	My troubles!

Instead, he felt fired, alive and excited. But he also felt drained and lonely, and troubled in this strange location so far from the city he loved.

With an original urge to improve, bargain, sell and make profit, he was at a loss. This place had nothing he had really sought for in life, except now it proffered a brief moment of isolation, and for the second time in a day he was thinking the word '*home*' as if it described this wholly inadequate building and its land. He reminded himself that there was no power, no communication and no people, and so therefore so little of what he desired. But there it was again, *home*.

The diver looked at him down a straight powerful black bill. It had drifted close to the shoreline and was gently cruising in its laid back fashion with a sigmoid neck that held beady eyes visible by their lunar-twinkle. Pied feathering made it a difficult form to hold in detailed view against the temperate lap of the salted water as it bobbed alongside the algae-encrusted pebbles and light shell sand. But its silhouette made this ethereal creature real again; a true motionless form layered over the ever-busy kelpies on the water.

Sol and the bird held each other's gaze and he knew in that moment that to develop the *Bothan* beyond its isolated solitude would be the end for a creature like this. Plans that had formed embryonically in his head, to build neighbouring properties, to use the headland to construct a lookout, maybe a café, to erect a series of chalets or loch-side attractions, they would all be wrong for this beast.

The bird raised its bill to the blue-smiled moon and whinnied one last elongated warbled call. Then *'flop'*. The water consumed it. The bird was lost in a back-arched dive that left only white-capped, cerulean-blue concentric circle ripples that spread outwards from its last surfaced position. The bird was gone, and somehow Sol was left wanting.

He neither knew the bird for what it was, nor understood the meeting they had had, but he was touched by it and something of the previously overwhelming city-boy character left him, and he regretted his text earlier to his dealer friend. There was a pang of guilt about his thoughts, for he knew too well that in this virtual world emails and texts left electronic ripples that spread from their point of entry in just the same way as the diver's last moment had been recorded and passed about the loch. His only hope was that once the ripple had started that it would soon lose its power and find the hard edge of rejection as the diver's had when they hit the shore.

Sol sat for a while in the peace that the storm had left in its wake under a bright lit sky of dust and aerial illusion, green and red. In the distance, far off, yet approaching, he felt the advance of dawn and somehow knew, whether as a memory or an instinctive thought that with the sun's emergence would come more trouble for the *Bothan*, but that he had now become its official custodian in the last few days, taking over from G.

Who was G? He needed to know. And, where could he find him?

Hating to break the magic of a timeless scene, Sol turned back towards the house, watching a play of colour dance over its faded white exterior. There was no doubt that the *Bothan* was part of this landscape and he knew that whatever sprites were responsible for casting this spell over him they dwelt there too in that basic rock, tile and mortar construct.

Sol was stiff from the cold night airs, and turned to re-find a bed he still hadn't made properly since his arrival several days before. He placed his hand reverentially on the prow of the upturned boat stroking it as he passed it towards the wall of the garden where the greening vegetable sprouts supernaturally rose up from the soil from seed so tiny that a Martian would find the concept of gardening incomprehensible. *How could such produce be derived from so small a seed, microscopic in proportion and featureless in its design? How could these tiny things give rise to plants of complexity, specialised in their adaptations and able to harness the vitality of the sun in a complex series of biochemical reactions that locked that energy into sugars and biomass?* No alien could be so conned. And yet it was true.

Mid-thought, he continued to philosophise on vegetation and the wonders of ecology as he rounded the back of the cottage to enter the porch door via the yard, when he was greeted with a loud, low-rumbled growl. It was delivered with ferocity from a large feline profile splayed to the ground behind the bucket containing the raw remains of the now-cooked bird.

Sol froze, unable to take back the last few steps that he would have completed with greater caution if he had suspected the supernatural presence of the wild cat.

Neither moved, but instead each contemplated the other with an electric distance of twenty feet spread between them.

The moon caught the animal's eyes and lit up a savage face, staring and unmoving with lips curled as it continued to snarl, teeth bared and facial whiskers erect. Even without the assistance of the sun's light Sol was able to pick out the impression of a capital letter M emblazoned in markings on its forehead, tiger-like stripes along its back, and a shorter than expected bushed up tail with concentric rings of black that ran broadly around it.

The cat spirit had returned.

After that indeterminate time that marks any moment where we are only able to guess whether it was long enough or not, the cat appeared to relax and confidently removed the head from the bucket of feather and entrails before it leapt off quickly into the moon shadows of the sheds and the wood. Three bounding springs was all it needed to check the yard and leave Sol behind, gawping and again lost for words of description.

He felt he was now part of a secret, revealed to him personally, a conspiracy of things he had to keep to himself to protect. He knew from reading G's notes that truly wild cats were rare creatures, but to have seen it twice in just a few days meant that at least one was living very close by and was assured enough to visit the yard where G had lived.

Something was awakened in him; something not sought for but delivered by his brief experience of the *Bothan*. Now Sol wanted to know how he could get to see this wonder of the night forest better and in clearer detail, more often and more easily. *Could it be contained or should it be?*

Sol quickly returned to the comfort of '*G's chair*' as it had become named, and covered himself with his sleeping bag, retrieved from the bedroom. It was like he was acting the spoilt child having its duvet moment on the sofa in front of the television when the parents were out. Already it felt familiar and comfortable to sit there when in the front room, and, once poked and restocked, the fire gave enough heat to reach that space, if only he needed to watch where the popping and hissed cast its embers to avoid either him, the chair or the bag catching fire.

Used to the sodium lamps of the city, his eyes felt an odd relaxation in the light of the burning hearth, even though its heat dried and scorched his corneas, desiccating them to a fiery heat. He breathed deep and fell asleep quickly with nothing electronic to disturb his slumber or awaken his brain with its emitted blue backlight or sporadic buzzes and vibrations...

His dreams took him to a wide expanse of water where the wild spirits dwelt above and below the surface, and jostled with those who gave life to the land and the sky. When he was able to explore in that strange slow way that dreams allow, he descended in close to find that they were the birds and the fish, the insects and the mammals. They told him many things and asked for his help, explaining their struggles with the encroachment of civilised man. Many of them had been lost and their numbers had dwindled, but some of them remained strong, even if they were losing their hold on the land, the water and the air.

It was if they were giving him a wild warning of things yet to pass. He knew about what they told him, from the news, from school classes and from the general understanding that the planet was suffering as a result of man's continuous onslaught and lack of foresight and care. For many years, like so many others, he had ignored these portents from the ecologists and the '*greens*', writing them off as the musings of scaremongers and killjoys. And after all, what difference could he make as an individual in the face of a whole species' neglect of their planetary stewardship?

But deep down, where most of us hide the truths we do not want to face about our own responsibilities, actions and consequences, he was fully aware that he had always known and had just chosen to ignore, humour and debase the obvious fact that he had not wanted to care, nor be affected, nor change his own lifestyle – he had it too good.

Sol travelled to the standing stone on the headland and sat in his dreamscape by the carved holy rock on the raised rectangle of land where G had obviously sat before. As on his walk today, he could see all around, the land and the mountains that grew behind, the loch and the extending seascape, even the *Bothan* itself, the woods and the cliff.

He was not alone, but instead joined a man who was already there. Sol guessed this indistinct person was his dreaming image of G, but he lacked features, as Sol did not know what he looked like. Together they sat and watched the water, and the birds that flew in and out of the loch, the fish and the other animals that swam, even the deer that pranced amongst the trees and heather. The wildcat stalked in the shadows and passed through the wood in glistening spirit form and a broad-winged eagle rode the thermals as predator over all. The diver paddled further out than the dabbling ducks and geese. It was instantly recognisable as it drifted with the frame of a rapacious organic battleship.

Those two men remained silent for a long time, sat side by side in the azure-tinted light of a full moon. Then the man spoke in a voice that carried lyrics on the wind. They were words that Sol did not recognise, but he knew their meaning even before they were spoken.

"Those that can will leave if we let them and they can't come back. Many will be lost if men come to the glen. Seek the wisdom of the earth around you, the salt of the sea loch and the light of the sun. Keep them fresh and remember the life in the waters of the brooks and the green of the tree, so that they all remain."

Sol was acutely aware that all things around him had stopped, the deer, the cat, the diver and the geese, even the fish that caught the now stilled current, and they all watched *him*. The man placed an icy hand squarely on Sol's shoulder and he could not help himself but to stare deeply into the face where no eyes met his gaze from a facade that remained unclear.

"Choose wisely," said the ghost figure. "More than *your* future depends on you."

He was cut deeply with guilt and a desire to help such that, when he suddenly awoke into the quiet of the *Bothan*'s damp-ventilated stillness, he was struck with a sense of foreboding for the future and a conviction that he, Sol, needed to help. It was up to him to act on behalf of *Bothan Faobhar*, as nobody else could. It was left to him.

Chapter 6: The Peace of Swans

(Scottish Symphony, Max Bruch)

The next morning's beginning was marked by a sun that rose cold but certain from the east, casting light over the hills in the west and scorching the heather cladding of the cliff tops an inferno crimson. The martins and swallows woke early to catch the insects that rode the thermals with the woodland shadows' completeness being ruined by the light-catching gossamer of arthropod wings as the daybreak's hatch took up their places in the sky.

Hoverflies held their position in motionless flight, their wings almost invisible with the rapidity of their beating. Wasps coasted by with the arrogance their size, sting and formidable black and yellow warning strips allowed, convergent on the same evolutionary designs as the striping of police cars. Smaller creatures flitted in between and the web-made parachutes of spiders took their silken-plumbed creators heavenward.

A large bumblebee tumbled through the ferns in search of spring nectar, defiant of gravity and superficially the laws of aerodynamics and aviation that claimed it could not fly. *Or was that just an urban legend?* The bee did not care and flew anyway.

Sol watched them through the glass of the front window and felt as if he had never noticed such detail before.

He brewed a morning coffee and went to sit in the rays of the earth-warming sunshine as it hit the plastic chair at the end of the woodland ride. There he could hear the babble of the brook and the lap of the shore, but the needle-cushioned flooring of the pinewood deadened all.

The trees had obviously been planted in rows through intention in some day gone by, but they had outgrown their use for timber now, being gnarled and copiously painted in lichen, moss, fern and liverwort. Tufts of grass sprouted from their over-bent branches and some, headless, had lost their tops to wind, rot and lightening.

Behind was near natural woodland of a mixed and open nature. The dying spruce gave way to oak and Scot's Pine, aged but elegant and without the formality of an introduced species regimentally lineated in its planting. These trees were not uniform in stage, shape or genus. Instead they gave an impression of diversity, in all senses of the word, and a richness of bird song escaped their light penetrated canopy.

Once a tooth-filtered mug of coffee was within him and he was warmed by the vigour of the sun, Sol decided that breakfast could wait until he reached the headland for a picnic. The sky was clear blue giving the gorse a bright lemon yellow and custard that contrasted well with the shadow of its grey-green spikes and stems. Together they looked like tessellated cut outs of colour that had been laid over each other to make up a contiguous butter and black cloud over the edge of the cliffs above.

Returning to the kitchen he packed his holdall with some fruit cake and an apple from Hamish's wife and he found a plastic bottle in his bag from the car that he filled with *Bothan*-brown water. Holding it up to the light he inspected its rich amber clarity and wondered at its chemical content and if it would pass inspection well enough in London to be allowed out of the tap. He strapped his violin carefully to his back and then headed up through the wood to the cliff path and on to the end of the rocks where that odd raised rectangle of land lay prostrate in front of the carved standing stone. Once convinced that the weather promised to be good for at least the present, and no storms were brewing on the distant horizon, here he sat to enjoy his outdoor snack.

Somewhere on the way up, he had grazed his knee and it had swollen up bright crimson and sticky, glistening as it dried in the hot sunshine. Only now could he feel it, but he was keen to simply ignore the sensations and tingles, instead wanting to enjoy this moment in the outdoors.

Seven swans crossed the loch in front of him as he unpacked his meagre supplies. Their long necks stretched out heads upfront and their gracefully large wings flapped heavily in whistling downdrafts like the arms of angels. They flew in a v-shaped skein, their heads held in exact position like tanks' turret mounts, ever facing forward.

He chewed the fruitcake noisily. It wasn't his usual breakfast as he was more of a coffee then gym followed by bacon butty type man and he would have done almost anything for a cigarette right now. But it was moist and full of chewy delights and a sweetness that he knew would boost his energies later in the day as his adventure in the wilds continued.

After a time of contemplation Sol removed his violin from its case and stood on the elevated strip of land that lay between the carved rock and the sea and he played a melody to the white angel-birds he had just seen. His performance was slower in construction than his tune of last night. It was eerie in places and was affected by the dreams and experiences of the darkness of the early hours. The diver was there with its trill call, and now the skylark that shouted from above the moorland, and the pipit that sang from within, all joined together, to end in the grace of the ballet of swans that had passed over and by.

He replaced the violin back into its open case, carefully ensuring that it sat comfortably and tight in the velvet soft moleskin felt of the interior. The sound of regular whistling downbeats caught his attention again as the seven swans flew back and then round and around above him, an elegance in flight. They crossed in front of the distant mountains and called melodically to maintain communication with each other and as if singing to the hills themselves.

Each threw shadow giants of swans onto the ground and was enlightened by haloes of sunlight from above, their wings cast like crosses against their outstretched necks and tails. They circled again and another time, and then, as one they fell from the sky in formation to drop clumsily to a lower thermal, which they then followed out and into the bay and towards the open sea.

From here they were little more than seven white specks now and Sol felt their drive to leave but was heartened that they had circled him by a second time. He tracked them as they turned north up the coast and then were lost in the wake of the mountains that provided a stately gateway to the loch before the real ocean began.

He knew from G's notes that they had probably left until the next winter, seeking migratory destinations to breed in, those regions where the ice was now receding, and productivity and opportunities returning.

"Did you see them, Sol?"

A surprisingly clear female voice broke across the moorland to greet his ears and made him start.

There was a woman running towards him through the blaeberry and undergrowth waving with one hand but with a large shotgun flung disturbingly over her left shoulder and held tight by the other.

She was attractive in a wild sort of way, with orange red hair that fluttered in no particular style with the wind from the sea, and cheeks that were flushed from exposure to the morning sun. Freckled and pale-skinned her voice was gentle but firm. She was dressed sensibly in a tweed jacket, underlain with a cream checked shirt, and her trousers were tucked deeply into high leather boots.

"Did you see them?" She asked again as if Sol was either deaf or stupid. This time she was more urgent and insistent.

"The swans," she continued. "Did you see them?" she broke the sentence up into individual words as if helping him to understand.

"Yes," he replied, the first word he had uttered to another human for more than a day.

"Are you only *just* eating breakfast?" she asked looking critically at the cake on the bag that lay on the floor.

"Yes," he said again. This was the second word he had said.

"Hamish thought you'd be lazy and late in getting up."

She smiled reassuringly as she neared him.

"And it was *you* playing the violin?"

"Yes."

"Do you say anything else other than yes? Hamish said you were strange."

"Yes," he answered. "I mean, yes I do. Yes I am having breakfast. Yes it was I playing the violin. And, yes I did see the swans."

"Did you see the swans before or after you ate?"

"What?"

"It's important," she hurried. "When did you see them?"

"Well, first, before I ate." He thought carefully looking at the woman in front of him who was gesticulating that he needed to give a fuller and more accurate description complete with timings which to him seemed irrelevant.

"Then I began to play and they came back."

"Excellent. Play what?"

"My violin."

"Yes, I know," she looked frustrated at his replies. "What were you playing on the violin?"

"Well, I was making it up and just playing how I felt…   …is that okay?"

"That's just excellent. Marvellous. Wonderful!"

"Why?"

"They've given you their peace," and with this she pushed back a leather bag that had fallen on to her right arm from her shoulder and stretched out her mud-caked hand to shake his.

"The name's Gerry," she explained. "Gerry Macleod. Pleased to meet you, Sol."

"And you too," he replied as his arm was shaken thoroughly to the shoulder.

Her grip of his hand was secure and strong.

"What peace are you talking about?" he questioned, being at a loss as to what this strange, wild woman was talking about.

"The peace of the swans of course," she explained, but it was soon clear that Sol did not understand the significance of this statement and so she explained.

"The swans. They were whooper swans. Well some believe that they are the spirits of the old religion, others that they are the early Christians. They were persecuted by the Norse and fled as swans now resting only where they feel at peace. That's why you should never kill a swan… …just in case."

"I really won't," he nodded. "I've never thought of killing a swan."

"Anyway, it is said that if you hear them before breakfast it's a good omen for you. How many were there?"

"Seven," he replied with confidence. "They were all flying in a v-shaped formation."

"That's seven years then."

"What like a mirror? Seven years of bad luck."

"No silly," she laughed. "They've just blessed you with seven years of peace in which you'll prosper if you listen to what they offer you. *Chuala mi guth binn nan eala.*"

"I'm sorry, I don't speak Gaelic - I presume that was Gaelic - beautiful although that sounded," he apologised.

"I heard the sweet voice of the swans," she translated. "*Chuala mi guth binn nan eala.* Somehow it sounds best in the native tongue. Don't you think?" It was a question that didn't need an answer.

Gerry was staring vacantly off to where the birds had flown up the estuary and out to sea. "That's the last we'll see of them till winter. Funny they left so late this year. I expect they wanted to check you out too and make sure that *Bothan Faobhar* is in safe hands." She pronounced the house name in a way that Sol had to work hard to recognise as his own cottage. *Bo-han*, where the o was harshly sounded as in the word 'odd' and the 'han' had a Welsh lilt to it, and *Ferv-a-rth* that sounded almost like the word fervour.

"You must have called them back with your violin," she continued. "Maybe they'd gone part way up the coast and then they heard you're playing and wanted to leave their peace with you?"

She turned to find Sol staring at her with a look of incredulity across his face.

"And you believe that?"

"Of course not," she laughed. "That was just a guess. They're just swans after all. But you can never be too sure up here where of all places in the world the spirits are still likely to be living and moving. Wouldn't you say?"

And then she looked at him and waved her hand in front of his gaping face.

"Do you always stare?" she asked.

"No. Sorry. But, what did you call the house?" Sol enquired pointing to the *Bothan*.

"Sorry?"

"The house."

She repeated its name. "It's Gaelic," she explained. "It means The Edge House. G liked to say it was because the House was on the edge of the known world, but I think it's because of the cliff edge behind it, that's an edge too. Others say it's because it's on the edge of the loch. There's a number of edges it can be named after but that bit of history is now lost in antiquity. People have lived there for a very long time."

Her accent was strong but nevertheless lyrical and Sol quickly decided he liked her, and not just because he hadn't spoken to anyone for several days. She was relaxing and yet had seemed to teach him more in the last few moments than he had taken on from someone in quite a while. Maybe he was listening better and appreciating the company. He tried the new pronunciation of the *Bothan*'s name and failed. She was patient and corrected him.

"Don't worry. If you are anything like G you'll be here long enough to learn more than just that little bit of Gaelic."

"So you aren't G?"

"Oh no, of course not. He was a bloke for starters."

"But you are the same Gerry who brought me the pheasant?" he asked.

"Yes, and the rabbit. I do hope they were okay. I suddenly worried that you being a city boy wouldn't know what to do with them. Couldn't have you getting ill in your first week could we?"

"They were lovely, thank you. I think I've worked out how to pluck, gut and cook them now, only Google isn't working at the House and so I had to guess a bit. Not done the rabbit though yet. The pheasant were great though."

"Oh good, because I've just come over the hill to give you some more pheasant. Thought you might have been starving down there," and she thumbed back towards the *Bothan*. "I brought you this too," she stated as she pulled two pheasant and a small blue cloth-covered hard backed book from her shouldered bag.

He took them, thanking her saying, "the cat will be pleased."

"Cat?" she questioned. "What cat?"

Sol went guiltily quiet.

"It is okay," she whispered. "The secret *will* be safe with me," and she pressed the point. "What cat?"

"The one from the woods. I think it's a wildcat."

Gerry placed her hand on the Pictish stone as he spoke and traced its carvings with her finger following their continuous Celtic designs round and round. Her brow was furrowed as he described the cat's features and size, and then at last she looked at Sol full on, quickly down at his bag and the rectangle of land on which they now both stood before taking in the violin and bringing her eyes back to meet his.

Sol stopped. "What's wrong? It was a wildcat wasn't it?"

"I just think the *Bothan* may have chosen well...   ...again. G said it had, although I'm not sure how – you had the briefest of communications and that was via the agent on the phone. It's a strange little place that *Bothan* in the glen."

She mused for a minute, misty eyed, whilst Sol stared out to the open sea.

"The peace of swans, the blessings of the cat...   ...what else have you seen?"

Sol thought for a while whilst he took the pheasants and laid them carefully into his holdall.

"I saw a bird on the water late last night when the sky was churning red and green."

"Really?" she sounded surprised and questioning. "What bird?"

"Oh, I don't know. It was low slung in the water, a bit like a patrolling surfaced submarine if you like, but with a chisel-like bill."

"Did it call to you?"

"Yes, it kind of whittled and warbled.... ....like this," and he imitated the call of the diver before feeling self-conscious and stopping.

"You saw and heard the sea herdsman, *mur bhuachaill*, the loon, under the northern lights. Magical."

"I'll give it magical, it played merry with my dreams last night. In them, I even ended right up here sat next to some old man talking about the wildlife."

Gerry went ashen white and glared coldly at Sol.

"Is everything okay?" he asked.

"Yes, yes," she muttered, but he knew something had affected her about his mention of the dream, if only for a second. Then suddenly pulling herself together she forced the book further into Sol's hand. He held it for a while before looking down to see what it was and then laughed, breaking the awkward silence that had suddenly fallen between them. It was an ancient recipe and cooking book for use with a wood-burning stove.

"It's a house warming gift. I thought it might help," she smiled reassuringly. But something had obviously bothered her and affected her humour still. "It took me ages to find and really you should have had it before now. We don't exactly have a lot of shops up here."

"No," Sol answered. "I've been looking for the supermarket for the past few days."

He looked at his bag before asking, "How much do I owe you for the pheasant?"

"What?" Thankfully she was beginning to relax again and more of her character shone back through her recent tenseness.

"Well I've got cash. Back at the cottage that is."

"As I said, there aren't really many shops around here so cash isn't that much use is it? Besides, strictly speaking these are your pheasant."

Sol gave her a look of confusion.

"I shot them up there," she explained and pointed back towards the moorland that footed the mountain. Sol followed her gaze blankly.

"You do know that you own all that land back there don't you?" she asked earnestly.

Sol tried not to make it too obvious that he did not know that the land was his, but struggled with the gravity of such a lie in front of a new potential friend.

"Sheesh, maybe Hamish was right after all. You don't know what you've taken on do you? 'Proper little city boy' he calls you. Still, we'll see you right and will make sure you survive longer than he thinks you will."

"Do I own this?" he quizzed, puzzled, looking at the moor on the headland.

"Oh yes. And a bit more."

"How *much* land do I own then?" Sol enquired. He knew he had purchased a house with some ground but he hadn't really looked into just how much actually was his. He presumed he just had a big plot and compared to London where his roof garden was a luxury, anything was large.

"Oh, about fourteen and a half..."

"...acres?" Sol finished impatiently not really believing his luck.

"No," she paused. "Fourteen and a half thousand acres. You *did* know that didn't you?"

Sol didn't. But truth-be-told he still could not put that measurement into any context.

"What's wrong?" she enquired. "Aren't you happy with that?"

"Well yes. But how big is an acre let alone fourteen and a half thousand acres?"

She thought for a bit.

"Well imagine a football pitch…" He could do this.

"Now, imagine you had more than twenty thousand of them…" He looked surprised.

"That's about how much you own. That includes that mountain back there, this headland, and the glen, and off to the other side there's a sheltered bay and an old chapel. Up there," she pointed back towards the mountain. "Up there is the header loch where your water comes from and it's full of fish…   …I might have poached those too, sorry. Oh, and everything you can see down the road up to the *Bothan* is yours as well."

"But how can I have afforded all that?"

"It's not everyone who wants to live all on their own like you do without power and everything else. It's a bit cheaper here than London I dare say?"

Sol had to laugh at that. "The *Bothan* does have her limitations."

He sat down. "Power, light, Internet - still I suppose I'll get used to it."

"So," she said. "How much do I owe *you* for all the pheasant I've taken over the years?"

Sol thought about it and gave an over-zealous expression to reflect such.

"Nothing," he added after a while. "So long as we can be friends."

"Deal. G hated them anyway. To him, they were just an alien introduced species and all. He thought they tasted nice in the pot though." And they laughed naturally together. Unusually, there was no competition to be better than the other, no intensity to impress or even a desire to be anything other than amicable companions. Quite surprisingly for Sol, there was not even a hint of tension. It was as if they had been friends for a while, proper friends even though they had just met.

Gerry suddenly broke the silence, "you've cut your knee! Look at it!" She shouted with the enthusiasm of a child who had discovered something new, and before Sol could answer that it was just a graze, she was up and off through the herbage.

After a few minutes she returned with a clump of vegetation grasped meanly in her hand and knelt down close to him, rubbing them together rapidly and bruising the leaves. She smelt them experimentally before placing the now strongly scented herbs directly on to the cuts and scratches. She then took a grasp of his hand and positioned it firmly over the mashed mass and asked him to hold it tight.

"What's this?" he asked, curious at the cool numbing sensation he felt in his knee.

"Herbs," she explained, and because he looked at her as if wanting more information she clarified. "Plantain takes down the swelling, and there's daisy to speed up the healing, and garlic will kill off any bacteria, but you will smell a bit. It's a poultice – an herbal remedy. Medieval or older probably."

"I just use antiseptic cream normally back at home."

"Waste of money and too much chemical in it." She spoke sincerely and he nodded in recognition that she was probably correct. "I mean, there are chemicals in everything, and not all herbs are good for you. But these have the right sorts of chemicals in them."

The coolness of the poultice spread through his leg as they both gazed out towards the sea, to where the swans had left off, until Gerry, filled with unexpected energy, jumped up from where she was sat.

"Right, time to go," and she threw out her hand to grab his to shake it once again, as robustly as the last time. "It's been lovely meeting you."

"And you too," replied Sol with untypical honesty.

She picked up her bag and gun from amongst the desiccated stems of heather and then turned to leave.

"Well, I'll be off," she said in a voice that Sol felt was filled with a sense of joy and carried the very sound of hope. "If you need me then just come up and over the headland, skip the bay where the chapel is and my cottage is hidden in the next valley. It'd be no more than four or five miles but 'd be *much* quicker by boat. You can sail?"

"Yes," Sol lied, but Gerry wasn't easily taken in.

"Just let me know if you are stupid enough to want to take the boat out. I don't want any accidents and I've heard about the car."

"I will," he lied again, blushing and embarrassed about his accident on the drive.

"*Now* say it as if you mean it."

Sol didn't answer.

"Look, we know you aren't from round here and it will take a while to work us out and for you to feel at home, but trust us. We don't want any accidents. Besides, I like you and, despite what Hamish might have said, we do want our new neighbour to live."

"Oh good," Sol replied.

"Oh don't get too cocky though. It's only because I see you can play the violin and we need a new fiddler in the ceilidh band that most people will even talk to you."

With that she smiled and bounded off through the heather throwing a drift of flies and bees up in clouds that quickly re-found the shelter of the shrub and ground behind.

"Promise me you won't go near that boat without me," she shouted over her shoulder.

"I promise," he lied.

"Promise me you'll get better at lying too."

"I promise," he lied again with a smile across his lips.

And then she was gone from sight but he still caught snippets of her singing voice drifting beautifully over the moor with the ebb and flow of the wind long after. The skylark sang a counter melody in harmony over the top of her tune joining her as avian accompaniment. Crickets added percussion as they stridulated from the grasses that fringed the moor. Their presence ended in flashes of yellow bird's-foot-trefoil and the lilac pompoms of the sea pinks that grabbed onto the edges of the splash-sprayed rocks tumbling down into the salt water far below.

A flotilla of ducks bobbed on the surface of the loch as dark specks and the Solan geese dived missile-like on gatherings of fish that Sol could distinguish vaguely by the silvered outline of their shoal.

He waited alone sat abreast the raised rectangular platform of dusty soil with that curious carved rock behind him.

Eventually Sol retired from the top of the headland and feeling adventurous he walked over to the next bay following a rough path cut through the heather and gorse from the standing stone and over the edge of the cliffs. It headed precariously but assuredly down through ledges and cracks that hung over the deep-greened waters that frothed gently, but powerfully, below and from which gulls dropped into flight. He could perceive a rock stack much further out in the loch, misted and spumed from absolute focus. The white and black of mixed seabird flocks drifted around it with waves crashing up from the open estuary in attempt to envelope them. The rock was guano capped after centuries of busy nesting use.

Finally, he set foot on the solidity of flat bedrock and then stepped out on to a coral sand beach that reflected the heat of the day with ferocious intensity. There were the remnants of an old farmstead in wall-outline only at one side of the glen that arose from the bay, and a small stone building built into the far cliffs that remained complete. It was erected only just higher than the tide seemed to end which leant it a certain precariousness, with it been constructed below the crumbling wall of the cliff and above the rising surge of the sea, and it was hemmed in even more by the presence of a tumbling river that happily wound its way down the glen and into the loch. It just did not seem the right place to build anything to last. But last it had for it was obviously old.

He paced slowly along the loch shore leaving imprint footprints in his wake to investigate this solid looking creation.

It was a basic building hewn from rectangular blocks chipped on site and mortared roughly together with an over-coat of yellow and black lichens where the sea spray hit it most and moss on the darkened side that saw little of the drying sun. A well-trodden path partitioned the short-cropped grasses into two sections that ended abruptly as the lawn fell into the beach and strand line of flotsam. At the far end was a jaggedly cut bell tower from which an oxidised-green and brown brass bell hung with a rope that passed it and down into the main building.

Sol was curious, even though he knew this was a chapel and he had not been in any form of a church for so long. Pushing on through the door he found a cold interior of white washed inner walls illuminated by a leaded window on both sides, and hard straight wooden pews for a maximum of twenty people. At the front was a primitive lectern of some type and a separate apse that led to a dense stone altar covered by a clean, white cloth that fell over its edges, upon which sat a large silver cross. Two tall part-burnt candles were gripped by cleverly cast brass stick holders either side, and although both were snubbed out they still emitted the scent of scorched wax that lingered heavily in the air.

'They would have been stolen in London!' he thought to himself. London was a place, like so many others, that if something had street value and was left out publicly, then it would soon find that value, only in the pocket of someone other than its rightful owner. Trust was not something that had served him well in his early life in the city.

He had always been taught to respect others' places of worship and even though he was much aged from then and had little interest in religion, he still stepped towards the altar with some reverence. Light glinted from the hard edges of the metal cross as it reflected back the view from smaller leaded windows on either side of the sacristy. The cross was a bold, simple, unnatural object.

There was a large 'King James' bible open on the lectern, the pages pinned down by a length of heavy red cloth with gold thread woven into it in the pattern of a Celtic serpent and eagle.

He couldn't help but read aloud to himself the way he had done all those years ago in church and in school. It was an almost automatic reaction returning him back to a bygone past, but he was interested too, just to see what the last parishioner had been focusing on.

"One Kings, Chapter 8, verse 22," he began, and then froze, scanning the awkward words of the highly prosaic King James edition of the Bible in front of him. Coincidence or not, someone had been reading about the King called Solomon, Solomon the Wise.

Hadn't Hamish referred to him mockingly as Solomon the Wise?

He read on intrigued.

Verse 22, Solomon stood before the altar.

Sol turned around and looked shrewdly at the simple altar, its plain cloth and the dazzlingly bright cross of silver on top of it.

Verse 26, there was a prayer by Solomon for wisdom.

He knew inside that wisdom was something he needed right now - that much was obvious. His city experience was not really going to sit him right for the future in a house with no power, no connection and no close neighbours however little time he really intended to stay in it.

Verse 29, Solomon asked for God to help him, the new king.

Any help would of course do. And although he had no interest in religion, or felt any spiritual spark, there was no doubt that he had the desire for some help.

Verse 34, there was a need for forgiveness of past sins.

Sol was not even going to contemplate his *'past life'* – not now. There was the usual long list of regrets and mistakes, involving friends, relationships and money. That was probably why he had ended up with and in the *Bothan* in the first place. He knew that although he wanted others to feel responsible for where he found himself and the past he had both enjoyed and, at times, regretted, it was his actions that influenced his future and he was of course ultimately in control.

Verse 39, God knows the heart.

He always struggled with this sort of religious mumbo, but had been conditioned enough as a child not to disparage it outright.

In all it was a prayer for wisdom and Sol had the compelling thought that someone somewhere knew that he would be passing this way and had left it open for him to read.

Sitting on the front pew, he took a few minutes to scan the chapel's interior, reverentially clean and white save for an age-darkened roof of wood that looked for all intents and purposes like a ship's hull that had been turned over and rested atop the walls. Roughly planed crooked timbers were layered with clinkered panels and then covered with heavy slates, each pegged securely in place by small wooden pins.

An interwoven rope hung from the roof and was secured to the wall by a brass pin, being hand-greased where it had been pulled over the years to ring the little bell on the roof.

Over the heavy door was a painted crest on a plinth of wood with a stylised diver rampant as its emblem bird. It was paddling in upright posture as if it walked on the waves of the busy water below it and there was a fish held in a beak that pointed backwards as it looked rearward from its red eye. Sol was immediately reminded of the bird in the cabinet back at the *Bothan*, the creature that had haunted his dreams and the real, live bird that had greeted him on the loch last night.

There was a small posy of drying spring flowers and grasses lain on the altar in front of the cross. Someone's homage had been made in the recent past.

Sol left the little church in a quiet mood of that type that only places of solace and long-kept respect can bring no matter of one's state of faith, belief or both.

The garden outside had been tended and he noticed that there were flowers that lined the simply beaten track that served as the entryway to the building. White pebble stones had been carefully arranged to make the path clearer.

'Scrarch!'

A beady-eyed black-headed corvid taunted him from the roof of the chapel, a living gargoyle that brought an element of sinister menace to the bay. It judged him side-eyed from the apex of the roof, where a basic stone cross had been added to prevent the resting of witches and other things of evil. It did not keep this corvid away though and Sol understood the malevolent portent these creatures were once believed to be in their twisted human appearance. It watched for a while before it continued to pick at the moss that encrusted between the overlaps of tiles in its search for grubs and beetles.

It was a disconcerting bird to be examined by, walking along the roof slates like some grotesque windup toy with an almost anthropoid expression of intelligence about it. Its wings were folded back across its spine in the serious pose of a waiting butler or pacing lawyer at the bar.

Sol left under the shadow of this avian justice and headed back across the beach to re-join the path up to the standing stone and the eventual route back home to the *Bothan.*

Half-way up, he remembered his phone and almost cursed himself for the mix of feelings this brought. First was the sensation of guilt that he had until now forgotten it, that draw on his attention and interference into his life. Then there was the anxiety as to what he had missed, and when he addictively switched it on what messages it would bring from his past life or that which might affect his present time or his potential future. There was also anger that the phone had encroached back into his psyche despite his sudden, new-found loathing of the device and his desire to be free of it and to just continue, isolated in his own little kingdom of *Bothan Faobhar* – which he now learnt was actually quite large.

He rested by the relic stone and switched the mobile on, waiting for it to connect with the network and to download the messages he had received. With anxious antipathy he looked at them as they appeared in their turns.

There was an acknowledgement from the supermarket that his shopping would be delivered by 4.30pm tomorrow night but that the lorry would go no closer to the Bothan than the end of the drive. Another message indicated that his possessions from London would be delivered between the hours of 9am and 5pm, as if that sort of time period was any kind of limitation and helped him with his life-organisation and ability to be in to receive it. In addition his three online purchases would also arrive in the same time frame and so it looked like he would be camping at the end of the drive for the duration of the whole of the next day.

There were other messages too.

She wanted to know why he hadn't replied...   ...he needed to get over it, as it was his fault...   ...could he not grow up and reply? ...did he not know how his lack of response made her feel?   ...it was really very childish to be like this and to make himself unavailable... ...answer!

Office calling for yet more details he could not provide about the deal with Tokyo...   ...did he not know how his lack of response looked to the office or the authorities?   ...it was irresponsible to do business this way...   ...if he expected references he had better think about replying... ...answer!

Therapist asking if he was terminating his contract with her? ...not a good sign that he was not writing to her...   ...maybe another session would help?   ...thinks it would be beneficial for him to call up... ...answer, please!

Friends concerned he was obviously feeling worse than they had initially thought...   ...still he could text...   ...fine, if that's the way he wanted it...   ....surprise visit?   ...where is this house anyway? ...answer!

'*Do not visit yet,*' he replied thumbing his message in efficiently with adept strikes of the touch-sensitive screen. '*Place needs work first and there are a few issues I will need to work on before I can receive guests.*
Sol'
The return text was quick in response. '*Oh, you ARE alive! Antisocial bugger. We'll give you a week then?*'
'*Maybe a month?*'
No reply.

Family hoping okay?
'*All well,*' he wrote. '*Just taking some time and the house needs more work than I thought.*
Love Sol.'

Authorities sending a list of questions to which he replied providing information, links and references to others where possible. There wasn't much material... ....not yet anyway.
Memory is never good when communicating in legalise, but he tried his best and gave them the details of the accounts and the deal that he could without access to a computer and his office desk and its attendant team of subordinates at his immediate disposal. It was not illegal, and he reassured them of that, but the paperwork would be slow and so he needed the authorities on side, but to be patient also. This was not a virtue he had seen much from them in the past and so he would need to work on buying himself time if they continued to press him for anything but the scant details he had already provided.

Solicitor asking him to please confirm receipt of the deeds to Bothan Faobhar which should arrive by courier on Tuesday... ...they ask if he could meet them at the end of the drive between the hours of 9.00am and 5.00pm.

'*Of course*,' he replied. '*I have nothing better to do than to wait at the end of the drive for eight hours.*' His answer was laced with sarcasm that he thought better of it only once he had pressed send.

'*Good*,' came the perfunctory reply.

There was also a message from his city friend Al, an independent entrepreneurial businessman who worked in hotels and food. His view of life was a very money-focused and jaded one, with value being a core principle to anything he was invested in.

'*Sol,*

Glad to hear you are alive. I'll come up to assess the property as soon as I can get out of the office. Things are busy for the now. Permanently have overseas potential buyers at hand and your place may be of interest. Typical you, always looking for profit. The view you have would add much to the money you could make. May need to flatten the house to make room for development.

Send list of books and equipment, pictures if possible, and I'll get them valued. Have friends at the auction house asking questions. Probably best potential if sell individually via auction or in collections of type and age. What do you think?

Get signal sorted as tried phoning you loads of times!

Don't get too lonely up there on your own you daft bugger – just looked it up on the map and can't even get street view to the end of your driveway.

Al'

There was no mention of Pete in the text and Sol's last message for Al to pass on news of the wildcat, and so he replied with some relief.

'*Al,*

I think I was wrong about potential as place is far too isolated. In fact it's in the middle of nowhere. Not much going for it. Think I was wrong about the books and kit too.'

He was suddenly feeling protective and defensive about *Bothan Faobhar* and its contents, selfishly wanting it as a whole and kept for himself. At least there was no mention of the wildcat.

'How's London treating you?' he continued. *'Hope the boys are misbehaving as usual?*

Sol'

He went on to the next text and took an intake of breath, deep and profound. It was from Pete, a mutual photographer friend obsessed by wildlife.

'Sol,

You daft sod! Al tells me you have bought a house up in Scotland somewhere in the back of beyond and that you've got wildcats roaming round the place. Is it true? Coming up to see your wildcat if it is! Could make money as an eco-attraction if you can get photographers in easy and get close up views of wildcats. They are ridiculously rare.

Give us a call to let me know when I can come up.

Pete

PS. I get first dibs on business enterprise – London boys would pay a fortune to see wildcats if marketed well'

"Shit!" Sol exclaimed and then quickly replied.

'Pete,

Wildcat not been seen for a while. Could have been a moggy anyway. Will let you know if see it again. House not ready for guests yet.

Sol'

The phone bleeped that irritating call to indicate a message had arrived and Sol jumped reflexively. It was Al again.

'Anyone would think you are trying to hide something up there. Send photos and let me decide on the value. Need pictures of house and grounds, views and any books or equipment. If you know the edition of any books, even better. Obviously first editions are the best. I will also require an estimate of the condition of each and every item.

Al'

As he started to reply, the phone bleeped twice more. This time it was Pete and *that* woman, the one he was trying to avoid.

'Worried about you up there on your own and besides, keen to see if the wildcat is genuine. Must be other good wildlife too? Normally is if they're about. Will get the boys up next week. Bring some bevs and make a drunken week of it?

Pete'

He scanned the message from the woman.

'Sol,

Pete and Al have both just told me you are on line. Why aren't you texting me? Typical of you, putting the boys first.

Your things are on their way up. I know I asked you to go but I am still worried about you. Are you okay? The boys say you have a house in the middle of nowhere.

You'll never survive without other people! Not you! You're not the type. Have you met the neighbours yet and do they seem friendly?

Let me know.

Sue'

What did she know? The anger boiled up inside remarkably quickly, almost irrationally, and erupted in a volcanic outburst that was only settled as he looked out across the sea, planted his now bared feet firmly into the dusty rectangle in front of him and felt the sun and the breeze on his skin.

He would survive!

He was the type!

He was happy to be alone!

He did not need the London crowd up here!

Instead, he needed to protect the Bothan and its contents and the estate!

He penned a short text to the three interested parties, Al, Pete and Sue.

'Dear all,

*Struggling with reception but will call you when I have improved
the situation.*
*Not ready for visitors yet as the house needs some work too. There
aren't many builders around here and so it might take a while.*
*No need to worry as I enjoying myself. Not really alone anyway as
the neighbours have been very welcoming so far, all except for one
old man. I am alone in the house but not lonely, and there is quite a
difference between those two words.*
Speak soon.
Chow,
Sol'

And with that, he performed the greatest insult he could. He
switched the phone's power off, dropped it into his violin case and
promptly tried to forget about it and the threat that messages on it
represented to his new peace, his new home and what he foolishly
considered was *his* wildlife. With the mobile out of sight the guilty
thoughts for his distant friends rapidly evaporated and he wondered
just what they had in common with each other and what bound
them together as *'friends'* in the first place. In some respects they
were little more than just passing acquaintances and drinking
partners and he started to count who were his closest actual *friends*
and those that did not just rely on him for a good night out and the
money to pay for it. Of course there was Al and Pete whom he'd
known for an age, and there had been Sue. But then the list ran
dry…

With lunchtime approaching his stomach lurched and he made his
way back to the *Bothan* through the heather, down the cliff path
and through the pollen rich atmosphere of the drying wood where
yellow dust fell from the pine and yew trees with every caress of
the air. Back at the cottage he felt warmed not just by the heat of
the high sun but the view of the twinkling waters where the light
reflected off the waves that gently lapped their way towards the
short grasses and flower stems of the machair.

A high tide out at sea had pushed the loch up so much closer to the house that the greylags, that '*quanked*' noisily, had come to crop greenery only feet from the low lying wall of the garden. Gulls hung effortless in the sky as if hooked by invisible threads, and the large silhouette of a bird, mostly wings and fingered end feathers, drifted at a height. This was the fish eagle, a return to the land after generations of exile and recent re-release following its British extinction.

It saw the world in opposing context to Sol.

Looking down from a position of elevation with the sun on its back, the bird beheld the little man on the shore who craned upwards, his eyes shielded from the glare. What he saw as distant this avian marvel watched in magnified detail with lenses designed to accommodate for the space between them. It was a hunter and he a mere observer, watching and taking in not seeking with an eye for the table. It moved without effort or display, wings held aloft and catching the passive currents of the air that the sun's heat baked and allowed to raise from the hot earth, whereas this man worked actively to fight against gravity's best and used effort inefficiently to move from place to place.

It was unaware of the concerns of the phone, of commerce and of friends. Instead, it drifted simply in search of food and in defence of the territory it needed to breed for another year.

Their lives could be little more different.

Sol quickly hung the pheasant in the larder to prevent them getting any higher than they already were and then prepared a simple lunch from the stores that others had provided. Next, he went out to consider a nagging thought that had tugged at his mind since his meeting with Gerry and he found himself stood next to the upturned wooden boat.

Something at the back of his mind told him that to take it out, however calm the waters, would be a mistake. But then there was another, adventure-desiring portion of his brain, the one that made him such a success in the world of business and allowed him to push the boundaries, extend his horizons and take the greatest chances. This was that uniquely male part of his psyche that coupled with the foolhardiness of testosterone meant he could face risks and adversity in order to attempt to succeed, when following advice would have been easier but would have led to less potential benefit and profit. This part of his brain lacked the capacity to consider consequence beyond the immediate gratification of its desires.

He looked at the boat for a long time.

Her name was carefully inscribed in white hand-painted letters on either side of her prow. *Sireadh-thall* (seek beyond) seemed such an appropriate tag for a craft designed to literally travel beyond the interface between land and sea. She, as she had already taken on a gender, feminine as boats usually were, was a beautiful boat hauled up here and laid gently on a bed of brash'd sticks that were placed over the cobbles and pebbles by the side of the house wall to avoid her wood being abraded by them.

A master boat builder in a workshop, using just traditional tools and techniques, had cleverly created her from nothing but wood. Her fifteen foot of timbers remained well varnished, a deep amber in colour, and she swelled in her mid-section to a beam of nearly five feet in diameter. A stone-etched keel ran proud of her hull from tip to stern. She was a big boat for one man but Sol was confident she was built for the single if required.

He tipped her heavy construction over to reveal a tenderly folded red-brown sail and a boom-less mast, with two great oars to connect into the loops on her sides.

He knew he was going to take this craft out, whatever Gerry had told him, and turned into the paddling geese by the wall and at the water's edge, with the painter rope in check, to see how best to get her safely to the shore.

Chapter 7: The Birds Beyond

(The Hebrides (Fingal's Cave): Overture, Felix Mendelssohn)

Lines are curious things.
Every piece of artwork is in some way a line. Be it painted, drawn, sculpted or marked, they simply represent the image that an artist tries to portray, or the observer perceives or studies. All scenes that we admire are lines whether they are straight, curved, regular or random. Even that famous cityscape, that takes us to any major conurbation, is a series of black lines punctuated with the lights of home windows and offices illuminated from behind by a day or a night sky.
Look into the heavens in the dark and our eyes make link-lines between the randomness of stars and space, forming ordered constellations between the pinpricks of light that have travelled so many million miles to hit our retinas. We find lines, interconnecting cities and towns as roads on maps, circumnavigating topography as contours, tracking the routes of rivers and showing the safest passage for boats and planes. We are line obsessed.
There is little as satisfying as typewritten script all in perfect alignment, the letters each created of lines themselves. Or, even the beauty of a handwritten letter where all the characters slant to the same lineated angle, keeping within a rulered margin on every edge, and maintaining straight parallel positions as the words cross the page left to right. There are then those Chinese masters of symbolic font or the Japanese artists that record words in pictures with a skilful deft hand use of the brush. Here every line and stroke, even its initial mark through its broadest elegant drift onto its last waning connection with the paper, counts towards meaning and accurate communication.
Lines even define the style of writing or art.

When vending a car or a house, it is the lines we market and sell. When buying, it is the lines we fall for and purchase, and when judging an ocean, it is the lines which deceive the unwary.

As Sol walked towards the pebbled shore where the low flat ranks of receding breakers hit the edge of the coral sand beach with their white topped *'swish'*, it was the straightness of the water and its linear calmness that gave him the feeling of safety and assurance that he needed and sought. They lifted a stranded line of blackened weed where their heights had made their uppermost insurgence towards dry land as they had worked their way slowly up the beach. Waves broke in threes before a relative peace fell on the water, then building up to a large greenish-silver swell that rushed in and crashed before another three smaller broke, one after the other. White foam tops laboured along the crest of each surge from left to right as the wave fell angular to the beach, another line intersecting, the breakers not falling all at the same moment.

Sol saw the perfect mark of the horizon from which the distant shore arose, as if the loch's waters, although chastened by the mobile sea, had found their level and stuck to it as liquid in a very large contort-shaped bowl. The lines looked good and welcoming, flat and calm, and he was reassured.

Then there was the craft itself, whose beauty came from the curvaceous line of her hull, from pointed prow, which blossomed to full beam mid-ship and then closed in as a round ended stern. Perfectly tessellated timbers lay closely abutted, with no room for a breath between them, to produce a thing of symmetrical harmony whose lines of wood lay as testament to the contours of her streamlined profile. She was made for water as every part of her frame testified, in the same way that a fossilised fish is so obviously created for life in the seas even though it is now found locked in a rock and stranded hundreds of miles inland. No geologist would be confused about its initial design brief. It was a fish. It lived an aquatic existence. Therefore the sea made the rocks around it.

Stepping out into the water, Sol tugged on the painter rope and was surprised at the sudden lightness of *Sireadh-thall* as she lifted up into the waves and the loch took the brunt of gravity. She slipped easily over the few cobbles on the sand until she bounced with each ice-brimmed upsurge that crashed with gentle abandon into Sol's legs, held tight by wetted trousers that clung in their salty stickiness. The hiss of sand on wood ended as a diminuendo of the rushing sound of the last grains, to be replaced with the gentle tugs and laps of seawater.

One moment's reflection and Sol pulled hard enough to launch the round-bottomed craft into deeper water and more or less fell over her bulwark and into her deep interior. Wide-based she was stable enough, although Sol was going to have to gain sea legs if he was to cope with the gentle rise and fall that the waves bid the boat to undertake.

Locking the two black-painted oars in he realized that *Sireadh-thall* was more of a twin man boat than a single and struggled briefly to gain control, only finally realizing that he would have to paddle backwards if he was to go anywhere. He dropped the rudder and then anchored the lengthy tiller with his foot, and turned the boat more easily than he thought he would be able to, stroking the active water surface to test his skill. She gave slightly and reluctantly followed his command, something recalled from distant holidays when he was young.

Next he got used to the feeling of the oar-resistant water and its control by scraping the blades deeper in experimental pulls, sending up showers of spray as he miss-timed one stroke or the other. *Sireadh-thall* quickly learnt to obey his instruction and he mistakenly developed that landlubbers thought that he could master the sea given time. Every seaman knows that no one rules the sea, least of all the one who fails to respect it, and many of these people have been trained for the water from birth with many generations of experience before them to give out warnings, recall success and remember the costs.

Gaining confidence, Sol pulled deeply backwards and drove her into the darker blue of the main loch waters, finding ease to his movement and stretching his back in a way no gym ergo could. Where there every stroke was identical in resistance and depth, here each one required readjustment and an ever-changing tension, depth and power.

He felt the temperature of the hull drop with the depth of the rock bed below him as the security of the edge dropped away and *Sireadh-thall* bobbed smoothly with the breakers. She cut them cleanly, white-frothed, at a right angle to their shore-centred linear onset. Afloat, he bound as rough a course as he could for the headland promontory that struck out broadly into the loch and sheltered the bay from the open sea.

There is an exhilaration that comes with sailing, especially when alone, that one caveat given by any emergency service and boat salesman being that you promise you will never do it. Something intangible comes from the pull of each wave as it lifts and drops the boat in rhythmical expression of the energy within, the rock and yaw with a feeling of hidden depth below. It is exciting and the skin prickles and the brain alerts.

An element of danger brings us to our senses as we quickly come to understand the power of the sea in comparison to our own humble, fragile forms, guiding and directing or destroying and smashing, all dependent on the current and geography. No one commands the sea, they simply occupy a miniscule displaced portion of it that their body or craft has squeezed aside, not making any appreciable difference to the mass of water around and beyond. To cut a wave is temporary and what your prow splits in two at one end will fluidly merge to re-form at your stern as if you had never been there. Water crossings are the only human pathways that leave no visible trace of our passage following and we are quickly enveloped and forgotten, leaving no trace of our journey behind for anyone to track.

The sea itself has emotion, something seen and described by painters and poets, and, before this retold by word of mouth in the aural history of humans which far predates any record. Its colour can be a reflection of the sky or a transmission of the water's bed. It can take on hues of its own and swirl to create brightness' of white, through green then blue to deepest black, and it can be as flat and featureless as the ball-rolled baize of a billiard table or as violent and chopped up as a tsunami with every texture, shape and upsurge in between. Always, it can be dangerous, and yet is the source of evolved life and still supports the greatest living diversity we know, in continuous range from the smallest bacterium to the largest creatures to have lived on Earth.

Its depths hold secrets only witnessed by the dead that have sunk with their ships in days gone by and the only limitation to oceanic biological design is often our own imagination. It covers mountains as high as Everest and submerges volcanoes that even today split the vast oceans in two, with the seas covering two thirds of the Earth. It has given us access to other countries, allowed empires to thrive and people to trade and travel. It has always been the home of the gods. And yet, the sea remains the most under-explored and poorly understood biome on our planet with us quite literally only ever scratching the surface when we visit or travel around it. Its very medium both attracts us and prevents us from ever truly knowing it.

But to ride the sea, to feel the power, and yet sense the freedom to explore and taste just that part which you can, is something that, like a fully matured addiction, sucks all of us in. That is so long as we can cope with the unseen depth below our feet and allow ourselves to be hung in the water, separated from it by only a thin covering of boat, suspended over fathoms of mystery, and in control of very little; that is certainly one definition of exhilaration!

Sol allowed the boat to float free and made himself familiar with drawing the water evenly on either side of the hull to make sure that he could keep her straight. He then practised turning using the paddles and next the tiller, a simple but strong wooden dowel that directed the rudder, with his foot. It all seemed easy enough, but today he would not go far. He had no life jacket, little understanding of boat craft and no knowledge of the tides, the currents, the winds, or even the rocks. He would simply turn her around and head back to shore.

But *Sireadh-thall* was keen to live up to her name and once committed to the sea, after little recent use, she was happy to explore again and to travel further. As Sol took her to the end of the headland the incoming tidal current picked up the small craft and gently teased her further out into the faster rush of the central loch waters. And then he found her rising and falling with greater height as he rounded the rocks, and, suddenly spinning into the wind, she was drawn out into the central channel.

The water, cast blue with greater depth, was stained black by hidden rocks below and was chopped up readily by the flowing stream of churning liquid. Within only a minute Sol knew that he had lost control and that *Sireadh-thall*, by the sea's volition, was now heading at an alarming rate out into the very middle of the loch, which now appeared larger than he had appreciated, but thankfully in a direction that opposed the open sea. He was gladdened that the tide was still coming in but it didn't do much to make him feel safer.

As paddling only seemed to aggravate the boat, unsteady her and make her spin against the prevailing current and airs, Sol brought the oars in and sat back for a while. He was less frightened than he thought he should be as he watched the little white cottage drop away from his view and become engulfed by either jaw of the diminutive glen by which it was it was possessed.

A wide opal sky filled the void from horizon to horizon. Sol could see rock stacks that leapt up out of the mouth of the loch, black with distance, which tried to reach the sky's blue whilst fighting steadfastly against the waves that broke themselves in foaming spray against them. White specks of milling bird flocks gambolled around and above, and three greasy green-backed cormorants torpedoed their way along the loch in low-slung flight that threatened to collide them with the water.

Sireadh-thall drifted over the surface towards the far shore, and strangely, after the initial fear that he might drown or become lost, Sol simply gave up and over to nature and a trust that if he had got himself this far then he was sure he could go on further. He had an unbidden belief that the boat somehow knew where to go. This was probably the gut reaction and nerve that had helped him so much in city business. However he was equally aware that this was also the sensation that had drawn him in to most of his historic trouble too and was probably the foolhardiness that led most would be sailors to their airless ends and a watery grave. He knew he was a fool to even be out here on the water. But then, he was also certain that he now had little choice other than to follow the boat's direction.

An ensemble of small streamer-tailed angel-like birds screeched their way into his consciousness. Each individual had a grace movement of its own, working as a singular, intent on the hunt of fish glittering in the waters below. And yet, this commotion of group effort made the flock a writhing ball of birds that moved as a collective, not just as individuals, shape-shifting at its periphery, but still holding true to the colony. Characters were played as the hunter dropped, the observer held back and the successful fed and screamed.

Black-capped heads all facing seaward, this frenzied mass of active birds steadily approached Sol in *Sireadh-thall* following the silver piscine bullets who raced the nutrients in the rapid current below. Birds dropped as bullets around them, plummeting with wings held back and beaks out-pointed. '*Poof!-Plagh!*' and the water enveloped each tern as he or she dived down on hapless prey that thankfully remained blind to the stalkers dropping in from the sky above. They were plucked up in vicious reddened beaks, sharp for the kill and wide for the snatch, and then hooked up and out of the water as the birds gulped them headfirst in wholes as complete fish, unprepared, other than dead.

The boat and Sol seemed invisible to the writhing throng of sun-halo'd terns, who continued to hunt and squeal around them, until the fish moved on and the birds went with them to a place beyond his sight and hearing.

Drifting for a while the boat seemed unsure of the direction until it picked up another current that carried it towards the cliffs on the far side of the loch. A slight breeze lifted and moved it with the boards underneath banging as if men were hammering from the underside. Sol did not enjoy the flexibility of the panels that seemed to wax and wane as the waters eddied around and under them making momentary fluid patterns in the froth etches on the water's surface, which endured briefly before dissolving into nothing as if they had never previously existed.

He had the feeling that the loch was alive.

Not simply as it was so filled with living things, but instead the waters themselves, joined by their salt-drenched sister molecules from the sea, or the burgeoning downpours from the clouds, or jostled by the outpourings of brooks, rivers and burns, some slow and lugubrious, others quick, cold and fast. The water played emotions in colour, texture, shade and scale. It reflected, it hid, it engulfed and in amongst it all, it had strength and yet consisted of nothing but an unsolidified medium of liquid. It was easily broken, re-fused, evaporated or precipitated. It churned and made noises inhuman. It stood still and remained immobile and yet also it was constantly on the go.

It *felt* alive.

An urge to move under the power of a light breeze swept Sol up into action. Feeling the prickly heat of panic sweat coat his skin he pulled the sail free of its binding and slotted the mast post into its wooden housing, securing it with a brass bolt. The sail hung limply, flapping when the wind's courtesy demanded it.

Tension, the sail needed tension.

Binding the foresail to the painter ring at the front of the boat and the rear of the sail to the stern he was surprised that the sail quickly picked up air and filled in one triangular blossom, dragging *Sireadh-thall* bodily and throwing her sideways in a pitch that threatened to dip her right side bulwark under the water. Instead it licked dangerously in its constant frenetic lapping, unsuccessfully urging the boat to capsize. But then the craft turned against the wind, and, catching more air it began to race across the waters in the direction of the opposite shore to the home he really sought.

Home was gone, a speck some way off, white on an otherwise dark planted-green of a shrinking shore. *Sireadh-thall* was a wind-possessed demon and coasted with abandoned care and purpose.

Eventually they came to a broad coral-white sandy beach shoreline in a valley not that dissimilar to his own glen. It too was sheltered by a headland, except that it was more open and exposed to the sun's heat. A white and grey stone house nestled up and away from the loch, huddled by a forest and accompanied by a river that tumbled down over rocks and joined the loch via a wide-mouthed estuary where fish leapt at the afternoon's fly hatch. There was a wooden jetty that extended out into the loch and with some concern Sol realised that he was on a heading straight for it but lacked the skill to avoid a collision. Worse still, on the end was a past middle-aged woman, white-haired, plump and ruddy-faced, fishing from the end of the pier.

She turned to look at him with little concern and waved nonchalantly at him before turning back to observe the end of her line, hidden somewhere below the surface of the riffled water.

The jetty came closer and Sol could only assume that the boat was travelling slower than it appeared to be when sat down in it and so close to the water's surface.

How to slow a sailing boat?

"Sail," he thought half out loud. "I need to drop the sail!"

He fumbled with the knots at the back, cold salt-sticky and tension-tightened, and once released, he watched the largest portion of tarpaulin immediately fall slack and he felt the boat lose momentum. Still she ploughed on, the gently lapping water offering little resistance, and he continued to approach the wooden jetty where the lady carried on fishing as if nothing were the matter.

Next he ran to the front and untied the hefty, effective but difficult to untie knot he had created at the painter ring. The foresail dropped uselessly after which Sol deftly lowered the mast and gathered up the sailcloth. Nevertheless *Sireadh-thall* continued, slowing in increments too small to avoid the collision.

"Paddle," he thought.

And so, placing himself firmly in the centre of the beam with his foot on the tiller as before, he used the oars to try and slow his progress towards the lady and the jetty, and instead attempted to aim for the ample sandy shoreline.

When *Sireadh-thall* eventually collided with the pier, after what seemed an age of back paddling and tense footwork, Sol was thankful that it was only a glancing blow. Somehow he had managed to steer the hull to near parallel with the springy wooden timbers, lined with old car tyres, and little if no damage occurred even though he was thrown backwards from the beam. A second lady, who matched the first still fishing without concern from the end of the jetty, had mysteriously appeared from somewhere and grabbed the painter rope that she used to direct the boat and then secure her to a post on the pier.

"Hamish said you drove everywhere too fast," she laughed and she rescued the pier from any further damage by yanking hard back on the stern rope making the now half standing Sol fall forward the other way.

"Hello," he said reaching out his hand from his final resting position seeming to have lost his sea legs. "My name's…"

"We all know who you are," said the woman laughing heartily. "You'd be Sol. Who else but a city boy would sail like that?"

"Oh dear, really?" he asked as the buxom lady pulled the boat in tight to the pier with limbs that were far better formed and muscled than his gym-softened forearms, and she secured his boat off for him in rapid winding twists of the ropes. She checked them for tension and, once satisfied that all would be well, she turned back to look at Sol in the bottom of the hull.

"You do know how to sail?" she asked watching quizzically as he stumbled ashore on to the safety of the wooden planks now ricocheting with the hollow bump of his feet on them.

"Keep it down will you," called the second women still fishing off the end of the quay. "Every noise you make will scare the f…"

"It's all about fish with her," explained the first. The she continued in a quieter gentler voice. "You don't know how to sail do you?"

"No," Sol admitted.

"I thought as much." She shook her head in a teacher-like manner; caring but judgemental. "Well, you are lucky to be alive and it's a good job *Sireadh-thall* knows the way here and both the sea and the weather gods like you. I expect you heard the blue men knocking on the underside of the hull as you crossed the tides?"

She looked for recognition in Sol's face.

"Well there was a knocking from underneath," he explained. "Something banging the timbers and making them shake. Is that what you mean?"

"Aye, that'd be them. They probably worked out you needed help and meant them no harm. They can spot a novice. They'll have pushed you on your way, which would go some way to explaining your speed once on this side of the loch. They are usually like that with newbies. Next time take an offering out and you'll pass more surely and safely. You don't want the '*Blue Men*' climbing up on to your boat, trust me!"

"An offering? Blue Men?" Sol was now completely unsure as to whether this woman meant what she said or was just joking. She had a friendly face, creased as it was so used to smiling, and he found her hard to read.

"Of course none of us believe in them, the *Blue Men*. But just in case, if we cross the sea loch to the other side we drop something of value to us over the edge when we hear the knocking under the boat. It's just a tradition but the ancients used to say that they were the '*Blue Men of the Sea*' or the '*Blue Men of the Loch*'."

"Who are they supposed to be? No one could live in the loch!"

"No one knows. Minions of some forgotten sea god probably."

"And, why exactly do you need to give them an offering?"

"Well for a start it means we show more respect to the sea if we do something sacrificial like that. It demonstrates that you are aware of something bigger and more powerful than yourself – that element, the sea, it kills hundreds every year." Sol looked back at the waters churning out in the middle of the loch where the tides mixed in confused patterns. "Let's just say, hypothetically speaking, that some idiot from the city decides to take a little wooden sailing boat out on his own into the loch without any idea of safety, no life jacket and probably never having been in a boat before. Just hypothetically speaking you understand?" She looked reproachfully at the blushing Sol. "Well, is he, or another hypothetical person so aware of the sea and its dangers that they drop an offering to it as they cross over, going to be safer or less safe?"

Sol look guilty back at *Sireadh-thall* as the woman's voice tailed off.

"Exactly. Just that moment of thought could be what makes the difference and keeps them safe."

She paused as Sol continued to consider the boat.

"Secondly, what happens if we were wrong? Obviously there are no blue men who live under the water. Anyone knows that. But a century ago nobody knew about computers and passenger jets and that everybody would have a car and a phone. If I told someone in the year 1900 that I could talk to another person on the other side of the world and have a conversation with them, they'd think I was barmy."

"You are," called the other women intent on her line.

"Thanks, Skye," called the other smiling at who Sol assumed was her sister. "Obsessed with fish she is," explained the first.

"That's because they make better conversation than you," laughed Skye.

"But you *kill* them and we *eat* them."

"Exactly, that's better conversation than we often have."

"Anyway," the other woman began again. "Talking about sacrifices. I've often wondered about pushing Skye overboard as an offering to the *Blue Men*, but she'd float too well, swims quite effectively and as she isn't worth that much to me they'd see through it in no time!"

Skye turned to face her sister and tried to give a hurt face, which was too screwed up with laughter to have any impact. They were obviously very relaxed with their banter to and about each other.

"To complete the reasons for offerings to the sea men. It's traditional too, and we've always done it here for countless generations. It must have been important to someone once and so why stop now? Just think," she started, her face scanning the choppiest waters, "there are probably hundreds of treasures buried over there in the middle of the loch where the currents change. Some idiot, no doubt from the city, will probably try to dig them up one day. They'll most likely get attacked by the *Blue Men* of the loch as they do it though, thus meaning that we are all wrong and the *Blue Men* do exist after all."

"I'm in," shouted Skye, suddenly leaping up to her feet with an energy that her frame suggested she was incapable of. "I told you I could catch tea before he got across."

Her barrelled-reel whizzed and whirred as she allowed the fish to race away and her line cut a pattern in the water's flat, calm surface. Then she leant sideways, with the rod tip bending with surprising flexibility, and started to guide the ripples of action closer in.

"Oh good. But sister, I hate to question your logic, only he is effectively already across the loch and you still haven't landed our supper have you? He got here before you landed the fish and so the bet has been won by me."

Skye twisted backwards whilst holding the rod taught and playing the increasingly excited fish below the surface. "He has not actually stepped ashore yet as he is still on the pier and so, dear sister, I believe the bet is still on."

She turned back to continue teasing the struggling silvery body that now leapt up and out of the water to produce contorted back-arching shapes in the air in its attempt to be free of the sunken fly nymph that it had fallen victim too. Hooked feathers and bound thread had conned it into attack.

"Sol, can you bring me the net please?" she asked as she fought on, but with little concern for anything but the tension of the line that now sang as the fish dived back down and under the broiling line cut surface. "You'll find it just behind me."

Sol obliged, hypnotised by the scene in front of him. He picked up the net and walked to a position alongside Skye, who took the net with her left hand and then passed the rod and line over to Sol from her right.

"Here you are," she said. "Now don't lose it. That's tea you've got on the run there."

The line flew freely out of the reel as the fish made a dash for it. But Skye was a good teacher and directed Sol clearly, a little like a parent instructing a particularly slow child. Initially worried and confused, not wanting to make mistakes or lose the fish, he started to feel the tension of the animal through the rod and make a connection with it.

It felt large, but what was he to know?

It gave him a buzz as it pulled backwards and forwards, and from its distant location he slowly found the creature being drawn closer and closer to the end of the pier. Skye had by now stepped away from him, and where she initially had been all hands and arms, physically directing his body and motions, now she used words only. Sol had the sense, rightly or wrongly, that although instructed, he was doing this one thing alone. *It was just he, a line and the fish on the end.*

It leapt up high and for the first time he appreciated its size. Two foot from nose to tail its scales caught and refracted the steadily dying sun's light into an iridescent rainbow of colours, prism-produced by each and every individual water-dropping scale. Fins of polished brass flapped and there were gills exposed as bright intense red as it aced its way back into the water in a plume of droplets frozen in time as his mind raced fast and his eyes stared with almost disbelief.

Heart pounding, he became aware of Skye shouting something to him.

"Rod up," she chastised. "Keep the end high. You've nearly got it."

Sol could feel the fight draining from the fish. It swished lazily towards the end of the jetty with him using the reel to take in the slack and bring it in close as it flopped sideways, left then right. The net handle was thrust into his left hand and he carefully eased the fish over the lip of it before lifting its heavy writhing mass clear of the water and gently onto the wood beside him. There it dripped water outwards and gasped reflexively.

"Here," said Skye matter-of-factly. "You'll need this." And she handed over a bone handled brass-headed hammer.

"What is it?" he asked, vaguely aware that he already knew what it was for but revolting at the thought.

"A priest," she stated. "You need it to kill it."

"What?" he questioned.

"A priest. It delivers the last rights," she explained.

"Me? Kill it? But that's inhumane."

"Have you never questioned where your food comes from?"

In fact, for a very long time he had not. Here there was no cellophane wrapping, no digitised label and no pristinely cleansed supermarket offering, ready gutted, dressed and finless. This was the real thing, still very much alive.

"I suppose it is bad for this one fish," she pushed, "but it is not as inhumane as leaving a fish alive out of water where it will asphyxiate like you are doing now." She was hard in her words but gentle in her demeanour. "Nor as inhumane as netting a few thousand at a time and then letting them be crushed to death as they are hauled up on to a huge fish factory deck just so that we can have very cheap fish for sale in the supermarket. Nor as…"

"Okay, okay. But what do I do?"

"Hit it here," and she showed him where, and so he did.

The fish continued to twitch reflexively afterwards as he stepped away rubbing his mucus-coated hands on his trousers. They smelt of the sea.

"Well," said Skye. "Hamish was wrong about you. He didn't think you'd have done that." And with this she reached out a large welcoming slimy hand and shook Sol's heartily. "I'm Skye by the way and I believe you've already met Iona."

"We're sisters," Iona stated in a curt way. "But you may have realised that as she shares so many of my good looks."

And Sol looked at them, taking in the vast array of similarities between them, and he could tell that this was exactly what they were; twin sisters.

They were both topped with a mass of mid-cropped white hair, which he suspected they cut for each other, and wore similar cable-knit sweaters, Iona's navy and Skye's brown. Under this their shirts were plain and unbuttoned at the neck. Kindly and round faces were flushed red with the effort of holding up their large but not obese bodies. Both wore thick moleskin trousers tucked into large rubber boots that were stained with farm mud.

"Identical?" he asked.

"Only genetically speaking," Skye bellowed. "The interesting bits are all different."

"Speak for yourself," Iona laughed. "I'm not sure you have many interesting bits dear!"

"Well now that you've caught tea we can start cooking supper," said Skye ignoring this last comment, reaching down and scooping up the large fish.

"What is it?" Sol asked as Skye clutched the glistening silver prize under the gills and gathered her equipment safely back in, clipping the now folded net onto her belt.

"A fish," she explained. "Now, I know they've got those in London. Sure, they usually come in plastic and without bones, but even you should recognise one of these. It's a fish."

"Yes, I know it's a fish. But, what type?"

"Salmon. And the quicker we cook it, the better it'll taste. Not your farmed rubbish mind you. This is fresh in from the sea. Come on, we'll salt it and then smoke it over the fire as there's too much on this one to eat just tonight."

They walked along the jetty back towards the beach and Iona looked down at Sol's craft.

"And," she said. "You've never sailed before? Never?"

"No," he admitted somewhat shamefaced.

"Well, you did well to survive and chose the conditions just right. I saw you row before you raised the sail, and then watched you control her with the sail up. You knew something of what was going on." She whistled to herself. "Either you're mad and were foolish enough to have a go, or you have read about sailing and have retained something about it. Or else you are just plain gifted in the water. Maybe it's in your blood?"

"What a genetic pre-disposition to be able to sail a boat?" Sol laughed incredulously.

"Well no. But maybe you have a connection to a past out here or even to the sea. It was interesting to watch you. I think you'll learn quite fast."

They walked up to the small house that the sisters lived in together. It was squarer than the *Bothan* and closer to the trees. Nets were left hanging over wooden structures in the garden. Between them proud red-pink wattle'd chickens, smaller than normal birds, yet firm-structured, with black and white barring so that they took on a grey colour overall, freely ranged and pecked at the ground. Their fierce eyes tracked Sol's progress up the garden and one defiant cock bird, easily identified by his plume of long tail feathers that drooped at the end to nearly touch the ground, stamped the earth up with his long white-spurred legs.

"Scottish greys," Iona explained. "That one's a prize winner for the breed. Problem is that he knows it and has the attitude to go with the position. Never turn your back on him. I am certain he'll have one of us given half the chance. Still the geese are far worse." Then she stepped over to him and picked him up in one broad sweep of an arm and tickled him under the chin, speaking to him softly in a language that Sol did not understand. The bird seemed to enjoy it, but it was difficult to tell if the cockerel was happy or not as its fixed expression gave no hint of a smile.

"*She* mocks me for *my* fish," explained Skye placing her rod at an angle against a wooden fence alongside a series of others and hanging her landing net up to dry. "I run a little Salmon farm out on the estuary. It's floating out there somewhere." And with this she pointed out to a yellow metal dot floating just visibly in the distance, possibly constructed of metal. "It doesn't make much money. But it's still a lot more than her birds."

"What birds does she have?" Sol asked looking at the small number of chickens milling around the somewhat pragmatic front yard space, where a large old green-rusted Land Rover dominated a small red tractor. Both seemed to have seen much better days several decades ago and nothing sang out about suggested wealth. He had always thought that most farmers were well off. Evidence for this was not here.

"Ah, these are her pets." Skye spoke with affection for her sister as she carried on walking up towards the house dangling the salmon from a hand that was buried inside its gills, looking back at Iona who was now surrounded by Scottish greys. They fought for her attention and the grain she obviously held in her pocket. "The real birds are in the next glen. She's only a small-scale farmer with a few hundred chickens. The valley wouldn't support much more. But she does insist on the old breed that our father used to farm. They look beautiful, they taste fantastic, but they are a bit small, grow slowly and produce the tiniest eggs for a chicken, however equisetic they might be. You see, its tough up here in the winter and only a hardy breed like the Grey could live through it. That's why the old breeds were bred in the first place. It's just difficult to compete with the supermarkets and to find a buyer who'll pay enough for them."

Skye looked back at her sister again as she lifted the salmon up on to a very clean metal table, well used and dented, but shiny with hygienic devotion. It abutted against a clean walled shed of some kind that linked to a series of others that ran down the hill.

"She's got about a hundred geese too. Again, they are old breed. Shetlands. I think they are just well-farmed Greylags really, but they do taste good."

"Greylags?" Sol asked.

"Commonest goose in the area. Big grey things with about twice as much meat on them as what my sister breeds. Tell me, have you been going around with your eyes closed? They *are* everywhere."

She selected a large knife from a rack on the shed wall behind and deftly gutted, de-finned and beheaded the fish, throwing the waste into a bucket. Then in a move that Sol struggled to understand, she flicked the creature, cleverly removing the spine and bones that then joined the slop in the tub. She was left with two huge fillets of orange-pink fish flesh, dressed in shiny silver-scaled skin that linked them together until she cut it to produce thick, symmetrical, flat sections.

"We'll never make money. There's no market for our scale of farming these days. It's for the big boys and girls who manage acres and acres of land and sell themselves out to the stores. However, we can afford to keep on living here and farm our old breeds so long as we don't mind too much about profit. It's become more like a hobby that keeps us fed, watered and housed. All I can say is, thank goodness neither of us went and had children. We'd never have been able to pay for them, and I hear they don't do a sale or return offer on kids these days."

After a hollow laugh, she next lifted the two sides of salmon and carried them into the first of the sheds. Inside, it was cool and again very clean. A red-painted floor was obviously regularly swept and mopped and the walls were whitewashed except for a single, framed hygiene certificate. It was well lit by large windows that had been placed cleverly enough to catch the light. Spotless metallic topped tables lined the edges of the room in the corner of which was a large shiny walk-in freezer unit that hummed loudly and vibrated noisily every so often when the pump switched on or coughed violently to quiet when it went off. There was also a large metal double sink in which Skye rinsed the fish until the waters ran clear. White coats and plastic hairnets hung on a row of hooks by the door over several pairs of clean green wellington boots.

Skye extracted a large metal tray from an under shelf and filled it with salt crystals into which she buried the salmon sides.

"Of course, it's not just salt," she explained, pointing at black flecks amongst the white light-reflecting crystals. "It's a secret recipe though and I would have to kill you if you found out what was in it. Do you want to know what it is?"

Sol shook his head. "Not if you'll have to kill me afterwards," he mused.

Leaving the fish buried in the salt, Skye took Sol out to the House for a drink in the garden.

"We've got the cattle too," she explained, as if the conversation had simply carried on from earlier. "But not many of them these days.

Eleven highlands live up on the hill and we rent the stud out to the locals to keep the genes circulating widely enough. We don't want too much inbreeding – even here!"

Iona brought out mugs of hot brew and set them down on a circular table, kicking out chairs for them to sit on. The sun was waning now, but still had heat to it, and Sol basked in the light and the company of these two amusing older ladies. They mocked his city ways but showed interest in what he had achieved, probing him with questions about his past life and how on earth he could exist in a world without a real garden, let alone any pets.

The sisters were at times brutal with each other but always full of good humour, and it was obvious that they got along well. Twins in their late sixties, they had simply stayed in the house of their birth, *Treabhair*, which meant 'Farm Buildings', and taken over where their elderly father had left off. There was no mention of a mother, and so, despite curiosity, Sol did not ask.

"So," Skye began, and she swallowed thoughtfully, pondering a distant spot somewhere off in an excitable horizon where the sunlight danced across the treetops and stained the hillsides golden orange. "After we've started smoking the fish, you must tell us what you are running away from and how you ended up here."

"What?" asked Sol. "I'm not running away from anything, am I?"

"No? Surely not." It was Iona's chance to speak this time, and she smiled warmly to see his surprise. "Then why in heaven's name have you moved up here? No one new comes here willingly unless they've got a reason. Is it a woman? Is it work? Is it the law even? You're now miles away from anyone and have little with respect to services. It's not the usual place for a city man to move to is it?"

Sol started as if to give an answer but was interrupted.

"We'll give him a few minutes to think about it," Skye finished. "Poor chap might not even know himself yet." She took him back to the fish in the shed, which she extracted carefully and then washed under the tap over the metal sink.

She explained what she was doing as she worked. "The salt heightens the flavour of the smoke but you don't want too much of it."

They then took the fish next door to a second soot-painted shed that housed a wooden construction on which Skye hung the fish sides using shiny metal hooks. The room, which wasn't large, smelt sweet and smoky, and there was very little light entering it except through the open door and a quite mucky looking window at the back which was heavily smeared with greasy black.

"I think we'll use oak and peat today," she said and set too under the fish making a smouldering fire out of wood chips she extracted from one of a number of large sacks.

Smoke quickly billowed up, tracing bulging patterns of grey-blue as it rose to encircle the fish and encompass the room in spectral finger patterns.

"It's a bit wasteful for just one fish but we do need to complete the job properly as we have a guest," she explained and closed the door as the fragrant smoke wafted ever upwards and towards the outside. In what felt like no time smouldering fumes wafted from leaks in the roof tiles as the room burgeoned with vapours.

"Now, take a seat," she said firmly once they had returned to the outside table. "What is it?"

"What?" he asked. He was conscious that there were now three glasses on the table, each filled half full with yellow liquor that looked and smelt decidedly like fine whisky.

"What are you running from?"

He had never meant to say anything, being guarded in his words and clumsy in the structure of his sentences. But it is strange how the warmth of companionship can act on a mind in turmoil.

After some pressing he told them about Sue and their relationship and where it had gone wrong. The whisky helped, even though he wasn't used to the burning sensation of it in his throat as it loosened his tongue and reduced his inhibitions. After the prickle of the first sip in his mouth he was lubricated and more ready to speak.

Then he went on to talk about work and friends and the deep emptiness he was experiencing in life, despite his successes – it was strange to gain the realisation that although he had so much, his life lacked meaning and was instead filled with a voiding emotional hollowness. He visited the Tokyo deal, knowing that it was worth millions to the company, but that although it was risky too, he knew that within the year they would all benefit and they'd be crying out for him to work for them again. He showed off, told stories where he was the conquering financial hero, and others that he thought would impress, and he dominated conversation with what he had achieved in the name of money. But he then broke off and thought. He suddenly saw no point in that life any more. There was a barrenness that came with too much money. It did not automatically allow him to buy everything, especially not an inner, lasting peace.

He felt a sense of being lost and of melancholy, and loneliness amongst 'friends'. He had a need, almost yearning, for something else in life other than the relentless monotony of business and life as usual, drinks after tea and rehab in the gym.

He even told them about his therapist and the compulsion he had had to escape and to seek a retreat; not just because she had told him to. And so, he had simply bought a house.

But he wasn't running from anything.

Not him.

"So," replied Sol. "If I am so obviously running away, then what are you two running away from still living out here?"

Iona smiled at Skye, and Skye back at Iona. They nodded.

"G *was* good wasn't he?" said Skye to the other. "The *Bothan*, she chooses well yet again, just like he said it would."

"But I don't think we are running away from anything," said Iona. "I think we are simply hiding from the new order of things yet to come and hoping that we die naturally before it gets here. Rather than run we are simply keeping it all at a safe distance if we can. Old G had run away from the reality of things a long time before now, clinging on to a world that never really existed anywhere but there in that old house of yours. He was so shocked by the depths of human depravity in the war that he simply left the big old house he had rightfully inherited, turned his back on society and instead he invested every waking moment he could in looking at the wildlife of the *Bothan*."

"Observing it," Skye added. "Always observing, recording, counting, painting and drawing."

"Painting," said Sol suddenly. "Thank you for you the milk and the flowers and the painting. They were lovely, especially the painting."

Skye beamed, abashed. "It's the least we could do. If Iona's chickens produced more eggs you'd have had some of them too. But you know how it is with chickens? Like a watched kettle they only do useful things when you are not looking and usually they do that under a bush where you can't reach the damned eggs anyhow!" Then Sol thought for a moment, "what is Gerry running from then?"

"Like most of us, I think that Gerry is just scared of the modern world," mused Iona thoughtfully. "She hasn't two pence to rub together the poor thing and moved up here a few years ago to avoid living in the real world. Something bad happened, that's true. And, as the local witch, she's quite frightened of reality."

"Witch?"

"Oh, not in any bad way." Iona was quick to reassure Sol that she meant no harm to Gerry. "She loves the land and uses the herbs, you know, does healing and things. She thinks of the animals and reads the weather. She's keen on myth and folklore too. Only witches do that in my book. But at least she's a white witch, a good one. She wouldn't have it in her to do anything nasty and everyone loves her completely just the way she is."

Skye stood up to go and collect the now smoked fish but Iona poured another half full glass of peat-amber whisky for each of them and she re-sat.

"Everyone's running or hiding up here," she meditated.

"So what about Hamish?" Sol asked. "What's he running from?"

"Oh," she said bluntly. "Except him of course. Hamish isn't running from anyone. They were all running from him and they just stuck him up here to keep him out of the way."

Sol laughed inwardly as he started to steadily drain his glass of liquor, feeling its strength easily overcome his own, and he gazed out across the sea loch to a distant place, another shore, where somewhere, tucked into its little glen sat his *Bothan*. There were birds air-drifting the currents in the dying light of a glorious day that fell in straight rays on to his beach. But he could not identify them from this far away. They were now simply birds in the beyond.

Chapter 8: The Values of Life

(The Ashokan Farewell, Jay Ungar)

There is a joy in being with people with whom you want to spend time.

They gladden the soul with their presence, and often that is even without the requirement for spoken words. A well-held silence, a prolonged pause or an electric moment of nothing, charged with the love and empathy that only friends and family can express, amongst the right sort, is as good as any sentence, however well-constructed or meant.

You can sit and bask in the simple knowledge that they are *there*, and that they will always be there, physically or metaphorically. They can be *there* even if not present and can even still exist *there* if they are now dead.

We rarely realise what we have in such people unless we come to lose them. That is of course unless we have never experienced that type before and suddenly we find ourselves in the presence of such people after an absence of a long time or possibly our whole life thus far. Then we are touched by something quite special and most probably unique.

Earlier that day Sol had realised that he had found an embryonic friend unlooked for in Gerry. He did not understand why yet, but he knew that they were destined to be close. She was attractive in her own wild-spirited way, but this pull was not his usual tempestuous urge and a physical romance had not crossed his thoughts. Instead, he was just comfortable in her presence, happy when he was talking to her and merely enjoyed the time with that stranger for whom she was.

And then, quite by accident, on a whim, he had left the security of the shore at *Bothan Faobhar* and found himself in the company of these two jolly women where he again felt quite at home and welcomed. His eyes closed and he enjoyed silence in their company without the compelling need to fill the natural spaces in between with unnecessary words or nervous outpourings. It was something he had little experienced back in the city where to leave a quiet moment would be unthinkable, and besides any gap would quickly be filled with banter or words designed to apply leverage and pressure, to broker a deal or extend a commission.

They all sat, glasses in hand, outstretched legs pointing radially under the half-rotted wooden table, eyes closed and heads back listening but to nothing in particular, thinking but not in any direction. They were at peace.

This felt new to Sol, but then he was revisited by a memory, long lost and presumed forgotten. He returned to that time in the past when an elderly hand held his as they walked on in peaceful accord with one another. Doves cooed from the tree tops announcing their intention to roost as the two human companions, separated by twin generations, lay down in the cold moist grass of the ride and stared up into a setting sky.

The air had cooled and moisture saturated it to a point where it felt heavy and wet to touch and the horizon dropped through the colours of late day to a green hue that eventually became blue. Stars appeared as the heralds of true night.

"Listen," came the kindly old voice from his side. "You'll find it with your eyes only if you search *first* with your ears."

He had no idea what it was that he looked for, and so he listened.

When the ears are allowed free reign of the senses and are given chance to dominate, it is astonishing what they allow us to hear. Sounds we never thought present are suddenly brought to the fore and a noisy unfiltered world is revealed to our minds; it was always there before but suddenly, when focused on nothing but that soundscape, our brains become attuned to the depths and volumes of so much more.

There is the rush of a gentle wind racing as a near-silent sleeper train through a non-stopping station. Then we become aware of the patter of leaf on leaf, like rain, but dryer, where each rattle can be identified as an individual collision. There is the camouflaged rustle of an animal trying not to be heard, walking on hooves or toes, and padding quietly and slowly in a land where discovery can mean death. Those birds close at hand have masked the ones far off and the sound of a distant road carries the space however far we try to separate ourselves from it.

A gurgled '*croak*' fell from the sky and that young Sol flinched for fear of what it might be.

"Hear it?" It was a supportive, gentle, calm voice – the voice of one who cared. This sound represented no danger or else that trusted voice would have registered urgency and concern.

This time the frog-call was elongated and almost comical, but was something strange and unknown; an amphibious call descended from the dusking sky itself cloaked by the darkness of the gloaming.

And then there was the flutter of a fat bellied bird, long beaked and stub-winged flying in erratic circular motion. There in the night sky was a silhouette bird, not a duck, but that quacked.

Sol opened his eyes. "Woodcock," he said sitting upright and startling Iona and Skye out of their half-slumbers. "There's a woodcock roding above the trees."

All three looked up above the woodland higher up behind the house where Sol pointed to a plump lengthy-billed wader who bounded on shortened wings round the treetops quacking.

"How *did* you spot that?" Iona quizzed.

"Easy," smiled Sol, proud of his discovery. "Someone once told me, that you'll find it with your eyes only if you search first with your ears."

They watched the bird skirting back and forth across the canopy top emitting its frog call, artificial, comical and toy-like.

"It's funny," laughed Skye, "we've lived here for ever and it takes the inexperienced city boy to point out what's under our noses and probably been here all the time."

They rested back into comfortable silence with each other again as the woodcock roded above and behind.

The first of the midges rose off a pool in the river and yet Sol resisted the temptation to scratch it as it drowned in whisky-scented sweat on his forehead. It would have ruined that chance to relax with others if he had paid it any attention.

The sun began its final set, the woodcock croaked in agitated fashion and the owl attempted its take-over where the day birds started to clock off from a light-delineated shift of territorial display and courtship. The latest of the Scottish Grey cocks signalled the evening with its chuckled *Last Post* and the early evening moths greeted the light of a singly lit window with fluttered joy as if they had happened upon the moon itself in their nightly migrations.

"Supper must be ready," muttered Skye after a while. "We'll eat inside."

Skye took Sol back down to the blue-smoking shed and in the half-light of the cast shadows they removed the fish from its peg and carried it on a clean metal tray back up to the house. '*Bàgh an Iasg*' read the hand painted sign by the front door under the porch roof.

"Fish Bay," Skye explained. "Actually it is '*Bay of the running Salmon*' to be exact and it's the name of the entire bay really. |But the house has rather selfishly taken the name on for itself."

It was a solidly built, clean yet cluttered House. It smelt of animals, but not in an offensive way, and it lacked the mustiness of the *Bothan*. Sol linked the smell with that of an older generation and assumed it was the scent of country folk. Everywhere was the cologne of the sea, both sweet and tacky at the same time in the back of the nostrils, and it seemed to cling to the fabric of the house, its furnishings and its people.

The flat plastered walls were often dressed in floral patterned papers which ended at the height of a tall man's arm reach with a white glossed rail on which pictures hung on lengths of chain.

Above this was plain satin magnolia - that accursed colour of the middle class, too posh for cream, too poor for pastel and too judgemental for white. The plaster-patterned ceilings were cornered by painted mouldings and centred by light fittings that were robed in elegant shades of stained glass, blackened metal and cloth.

A polished wooden stairway ran up from the deceptively long hallway with a dark patterned runner, which mimicked the rise and flat of each step, held in place by brass rods at the crook of every stair. It was well walked and threadbare in places.

But one feature of this front corridor suddenly hit Sol. It was light.

"You have electricity?"

It was a simple enough question and one that he would never have thought of asking before venturing up to live at the *Bothan*. It was one of those things that everyone in his world took for granted, a necessity and expectation of life, or at least of life as we now know it. There wasn't a city without it, a town without it, and until a few days ago he had presumed a house without it. But then he happened upon *Bothan Faobhar*.

"Electricity?" he repeated.

"Yes," said Iona, "isn't it clever?"

"But," Sol started to form words, drawn in as the moths at the window to the warmth of light and succour of heat from the iridescent filaments glowing within each electron-agitated glass miracle.

Skye butted in. "Of course, G never saw the use in it and so never had the mains connected to the *Bothan* when he was given the chance. That is going to rather set you back if you need any power."

"Do you have a phone as well?"

"Yes," finished Iona. "A landline. I'm certain they still have those down in the south too. Don't they? And the Internet? Just because we live all the way out here doesn't mean we're completely backwards."

"Unless you live at *Bothan Faobhar*," said Skye quite bluntly. "You don't have much there do you? No power, no phone and probably no signal for a mobile. I don't what you'll be doing with yourself."

One part of Sol was jealous, wanting these resources from across the loch for himself. The other part was more cautious. He had survived so far all right and he was plotting his plans to improve the situation. But how much of it did he really need as soon as possible and what was the cost to the environment and himself of introducing too much technology too soon to the *Bothan* and its valley?

He was led into the front room where a thick wood table dominated a bulky space with four solid straight-backed chairs. There was an outsized mantled fireplace on which stood a clock that ticked the seconds away aggressively as a black hand cranked its way around, marking time. The fire was ready set but not burning and the hearth was deep and black sucking the light from the room and attention from the observer. Cobwebs suggested it was rarely lit.

Skye disappeared into the kitchen whilst Iona laid table to a strictly cultured conformity, extracting the tools for display from an under drawer in a large oak dresser. Sol was asked to sit in the bay window seat on a wool-covered cushion from which he could watch the careful choreography of this strange class-based dance whilst woodlice, greyer than he remembered, walled along the edges of the room and competed with silverfish that crept through the pile of the carpet.

Placemats central, forks to the left, two. Knives set to the right, one larger, one smaller. A spoon and a fork were laid to rest in opposite directions above, a strange crossed sword emblem. Glasses on coasters were arranged to the right and beyond the settings. A tumbler for water, a flute for white and a round for red. A serviette, each rolled into a tapered tube, was secured with a fish crested ring and placed on a delicately floral-patterned china plate at an angle of forty-five degrees, no less, no more. Plates two inches to the right of the placemats, each a hand-finished painting of the loch, the house and the sea.

Iona stepped back, focused and alert, checking a mental list and acknowledging those items she still needed to collect. She left and returned with butter, with cheese, with bread and with salad, and finally with Skye who was now carrying a green and brown leaf-decorated fish platter, thick glazed and rustic, arranged perfectly with herbs, pepper, lemon and lime.

They stood behind their chairs offering Sol the head position at the top of the table. There was silence, with there being no need for words. Body language ruled and spoke all.

Sol pulled out his chair before he realised that neither of the other two had moved, but instead they remained stood quite still behind their places, hands placed firmly on the stiff wooden backs with their heads bowed low.

Sol stopped, felt a moment of sudden panic with his half move to sit, shifted uneasily and then bowed his head to look uncomfortably down at his chair's seat where his gaze was drawn by a padded woollen cushion embroidered with flowers and a never-ending, interlaced Celtic pattern. He waited, unsure and suddenly ill at ease.

"God doesn't mind what we are thinking about, or what we do," said Skye with an amused chuckle in her lyrical voice. "We do this mostly because we've always done it. We should have said we say grace every mealtime. That was unhelpful of us. Sorry."

Still unsure but suddenly more relieved, Sol kept his head bowed low, half expecting someone to announce that this was all part of an organised joke. In his book, grace was something for school dinner halls and Sunday school and not for every day meals.

Then Iona spoke in a clear, controlled, but almost murmured voice, quietly as if half to herself and for the benefit of another unseen in the room rather than for the gathered few. Sol craned to hear the words in the Gaelic tongue. But he knew so little of it that he struggled to define any words, sentences or sounds, and he knew he would have difficulty if asked to repeat any of it back. Like the struggling child at the back of the French classroom, he worried about his lack of understanding and hoped that his ignorance would be overlooked. And so he listened and instead tried to gather meaning from the sound, emotion, intonation and harmony, the universal languages of the world.

"*Dhe bi maille ruin*
Air an oidhche nochd,
Amen."

"Amen," he repeated, recognising that final word.

The two ladies sat, relaxed and smiled, and Sol joined them with quiet relief.

"It means, God be with us on this night," explained Skye. "Wine?"

They ate a fine, delicate meal of home cooked produce which Iona and Skye described to him as he selected it for his plate. There was a malted loaf containing bladderwrack seaweed and a lightly salted locally churned butter left out of the fridge long enough to take on a glistening sheen and to be as soft and greasy as hot polish. The cold smoked fish, flaky and muscle-block contoured, was served with salads and recently picked new potatoes dug up from behind the house. Everything had its own tender complexity of flavour and texture, whether it was the crumble of the orange-pink fish with its peaty, sweetness and salty smoke, or the waxy skins of the firm creamy potatoes and the taste of the sea captured in the bread or the salt of the butter. The hard-boiled eggs were small and turgid with deep orange yolks, the colour of sundried apricots sold from a Mediterranean road side. Their taste was rich, and he knew as he bit deep, that these were the eggs of the Scottish Greys now roosted in the yard and the glen beyond. He could not help but wonder what a deli in the city would make of such produce and his mind flashed with typical imagery to money and profit.

Next came a cheese board of firm full fat triangular blocks and blue-veined, sweat-moistened shapes that oozed at their edges as they warmed in the natural accumulation of heat from the bodies in the room. Again, he was not surprised to learn that their providence was all very local, their flavours all unique and their production remained small scale.

Then finally there was a rich fruity cake, moist and almost black inside with sticky, caramelised dark sugar crisped to its crust, which was sliced thickly and smothered in yet more butter. Its life journey had started in the steamy kitchen of the sister's house and its carbon footprint only stretched as far as here to the next room; it was as environmentally good as it could have been.

Once he had overcome his fears of the rules of the table and the order of cutlery with which to attack this minor banquet, Sol enjoyed fine simple food and quality rich wine; some homemade and some bartered for in the hills around. Before long, the day had faded, and tiring, his thoughts returned to home and the long journey back in the dark across the loch. He looked to the window, viewless with the night, with worry.

"Well," said Iona as she stretched in satisfaction. She took in his glance to the glass in the bay window and the darkness that lay beyond. "It'd be safer to get you back over in the morning. But if you want to sail now we can always take you."

"Sorry," said Sol.

"Oh don't worry. Anyone would recognise the face of someone whose home is calling them from across the loch if they took the time to look for it. The *Bothan* calls you doesn't she?"

"But you'd have to sail there and back if you were to take me," he protested.

"That's why God allowed man to invent the outboard motor. Besides Skye will happily fish until dawn if given half the chance." Skye nodded her approval. "She'd be happy whichever way you choose to go. There's a bed here and there's a boat there. She'll probably fish from the jetty all night if you don't go or will use a boat if you do. So, which will it be?"

Sol was used to quick decision, but only if it didn't involve his own life plans.

There are types of people who can turn any situation into an opportunity in the briefest flash of a second. They can deal, see potential, use that chance, and then off they go as they trade and adapt. There are others that prefer time and fact upon which to base their life's choices. Pondering, they often miss some great '*thing*' or lose out on some of the benefit of what is being proffered. But they are cautious and safe, or at least gain security from the knowledge that in the end, however long it takes, they know they are doing the right thing. Of course the most stable strategy lies somewhere in some flexible and indescribable place between the two extremes, and like in every good controversy which response is right for any given situation is a grey area that floats randomly between the black and the white. Its final position relies on a number of factors including which shade of grey you actually prefer. It is an impossible tone to determine until the decision is made, and it may never be right, or always be right, or simply be an arbitrarily assigned contrast to the two extremes.

Those who make rash decisions can be wrong but are often convicted by such confidence that they are protected from seeing their inaccuracies or may not care. And once they have jumped in one direction or the other their protection becomes defence, and defence is then strengthened with every challenge, or they spend too much time explaining and protesting to make sure that their '*correctness*' is recognised and unquestionable. Dogma, if well marketed, becomes the only way to think and after all, *who would question such a confident stance? They must be right!*

He who shouts loudest often wins regardless of their moral, factual or even their precise position.

But then there is a further interesting correlation between decisions made in the public realm and choices that take place in the private lives of those same people. So often there is an overcompensation being created in the outward confidence of the least personally secure and dig down just under that perfect surface, or take them just outside their comfort zone, beyond where they want you to see, and watch the effect on their decisiveness; an experiment only to be carried out if you know it is ethical and safe, as all good science should be.

Making assertive decisions for the lives of others, or regarding the money of faceless institutions and nameless individual investors, dealing with the woes of those you do not know or writing at arm's length guidance, news reports or policies, what do these all say about *you*? Is it that you are a good decision maker, able to deal with the problems of many, to make the right choices for and on behalf of them, or to find the right path for society, your company or your group? Or, is it that in the confident selection of others' direction, preferably out there in the public eye, you are seen to be empowered and decisive, and, above all, confident yourself? *Are you simply trying to hide from view your real state of personal esteem?*

Putting distance between decisions for the greater good or making choices of importance that affect the business or community, it buys you time from either letting others see into your own personal crises of judgement or, more importantly, letting you yourself venture anywhere near them, even accidentally. *After all, how would those others judge you if you appeared anything less than perfect, or anything less than secure, and anything less than absolutely right in everything you did?* It's a distraction we all succumb to and society is awash with it.

He was now just Sol, that ex-city buyer with nothing much to his name at present.

This was Sol, initially arrogant but recognisably over compensating, with little personal confidence of his own.

This was Sol, no longer with large desk, large office nor large ego. It had all gone now and he was desk-less, between offices and in a world very different to the one he had engineered back in the city;

the one that kept his own angsts safely at a distance from anyone and everyone, including himself.

This was Sol, without his city pad, lost in a world he had accidentally stumbled into and seeking new relationships with people he did not want to disappoint.

He craved to do what was the right thing in this situation but had no anchor upon which to secure his choice, no beacon of experience to guide him and no distance from his personal feelings to keep his choice purely objective. Should he return back to the *Bothan* and be alone but in *his* space, where he could relax and sleep easy, spread and let down his guard - be himself? But to get there he needed help as there was no way he could cross the loch safely in the dark in a boat that he could hardly control. His other choice was to stay, which was equally attractive with these two older dears who would no doubt pamper and mother him for the evening, feed him well in the morning and give him a comfortable bed to sleep in for the night.

Oddly his heart raced and what seemed like an age passed where the steady beat of the second hand on an old clock somewhere in the corridor amplified to an extreme, and the creak of its pendulum echoed within a long, resonant, wooden chamber to become unbearable. Time extended interminably before he could speak again.

But, eventually he did.

"I had probably better go," he said.

They nodded without judgement and gathered together the plates and the crumbs, undressing the table in their regularly practiced regimental dance, this choreographed around each other like two floating feathers spinning in the wind on the surface of a still pool. And then the three of them departed from the house and walked down to the jetty where *Sireadh-thall* waited, patiently bobbing in the dark waters and unable to contain her excitement at the chance for further adventure.

Skye switched on a bright-beamed torch and took off to a red-rusted tin shed that stood proud of the loch, up where only the splash, spume and spray ever dared to reach. Entering by a side door that struggled to open on the straight, she appeared at the front through double doors, slowly lowering a long wooden boat down into the water on the end of a hand turned winch. It creaked rhythmically as the boat's belly scraped water-wards on the angle of a launch, so old that the sea had carved it into shapes not dissimilar to the rocks nearby and the barnacles had covered all but the roughest sections in knife sharpened pin pricks of white calcareous shell. Then the wooden hull met the enticing waters and was dragged out by the receding tide until it had picked up its slack in the rope and then jostled amongst the dark brown sea wracks that floated with the buoyancy of their gas-filled bladders.

"I don't want to cause any trouble," said Sol, a feeling of guilt creeping through his body for the fuss these ladies were going to just so that he could return to the familiarity of his own home.

"This isn't trouble," explained Iona fitting a heavy lamp she had extracted from another shed to the painter ring on *Sireadh-thall*. "There are times in any community where we each need to go the extra mile to help each other. It costs us nothing and you would do the same for us if we needed it – that'll be after we teach you to sail of course!"

She forced Sol into a bulky old life jacket. Smelling of heavy oil and grease, it still gave the impression that if forced to it might float. In the poor light it was difficult to understand its colour, but to Sol it felt orange.

"You catch up," she called over to her sister who was still securing nets into her launch now that it was out in the water. "She'll take ages getting her fishing kit together anyway. We'll probably drop nets and lobster crates on our way back and then return for them tomorrow."

They both climbed in as Iona untied the moorings and pushed *Sireadh-thall* away from the security of the little wooden pier. The boat immediately picked up the rock and yaw of the loch's water. They paddled side by side for a while; one on each oar. There was just the sound of the wave's lap until Iona sat up, felt the wind and suggested it was time for the sail.

Whilst she unravelled the rolled up canvass, more by touch than sight, Sol sat back in the stern, where the boards formed their perfect symmetrical bowl end to the boat, and he held the tiller loosely as he scanned the loch, the land and far out to the sea.

The waters sang their rippled delight at meeting *Sireadh-thall*'s prow as they gently tugged and caressed her sides and waywardly licked up and down. The last vagaries of the sun had long drained from the sky but left their trailing stain as a halo of deepest blue that clipped the mountainous horizon. The loch obediently reflected it back, but like the sky it remained moonless but star struck.

A black silhouette bird cruised across the undisturbed surface of the loch, breaking it with a perfect straight wave line that fanned out in its wake. This was the white-necked cormorant, black now with night, the nocturnal fisherman. It fished for a while, unperturbed by the steady work of Iona, raising and securing the mast, tying the ropes and setting the sail, and a loon called for a moon that just was not there.

Sol watched the cormorant surface with a struggling flatfish in its grotesque beak. It shook it, stunned it and swallowed it whole, headfirst. Then it was gone, diving again to fly under the water using backward webbed feet in neck-flexed hunt. He could trace it below the water and under the boat as a string of pearlescent air bubbles that rose up in reverse fountains, fishing in the light of the painter lamp where its silvery quarry had collected and become mesmerised.

And then, as the northern lights started their nightly silent illuminations above and across the highland world, Sol watched the cormorant returning to the surface again now fluorescing as if painted in bright green. It was a bioluminescent bird perfectly lightened up under the water. He watched its neck dart and stab at small piscine bodies that flashed in schools to avoid its deadly snare. Paddled feet powering, Sol could see the bubbles of oil-trapped air that shone and shimmied around its bird-human form. But throughout it was brightest green, radiating an unholy, unnatural green-hued light.

"Iona," he called as the sail took the wind and the little boat pitched into the water, struck a course and started its run towards the *Bothan*'s cobble beach. "Iona, that bird?"

"The cormorant? That's the old Sea Crow or *Geòcaire*. That means 'glutton' in the old language. Milton didn't like them much either. He thought that they were Satan in animal form. A voracious hunter of fish too, so not that popular with the fishermen. What about it?"

"Its fluorescent green…   …under the water."

"The bacteria and algae in the water give out light when they are collided with. It makes them glow. G called it bioluminescence. Look at the bottom of the boat and you'll see what I mean."

Sol leaned right out on the end of a rope proffered by Iona to where he could see the underside of *Sireadh-thall*'s prow. It was eerily bright green and glowing where the water compressed up against her hull and keel.

There was magic out there on the sea loch. Nothing was actually supernatural. Instead, there was a biological enchantment, something entirely wild and normal, but unexpected and mystical as a result.

As the boat gently illumined the water below them and they headed on a good wind with the cool night-air bracing them from behind, it felt to Sol as if they were floating across the sky and into the northern lights themselves. There was a continuum of colour from within the sea, through their craft and up into the firmament of the very sky above. It was a dreamland and Sol's heart ached with its beauty.

He missed Iona's watchful glances at him as he sat in the stern and leant backwards on the tiller, a man unusually in control of this small part of his destiny. He was a man who briefly felt he could fly.

They passed over the change of current where the sound of the unreal Blue Men dwelling in the loch beat heavily on the bottom of the vessel, banging with their fists to demand a payment for the crossing.

"They won't forgive you this time," laughed Iona from the rope she pulled to control the craft's sail and she tossed slices of cake over the side and muttered a murmur of prayer. "I love cake," she explained, "and they know it. Therefore it's a good offering. What'll you throw? It has to be worth something to you? And remember, they don't care what it is, just its value to the person who throws it. Money means nothing to the *Blue Men.*"

Sol dug into his pockets to find what he could offer up in sacrifice.

His hand touched his phone and he instinctively pushed it aside. *No too valuable!*

"It has to be something dear to you," shouted Iona, "and you'd best hurry. They won't wait long."

The banging continued, heightening in its timbre and tone as the undercurrents fought and collided.

Sol searched his pocket more, furtively. *Not the phone.*

He dug deep and then his hand touched something gentle and soft, a feather that must have stuck there whilst he plucked one of the pheasants. *But it had no value and so surely it would not be suitable.*

His finger brushed it again and it suddenly brought back a pleasant thought story of memories like a silent reel cinema film.

His first meeting in the kitchen with the brace of birds gifted to him by Gerry.

His abhorrence overcome when plucking the first bird.

That first wonderful meal home-cooked at the Bothan.

The Bothan, his first house.

Those first flavours and that first gift of vegetables from Hamish and his wife.
Gerry, his first friend here.
These memories had value beyond price and thus the feather had intrinsic value despite actually being worthless. *The feather was a laudable offering to these Blue Men after all and he knew that this was the gift he would give – not the phone!*
He held it aloft in the current of wind as the banging on the underside continued apace.
"I'd do it quick," shouted Iona over the bucking of the current change and the anger of the sounds underneath. It was no wonder that the past peoples of the area had worried that these were the incensed outcries of mystical marine monsters or demi-gods in the water. To them, *Blue Men* would have been a credible explanation for this unnatural noise caused by something as insubstantial as water.
"They don't sound so patient tonight," Iona continued with the exhilaration of the boat's bucking response running wild in her veins.
He let the feather go. Up it floated into the air as if ready to join the rainbow light and dust in the sky. Then down it tumbled, smooth and weightless, to be entombed in a watery grave of bioluminescent froth.
And the banging stopped as they took to the other current and the *Blue Men*, satisfied for now, swam back to demand their sacrifice of Skye's boat behind.
"That was some offering you must have given," Iona commented as she attended to the sail and kept *Sireadh-thall* on course. "What was it?"
"Now that would be telling," laughed Sol.
"You don't have to tell me," she added, "but that meant something... ...to you. The *Blue Men* simply went! If they really do exist, then they knew the value of whatever it was. It meant more to you than cake does to me and that says something. Or else

it was simply a coincidence and we passed over the current changes at just the same time as you dropped your offering in. Personally I prefer the *Blue Men* idea."

Two fluorescing dolphin shapes sped up from behind and suddenly leapt alongside the boat, only visible by their irradiate outlines of bioluminescence. Sol stood, dumbstruck by the unnaturalness of this natural world. So much he had never known was there, right now, presenting itself before him.

"I'd like to think these two were the *Blue Men* of the sea come to escort you back home." Iona was as affected by the dolphin's appearance as Sol was. The natural world never failed to amaze her. "They obviously rated your gift young man!"

Iona gave him a wondering stare. "I'll only ask once more, what was it?"

She read his silence and did not ask again. She knew that it was of value to him, and him alone. Only the *Blue Men* needed to know exactly what it was.

They rode across the flat of the green and red reflecting water which continued to imitate the spectacular folding and withdrawal of the sky-arms above, with the waters glowing at the prow of that happy little boat, little changed in design from its Viking forebears. They were shepherded on either flank by their dolphin attendants. The dark mountains rose as jagged black obscurities against a bluer ink sky, sentinels to the loch as it opened out into the sea proper. The sky was a drift of stars; the Milky Way a soft hue that taken in as one was a simple airbrushed strip overhead from horizon to horizon, yet when studied closely was a myriad points of brightened lights coalesced into one. Shadow birds passed as silent silhouettes, black winged forms against midnight blue, occasionally painted by the churning northern dust lights; geese to the shoreline, ducks to the sea, cormorants to the fishing and gulls to nowhere in particular. They were now just passing spirit birds.

Sol could have been leaving this world and entering the gates of Valhalla.

All too soon they made the shore, faster than he remembered the journey in the opposite direction. Conversation had not been necessary, if it had been possible against the sound of the wind above and the water below. The single sail was released from its chores, dropped and carefully folded around a fallen mast. The oars were employed and then Iona jumped ashore, sending biologically iridescent seawater in her wake where the crests of waves were dipped in brightest green as they broke.

She towed the painter as Sol lifted and secured the rudder, fell neatly over the stern and pushed the boat ashore from behind. Towed up to the landing site where sticks and brash lay faithfully waiting to protect her wood from the ground, they turned *Sireadhthall* over and laid her to rest from her adventurous day. Sol placed his hand on the wood of her hull and felt her sadness now that she was ashore again and her exploits would have to end for the now. In silent prayer, he promised her that he would learn how to sail her properly and that together they would return to the sea soon, but more safely. He knew that, inanimate as she was, she understood and their pact was made.

There was a second boat on the beach, similar to his own. It had been left upright between the loch and the house wall and it still wore its mast tall and straight, secured in the upright by ropes that '*flacked*' in the breeze and topped by a bell-like sound tolled. Its name was difficult to read.

"That'll be '*The Tern*' that boat," Iona explained handing Sol a paper bag she had extracted from under *Sireadh-thall*. "It's your good witch's boat. She'll have been worried about you when she saw *Sireadh-thall* gone out on to the loch. We phoned her when we first caught site of you on the water and so she knows you're safe. She's a good one our Gerry. Look after her. She is undoubtedly going to try and look after you, the first newcomer in quite a while. That is unless you drown yourself by misadventure of course!"

Sol looked at the bag.

"What's this?" he asked.

"What do you expect? Eggs. Not that many, as you *would* expect from our chickens of course. But there should be enough to make a good omelette for you both at breakfast."

"Thank you," he said cradling the crispy paper gently. And then Sol thought for a moment as he heard the hum of Skye's outboard motor approaching them from over the loch, now just a small disturbance in the air and a dot out on the water. "How much do I owe you for helping me back across to the *Bothan*?"

Everything in his world had a financial value, possibly even his friendships that seemed to survive or fall on the basis of his financial means, and his community. That was the rule of Sol's world.

"Owe me? But what for?"

"Your help."

Iona laughed as Skye's boat skipped the last few yards to shore and then sank down to the normal as the engine cut.

"As I said, owe me? That's not what people do round here. It's not like the city, Sol. We don't have to pay for everything. Most of the time none of us would have enough money to pay for what we gain from others around us anyway. Sometimes we act like this because we want to and it's a kindness. That's how our community functions and why the city-mind can't easily sustain our sort of an existence and deep enough friendships. It's also why we couldn't live in the city. But then, each to their own." She checked that Sol's boat was secure and then started the short walk back to the beach where her sister waited in the darkness of the water. "If you pay for someone to do it then it might have financial value and be guaranteed as a result of the exchange of money, but it means little enough to either party. You've bought it. You expect it. They *have* to give it. But no one cares about it or means it. Not from the heart." She waded into the shallows and placed her hand on the prow of the other boat. "But, if you choose to do it because you want to, then you invest in the other person and they know it too. You've done something at cost to yourself that benefits another.

You're friends. Surely that guarantees a lot more than a bit of money can?"

Sol understood even if he wasn't sure he totally agreed. Sometimes, he felt, he needed the guarantee that only money could give.

Iona rolled over the side of the boat and as Skye pulled the cord to restart the motor she called, "Goodbye Jake Solomon. It has been lovely to meet, greet and return you safely back to shore. I'm glad we're all friends now. And remember, it's not all about money. But..." She considered her thoughts for a while. "I think G was right. The *Bothan* has chosen its next guest well."

The sisters both waved as their boat lifted up and then skipped off across the wave tops in a bioluminescent water cloud to seek the *Blue Men* of the loch another time and a fishing ground hidden somewhere out to sea. Sol watched them until they returned to become but a blotch on the horizon and then turned back to the *Bothan* with a feeling of welcome from its solid, friendly structure.

The air was tainted with the scent of a good wood fire and the front window glowed an array of heart-warming orange rays from the flames that flicked in the hearth. Entering through the back porch he found a paraffin lamp glowing weakly on the table and a plate of what looked like home-cooked biscuits next to it under a fabric cover to keep the vermin off of them.

The house was warm-damp and enveloped him quickly in its homeliness. He knew it was *his* and could sense its welcome of him on his entry as if it too had worried about his safety whilst he was out there on the water.

In the lounge he found Gerry asleep by the fire in the farther of the two easy chairs by the fireside. The light of the flames warmed the colour of her skin and her hair took on a raven life of its own as the shadows pirouetted their fantasy journeys around the room following the guidance of the glowing sparks rising in the grate.

Taking the kitchen lamp through to the bedroom, he found an old woollen blanket in the bottom drawer of the dresser and carefully laid it over her sleeping form to keep off the coolness of the night as it began to grip the room. Dropping the life jacket off onto the kitchen floor, he pinched a biscuit and then extracted his sleeping bag from the bedroom before snuggling himself down into the comfort of G's chair. Under the sleeping bag he smelt that tobacco whiff, which to him was the essence of the *Bothan,* and felt the warmth of the fire that reached its ray fingers as far as where he sat. The motion of the sea and body memory of the rise and fall of the waves accompanied him to sleep as he continually felt its motion in his body. It would be there in his dreams tonight.

He yawned, killed the lamp and then quickly settled.

He had companions he had not looked for in places he had not expected to visit and for the first time, for a period he could not measure, he understood that value was not just measured in currency but had a far greater meaning. Some value was immeasurable and he was suddenly aware that from abject poverty he had become a very wealthy man.

Chapter 9: The Reason of Roads

("Gabriel's Oboe", Ennio Morricone)

Sol woke slowly, his mind drifting through a string of ideas and recent experiences that had been slung loosely together in the way that the only the human mind can, as a dream. His was of a story he would not be able to recall again once awake save that he was out at sea. Instead, although he was certain of its reality whilst he was there living it, for all its authenticity at the time, it was destined to become an ethereal shadow that he would not quite be able to recall or reach.

There were birds on the water and the cormorant below fished aquatically, beating the water with flipper'd claw feet and using a sleek snake-like neck in arching motion to secure its glistening prizes in a robust and lengthy scissorbill. All was calm until Sol became aware of a boat that approached from further down the loch. It was large and it was noisy, and through its nature it was abhorrent to the peace of the scene. Just a long black profile of a hull was visible, with lights blazing brightly along its over-lit frame. Electronic music blared and people cheered and jeered from within its hedonistic deck top activity.

Then with clarity achieved, he vaguely recognised a past self in the crowd, centre of it all and with uncorked bottle over-spilling in hand, dancing. He was not noticing the birds slip away on silent wings, the seals dropping noiselessly down into the security of the deeps and the cormorant move on after a shoal of escaping fish that sought serenity at a distance. He did not even see the loss of the darkness as the ship's energy-enriched lights glowed and beamed, nor the snuffing out of the night sky's stars.

In a dream you can rarely shout, and Sol found himself frustrated by the other him on the deck in the crowd.

Why did he not notice?

Why could he not see?
Why did he not care?
And he knew the answer. He was looking inwardly with only an egocentric view and attention. He was unable to step out of the personalised arena he had selected at that time and see beyond his limited experience.
How common a disease was that?

As he forced himself forward in time to the waking world, he recognised and appreciated that this was just a dream, and he dallied for a while trying to stay asleep longer. But something called to him, reaching down into his nether world, and interrupted his thoughts. It was now making the vision he was having impossible to cling on to. He felt his grasp of it loosen, its clarity fade and already its memory diminished and greyed.
'*Sol?*'
Slowly he moved from one world back into the next, convinced at either end of his journey that he was in a real place and that it was everywhere else that was a dream.
"Sol?"
He opened his eyes, looking into the dead space of the burnt out hearth.
"Sol?"
He looked up and there was Gerry, looking down at him from the kitchen door with a mix of emotion encrypted across her face.
"Yes," he muttered stretching into the body-shaped crevasse in the cushions of G's chair and identifying a voice in what he had become accustomed to as a quiet house full of unsocial solace.
"Sol?" She smiled, but she was insistent, obviously wanting his attention as soon as he awoke.
"What time is it?" he asked in muffled reply as he made an attempt to move his limbs. It was still dusk outside but he could hear the toil of the early birds breaking out in the trees of the wood behind the *Bothan*.

"Five," she replied nonchalantly re-entering the kitchen and clattering around.

He looked up in surprise, instantly wide-awake although convinced he shouldn't have been, and questioned. "Five?"

"Yes, five."

"In the morning?"

"Yes, five in the morning. You don't think I'd have left you sleeping all day do you?"

"But I'll only have been asleep for a few hours."

"And sleeping is for the dead. For when you've got as much time as you want to do it!" Her reply was straight.

Sol stood up, his body slumber-drawn, and staggered towards the kitchen where Gerry had started preparing a hearty breakfast. Evidently she had been up a while already and the air about her smelt of soap as if she had just had a wash in the dark up at the bath shed.

"But why five? I don't remember getting up at five for an incredibly long time. In fact that used to be when I came back in sometimes."

A wren sprang into life outside of the porch door. It had been flung open to welcome the early morning sun, air the cottage and let the freshness of today's sea breeze in to have its cleansing effect on the sterility and mustiness of the cottage.

"Well, if you really do intend to get to the end of your driveway by half past eight this morning, as you informed me yesterday you wanted to, I suggest you do need to get a move on! It's a good few miles and you don't look the type to walk speedily, with all due respect." Her words were harsh and there was an edge to them.

They enjoyed a good breakfast of runny-yolk'd eggs then porridge, with curt conversation that Sol found hard to understand. In the end he felt the need to soften the tones between them.

"Thank you for waiting in for me last night," he eventually said, and she nodded before she spoke through a mouthful of wet oats.

"Just don't kill yourself before we've had chance to teach you how to be safe round here. I don't want Hamish proven right, okay?"

"Okay," he agreed. "Believe it or not, I don't want Hamish proven right either."

"It's just that the city is a different place. If you get it wrong here then there might not be someone there who can help."

"There might be a lot people back where I come from, but they wouldn't necessarily help you if you needed it either. Someone like me normally has to pay my way out of trouble."

"Well," she warmed, "that's unlikely to be much good out there on the waters of the loch."

They washed up and left the House at seven. The sun had already beaten them rising, but the day was still fresh cold.

Once certain he was packed up with food for the day, Gerry left Sol to walk alone down the track up to *Bothan Faobhar*. She had errands to run down in the town, which she explained would be quicker to achieve by boat. They agreed that she would stop by at the end of the drive around late lunch to see how he was getting on with the various deliveries and appointments he had, which they decided were all most probably to be made by the '*no access*' sign at the end of the track.

In a good headwind *The Tern* rapidly wafted her from sight and Sol was left to trudge his way towards his day's goal alone. But he was happy that Gerry had cared enough to check he was home safe last night and that she was concerned enough to keep an eye on him for the day and for at least the near future.

It was reassuring to know that someone had his safety in mind at this time; even if it appeared he did not.

There are days when the weather looks as if it will somehow be different to what it actually turns out to be. The sun shone that morning in a bright blue sky, but it was cold and the wind wicked away what little heat the early May could afford the land. The sky was azure-skinned with the occasional pompom wisp of grey cloud that portended snow for anyone who knew what to look for. For all intents and purposes the intensity of that burning yellow star and the freshness of the air and clarity of the heavens above should have suggested a dry, possibly frost-crisped day. But no, occasional snowflakes fell, big and heavy, cold and crystalline, melting on contact and hitting the eyes to make them cry ice tears that ran down and stung the cheeks.

Sol walked at a pace, sweating up within his clothes.

A round fluffed bumblebee, yellow and black haired on its concentric ringed abdomen, staggered its way through blossoms of lemon buttercup and the pale pink of emerging smock flowers. It passed in its lumbering flight through patches of sunshine where the light escaped the bursting canopy's photon absorbing grip and then into steady drops of snow that hammered it towards Earth in its weak yet drifting gravitational plummet.

The wren whirred from the ditch and scratched its call of alarm and a jay cackled confidently from the safety of the pinewood that enveloped the track for a while. Then above, the skylark hung, tethered to the sky in its song flight of praise to the world.

As he walked Sol applied his musical ear to the soundtrack of life.

It was in the buzz of the insect, the hammer of the woodpecker, the flute of the birds and the lap of the water. It occurred to him that there was a symphonic masterpiece to be written, one that had not yet been penned by any of the greats. They had had their turns but they had still each fallen well short of capturing the imagery playing over his mind's eye. As humans, they lacked the skills required.

'*Maybe,*' he thought, '*just maybe, I could have an attempt at composing a piece.*' He would sit at the *Bothan*'s front window and create it using its close proximity to the wild shore of the loch as his inspiration, with the windows flung open to sense the air, hear the sounds and fill his attention.

He found that he had slowed in his pace, distracted by thoughts of composition, and as his eyes were drawn hither or thither by the movements of flies, birds and even the rocking of flowers and grasses in the breeze. The melody was sweet and rich and warm. But every so often he reminded himself not to be taken in by this trove of sound, sight and smell, and he pushed on ever forward in an attempt to make the end of the track in time.

His first surprise came when he reached the corner where his sports car should have lain forlorn and up-ended in the ditch, stranded when traction had left it to dance on the muds and end in the dyke. The deep runnel tracks in the dirt remained, now filled with miniature reflective pools of fly-hazed water. He was shocked to see frogspawn in the base of the deepest, jellied and transparent, each clustered in its misted grape clump with its single foggy-black centre and bubbled outer case.

There was an algal base to give the muds below a green-black sheen that had been etched by the radula of snails in erratic and random grazing pathways. It was as if the snails had no directional commitment with their winding psychedelic tracks giving no indication of purpose. *Have algae – will feed – direction optional.*

Grasses jutted above the surface and cast lines of shadow that refracted at obtuse angles. The shallower scratches to the surface were cobbled with stone, tessellated by the round lineated leaves of the plantains and the jagged rough-cut edges of the dandelion that had now recovered from their scraping by the car's tyres.

A marmalade hoverfly held its position over a single white flower, trying with all its effort to give Sol the impression of danger, a potential sting and the overall visage of *'bee'* or *'wasp'*. Even he was not taken in with its gentility of form and immobile, stationary air hover, but evolution dictated that more than enough of its predators were fooled to allow it to survive, breed and its genes to succeed for another generation of steady incremental improvement.

There was a gouge in the dyke and a dent in its silted cliff edge where an old ash root had become dislodged, fallen and revealed a complex divergence of miniature tunnels that ants had spent their previous season excavating around it. This colony had now moved on but their city's underground transport network had remained as evidence for a future entomological archaeologist to uncover, describe and interpret. It made Sol think of London and what it would look like if a huge digger scooped down and under the streets to reveal the sewers, the underground and everything else the city hid from sight but depended on.

Alien *Carex* reeds, tubular and viridian, spiked up from the gentle stream that tickled the pebbles and earth at the base of the ditch, and split-leaved water plants broke the surface. The fresh scent of bruised spearmint permeated up and into the air from his clumsy footing, heady and strong, yet fresh and awakening.

But, there was no car.

It was as if nature had cleared up the accident behind him and except for a few scrapes in the earth, tracks on the ill-metalled road and one deep furrow that was now water-filled and recycled for natural purposes, it seemed that Sol's car had never been here. Soon there would be no evidence at all. His had been such a fleeting impression on the land and if he had died, there in that crash, the world would have continued, his tracks would have been covered and the sun would have come up each and every day thereafter. He had an impression of the transitory nature of his time on Earth and the fact that not long after he had finished using it, the Earth would care little about his impact, or whether he was worth something or not.

He had always felt a big fish on this planet, moving large sums of money around and banking on his own success. If he went, taken away into another existence, if in fact there was one, he had always considered he would be missed and that he would have left some legacy that others would have cared about. But now, in the face of nature's unconcerned continuum, he was less sure.

There were deeper tyre track marks further up the drive and so he followed them on back towards that welcoming *'no access'* sign that had greeted him at the end of the drive on his first night at the *Bothan*. Sometimes they were clear, with their well-marked tread digging down into the muds leaving a deep impression of their passage. At other moments they would disappear and simply become an integral part of the landscape, leaving little evidence of their course. In addition, Sol became aware of the strengthening offensive smell of oil and diesel mixed into a mechanical concoction that made him associate it with agriculture and farming. He was convinced that at the end of this trail there would be a Land Rover or a tractor. *What else could it be?*

Spots of black viscous material began to appear with increasing regularity as Sol approached the end of the drive to where the track left the tarmac road and ended in its aging signpost. And there, sat patiently, if with the occasional scratch to the white paint and mud splattered up and behind its wheel arches in red sprays, was his car. It looked dejected and forgotten, tucked away there amongst the vegetation on a stony pull-in at the end of the drive and he laughed almost with relief to see it. And, it was all in one, if slightly injured, piece.

The time was eight forty-five in the morning. He was later than intended but hoped that he was still earlier enough to catch each of the couriers and delivery folk as they came by.

Then the second surprise hit him.

On the far side of the car was a heap of brown cardboard boxes. They were neatly stacked and labelled with those at the bottom having become wet from the dewy ground, heartily soaking up the moisture from below. At least two were upside down with the deliverer having ignored the clearly printed arrows and the black font that stated they should be *'this way up'*, now pointing down. And beyond these was a large framed cherry wood construction that he immediately recognised as his own, even though he could only see a small corner of it poking out from behind the stack of boxed up items.

He walked around to face its front where a supported section stuck out across its whole width. A dark metal key had been left in the little inlaid brass lock, holding its lid down, and its matching red cushioned stool had been tucked neatly under as if this made it look more at home sat there where the grasses rocked gaily and beyond which the sea loch waters lapped incessantly and gulls cried.

It was square and angular compared to its natural, wind-caressed surround and contrasted completely as an item man-made, despite most of its component parts being conceived from once-living biological products.

It was his upright piano.

Of course these were his belongings and Sue had simply sent them on up as she had promised she would. The courier had left a transparent plastic envelop with a message in it stating that they had accidentally arrived earlier than expected, had waited a short while and then dropped the items off as requested by the lady in London. In his mind, he had done his bit, travelling hundreds of miles through England and then Scotland, running close to breaking the law with respect to hours slept when driving for long lengths of time behind the wheel, and he had found the postcode that the lady had instructed him to deliver to. The items were delivered and although it was a pity no one was here to sign for them, he had dropped them off. But then, the lady had suggested that Sol might be late, as he often was when being relied upon, whatever time the driver arrived.

Sol looked at the packages and was shocked how little there was if this was his entire life in boxes. Five even-sided recycled cardboard cartons, a piano and a stool.

Was that all he owned? Was that all he was? Was this the sum of his portion of this world?

Somehow, seeing his few earthly possessions here, boxed up and stacked, brought some finality to his and Sue's relationship and the end of his life in the south. Really he had known that it was finished when he had left the flat. But this scene made it clear to him as a visual indication of closure.

Was this all he meant?

A few boxes and a little-used instrument more often employed as an over-sized plant stand, bookcase and mobile cocktail bar than a piano; that was it.

Everything was brought even closer to home with the presence of that solid, heavy, cherry and rose wooden item that stood so out of place in the cobbled muds and plant life on its inappropriately small brass roller wheels, the piano; *his piano*. What a metaphor it was. All perfectly planed and straight-edged, polished and clean, now with beaded drips of rainwater where the snow had melted and repelled into minute dew drops on its hydrophobic wax skin.

It was a smart, elegant thing. An item designed to entertain the middle classes and to give an image of austerity and sophistication. Its mere presence suggested musical ability, training and spare time well spent.

But it was lost.

It had been transported well north of its ordinary environment and been dislocated out into the wilds of the countryside of another country where it simply did not appear to belong. But there was mud appearing already, in smears put there by the heavy hands of workmen, and at least one bruise where the clumsiest had obviously let it slip.

It still looked oddly out of place where it had been left below the needle-clad branches of two overhanging pine trees, as if they would afford it protection from any incoming weather. But given time, thought Sol, they both would become more naturalised to their surroundings, taken back in to nature and yet still retain the ability to make beautiful music even if they did need the occasional retune.

Sol snapped out of his malaise, stepped forward and pulled the stool out from under the keyboard, scraping it against the rocks and mud of the track as it went and adding fatigue to the patina of its lower legs. He sat down as if at a grand piano, unlocked the lid using that little brass key and raised it carefully, looking across the top and out to the expanse of the loch, that small pretender to the greater sea.

He breathed inwards, taking inside the essence of the view and the scent of the land, and with it the reality of this place.

An index finger hovered over middle C, and then he thought out loud, '*no!*'

He moved the digit right, over D, E, F and then G. He would start to write something in G. G for...   ...whoever that mysterious previous owner of *Bothan Faobhar* was. It would be a symphony in G, for G, about the *Bothan* and the glen, the loch and the countryside all around. That would be his naturalistic symphony!

He thought for a moment and then closed his eyes, pressed the sustain peddle gently down with his booted foot and held his breath before dropping his finger decisively down on the fine white key that obliged to its played angle. A hammer fell and a double strung metal wire was hit so that a vibration was created and resonated inside the back box before it travelled the short distance to Sol's ear and the note was played and heard. And then it was maintained by the sustain pedal under his foot.

It was recognised within his harmonic memory bank as a sound he knew and could recall. It was the note G, 391.995hertz.

"What the bloody hell are you up to now?" came the immortal voice of Hamish from behind, now chuckling to himself as he caught Sol in that moment of ecstasy that any performer will recognise as essential before they are about to become most creative.

Sol froze, lifted his foot quickly from the pedal and then stood to his feet to face Hamish whilst the piano stool fell over backwards to become hidden and a part connected to the foliage.

"Just checking it still worked," he explained less than convincingly, both embarrassed and annoyed.

"In the middle of bloody nowhere?" the old man chided as he stepped forward with a self-satisfied, mocking expression painted clearly over his face.

Sol looked around. "Well, no. Not nowhere exactly. At the end of my driveway."

"So, let's get this right. This is usual in London then? Playing the piano at the end of your driveway? In the middle of nowhere?"

"Well, no. Not really. No. I *can* explain."

"Not necessary really. It's your business what you get up to on your land. Just don't do it on mine. I can't be doing having a piano sat at the end of my drive with some daft city boy playing it... ...well bashing just the one note."

Hamish was enjoying the moment which Sol did not like and he felt an angry explosion building up within him.

"They delivered it here." He defended himself, feeling the urge to explain.

"Who? The fairies?"

"No the delivery men."

"Don't worry, I'm pulling your leg." Hamish paused for a minute. "Fairies are too small to shift this lot."

Sol smiled and tried to remember that Gerry, Iona and Skye had all told him that Hamish, despite his outward character, was the most helpful of people inside.

"You'd need giants for this kind of job."

Sol looked up and noticed a sharp, wicked twinkle in Hamish's eyes. There was no doubt that the older man was testing Sol.

"I met your driver when they came down the road earlier," Hamish continued. "They were completely lost and so after they'd driven up and down the road several times I stopped them and asked if I could help. It was a London lorry and so I made an educated guess. Told me about some woman in London... ...Sue?" He watched Sol flinch and made a mental note to be more cautious than he normal would. "She wanted your stuff out so that she could move on with her life. Described you as... ...let me quote '*a selfish*

prick who had buggered off up to Scotland and dumped all his friends running away from a messed up business deal and...
...something unrepeatable about another woman'. I thought you suited that description quite well. After all, you're the only selfish prick up here that I know. Well not the only one. But the only one from London."

Hamish winked at Sol who was trying not to look back directly at him for fear of any of the truth being acknowledged or finally sinking in.

"Anyway, I told them I'd wait nearby in case you forgot to come and pick your things up. Sue had told them you probably would. I told them you were no doubt dead by now and so there wasn't much point waiting anyway. But they were adamant that it was their fault that they got lost and they were very early. Not sure of that logic though. I'm normally late when I get lost. I might even suggest that they didn't really care much about the time anyway. They just wanted to get off. Must've been the jokes I was making..."

"Well thank you for waiting." Sol was honest in his appreciation for Hamish being there.

"That's okay," said Hamish smiling through his gummy tooth line, "I thought that if you were dead already I could steal your piano. There wouldn't have been many witnesses to the drop off and you know..." He trailed off to see what response he was getting from Sol.

"Do you mean any of what you say or do I just have to laugh when you speak like that?"

"Oh, I only mean a fraction of it."

"Good."

"About eight tenths though," Hamish said and he broke out into laughter. Leaning back on his old wooden stick he pushed deep down into his left jacket pocket and extracted a bulging pipe that he quickly stuffed with tobacco and lit whilst cowering with it from the search of the wind and cupping it in the palm of his hand. Once satisfied and surrounded by a smog of swirling fume, he tossed the still smoking match into the ditch at the side of the road where it landed with an extinguishing hiss having trailed a blue arc of burning mist behind it. He breathed in deeply and enjoyed the first moment of its taste whilst Sol drew in the wind whipped smoke, licked his lips with anticipation and coughed. He hadn't had a roll up for days and the temptation was great within him.

"You smoke?" asked Hamish contemplatively.

"Not for the last few days, I ran out."

"Good, it's bad for your health," Hamish sniggered.

"But why do you do it then?"

"Ah, well I treat the smoke with whisky every night. It removes the poison you see?"

Sol started to question the logic. "But…"

"I know, I know," muttered the old man. "The misses, she's always telling me off for it. But then, I treat the whisky each morning with black coffee. That washes out the whisky toxins you see?"

"But…?" Sol didn't see but felt suddenly warmed to the humour and character of the man that this revealed.

"Which means I need the pipe to replace what's been washed out. They do say that a little bit of poison is good for you."

"Yes, but not a little bit of three different poisons!"

"Really?" Hamish feigned shock.

Sol played along. "And, surely if you didn't smoke, you wouldn't need the whisky nor the coffee…"

"And wouldn't life be boring? And just think what would happen to the economy if everyone thought like that? If everyone stopped drinking whisky the shops wouldn't sell it and the distilleries would all go bust and there would be no market for the malt and the farmers would suffer. It would be terrible and that's before I've considered the coffee and the tobacco. The country should be thanking people like me."

Sol was amusingly stumped. "But what about the health effects?" he tried.

"My goodness, you're right." Hamish squealed. "I keep the health people employed too, and have we mentioned the taxes I pay yet?"

"I'm sure you've justified it for yourself, but..."

"Anyway," Hamish interrupted, "your car seems to have moved itself and it's about time this here piano shifted itself too. Where do you want it? Skip, my house or yours?"

"What?" Sol clasped Hamish by the hand, "I never thanked you for moving the car."

"No worries. I think it'll still work. Amazing what a Land Rover can pull and a bit of glue can stick back together. So where's all this stuff going?"

"*Bothan Faobhar* if possible."

"Okay," Hamish replied and turned to get stuck in as if this were a minor request, would not involve much hardship and could be achieved in only a few moments.

"But how much do I owe you?"

Hamish wheeled round on a rubber-booted foot, craning in to get a better view of the city boy now in front of him. "Owe me for what?"

"Moving the car, helping with the piano, anything and everything really. How much do I owe?"

"Oh Sol. You really aren't from round here are you?"

"So people keep saying," Sol replied.

"You don't get it. The sisters and Gerry, they've all said you did the same. Listen. So long as you promise me that when the time comes you'll help me out, help the others or look after what's precious to us, then this is a favour done for free. Besides, I'm not helping you."

"You're not? How so?"

"There's no way I'm letting some city boy get in the way. I'll do *this* job alone. Helping won't be an issue."

"But, what am I supposed to do?"

"Bugger off. Meet the locals. Town's that way," and he pointed an arthritic finger down the lane towards a few houses dotted in ribbon

fashion along the end of the loch. "I'll be here for a good hour if anything else gets delivered and so you needn't worry about that."
He turned to go, repeating that he needed no help when Sol started to protest.
"Or," Hamish suddenly considered, "back the other way is the stores. Sells bits of food, seed and hardware mostly. It's owned by James and Liz. You'll need to meet them sometime soon. But don't go in that though," and he indicated towards the white sports car resting behind them, dejected and laid down with obviously dented pride. "They saw you speed along past them on your arrival. They might judge you badly if you arrived in *that* thing. Besides, we've not checked if it still works yet have we?"
Sol stood in indecision.
Hamish groaned then continued. "If I were you, I'd try the town first of all."
Sol thanked him and left, walking in the opposite direction to Hamish who went in search of a vehicle large enough to carry a piano and the boxed up life belongings of Sol. The collie had appeared as if by magic at his heels, delighted that its master was on the move again, and Hamish gazed down to talk with that genuine immense love that only one man and his one dog can share and that the non-dog owner cannot even start to comprehend.

The road was just slightly wider than a single track; giving any inexperienced motorist the deceptive thought that it was big enough to drive at speed and that to overtake would be easy. But it was far from being that safe.
On the left was a narrow pebbled beach, occasionally littered with seaweed and drifts of white-golden sand. It reflected shell-colours brightly, distracting the driver's eye, and on closer inspection revealing the flicking movements of the sandhoppers amongst the flotsam and the pipits and wagtails that chased them between the weeds. Beyond this stretched the widening expanse of the sea loch,

dark and flat, inviting and alluring; an easy draw for the gaze of the traveller and another pull from concentration on the road.

Out there in the middle, appearing to float on a cliff-edged hull, an island erupted, tree-sprouted like the poorly tended hair of a submerged giant. Conifers clung to its shallow soils and spilled their roots where they dripped down in waterfall shaped cascades on meeting the end of the rock and the beginning of the air. They grappled with the lack of solidity, altered their trajectories and then descended seaward as gravity instructed them to.

On the right, the attendant dyke drained peat-stained waters, coffee black but clear, from the rocky moorland that tumbled upwards and away to greet the foothills and become the mountains, ambling way off behind to where the weather gods contemplated their next moves. Crags sprung from nowhere and jagged cairn-piled rocks, climate tainted and lichen flushed, revealed the difficulty of finding this track in the depths of the worst winter. The metalled margins crumbled downward or simply dropped and there were spreading swathes of rubble-topped tarmac where the waters had broken free from innocuous-looking brooks that obviously knew how to party recklessly should the rain allow them. Here, pebbles were strewn in sloughs of mud that washed the grey of the road, white, red and black, and camouflaged its traction from the tyres of passing vehicles in slippery masses of texture filling silt.

The road was a quiet danger - a sleeping menace.

Hidden in its geography and rustic charm, as it cut its ambling, sinuous, ancient way through the highland countryside, it wooed the inobservant motorist into a false sense of security from within their aluminium and plastic accessorised shells and gave them the dangerous confidence to push forth, faster. This was a green lane designed by the steady evolution of millennia of footfall. It had only ever wanted to be a cattle, a sheep or a goose herding droveway created for the markets that existed when the furthest one had to travel was the distance you could walk. A time when a friendly inn would serve a simple beer and a good plate of food, prepared only from the produce that could be harvested within the locality. This was a lane along which the fish were transported packed in salt made from evaporated loch water in the back of a pony trap to be sold several days' journey away, and where the stone was panniered to donkeys to construct the buildings out in the hills, even *Bothan Faobhar* itself.

In its long history it had existed as mud and cobble, and only recently, in comparison to its age, had it received the attention of bitumen and chippings.

This road did not understand the motorist or the pace of the car and many had paid at their cost for a lack of appreciation as to where this track had come from, save the obvious. Like all good roads its history could be read if time was taken to analyse and read it. Like all good roads it came from more places than the last house, village or town. Like all good roads its own journey was far more interesting than the one we are often on when we travel it. Like all good roads, for the time that each person is on it, it transports each and every one of our life stories with us. And, like all good roads there are a number of ways of ending our journeys on it, not all finishing at the earthly destination we intended.

Sol passed a single cut rose stem, left in halted full bloom, red but fading. It was laid on a difficult quick corner on the way and he knew that someone's journey had ended here in that ditch. He instinctively nodded his head towards the spot and then walked on. *Driving here in a recent past life that could have been him.*

Mixed gulls dropped on what appeared to be plastic litter floating on the sky-tinted surface of the water. He would have written them off as the litter he presumed they were if one had not caught his eye by moving. A pulsating pseudo-bag passed the road where it was raised high enough for Sol to be able to look down into the loch's depths. The bag was red and pink, with a brain-textured centre that ballooned and mushroomed in the way that 60's comic Martians' minds did. Short bulbous tentacles of a rich red descended and wafted dangerously, hidden momentarily before it drifted side up and turned with the tide. Then he saw another and another, so inert looking and innocuous in their wave directed motion. But still Sol shivered as he imagined the sting of these jellies.

Further away there were a few boats where rectangular stonewalls marked a port of some sorts and a rock jetty and slipway indicated a once bustling maritime history that seemed now to have faded from the site and given way to a tranquillity that could have graced a Cornish postcard. He felt he recognised *The Tern* amongst them and put on a burst of speed in the hope of catching up with Gerry.

The first building he came to was a large square tin shed, poorly painted in red-lead which almost reached the corroded edges of its sun-weltered walls but seemed to have missed the skirts and eves. Its roof was corrugated and dented as if it had made too close a contact with the few wind-beaten wispy birch trees that surrounded it shimmering in their elegant stances. There was a marshy pool behind into which the light fell but failed to escape giving it the impression of having an immense, possibly unfathomable depth. It was marked by its flylessness, stillness and featureless shape in a way that even Sol recognised as unusual and disturbing.

Clusters of *Carex* grass, viridian and tubular, topped with a tuft of flaxy yellow, ejecting upwards in search of sky interfaced the peat hagg'd boundary which was quickly overcome by the moor, the rock and eventually the creeping blaeberry, small in leaf and stature. But no reflections were cast as if the pool sucked in the light, absorbed it into its humic acidity and cast out a counter mirror image of the world, one darker and colder than that above. Its glass finish gave the impression of a highly polished obsidian disc, refined by the hard labour of many people; of the likeness that occultist John Dee would have sought for his '*seeing*' of the fallen angels. There was a deeper and gloomier world trapped below the surface, one that Sol did not wish to disturb. No beetle larvae, no nymphs. Just an unreal clarity that rapidly took the eye down to a tea brown sludge that fell away into depth as his gaze left the edge.

There was the smell of sulphur.

It is strange how a spot in nature can give or hold an emotion. There are caves that for their spine-tingling impression on the physical and emotional state of our bodies have been employed as catacombs and plots of land so icy that they are enrolled as graveyards. There are places and views that fill you with awe and wonder or top up that elemental aspect of joy that gives our life significance, purpose and a future hope of better things to come. These locations are preserved or have the special attention of conservation, find meaning as viewpoints or become the position for benches or pilgrimages. There are even those sites that draw the unwary to suicide and an end to it all or that immediately lend themselves to a holy dwelling or building. We are affected by the past experience of the land, our own life journey as we arrive, or simply the shape and natural design, which may or may not have been ruined, enhanced or interfered with by that ant-like constructor and tinkerer, man. But affected we are.

This pool troubled Sol, disquieting something in him for its geography and the forlorn shed that stood sentry to it and he walked on as the curlew on the shoreline stammered their rising flute calls in mourning. It was an eerily timed soundscape to accompany this water.

And yet, in the ray of a sunbeam and the movement of a grey base-tinted cotton ball of a cloud the emotion of the way changed and just around a schist-bound corner beyond the sad and lonely black pool and its forgotten hut, the vista of the port town revealed itself to Sol. He was warmed by it and quickly forgot the spine-tingle brought on by the shack and its pond behind.

A lichen-encrusted sign announced that he had entered 'Old Town'. It was not a very profound name and it did not need semantic analysis, but it described the dwellings clustered on the sea front well.

He imagined himself as a traveller on the road and felt the joy of now being so close to his journey's end where the bright painted houses clung to the road that separated them from the green of a sheep-cropped, daisy-dotted strip of lawn and a harbour wall. There, a diminutive cannon still pointed out to sea. A bell clanged metrically at the mast top of a little wooden boat that bobbed idyllically next to where *The Tern* rocked in its time too to the rhythm of the passing tide waves. In all six larger craft made up the flotilla with smaller rowing boats secured by ropes and chains to algae-stained buoys, the pier or the barnacle-encrusted seawall.

Gulls '*ca-gulled*' their distrust of the shabby figure of Sol as he entered the town in the hope of finding a coffee shop, a cash machine and the other vitals that the city boy gains comfort and security from.

At the head of the slipway across the road, which was marked in near-straight sun-warped metal runnels of railway track running perpendicular to its direction, was a large wooden workshop shed from which the sound of sawing and sanding could be heard. It emitted the smell of well-worked wood, of varnish and polish, and the aromatic pleasantry of wax and glue mixed into the heady scent that draws many a moth into its destruction. Grimy skylights, mostly overgrown with moss on their upper surfaces, punctuated the corrugations of the flimsy roof to send shafts of sunlight down into the dark vacuous room below and through the sawdusted air where it picked out the hulls and bodies of boat after wooden boat. A sizeable steel bar was suspended from the roof from which chains and pulleys descended to connect with and lift each land-stranded marine victim of conservation and repair.

Above the expansive doorway, where the iron panels almost fitted together, where they were knit decades before with a welding tool and little desire for perfection in its build, was nailed a crooked tin sign. It was hand-painted in white gloss and lettered boldly, if now neglected. '*James Nevin and Sons, Traditional Boat Builders and Repair, Est. 1841*' and there was a phone number below which had been altered by hand at least twice before.

Sol could hear conversation within and the sound of rough sanding became a whistle and then a muffled hammering and a crescendo of blasphemous swearing.

There were only five houses along the sea front and a few dotted up on the hillside where Sol could see the antlered trophies of a herd of red deer, curiously deep brown and pale muzzled, migrating up the slopes in stuttered ensemble. A collection of twenty or more heads, always one was on the lookout whilst their group fed and then moved on. There seemed to be no pattern in their behaviour but their numbers gave them safety and it was easy to see that some were more attentive to the potential of danger than others and through their individual differences the whole herd was protected. Some twitched their ears in irritation at the flies that accompanied them, all snorted and at least one twitched its tail and hind quarters in a nervous tick.

Wild-looking curled-horned sheep milled around the houses, goat-like in their straggly brown-patched fashion and many in need of a trim where wool hung loose in tufts that a good pull or scratch would remove. The houses had gardens at their backs that were hemmed in by tall fences to protect yard plots from the browsing attention of livestock and wildlife.

One house claimed to be a shop and had a wider window than the rest, and so Sol stepped down inside through the stiff door to be announced by the jingle of a bell that hid behind it. Dark, damp and dominated by the drilling sound of a fridge-freezer unit, the room expanded well back from beyond a counter top crammed with produce and half hidden by sacks of vegetables. There was a hand-written note on the counter written clearly in felt-tipped black capitals that had become smudged by the ring of a teacup and yellowed by age and multi-use.

'*Gone fishing. Back by 10pm. Leave cash in back room or next time you are in. Please turn lights off when you go.*'

Sol stared incredulously at the note. Never in his existence had he seen evidence of so much trust; a shop left open whilst the shopkeeper was absent. There wasn't even any expectation that the money was immediately forthcoming.

How could this work?

This was not like the city all!

He selected a chocolate bar and threw coins on to the note, half concerned that a camera had picked up his actions. He required change but did not want to seek any and so he left and stepped out into the sudden brightness of sunshine which strained his eyes but in a pleasant way. Walking over to the harbour wall he sat down for a minute to rest his weary legs, dangling them over the side and pointing his feet down to the lapping sea so that he could feel their flesh swell.

The curious black silhouette face of a seal broke the still waters below him and rose up enough for its dappled whiskered face to take this newcomer in. Its large glassy eyes seeped weeping emotion and it sniffed the air through prehensile nostrils that broke open as deep holes in its otherwise hydrodynamically smoothed skin. Only ear holes marked the otherwise iron-flat surface of its head. It puffed air hoarsely and sprayed breath-tainted spume before closing its dewy eyes and nostrils and disappearing down into the water leaving just a series of ripples as verification of its presence.

A green-headed merganser tested the water out on the loch and dived for fish.

Gulls hung effortless in the air.

Up there was a dot giving enough of an outline to be identified as a drifting eagle if only Sol had the capacity and knowledge to know.

This *was* a different world to the one he had come from, but as he chewed the refined sugars and milked cocoa of his chocolate he pondered, and he was certain that he liked it, however different it was to where he had come from.

He removed his shoes and socks, placed them carefully next to him and then lay back in the grass, disappearing backwards in memories brought on by the sound of the loch, the smell of the sea and the feel of the sun-warming plant life and moss his head nestled into. His mind's eye took him again to a time with that elderly, weaker hand holding his firmly and the two of them sitting beside each other on the cliff tops overlooking a calm, sun blue'd sea. They had pretended to fly like the birds on the crags below, leaning out into the wind with arms unfolded and flapping, and now they were playing a game of counting - the number of birds, the species of birds, the behaviour of birds; thousands, hundreds and infinitely varied.

Eyes closed, he listened to that continuing symphony of the ecology.

Sol felt an urge rise up as unbidden as the seal who had appeared in front of him, and he gave it chance to surface so that he could consider it more fully. He could sense that there was another life yet to be lived inside of him and that of the city-bred, merchant had the potential to die or move on, if it had not already been fatally poisoned or injured by the world he was seeing and experiencing in his *Bothan* retreat. His life road had accidentally taken a different turn recently and he had now started to look at the new junctions ahead, ones that led to other unexpected destinations. He just needed to commit to one pathway or choose to return back the way he had come to settle where he was going.

Chapter 10: Ripples

(O Magnum Mysterium, Morton Lauridsen)

There is a place between every medium where there must be a change.
When light hits glass or water it refracts towards the normal so that it appears to bend so that you can use a thick window to see further around a corner and a fish is able get a better view of the bank side fisherman. As volatile chemicals meet their interface becomes a reactive front marked by a change of colour or heat, even as a precipitation out of solution of some new thing. Weather fronts too meet so that one rises, one falls, and storms amount out of nothing but apparently empty air. Plates shifting the world around in their tectonic motion push up mountains, erupt volcanoes, shake the Earth or subduct rock back down into that unimaginable inferno of the magma furnace. Even the sea as it slips up and down in tidal ebbs impacts with the land to take away rock, inscribing its presence through erosion, and wind can undermine the very ground we plant things in and even sculpt solid rocks.
People too undergo marked changes moving from one medium to another and it causes much turmoil in our lives as we approach and pass through from one side to the next. A new location or school, work places evolving and practises flexible. Sometimes we are left high and dry, floundering on the beach of our own existence as the familiar seeps away leaving us exposed in a land where we feel insecure, outmoded or unprepared, the opposite of out of our depths. But then, some seem to thrive on the new, being spurred on by its opportunities, challenges and unforeseen consequences. Like evolutionary mishaps, some variants can always take advantage of serendipitous happenings.

Sol further unwrapped his foil-enclosed chocolate and chewed mid-philosophy, digging down to extract the crumbs at the bottom of the wrapper where they had become one with the silver.

In only a few days he felt he had started the process of forgetting the past life of deals and an obsession with the phone, being purged and cleansed in some odd retreat ritual, immersed in isolation but not left alone. He caught his reflection in the still waters below and could see the physical affect, where a scruffy, well-stubble'd, but relaxed figure looked up out of the water and smiled back to him. He wondered when he had last washed, how he would now smell, what his *'friends'* in the city would think if someone like him passed them, each of them sparkling, manicured and perfumed. *Would they even notice him? And if they did, would they give some repugnant remark, move away or pretend not to have registered his existence?* He thought back to the last time he had used a credit card, eaten out or drunk expensive coffee in a restaurant. He thought back to a time when he had felt that he was really living. *But had he been or was he now?*

Then his mind considered his recent purchases made on the phone in a state of desperation in a bid to re-join that rat race, to improve his situation and push back the frontiers of the wild. It was odd that he wasn't sure if he wanted to yet, but neither was he ready to just let go.

With no one to compare to and no one to impress or better, he hadn't been out there in the shops or on the Internet buying in the comforts of the latest fashions, ideas borrowed from those that pretended they knew more of what he needed for clothes, for housing, for holidays and for transport. From here, all this, now that he was left behind in a different country, felt false and unnecessary. But he also knew that if his friends and colleagues from that other land could see him now they would be looking from the other side of that interface and be wondering about him, concerned for his welfare and questioning his lack of sanity.

How quickly the mind of a human can bridge the gaps from one place to the next! How far one can travel by not really moving that far.

He sat upright, replaced his socks and boots and then stood up smartly, scaring fly-accompanied goat-sheep to trotting gallops as martins also skimmed the ground but in reeling pursuit of insects. This was not the bustle of city life and the thing he missed most was the constant distraction of others. He wasn't used to there being nobody there when he needed the reassurance of presence. Here he would have to face his own thoughts all of the time and the biggest change in life he now feared was the lack of security he often experienced when living so closely with himself and his own mind. Unlike in the city he would be unable to hide himself from his personal thoughts simply by becoming busily involved in managing the lives and money of others.

The dorsal fin of a large fish, fat and grey, with the skinned texture of crinkled foil, broke the still surface film and Sol watched the travel of the perfect ring of miniature wave after wave as they spread and dissipated through the bay, between the boats and up to the wall. Every action here had a consequence and set up ripples that met with new experiences, sometimes colliding and reflecting back, but always scattering out and fanning their range of effect.

A milk-yellow butterfly skipped the air passed him and he was reminded of that philosophy of a butterflies wings beating setting up cascades of amplified changes such that they altered the weather patterns thousands of miles away. Everything that was distorted now in the present impacted everything there ever would be again in the future.

The butterfly continued on its judder-halted journey, strong enough to fight the breeze but weak enough to appear fragile. For a moment Sol considered the complexity of such a small and insignificant living thing; cells and tissues, organs and systems coordinating movements and actions, eventually manifested as flight with the eventual outcome of genetic success or failure.

He went back into the shop, found a small bottle of single malt, over paid at the counter and walked back the way he had come, successfully working hard to ignore the temptation to buy tobacco at the same time or to sneak back in after he had walked far enough away. There was a small stone church beyond the town with an incumbent green tin-framed shed for a hall and he was becoming increasingly aware of the evidence of the people. Cars, usually old and rustic, littering the road and the tracks behind, washing flapping steadily from where it hung, not always clean, tools left for further use or to rot under a future rain, a toy tractor, plastic and faded, but obviously loved and cherished as all good toys should be. It was all there to be seen, the blemish and litter of humans on the landscape.

Beyond the headland was another collection of houses fronting onto the sea loch in the continued ribbon development of the little town. Each was brightly splashed with pinks, yellows and oranges, painted years before but still bright despite their over coating of algae and lichen crusts. Some time ago each owner needed to mark their position on the harbour line so that the returning fishermen could see their homes from far off the shore and know that there was a place and a family waiting on the land for their safe shoreward arrival back.

Wagtails bobbed long streamer extension-feathers behind them as they hopped the wall and '*chicked*' amongst the house sparrows that flocked the ground and rooftops. Sol listened to the oily feathered starlings that crowded the boat builder's shed ridge tiles. They whistled and peeped, called and laughed, each serious-face starting with dark glossy eyes staring anger-browed down their sharp chisel-beaks. He stopped to laugh at their comic robotic behaviour and gestures, and the squabbles that so often broke out between them, huddled in their hundreds as they enjoyed the warmth reflected from the roof panels.

He had never stopped to consider a starling before and marvelled at not only their architecture but also his previous blindness to this common birds' beauty. Dark, star-spangled feathers shone and refracted pink and yellow astral designs. And their song was an impossibility to describe it ranged and changed so broadly.

A man, well-built but care-worn, stepped out of the shadows of the boatyard and the starlings anointed the sky in an immediate retreat of wing-bound bodies and the noisy murmuration for which they are famous, and from amongst them a single feather dropped. He was armed with a string of tools hung round his boiler-suited waste and was followed in deepest conversation by Gerry who was carrying rope and some sections of wood. She was obviously hanging on each word the other uttered and was intent on the blunt message he communicated. They headed for *The Tern* where the man lithely dropped down into her hull and started an inspection of some part of other, and from where he shook his head despondently.

They were animated but not happy in their discussion as Sol drew up to join them.

"Hi there," he called over as he approached the harbour wall with an air of nonchalance that he hoped would diffuse the atmosphere.

"Sol," replied Gerry. "This is Sol," she explained to the man who smiled coldly and then withdrew somewhere inside of himself with a visible flinch.

"Yes, I know," he said. "Hamish has told me about him. Southern fool who thinks he can run *Bothan Faobhar*. Poor chance of survival he says. Don't bother to get know him, he'll be gone or dead soon. That's what Hamish said."

There was an awkward moment of silence, one whose passage seemed to drift all too slowly with the last comment hanging just long enough to prevent an easy bridge being made between one statement and the next.

"But of course, Hamish didn't actually mean that did he...?" and Sol paused enough to suggest he wanted a name of the boat building man.

"This is James," Gerry tried. "James Nevin, son of James, grandson of James and great grandson son of James. Well, you get the picture?"

She hadn't meant to belittle the man, but the effect was obvious.

"What we have in ability and craftsmanship we lacked in imagination over the years," explained the man not really looking at Sol as closely or intently as Sol would have hoped on first meeting. His jaw suggested a stressed and angry interior and Sol wondered if it was him or Gerry that was fuelling it.

"He's a master boat builder like his father...," she said again.

"...and grandfather and great grandfather," finished James Nevin curtly. "Yes, as I said, what we have in ability we lacked in imagination. Pity really, another trade would probably have paid better and stand any chance of longevity. Still, at least I'll be able to claim that I was the James Nevin at the helm when the company finally went bust."

He stared back at the boat yard shed and shook his head automatically.

"He's fixing my boat," Gerry explained.

"Well would be, if..." and he trailed off raising his eyebrows at Gerry.

"We're just discussing payment," Gerry admitted. "Cash isn't so easy these days. And that's for either of us. Things don't get done on credit like they used to." She looked injured as she talked, addressing Nevin as much as Sol. The man ignored her and chewed on something irritably, probably gum.

Sol leaned over the boat seeing a rotten section on the hull, a patch that James appeared to caress with his hand like a good vet with an injured calf or a doctor with a frail mouldering patient who felt the pull of the grave. The sea was winning its battle with the timber and a stain of black-green was growing through it and under the varnish in a fungal necrosis.

Sol whistled through his teeth. "How much?" he asked falling rapidly into business mode and spotting the talents of a man who obviously knew what he was talking about in front of him.

"Well," James considered the growing scar under his fingers and rubbed it. He passed his fingers behind and then down into the water. "She's well-made and may last another season. It's good wood after all. But the rot is there, as it was last year... ...and the year before." He ran his hand over the rim again and tapped it gently, the hammering resonating on all sound boards but sounding dull and heavy when it beat the blackened sections. "If it had been treated two years ago when I first saw it and offered to do it for free, then..." Nevin paused, watching Gerry grimly.

Sol was aware of some politic reason for this, but feeling belligerent he decided to push the deal forward anyway. Business waited for no man. "I said, how much? It's a simple request and I don't need the history. Just the price... ...please."

"We don't rush things round here Mr Solomon." James stared furiously into Sol's impassive face. "We take our time. We consider what needs to be done. Then we consider the alternatives. All that before we rush in."

"And by when the business has gone elsewhere?"

Sol was not sure why, but he felt something hung in the air between him, Gerry and this new man. There was a limpid flavour to the conversation that he knew meant he had missed something. *But what?*

Jealousy?

A past relationship between the other two even?

Concern over the newcomer?

"All wood succumbs to the sea eventually," the man explained. "Like relationships, they can look polished and glossy on the outside with all the right grain running through, but still be rotting from within. Then suddenly out it comes and the whole thing spoils. Without the work, before you know it…" Nevin was talking to Gerry who glanced away with guilt, and something in Sol engaged with the problem between them all.

There was a relationship.

"It'll need dry dock eventually and more than this little patch up. She's not as young as she used to be, I'd say a good seventy years – a good design, made by my grandfather."

"But, how much?" Sol demanded, less patient but keen to press the man to see what else his behaviour would reveal when stressed.

"Six hundred."

"Is that the best offer?"

"As it's for Gerry, and we've known each other so long, five hundred and seventy five."

"But…" Gerry started and the man continued to avoid Sol's gaze as Sol silenced her with a motion of the hand.

"Five fifty and you can have the cash in your account tomorrow," Sol was cold, calculated and held the man on the deck below in his full gaze.

"Sol…" Gerry tried to interrupt again.

"When can I have it in cash?"

"Two days I suspect."

"Jake Solomon!" Gerry protested, but was ignored yet again.

"No sooner?"

"If you start work tomorrow then you'll do the job for five hundred cash?"

"Done."

James leant forward and shook on it, grasping Sol's diminutive, softened hand with his dry, hardened, expansive one.

"The boat can be here tomorrow?" he asked of Gerry who clambered up and out of the boat sweating hot red with concern.

"Yes," she replied quickly thanking James and bustling him back towards the boat yard as she fixed Sol hard with yet another stare and whispered angrily to him. "I *can't* afford that!"

"But I can," he whispered back with a smile that he thought would ease her.

"But how am *I* going to pay *you* back for it? As I said, credit isn't a good option either. At some time I need to pay it back and I'm struggling to do that with the debts I already have!"

"I thought you were from around here?" Sol quizzed.

She stopped dead. "What did you say?"

"I thought *you* were from around here?"

"Okay. *Why* did you say it then?"

"Don't people round here do favours for each other? You know, look out for each other? That's what everyone's been telling me ever since I arrived! Hamish, you, Iona, Skye. You've all told me that favours are done and people help out."

"Well, yes, but this is five hundred pounds or more."

"So far you've fed me, checked I'm still alive, been the first friendly face I've met and seemed just that bit concerned whether I live or die out on the loch or up a mountain slope. You said I would pay you back when the time came. Well the only thing I seem to be any good at is in dealing in money. It's what I do... ...sorry, did, for a living. And, I'm only any good at it when I'm meddling with other people's affairs. So I'm just doing what I do best. I'm meddling and with money. I've just chosen to meddle with yours for a bit."

Gerry was silent a moment and then leant forward and kissed him on the cheek and ran off to the boatshed to finalise the contract shouting, "thank you, Sol. I don't think I understand your ways at all, but thank you. I will pay you back."

"But," he started as she passed over the road, "you don't need to."

She disappeared into the cavernous tin-roofed yard from where Sol heard a final shout, "if you wait ten minutes I'll take you back round to the track up to the *Bothan*."

Sol stood on the harbour wall, static whilst the water below bobbed and cajoled the wooden flotilla at his feet. *The Tern* waited its mistress patiently whilst silver bullets of fish swarmed her prow and played flashes with the sunlight. He felt his cheek, red and flushed, and sensed a growing depth of emotion for the woman that the boat and he both awaited.

It was a strange mix. Attraction but not in a way he had recognised before. Here was a friend and nothing else. *But what more could some other person be?*

The journey along the bay was quicker by sail than foot and they rapidly made the beach by the end of the track, skipping the waves and forcing the dabbling waders by the froth line up into frenzied flocks of black, grey and white panic. There was now no piano or pile of boxes, but the white car was still there looking for all intents and purposes like a burnt out remnant of some brief and ill-fated joyride. Hamish had been good to his word and except for the deep rutted tracks of the Land Rover there was little evidence of Sol's belongings left at the track's end.

There was however a new box lying lonely alongside the car – yet another item dumped by a speeding courier too busy to care and too hurried to wait.

Sol sprung ashore as *The Tern* ran up the shingle of the beach and pulled heartily on the painter rope to tug her into a line set at right angle to the water.

"You're getting the hang of this sailing business aren't you?" Gerry commented from the stern, dropping the sail such that its billow slumped and the thick material flapped weakly, losing its grip on the air. He grinned back and walked on to investigate the coffin shaped cardboard package awaiting him.

"It's item number two of three," he called back, "but I'll never shift it up the drive. It's bigger than I thought it would be."

They discussed the way forward.

Gerry would wait for the deliveries, a further two boxes and Sol's groceries. She would then ship them up to *Bothan Faobhar* where he would join her with any other outstanding post. Gerry agreed to cook the rabbit, still hanging in the larder, which she described as

being as easy to skin as undressing for bedtime, but only if
undressing someone else... '...and when they were dead'. She
also suggested that it was probably now *'higher'* than the average
Londoner on a Friday night as Sol had left it so long. She just
hoped he liked his meat *'gamey'*, whatever that meant in reality.

They sat for a while on the beach and skimmed stones, drinking
whisky straight from the bottle and discussing their different life
stories in perfunctory detail, missing out those parts that really
mattered and yet still giving enough to maintain interest.

"Why is James so frosty?" Sol suddenly asked.

"Long story," she answered, keen to keep it short. "When I know
you better, I might tell you, but it'd require a lot more whisky than
this."

He snorted, that last sentience carrying far more information than
she had intended. He would have probed just that bit more, gently
and conscientiously, when a square white delivery van, emblazoned
with fruit and the smiling photographs of inanely-happy and
healthy airbrushed people on its sides, pulled up on the road above
them and sent the road-accompanying linnets up in a flight of
'twitters' and scolds.

"'Scuse me," called the poorly-shaved driver cutting the engine and
coughing heartily from his smoke-fumed cabin through a shabby
looking window. There was little to maintain a feeling of a healthy
atmosphere. "'Scuse me. Can you tell me where I am? I'm
completely bloody lost!"

"I suspect that means you're in the right place," Sol shouted up to
the driver who was now scratching his black sweaty mop of hair
that topped a deep red, angst-ridden face.

"I'm looking for Bow-than Fay-ob-har."

"You mean *Bothan Faobhar*," corrected Sol, amazed what just a
few days was doing for his local language skills.

"If you say so. But all I can find is this here track."

"That'd be it then. I'll sign for the goods if you can put it in the
boat for me," and he pointed down the shore.

The deliveryman looked curiously at Gerry, Sol, the boat and the loch with a question in his face.

"The boat?" he asked.

"Yes," they both replied as if this were the most normal thing in the world.

Sol scrawled something that approximated to anything but his signature on the handheld silver-screened device the man proffered him. It didn't really matter how he signed this sort of machine. The screen was never sensitive enough to pick up what he wrote and Sol suspected that no one would ever check it anyway. The man pocketed the device before explaining about the items that had been forcibly exchanged due to their absence in the most local stores and warehouses, still some forty miles away.

There was a red wine at twenty-one ninety-nine that was no longer in stock and so it had been swapped for a more expensive one now charged at the same price. *Did he mind?*

'No,' explained Sol, 'the grapes are just as good in that one, and it has a better vintage. That'll be fine.' But Gerry looked dumbfounded and walked up to inspect the wines being loaded on to a metal trolley that clacked as the cases were pinned securely to it and the bottles clanked together, bell-like and clear.

"Why are you paying that for wine?" she asked.

"It's good," Sol replied nonchalantly scanning further down the list of items and changes.

"But the stuff I make in the porch back at my house is perfectly adequate and you can buy other wines for a fiver at the local stores on a *'treat'* day."

And so he explained his logic in that over-compensating way of an adult justifying their own addictions and compulsions to a naughty child who cannot understand why they never get the best of anything. "It's what they all drink back in London."

"Yes," she replied, "I understand that, but do they enjoy it more?"

"Well…"

"Can they, or you, tell it's a better wine, or is it the label that makes it better?"

"Well…"

"Or do you just drink it because your friends tell you that you should?"

"Ah…"

"Have you tried my homebrew?"

"Well, no…   …but I will."

"Do you want the wine sir?" asked the deliveryman politely interrupting, looking from Sol to Gerry and then back again.

"Yes," said Sol looking from the deliveryman to Gerry and then back again. "I'll save it for after I've tried some of Gerry's homebrew. It can be an alcoholic mouthwash."

The wine went into the boat in stacked boxes of six with the driver struggling with the trolley down the cobbles of the beach with its large wheels, thickly enveloped in black rubber tyres better designed for the town than the seaside. The deep green bottles clanged noisily.

Some of the cheeses were alternative brands too.

"Are these the cheeses they eat in London too?" asked Gerry of the intent Sol.

"Actually no, not these," he replied. "These are all exchanges."

"Good because this one is made by friends of mine across the loch and I should hate for no one to actually taste it and only eat it just because the people in London tell them to. They go to a lot of effort to get that flavour."

"What?" Sol quizzed.

"The breed of cow, the pastures they feed on, even the culture for the cheese itself and the maturation process. It's all carefully controlled and unique to their wee glen."

"And?" he pressed.

"Well, the label is a bit boring and unlikely to impress your friends. But you wait till you've tasted it. You should use your taste buds more often and not your eyes when shopping. You never know, you might find something *you* enjoy."

"So," butted in the deliveryman, "do you want the cheese?" He looked from Sol, to Gerry and back again.

"Yes," said Sol taking both of the others in with a glare.

The cheeses went into the bottom of the boat.

"And then there's the bread, sir?" added the deliveryman.

"What?" Gerry quizzed.

"Bread," he repeated.

"What are you buying bread for?" She fixed Sol in her mightiest glower.

Sol had no clue as to how he should reply. "Because I want bread," he eventually answered exasperated.

"You don't *buy* bread," she scolded.

"What do *you* do with it then?" Both he and the deliveryman were with each other on this one.

"You make it."

"Make it?" Sol gestured wildly with his hands. "Make it? How?"

"So you don't want the bread?" asked the man raking back up the beach with his trolley stacked with near-empty green baskets clipped securely down, the bread on top.

"Yes," said Sol, but "No," said Gerry.

"That's a no then," agreed the deliveryman. "I'll knock them off your bill."

"And take these too," continued Gerry rifling through Sol's bags. "He won't need this meat, nor these mushrooms or the veg," and she threw them out of the boat onto the shore.

"Why not?" asked Sol, pride beaten and somewhat crest fallen and a large part confused.

"Because we can get you the meat off your own bloody estate for free, there are mushrooms growing all over it for free too, and have you looked in your own sodding garden?"

"No," he admitted truthfully, "no I haven't."

"Well at least I know what we'll be doing tomorrow then."

The deliveryman starting picking up the goods cast out onto the beach amongst the stones and placing them back into the green baskets on his trolley. He then struggled to tug it back over the cobbles, the wide wheels being sucked down by the sand and sinking between the grains, or competing badly with the cobbles and pebble stones. Eventually he made it back up to the road where Sol joined him at the van and signed for the goods that had been returned.

"I say," Sol began, "I am sorry about that. It's just that I'm not used to doing the shopping and..."

"Marriage takes all sorts," replied the man.

"Oh no, we aren't married," explained Sol.

"No," finished Gerry. "He's more like my brother. My *little* brother. And as *big* sister I have to help him out from time to time." The driver left quickly and the two sat back down to enjoy a more local cheese than Sol had intended and a more continental and expensive wine than Gerry had expected along with finger-spread homogenised butter from an unknown source that '*offended Gerry to the core*' and biscuits of a type that '*everyone in London was eating*'. By the end of the first bottle, however they had started out, neither of them knew what was a good cheese, a pleasing wine, a poor quality butter or a popular biscuit, but they were full and they were happy and laughing when the next delivery arrived unannounced.

They were lounging on the cobbles taking it in turns to draw from the bottle, its cork cleverly removed using a gnarled wood-handled knife with an oily blue and tempered blade taken from the essential tool kit aboard '*The Tern*'. This time there were two smaller boxes that were quickly stowed away before the lorry driver left the curious, half-cut couple he had discovered in hysterics on the pebbled beach.

Gerry set sail soon afterwards, seeming to be perfectly able to control her craft despite being unable to walk as well as earlier. She claimed that when she had had enough to gain sea legs on the land then her brain was thinking about right for trying to stand upright on the sea. And then Sol found that he was on his own again with just the loch water, a flock of fat grey geese that joined him for company and the smaller whimbrel that probed deep into the yeasty ferments at the water's edge. The clouds ballooned upwards over the sea, stretching like giant pillows that sought more space and the chance to burst, and the wind pressed into his face cruelly; he knew there would be rain and only hoped that the last, probably most important delivery yet to come, would arrive before the downpour.

Time is the one immeasurable. We think we have a grasp of its passing using clocks and watches, phones and IT. We believe that global misconception that there are twenty four hours in every day, each separated into sixty minutes and subdivided again to make sixty seconds a piece. And yet we could go further and, like the physicist, fraction time into its milliseconds, then micro and next nano. But why stop there? This supposedly easily defined unit of measurement is simply a manmade construct and we could have chosen any convenient passage as the second, the minute or the hour – we certainly would have done if we were metricised prior to the invention of the second and its curious units of sixty.

And time changes, despite it being considered an absolute.

One man's minute is another man's second and a young child's hour. Time alters depending on our season in life, whether we are new to this world where every second is an impetuous lifetime, or near to our end where the passage of our time means that even hours and days are less significant than they used to be and the only thing we have really learnt is patience. An hour in the arms of a lover can flit away as if no time had passed at all, and yet those moments we dread, or when we are bored or ill-occupied, can stretch minutes to fill vacuous spaces in our minds, seeming to drag on. To a tree time is nothing and yet even this portion is fleeting when considering a sea, a mountain or a planet.

Time changes.

It changes with age and state in life, emotion and desire. We start out our life with so much of it that we feel invincible and eternal, full of energy and enthusiasm. We end it in the knowledge that time has been squandered and we have run out and few are fully satisfied with their allotted amount of it.

Sol counted time.

How long would the courier be?

Of course, the mind-set that asks such a question, unless distracted, is doomed to find that time drags even though our carefully tuned watches tell us that it simply passes at the same speed as it always does and always will do, everywhere and at any time.

He counted geese.

Seventeen.

Large and round, their melancholic feathering was far grander than he had first appreciated. Time allowed him the chance to observe their finer detail. It was not the homogenous 'grey' he had written them off as. A pale head sported a bright glassy black eye that was wet and reflective, and each held a friendly white tipped, pink bill with an upturned smile. Their thick necks were striated with black fluting that sinuously swelled into a deep chest of hoary sienna and then became increasingly well striped as it fell back to meet the pink of the legs and the white of the rump. Over all were folded two dark wings with white fringing demarcating each feather in its firm-held place.

They sifted the water, craning their necks low and sampling the liquid for dissolved life as they raised their bills in critical pose. They crackled and commented on the content and flavour in gregarious conversation as if they were critics or connoisseurs at a wine tasting conference not geese dabbling the shallows.

Twenty minutes had gone – lost, but well used in the space of time Sol now considered to be but five minutes.

The whimbrel was joined by godwits, straight-billed and rufous bellied, and a bandit-eyed ringed plover picked the seaweed flotsam at the high tide mark by Sol's feet. And then, in the same way that from a magic eye puzzle a three dimensional picture suddenly emerges which the observer cannot help to notice every time they see the image again and yet struggled to recognise it for what it was before, he suddenly became aware of a mass of avian life just beyond his outstretched feet. Amongst the rocks and pebbles, the sand and the littered weed were cleverly camouflaged birds, some black chested white lined and speckled gold and brown on their backs, others less well patterned; golden plovers and turnstones.

He counted them.

Fifty-one birds.

Had they been there all the time unnoticed?

It is amazing how we can only see what our eye is looking for. It is a consequence of us being bombarded by so much information all of the time that we can only ever be fully aware of a small portion of it. Try closing your eyes and listening and it is incredible what you become aware of. Try not listening and instead simply visually searching the world around you and it is awe inspiring what there is to be seen. Why does the twitcher spot the bird even when driving the car, or hear its song despite being part of an intense conversation? It is a heightened awareness brought on by interest, one that means they are searching for that thing, or at least its type. And once the floodgates are opened and the filters removed, when the sensitivity is increased for sound or sight, then there is no stopping it.

There is an object on a distant branch that does not move the way the tree sways with the wind revealing an animal, or a bird that flies differently to the rest or has a colour that matches a picture seen in some forgotten book. Then there may be the flower with the altered petals, or leaves or stems that just doesn't counter with the others, or the insect that hovers rather than darts. There are so many skills the field naturalist employs that we all had at birth and is only ever encouraged in the world-explorations of the very young. But once disregarded they are difficult to recapture and re-learn. In effect, naturalists just never grow up and carry on with an interest in the world around them that most have forgotten they ever had.

The plovers sat tight, huddled as a flock of sleeping cryptically-coloured bird forms with their heads tucked under their wings and their backs all pointing in parallel to the wind that swept up the loch and tussled their down. The turnstones picked and prodded between them.

Sol decided that they had always been there and only now did he have the sixth sense required to see them.

The '*phut-phut*' of an approaching motorbike scattered the birds to the air in one synonymous flight of creature that headed rapidly on black-tipped wingbeats down towards the town to find respite amongst the cobbles further along the loch.

The spell of nature broken, Sol left the beach and headed back up to the road where a leather-clad youth was contemplating the '*no access*' sign at the bottom of Sol's drive. He had left his red bike, small and powerless, turning over and was referring to an electronic device on the handlebars.

"Hello," Sol called, "is that for Mr Solomon?" He indicated to a large brown envelope that the young man held protectively to his chest as if it would shield him from this dishevelled, wild-looking stranger emerging off the shore. It was A3 in size, padded and caught by the light wind it rattled.

"Yeh, but I don't seem to be able to find where 'e lives." The youth's accent was of London origin. It was familiar and friendly, but not all too welcome to Sol who was keen to move on from that episode of his life for now.

"I am he," he replied formally.

"How do I know?"

"What?"

"This needs signing for and I need ID."

Sol took out his wallet and sifted through his cards where he came across no photographs save for a few of Sue that after a moment of thought he let fly away into the breeze, sailing off to meet the distant water as a handful of feathers might. He kept one, closing his eyes momentarily as he thought back to the happy moment it instantly returned him to, tugging at his heart that beat quickly. A few minutes of Tomfoolery in a photo booth – that was a good memory.

"I have my credit cards and that's about it," Sol explained curtly.

The man looked around nervously as if he expected the long arm of the law to stretch out to this barren junction on the road and catch him considering the thoughts that flashed through his mind's eye.

"I'd lose me job for it, but you can 'ave 'em for a fiver mate, and I'd jus' say I'd seen 'em pictures."

Sol handed him a crisp English five-pound note, the monarch sternly smiling off the paper.

"An' andover anuver fiver and it'd mean you cud witness your own signature for the return paperwork. See 'ere. It's says we need a witness and there don't seem that many witnesses hangin' about, mate." It felt ludicrous but was somehow real.

Sol handed over a second five-pound note and signed for himself and then witnessed for himself, making up the name of Gerry Gee.

It felt akin to some ominous scene from a gangster movie, where in the middle of apparently nowhere a youth on a bike had appeared along the remote track through the hills and moors, where a scruffy man had met him, a lone figure who had wandered up from a desolate beach where he had been loitering for the drop off. At this rendezvous point, a slight bend on an otherwise continuous road, there was a sign that threatened '*no access*' to a track that headed up into the woods, now drear as the rain poured down and dripped. The younger of the two, huddled against the wet in damp leathers and with a face muffled by a yellow scarf on which his replaced helmet fitted tightly, handed over an envelope in exchange for cash and a signature on a flimsy piece of paper that was stuffed by gloved hands deep into the folds of a zipped pocket. That cash would not see the light of day with respect to taxman or employer.

The bike left and Sol stood at the end of his drive as the approaching rain evolved into something harder and steadier, with his precious A3 padded envelope tucked under his borrowed coat.

As the plovers returned, Sol bowed from the road and left to walk up the long drive back to *Bothan Faobhar* where he hoped Gerry had managed to return safely already. He was more sober now due to the cold and wet than he had hoped he might be and he knew that soon he would need to do something about the inconvenience of his driveway, or at least buy a different car.

An oystercatcher shoed him on his way as it soared the loch surface behind and a cormorant dried its wings ineffectively on a black rock stranded out on the choppy water.

Rain is a necessity for British wildlife although it is something we rarely brag about despite it being the only reason we enjoy our green and pleasant land. Try as he might, Sol was unable to appreciate it at the start, but even he knew that if he were without it for only a few days, the land would dry, the crops would fail, the other plants would die back and the animals would be without food. It seemed that the newspapers were obsessed with rain. Too little and a drought was called, the water boards were taken to task and the bills we all pay for supplies and disposal would be questioned once again. Even though they could do little about the dryness of one season's climate, some boss somewhere would probably fall on their sword and resign, later to be the subject of further press enquiries when their pension pay-off finally made the news. Too much rain and there would be floods bringing the limited resources of the environment agencies back into question even though it is our lack of trees, over tarmac'd surfaces and the supreme efficiency of our drains that probably caused the issue in the first place, not to mention the number of housing estates now built on natural floods plains, wet meadows and other damp features of our nations. No one seems to notice the clues in the names of towns, roads and houses when they purchase them. *The Floodmeadows Estate, Mill*

Lane or *Mill Flash House* – surely there is a hint somewhere in there? But one could be forgiven for the continued use of ancient words in a place's name such as *Carr* (marshy wood) *Fleet* (small stream) and *Ghyll* (ravine or waterfall). *Ford* and *Well* seem too obvious as do those towns that announce they are '*on*' or '*upon*' some river. But still we buy these houses, still we insure them and invest, and still they get the worst of it when the rains do come.

A typical seasonal climate to a human is the last few years explaining why we have so many statements about the coldest, the wettest, the driest and the warmest since records began. One day we might realise that what we see in a lifetime, and consider as the norm, is only a very small portion of the seasons and their climates experienced and survived by our wild things. In essence, our records began too late and we forgot the aural history passed on by word of mouth by our forebears, probably those same ones who left the words *carr, fleet* and *ghyll* in our place names. More in touch with nature, they needed to know where flooded for the fertility of the land relying on it, where was dry for safety and security, and where their food would be and what could be harvested in its season. The modern human still thinks they can bend nature to fit their will and succeed. The ripples set up by the agricultural revolution of our little group of islands continue to spread outwards, affecting our food, our species and our wild things, tainting our waters, flooding our homes and drying some out, but always changing, in many ways for the better, but not in all.

The trackside vegetation welcomed the wetness as did the spring-fed brooks and burns who gurgled back to life from their day-drained low ebb. Sol saw the being in them in its purest sense as the lengthening light of an ending day gave way to the closure of night and the droplets of water built up into dripping suspended diamonds. He was now pleased to be walking in spite of this affront of British weather. He was on a track, familiar, moving towards a home, now accepted, to meet a friend, now confirmed, to share a meal, yet to be tasted. He knew there would be warmth and companionship.

He made the last few miles quicker than he expected and was happy to smell the wood smoke in the chimneystack burgeoning grey and blue in wispy clouds that whipped up to become one with the sky or dispersed on the air. There was the smell of stew in flight that passed unnoticed by the last few martins and swallows who hooked evening rising midges whirring around his ears and making his skin itch where their females found access, bit and sucked blood to feed their developing eggs. He scratched at the round scarlet welts as they rose and was glad that malaria was not a feature of the Scottish wildlife scene.

The Tern was pulled up on a shore that had receded quite a way from the rocks, pulled yonder by a distant moon that now smiled on another quarter of the planet. It sat beached on the shell-yellow sands, marked opalescent by streaks of accumulated mother of pearl, a beach cleaved between two scars of sedimentary strata. These rocks had been upturned by eons of subterranean tectonic activity and left exposed as their softer counterparts were ground away by the twice daily devotions of the sea loch's water. Seaweeds, black-brown and dreadlocked, hung limply to give the boat a protecting cover and a lubricated launch when she eventually moved. Then they would burst their jelly filled mucoid vesicles.

The mast was up and so Sol knew that Gerry did not intend to stay tonight. His mind was in a strange quandary about this. He was enjoying his own space, the chance to read and be himself in his own plot in a way he had not known for a very long time, if ever. And yet, he also craved the companionship of others, but on his own terms.

In some ways it was a selfish thought, but in others it was a very real and necessary thing. He had not had time to think in his own space for such a while, but he now knew he needed to spend all the more time doing it. Like prayer, this thought time, often avoided by the modern human so busy being distracted by that going on or engineered for themselves around them, is an essential, spiritual thing that all people need to do. A few days alone in the *Bothan* was what Sol had required to realise this. How fortunate he was, as so many spent their entire lives, its time, its finances and its opportunities, seeking just this solace but not investing the right time alone to find it.

But then, that word *spiritual* is one that the modern human would rather not address anyway, confusing it instead with *religious*. Sol knew his connection with the land was becoming deeply spiritual, although only a few days ago he would have denied that he had the capacity to be spiritual at all.

By the porch, Gerry had left the bucket with the rabbit's skin, head and some of the bones. She had listened to him when he had spoken about the wildcat and had prepared his sacrificial container in readiness for the vigil she knew he would want to engage in later tonight. There was a second pail next to it, full of peelings and vegetation, as she also intended to teach him about compost, the great green revolution that the civilised had forgotten, and the essential recycling of nutrients back into the ground to be reborn as new life.

Returned to the warmth of the kitchen, Sol felt immediately encompassed into that place he knew as home.

A bottle of too expensive red was open on the table and left to air, and the scent of rabbit filled the room. They enjoyed fine food and company and Sol was mocked for his paucity of possessions dropped off in his bedroom and the upright piano delivered, all by Hamish. The piano was now placed under the window at the front of the cottage and the desk pushed to the side. It fitted, just.

The two of them retired to the living room where the fire crackled in the hearth to draw attention to its ember'd activity. It emitted a weak red light that cast long shadows deep into the room, but its heat had circulated beyond the backs of the chairs and taken with it the smell of good, clean, dry wood.

Sol looked at the three boxed up parcels on the living room floor and the A3 padded envelope delivered by the young motorbike courier earlier at the end of the track.

"You aren't going to tell me what they are, are you?" asked Gerry of the packages lying behind the table. Their labels were curiously unhelpful and she had tried to draw their contents out of him on several occasions that night.

"No," came his reply as he carefully cut open the envelope and pulled the documents within out on to the now cleared table top. "But I will tell you what these are. These are the deeds to *Bothan Faobhar*."

He sifted the papers outwards fanwise.

A letter from his own solicitors, countersigned by G's solicitors, but no information about the former's name, simply referring to him as 'the occupier'.

There was a document outlining the history of the House together with a bundle of handwritten papers spanning back in time. A stretched out chronology reached to a time when the Bothan was first constructed. But it was an eon when people did not think that the dates and times were important and so no absolute could be given, just an approximation.

A series of letters of transfer were hustled into a string bundle, which crossed both fore and aft, and were secured with a tight bow across the front. The final type-faced letter had both G's spindly yet ornate signature on it, dated a few weeks before, and a space was left for Sol to sign and date himself. His particulars had been recorded but G's remained mysterious.

And then there was a map of the Faobhar Estate with a handwritten description in ink across the top. The map was drawn in nib'd pen and took in part of the loch, the chapel and a variety of dwellings across the hillside. It encompassed the mountain and moors and dotted around were a range of shelters, bothies and folds for deer, sheep, travellers and gillies. It extended down the drive where there was a building hidden in the trees with its own track up to it. This was labelled 'garage'. His land ended at the 'main road', as it was called, that ran along to the town.

"It's more than I thought I'd bought," Sol commented trying to give the map scale in his mind.

"I know," she replied.

"I'm going to need some help looking after it."

"I know. We all do."

"I'll need to introduce myself to whoever lives in these cottages," he said pointing to a variety of dwellings.

"I know. In good time."

"I'd better explore the land too."

"I know. And I'll talk to you about the rent in the morning."

"What rent?"

"The rent for this house here," and she pointed to a cottage on the map several bays closer to the sea than his own. It was labelled *'The Boat House'*.

"Why?"

"Because now you are the local laird, you own it and I'm a tenant." He whistled through his teeth, "oh."

"You'll have to haggle that one with all the people who rent cottages from you."

"I'll need help with that too won't I?"

"Yes, and good luck with Hamish."

"Is he…?" But he never finished his question.

"Yes, he's a tenant too."

Sol sighed.

"But how much money does anyone have around here? To pay the rent?"

"That's the biggest difficulty about these parts for any of us. There just isn't any money."

"It's not going to be like London rent is it?"

"No," she said reassuringly. "I think you are beginning to understand that now."

"And?" he asked. "Who is responsible for the upkeep of these properties?"

"I think you need to read your deeds Jake Solomon. The houses are yours – all of them. Only one person pays for their upkeep."

"Shit," said Sol. "If I'd have known I was buying an entire estate…"

"Probably would have been good to have read the small print then?"

"Probably," he agreed.

Then Gerry took her leave and Sol was both sad and happy to let her go.

He helped push the boat down into the water from where it took off quickly and headed further up the sea loch. Sol returned to the darkened house, placed the bucket of rabbit remains gently in the middle of the yard and, after wrapping up closely, he positioned the plastic chair at some distance away by the back porch door. Now, like so many other ventures in life, it was just a waiting game.

And Sol, in the warmth of a cloud-covered night, that if it were day would be a non-descript colour of off white, now dry with a slight offshore wind, fought sleep so that he could meet with the night spirit cat of the woods one more time.

He sat and he waited.

Chapter 11: Not Seeing

(Tros y Carreg "Crossing the Stone", Karl Jenkins)

"Where's all the nature then?" they ask expecting the wild things to be there, visible for all to see and whenever they want to see *them,* those other species that often have to make do with being slotted meanly in between our conurbations. *Surely that's what a nature reserve is for?* A place where the natural is on everyone's doorstep, regardless of their skill or interest, so that it can be seen from the comfort of a, preferably heated, double-glazed hide with good, rich coffee available and plenty of cake.

How few seem to realise that the wild things in life are often the furthest away from such people and places, ill-suited to be confined to the pleasantries of a neatly built hide and the often micro-scale nature of a reserve. It needs quiet observation and knowledge to see many of our wild relatives, the ones who evolved to live on this archipelago of islands well before any of us arrived with the receding ice – more than is often conveyed by the armchair style of nature programmes on the television which lulls all viewers into the expectation that nature is just there to be seen if only we spent five minutes or so looking for it.

Too often people leave a wildlife preserve disappointed that they have not seen *that* wild thing. Or else they invent *that* story of what they have seen, many even believing it for themselves. It is incredible the number of new naturalists, or those people just out for the day, who claim to have seen the more reclusive of species, the harder to spot or the downright rare and uncommon, and that is even when they have lose dogs about them or complaining children in tow. The question remains, '*if they are so easily spotted, then why are they labelled rare in the first place?*' Gone are the days when people would be forgiven for thinking that the lesser spotted woodpecker was rare simply because its name suggested it was - being less often seen than the greater spotted!

Instead, we often see the mundane, might see the uncommon and only occasionally spot the rare; it's the way of things. But this can leave some dissatisfied, especially as we expect to see things easily and quickly in our modern rush to experience everything and then quickly move on. Surely a better mode of operation would be to enjoy being out, the process of '*looking at*' being more beneficial and the actual '*connecting*' with nature being that part of the event that improves our moods, develops our patience and eases our too regularly troubled souls. Not seeing is part of the hide and seek game so that when we do spot something out of the ordinary then we can be justifiably content in our achievement and the grace that nature has offered us in allowing us to be there and then in the right place to see it, however briefly.

After all, every view we see and every wild thing we experience, we must remember, we are the only ones seeing it, breathing it, smelling it, touching it or embracing it in that place and at that moment, and that is even if it is not rare. And, if this is our method of natural history then we can wonder at it all, quizzically find out more, and have every reason to explore the literature and expand our knowledge. But above all, we will enjoy it, whatever we see, even if for too many it would be considered as nothing or not much, a disappointment.

Sol sat in his plastic white chair and watched the bucket till sleep threatened to overcome him, the midges bit deep and his will drew him inside to a fire-warmed easy chair and some of G's notes to read which had been calling to him for most of the day. He had a desire to find out what G had seen at this time of the year in the past. In short he wanted to be informed and therefore ready, as intelligence and preparation are of course some of the most successful elements of any attack or deal. He knew that as a businessman and could apply this logic easily, especially as the night air cooled to that point where shivering played no role in keeping him warm.

Leaving his watch post, one thought could have been that he had seen *'nothing'*, or at least not that which he sought. But his greater part knew that he had watched the bats reel the night sky in circles and dashing arcs for an hour, he had surveyed the moths' dance of the moonless night in random erratic searches for the windows, he had heard the deer bark in the woods and the night owls screech and hoot; he had seen and heard much even if at times he could not identify it for what it was. But he kept his mental records for reference at a future date, extending his expectations of his mind beyond that which he had become used to.

A star pulsated slowly as a bright pinprick in a clear patch of silver-cloud edged sky. He had watched the break in the otherwise continuous cloud-veil drift from horizon to horizon revealing a small fathomless section of the heavens above and their millennia old light display. It was odd that he forgotten how to look up during his years of city focus, where the orange glow of sodium and the irradiance of halogen bulbs had seemed to hide and replace the rest of the universe; he had failed to remember its existence nor notice it masked behind the lighting of a cityscape. Millions of people would be oblivious to the rest of creation this evening, but it did not stop it being there and its reactions, motions, explosions, expansions and contractions would carry on regardless maintaining and encapsulating everything we knew or would ever know on this little planet. Humans wouldn't even see the coming of the end of their own species if it were obviously indicated; and it probably was.

He became cold and his spine shivered that erratic body lurch that no one likes to feel, from the base of his back and electrically up to his neck, but the cat did not visit. Instead there was a screech from the wood's shadow, a deep less blue black than the nights' own depth of colourlessness. Surprisingly the geese still squabbled out on the water and there was that emotion-filled *'tu-wink'* of a lone redshank to send his thoughts inwards - surprising as it still cried at this late hour. Even the *'chuka-chuka'* of the roosting partridge and the smoker's coughs of the pheasant had now died low, their composers asleep. But the shorebirds still conversed until early into the morning.

Moved somehow, he returned to the kitchen and with a glass of luxuriant red in hand he walked on towards G's chair into which he slunk with the next volume of handwritten notes to digest. Tomorrow he would add his own observations to the record, just to keep up the tradition started by this G. It was the least he could do after G's confidence that the *Bothan* had chosen him for this purpose.

Eventually sleep won its battle as the fire's warmth ebbed into his soul and the comfort of the cushion's shape enveloped his body into dream-filled slumber. He was serenaded by the hooting of the tawnies from the wood, one stood atop the gable end of the cottage where its talons clawed scratchily at the roof tiles and excited the beetles in the moss that scurried and fell prey to her hooked beak. Her sounds entered his imaginings, but even in that night world there was no wildcat.

The next morning found him up and out early.

It is a curious thing of being human that removal from the illuminating blue-light of the computer screen, phone and television leads us back to a more biological diurnal rhythm, one where we wake up with the sun and fall asleep as it leaves our part of the planet. We return to a natural state of rest and no longer feel the tiredness brought on by disturbed sleep and the unexplainable fear of the need to rise out of bed early and thus suffer the anxiety that prevents us from getting proper respite. We relax, and our bodies and minds accommodate for the changes in the length of day with the seasons – we sleep more in the winter and less in the high summer, our diets are different and the very energy we enjoy waxes and wanes just like that of our wild cousins'.

He checked the bucket of rabbit remains as he travelled that cold wet distance to the toilet. Sure enough the cat had been as thief in the night and removed most of the carcass. But, not sorrowful for missing that spirit of the night this time, Sol was instead happy at the thought of it being there, safe and secure, well fed for another evening. There was a satisfaction felt in him being the provider.

He wondered if it had a mate and if female if it were due kittens soon.

His own breakfast was an entirely different affair to that of the cat. He had bread dried on the embers of the fire to make near-toast, richly buttered and then smothered with thick cut orange shredded marmalade, a hangover from his grandmother's day that had refused to die. It dripped fatty yellow liquid down his chin that made him suddenly aware of the prickled density of his shaggily developing grey-white highlighted beard. He would have to address that before any guests arrived, and he wondered just how rough he must now look in his borrowed clothes, him poorly washed and with little manicuring of any kind. In so many ways he was falling back to nature. But without the drive and press of commerce he felt little desire to conform to what until a few days ago had been the 'ideal' way to look and impression to give.

He made coffee from pre-ground beans delivered by the supermarket the previous day, and with careful filtering through the tan-stained cloth he was able to extract most of the grouts and bean remains. It was as if a luxury had been delivered by heaven itself and although it was not produced under the pressure that he had been assured by friends and the city fashions was essential to make good coffee, this *was* good coffee and his taste buds relished its dark bitterness and his mind lurched with the caffeine kick it induced.

The rain fell in incessant patters on the ground outside and the weather looked set to continue wet through the day with the hills across the sea-choked valley invisible through the sheet of water falling. Gulls and eiders bobbed in asynchrony out on the loch as the waves jostled their unaffected buoyant forms and he smiled to see the ineffective wing-drying efforts of those reptilian silhouettes, the shags, hunched and gremlin-like, clung to a rock rapidly disappearing in spume as the tide rose. They rocked with each white-headed crash and from this distance took on the guise of sailors on an unholy craft, just proud of the surface, rowed by haunted apparitions that floated in and out of an active sea mist.

But Sol had work to do and eventually turned away from this window-framed view, tearing his eyes from the unfolding stories of the loch's life. He busied himself emptying box after box of delivered items and possessions sent up from the city.

He slid a rough-edged knife along the brown-taped edge of the first of his three smooth-sided cardboard packages. It was the coffin length rectangle dropped off at the end of the drive, and from within it he extracted its rod like contents from amongst the plastic, the air-filled bladders and expanded starch. He then searched for the instructions before braving it across the yard and collecting the tools from the shed that he felt he needed.

The next hour was replete with blasphemy and swearing as Sol attempted to build something from the contents of the boxes and eventually resorted to that male tradition of ignoring the twice-translated guidelines, that made little if any sense anyway, and following his own thoughts on the process of construction. Slowly it took on the form he expected and which matched the illustration on the front of the explanatory pamphlet. Then he crossed the yard again and walked about feeling the wind with his finger in the air in a strange way resembling a human weather vane. He wanted to judge the direction of the predominant currents but this boy-scout method was never going to work without a cessation of the rain or the local knowledge required to predict the weather each and every day.

Confounded and cross, he returned to the porch and pouted. How was he to succeed if there was no help to be found? Today it felt as if the *Bothan* just did not want to be dragged into the latest century and instead was happy to wallow in its pre-technology heyday. It annoyed him that something as simple as wind direction was so difficult to predict or determine.

Water dripped down into the kitchen from a leak in the roof and he was aware that a draft running through the cottage probably meant more work was needed on it in a part of the building he had not already realised.

'*How am I supposed to help you?*' he asked in his mind of the building around him pacing a hand on a patch of plaster peeling in a way he had not noticed before. '*I'm going to have to do some of the things I used to. They weren't all that bad and some might even help the glen and the loch and keep this estate going, if only you would let me.*'

He caught himself for a moment and watched the swifts, swallows and martins flying low to accommodate the air pressure and the ground-hugging flight of the insects that drifted with it. They did not stop for the wind or the rain. They *could* not stop for the wind or the rain. They all had their allotted time here to lay, feed and fledge their young before they returned to Africa on their immense migratory flights. They did not have the time to waste worrying about the wet and the direction of the wind. Instead they had to make do and feed while the insects were on the wing, and more importantly hawk where the creatures actually were, be it high in the thermals floating on the breeze or low to the ground and pushed to the Earth.

He tracked a martin tacking the air and hugging the canopy top.

It was then that the outlines and shapes of the trees in the glen suddenly came to the fore of his mind and gave him a clue from the wildlife itself as an answer to the question in his mind, '*from where does the wind come?*'

Each was bent away from the shoreline, those closest to it bonsai-like, gnarled and resolved to the severest of angles. He looked again, unsure as to what the significance of this serendipitous observation could be, but certain that it was important as volley after volley of birds chased the invertebrates up from the shore and over the woods.

If the trees bent away from the loch and the distant sea then something must push them. *Where from?*

If those closest to the bay were contorted the most then it came from the loch. *What was it?*

If there is a force from the sea that changes the growth of terrestrial plants it was the wind. *The dominant wind comes from the sea.*

It was a simple logic and an obvious inference. Nature knew more about the climate than any human. Those abiotic factors we spend so much of our lives trying to overcome were the very same variables that determined what life could succeed, feed and breed; the very same things that shaped life's evolution.

Sol ran to the front window of the cottage, rubbed away the condensation with his wet shirt cuff, leaving circles and beaded water in swirls as he cleared it. He looked to the east where the trees were each gradated up the hillside as they pointed away from the sea. He looked to the west where they mirrored this image up the glen and then behind from the porch he could see in reverse the forest cowering its way up the valley with mosses clinging to the moistest, most exposed sides; the windward.

Out on the water the bobbing ducks and gulls were wind faced with beaks directed into the worst of the gusts. They had aligned with the currents of the air to offer it their least resistance. By the lapping water the resting geese and waders each had their backs bent to face it, feathers tickled into lively action but giving the bodies of their owners the protection they needed as they slept whilst they waited for an exposed shoreline to reveal itself again, ready for the picking and the next life-giving feed.

He had the first answer he needed for his new box of tricks and the *Bothan* and her glen had helped provide the answer. *Maybe she would welcome the technology he desired?*

Sol returned to the front room where two metallic constructions of interlacing triangles lay bolted together like the sections of a fallen miniature electricity pylon. He had never considered himself that handy a man at the best of times and whilst his mind tried to recover from the effort of having concentrated on something so practical for this length of time, his fingers and arms ached with the effort. He knew that he needed to do something different, less purposeful and pragmatic.

Looking back to the table, there lay his battered black violin case, but the skin of his finger pads smarted from the morning's efforts and he knew he would struggle to play. He scanned the room until his eyes rested on the piano. *Today, the piano would win.*

He eased the stool out from underneath the hood, pushing back spilt packaging that had escaped and spread like chaff from an explosion, and he sat quietly and contemplatively, listening for the cues of nature to find some form of music from within him. He had never been a good one for reading the manuscripts of others and so he knew full well that there would be little or no compositions inside the stool where most people stored their music and practice material.

There was the patter of the rain, a barrage of related taps that harmonised perfectly despite the millions of beats that took place every second. Some were deep and heavy as they caught the ceiling, or dulled by their impact on the glass. Others were light and sharp, slapping the ground or the wet leaves of the opening canopies, or they were diffused by their falls through needles and the cones of pines. Yet more hit water in the puddles or the loch, penetrating the thin glass of the *Bothan* that let in both sound and the cold of the day's descending temperature and rising humidity.

The emotion of the loch today was forlorn and only the sea ducks seem at ease.

He closed his eyes and started that familiar pattern he had to playing music, searching his mind for a tune that he could play, part improvised and part recalled. And then it came. A flowing melody that spoke of water and its journey to the Earth as drops, each balanced and perfect in its formal shape, plummeting to be one with the ground until it met the rivers, the loch and the sea. It was a glad piece, but with an underlying melancholy, for the water knew that at some time it would leave and re-join the skies and their burgeoning clouds to later again fall in cyclical completion.

At times it was Mahler, then it was Sibelius, next it was Debussy, but always it was the water, sky, river, loch and sea. It kept going around. And there, he realised, was another unanticipated thought for Sol's mind to ponder, in answer to his difficulties of introducing technology to the *Bothan*.

He finished playing as the rain eased, and pushing past the strandline of boxes and material he had strewn across the room in the same haphazard yet organised way the sea did each day, he returned to his note reading at the desk just within the heated sphere of a newly stoked fire. His mind was finally at ease as he had given it its creative opportunity to express itself in music.

There were geese out on the loch now, returning to graze the shallows in their grey bodied masses and he could hear the steady happy chirrup and chirp of goldfinches in the trees with their warbled canary calls and whirrs carrying easily from the wood through the open porch door. One leapt from its song post screaming '*chiseck-cheek, chiseck-cheek*' as it abandoned itself from the springy bud top of a spruce, pre-empting the attack of a large black and white barred grey hawk with burning orange eyes that cut the air in failed pursuit. She glided to within a wingtip's brushing of the burgeoning bracken's and dancing grasses, and then floated with the grace of a buoyant bullet around the *Bothan* and out of sight, hanging from the air with little effort.

The dispersed songbirds returned quickly as if no danger had passed their way and Sol marvelled at how quickly a near-death experience could be forgotten and written off. Then he thought of people and the shortness of their memories when times were less hard, stressful or dangerous, and how speedily they too seemed to forget and move on. There was something innate in the ability to leave well behind, to seek out sanctuary in an amnesic way and to move on, confident and ignorant. It was a survival thing without which we wouldn't continue to live, to feed or to prosper.

Sol sat for a moment at the writing desk and looked carefully at the last notes written by G. He felt an urgency to write something of his own. *But what should his entry be?*

He lifted the ink pen and checked that it contained ink.

It felt heavy and solid, and he believed it was well made even though he knew nothing about pens or the fabrication of the one he held. It simply gave the holder the sense of quality. Like the presence of a great person when they enter a room unannounced, something is obviously special; the pen offered something discernibly different.

There was a pot of black ink, '*Quink*' named after the noise made by the Brant Goose because it made the best feathers for ancient quills. He was bizarrely nervous about what he should write, then started as he would do an improvised musical piece. He closed his eyes and thought. His mind took him to where he *felt* he was, he spent a few moments considering the creatures he would describe and then he gently placed the gold-plated nib down on the rough, fibrous-thick paper of the notebook and started to move it so that it left a smooth, wet, glistening black line behind it. The flow was almost painful at first, slow and ungainly, requiring a movement of the hand and wrist that took him back to the age when he was at school and learning to write. First this had been by pencil and then, when he was considered advanced enough, using the now obsolete ink pens collected from the teacher's desk where all authority began and ended. Sol remembered well that day when he proudly took his first pen and pot from the front.

Soon he felt the nib lead his letters, characters that naturally fell into a Victorian rendition of English script, with ornately curled letters and joining flushes that made the words almost beautiful to read.

'*I have been here at the Bothan for a few days now, already forming what I hope will soon become friendships. The loch expresses different emotions each day. Today it is sombre and grey but I am pleased that the sun is now burning through the cloud and the geese have returned...'*

He wrote far more than intended and listed birds he had seen, looking each up in the books that G had left on the shelves and simply describing them when he was unsure. Eventually he signed off with the date and some notations on his musical thoughts in preparation for the symphony he now desired to write. He recorded a simple melodic stanza as an endnote to his entry, then carefully replaced the ink pen's lid and placed it on the notebook to let his writing dry.

Sol felt a relief that he had finally done something in G's notes and only hoped that he could continue with it on as regular basis as he could, and secondly that it would be of the quality with which G had previously written.

Sometime after lunch Gerry appeared unbidden but not unexpected at the porch door.

"Hello," she called hopefully before wandering in. "Are you still good for the money for *The Tern*? I can still call James if not. I would completely understand...   ...besides, I've worried about it half the night."

Sol looked up from his note reading, genuinely pleased to hear Gerry's voice. Of course he had forgotten his promise to her, but he was not going to admit it.

They agreed to sail the two boats (*The Tern* and *Sireadh-thall*) down to the town and the boatyard with Sol in tow and listening to every shouted instruction to avoid accident and potential drowning. The water was now calm and so Gerry was confident that they could do it even if there was an element of danger throughout. Then, Gerry would take charge of *Sireadh-thall* and would sail them both back to Sol's car from where they would drive on to the next large town for Sol to get fuel and cash before returning to the beach. Next, parking the car and sailing *Sireadh-thall* back to

Bothan Faobhar, Sol would be taught on this journey the basics of sailing and the dangers and curiosities of the loch. Gerry could then borrow *Sireadh-thall* to get home and the next day she would return in order to take Sol around the estate to meet his tenants.

It all sounded so much organised and it was a pity it was doomed to some form of failure from the start due to its complexity and inelegance.

With both boats out on the loch the wind amused itself and turned to the east and pushed them too fast down towards the town. *Sireadh-thall* was a good craft and once free on the water she was keen to tow and not be towed. She kept leading the way and straining the ropes, tying them in interesting wind-knots that Gerry later struggled to undo. They avoided any real collision, but they were both sure that *The Tern* would be costing more to repair by the time they reached the harbour slipway at '*James Nevin and Sons*' than it would have done if it had been left there yesterday.

The journey allowed Sol little opportunity to take in the views as they opened up out of the rising mists and the clearing cloud. But he gained glimpses. There, the majesty of cliffs and their encrusting lichen diadems, weedy stone beaches draped in fucoid strings and the bright coral reflections of sandy shorelines replete with broken shell flotsam; all could be spied. But the pace of his craft and the tossing of the stern in the current crests kept his focus, and by experience more than instruction he became a better sailor.

"How much of this is mine?" he shouted over to *The Tern* as they came dangerously close to each other yet again and he leant heavily on the tiller in the opposite direction to Gerry on hers.

"All of it," she called back.

Sol scanned back to the land that crawled out of the mist-footings of the loch where the seals lay beached on mystic thrones. And then he allowed his eyes to range up onto the moors and somehow to the cloud-hidden mountain as they slowed into the slack pool of the harbour where they were soon tethered safely. The thin strip of visible land behind was sandwiched between steaming masses of humidity; a visual appetiser for what he owned in total.

James was summoned and then took charge of *The Tern* having her attached to the chains of the winch secured in his sheds at the head of the slipway. They left in *Sireadh-thall* with a tear-eyed Gerry looking mournfully back as her craft was slowly tugged up to be stranded out of her element, water-dropping as her life-giving medium slipped away, up onto dry land. Gulls flocked about her in the ill-conceived expectation of a windfall of hull-encrusting wildlife being revealed and released from her wet underside. But *The Tern* was too well kept for that and they left disappointed in squealing revolutions, balling and dispersing.

Sireadh-thall was hauled up on to the pebbled beach by the end of the *Bothan's* drive and the two then transferred to the relative luxury of Sol's white sports car, still laying dejected by the roadside at the end of the track by the sign that still failed to welcome even Sol to his own abode.

The car looked out of place, white in spite of its dirty covering. A manmade device indicating wealth and power that didn't belong here amongst the wealth of wild things and the raw power of the scenery.

"I really will need to change my car won't I?" He asked the questions without real meaning as they sat down and back into bucket seats better adapted for the motorway but impractical in every other way for life near the *Bothan*.

"I suppose so," she replied struggling to locate the seatbelt from where some European engineer had cleverly had it hidden so that it didn't affect the internal lines of the vehicle. "But you could just use the Land Rover?"

Sol stopped and turned to face the surprised Gerry as she finding the clip had forced it home.

"What Land Rover?"

"The one G left you in the garage." Her answer was matter of fact and abrupt.

"What garage?"

"You've not read that bit on the map then?"

There was a silence for a moment as of course he had not.

"G left you his old Land Rover up at the garage. I'll take you there some time. Unless you want to go today?"

But Sol knew they were in a hurry and then took the fateful decision that he would take the sports car for now, whatever car remained waiting in the garage for him to use in future.

Gerry informed him that the main town, New Town, lay about fifteen miles away. When the car revved up with its typical loud roar, the red indicator light and the digital display suggested they should just about make it before running out of fuel.

Sol was never the most efficient of drivers, but then few of us ever are. We fill our driving with extra weight than required, speedier revs than necessary and a lack of understanding as to how to achieve the most miles per gallon despite the increasing costs of that precious liquid; the millennia-fermented remains of Jurassic life. In addition we use the wrong tyres, poor fuel and have a desire to go too quickly regardless of speed limits and the advice given by vehicle manufacturers – *after all, who actually reads their new car's manual from cover to cover to find out such information? A car is to drive not to study!*

At ten miles to go they got stuck behind a road packed full of sheep, nose to nose in a continuous dog-induced flock of wooliness that extended along the lane as far as the eye could see. When he realised his petrol predicament, and following Gerry's patient guidance to encourage the flock to move on, Sol cut the engine so that the sheep felt more able to flow in their drift of woolly bodies around the car before reforming the gargantuan flock on their stern side. Matted and fluffed up bodies brushed up against the vehicle and filled it with the damp smell of lanolin, and short-haired black faces reached up and into the cockpit breathing wheezy grass-scented breath onto the passengers through mucus-loaded nostrils. Pied wagtails flitted amongst their bodies and picked at escaping black dots of life whilst corvids '*carred*' at distance and tracked the crocheted throng.

Gerry was nonplussed and fussed the occasional white-eyed, black slit pupiled face as it came too close. Instead, Sol cowered away unsure as to how to respond to these dim-witted cud-chewers who occasionally tested the leather upholstery with their damp, mobile lips and chisel-like yellow-enamelled incisors. Their breath hung in the air, a damp and yeasty grass aroma. There was intelligence in their faces that he had previously refused to acknowledge and now disquieted him as he saw their sporadic terror at his presence.

For a while, the car, buffeted and rocked by bodies and surrounded by a rippling sea of wool, felt like it was stranded out in a thread-fluffed sea. Bleating waves passed and passed, and all Sol could do was to wait and listen to the cooing of Gerry and take note of her patient tone.

Flies hummed in irritated profusion getting caught in the small back window of the sports car where they zither'd in anger at their entrapment.

"They'll be moving them closer to the farms for more lambing and then moving them on again to shear them in a couple of months," explained Gerry running her fingers deep through the wool of one clammy body as it scuttled past. "They've been using this track for that purpose for centuries. Up and down they'll go so that they can spot the ewes in trouble and find the lambs that are on their own. They'll then sell the meat as lamb and mutton, and wool at the market if it's worth it."

Her voice was melancholy and seemed distant.

"What's the wool worth then?" Ever the entrepreneur Sol was interested in the potential for profit.

"Almost nothing," she carried on. "It's cheaper to buy wool in from overseas and so they'll only bother taking it to market if it's worth more than the fuel needed to take it. That and no one wants as much wool these days. It's all artificial and made out of recycled plastic bags. There is an old knitting shed down by the black pool in Old Town but almost no one uses the looms in there anymore – no one buys their produce and so they do it by hand back at their homes, knitting for just the people in their families that need, or in fact, want it."

"What happens to the wool then?" He was genuinely stunned, as surely *British was best?*

"It's dumped, given away for free to those who want to make anything out of it, or it's burnt. Otherwise it isn't worth the diesel it costs to move it and it ends up costing more to transport than anyone gets back from it."

"But what a waste. Surely someone wants it somewhere?"

"If you can find a market, then go ahead. Shepherds don't make much money these days."

Two shepherds brought up the rear on mud-splattered quad bikes, whistling to their dogs as they stood up as if in stirrups on mechanical horses, which once they probably were.

"Hiya Gerry," called one. "Hello to the new boy too," and he nodded his head in Sol's direction.

The other waved and then accelerated away after a straying straggler missed by the sheep dogs. Sol recognised the stern focused stare of Hamish.

"Is Hamish really a tenant of mine?" Sol enquired.

"Yes," Gerry replied, "as is the other, Euan. Usually his wife would be out with them but she's expecting a baby. They don't think it'll be a shepherd though and that's even if Euan is at least sixth generation shepherd and thinks of being nothing else himself."

"Why?" Sol asked. But he knew the answer before it came. "If there's work for people to do then why doesn't anyone want to do it?" His view sounded so much like the sentiment often given in the more opinionated broadsheet papers that he felt the cliché even before he had finished speaking. He knew his logic was too simple, too short, too uninformed.

"He earns very little money and the hours are long and conditions poor. Not everyone earns like you Sol." She smiled coldly and looked out at the flock as it trundled onwards.

"Well, technically speaking I am unemployed for the moment and am therefore not earning anything."

"But are you still earning money? I mean in interest and on shares?"

There was an awkward silence and then they drove on again.

At six miles to go the engine started to splutter and the indicator now said that they had less than five miles of fuel left in the tank. It is curious that cars seem to become less accurate as to the amounts of fuel that is left in them with the less fuel you have and no one is ever confident that they know how many more miles the engine will continue to turn when close to the last dregs.

A gentle drizzle found them on the lee side of the next hill as the town came into sight still down in the valley where foothills ambled and green grasses were painted in tessellations of light and shade. The engine coughed and misfired with increasing regularity until it eventually went noiseless at about half a mile to go putting up a single magpie, variegated and humanoid in its expression.

"One for sorrow," muttered Sol as the car hushed to a stop with only the limited grip of the tyres biting the road's tarmac for sound. The time was just after four in the afternoon and they were keen to get back to pay James the cash for the repair on *The Tern*. The march was wet and determined but they kept their spirits up as best they could by joking about each other's differing backgrounds and experiences, accents and expectations. Clearly Sol was a monetary-orientated man keen to succeed, but Gerry felt there was hope for him yet. Gerry on the other hand was not interested in wealth at all but favoured learning about the wild and experiencing what she could; almost living in the now. Sol was convinced that he could make her more money wise until he discovered that she earned almost nothing.

"But what do I need the money for?" she asked honestly.

"Well what *do you do* for a living then?" He stood in the pouring rain wondering how anyone could do nothing much. He was a man in a hurry in life with metaphorical ladders to climb.

"Well, I've got some savings I brought up here with me and I sell some art work every so often. And, I do odd jobs for people about the estate and around the loch."

"And what is your web address for the website you have for your artwork?"

"I don't have one. People see it in the gallery down by the harbour and some buy it if I'm lucky."

"What about you're advertising for odd jobs?"

"Word of mouth is enough."

"Do you have much in savings then?"

"Not really."

"But what about your investments and assets, do you have any of them?"

There was silence which told Sol a lot more than Gerry wanted to give away.

"Sol," Gerry said, "you are very different to people round here. There isn't much money and quite a few people are struggling because of it. Just don't be too flash if you are sitting on a fortune."

"Well the fortune won't last long that's for sure. But we both need the same things though; food to eat, water to drink and a place to live."

"Yes, but you pay more for yours and the folks round here only have so much of it, often not quite enough of it, and it isn't as if they could work any harder. Look at the shepherd's lot. It's not a life for everyone and fewer people want to do it now – especially when lamb can be bought cheaper from overseas."

They turned and walked as fast as they could towards the edge of town, both certain they should have packed coats and wet weather gear. The single magpie had become two and they nosily followed the progress of the humans as they passed them on the road from the security of a bare-branched fruit tree that was warped with age and illness.

"Two for joy," Gerry chided as the rain dripped off her hair dragging it downwards and into her eyes.

They soon came at a trot down to two fuel pumps housed together under a wind-creaked canopy of corrugated tin that wrenched itself up and down on an unintended hinge with the shed it was attached to more by faith than weld. The pumps' colour had once been white but corrosion had played its patient game and was beating the paint work away from its surface in orange-red streaks of rust that fell like tears from a glass fronted gauge that would have graced a museum to the history of motor travel. A khaki-dusted forecourt was littered with oil cans, coal, lump wood bags and the local news, and there was a fine selection of snow shovels, rock salt and tyre chains to choose from.

Although this was obviously a petrol station and in its own way abhorrent to nature, it was interestingly being taken back in by the wild itself and was now losing the steady battle to remain dominant, clean and human. Sparrows huddled under the canopy on green moss'd beams and they 'cheeped' in communion with each other, their voices echoing off the roof.

Gerry pushed on through a wooden door into the shed where her entrance was announced by the ringing of the attendant bell that hung behind. The lights were off and no one was in, but she was confident that she could find someone if she shouted loudly enough. Inside were rows of spanners, grease and spares, and a black, gold and brown stained worktop with an expansive silver-metalled cash till. Through the back window of the building Sol could see the piled up remains of a variety of old cars, heaped according to their make and age, and in some places the colour of their parts. There were a large number of tractors and off road vehicles stacked in various states of decomposition, sinking slowly into the dirt of the hillside and out of which grasses sprouted and spindly saplings had taken root.

Gerry called again, this time using a name. "Simon!"

An oily-capped head, stained darker with the wet of the rain, popped up from behind a rusting red pile of tractors. Its face was old and wrinkled and sported a beard that would have suited the pilot of an ancient fishing trawler or whale boat. He was dressed in denim dungarees with patched knees where the fabric was most worn through and his once white shirt revealed highly tanned hairy arms and a chest to match. He had a friendly, welcoming expression and his eyes reflected pleasure at the sound of his name being called.

"That you, Gerry?" he shouted in reply with the coarsely-accented voice of the antique mariner his faced suggested.

"It's me," she called again.

"What brings you down here my treasure?" he asked as he hobbled up to the front of the shed and dropped his tools in a heap of oily steel and aluminium.

"This is Sol," she explained. "He needs fuel."

"That's lucky."

"Why?" asked Sol.

"Coz that's what I sell," and he grinned. Sol laughed as the man gave him a wry smile and grabbed his hand in welcome. "So, what's your poison, petrol or diesel?"

Before Sol could reply, Gerry barged in and spoke for him. "Both," she said, "in cans, as we ran out up the road."

"Both?" questioned Sol and Simon together.

"Well the sooner you get rid of that white sports number the better."

"Ah," said Simon knowingly, "you're the new boy then."

"Sorry, yes," apologised Sol and then he turned to Gerry as Simon waddled off to find cans whilst chewing his gums noisily. "So why do I need diesel?"

"For the Landy G left you in the garage. It'll be far better once you've got used to it."

Simon returned and started to fill the first can up with petrol from the first of the two pumps. "G loved that wagon but got too old to drive it. Series 2A, '64 plate. It'd go anywhere on the estate. Not been used for a while though. I'll pop up and check it in the morning if you like. If you give me a lift back here I'll drop it off at the *Bothan.*"

"Thank you, but how much will that cost?" asked Sol.

Simon stared at him "Hamish was right wasn't he? You're not from round here are you? Just buy the spares from me in the future and we'll see you right."

Simon topped up the second can with diesel which he marked with a large white D.

"D is for diesel okay? Whatever you do, do not mix them up! Your sports number will be worth even less round here if you do that. Mind you, from what Hamish says about the way you drive it..." he trailed off and simply smirked placing the cans on the floor. Then he walked into the shed beckoning Sol to follow and rung up the bill on the till, hammering each heavy key with a single finger so that numbers and decimals were flung up into a glass chamber that topped the machine.

"Do you take a card?" Sol asked reaching for his wallet.

"Why would I do that?" was Simon's basic reply.

Sol stared, holding his usually very powerful gold credit card out towards the long-suffering face of the vendor.

"Doesn't everyone?"

Simon shook his head. "Not round here they don't, no."

"Oh, well I need to get cash from somewhere to pay Nevin for the boat anyway..."

"Well, you'd better do that quick then hadn't you?"

"Why?" asked Sol.

"Bank closes at five. Pick the fuel up here on your way back as you've got six minutes to get down to the bank and it's still quite a way."

Sol thanked Simon before Gerry and he ran off into the rain for the second time, this time quickly making the outskirts of the small town where houses started to spring up from the roadsides where man had left his constructional mark. It was a ribbon development with all the houses clinging to the one street with little behind. When they arrived at the bank, dripping on the stone-columned steps, that mockery of classical architecture that even the smallest of banks seems to have inherited from a bygone age, the clerk was about to lock the large wooden door.

"Stop," Gerry called as she panted to gain breathe enough.

"Oh... Hello Gerry," greeted the primly dressed lady who ran the bank, the post office and the shop that had all evolved to take over the rooms behind her. "Cutting it a bit fine aren't you?"

"Yes," Gerry admitted.

"I'm sorry," said the lady sternly. "I won't have the time to organise an overdraft for you today. If you still need one, come back in the morning."

"No, not that." She cast a side glance across to the ever-alert Sol. "Not this time. This is Sol," Gerry announced, "and he needs cash quickly."

"Tourist?" asked the lady, eying him up suspiciously over her severe glasses.

"No," Gerry replied, "the laird."

The lady looked at Sol in a moment of dismay, dropping her regal façade, and then rapidly unlocked the secondary door with a '*clunk*' and a '*thud*' and opened it wide. "I'm sorry," she said. "I'm Erica and you must be Jake Solomon."

She bustled them both back into the shop, dripping and bedraggled on the coconut mat, and then ushered them on so that she could switch on the lights and open up the back section which served as a glass-fronted banker's desk. She apologised and muttered the length of the shop.

"How much will you be having then Mr Solomon?" she asked in a now pleasant and relaxed voice from behind the security of her booth.

"I'll just take out a thousand for now," said Sol matter-of-factly.

"Pounds?" asked Erica, somewhat taken aback, again losing her professional front.

"Yes, if that's okay?"

"I don't really know how much we've got in. That's not the usual amount people take out you see."

She bent down to check the under counter safe and after entering the code, pressing buttons that bleeped their complaint, and twisting its handle, she started counting out notes aloud onto the counter behind the glass screen at the back of the office.

Twenty, forty, sixty, eighty...

Sol turned to Gerry who was looking as equally flustered as Erica.

"A thousand?" she asked.

One hundred and twenty, forty, sixty, eighty...

"Well yes. Five hundred for James, money for the fuel and spending money as required."

"That leaves about four hundred and fifty for spending money?" announced Gerry.

Two hundred and twenty, forty, sixty, eighty...

"Oh, do I need more?"

Erica looked up cautiously and slowed her counting down as she took in the conversation.

Three hundred and twenty, forty, sixty, eighty...

"What are you going to spend it on?"

Four hundred and twenty, forty, sixty, eighty...   ...five hundred.

Sol thought for a while as Erica ran out of twenties and moved on to tens.

...and ten, twenty, thirty...

"Make it six hundred then please, Erica."

...and forty, fifty, sixty...

Erica counted out five pound notes.

...and five, seventy, five, eighty, five...
Erica ran out of notes and then finally made up the difference in pound coins and Sol completed the transaction using his card and a roller that copied his details via a carbon paper insert. He had never seen anything like it before and marvelled at the simplicity of its design and technology. Nothing electronic was required.
"It works even when the power cuts out," Erica explained as she let him inspect it.
As they left, she asked Sol to warn her if he was coming in again, whilst standing at the door as if to see them off the premises and well away.

"Well, she was very nice," said Sol as they started up the road again, heading back towards the petrol station and scrap yard. He did not see the consternation in Erica's face as she watched him go. When they arrived at the garage the wind had joined the rain, but even so the martins whooshed the sky, dive-bombing low in their continual search for insectan delights. It was as if the height of their feeding, dictated by the present elevation of their food, was a physical, visible indication of the emotion of the weather; grey and low. Streamer-tailed swallows whipped between them chirruping their fart-songs as they skirted the rusty buildings where a dilapidated yellow sign stated they had entered '*Simon's Scrap - where your waste is my wage*'.
They couldn't find Simon and so left money on the work surface before collecting the two fuel cans, both black and now wet, one for diesel and one for petrol. Together, the trudge up the lane was better than it would have been alone. They tested the relative weights of a can of diesel and petrol to keep themselves entertained; being convinced that there was a difference. They swapped cans regularly to keep their spirits up and their bantering chat kept their humour alive.
The wind gently eased them on in gusts that met their peaks every six before they fell back down to simple shuffles of the air, then

building up to a new crescendo in the next six-series. The large drops of wet, clashed with their dripping clothing, which was now sodden to the skin, and leaked unremittingly down into their boots, that flopped and slurped as the deep pools of murk inside of them clung to their feet and then released it like the water drawn up in miniature engine's pistons.

They made the low sports car, stranded by the roadside where it lay surrounded by sheep droppings and clagged with soggy wool strands, and Sol fought the petrol cap open with cold fingers that hurt.

He checked for the now rain-washed white diesel mark and found it on the first can. "Not this one," he stated quite simply and swapped cans with Gerry before extracting the petrol cap on the tired-looking once white but mud-splattered, heavily dented car. As the fuel glugged and jockeyed inside the can, down through the car's insides into its tank, he recalled to Gerry how much he had loved this car and its purchase.

"She isn't going to last round here though."

"No," came the terse reply, "she's probably alright for the city but even after a few days she's showing a distinct lack of compatibility with life at the *Bothan*. What are you going to do with her?"

"Sell her or trade her in for something more suitable probably."

The fuel came to an end and after they had stowed the diesel can and the now empty petrol one under the bonnet hood they sped noisily off back towards Nevin's boat yard. Rounding bends too quickly, Sol slowed to a more leisurely pace as he passed the flowers laying in memoriam by the side of the track. He noted a whining from the engine, slight at first, but rising. There was a judder to the pedals and a faint trail of black smoke coming from the exhaust. *It would pass and was probably just the result of them running out of fuel back over the hill.*

As Gerry talked about something and nothing, as only a good friend in relaxed company can, Sol felt the car get worse and the smoke become more insistent and increasingly difficult to simply ignore. *Surely, it would clear soon.*

Therapists could do a lot if they took their clients out with them in cars and drove them about. A simple excuse is all that is required for a short journey and so long as the passenger is travelling with you by their own accord, it is incredible what security that short distance between you and them can afford them. And, they will naturally speak out their thoughts, about how they feel and what is on their minds because you are unable to look at them and make eye contact in the way you would back in a room. Not put off by the analysis of a stare, they talk.

It was as if a lid had been taken off Gerry's private thoughts for a while in that way that a good wood fire can help someone who does not normally or easily do it and talk, and why friendships can be forged around the hearth.

She told him about a distant past and another community where her art was respected, and although she had not made much money in Sol's terms she had managed a good living, moved to the city and done well enough. But family feuds, problems with men that wanted to capture her creative spirit, control and eventually destroy it in a way that they each considered caring, and a growing resentment in relationships, had all finally driven her to the town at the end of the loch to where she had first met James Nevin. All had gone well, but then it had developed too quickly and she then had another fleeing escape into the care of G and the Boat House up the loch.

The smoke turned blue-black and the engine stuttered badly as they passed the black pool.

"Is the car alright?" she asked as the revs died and they drifted powerlessly down into the street by the harbour just outside James Nevin's boatyard.

"No, I'm not convinced it is. In fact, I think it's very sick. Which fuel did we put in it?" He felt that once again he was asking a question the answer to which he already knew.

They secured the car on the handbrake and then climbed out before checking under the bonnet. Both black cans seemed to have rain-wet white paint marks on them probably smudged one to the other as they tested the weight of the different fuels on their walk back to the car.

"What's the effect of running a petrol sports car on diesel fuel?" asked Gerry thoughtfully.

"Well, I don't expect it'll be good for it," Sol replied as James came out of the yard from behind *The Tern,* now up in dry dock under the corrugated roof of the boathouse.

"I'd say," said James with a sneer, "that a car like that is beyond repair. That'll be five quid to park it there overnight too... ...cash."

"You really don't like me do you?" muttered Sol taking a folded wodge of cash out of his back pocket and counting out notes for James.

"No," was James' reply. "You don't belong here. You're just a city boy who's done well for himself. What could someone like you possibly give to a place like this?"

"Well let's start with cash," Sol answered obliquely. "Five hundred and four pounds."

"There's a pound missing." James held out his hand and waited, impatience spreading over his face.

"Gerry?" Sol asked. "Do you have a mobile phone?"

She nodded and took a small black plastic device out of her pocket. It was either old or very retro in its design.

"Does it have a signal around here?"

She looked at it and nodded again.

"Good. Call Simon and ask him to collect my car. He can sell it for spare parts. Tell him that if he picks it up tonight that not only does he save me a pound in parking, but that he can have it for fifty percent of what he thinks it's still worth. If I'm to drive around here I need him at least on my side."

Gerry hesitated and then started to make the call.

"Oh, and Gerry?   ...tell him to bring another can of fuel marked with permanent ink this time. We'll need some more for the Land Rover in the garage." He then turned to James as cool as he felt he could. "And you...   ...do a good job on the boat will you? Otherwise you'll be offering her a discount and this time it'll cost you more than a pound. It'll cost you your reputation as well."

With this, the rain-dripping off his poorly-shaved chin and badly washed face, but still absolutely proud, Sol turned on his heel, trying to look as unruffled as possible, and stormed back up the country road to go and find his boat. Thankfully he only slipped once, and only when out of sight of the stunned Nevin and the busily phoning Gerry who jostled along behind him.

Chapter 12: The Native

(Adagietto from Symphony No 5, Gustav Mahler)

Emotions are a funny thing. They are often said to be neither right nor wrong, just the way we feel at the time. With age we learn to control them and are expected, with the development of manners, to keep them tethered so that others cannot always tell what it is that we think or feel. The confident poker face of the business trader can hide much insecurity in the hope that others will buy, invest or otherwise part with their own money to help bolster and increase yours.

There is something innately reassuring in presuming that the next person knows more than you do because they act like it, that they have a greater knowledge of the future because they tell you they do or that they possess or earn more because they spend in a way that suggests they do. How we learn to resent them for what we think they have, believe them when they appear better equipped or moneyed than we are, or trust them with the advice they give us. And, how quickly we are made to feel inadequate or in some way inferior – it is a human condition and one that allows others to take advantage of it if they know how to.

It is an insecurity unknown by the wild things of this world.

James Nevin stood angrily outside his own boat yard, in his own town, on a street that generations of his own family had successfully trod for centuries before him. He had knowledge of boat craft and seamanship that would have earned him praise and honour in times gone by when there was a greater reliance on the sea for transport, communication, food and commerce. Here he was, old blood, defiantly trying to stay afloat against the odds and the tide of finance and devolving emigration against and away from his beloved rural community. He had roots here and had chosen to stay as others had fled to the bigger conurbations in search of more lucrative enterprises, better prospects, finer housing, and greater educational options for their offspring, shorter working day lengths and a more secure future for their families.

James could not blame them, struggling as he was with mounting bills, falling work rostas and simply too few boats out on the water. Gone was the fishing fleet and the yachts now used the city marinas. Few people fished from a wooden boat and almost no one knew or cared about the beauty of the traditional built *Birlinn*, the *Monach* and other island craft slowly developed and evolved in design. They were the craft of his business, built to exacting standards from local wood to cut synonymously through local water in a way that would have been recognised by the Viking invaders of the north; those who arrived from the sea, who settled locally and from whom he could also claim direct blood birth rite.

His emotions ran as deep as the base rock below his feet where he felt a genetic link between him and the land, as primal as his desire for another where a relationship had been denied, cut-off before it could blossom. It was as broad as the magnificent landscape that surrounded him enclosed by the potency of the hills and their castellan mountains, out to the seascape that literally extended beyond the open door in a vastness of water that became one with the sea running back to his decrepit inherited business. The boats behind were mostly left unclaimed due to debts that could not be paid, flotillas that had folded, fisheries that had dried up or simply those left by the long dead. True, there were craft in there that could be saved and sold, into which the piscine life of the sailing vessel could be breathed back, and they were all rightfully his. There was beauty in the lines and the clinkering that held them tight, some with beams and timbers that were so well seasoned that they would forever remain watertight and buoyant.

But who wanted them or would pay for them?

In common with the land rich laird, he had so much of value that he could claim was his, but could not release the value to be of any use to him.

To James, boats were like people in their abilities to weather the storms and ride the waves, and even to handle the most simplistic of water and the most complex of shorelines.

Some lasted the seasons and coped with everything flung at them by nature. With a good hand at the tiller and a sensible sail managed by a crew that learnt from experience, listened to the old-timers and continued to take advice as it was offered by nature or by man, it was a boat that would succeed, never tip and rarely sink. A good boat was like a good body, it was a worthy vessel that carried the soul safely throughout all of life's trials and managed whatever was thrust at it so long as the crew remained steady handed, confident and well guided.

Lose that and the boat was as good as lost.

Lose the confidence of the crew or the faculties of the skipper's mind and then it would hit the rocks, drift off course or tread water in the doldrums for years on end, wasting that wonderfully designed thing – the body, the hull.

Lose sight of the destination and who knew what would happen?

Of course, there was always the chance of that freak wave colliding broadside that might send her off course, cause irreparable damage or eventually drag it down. But then life did that sometimes and there was never a good enough reason or religious explanation that could really provide sufficient explanation. Stuff just happened, and in the same way that no good sailor presumes they control or fully understand the sea, however expert their abilities are claimed to be, no human presumes they control or fully understand life and the events they meet in it.

A well-built boat is a beautiful thing. The human construct is also a beautiful thing.

But today we are satisfied with less. Plastics, composites and fibre-glass replace wood, metal and leather, and the very fabric of what makes '*boat*' has changed from the organic, which behaves in sympathy with the living, to the abiotic which confounds it. The cotton of the sail and the twisted fibres of the ropes, each of which creaked and spoke of the tension in them and the force of the wind, are now technical synthetics which do their jobs impersonally and near-silently, dumbly following command and current. Even shape is a compromise for stability or speed, computer-aided design having bypassed and lost the careful inventions that result from millennia of incremental improvements. A boat becomes a recreational toy and not an inheritance upon which your trade and survival might endure and with its added digital technologies it becomes bionic in its own right.

Much like the modern human, still a caveman in so many ways, physically, emotionally, mentally and in terms of survival need and desire, the boat has become a superficial yet advanced, limited yet specifically designed, ghost of its former self. And James was a man of the old world, unsure of which way to turn, how to compete and continue and mixed up in the way that he felt about it. Both he and his business were old before their time and yet he was acclaimed as a highly skilled, rare-breed craftsman and sailor. Articles were written about his ability to build up a traditional wooden sailing boat from scratch, made to order, or to bring an ancient craft back to life. And yet, the orders were drying up, the calls for his services diminishing and, worst of all, it could not continue.

Beyond most things, he hated the idea of the city, and yet here he was with money in his pocket for a small repair that had come directly from a man who represented in his mind everything that there was to detest about that modern world. There was a man who could simply buy it. There was a man who had the power of hard cash behind him. There was a man who was successful, able and confident. He had the arrogance to travel up here from the south and claim that he owned an estate, a loch and a mountain simply because he had the good fortune of money.

Evolution is so very red in tooth and claw, where selective edge, accumulation of wealth and ability to predate on the weak are all encouraged, honed and developed.

Worse still, that man had Gerry with him, and even though James knew full well that nothing was ever likely to develop between the two of them again, he still help out that little candle of hope – however slim; after all, what are we without hope?
James Nevin stood and watched Gerry disappear towards the lonely shack by the pool at the end of town and coveted Sol for so much of what he had, and he hated him for what he represented. This angered him even more, as did the nodding crows that mocked and taunted him as they stepped about knowledgeably, as if conceiving plans against him, pacing the close-cropped grass blades where they picked at the straggly wool of the sheep; they were the portents of ill tidings well known in the history of folklore.

Away from the town and route marching towards the beach, Sol made sure he was well away from view before he collapsed in a heap on the floor to gather breath and bring his thoughts together. Panting, Gerry caught up with him and threw herself on the ground beside him. She was laughing.
"Simon says that he'll give you twenty quid for the car," she giggled landing next to him on the bracken-cushioned floor. The fronds unfurled to form a miniature Amazon about them, flicking back skyward so that they were hidden from the road and emitting that all too familiar carcinogenic odour that historically gave ancient bracken bedding its in-built insect repellent. The springy wooden stems gave strange support to Sol and Gerry's bodies so that they floated clear of the dampness of the moss and the gravity-fed trickle of the soil water. Down here in the shade of the fern-jungle canopy, where the dewdrops of the morning still clung, dripped and fell, was a coolness and humidity to the air such that the slugs remained active despite the emergent warmth of the season beyond.
"That much?" Sol replied with the thoughtful voice of someone distracted. There was a beetle walking the length of one bracken arm. A rusty orange with clear white near-perfect circles daubed

over its polished dome of a body, it trundled onwards on its reddened legs with purpose and yet seemed to be going nowhere in particular.

"He'll get it traded in for off-road and tractor parts next week but is coming to pick it up now. He's no idea about its worth but'll try and get you the best deal. He's good like that."

The beetle continued until it stumbled on the leaflet pinna and the smaller lobes that made it up, each a pinnule; a pinna in miniature. Here it stopped, considered the wind and then raising its wing cases high and abroad it unfolded brown-etched origami wings that reflected light blue, white and oily, and lifted upwards, humming like a diminutive helicopter across that human-stain of tarmac, the road, and towards the sea.

Sol followed it, lost it to its freedom, and then surveyed the loch.

"He is lucky you know?" he spoke out loud, less for comment and more for what was passing through his mind for him to hear spoken himself.

"Simon?"

"No, Nevin."

Gerry went quiet and stopped laughing. She didn't understand Sol's train of thought and couldn't read his expression for the myriad stems and leaf-dappled shade that enveloped and camouflaged him despite his physical closeness.

"He has all this," and he sat up and gestured towards the shoreline and the loch and the distant sea where gannets were diving beyond the mid-island.

"What, a failing town and a destitute population with an encroaching sea loch, not to mention a surplus of wool and nothing for miles but heather moorland?"

"No," said Sol flatly as he stood up. A startled wren whirled from a nearby rock shelter and rapidly became invisible in amongst the vegetation that crawled over the boulder-strewn hillside behind them. "He can make a boat, mend a boat, sail a boat. I have to buy a boat, pay to have it fixed and give money to be trained as to what to do like some child or boy scout. He probably knew how to do that when he was a kid!"

It is that irony of life that each person on either side of a divide can feel that the grass is always greener on the other side of the hedge and that there is a genuine belief in life that it is everyone else that has it best.

"But you went off and did something else. You learnt to make money and earn it for others. Not everyone can do that! And I bet you've got qualifications and went to university? None of us have done that either!"

"But, I'm just a pebble counter," and he crossed the road to the deep shingle line of the beach with Gerry in tow. "And I'm good at convincing other people I've got more pebbles than I really have and that if they give me their pebbles they'll get even more back." He kicked stones up with a booted foot.

"Ah, I see." Gerry smiled reassuringly as she joined him. "We have the sea for that of course. It gives us loads of pebbles. Problem is that none of them are worth very much."

She picked a wave-rounded stone from the mound the sea had carved into the long wide bay and turned it in her hand.

"What's the history of that pebble?" Sol asked out loud watching her thumb it over and over again. "What made it? How old is it? Where did it come from? What's it even seen?"

"Sol," Gerry interrupted, "it's just a pebble on a beach. There are millions of them." And with this she tossed it across the waves so that it skimmed, bouncing three times before it caught and refracted down into the abyss.

"But are you sure?"

"What?" she turned to look at the philosopher next to her.

"That these pebbles here aren't worth very much?"

"What? You're not going to sell our pebbles are you?"

"No. But look around you. You could sell this," and he gazed around at the land about him, turning in a broad sweep that scrunched the nuggets of stone accumulated around his feet and allowed him to pan a full three hundred and sixty degrees from mountains and land through sea and loch and then back again to the mountains. It was the view he imagined a woodcock would have every moment of its waking life with its eyes wide set on the side of its head. "You sell the idea that it's all as perfect as it looks and I'm sure they'll come to take a look."

"The locals would kill you if you sold it all. They already think you are either going to die in a few days' time, starve to death, or sell up for some huge profit, break up the estate and leave. Don't sell it! You wouldn't have time to starve before they hunted you down and killed you with their bare hands."

"No. I couldn't sell it. Not now." He paused as if to formulate the words to explain how he felt about the land and the water and his strange feeling of responsibility for the *Bothan*. But then somehow communication failed him. "I just couldn't," was the only explanation he could give. And Gerry wondered before he carried on. "Instead, if we could just get *them* to come here, the people who have finance behind them, to give their money to the community in some way, invest without really knowing it and then leave... ...after they've seen the pebbles on the beach of course..."

He sat down for a moment and considered the geological history that had brought these stones here to this pile on this beach as whips of volcanic cloud boiled over the mountain tops and a flock of spring-maddened linnets tumbled behind them from gorse to gorse. The two then got up and wandered back up the road towards *Sireadh-thall* who waited patiently further on, stranded above the line of flotsam.

"But," Gerry asked, "won't that ruin the place? Having lots of people come here to... ...to see your pebbles?"

"Not if we do it properly. We'd keep most pebbles for ourselves and make sure that the other locals got the pebbles they needed too. Iona and Skye have eggs, chickens, geese, fish and cows to sell. James has boats and a boat yard. There's a shop. Hamish has his sheep, their wool and their meat. Your friends have cheese. And you...?"

He stopped short and stood stock still whilst Gerry paled and felt the nerves of the unskilled, uneducated and unconfident. He scrunched his face up before continuing. "Well," he said, "can I see your artwork sometime?"

"I'd stop there before you get carried away." She was relieved that she hadn't been left out of his equation. "I have to warn you. If you start talking like that to the locals they're not going to listen to you. Blood runs deep around here and until they think you're one of them, then there's no chance anyone's going to listen to you. In their minds you've only been here five minutes and you've not even met most of them."

"But what happens if we make it their idea too?"

He was serious and animated by excitement. The Sol of the boardroom and business deal was momentarily alive and re-energised. "We could talk to them and get them onside. If they too could see the benefits to the community, then just maybe? What do you think?"

Gerry silence voiced much.

By the boat was a hunched up grey heron, sharp straight beaked, beady eyed and focused, hoping to convince the fish life that it wasn't there. One leg was held up into its downy chest where straggly streamer feathers descended, fell and curled at their ends hiding dangerous talons and a deadly intent. It stood its ground until there were nearly upon it at which point it launched itself on heavy hooped wing beats, pushing out a deep proud chest, 'scrauching' its disapproval as it left in saurian flight.

"The heron," said Gerry nodding. "*Corra-ghritheach*. That means the 'old screamer'. I think you could learn a lot from what the old people thought of the heron."

Sol watched it fly off to find another more secluded site to ambush from. "Why?" he asked. "What did they think?"

"That *corra-ghritheach* was intelligent because it knew patience and knew when to wait before any action. Its success was down to its patience."
He knew what she meant even if he also knew that he would find following her advice difficult.

The journey back was tough with a wind that did not feel it wanted to be helpful. Instead it played boisterously with the sail cloth and tossed them in and out of coves where torturous willow trees danced with the breeze on cliff faces that seemed impossible to hang off. As they skirted the rocks seals dropped into the water with much bemoaned barks and bellows, revealing their canine ancestry better than their maritime shapes and blubbered forms.
For a while a puffin joined them, cheerily adding some colour to the water's processed froth with its over-large, bright-coloured bill and penguin-striped body. Sad eyes watched their passage tearfully from within their triangular sockets before the pocket-sized bird, so much smaller than Sol had imagined, flopped down below the copper-green sea surface leaving nothing but a trail of bubbles behind it as it flew for its piscine supper.
Gerry broke the silence between them. "I painted the deer in your living room," she called as the pre-rain wind flogged the flapping sail she was harnessing and tightening yet another time. "It's a bit big, but G always said he wanted the wall to look like part of the scenery. It was my thank you to him for letting me have the cottage and taking me in." She was considering him regretfully over the froth of the waves hitting the prow and spewing up into their faces. "That stone up on the headland...   ...it was his favourite place. That's why I was so surprised to find you up there that day I first saw you. It could have been him, what with you dressed up in his clothes and all. I heard the violin, he played that too, and well it took me back the few weeks to before when he left."
The words hurt somehow. "I really did think it was him, but then..."
She trailed off.

"Then, what?"

"Well. He's gone."

"Gone where?" Sol knew she wouldn't really give an answer but he had a desire to know where this man G had gone to.

"Well he just left," and the conversation ended for now and they did not speak until they beached up in front of the *Bothan* and the two heaved *Sireadh-thall* up and out of the water.

"Do you want to come in?" Sol offered, but the still thoughtful Gerry declined and started to get ready to walk back to her own house. Sol's heart dropped slightly and then he made a second proposal that he thought would secure their friendship just that bit more. "Take *Sireadh-thall* and sail her back home." He patted the boat's hull soundly as he spoke. Beached here she looked more like a small wooden whale out of water, something designed for some other medium; anything but dry land.

"Pardon?" she asked, unsure that she had heard him properly over the crashing of the waves on the rocks behind where the gulls stood and preened or slept on one leg.

"Take the boat, sail her back home, bring her back when you visit tomorrow."

"Tomorrow?"

"Look Gerry. I know you'll miss your boat and I need you to teach me to sail this one properly before I do something silly or dangerous in it. I also want you to introduce me to my tenants if you have time? That can be payment for taking my boat."

She nodded before he went on. "And well," he paused, "I think you're my first friend round here and traditionally I've been pretty damn rubbish to most of my friends over the years – I'm not even sure I've got many, except for the ones that care more about my cash than me...   ...and...   ...I know I am going on, but..."

"...tomorrow," she said, rescuing him from his own rambling. "I'll be here by seven and I'll bring breakfast too."

"Excellent and..." He thought for a moment as if to check in his mind that it was alright to speak out loud the words he thought. "...thank you."

She stared at him hard. "Thank you, too."

Gerry pushed *Sireadh-thall* back out into eddies of the tide, jumped in and twisted the tiller expertly to make the boat rise as the wind, now behaving perfectly, caught her tightening sail. "And Sol?" she called over the pitch and flush of the next tidal push.

"Yes?"

"You are a friend too. Thank you for all that you have done for me so far."

He smiled and then watched her go off in her borrowed boat until she disappeared around the headland, the second man to do that in the one day.

In the hour, Sol found himself engrossed in the tasks of managing his house, preparing his dinner and of completing the construction of yesterday's delivered items. Using the windblown trees as his guide, he fixed the two metal assemblies together to produce a large aluminium tripod which he stood out of sight of the house and, where possible, from the loch but in the full force of the wind. This he secured to the ground with bullet-grey wire guys made of coiling metal threads that cut his fingers when they sprang lose. Next, working through the wet and the dropping light, he attached a plastic propeller to the head. It immediately started to spin and jockey with the power of the wind and quickly demonstrated his wind direction inferences were correct. Finally he connected this to a small generator behind, positioned to the rear to steady the propeller section as it rocked on a rotational axis so as to greet the wind more efficiently. Playing out plastic-coated copper wire back to the *Bothan* via the sheds, where he set large greasy-black battery packs, and across the yard, he worked it neatly into a terminal plastic box which he fixed to the inside window ledge of the kitchen. There was a three-pin socket on its side and into this he plugged his mobile phone charger and prayed that the money and time had been worth it.

Several seconds passed and by some small miracle the god of portable technology blessed Sol in a way he part-thought it never would and the device acknowledged that it was receiving enough power to be charging for the first time that week.

Grazing on food as he passed in and out through the kitchen Sol opened and collected the contents of the second delivered parcel. It contained a fold out metal dish that fanned around to produce a complete parabolic circle which attached neatly to a wall bracket also in the box. Trailing across the yard again he found the ladders and tools required to connect this to the porch woodwork where it was not as rotten as the rest and he ran a connecting wire along a ceiling beam again to the kitchen which he then plugged into his phone.

Running his fingers along the underside of the beam to hide the wires from view, their tips caught briefly in the Teflon stickiness of old-web and his spine tingled as he imagined the long hairy legs of spiders withdrawing into the alcoves bored out by past generations of beetles and bugs that had left now that most nutrition had been removed from the timber. Feeling a powdery textured material crumble in his hands where he dredged them unseeingly, he retracted quickly to find a glistening grey wood-dust bell construction built internally of about a hundred tessellated hexagonal cells knitted together around a central entrance chamber and folly. This wasp nest he carefully placed on the work surface where the potted plants were growing rapidly in their search for that rarity of the north called sunlight. Each plant was leant in parallel to its neighbours showing the prevalent direction of light and the seedlings' expectation that the same would be repeated day after day unless Sol fooled them by turning their pots through an angle.

He then positioned the phone so that he could see the screen whilst hanging off the dish and standing on the ladder on one foot. He reached out as far as he could to push the dish left then right, up and then down, always checking back with the phone screen to see if the signal bar changed at all.

No bar of signal.

First he nudged it left a fraction so that it now pointed out to the loch.

One bar appeared and then sank back down to none.

Then he resorted to right.

Two bars, one bar, none.

And then back again.

Two bars.

"Hello, Sol," called the familiar voice of Hamish from inside the house. Intended or not, it was laced with the sweet sarcasm of one who had discovered yet another delicious morsel to make fun of. "Now what the bloody hell are you doing?"

Sol fell off the ladder and clattered somewhere off into the darkening yard before recovering and reappearing at the porch door.

"Hamish!" he said.

"They do some funny things in London don't they? What may I ask are you up to? First you try killing yourself with your questionable driving skills. Then you're off on a boat you can't sail. Now you're hanging off a ladder. Is suicide a dream of yours or are you just completely stupid?"

"Thanks, Hamish but…"

"You *can* just ask me to help." The old man stepped forward to give some assistance; an obvious natural at being there for the aid of others. "A problem shared can be a problem halved. Unless I'm feeling unhelpful?" And he laughed, and Sol felt he could too.

Hamish picked up the mobile phone and held it so that Sol could see better and together they managed to get the greatest signal possible, although strangely it seemed to change with the direction of the wind, the spinning of the wind turbine and the mood of the two men working close to it. It was as if something unseen could influence the airwaves around them. Sol liked to think jokingly that the smaller the technology became then the more it could be affected by external factors around it, as if IT could develop its own personality and response, or worse still a personalised sense of humour working antagonistically against the operator. *And why not? If the distant, small lump of stone we call the moon can alter every tide in the world twice a day? Then why not indeed?*

They settled for three bars then sat down in the kitchen whilst Sol's mobile pinged constantly as it received the tens of new messages that he had missed over the last few days.

"Popular bugger aren't you?" muttered Hamish fascinated at the waste of time he considered this to be.

"That's not always a good thing though," Sol explained full of instant regret as he saw the burgeoning list of missed calls, unanswered messages and emails. He had craved contact with the outside world, and now that he had it he immediately longed for it to be gone.

"I can understand that. Lucky if I get one message a day. Usually don't even want that."

"So," said Sol, "how are the sheep?"

"Fine, fine. Well a bit tough today really. They don't like the wet. The lambs are coming through at present and they get cold. I've left the other shepherd with them so you needn't worry too much."

Sol looked up. "Worry? Why should I worry?"

Hamish's eyes glinted roguishly. "Your land," and he chewed his lip, "your sheep."

"Oh. I probably should've expected that really shouldn't I?"

"Yes." Hamish's answer was perfunctory and to the point. But it lacked the edge of their first few meetings.

There was a pause before Hamish carried on, "I've come to give you an invitation."

"Another one? You've already asked me to dinner next week."

"Yes, but I might have been a bit hasty really the other day... ...in writing you off. You're still alive after all *and* you haven't left yet."

"No," Sol agreed. "Sorry if I've disappointed you. Have you lost your bet?"

"You might have cost me some money, but...   ...Gerry says you play the fiddle."

"Violin."

"Aye...   ...fiddle. She says you're not too shabby at it either."

"A wasted youth at music school I'm afraid." Sol loved to show off about his music and was proud of his musical education.

"No need to apologise. I'm sure we could un-teach anything they taught you."

"We?"

"The band. We meet on Thursdays when we can. Want to know if you would join us...   ...for a trial like?"

"Well, yes of course." Sol found himself agreeing all too eagerly. He knew nothing of the band, who played, what they played, how they played or even where they played. But it was a chance to meet musical people; any people!

"Good. I'll come by at seven and we can have a bite to eat at the pub in the old town after."

Hamish turned as if to leave, then re-faced Sol squarely. He looked thoughtful and some of the judgement was gone from his creased brow.

"The boat...   ...thanks for what you've done for Gerry."

"That's okay. I like her."

Hamish continued to measure Sol up with a direct stare, his bright eyes piercing deeply. It was obvious he had something else to say but that he was gauging how to word it right or was struggling with the terminology to express what he felt. No one ever knows how they form words from the thoughts in their minds and yet we all do it, only becoming consciously aware of how difficult it is when we concentrate on trying to do it or lose the ability through illness, age or accident. It is like the animal faced with the indecision of making the first move to impress a potential mate. Communication becomes difficult and actions well-learnt suddenly distracted and clumsy.

"Look after her," he eventually said with raw feeling in his simple yet calculated words. "She's been hurt too many times before." He paused again and then added, "I've seen plenty of people around like you, believe me. Plenty of money but not much sense. Money gives them power where *they* come from and can even temporarily buy things for them around here. But it *doesn't* save your life in a hard winter, it *won't* keep your sheep in good condition for the new season, it *can't* get you water when you need it and it *doesn't* buy you the right sorts of friends to be going on with."

"I know that," Sol replied humbly in his defence.

"People like you tend to come and go and they don't stick around. Our Gerry likes you and so I suppose I'm going to have to one day too, but...   ...time will tell. You seem better than I first thought. Just look after her that's all, and when the time comes do the thing which is right for her and...   ...and not just for you. That'll be the day when I get the measure of you."

And before Sol could answer, Hamish span around and out into the dark beyond the porch where the weather was churning and yet the owl still hooted through the necessity of its desire to mate.

Sol stood for a moment, thoughtful, and then paced around to the front of the *Bothan* to watch the rear lights of Hamish's Land Rover glow red as they headed on and up the track with the beams angling out in rays that lit up every drop of rain falling before them. Then he was left in silence and the dark, yet not silence with the calls of the wild, the rustle of the trees, the lapping of the shore and now the gentle hum of the rotating wind turbine.

At the head of the immediate drive by the side of the *Bothan* was a large silhouette of a vehicle. It was black against the gloom of the descending evening, cut square, solid and lightless over the backdrop of the cobbled yard sheds, stone hewn and irregular with their ever-present fern shadows and moss blemishes. Its pickup back extended long to the rear with chunky-treaded tyres fore and aft. Simon had obviously come good and delivered the Land Rover. Two eye-like headlamps were sunk into the alcove between the algae-painted wings where a basic grill with leather muffler was held upside-down t-shaped. Un-lockable doors meant that Sol could easily climb up into the cab where he sat high up on firmly sprung elephant-grey hide seats with a large round black wheel, cold to the touch, and a primitive dashboard ahead. It was antediluvian when compared to the sports car, but at least it had made it further along the drive and its elevation gave him a feeling of safety and security, strength and ability, despite its rustic charm.

He gaped out of the two split sheets of flat glass where the wipers hung off their large inwardly projecting motors across the spare wheel strapped to the expansive bonnet and down the drive and imagined what it was like to drive this beast.

There was a scrawled note to him tucked into the driver's air vent that he hurriedly removed and unfolded. The letters were basic and large enough to read in the dying light.

'Car delivered as promised.

Have spares if she breaks down – just call.

G loved her – called her 'Addie'.

Simon'

His belongings from the sports car were neatly stacked on the passenger seat, a laptop, some papers and a few bags – mostly of sweets and a packet of tobacco that he chose to ignore.

Sol sat for a moment and in spite of the temptation to turn the keys in the dash in front of him, he decided against it for now. They looked more like front door keys than any car keys he had seen before and it amused him how crude everything about him appeared, taking on a historic twist. He fiddled with the switches in front of him until the headlights sprung on to produce beams that cut through the swirling of wet and misty dusk ahead.

Light caught the dropping beads, heavy jewels of refraction which then broke into the puddles and runnels of the track highlighting their splashes in the yellow and blue of the lamps' filaments. It drummed on the roof and bonnet.

Movement beyond the *Bothan's* yard drew Sol's attention.

Small rodents were scurrying down the track's edge, walling along the grasses and wild flowers that he could see rocking unnaturally as they passed. Through the open vents he could hear their high-pitched squeaks of communication, as if they were expressing themselves with gleeful pipes. A fracas broke out between two of them and they rolled angrily into the lane until they bowled indignantly into a puddle and threw themselves upwards with the shock. They then backed off from one another with much posture and threat, anger in minute.

An owl was hooting in the distance in a language that Sol did not understand but which was comprehensible to its mate and those sat in other territories as they howled and called their replies from around the glen.

And then, the cat appeared again, materialising out of the twilight-toned trees, the shrubs and the grass as if some ghost of the moor had vaporised into view before him. One minute there was an empty track, muddied, boulder strewn and rutted, and then within a second a silent apparition of cat form was there too.

With the beams on full this was the first time that Sol had fully understood the scale, shape and colour of the wild cat as it disdainfully considered the Land Rover and its staring occupant. Surely this was the tiger of the Scottish woodland – muscular, angular, brindle-striped, and short tailed, it was alert.

It padded to where the rodents had fought, sniffed the ground and next the air and then vanished. Once more a spirit, leaving only a memory of cat imprinted on the mind of Sol who barely understood how rare an event this was that he had witnessed so often and easily.

He sat and contemplated rain, rodents, cats, friends and the *Bothan* and knew that he was blessed.

Back inside, Sol cleared the packaging from the turbine and the dish, coming across the third cardboard box delivered the previous day but forgotten. It was much smaller than the rest, but as he cut the tape that held it secure and spilled out its over-zealously filled innards of inflated plastic padding and expanded corn starch, his heart skipped in a mad rhythm enough to impress any musician of any genre. At the centre, lying on a sumptuous bed of wrapping litter was a shiny glass, spouted cylinder held tightly in a copper frame with three spread feet at its base. A polished copper dome at the head held a descending mesh plunger caged inside. It was that thing that every bachelor without much electricity, living in the middle of nowhere at some point would come to realise he could not live without. A cafetiere! And now breakfast *would* be a success.

Pushing boxes aside, he found his violin placed respectfully within its sumptuous case and took it up to his chin to play, taking advantage of the speeded heart rate this pre-caffeinated discovery had gifted him.

"Fiddle," he thought out loud derisively. "*This* is a violin, not a fiddle. Seventeen thousand pounds at auction in the eighties for a fiddle!" And he began to play in front of the window as the darkness sloped around the cottage and the fire's glow intensified to enlighten the room and then guide the passage of his music.

Sleep was slow in coming, but as if the wildcat had left something of its spiritual self lodged inside his mind, Sol took it with him into his dreams as he descended down into that other world. He padded along with the cat through the woods and away from *Bothan Faobhar*, and eventually found himself up on the headland by that relic stone where he once again joined the man sat there watching the waters.

As they spoke the wildcat lay and licked its paws before settling down at a cautious distance. On waking he could not recall the conversation with the faceless man he knew to be G in a dream.

Neither could he remember how he had returned from the fantasy world's stone on the headland promontory back to the chair in the *Bothan* where he sat sleeping with G's own notes animated in sight and sound by the crackle of the fire.

He was called into the realm of wakefulness by the chime of a text arriving. In his rush to produce power for it and to obtain its slender signal enough to communicate with the outside world Sol had forgotten cleanly about the phone itself and forced himself to sit up, muddy headed and misty eyed.

The mobile *'pinged'* again, its reminder that a text had come.

Staggering to the kitchen, Sol poured a glass of *Bothan* brown out for himself, cold, rich and heady with beery bubbles, and then struggled to focus on the small blue-lit screen.

42 messages.

He made the mistake of opening the first one up which immediately set his mind into action and banished sleep from his thoughts completely in that way the mobile's curse does whenever we are lulled into using it too late at night.

She angry...   *...she did still care...   ...but wanted to move on... ...how was he?   If he wanted her to come up and see him? If he needed somewhere to stay in London...   ...just call...*

He declined the offer and waited for the next barrage of texts. His life was now firmly planted in the north and he had an obligation to the *Bothan* to complete on.

Office contract now terminated...   *...still nothing on the Tokyo deal...   ...shares dropping and transaction appeared to have soured...   ... authorities struggling due to lack of paperwork... ...Sol not helping...   ...no text, no contact ...   ...final bonus transferred...*

Sol replied to say that he was thankful to the company for their support through the years and expected that they would continue to honour his commissions especially with respect to the Tokyo deal. He was confident that things would change and that the company would return to him with their tail between their legs – it was important that whatever they thought, they remained convinced that he was feeling positive about the deal and what money it would yield. They knew he was just gambling, but he did not need them to see any chink in his determination armour.

Concerned, he plugged his laptop in using his phone as a signal generator and checked the markets. They were down and had continued to tumble markedly through the past few days. It was a broad-spectrum drop and the money he had left England with was now only worth a fraction of what it had been. Still, he was comfortably rich at present and could afford to remain smug for the now. He just did not know how he was going to continue to remain with enough money in the long term.

Therapist *trying to extract money one last time...   ...considered the contract between them was now null and void...   ...he could contact her if he needed it in the future...   ...but he had better rush as she was busy...   ...still one more session available this week... ...maybe next week, but her diary was filling up quickly and he could not afford to delay much longer or else he might miss out... ...did think he should call her, as she was a little worried about his state of mind...   ...maybe she could help?*

In a mood to burn bridges behind him, Sol wrote back to the therapist and thanked her for her time and set her three questions to consider before she wrote back.

> *1.   What tangible thing had she achieved with Sol over the past few years? True, he had enjoyed his visits and had talked through much material. But what had changed and why whilst he was still in the city? Did he still rely on her and carry on making the same wrong decisions in life and still feel pent up and allow his emotions to run away with him? One week in the countryside of rural Scotland and all these feelings had gone and he no longer felt the desire to see a therapist like her. Surely, she should be suggesting to her clients that they should spend a bit of time out of the city, relaxing in the wilds and reconnecting with the wild*

things? This, Sol felt, was a better solution to his stresses than the non-directive, highly expensive talking therapy she had given him so far.

2.   What exactly was she charging for and how was she qualified to do it? Sure, she had talked with him and made him feel at ease with her, the coffee she served was exquisite and proffered to him in beautiful cups, and she had a lovely office in an expensive part of the riverside district. But why did it cost so much for an hour's consultation when fully trained and highly qualified therapists working for the health service provided it for free or, at the most, a fraction of her price? It had begun to bother him and he was interested...   ...just interested. A breakdown of costs would be quite helpful.

3.   If she was so very busy, why did she keep telling him and yet still have sessions available in her schedule? Was it that she was not busy at all and was simply trying to encourage him to book in by pretending that she was busy, using the same sorts of pressure tactics as an estate agent does if keen to sell a property or a car salesperson wanting their commission regardless of the suitability of the vehicle you were looking at? He too was a salesman of sorts, a trader of people's confidence in any given company, its assets or shares. He knew all too well that the most gifted in his career were those who made others feel that they had to invest, that the potential benefits were obvious and that time was running out. Was she the same?

With only slight guilt as to what he was writing, Sol thumbed the send icon.

Friends, *though less than before...*

It is interesting how quickly you can be forgotten and your phone, mobile and other communications tools become only for outgoing messages and not regularly used for incoming ones after you leave a district.

Family still keen to visit... ...we won't bother you though... ...not until you are ready for visitors... ...hoping you are still okay?

He reeled off just a quick reply. Although they say you cannot choose your family and that you are stuck with what you've got, it is good to know that they are always there and are often only those who learn to give you the space you need at times. After all, they have had a lifetime thus far to learn about you already and will be with you for the rest of a lifetime.

Authorities acknowledging that there is still no case to pursue yet, but annoyed that the paperwork is so slow in surfacing... ...although it does all appear to be there... ...so far.

He sent thanks for their continued patience and reassured them that all would be well in the end, given time.

Solicitor giving perfunctory thanks for the signature on Sol's receipt of the deeds... ...if he needed other services please call...

Bothan Faobhar and the estate were now officially his.

Then there were messages from his London friend Al.

'Sol,

Gone mad up there yet? Not heard much from you.

Pete and I can make it up next week. I want to suss the house out and look at that equipment of yours before you turn native. Have done some research and it might require a large investment to turn the place around so don't burn any bridges at work – you never know when your ability to sell anything to anyone might come in handy.

Pete is bringing up his camera gear and has a buyer interested in a story on the area, especially if there are good photos of the wildcats.

What's the local bar like? Are there any good restaurants or hotels we can go to and eat at? Or anything with potential I might want to buy? Need a house warming party?

See you next week,

Al

PS. Sue is worried about you. Strange, she's actually missing you as well – that's a first! Shall we bring her up too?'

Sol replied whilst his mind was filled with the horror of his old friends coming up, worse still Sue. For some reason he did not want his past life following him up from the city. He knew that he was already a different character to the one that had left a week ago, even though he did not really know why and how he had changed. All he was aware of was that this little cottage and its glen had cast some spell over him and he once again felt the pang of a need to protect it if he could.

'*Al,*

All fine here but still a lot of work required on the house. Bought more than I thought I had and only just scraping it into this century – finally got a signal sorted in the house but can't guarantee I'll keep it.

Officially unemployed now, but am sure I will be able to make a go of it on my own savings – I'm an investor for god's sake so should have enough put aside. Have tenants and so will be able to make enough on rents.

Not found a local bar yet and house is a bit quiet for a house warming party.

Don't rush up if you have other things to do.

Sol'

He signed off and pressed send.

The time was twenty past three in the morning and a lazy sun was burning its volcanic halo over the eastern hills. Switching the phone to silent Sol discarded it on the kitchen table, brewed coffee and took an algae'd plastic chair from the bathroom shed to sit out on the beach. He caught sight of himself in the fractured mirror of the room as he swept by it. His grey-tipped beard was at that length where it was somewhere between being poorly shaven and intended, existing in neither realm properly and thus giving the impression that he cared little for his appearance. Hair adrift in its own way, it had been released from any kind of format and as a result lay scragged up in what can only be described as the *'preppie'* style. His skin was more tanned than he remembered it, but was loose and relaxed and he knew that neither it nor his teeth were as clean as they should have been and he wondered critically how he must smell.

"I'm becoming the scruffy bugger," he commented to himself. "What Al would describe as turning native," and laughed out loud.

Wrapped in a thick grey-white Arran sweater patterned in cable-knit formations over its front, he sat down on the chair, plastic and unyielding, in the middle of the shore to absorb the unfolding of the dawn.

Geese flapped noisily in with wings that *'hooped'* as they swiped and cut the wind. They skidded to a halt in foamy splashes as they used their fanned webbed feet as water brakes that cut their descending speed and threw their bodies down and forward. A flotilla of scoters, velvet black and with curiously colourful oddly-knobbed bills, bobbed further out where an unidentifiable diver lived up to the description of its name and snorkelled for fish at depth.

Mackerel, silver green and striped, flew upwards into the air fleeing an unseen predator below the water that thrust itself through their school, and terns that hovered the sky on fluttering wings held in angelic poises dropped on sand eels.

Slurping in a way he only did when alone, enjoying the schoolboy humour of doing something that he would never do or get away with in company, Sol watched attentively. He was now making mental note of the sea scents, the tidal sounds, the animals, even the plants that until recently had only ever reached the periphery of his consciousness before and to which he been blind, travelling the natural world oblivious. He would write about these in G's diary, keep a record and record it for someone else; the next incumbent of the house. Turning his thoughts, observations and experiences over in his head, he visited the way it made him feel and found a melody that he felt best described them. He knew it was in the key of G before he even tried to imagine how it looked written on a manuscript and was certain that he had found the core stanza for his symphony. He could write the loch into it, the river, the hills, the sea, the land and the sky, and suddenly there before him was music that he closed his eyes to enjoy and orchestrate. That stanza was the loch, and it depicted the centrality of the water.

The coffee was warm and good, steaming into his nostrils and scolding the back of his throat, and its chemically-controlled bitter contrast to the fresh remote air found his lips with ease until it was finished. Then he acted out conducting his newly found piece with his free hands.

When he opened his eyes, the otter was attending the shoreline searching for washed up debris and crabbing amongst the weeds. It wound its way sinuously in bounding fashion, smelling the air every few minutes and cautiously surveying the beach. Crying gulls disturbed it and so it slipped away and was gone save for a head that rode the water for a while.

Sol was convinced that it had neither seen nor smelt him. *Maybe he had turned native after all and he was becoming more accepted by the wild things about him?*

He sat and he waited and he watched.

Nature continued to enact its on-going drama with each character coming in from off-stage to play its part, sometimes deadly and predatory, at most other times peaceful and herbivorous, and then on occasion active or else mundane. Sol had not missed television yet and for the first time realised that he might never need it again as a truly settled *native* living amongst the other *native* things he shared this place with.

Life, it was infectious and engaging, and he had caught it.

Chapter 13: The Crossroads on the Bealach

(Andante Festivo, Jean Sibelius)

There is a wonderful depth of self-discovery available in solitude that many fail to understand until they have spent enough time alone with themselves. Rarely do we devote a great enough period in that place where we can meditate long enough to learn who we are, what we want, where we have been and where we are going, let alone who we actually are, not to a deepness that allows us to be truly at peace with the one person that actually makes any difference in our lives and on our satisfaction in life itself, ourselves.

It gives us a chance to empty our minds of the clutter that builds up through any and every busy day and to sort out those things that matter and, just as importantly, those that do not. Some we can simply dump, forever, lose and let go of; although it is always a surprise what we can dredge up when required or more often when we least want it. Then they can bother us no more, we can move on and our lives can be freer, lighter and more mentally nimble, not weighed down or dragged back by the past wrongs that we have inflicted or have been inflicted on us. Suddenly, our central processor, the brain, is able to focus on the things that are of importance rather than trying to multitask on those articles that we should have forgotten. We forgive and we are forgiven – and we are free! This is the truest definition of redemption; to be at one with ourselves.

It is also that opportunity for us to sort out how we feel about decisions and directions as yet to be chosen and committed to. So often we launch into new ideas that seem so good on first appraisal. With reflection we are able to take stock, make informed judgements and to do the right thing for us or for them, knowingly weighing up the costs, the benefits and even being able to make a wise compromise when the time counts.

And then, when thoughts have passed and our minds are looser and more relaxed, when we reach that point of time where we are happy just to be whom we are and to be content even if we are still a work in progress, finally we can befriend ourselves and just enjoy relaxing in our own company. We do not need to prove anything as we know who we are. We do not need to talk at length or be funny as we share the same thoughts. We do not need to impress, display, teach or learn as we already know all of these things. But we can look inwards on ourselves, or outwards at our world, in a way that is neither critical nor self-satisfied, but that is relaxed and at one.

Himself at peace, in a way he had not felt for many years, Sol sat within the arms of his plastic chair with the incoming loch water rising to touch his now bare toes in its frothy tideline. His boots and socks had been moved up to the cottage wall and he felt secure that he was safe as the water lapped up to be around him, a strange form sat in the sudsy clear-green like some modern day King Canute. He however knew that he could not control the tide.

The water's clarity allowed him to see depth as shallowness with the refraction of the light being bent to give him an opposing view to the fish in the further puddles. He could see them, eyes positioned to scan upwards as they gambolled along sands amongst now submerged rock pools that had re-joined after their tidal fragmentation brought on by the water's retreat. What had been stranded in diminishing salted tarns, unable to affect the happenings in any other, now became adjoined through Siamese extensions of connecting water and an eventual flood as the sea over-ran and finally swallowed all up in its unremitting advance up the beach.

Orange and green crabs scuttled sideways pincers adept as they swashbuckled at transparent grey shrimps who skipped on their many legs out of and into the shadows of weeds where they became invisible but active. They flickered between perceptible and not, shooting backwards in tail twitches when their elongated antennae detected the slightest disturbance in the waters they analysed, filtered and explored.

A stone-sand camouflaged flounder flew past the chair legs as a graceful, sinuous be-speckled plate, its awkward double eyes placed close together in their *'forever upwards'* stare. It sunk into the silt under the white plastic using the shade it provided as cover, burying itself into the coral dust and suddenly disappearing from view, an ambush now set and waiting as its syphon-like gills blew the silts into mock ripple-prints to complete the disguise.

The shells of limpets and winkles slowly grazed their way in spiralling random motions leaving hieroglyphic patterns of cropped algae etched into the rocks where their radula tongues had scratched the surfaces clean. White dog whelks, the predators of the molluscan shore, pursued their quarry in slow motion in a death chase that could take hours to play out to its end, and the shadow of a larger fish passed within inches of Sol's seat as the clear water continued to rise.

Urchins wiggled their spiny routes over the sand and bruise-purple jellyfish drifted harmlessly pulsating in with the tide that lifted the limp iodine-black seaweeds into living jungles of gently wafting plant life. These took on new hues and unimagined shapes so very different from the land-flopped dreadlock contour-forms they were left as when stranded by the low tide. Here tiny silver darts of fish flocked and schooled and petite pipe-shaped dragon fish, cryptic weedy-finned and camouflaged, behaved as if they were part of the sea-elevated flora themselves, even moving with the rock of the tide as they sucked up passing invertebrates and tested the water for suspended creatures.

There is a complete world in a rock pool and a galaxy in a shoreline and a universe of life in the sea, and yet again Sol understood that he knew little of what he shared this planet with, drawn through fascination to each moving thing that ripped his attention down and to the sides.

Gerry found him that morning half-submerged in the rising water, sat slumped on a near-floating plastic chair, which was pushed and pulled by the tidal flow, staring low into the water, nose in contact with the choppy, rising sea. If she had not been more aware she would have hit him as she raced *Sireadh-thall* into the cove at *Bothan Faobhar* and was quite concerned that he might have drowned or just sat out and died there last night until she saw him move. A man fixated with the interest of a child on discovering nature for the first time.

"What are you doing?" she asked as she pulled the boat up alongside and leapt out to pull on the painter and beach her.

Sol whipped his head up and out of the water.

"I need a mask," he said as if in reply, salting dripping down his sea-reddened face from hair that hung long and twisted over his forehead where it gripped his scalp in wet, oily straggles.

"What?" She had the boat up on the rocks above. "Why?"

"To see under the water." His reply was innocent, vacant of thought for what was passing the other's mind. "Goggles would do, but a mask and a snorkel...   ...I need to order them today. I'll get flippers too." He was incredulous that she didn't understand as we so often are when we are preoccupied with our personal thoughts and forget that not everyone has travelled with us on our own mental journeys.

"And a wet suit if you don't want to die the death of cold!" she grinned securing the mast and wrapping the sail. "What are you doing?"

"Have you ever looked down there?" he pointed down in to the water as fish darted in a dispersive school that parted from where his finger would have hit had it been a predator. The silver-bodied bait-ball remade itself and twitched its sinuous way over the submarine terrain and out into deeper water where it became one with the blue-green.

"Yes, but only when the tide is out to collect seaweeds for food, medicine or fertiliser. Even that's considered unusual and just slightly nerdy. I've never read of anyone using a plastic chair to do it though." She returned to the edge of the water, to where the surf crackled rhythmically against the blackened bedrock and where only the channel wrack, a fucoid brown crepuscular weed with multiple gullied fronds, hugged the ground, left exposed to demarcate the upper most reaches of the intertidal region. Zoned, each to their type and their exacting requirements for biotic and abiotic factors, the seaweeds changed in species depending on their position on the shore. Such zonation is a well-known and predictable fact of ecology, but like so many things, it is only obvious and familiar if you know about it.

"It's incredible!" he exclaimed. "There's so much life in there, and so close to the cottage. Fish, shrimps, weeds..." and he held a grasped handful of saw wrack up in his hand, deep black and serrated along each thalloid border.

"Helped by a lack of pollution and no disturbance... ...except of course for the lunatic sat on a plastic chair ripping up sections of seaweed. Sol, most people stop rock pooling when they are about eight or nine years old. What are you doing?"

"Revisiting my past I think," he replied. "Going back to being eight or nine years old. I think everyone should do it. I've been out for hours and, well... ...well, I've seen loads."

He left his throne-like position and pulled the rocking plastic chair out of the water before together they dragged *Sireadh-thall* further up on to the beach and away from the tide and Gerry replaced the plastic chair high up on dry ground to drip. It was well beyond where the sand hoppers skipped between piles of seaweed detritus and the pipits and wagtails chased them. But the zonation of life continued up the shore, through lichens and then terrestrial plants, the thrifts and the grasses, before replacement by the woodland proper; a gradation of complexity, colour and diversity.

Halo illuminated flies caught the glare of the morning sun and lifted steadily in breezy patterns to rise in growing clouds of ethereal light-crystallised wings, and the outline of a small hawk floated an effortless course just over the tree tops behind the *Bothan*. Except for the trace of a jet's white-clouded vapour trail, high up beyond where the buzzards had started their daily ascent in wandering thermal pursuit, and the presence of the house itself, no one would have suspected the discovery of this land by humans, or at least they would have been forgiven for thinking that they had forgotten it. There was the stain of past anthropomorphic activity, of course there was. But it was limited and had been here long enough to take on an organic nature of its own.

Gerry extracted a cotton satchel from the boat and a willow trug covered in a check-patterned tea towel, red and white.

"Breakfast," she explained seeing Sol's questioning look as they returned to the kitchen where she set a good fire for him to warm up and dry by. His wet clothes were already steaming in the early sunshine out on the line in the yard, having been pushed through a mangle she had discovered under a pile of equipment in the sheds. "There's a few supplies in there for the day too," she added as she bustled through her basket and bag producing a loaf, oatcakes, butter, cheese, fresh and desiccated mushrooms and herbs, speckled eggs, and piled slices of red-brown fat-marbled bacon, thick-sliced and home-cured. "All produced or collected from within ten miles of here," she stated with a grin. "This lot has a smaller carbon footprint than anything you can get from the supermarket, whatever they claim."

Her smile quickly faded as she saw the state of the front room, the litter of boxes, packaging, plastic and tape. It was the spoils of a war with modern deliveries and our current obsession with wrapping everything up too well for fear of damage.

"Sol, what's going on here?"

"Packaging," he replied shivering.

"Yes, I know. But what are you going to do with it all?" and she started to sift through it critically. "In the city you might have your rubbish collected, but not here. It needs sorting into compostable, recycling, burnable and unusable for landfill." She turned and was met by incomprehension on Sol's face. "What I mean is, it's *your* job to sort it out and to dispose of it. No one else is going to do it. Compost goes behind the sheds, recycling you need to collect and then take down to New Town when you have enough, burnable you keep dry in a shed until you need it for the fire and landfill needs bagging up and leaving at the end of the drive every other Thursday. If you are lucky and the council remembers we're here, they will collect it for you and take it well away. Where else do you think it's going to go? And," she returned to the kitchen to check something she suspected she would find there. "Yes. I thought so. You can start by sorting that out too." Sol followed her finger to the brimming kitchen bin and a shiver of revulsion passed up then down his spine.

"But, that's disgusting," he moaned.

"Yes. But it is also yours and nobody else's and so you get the pleasure of sorting it out."

"I'll need gloves."

"And where do you think you'll find them? And if you did find them wouldn't you need to dispose of them too?" Sadly, Sol knew that he was beaten.

Whilst Gerry cooked over a glowing stove, producing the most appetising and welcoming bacon aroma, the one responsible for the fall of so many vegetarians, Sol spent a miserable few minutes, still with iced fingers and toes, and a cold-blue nose, collecting and dispersing rubbish. He was eventually left with very little that would need taking down to landfill, more recycling than he thought he would have and plenty to burn or start a fire with.

"In future," said Gerry with the air of a disappointed teacher who knew better than her failing student, "sort it out as you produce it. The kitchen bin really is the worst invention!" She then handed him the bacon rinds. "Hang these in the trees behind the sheds next to the bird feeders and see what birds you attract."

Submissively he went round to the wood side of the sheds, with the aromatic smell of cooking continually drawing his nose back towards the kitchen. Here he hung the bacon strips on strings already tied to branches with blunted fish hooks knotted to their ends like some macrbre outdoor butcher's shop. Knowing that breakfast would still be a few minutes he then returned to the seed shed and collected seeds and nuts to fill the other feeders.

Even before he had finished he knew that the birds were aware of his presence and what he was doing. With an obvious sense of expectation the blue tits had started to *'whirr'* ever louder in their readiness, and they in turn had drawn in the other songbirds that chirruped and called, squeaked and whistled. As he crept away backwards they flew in from every angle, some to the feeders and others to the scraps he had dropped to the floor. Squabbles broke out despite there being plenty and he had to laugh at the selfishness of the few trying to dominate the ample resources. It was like watching the market traders on a good day, attempting to guard the best for themselves when there was so much available that everyone could have some if only they didn't squander it. But, the most dominant didn't always win even though they defended their little spaces well. They were overwhelmed or cheated and Sol wondered about his own overall success in the city.

Where had these birds all been until now? How long had they been waiting? What had they done in the meantime? How did they know that the feeders would have been filled at some time?

A call from the kitchen sent them flying back into the canopy and the shrub layer, and propelled Sol himself back to claim his breakfast, butter fried herby mushrooms, a unique Demerara-flavoured bacon, slab-cut grainy bread and yolk dripping fried eggs, two each. They ate off their knees in the middle of the yard on a tatted rug cast under a sun that competed with the cobalt of the sky and the blackness of the silhouetted forest. It was bliss and Sol knew that Gerry was right in that they had become brother and sister in that way best friends really do. He sensed it in their companionship and conversation, in the way that she gently directed but chastised him too, and he felt it deep within his soul.

After the dishes were cleaned as near to spotless as the peat-brown water would allow and Gerry had instructed Sol to clear away the still-packed belongings he had left boxed in his bedroom, she showed him the dried herbs and mushrooms that she had brought him and explained what they could be used for. Then she gave him a brief lesson in finding some of them within just a few feet of the *Bothan*, believing that '*if you can teach a man to fish he will feed himself*'. Next she instructed him to wash in the bath shed, regardless of the temperature and suggested he shaved or at least brushed his teeth and combed his hair. He was after all about to meet his tenants.

Following a standing shower in the bath, which was only just this side of freezing and made him reflexively gasp an intake of air as the water hit him, and the embarrassment of having to call for a towel as he had left his in the house, he went to shave but found that his electric razor had lost all charge. Gerry came to the rescue and trimmed his beard using scissors and by running a comb through it whilst Sol watched red squirrels descending on the peanuts in the feeder hanging behind the bath shed and jays picking up the windfalls. The wild things had no interest in the human beings, being too preoccupied with those things that kept them alive or prepared them for the production of future generations.

Next he went to brush his teeth, but the brush had by now lost power too, its battery being old and him regularly forgetting to charge or replace it. His dependency on power provided through the magic of the copper wire was excruciatingly obvious and he fumed, then worried, before Gerry appeared at the bathroom door concerned about the time he was taking. Gone for a few moments, she returned back holding spearmint leaves to chew on to freshen his breath and a splintered greenstick she then asked him to scrub around his mouth after wetting it and then mixing it with a paste she had created out of bicarbonate of soda found in the kitchen stores.

Not prepared to wait much longer, she combed his hair and then sent him to the bedroom to put the borrowed clothes on she had selected for him to wear and left folded and spread on the bed.

"Don't expect it every day," she called after him. "Oh and you've been so long that I've washed the things you've been wearing up until now too. Please tell me someone taught you to wash clothes without a washing machine before?"

He gave her a withered look as he crossed the yard in only the flapping wool towel like some Egyptian slave of a long past era, to which she sighed, not for the first time, in reply.

Eventually, with the sun high in the sky and the morning's dawn chorus lulled to a quiet ebb, Sol found himself ready for the day's adventure and prepared to meet his tenants. He was far more presentable than he had been and Gerry felt that he would cut a more dapper figure as the new laird looking the way he did now. She was almost proud of what she had achieved in so short a time – a far cleaner house and a much cleaner man.

Sol sorted insurance of the Land Rover over the phone and was shocked at the saving it incurred from that of his now abandoned sports car. He had to re-check that the clerk was being serious and then agreed to accept the money back into his account, a feature he had never experienced with insurance before.

Gerry opted to drive the Land Rover and show Sol how to handle the primitive vehicle, its clutch and old-fashioned gears, the low and high ratios, the road and the local terrain. She talked him through the heavy steering, the track's camber and the way to overcome a ditch and a rise, and then almost without warning she veered off right up a barely discernible offshoot of the drive and headed for all intents and purposes through a clump of gnarled, lichen-weighted pine trees and out on to the hillside.

"You know an awful lot about cars," Sol commented as they were thrown bodily about the rustic cabin.

"Need to if you're going to drive round here." She replied as matter of fact, shouting over the roar of the engine. "Else what happens if I break down or crash and there's no one about to help me?"

"Call someone else?" he offered, still suffering from the assumptions of the city.

"Who would I call? And what about the signal?"

"True." They cut on upwards on a track that made Sol feel as if the car would tip if they leant too far backwards. It launched itself in a steep rising snake that cut deep through the plant life forming a gorge which ended where the tyres found water-streamed rocks that were sunk into the mud. Between the gaps sheep-cropped grasses clung and mounds of wheel-gripped moss formed dense cushions of viridian and lemon yellow. Pink-chested linnets kept look out from the whin bushes that threatened to roof in the lane at times and a kestrel sky-gripped the air below the clouds before it swooped on to another stationary site further along.

Several times they crossed rickety stone bridges that gripped the steep-sided burn-flooded valleys whose fingers extended between the mountain's outcropped extensions. The unkempt ill-edged road, if that is what it could be classified as, had age and sung a history of well use over many years.

"Where are we going?" he asked after a time of silence.

"We're about to pass your garage and then we're going on up to see the first of your tenants, Euan and Sarah McCann. Nice people, both of them shepherds." She fought the wheels' natural desire to spin them off to some unknown grave far below until they passed a large series of interconnected barns that had once served as stables for a large farm or property nearby. Tyre tracks, which no doubt matched Addie's in reflection, led out of the largest stall suggesting that this was Sol's garage.

"More storage for you if you need it," Gerry confirmed indicating the impressive court-encircling buildings.

They continued along the rut-track until they came across a small but adequate house built into the crags of the hillside for protection.

It had a pretty, well-kept garden, walled in from the livestock, which was over-sown with the flapping of the day's washing that flicked in the wind on a tightly strung line. They were firstly greeted by the exuberance of two collies that ran out to welcome them in that near-aggressive but enthusiastic and tail-waggingly friendly way that only a hill-farm dog can. They scared the wagtails up into agitated bob-flight, dragging their tails feathers behind them as they limped the air to the security of a wall top and a shed, and a robin sensing an interesting turn of events, held its position on a fence post so that it could watch these human proceedings; always ready to take advantage if the chance arose.

A young, heavily pregnant, fair-haired woman came to the door and raised a smile in acknowledgment of their arrival. She wore dirty jeans over hole-adorned trainers that had scuffed rough in places and was draped in a dark blue woollen jumper, badly fit and two sizes too large. Sol and Gerry were rapidly and almost silently ushered past an antiquated tractor and a rusting car as soon as they dropped out of Addie, and then it was quickly into a warm dark kitchen that smelt of food and was humid with cooking.

"This," Gerry explained, "is Sol," and she pushed him forward as if for inspection.

"I guessed as much," replied the lady sitting down at the clean table in the well-appointed room, poorly lit by the open door and a small window over the sink. "I must say, you move fast Gerry." But she was quickly cut down by a hard stare from across the table where Gerry leaned and fumed.

"Hello," interrupted Sol reaching his hand forward in open greeting and attempting to stop the only drama that could result from such a start to the conversation. "I just wanted to come up and say hello really…"

"And to discuss the rent I presume?" the other stated sombrely.

"Of course, yes. But all in good time."

"Well, Euan's out with the sheep but left this letter for you in case you arrived. It outlines everything," and with this, she pushed a scruffy envelope over to Sol, purposefully away from Gerry. "I don't know what it says. Can't read so well, nor write."

Sol was shocked but didn't want to show it. He had enjoyed a privileged education and had presumed that everyone had at least the most rudimentary skills with words and numbers.

"Thank you," he said as he picked it up and read the biro-scrawled writing on the front and he opened it up to reveal the hard-won letters that formed the well-worded, formal message inside.

'*Dear Mr Solomon,*

Welcome to the Faobhar Estate.

I hope that Sarah and I can remain as tenants of yours at our cottage Bothan Fáire. The last laird was very generous allowing me to continue as shepherd after my father, and we are now expecting our first-born soon. I hope that I can carry on this role as it is all I am trained to do and one that I greatly enjoy. Sarah used to clean your house and would gladly do this again when she is able to.

The last laird bought me the dogs and we hope to have pups from them this year. They are good workers and have done well in the local trials. If you want one, let me know and we will choose you a good one out of the litter.

I am not sure what the rate of payment will be but we are currently paying rent at £10 per month so long as we keep the moors well-trimmed for the bird life and burn it on rotation when we can. I also provide 6 lambs a year for the table and several that I have been keeping, and my father before him, for the old laird, as G never wanted them. You currently have four hundred and twenty sheep in my part of the flock, many of which will lamb soon, which we will sell if and when you need us to. The wool is not worth much and there is no great market for our lamb or mutton either. Currently Hamish and I sell enough sheep to manage the stock and keep our families fed. I manage my own thirty sheep too as per previous agreements.

Please let me know by return of letter if this is still okay or if you need to change any of the previous agreements.
Yours sincerely,
Euan McCann'
Sol sat and read the letter slowly, fighting the twisted script to make sense of the words as the fire crackled in the hearth and Sarah stirred a cold cup of tea round and round, noisily scraping the side of the porcelain with her spoon. There was an over-thumbed second hand book of baby names left open on the table, pages down to damage the spine, clutter around the place, but it was clean, and a quiet ewe-less lamb lay curled up snug in front of the cooker in a box and under a crocheted blanket. Hung from the wall opposite the range was a medium-sized painting of a shepherd tending a flock of sheep tinted orange-red by a fiery setting sun. On the rocks beyond a beautiful woman sang, combing her hair and staring out across the sea.
"Cailleach's sheep," said Sarah, answering Sol's embryonic question before he could ask it. "She watches over the shepherds who tend her flocks. She's one of the old religion."
Sol nodded his thanks and then re-focused, taking in everything he could in the way he had done when buying up new stock, profiling them, learning about them, calculating the value of assets and potential. There were a million distractions to Sol's concentration but he busily measured his surroundings, weighing them up.
Nothing spoke of wealth or excessive spending. If they were making money then they didn't show it. At ten pounds a month, they were living almost rent free and G had obviously intended only to charge them so that they didn't feel that they were being treated as charity. There was a baby on the way and they would need things for it.
A clock ticked remorselessly in the background drilling holes into Sol's mind, and for a moment he was taken back to his grandfather's house in the country. He was never rich but never without. He lacked plenty but was not short of anything. He was

wise and knowledgeable but not recognised for it. His home was on a farm but it was never his.

And then he thought of his own brother, just fleetingly. Eventually Sol spoke.

"Do you have paper Sarah?" Sarah collected him a sheet of paper and a pen, a cheap rollerball probably free from somewhere. "And I would love a cup of tea if there is one?" He almost asked it as a question but it came out more as a command and he chastised himself internally as he pulled up a heavy wooden chair to write.

Sarah seemed glad to have something to do. She looked worriedly down as Sol began to pen his thoughts. He knew she was concerned that he was about to raise the rent to that which they could not afford and at a time when they needed a home and some money the most. She made a mug of tea for both Sol and Gerry and then sat back down wringing her fingers through her hair and apron. Sol felt her distress.

'Dear Euan,

Thank you for your welcome to the estate. I little knew how much I had taken on a few weeks ago when I first looked at Bothan Faobhar.

I am pleased that you want to stay on as shepherd at Bothan Fáire and gladly accept your offer to do so. Please do come down to Bothan Faobhar whenever you are passing to keep me informed as to how the flock is progressing and anything you need to keep them in good health. I am keen to learn about the animals of the moors and so need you to tell me what birds and other animals you see and how we can conserve the wildlife that is on the estate. I encourage you to advise me as much as possible as up here is very different to London. You are always welcome in for a drink too.

As for cleaning, once Sarah has had your baby please come down and let me know so that I can congratulate you both in person and only when she is ready should she come down to start work again. The house needs a cleaner and I can see from your own house that she is good at it. I will leave £50 with her to secure her cleaning services in the meantime. Please put it towards baby items and clothing.

As for rent, if you feel able to change I would like to alter your rent to £5 per month whilst Sarah is not working and to increase it back to £10 once you feel able.

Please watch the moors for me and once lambing is over I would like to have you and your family down to Bothan Faobhar for dinner and maybe to see your dogs working at a trial.

Thank you for your work on the estate.

Yours sincerely,

S'

Sol slurped tea and folded the letter up before handing it and £50 in notes over to Sarah.

"What's this for?" she asked.

"A retainer," Sol explained politely but firmly.

"What for?"

"To clean my house once you feel ready…   …after you've had the baby."

"But…" and she looked at Gerry.

"Trust me," Gerry interjected, "he needs all the help he can get."

"So you two aren't?" Sarah asked with a strange relief.

"Oh no," laughed Sol, "she's just my sister…   …well, like my sister anyway. True she has just cleaned my house, but it was more out of pity than anything else. I really am quite useless at it."

Sarah relaxed a little more, then as Sol finished his tea and headed to the door she asked, "and what about the rent?"

"What about it?" Sol replied turning from the light of the outside to the dark confinement of the kitchen, feeling an odd pull to be free of buildings and out there on the moors and within the life of the land.

"Has it changed, as we can't afford much?"

"Yes, it has."

Sarah's eyes widened. "By how much?"

"Five pounds."

"Oh. I was expecting more."

"Five pounds down," he explained, and with this Sol vanished from the kitchen and he and Gerry left as quickly as they could.

In the Land Rover, Gerry fired the beast up and they chugged happily over the moors following the track upwards to a crossroads from which they could look up to the mist-capped mountain that marked the end of Sol's land.

"Are all the rents in that range?" Sol asked as they pulled up to the side of the lane as it levelled slightly, Gerry braking so as not to disturb a padding group of Black Grouse at a lek.

"Probably," Gerry replied.

"What's your rent?"

"I used to pay in pheasant, deer, plants I collected and specimens for G's notes or collections, and any food or medicine I gathered for free. Like Euan, Hamish pays in sheep and news of the moors. He's also a useful handyman. Old Joe is nearly blind but somehow still manages to get fish enough to pay his way. He finds salmon, trout, grayling and occasionally comes up with pike and eels. He'll bring some fresh for you some days out of the blue and at other times he'll home-smoke them and bring you a whole batch. No one knows how he does it, but then he is still officially the gillie on the upper loch and rivers. Sally runs your woods and uses the old hunting lodge. I already know that she's concerned you'll use up all your wood before the winter. She'll pay in fuel and build anything you want...   ...so long as it's made of wood. There are some occasional workers up with her too and the gossip is that she takes a fancy to one of them every so often. Again, she's not making much but creates bowls and chairs in her workshop during the winter out of interesting bits of wood she finds. Sells a few from the side of the road and at trials."

Sol considered what he was hearing as a fine gloss-feathered black grouse that was belly flopping in the dust of the track suddenly started clucking to himself as another bird approached. Flattened to the ground, they circled each other with tails erect and wings arched backwards and spread. A warbled gurgle erupted from within each of them as they orbited in robotic posture, ballooning their throats and erecting their scarlet eye wattles. Brown female heads lifted from the surrounding heather stems, interested.

Gerry continued to speak and cut the engine to enjoy the grouse display.

"There are a few outlying properties where folks have settled. They'll give you fruit at the proper time – strawberries, raspberries and blackberries, currants and apples. You'll not be made rich by living here, but you'll never starve either! I just hope you didn't expect any money from the estate. She won't pay well."

One male suddenly gave a dominant chuckle and chased the incomer away and into the shrubs of the moor where it scooted into the shelter of the craggy rocks. The former, puffed up with pride, lifted its head and ambled into a swooning crowd of female onlookers, the wags of their species. His chest was out, his power obvious, his resource and resultant sexual prowess without question – *Sol had been there before, but how strange that even though he felt in some great position of power now as owner of this estate, patrolling it with Gerry, dominance was the last thing on his mind.*

There was a tall wooden post at the head of the crossroads just ahead of them made into a shape that suggested intended, possibly morbid, design by the addition of a cross strut supporting a perpendicular bar.

"What's that for?" Sol questioned.

"That," Gerry explained, "was the gibbet from which they used to hang offending people and ravens. It was built on the crossroads so that it gave the spirit of the dead four choices of which way to go and reduced the chances of them coming back to haunt the executioners or judges."

"But why ravens? They're just birds." The grouse had cleared the area leaving only their telescopic-necked heads visible and now chuckling from within the heather.

"Not any more. G put a stop to that. Except for the rain and the cold, the ravens are still the shepherd's worst enemy. The Corbie as they are known around here will pick the eyes out of lambs and any stranded sheep. They couldn't hang the rain out on a gibbet as a warning to prevent more rain so they used to hang the ravens here as symbol to other ravens not to hang around."

The crossroads felt cold and spiritually negative with its lonely half rotted scaffold. But then Sol spotted the white stains of guano dripping dried down its sides and knew that at least some wild thing was taking advantage of even this item of torture and death. Bright yellow ringed mushrooms at the base, sprouting from where the sward grew thickest and greenest, even suggested that the timbers themselves were being reclaimed.

"Did it work?"

"Well no. The ravens used to come and eat the dead ravens as a snack in between lambs. But you try correcting a shepherd when they've got a thousand years of folklore behind them!"

Bees and flies hummed resonantly over the sprouting moorland where cottony heads were beginning to show and the occasional creeping willow was coming into leaf as it stalked over the ground religiously following its every contour. The red-green oval leaves of blaeberry were breaking the surface in clumps and the bog grasses and spongy mosses took over where pools had formed and water trickled its way down into the glens; the terrestrial trying to overcome the aquatic.

There was still the outbreak of snow here and there, now clearing up like a summer-cured form of acne on the landscape, and Sol was surprised to see coal-dusted butterflies casting shadow puppets over it.

High above the lark patriarchs of the sky held their positions and skilfully sang in twiddled melodies that helped Sol recall the days of playing Vaughan Williams' descriptive pieces for violin. Meadow pipits and linnets flitted amongst the fading gorse and a thrush tapped out a snail from its shell on its anvil stone. Sheep bleated and bayed and a distant herd of deer watched with the comfort of knowing no danger was imminent if the humans were parked up so far away but still kept a healthy watch on the two humans as they spoke.

For a moment the mountain cleared enough for Sol to see the top.

"It's a dangerous place that, so do beware," said Gerry following his stare upwards. "I know that in telling you that, you'll be up there in no time. But trust me, you need a map, supplies and a bit of local knowledge. I'll draw something up for you as no doubt you'll try it alone some day!"

If 'sea fever' is a state that drives humans to recklessness in pursuit of the water, then 'mountain fever' and the enchantment and exhilaration of the climb must also exist as a genetic-borne predisposition to seek thrills at height and to achieve every peak possible or otherwise, and at any cost. Sol's heart skipped an unheard medley within his chest as he took in the cragged and shadow daubed iced ridges that ascended and bordered the massif up to its crescendo and connected it in an arc through its range and then back down to re-join first the boiling firmament of cloud lands and then the real Earth.

'I will have to climb that,' he thought in a voice he kept inside but it found itself sounded out loud in the expression it painted across his face and body, and Gerry knew that she would need to act fast to equip him well enough to keep him safe from his own self-belief. Too many die needlessly on the mountains each year. She did not want this man to be one of them.

They had approached the crossroads from the south, meeting an intersection of mountain paths coming in from either side across the moor in a broad corrie between peaks. For the rest of the day they visited tenants taking one or other of the tracks except for the more northerly one. Every time they returned to this place Sol realised that his ambition of funding the estate through rent was becoming slimmer, but at the end of the lengthy moorland driveways he found the nicest of people living. They were surviving without many worldly goods, but inhabiting very complete and filled lives crammed with things which required little or no money or could simply be found or supplied for free; value without value.

The Land Rover cab slowly filled up with home grown food, homemade produce, knitted jumpers and even a hand carved bowl given in thanks for Sol's kindness in keeping the rents low and accepting other payments in kind.

Sally at the wood yard promised him a chair, continually slapping him on the back and making him feel subordinate in a way he had become unaccustomed to but basically had no choice but to accept. She showed him her workshop where half-completed seats and turned bowls were stacked up in her slow production line waiting for the winter and the time for her to finish them. It was the ultimate snail's work space where nothing was hurried and little was complete, everything biding a future time to face its final reckoning. And yet, like the inch-progressing tortoise in its race against the hare and the persistent grass that outlives the gardener, patience was winning out, natural shapes were etched up and out of the knots, twists and grain of organic material. And something beautiful was emerging in each rustic construction as if it had been guided by the hand of the environment by some master craftswoman who spent the time listening to its instruction. Even the mucor'd stain of a fungus' hyphae was accounted for and utilised in her artistic pursuits.

She proudly toured him around the yard, the stacked timbers and a variety of mushrooms, some edible, others not worth the trouble and yet more deadly, many of which seemed to look the same to the bewildered and slightly over aught Sol. Identification cues unlearnt, he knew that there was much more to acquire about these mystic non-plants that had received only the briefest of mentions at school where classification was dominated by the animals and even then only by the mammals and in particular that one dominant species *Homo sapiens.*

They left by an airy barn door by which hung framed photographs of gnarled old trees, ferns in unfurled glory, dew-dropped leaves and a work in oil of a tree in to which was cleverly introduced the body and face of a female wood spirit.

"The green man re-worked as the green woman," Sally explained following Sol's gaze. "I wouldn't have it any other way."

Seventy-three year old Joe, the gillie, sat quietly in his dimly lit shieling cottage by the upper loch remaining ever-close to an old picture, faded with the sunlight, of a well-dressed lady from a different age. On the wall Sol saw a painting in the style he had seen in each house already. It was a fine oil of a great-horned bull emerging from the loch, water dripping from its well-muscled flanks. He recognised the loch from the waters still visible through the old-dusted kitchen window which had accumulated the blown sediments of the land, the space dirt of the universe and the skin sloughs of a generation; the dust that normally only becomes visible when we break open an ancient mattress and witness the mite-supporting fragments that have been deposited within. Sol did not ask what the picture was of, too embarrassed at the old man's weak sight and finding his past-sight way of looking across rather than at anyone speaking to him uncomfortable. Emotion and manner were difficult to comprehend with unfocused pupils that stared somewhere over your shoulder.

He worried about this man and questioned in his mind how he could maintain himself so far up on the hillside, under the shadow of the mountain in isolation and without sight. All he had was this house to rent and a poor view of a loch, a mountain and a moor. Sol pitied him his presumed loneliness, lacking vision, lacking companionship and lacking technology of the type that could assist him in any way. He left moved, if unknowingly wrong in his initial assumptions.

But the man seemed content, if quiet, contemplative yet somehow at ease as if he had given up on any greater achievement than his lot in this world. As Addie took Gerry and Sol back towards the crossroads Joe hobbled to a wooden bench at the back of the gillie cottage where he painfully sat and then relaxed, leaning his chin on a wooden walking stick and taking on the posture and gaze of one watching and waiting for something coming from over the loch, over the mountain or over the moor.

The others they visited either nervously ushered Sol in or around their houses pointing out the problems, sat and listened whilst he guided their conversation, or just seemed glad of a bit of company in their far flung locations. Like the visiting vicar travelling their parish, he was filled up to leaking point with tea and crammed to capacity with cake. He could see that the estate was managed well, if mainly on good will, and that so long as he could fund it, he could spend the time continuing with G's research and study in the certain knowledge that there was a genuine love for the land, its wilderness and its perpetuation.

But money was one thing that was lacking in the area, and he was fiercely aware that his own finances would themselves become rapidly limited by unemployment, market slumps and a lack of confidence in his latest loan-stretching transaction, the fateful Tokyo deal. At first sight, many of the properties required attention and modernisation, each falling back to what nature would rather they were, and he guessed that these costs fell to him too.

"Well," broke in Gerry over his train of thought as they approached the crossroads for yet another time, whilst a buzzard drifted lazily at a distance, its 'ker-chee-yar' mews bounding the moorland to greet them. "That just leaves Hamish and me. Where to next?"

The mountain was in full view now. Its crags reached up high to connect with the sky and then fell steadily back in a sweeping sun-shaded horseshoe that encompassed the upper loch where Joe lived all on his own, quiet and satisfied, but isolated. From there, Gerry explained, he watched the fish through his near blind eyes and used his ears to see them better – or so he said – and the smell of the wind to determine the portent weather on the hillside.

Chough '*chacked*' under the crags, and Sol liked to think that the broad-winged raptor cycling the cloudless cobalt blue above it was some form of eagle, utilising its extended feather tips to draft on the rising thermals and scan the ground for carrion or prey. As his eyes fell down the hillside he could see the zonation of flora change from the windswept, snow-clagged rock faces through a region of lichens, mosses and then alpines that evolved into grasses and shrubs and then moorland which then scooped into the marsh and then on to here abutting up to the crossroads.

"This is the crossroads on the bealach," said Gerry, "from which you need to make a decision. Where do you want to go?"

"Bealach?" he asked, unfamiliar with the word.

"It means mountain pass. *Bealach na Crois-rathaid – the mountain pass of the crossroad.* It's the only way through to the houses in the winter when the snows come. Joe is cut off every year as he lives in a summer shieling all the year round. One day he'll die up there and no one will know until spring. But he doesn't seem to care about it though and is quite happy to wait until then. His wife died in that house some years back and he's just satisfied to wait where she left him until he can join her. He believes that one day the water bull, *Tarbh Uisge*, a good spirit of the loch, will rise up from the water and take him off to be with her. Every night he listens to the sound of the fish jumping in hope that one of them will be the bull. That's why he won't leave the summer shieling – he doesn't want to miss his chance to go with the bull. And that's why he always sits on that bench. He's waiting."

Gerry stopped talking and turned to Sol.

"Which way?" she asked abruptly. "It's your decision."

Sol was unsure. He forced the simple glass side window back against its will in the runner and it squeaked rudely through ill use.

'*Go-back, go-back*' clucked the red grouse from the heather mass and Sol drew in breath through the open window to test the honey-scent of the air and enjoy the aromas of the sea that blew from off the loch below. He went back in his mind as directed by the birds and walked with his grandfather across the farm that the old man had subsisted on.

He was a proud man but poor, herding the cattle and milking them for the farmer. He knew where to find the flowers in their seasons and when the migratory birds would return. He missed them when they left and counted the days until their return. He recorded the first bee's busy appearance and noted changes from year to year when buds burst, butterflies capered amongst the dapple light of the rides and if the weather was beyond the usual.

His life was an encyclopaedia of the old sayings concerned with crops, cattle, climate and wild things, and even when he was dim with age he was the first to hear the cuckoo and notice another sound, to break off mid-sentence and to pronounce what it was that had ripped his concentration away. He could smell the onset of rain and feel the vibration of distant thunder, identify friend or foe in the differing pitched buzz of a wasp-mimic fly or the real species it was modelled on without even seeing it. He had the skills to alight the taste buds with something fresh from the hedge and he could seal a cut or diminish pain with leaves, twigs and flowers. *How could the next two generations forget so much in so little time?*
'*Go-back, go-back*'

Sol felt the age-old significance of crossroads: both physically and metaphorically symbolic; always representing a meeting of many pathways and giving a choice of some kind, even if it is simply to turn around and go back the way you have come. He was disturbed by the lack of direction given by this meeting of roads in the middle of nowhere.

In life, we meet our journey's crossroads in much the same way as a traveller on the road or a walker on the path. Much depends on our state of mind, our life's goal, or the experiences we had when developing or else that happened just a few moments ago. Like *Pilgrim* on his progress, we don't always know which way is right, which will be hardest or which looks easy but leads either the wrong way or to somewhere unintended but perhaps equally as interesting.

We meet them, we deal with them, and we choose or else we just drift, take the recommendations of others or follow the most tempting, but not necessarily the best, routes. Each path we opt for leads at some point to another junction which could eventually lead to some place we never dreamt of or intended, through its many contorted decisions and diversions, future crossroads and track ways, some well-trodden and cutting deep into the ground as drove ways and hollow ways, others hidden by overgrowth and little explored.

Sol sat, stunned by this point on the estate in which he found himself.

The purchase of *Bothan Faobhar* on a whimsical midlife crisis decision had brought Sol to this crossroads on the moor from which he could see the land. *But was it really his? Could he buy a mountain, a loch, a moor, a river and the lives of the people and wildlife that depended upon it? Was that purchasable like one of his deals? Or was that all beyond price?*

He knew that many of the locals, whose ancestry in these parts extended well back to the Norse invasions of centuries ago, would not feel that he deserved any of this. He was also certain that one day, they would accept him if only he continued to take the right roads at the crossroads he came across.

'Go-back, go-back'

"We'll go back," he said. "We can leave Hamish until another day."

"Okay," Gerry answered as she turned the Land Rover south and they dropped down past Euan and Sarah's and then on to the garage where electricity wires fed power across the countryside, before they met the drive up to the *Bothan*.

"There's electricity to the garage?" quizzed Sol looking back at the starling-decorated wires suspended in loops from pole to pole.

"Yes, it's the closest that G would allow them to *Faobhar*."

"That's worth knowing."

"I'm sure it's not live, but could be switched on quite quickly if needed."

Then, after a period of silence, she stopped the car, turned to him and held him directly in her gaze. "But what about my rent?" she asked in earnest.

"How much is it?" he questioned in reply.

"Well I painted that picture of the stag and kept G supplied with pheasant, grouse, partridge and deer. And I was always bringing him plants to eat or collect... ...I also tended his garden. I've been doing it since too."

"Thank you. I didn't know."

"Gardens don't do themselves you know?" she laughed at his naivety. "They need weeding and feeding and planting out. That's why there are seedlings in pots in your porch ready to put out as it warms up."

"Thank you...   ...again. I've always got my veg from the supermarket wrapped up in plastic before," and he sniggered at how simple he knew he would be sounding. "Some came ready chopped."

"Well, if you order the plastic, I can wrap it up for you if it helps? But it's you who will have to recycle it! I'm not the greatest fan of plastic. Litters the place and takes millennia to break down."

"So what have I got growing in the garden?"

"You've done well this year so far. Carrots, beets, potatoes, swede or neeps, sprouts, broccoli, kale, cabbage, peas...   ...they can all be wrapped in plastic as I say! If you want it?"

"Only if we can have labels too!"

They both snorted as the vehicle rocked its way homeward, a terrestrial boat that rode the currents of a rubble'd trackway down into the valley.

"On the rent," she said and the laughter stopped. "G refused to charge me until he fixed the house and said that as he was never

going to fix it if I was rent free... ...so he wasn't going to fix it...
...I have no idea what your thoughts are on that?"
Sol thought for a while. "Paint me a picture," was his unexpected
answer.
"Well, it's a small cottage with a shed at the back that I use as a
gallery and it's in a bay like yours..."
"No," Sol interrupted. "Paint me a picture of something that makes
you think of me. There's the stag in *Bothan Faobhar*, that's one of
yours but it was for G and not for me. And, I saw paintings in each
of the houses we visited today and suspect there'll be one at
Hamish's too when I get there. They mean something don't they? I
mean, the stag in the *Bothan*, he's falling to the ground up on the
headland where G loved to go and sit. Joe had a Bull coming out of
the water, that's his water bull. Euan and Sarah, they had the sheep
hanging on the wall with the goddess of sheep watching over, and
he's a shepherd. Sally's was the green man of the woods only you
made her the green woman because there is no way that any green
man would get an upper hand over Sally. Am I right so far?"
"Yes," said Gerry humbly.
"So, do me a picture. Think about it and make it significant to what
you see in me – but don't paint a market trader whatever you do!
Your rent can be your commission. Take your time and let me
know the cost of the materials. You do plenty else for me in lieu of
rent and you're a friend."
Gerry was quiet for a while.
"You aren't quite the person we were all expecting." There was
another pause. "You do know that don't you?"
"Thanks... ...I think I do."
"We knew you were from the city and that making money was
what you did, but G obviously saw something different in you. It
appears he might have been right. You've a long way to go, but...
...well, there's some small hope for us all."
"Thanks... ...I think, again."

Journey's end found *Bothan Faobhar* patiently waiting for their return, tinted orange by a burning sun that was rapidly slipping below the curtain of the mountain horizon. A score of geese cut the air in a skewed skein that held them loosely together in aerodynamic union. They rolled around in finely-choreographed unison to ensure that each only stayed at the head for a short while. Sol almost wished that he could do this with the ownership of the *Bothan's* estate.

The geese vocalised in '*quaink-quaink*' branks as they passed comment and communication between each other from wisely furrowed brows over pink-veiled bills with the observers on the ground wishing they knew what advice and insight they were offering from so far up.

A woodcock roded somewhere nearby and the last woodpecker '*chipped*' night-thoughts that silenced the ever-present coal tits.

There was a lamb-soft fleece on the doorstep with a brief note attached to it written in spidery biro'd writing.

'Sol,
Thank you.
Euan and Sarah McCann'

Sol was glad to be home and to have the chance to rest his aching back. Once the fire was lit, the pot was on and the natural light felt near to its final drop, he waved to Gerry as she took his boat back to her own abode for the night. He was charged with that double emotion of sadness that she was leaving him and gladness that the place was now his alone again.

He left the phone on silent and ignored the missed messages and calls it retained ready for his next venture into its digital world, and went instead to leave his bone, skin and dinner-remnant sacrifice to the wildcat outside. This time he would place the bucket where he could easily watch it from the front room. And then, whilst the rich stew of roots, leaves and chunks of meat, all given to him by his tenants, cooked itself in the oven, he took off his shoes and socks, sank into G's old chair and enjoyed the feeling of warm, plush lamb's wool between his toes.

The tawny owl launched its first haunting assault on the night air and the ultrasonic screeches of the bats could be detected in the back of his skull as they penetrated through the open porch door. The scrabble of mice was easily ignored and the squabble of ducks and waterfowl out on the loch listened to attentively.

With a less than elegant glass in his hand, he supped homemade red wine as the fire fought off the cooling of the night air and the first midges found their way into the living area. Later he would face them in full force and sit a vigil to spot his wildcat friend.

Sol sent thoughts of money flying from his financially trained mind, a poverty cat sent amongst note-shaped pigeons. He was not going to be worth very much, but from now on he was going to try and value everything he had in a different way and probably become a much wealthier individual.

Chapter 14: To a Different Tune

(Scottish Fantasy in E-flat major, Op 46, Max Bruch)

Expectation is so often more important than outcome.
When we expect something but gain nothing we are left bereft and disappointed, demanding something in recompense for the way we feel. It can lead to a desire for revenge or a charged emotion that makes us more likely to justify some poor action or behaviour. If we expect too much, then we are doomed in some way, even if those we expect something from have no way of knowing what we want or need from them.
When we expect nothing, or very little, yet gain something, we are consistently pleased with the result. We have something, someone cares or the world is a good place after all in which to live, and we have achieved where we thought we could not. Low expectation may be a result of a past disappointment and could be an inward expression of our outward view on life and those we share this planet with, but it does mean that we benefit and can be happy on receipt of any gift, kind act, financial gain or improvement.
When we have no expectations at all then our lives are without ambition or desire and we are rendered partially inhuman as a result of poor vision of others, of life or even of our selves.
But when we have them and our high expectations are met, or surpassed, either through our own ingenuity or as a result of others, or even just pure chance, then we have a moment to be savoured, enjoyed and possibly to be built upon. It is this scientific development that has driven many an engineer on in their pursuit of a soluble design brief, using a logical and sometimes serendipitous method to predict results from which expectations can be tested and a theory given confidence enough to be a success, or in the least be deemed acceptable.

Sol chose to sit out in the front garden awaiting the wildcat with a mix of expectations. He knew what he wanted to see but was also acutely aware that the chances of its passing in the night to within just a few feet of where he sat was something that many would never experience. However, he was also lucky to be sitting in a place where the cat had passed before and he had tipped the odds in his favour by being right here, right now in the un-comfort of the cold, with food provided as bait for the potential animal, to lure it in despite its natural timidity and fear of man. But he could not take for granted that the wild would do what he desired, for by its very nature it had its own selfish gene approach to survival, and so his expectation were neither high nor low, but wavered with anticipation and excitement somewhere in between.

Spreading the carcass remains from supper along the wall and on a lumpy stone half-embedded in the well-tended vegetable rows, where the rock had been left either due to ancient significance or else its huge size and weight, he placed his plastic chair up against the front wall of the cottage. It was still crystal sticky from the sea's dried salt and the normally malleable arms felt brittle to touch in the drop of the air's temperature.

Dressed to snub the penetration of the ice-fingers of the night, he collected binoculars from the tool shed, his phone now set to 'airplane', biscuits from the store to keep him fed, and, wanting to add a moment of class to the event he re-filled his tumbler with red, before returning to his plastic throne for the vigil.

He had done all that he could to improve his chances and sat and waited.

The northern lights were not as distinct tonight. Their show was still huge across the clear sky, printed in the brightness of constellations and sparkling stars that twinkled from white through ruby or sapphire. But somehow, the vastness of this evening's heavenly display limited its unfolding extent to the northern mountain horizon, as if the pole wanted to keep its secret for itself and it was being sucked back up north for another year. It had millions of years in which to wait and re-enact its annual light display.

Heat from the land dissipated swiftly leaving the spring-warming water's humidity to replace it so that soon Sol was aware that as the land cooled the loch remained constant and emitted a radiant energy of its own. On its bobbing surface the geese and ducks had drifted away from the beach for security where they oscillated in '*gurgling*' armadas of mixed species, the larger attended by the smaller, and the piercing, descending moan of a wader was trumpeted forlornly from the ragged rock edge of the shoreline.

Woodcock croaked in roding performance over the woodland and the tawny owl drifted twice low over the garden in its chase of the whispering mice that skittered over the walls and climbed the sides of the *Bothan* in a way that Sol had not thought possible. There was a hedgehog, snuffling and snorting, trundling along the hoed rows of the vegetable patch trailing the glistening star-lit trails of mucus left by the over-numerous black arion slugs that emerged as if from the soil and walls themselves. Sol could hear the discreet crackling of these molluscan pests as they oozed in pursuit of his future crops and he realised that animals he thought were silent had noise. And then, once caught, they were squeezed and popped in sharp toothed jaws and noisily chewed with open mouths by the rapturous hog who appeared to settle back on to its haunches to enjoy these hideous feasts with lip-smacking delight.

After that time required to get the eyes used to the darkness of the night and for his retina to forget the glow of the now dulled paraffin lamp left in the kitchen for later, Sol began to use the clear-bright blue reflected light of the ever-smiling moon to pick out detail. The highlighted tree leaves rocking in the wind that made them hiss, the branches cast in one-sided clarity and the ridges of the rippling waves that came in with the power recalled from the sea's distant fetch. Illumined bats flitted in eccentric torturous routes as they ticked and squealed in moth-hunt flight paths. There were at least two different sizes, with the largest tending closer to the tree canopies where they exceeded the scale of the open sycamore leaves, and the smallest tattooing the yard, the house and the garden. Here the moths pranced in lunatic circles and bounced on the fire-glowed window leaving moth wing-dust ghosts on the glass.

On the horizon a silver lining of tomorrow's burgeoning storm clouds, reaching high in mushrooming shapes to encompass the cheerful moon, took on a sinister form, a snake eclipsing a lit sky-borne egg. Sol decided he had half an hour's moonlight left to see and sensed the opportunity to watch the cat, *his* cat, passing. But no amount of panic, emotion or hurry would increase the probability of a sighting and so he continued to sit patiently, and waited.

The tawny alighted on the far wall, wide, glassy, wise-eyed and human faced. It looked through him as he scanned it with the binoculars slung round his neck, his movements slow and measured, cautious and tight. They faced each other across the garden.

What did it see? How did he appear to it? If it was a human-faced bird with its plate-round face and large, academic eyes, was he, with his binoculars raised, an owl-faced man with a glass lensed expression? Was it really wise or did it just give that impression because of its human-like appearance? Was it wiser than a human? They continued to consider each other for several minutes, separated by a small physical distance but a chasm of evolution, as the clouds carried on their march towards the heedless moon.

Sol soon passed from the bird's conscience and it craned its neck down to watch the passage of a rodent between the plants. Even Sol could hear its clumsy progress, a mistake that cost it dearly as the tawny dropped with talons outstretched and plucked the squealing life from it with a nip of the bill behind the neck, and it then whipped it up into the air in drooping saggy form, head limp and tail plumbing behind. Life was gone without the mouse knowing, all chemistry and organic structures still present and warmth contained, but dead. Killed to keep another alive.

The owl was gone in a silent night flight that took it back and over the *Bothan*.

Sol dropped the binoculars, to be surprised by the presence of the wildcat licking the wall in front of him. How it had slunk up without his knowledge he did not know. But it was present. In the seconds he had he used the camera on his phone to snatch the best shot he could and was taken back himself by the blinding flash it produced as the photo took.

Like the mouse moments before, Sol immediately regretted his ineptitude and lack of stealth as the feline form, turned, took him in, dropped behind the wall and was gone, lost to the night as the clouds finally enshrouded the moon taking its light with it. Just a shrinking half sky of stars remained and the passing shadow shapes of moths and the bats whose blind sonic-sensed flights were unaffected.

All chance had now evaporated, snuffed out like the stars of the sky.

Cursing, but pleased with his evening's observations, Sol sifted fly-floating wine through his teeth, ate biscuits, listened to the patter of approaching rain smacking the loch in its advance on the glen and returned to the warmth of the hearth and the hope of a good, satisfied sleep. This, he decided, was a night that exceeded expectation, even though it had ended with the loss of all future hope for this evening.

Looking at the blurred but identifiable picture he now had on his phone, he knew he wanted better views of the wildcat, but that would come with time and a more cautious approach. Under their angry furrowed brows the cat's crystal clear eyes were captured in yellow brown, wetly replicating an impression of the phone's dazzling flash and its black dragon-pupils were reduced to thin vertical slits. Those eyes, arched over a small symmetric nose, stared back out of the phone's liquid screen. Huge, unfocussed canines descended from a hissing pale-framed mouth and flashes of exploding whisker bent away radially. Alert, incensed ears were just there in the shadow of the head, flattened and aggressive. But distinct in the centre of the forehead, amongst the mottled brown and greys, a feline agouti, was a large black capital M imprint of stripes.

It was not the best photograph and only showed the face highlighted in the blackness of night, but he had captured a wildcat in digital copy and he felt the same thrill of success as the ancient hunter-gatherer within him would have if it had killed its first deer to feed the clan. He recognised that character that, despite any amount of evolution, technology and development, no man will ever truly be able to leave behind. As, after all, we left the cave, but the cave did not leave us and never will, and that's for all our advancement.

Back within the *Bothan*, he checked a description of the Scottish wildcat on his laptop, trying to ignore the automatic reference to his dropping share prices and momentarily regretting not being on top of his investments and managing them as attentively as he so recently would have done. His picture record was a dead ringer for the species and the hunter-gatherer was fully satisfied, with an adrenaline-fired accelerated heart beat and a well sweated brow, as he had now exceeded his already high expectation and could hope for little more.

Reading on, Sol was surprised to learn of the plight of the wildcat, its rarity and the threats it faced of interbreeding with common moggies, illegal poaching and fear of the encroachment of man. He hadn't realised the significance of his find here at the *Bothan* and a growing electric bristle of excitement spread through his body, rippling up from the base of his spine to embrace his whole frame.

Sadly, there are moments in all of our lives when we act impulsively and without thought. It can simply be that, we do something hastily and the most ancient of brain programmes, the limbic system, jumps in and makes us act in a foolish, less cautious, frightened or manic and hassled way. We are all too familiar with the fight, fright or flight mechanism that saves us or sometimes, especially if chronic or a result of our lifestyles or work, shortens our lives, increases its stress and makes us behave rashly. At other times we do things whose only explanation can be to increase risk in our lives, to get ourselves noticed or to escalate interest in our otherwise miserable, mundane or ordinary lives. After all, *who wants to be average?* This comes in so many guises. But commonest of all we just show off.

Sol skimmed through his messages, fewer still than the last time he had looked; gladly for now, he was being partially-forgotten and the un-remittance of time was forcing him from the memory of many he had associated with or called 'friend'. On noticing a cheery text from Pete, excited about the chance of photographing a wildcat next week on his proposed expedition north with Al, Sol replied attaching the picture he had taken moments before.

It went all too easily and irretrievably, as our e-world allows, sent through the virtual ether and immediately beyond control. It was an instantaneous regret that he experienced. But then, he supposed, the secret was already out anyway. Yet more ripples were spreading out from the little *Bothan* in the glen.

Sleep came with difficulty that night as it usually does when the hopeful dreamer desires it most or a good rest is recommended ahead of an important engagement, meeting or event. It is a strange thing that the mind can distract us from what it needs for the best health and full focus.

The rains slashed the windows in their loose frames and the wind found the slackest tiles and lifted them in xylophone notation from where it sought the warmth of the fire and slighted it before it could heat the room. The demonic wails of the storm whinnied in the chimneystack and drew what succour there was left in the grate upwards.

The constant in-house drip of every wet day so far gathered pace and Sol discovered that there was a hole in the eves at the back of the spare room that would need attention before the winter. For now he collected the drainage in a dull-metal bucket from the kitchen and the sounds changed to the '*pink-pink-pink*' of drops on metal until it filled enough to give off a more pleasant poolside noise, that of a slow-styled water feature.

In his mind, as slumber finally overtook at an hour well into the morning, he was faced with the flash-caught snapshot of the wildcat. It hissed at him and padded its foot, demanding he back off and leave it alone. Sol found himself in strange conversation with it, part of him pretending not to be there and the other trying desperately to encourage it to stay near him. Then, by some fluke of the dream, he materialised up on the headland again where the man he supposed was G was sat puffing on a tobacco-filled pipe that smoked in breath-powered billows to fill the still air in rising clouds of grey-white and khaki. Sol enjoyed that smell which transported him to a boyhood of scouting and elderly relatives who used the necks of pipes to give emphasis to conversational points.

The other remained faceless, that detail being denied to Sol by a lack of knowledge as to what G looked like, and a thick billow of fragrant pipe smoke surrounded him. But G mostly looked away over the sea anyway and as a dream-figure his face did not matter to the sleeping Sol. His brain gave only the details it needed to help sort the experiences of the day.

"She won't be tamed, the wildcat. It's in her name," G explained. "You can never tame the wild. But the wild can turn you if you really want it to. To see the wildcat, think like the wildcat, go where the wildcat goes and let the wildcat take the lead." The man nodded to himself, drawing in deeply another time. "Don't try to dictate what it does. It's wild. It will either leave or else get so frightened of you that you'll never see it again. She moves silently and slowly and needs to feel comfortable around you if she is to live with you and remain your companion."

Sol sat down and leant back on the carved standing stone so that he could then enjoy the taste and scent of tobacco. He both missed it and he didn't. He wanted it but he didn't. Mostly he needed to hear the old man, almost to *be* the old man, so that he could learn to find this wild exciting creature all the more easily. He knew it was something he couldn't buy and that it required the acquisition of skills he had seemed to forget, however obvious they may eventually turn out to be.

"Give her space," said G and turned his featureless face to Sol to hold him in his eyeless, haunting stare. "She's one of the last of a dying species and her family will need all the help and protection you can give them. They simply won't be able to survive around people if they do come and settle, develop and expand."

Sol nodded, but as is often the way in a dreamland he could not speak, remaining frustratingly dumb with a hundred eager questions left unasked and unanswered. Instead he turned and watched the diver out on the water singing its haunting song to a moon now hidden in cloud and a mate unseen somewhere else out there on the loch.

"See what happens if you give her space," said G, and the man faded away, the headland was gone and Sol was left sat on a wet bank watching the cat and two kittens mewing and growling like miniature tigers amongst the dead roots of a moss-ridden stump. Thoughts raced and inferences evolved.

If the cat was a female, then the cat could have kittens.

If the cat had kittens then there was still a chance for wildcats, however slim, in this area.

If the cat needed help, then he needed to make sure she was well fed.

He had a role to play.

Unseen on the headland, up by the standing stone, sat on that curiously flattened piece of land, G nodded his dreamt approval and stroked the wildcat affectionately and tickled the kittens that played by his feet. Behind him, a stag stood rampant and brayed towards the sea.

Sol awoke late and before anything else recorded the last day's observations into G's diary and notes, ending with that few seconds with the wildcat caught on a phone's pixilated screen; an image that brought back instantaneous reminder.
Making breakfast, inside as the weather continued unabated, his phone, still on silent, lit up to signify that a message had arrived, at which point his heart sank and his brain tensed. Questions surfaced as he reached nervously for that little plastic device that was the source of so much, both good and bad.
As he feared, it was Pete.
'Sol,
Photo of a wildcat on a phone? Flip Sol, that's incredible! I've sent the picture on to a few people and they are keen to come up as soon as they can. Definite wildcat!
I've told them you've turned native and have become a miserable bugger up there on your own for a week and so you'll be glad to know I've put them off for now and they don't know your address anyway. I'm packing quite a lot of kit and should be able to get a good article out. One publisher is asking for a blog whilst I'm with you. Do you mind if I get started on it? Too late if it bothers you. The blog's already live.
Can't wait.
On a phone camera! That's unheard of. Flip!
Pete'
"Shit!" Sol shouted. "Shit, shit, shit!"
What had he been thinking of when he posted that picture off?
Nothing could be done about it now. But what was important was that he thought of how to provide for the wildcat to make life as easy as he could for it, especially if it did turn out to be a female and did have kits to be looked after and fed as he had dreamt the night before. He needed supplies, and so grabbing his wallet and an

old coat he took the Land Rover along the drive and towards the road up to the crossroads to find Gerry's house and some welcome advice.

With much difficulty he worked out how to control the heavy old vehicle as it slipped on the scree and wet muds of the track, working its handling out by the time he had passed the McCann's, who waved from their door and shouted greeting, and he made the crossroads at the Bealach in good time. Simon had given the car a name, Addie, and in doing so had given it a character of its own. Sol wondered at the significance of this name. Everything seemed to have meaning, the house's name, and the boat's name, even the crossroads' name.

Addie?

He settled simply for 'adventure' as that was what he intended to have here in her. This name and meaning would stick regardless of its real Gaelic etymology.

Curlew crossed the sky ahead of him. Long curve-billed, their white rumps and extended legs gave them each an elongated shape as they hugged the moor and finally came to rest where the heather cleared and a dark peat-rich mire denied the plants oxygen enough to root.

Taking the crossroad exit that headed north towards Gerry's house, he saw how each of the four spurs broke into a network of water-filled rut tracks like those of interconnected leaf veins that spread from a midrib vessel or a delta viewed from the sky. It felt as if the crossroads, *Bealach na Crois-rathaid*, was the vascular centre of the estate with *Bothan Faobhar* its beating heart.

A harrier wobbled in the wind as it glided feet over the moor cutting that characteristically shallow v-shape in its flying form, head crucially placed down-facing such that it could scan the shrubs and dwarf rowan and scrub willow trees for prey. A flock of grouse squabbled their way out of sight as the rain pattered and curtsied up and over the split screen. Ahead Sol caught sight of an unaffected herd of long-horned highland cows who chewed the cud thoughtfully in windswept ginger coats of lengthy brown hair about which black clegg flies buzzed. They watched his passage vacantly through sightless eyes hidden under dreadlock fringes keeping bundled calves behind them in their contemplative stances.

The track dropped steeply into a dark and densely planted fir wood of viridian green that eventually gave way to a less regular open deciduous-pine mix carpeted with spring flowers and travelling carefully along its lengthy drive of rutted mud wells and stony cobbles.

The rain clouds clung to the headlands on either side of an expanding bay and eventually Sol found himself in a yard, carefully hidden behind an outcrop, with a wooden and stone cottage and barn beyond. It was rugged and slightly forlorn, and it was undoubtedly in need of serious repair in places, but its artistic accompaniments, hangings, plantings, and decorations, and even its location, all screamed out *'Gerry!'* from every inch. As if to confirm his suspicions, there was his boat, *Sireadh-thall,* hauled up on the coral shore with the painter tied off to a sand-stranded buoy.

Dismounting from Addie's cab, he silenced the engine and sauntered to the house that was Gerry's dwelling. Stone-based it had wide windows that faced the sea loch behind the protection of a cliff-lined headland. Machair grasses and flowers were beginning to bud and burst on the approach from the cottage front to the water's highest edge. The white-painted window frames were well peeled and rotten, and more than a few wobbled with the wind, in spite of the glen's sheltered position. A large wisteria hung over the doorway and threatened to engulf much of the property and from its branches feathered and leaved charms and painted models hung alongside bird feeders and drying bunches of twisted herb. In front, where the sun would obviously send its ray the most often, was a pair of metal chairs and a round table inlaid in a mosaic pattern made up from the tiny fragments of broken pots now given new life, being tessellated to form a Celtic image of intertwined plants, snakes and flowers.

But it was the roof that drew Sol's eye. Threadbare in places, the tattered remains of an ancient thatch clung to the rafters and he knew before looking, that inside it was simply a large boat's hull turned upside down, with two chimneystacks poked through it and covered roughly with twigs tied down in bunches with rotten strings and wooden pegs. There were two nests obvious, buried deep in the pile of the roofing, and from within the twitter and whistles identified that many young had hatched and were demanding food from the busy blue tit parents who flitted in and out with beaks full of worm, caterpillar and still-winged insect.

There was a hailed greeting from the barn behind from which Gerry appeared looking with some embarrassment at her house.

"Hi," she said, "you should have told me you were coming and I have cleared the place up. Or re-built it!"

"I'm not here to inspect it for you," he laughed. "Besides, it should be me as landlord who tidies this old place up. How many leaks does it have?"

"A few," she smiled. "But I've grown familiar with most of them. They can be good company on a bad day."

"And the windows?"

"Noisy if it's windy from the west…   …like today. You really are seeing it at its worst. So don't worry too much. You've got enough to think about."

She wiped her smudged hands ineffectively down a paint-splattered apron in an attempt to make them cleaner.

"Best time to find out what's wrong with it then." Sol paced along the front of the building and prodded lose twigs on the roof. "Can Hamish fix any of this?"

"No, but…"

"But what?" he asked.

"Well, there's only one man around here who can fix a boat like this one," she said, patting the wood of the upturned boat where the thatch now failed to cover it. Reddened beetles, highlighted in etchings of a drear grey-black, scuttled away in fear as she exposed them to the shock of daylight. Woodlice huddled an algae-moist wood knot in a herded gang with antennae held aloft for information as to the angle and type of anticipated attack.

"Nevin," muttered Sol with some resentment and Gerry nodded.

"The same, and he'll never fix this whilst I'm living here."

There was a pause as Sol listened to the rain pouring into the property from the open-holed roof and counted the number of breaks he could see.

"Then it's obvious," he blurted out to her surprise.

"What is?"

"Move in with me whilst he fixes it for you. It won't be for long... ...and you could sail back to work in your...   ...barn... ...workshop..."

"Studio!"

"Sorry, yes, studio."

"How could I move in?" she asked, quite taken back by the proposition; its generosity and its potential. "People would talk and that's what happened last time."

"With you and Nevin?"

The silence said it all.

"Okay," said Sol. "Move in, but make sure everyone knows, especially Nevin, well in advance, that it is a temporary thing and that as we are just about brother and sister now, it's as friends only. Nothing else."

There was another pause when Gerry spoke again. "And, why are you doing all this for me? Are you wanting us to be more than brother and sister?"

"No. I don't want anything more. I don't know why. But for once in my life I don't want to mess up a perfectly good relationship before it's had chance to start the right way. I own your house, not you, and you need it fixed and I want your friendship...   ...as a sister, if that's what we want to call it. But I am happy to call it by its proper name...   ...friendship. Just friends."

"Okay. But you talk to Nevin. I can't see any way you'll get him to work on any place associated with me…   …or you for that matter! But you stand more chance of getting something than I do."

Over a damp cup of tea in front of an inefficient wood burner that hissed as water poured down the chimney pipe to meet it, Sol told Gerry about his messages to Al and then Pete and the photograph taken on his phone, which he then showed to her.

"She's a beauty though isn't she?" said Gerry in reply.

"So you aren't cross with me?" He was pleased that she didn't seem disappointed with his rashness.

"No, should I be?"

"Well, what about the wildcat? You said I should tell no one about it."

"I'm certain something will work out right from it. Besides, there's only one issue really."

"And?"

"If they really are the highflying London type, then where are they going to stay when they come up? Will they cope with life at the *Bothan*?"

Sol thought this through.

"Al might struggle, but Pete is always off roughing it somewhere or other to take his wildlife photos. He only does the gallery shoots to pay his way until the next expedition. Truth be known, he'd give up all the popular stuff if he could afford to live in a tent and watch wildlife all day. Al is more a fast car, fast women and fast profit man. It'll be interesting if he stayed at *Bothan Faobhar* to say the very least. He owns a string of hotels and from the free nights he's offered me in the past, old *Faobhar* is going to be a shock for him. What hotels are there in the towns?"

"The Inn at Old Town and a few shabby places over in New Town. Let them choose if they want to come up. Then we'll think about your wildcat."

"I just hope they come in Pete's car and not Al's. The four by four will win every time over the sporty number." But he chose, regrettably, not to warn them.

The day passed quickly once returned home.

With the reappearance of the sun, the wildlife resurfaced from where it had vanished into shelter. But between showers it played hide and seek, with one minute flies being aplenty and a buzz in the air and the next them being replaced with a cascade of water drops. At the same time Sol would retire to the front room to play piano or strum the violin. On several occasions he returned to the feeders to record what was there and armed with yet more pheasants from Gerry he then focused more on entrails and carcasses for the wildcat, and its potential brood, than for his own food.

There was a haunch of lamb deposited by one of the shepherds' helpers as a home warming gift that Sol hung on the hooks in the larder, and, obviously the ladies from across the lake had been worried about him as they had left a handwritten message and a string of numbers he could call them on if he needed too. He felt cared for, but from a distance – a strange comparison to the life in the city where he had rarely felt cared for but was aware that everyone was so close.

Checking his laptop he found that his share prices had dropped yet again and he wasted an hour worthy of more profitable work on the Internet and thumbing through messages.

Sue *seen his photograph which was now being circulated in the wildlife quarter and causing quite a stir...* *...missing him being around...* *...did he want her to visit? She did forgive him for everything...* *...but she was still angry ...* *...missed his bank account too! Ha ha!*

Office *agreeing he would retain his commission...* *...authorities gone quiet but they were unhappy with the costs ...* *...they would pick up the bill...* *...nothing on Tokyo deal!*

Leslie A Kent

Therapist finding business a little difficult at present in the current financial markets...   ...a consummate professional...   ...Sol's three questions suggested the need for more therapy...
Sol declined the offer.
Friends and family *little contact now.*
He wrote to his brother, the favoured child, and explained that he could visit in a month if he was still in the mood for it.

A white-tailed sea eagle distracted Sol from his mobile, which he dropped immediately in his rush to observe it better, something the past him would never have done to this item he had previously considered so sacred. The bird glided low over the cove and tipped around in effortless circles with the merest of alteration of its outstretched wings and the contours of its aerofoil that took it up towards the headland.
Giving it chase, he headed on up through the woodland track following its meandering progress and using all his senses, the '*squall*' and '*mew*' of its cry, the shadow cut out that passed briefly over forestry rides and the random breaks in the canopy where old standards had fallen to a rotten moss'd grave. Along he raced, head up for glimpsed views and then down to counteract a stumble or trip, to the crags via the gurgling river who still held the dead stag firm in the rocks. Its flesh had started to stretch and peel to reveal the ribs below and release a noxious stench that offended the nose but attracted the larger fizzing flies who swarmed to it in decadent mobs. Its retracting flesh was hollowed below, a writhing maggot liquid that sought out the earth, heated by bodily respiration.
Up the rocks he slipped until he made the heather moor above. He ran to the standing stone and the flattened land where he had met with G last night in his dreams and there was the eagle lazily slanting its wings in reverence to the fresh wind that brought with it the next storm in from the sea. From here he looked down on it as it searched the flotsam of the exposed sand of the beach below.

A white-feathered head sprang forward from a deep golden brown chest and a darkening body and wings with the spread of a house door. Behind it was balanced by a tail splayed like an Indian brave's headdress from an old time game of *'Cowboys and Indians'*. Beyond, serious forward-pointing eyes pupil'd round and black, was an immense horny beak matched in yellow colour by lengthy, dragging pitch-talon'd clawed feet. This bird was enormous and even the mobbing corvids that *'cawed'* and *'crarred'* at it seemed insignificant and below it in terms of their dominance; a king of birds.

Then it switched flight path and yawed towards the sea, angling in a rapid descent that took it frighteningly close to the waves. It tracked along the tidal race inland and up the loch, flicking its talons unsuccessfully at silver images of fish that lay safely below the froth and the waves. Then, more determined, it returned to the cliff's height and scoured the busy ripples below it in hovered circles of increasing diameter.

Claws unfolded, talons loose it sped down and down through the zone of mist that the water threw up and then in a backlash of wing and a raising of the head it blindly grabbed at something silver in the water and left in sweeping wing beats with a well-earned fish prize. Water dripping, the limp form hung, snatched firmly from the loch.

Sol stepped back as this leviathan of the air struggled with height and then flew straight back over the headland, undoubtedly to an unseen nest sight back in the woods.

Who in London sees this on their doorstep? Who anywhere is this privileged? How was he so fortunate to have earned this moment here and now? And, he was immediately glad that Pete was coming soon and could share in this experience with him.

The evening came quickly after his hurried return home ahead of the next storm and he heard Hamish's approach in his Land Rover well in advance of his arrival. The light was not yet gone when the headlamps lit their way brightly and viciously into the yard. Sat in the front was Old Joe, the partially sighted man from up by the upper loch, who hardly turned to acknowledge Sol as they greeted each other. He was forced to climb up into the hard-cased back where he found a collie dog spread happily amongst tarpaulins and ropes, and a violin case with a few other black but bruised instrument bags spread about in haphazard fashion.

"Forgot to mention my guest," Hamish shouted over the noise of the growling engine as they headed back up the drive plunging the *Bothan* back into the darkness she was more accustomed to, with Sol having left carefully laid entrails out for the wildcat and any other creature of the night that cared to sample them. "I believe you know Old Joe?"

"Yes," Sol called as the engine roared inconsistently and the wheels fought the road for steady traction. A startled deer leapt the track, followed by two other hinds. From the rear of the vehicle, sliding up and down the bench seats, trying not to sit on the wet, mud-stained dog and clutching his precious violin to his bosom, Sol saw little of the journey, and heard less of the front seat conversation. He was only too glad to get to the pub in Old Town where they were due to play together. Although the road had been better than the track, he was still isolated from the quiet cab-fronted conversation where driver and passenger could not help but to keep their backs firmly towards him from the comfort of their well-sprung seats. He made a mental note to ask to be dropped off at the end of the drive on the way back – he could walk if they weren't too late.

Once there, Joe alighted lightly from the cab and opened the rear up for Sol and the dog to escape the piled materials inside. Without looking, Joe felt about the back of the van and grabbed his violin and Hamish then came to find his cases and to help Sol out from his entanglement between the instrumental and agricultural material within.

The inn was a rustic affair in a section of the town that ribbon-flowed its way around the headland beyond Nevin's boatyard and the shop he had visited a few days previously. It was welcoming and warm, comfortable and with the smell of oak burning in the wide beamed hearth and food cooking in the back kitchen. The interconnected rooms were dark with tabled niches off to every side for eating and drinking and that dim light afforded by black smoke-stained wood and not enough bulbs. Low beams were littered with horse brasses, sailor's kit and fisherman's hooks, and the walls were given a second layer, beyond that of their whitewashed wattle and daub, of photographs, pictures and handwritten poems in a language that Sol presumed was Gaelic.

A large plaster fish, a cast of the record-breaker it represented, was suspended above the doorway along with the plaque to the champion who caught it and there were trophies of past battles with harmless nature in cabinets and attached to wooden shields.

A generously apportioned man and a buxom woman, both ruddy-cheeked and jovial in form and feature, propped up the rear of the bar where they hand-pulled frothing pints of local beer and served up crisps, nuts and '*food*' as it was called forth. Glasses and bottles lined the walls behind them and when they were asked jokingly for a glass of white wine and soda in an overly played English accent everyone burst into hysterics and looked knowingly at Sol who blushed.

The place was humming with activity and Sol wondered when they were due to start their rehearsal.

"Hamish?" called the portly woman at the bar. "Joe, the usual?" And without asking she pulled two pints of tarry liquid that frothed yeasty bubbles at their heads into glasses that bulged at their top third. "And for the stranger?" The hubbub of the pub cut silent as an air of murmured anticipation spread like wildfire around the room. Only the fire crackled, a fat gingered cat purred as it meandered between tables and feet shifted giving a noise.

Hamish turned to Sol inquisitively; who knew instinctively that on whatever he chose now he would be judged.

"I'll," he stammered, swallowed awkwardly and then considered. "I'll have whatever they are having." He was quite surprised that this was met with a hearty cheer and a warm reception with men turning back to the bar and their halted conversation as if nothing had happened, no one had appeared and no judgement had been made. In the same way that the loch water forgot the passage of the boat, his entrance to the inn had passed on and he was in.

Collecting their pints, Sol slurped noisily as he was led through the throng of rowdy country folk to a larger back room where the stools and tables had been pushed aside to create a space as a bucolic stage.

"What's this?" asked Sol, as he tasted the first rich mouthful of dawdling black ale that slowly and easily slipped down his throat and warmed him inside.

"Local brew made round the corner," Hamish called back opening his smallest battered black case and removing several darkened wood tubes from it which he inserted one into the other before fiddling with the reed at the end of one. Sol took another swig. "It's made from fermented sheep's eye balls and strained through wool," and with this Hamish turned to grin at him. "Stop worrying," he added, "the water's off these hills so there may be some sheep in it but it is made the normal way beer is, except that everything in it is grown within twenty miles of this pub. They make it here."

Sol nodded and returned Hamish's raucous smile. "It's good," he called with genuine approval.

As Sol took his polished and well-kempt violin out of its case he saw that Joe had extracted his own, a dusty aged instrument, from its tattered leather bag and that he was preparing an old bow strung with what looked like hair with the spilt ends of a poorly treated mop. It looked old and shabby in comparison to Sol's and so he stood smugly enjoying the feeling of superiority that comes with confidence, training and the sentiment of wealth and power, and the ability to wield both.

Hamish had now attached a dark-coloured felt-covered bag to the tubes, of a shade indescribable in this light, but unlike bagpipes Sol had experienced before, this set when completed was small.

"Scottish small pipes," Hamish explained caressing the diminutive bag and drones into a semblance of the instrument as inflated and played. "Better for a smaller venue like this. Or else we all need earplugs because of the volume. I leave the big set for the battlefield or when I'm out with the Missus – similar situations really." Again that wry smile shone through his face and eyes and Sol felt himself warm to Hamish still further. He knew he wasn't trusted yet but he sensed that Hamish was more forgiving of him than when they first met.

"Careful Hamish," laughed a friendly voice from behind ahead of a short, stocky man with a guitar, who then squeezed through the crowd, "my Alice has brought Mrs Hamish down with her tonight."

"...and she heard what you said," called a mature yet musical woman's voice from the throng. To Sol's ear it could only be described as that of a pure '*singer's*'. Lyrical and light, yet fulsome and tuneful, it held the warmth and rarity of the turtle dove's resonant warble but recast in human speech.

"Mrs Hamish," announced Hamish, as a grey haired woman, grace-filled in motion, came through and gently slapped her husband jokingly across the shoulder. She was like a past film star in her upright posture and measured movement, glamourous in her old age. "Dearest, this is Sol. The man from the city I've told you about. The new laird."

"Charmed," smiled Mrs Hamish giving Sol a greeting hug. "Sorry for the formality but everyone calls me Mrs Hamish. I'm the cultured half of our relationship and I do hope my husband has been good to you so far. If he's been grumpy that'll be his age... ...possibly his hormones." She smiled beauty through perfect lips and half closed her eyes in recognition of Sol's response.

He was bowled over by the contrast between the tight-faced, crooked man that was Hamish and the fluidity and charisma of his wife who had all the refinement and poise of an elderly fashion model or ballerina and a balminess of voice that he had not experienced often before. She was musical in the way that she walked and how she talked. She was either trained or simply a natural in attracting attention and controlling the room.

"Graham," introduced the man with the guitar, interrupting Sol's momentary thoughts. "And this is Mark on the harmonica. Excuse the size of his case. He says it's to carry all the different instruments he might need. But we think he's compensating for other things."

"Hey!" shouted Mark as people joined in the banter. "Just because yours is full of air and's empty," and they laughed raucously as others pushed in to the increasingly claustrophobic space, its low ceiling beams adding to the effect of compression. The beer swilling populous seemed to be swelling the pub more each minute.

"Just need the whistles and we'll be ready," commented Hamish sitting down astride a short, threadbare, cushion-capped stool. He tipped the third of three legs backwards and rocked slightly as he tested the pipe bag and filled his cheeks with air to force down the narrow chanter mouthpiece.

"I say?" whispered Sol across to Hamish as he too took up a stool, and he edged further forward. "Is this a practice or a concert? I mean I don't have any music and don't know what you're playing yet. How will I know what to do?"

"Well that should keep it fresh for you shouldn't it?" Hamish chided. "You see we just make it up as we go along."

Sol looked closely at him to see if this was yet another joke. But there was no hint of it.

Hamish continued. "Join in as and when you can. Relax, it's not *'Top of the Pops'* we just... ...jam a bit that's all."

He gave Sol a reassuring pat on the arm when two faces appeared amongst the crowd. One was holding a shiny silver flute aloft above the seething heads of people, and the other a cherry red wooden whistle that looked like a modified form of the recorder with an oboe-styled reed. Its mouthpiece made it a very different object to the plasticised things Sol had been forced to play in primary school. Satisfied that the band was complete, Hamish pushed Sol to the side and shouted out introductions over the inn's vibrant sound. "Louise and Ben," he called in welcome. "Always late, but... ...but never missed... ...a gig... ...yet!"

The two sat down and after first feigning offence, they then sniggered and started to tune up. Sol looked back at the '*band*', one that combined to form an eclectic and motley grouping of a type he had never seen before in musical circles. All kitted in a uniform of drab trousers and thick knitwear jumpers, this was the only part of the group that seemed to fit in to his well-educated mind's view of what a band should represent.

Joe and he stood on one end with their violins, Sol's reverentially supported under his arm as befitted such a fine instrument and Joe's slung from a swinging hand with little due care. Next was Graham with his guitar not held in the usual fashion upright to the chest, but flat on his knee, strings facing up, and he held a rubbed and scuffed coin as a plectrum that looked as if it bore the hallmarks of having once been a Victorian '*bun penny*'. Hamish was pumping air into his pipe bag and checking the chanters were in tune, with Mark stood behind selecting one of his many harmonicas from their overly large presentation case. Then finally the whistle and the flute pitched up on the end.

Mrs Hamish brought a tray of drinks and placed them on a small round table in front of the band and as they all reached forward, grasped a glass and relaxed to drink. Someone took a picture on a mobile phone that caught the moment in a flashed image, bright and white. This new version of an old band was captured just prior to its first night of performance.

Hamish stood, called for quiet and then spoke with his eyes closed and head up.

"Tonight we bring you our latest reinvention, and should he survive the week..."

"Hamish!" snapped his wife.

"...our first concert featuring the new laird of *Faobhar,* Mr Jake Solomon on fiddle." There was rapturous applause, foot stamping, hand clapping and table thumping until Hamish called again for silence holding his hands high symbolically. Only one bumbling fly broke the quiet air as hush fell on the audience, now spilling out on to the street, like some vocal Mexican wave.

"A musical scholar in his day, this will be the first time he has played with a real band," there was laughter, "and so we will be forgiving of him this time. But let's begin tonight's meeting with a bright and breezy jig..." He turned to the band either side of him and muttered something quietly in Gaelic and all but Sol nodded their approval and broke up and away from their sports 'team talk' like huddle.

Hamish re-sat and took up his pipes before uttering the one name.

"Joe, over to you."

Joe, eyes unfocused and unclear, stood unsteadily and stared up to the rafters, slowly raising his violin to his chin. Sol watched fascinated, wondering why this old man with his well-dusted instrument should be asked to start, speculating that this might just be a courtesy or tradition. Maybe the oldest played first.

Many a pint of beer was lowered in anticipation and the band waited for the old man's lead.

Next Joe tapped his foot three times and then dropped his bow nimbly onto his strings and plucked the first notes of a highland dance. The clarity of play, the speed of production, the instant desire it gave everyone who could hear it to launch into motion was indescribable and Sol, who had just written this player and his instrument off in his youthful arrogance, could not believe what he saw or heard.

He knew immediately that he was in the presence of a master fiddler, not a violinist, as Hamish had tried to correct him on several times. And he could hear in the richness and depth of the notes produced that, not only was he skilled and well-taught, but that his dusty old instrument was something special also. *How had nobody picked this man up in the last seventy-three years? How had this man remained hidden up on the hill at the gillie's cottage?* Sol's foot impulsively began to tap and his fingers itched to join in as he deconstructed the piece in his mind and started to search for his own element to add. Slowly each instrument picked up the jig, finding their own harmonic tune or counter melody, the rhythm kept by the padding of Joe's feet and the movement of the audience who pushed in closer in their sweating humidity.

Minutes in and Hamish burst forth with a sound from the pipes that took Sol's spine and played merry with it in electric vibrations up and down where every hair on his body was excited and raised. His mind was on the shoreline and in the hills, it lifted to the sky and then fell to the loch. This music and its sound had evolved here organically over millennia, stretching backwards to the invaders from the sea, and he knew it. It had grown from the land and was a musical tribute to ecology and highland life.

Opening his now half-closed eyes, Sol raised his bow to his violin and caught the unmistakeable glint in Hamish's watching focus, knowing full well that this first note would be that make or break moment for him here in this land, and he began to play, finding his melody too. And, even though he couldn't see it clearly, he knew that Hamish was smiling.

Sure, endings were ragged and the whole performance was less than fully polished, but it was music live and music alive. The crowd, spilling further onto the muggy street outside, with the windows flung wide to let in air and let out sound, were thrilled with the gig as were the landlord and lady who wished every band night was this profitable.

"Not bad for a beginner," chuckled Hamish between pieces. "But could you teach him Joe?"

"Aye," said Joe, knowingly, "if he'd listen. But he's not so used to doing that as talking."

Joe played a slow fiddle solo next. It was bleak and described the dark waters of the loch where he lived in which Sol could picture the mountain behind and the desolate moorlands about. Each note penetrated deeper into his soul, dragging something hidden back up with it, and he felt moved almost to tears as he imagined the Water Bull, *Tarbh Uisge*, breaking the loch's surface to claim his willing servant. There were fish there. He was sure of it from the notes Joe played, and one that leapt skyward in pursuit of the fly.

Later Hamish gave his own recital on the small pipes. Three shepherding tunes intertwined to send the listeners back to a distant age when poverty was the expected, but somehow when a more innocent relationship existed between men, women, domesticated and wild things. It was ancient and it was scenic as a descriptive performance. On the third tune, Mrs Hamish stepped forward and joined him in song, as natural as anything, as if this was how the two of them spent their private time together, wooed each other and connected. Sol became aware of a depth of companionship he had never witnessed in his own shallow relationships. The two together were hauntingly beautiful. He was both mesmerised and jealous as she ended her song and they both held their last lengthy note smiling at each other, the sound of which left Sol somewhere off in his mind's eye in the glen behind *Bothan Faobhar* or out on the water.

The inn heaved at the interval as more drinks were delivered on tray after tray to the small table in front of the band.

"Where are they all from?" Sol asked Hamish between sips. "There's no houses nearby. Well not this many."

"Everywhere," answered the old man, "it's not every day that a newcomer joins the community and they want to see what you are like."

"And?" Sol asked earnestly. "What do you think they think?"

"Do you really not know? Are you so blinded by city life? Look around you...   ...they thought some plunk-head from London was coming up to take over *Faobhar* and was going to ruin it. They were right, but at least you can play the fiddle..."

"...viol..." Sol didn't finish. "I mean I still need to practise to play fiddle."

The two chuckled together.

"But, seriously," said Hamish, "look around you. These people are desperate to hold on to this land, to preserve it and to farm it. They've come to see if you're one of them or one of the others. You see, the time that they can still do what they've always done is passing and the modern world is taking over and pushing the old ways aside. Money is what they need, but we haven't anything to sell if we're to continue with the old ways, and so they know that something has to change. Either the way we live and farm or... ...well, we don't know. This music... ...it's a way into the past and a connection to our ancestors. I know you sense it too because I was watching you back then as we played, and..." Hamish thought about his words. "Well, it affected you. There's more to you Jake Solomon than even you know and I've a sneaky suspicion that that old daft bugger G knew it... ...we'll see. Can you save the estate? That's the big question. But at least it looks like you've got most of the locals on side... ...for the present."

And then he broke off, interrupting any further conversation, stood up and announced another piece and the band played on this time in unison with the whole crowd singing an old highland fisherman's song in Gaelic. Sol hummed along to the simple repetitive tune for lack of words. He was an outsider, he did things differently, but he could join in and learn.

They drank well afterwards and glasses were struck together.

"A solo," called a man's voice through the applause and cheers that followed the next piece, "a solo from the new man." It was James Nevin fired up with beer and keen to reduce Sol in public if he could. "The man...," he staggered forward onto the table and knocked drinks away, "the man with all the... ...the money. Let's see what's he's like on his own shall we? Without a band to hide in and where money doesn't count?"

Hamish stood up and held Nevin up and aside. "Nevin, you're drunk and you're embarrassing yourself. Sit down and leave Sol be. He's a good man. It'll just take time for him to learn our customs." Nevin turned to the crowd. "A solo?" It was a question really. And then he crooned round on Sol. "If you can new boy? If you think you're so good?"

Uneasy at first, a chant for a solo started up in the crowd, individuals joining each other to a crescendo in the way the bully builds up support in the yard until one or other snaps and a response is given. Hamish stood, but before he could re-settle them, Sol was on his feet and plucking strings. "I'll match your solo," he challenged Nevin in reply, who stood unsteadily on beer-jellied legs. "But only if you will honour me a request...   ...if the crowd think I play well enough?"

"Okay," slurred Nevin.

"You'll start work on Gerry's roof on her cottage as soon as you've finished the boat. I'll pay you well, but I want the job finished by the end of the summer."

Nevin swayed and thought about it. He knew he did not want to agree with the challenge but was also aware that with alcohol streaming his blood, his brain fuddled and his requirement for paid work, he was incapable of arguing against Sol now, even if he had been brave enough to back down after demanding a solo.

"The audience will be my judge," said Sol quietly enjoying the moment of show. "Do you agree?"

Nevin looked away.

"Do you agree?" he asked the crowd, who nodded and cheered. "Then I'll match your solo, Mr Nevin."

Sol took centre stage, stepping in to that cleared lit space between the crowd and the players, and the band sat closely around him with their ales in hand. Mrs Hamish sat on her husband's knee and Joe perched silently against a wall post with his far off, distant-focused stare. There was something of the magic of the old land he remembered in the charge of the air and he savoured the emotions on display and breathed in deeply the humidity of the heaving bodies and the scent of tobacco smoke wafting in from the blue-light night outside. He couldn't remember the inn being so full for a long time, and he felt the curious seeds of change sprouting green shoots everywhere. The people who normally stayed at home had come here, the locals and those from further afield. They were together for the first time in a long while, having left their television addictions at home, and save for the ramblings of a drunken fool, something was happening and it felt good.

Sol coughed and cleared his throat to make his preamble speech.

"I don't know old G who owned my *Bothan* before me, not like you did." There were disquieted murmurs amongst the crowd. "But, I am learning about him through his notes and what you good people tell me. Yes," he added looking at Nevin sitting head down at the front of the gathering, "I am a new boy and from another world. I am an alien if you like; a migrant." There was a laugh or two around the room. "But this is a piece I have started to write to try and describe the land, the water and sky of *Bothan Faobhar* and the rest of the estate. It is just a work in progress, so forgive me if it's not perfect. But one day it will be written down properly and finished, and then I will dedicate it to this beautiful land. I call it *'Symphony for G'*."

He shut his eyes tight and imagined the glen, the *Bothan*, the lake and the sky, the moor and the heather, the river and the loch. At last he fixed on that stanza he had written into his notes in G's wild diary and that poorly taken image of the wildcat came to the fore of his thoughts. He breathed deep, he relaxed his shoulders, he raised his violin and he released the bow on to the strings as his body intuitively instructed it what to play.

Chapter 15: When One Becomes Three

(Violin Concerto in E Minor, Op 64, Felix Mendelssohn)

He started the melody as a simple riff that wandered about his cottage and its grounds, sweeping majestically through the woods to the headland. He ascended through the river to its source and fell back down to the loch before he was swept out into the tides of the sea. There was the bright beaming moon on the heather moors and the ice peaks on the mountains that reflected back the sun's light in hues of sheer cold blue. Clouds built up and the mountains leapt to meet them, and there was rain.

In each place the wildlife crept into his mind and forced its way into his music. The geese that haunted the shoreline and the waders that scuttled amongst them, the birds of the wood and the dark silhouette predators of the sky who tore at speed or drifted from their positions of height. He played until he was spent, and, sweat-browed and armpits wet-patched and dark, he dropped his bow lose in one arm and the violin in the other and stood in silence unsure as to what impression he had made. He barely dared to lift his head.

There was nothing.
No damming comment.
No sarcastic retort.
No drunken outcry.
Not even an awkward cough or foot shuffle.
There was just the whispered sound of the sea air floating in through an open window, the clanging of the mast bells and the cry of the night birds and the gulls that milled playfully about the water.
It was as if the pub was empty and the crowd had crept out during his composition and so he dared to look up to catch Nevin's eye as he sat slumped at the fore of the gathered crowd. James was crying quietly to himself and across the room Sol could see Gerry edging

to get to him to console the poorly dejected man. Sol felt guilty about his challenge but was still keen to know what the people thought.

Maybe it just wasn't the place or the time to have played a snippet of a symphony on a violin? Maybe it wasn't as good when performed out loud as he had thought it would be when it was still contained within his head?

And then it happened.

A spontaneous ripple of clapping and applause broke the deafening sound of silence and one old man took off his flat wool cap and grabbed Sol by the hand, shaking it and him violently. "G would have loved it," said the man, "before he left us."

Hamish shook his head despairingly. "Now look around and see what you think." He chuckled and his eyes twinkled with that wicked glint. "What do you think?"

He and Sol exchanged a look of comprehension

"I can't believe it," he continued. "After all I've said, they *do* have emotional responses in London...   ...or these days do you just have to connect with your audience using texts and tweets and things?"

More drinks arrived and there was the tinkle of congratulatory cheers and the call of thanks to whom ever had bought them.

Eventually the gig had to come to an end and the mob spilled out and away as water does when it escapes a dam, with joy and energy at its sudden pent-up liberty. The band cleared up their instruments, glasses were drained, cleaned and stacked, and tables re-set with the attendant stools upended on top. Gerry hauled the vaguely-responsive Nevin away and said she would get him home safely and Sol watched them go with a mixture of emotions, predominantly responsibility and an element of guilt. He did not want this man hurt, he needed him too much.

Mrs Hamish forbade her beyond-tipsy husband from driving and ushered the jovial singing musical group of Sol, Hamish, Joe, and a few others to be dropped off on the way back, into the horse-straw scented pick up rear of Alice's off-roader whilst the ladies and the dog took the cab seats and warmed themselves on the grinding gearbox. Protected from the noise, they shut up the windows and had their conversation whilst the men folk sang their hearts out to the night if only it would listen.

A fox slunk away gingerly from the bins to the side of the inn and was quickly and silently absorbed into the night which denied any observer even a hint of its red-bright colouration. Only its bitter, musky scent lingered behind, yellowing the air with its unmistakeable offence, and only then was it the dog on the lead, the sheep in the pasture and the rodents amongst the litter that stopped to notice, to take heed and to act warily and accordingly as their genes directed. The fox left the scene in stark contrast to the humans its diet depended on. Softly padded, noiseless and ever aware, it watched the people depart as it sloped through its shadowed land filled with human-hidden olfactory information, tongue lolling and breathe condensing ahead of it. The Land Rovers pulled away in engine-voiced convoy, ripping tyre tread into the mud and trailing the stench of fumes, oil and diesel in their wake as they sped angrily off with white lights beamed ahead and bright surreal redness following on behind.

The fox returned when only the orange-yellow of the street-glowing sodium lamps remained and the last light of the inn bedroom windows was silenced.

Sol fell from the pickup, thanked Alice as best he could and staggered his way to the front door of *Bothan Faobhar*, swinging it shut with an uncontrolled flourish. Somehow they had made the length of the drive, a journey he could hardly recall from the cramped interior in which they had been packed and jostled and from which they sung with gusto. Carefully putting his violin case on the living room table he looked through the dark window to where he had left the cat's food but could see nothing and so he span around, tripped forward and dropped into G's chair with a loud gratified sigh and grunt, rapidly descending into the nether world of sleep.

He was satisfied that there was music for him here in the area and knew that, however guilty he, Sol, felt for entrapping him, Nevin would complete the works he wanted done on Gerry's cottage. But he was also haunted by one thing in the melodies he had heard that night and his muddled mind struggled to put his finger on it until he was in deepest sleep.

For a while he searched unsure what was directing him. It was not the sound of the pipes, nor the whistles, but his senses peaked when he recalled Joe's playing on the fiddle, and slowly a thought crystallised about what he had heard. Joe's style and skill interweaved into his dream and for a moment, Sol couldn't help himself but to lean over and look more closely at the violin Joe had in his arms.

It was a dusty aged instrument, little cared for despite the love Joe afforded it, and so Sol reached out with a dream-slow finger and wiped across the thick black, greasy coating layer to leave a clean chocolate and red brown wood below. He could smell the materials, the thin sheets of laminate wood, their varnish and the glues used, even the wiry threads of the strings, and within the dream he could see into the f-holes either side of the bridge over which the strings were held tight. Despite the darkness of the pub light Sol could see a scrap of papery card glued to the inside of the battered old casing on which was a handwritten note in an old flowing form of Italian script, a signature with an indecipherable date.

He then heard it play and in his delusional, beer-stoked world of slumber he started to question what kind of instrument made that tone, produced that voice or created that resonance in the listener's mind.

Joe's violin...   ...what was the chance of it being worth even more than Sol's?

What was the possibility of it being some long missing instrument, lost centuries before and presumed destroyed, or never even being

remembered, and which had just turned up in the middle of nowhere?
Was it possible?
If it were, then it could be worth a fortune!
And he sprang awake in surprise to see that the dawn had risen already, the birds were chastising him for being slow up and his head rang as if it had been hit by a shovel, he was so hung over.

Breakfast was a simple coffee-led affair, partly through necessity as his body swore it could not take anything else. It took little convincing in the end as hunger had its way.
Spread backwards over the desk chair by the window, he watched the loch in its mid-morning display theatrically lit by a bright sky. There were birds chasing the invertebrates in the seaweed and bright-legged redshank '*pee-ewed*' as they fought for supremacy of the largest piles, mostly ignored by the stark-billed oystercatchers who contemplated this juvenile behaviour over their down-pointed snouts as judgementally as the top-ranking officer with the new recruits. Turnstones turned weed and the pipits irritably '*pipped*' from rock to rock establishing their own territories against the scolding wren.
Sol was pleased to see that the cat had taken its spoils and left a huge paw print in the muds he had placed the food near too. He took a quick photograph on his phone and then sent it on to Pete along with pictures of hair tufts trapped in the brambles and a panoramic of the sun-illuminated bay. If Pete was visiting next week anyway it couldn't hurt too much sending a few more tantalisers to whet his photographic juices.
Late starting out, he had a few things he wanted sorted by the end of the day and so fought to catch up with where he wanted to be, time not attempting to wait or assist him as it seldom ever did.
He twisted the keys in Addie's ignition and she coughed up into life in a plume of blue-grey exhaust, before he forced her along the

driveway in steady crawl until he reached the main road and then took off towards Nevin's yard.

Pulling Addie up in front of the wide open doors that gave way into the vacuous cave of the workshop, Sol stepped out of the seaside postcard harbour view, sun-licked and raucous with the wheel of gulls squabbling as a diminutive fishing boat brought in its catch and they each presumed their unfair share.

Large wooden doors were rolled to the sides to cover wire-caged windows hemmed in by what appeared to be grey moss-grouted Victorian brick, slightly too ornate to be from any other age. An iron-red staircase spiralled up to a suspended crane of looped and descending chains above that could be moved along loft girders daubed with chalked loading weights listed in multiples of tonnes.

The boatshed was wide and tall, seeming to extend well backwards as a tessellation of shadow boats of descending scale. Each was illuminated in grime rays under roof lit skylights that allowed the hot, bright sun to penetrate the tin roof into this maritime memorial to wooden boat history. Echoes of pigeon '*cooed* and '*throttled*' from the iron beams that loosely held the corrugated sheets in place and they had left the meagre remains of their shoddy nest building as guano painted twigs poorly piled in evidence of their past mating. Sparrows '*chipped*', with each first syllable being offensively loud in this man-cave's interior where rags and tools congregated under the patches of light that reached the floor or steadily tracked across each boat in unison with the sun's daily route across the sky. Perched on bulkheads and mast tops, the boats had provided well for the sparrows as oversized communal nest boxes with cavities and cupboards packed full of twig, moss and feather to create cups to secure their precious eggs. This gregarious species was very happy with the declining state of the boat trade as were the speckled starlings who lined the roof struts and tested the gaps in the construction along with the blue tits clinging to the crumbling white of asbestos and rust-brown of the metal.

Like spilt pots of white, gulls had left their mark where they too had found dry shelter and there was the characteristic perfume of rat ammonia mixed in with the heady scents of varnish, glue and freshly minced wood, odours that were as much tasted as smelt.

Sol stepped carefully between the graveyard-stranded vessels, some on the ground tipped to their sides, some supported on joists that held them upright and several hung from chains from the high ceiling above. Following a clear path through dust and wood shavings he came to a window-enclosed box, an office, with dust-smeared shutters down denying an observer a view in. The door was ajar and so he pushed cautiously on it upsetting the static entrance bell behind and here he found Gerry sat by the desk still nursing a very poorly young man who was only unable to escape Sol's attention by him being too slow to stand up and stagger back passed him and away.

"I'm sorry," said James with his dishevelled head held low. It was all he could think of saying even though it came no way near to how he felt.

"It doesn't matter Nevin," Sol replied. "I was cruel. I never told you I could play the violin. I'm sorry too." He leant on a paper-lose desk and sheets slipped in liquid fashion off of the sides in waterfall cascade.

"But I shouldn't have tried to stitch you up." Nevin groaned.

"Its fine," chuckled Sol. "Effectively you only stitched yourself up. But no real harm's done." He scanned the workshop office. It was untidy, disorganised and voiced Sol's suspicions about the state of the business, being far better than any words could have been. Gerry left trying to send an unspoken message to Sol to ask him to be careful in how he treated Nevin.

"I can't afford to do up Gerry's property. The business is pretty much sunk as it is."

Sol patted him on the shoulder as he started to sort through accountancy files into a better order.

"A boat builder sunk?" he chided. "That's the best pun yet. Well, you're not doing the job for free. That wouldn't be fair would it?" and he looked across at the man to see if he could catch his eye. "It's too big and expensive. So, I'm paying. I just need *you* to get a team together, to source the right material and to mend the place. The roof... ...it is just a boat isn't it?"

"That's why it's called the Boat House," said Gerry returning, bustling in with cold water for both of the men to drink. "James, this will sober you up. And Sol, should you have been driving this morning, the laws tighter up here than where you come from?"

Sol ignored her. "Anyway," he said, "I want you kept afloat."

Nevin looked up curiously and looked sternly at the city boy. "Is that another boating pun or is there a serious point here?" he asked slurping water loudly and wiping his hand on the back of his beer-scented sleeve.

"Only you can keep the boats sea worthy and mend Gerry's house. It means you are a whole lot more useful than I am. You asked the question before, but what can I do? In this case, nothing. And, it helps out Gerry and she's a friend."

"Just a friend?" asked Nevin looking intently at one then the other.

"Yes," they both answered and Sol only felt the smallest pang of disappointment but sensed that moment of hope he had wanted to instil in Nevin for different reasons.

"And you can pay for it?" he asked again.

"Within reason. The money I have isn't going to go that far, but I can afford to repair Gerry's house and still work on some of the other properties. Rents aren't going to cover the costs the way I thought they would though. As for the long term...? Well, I need to work on that. But I am reasonably confident we can do something if we all work on it together. I'm investor. Surely I can think of something?"

"So you might yet be useful?" This time Nevin smiled.

"With help, yes."

"But, I thought you were a one man band?"

"We might all need to change a bit. Even me. Think about it, even soloists rely on an orchestra to accompany them. Otherwise they are just a lone instrument playing one strand of a piece. Compositions are always more interesting when they have more than just a melody."

Sol stretched out his hand to James. "I think we started out wrong. Friends?" he asked.

"I think so. Friends," answered James and he took Sol's hand firmly in a grip of sinewy strength.

"Do a good job on the house though. It needs to last a few more hundred years if it can. I can't afford to pay for you to mend it again whilst I'm still alive."

Sol put the sifted papers back down in a neater pile. He had revealed a telephone and an old radio set that looked pre-digital. Next he harvested the escaping pens, lidded those he could and placed them in their colours into a range of pots on the back of the desk. Nevin made small talk and started to explore the state of the Boat House with Gerry whilst Sol took mental note of the direction of the conversation and the changing mood in the younger man. He was warming to the discussion, thawing towards the person and becoming increasingly animated.

Sol had the sense that he could make a positive difference here and he allowed his mind drift out to the boats in the yard and the potential they represented if rescued from the nests and guano of the birds that lived there. He released the blinds to view the workshop and startling the jackdaws who fled from one upturned hull up to the high beams above from where they shouted '*chuck-chi-uck*' in disgust.

"Boat's nearly finished," James suddenly announced, remembering himself and jumping to his feet. "Do you want to look? I think we could sail it up to the house to start looking at what needs doing… …if you fancy it?" and the three of them entered the dim yard to look closely at how *The Tern* was progressing towards the rear of the shed.

Gerry was enthralled to see her boat looking so clean and sound, out of the water, and she ran a caressing hand down the rounded hull, tracking her smooth lines and tessellating timbers. Sol could see that James had nearly completed a fine job of the repair, and emitted an enthusiasm and vigour as he began to describe what he had done, extending well beyond the rotting patch that required his attention. He had taken this job on with care.

"Now, I'm sorry to break up the party," Sol declared when the repair had been well checked, the varnish described and the finish discussed. "But, I need a toothbrush and a razor and have another errand I want to run before the day's end." He wished them good day and set off towards the shop up the street from the sheds. There was a good feeling that came with having helped another person.

As he left the yard, Sol sighed - a satisfied sound that made him feel buoyant and good. There was potential in the people here. They were skilled and willing, if only he could find financial interest. He thought of his pebbles conversation with Gerry.

Could he get others to come and view or even buy the pebbles?

A flock of martins raked the sky in swarming, determined pursuit of flies. *If they could travel all the way from Africa to be here right now to add to the natural resource of the area, then surely Sol could attract in a few city folk too? After all, wasn't selling things Sol's main calling in this world?*

Potential is such a crucial thing in life.

We have to see it in others or else all is lost. If a parent can envisage no potential for their children, or a teacher lacks vision of what might become of any one of their students, or a government cannot realise that there is potential out there in their workforce, the young people, the mothers or the fathers, the elderly or the young, then our world is without hope. The author would have no storyline, the artist's canvass would remain blank and the musician would falter at the very first note. There would be no case to win or lose, and no future to be optimistic about, to gamble on or to fear.

In short, our world would lack colour and depth and be a drab representation of what is in fact a wonderful, varied life. Too often potential is reduced to what we can get out of something, how much it is worth or what we can save, when the most important things may just give us happiness, have unquantifiable value or save our souls more than the pocket. They lack value as they are priceless, and this includes the potential for friendship, success of another even if it is at cost to ourselves, families and a diversity of beliefs, cultures and interests, not to mention those things costly beyond description such as our wild relatives and the diversity of the organisms we share our land with.

How much do we value the oxygen produced by a tree, the relaxation offered by the green of its leaves, the humility brought about by its age or its size, the splendour a woodland walk gives us, the food chains that rely upon it and undoubtedly help feed or protect us in some way, and the fertility that is brought to the soil? *And, what financial value is this all worth?*

And yet, a millennia old tree stands in the way of development and down it goes. An ancient forest is fragmented by a road and out it is grubbed. Or, we allow the deer to over-produce, as a result of sentimental misunderstandings of the power of key-stone species and management, and the wood cannot regenerate, to be lost as a childless aging population of rotting denizens.

How much do we value diversity?

Sol watched the terns diving on sand eels within catching distance of the harbour's pier end and marvelled at the technology and science they had mastered to hold the air motionless, to sweep with control and to plummet with accuracy to fish accounting easily for the refraction of the light from the air into the water. And yet to the uninitiated they were just white birds, probably mistaken for gulls. They may even be an interfering noise that disturbs their music, texts or communications; an irritation.

In their turn the gulls demanded his attention. The large, grey backed lesser and the occasional greater that dwarfed them. There were domineering, lecherous herrings and the diminutive screeching black heads, which seemed to have chocolate brown faces and not the complete black their name suggested. There was another gull amongst them, that Sol would later find was the common, and as he searched through their masses, some perched, some surface floating and others ambling around with no care but to drift on the breeze, he started to notice difference, diversity.

These were not just white birds, not even simply gulls. Instead, they were a varied assortment of similar designs, each specifically adapted to that small niche they had been honed to adopt, survive and excel in. The evolutionary craftsman of time had worked its magic so that through incremental improvements and the removal of the anomalies that cost them life or the potential to breed, the species had moved on, differentiated from all others and taking on a new form, behaviour or feature, but never standing still.

Back to Addie, Sol took her up the track and then steeper still towards the crossroads, turning again to follow the ill-beaten trail through the moorland heathers up to Joe's summer shieling, the gillie's house, located on the sand bar beach by the upper loch. Climbing down from the cab, he silenced her well-heated engine so that it chugged to an awkward end and simply hissed as the radiator liquid boiled somewhere within. He grabbed his violin case and swept over to the cottage, rapping eccentrically on the door, trying the patience of the stooped heron huddled close by who eventually took umbrage and left to find quieter waters to hunt.

"Joe?" he called poking his head through into the darkness of the kitchen where the still air felt colder than the outside temperature. "Joe? Are you there?"

"Out here," came the crone's voice, and Sol found him sat on a bench that faced out onto the stillness of the loch's water in the lee of the craggy mountain above only feet from where the heron had just stood. The sun struck where he sat and Sol understood that the spot had been chosen wisely for the view of the water and the light's warmth. "I'll always be up here," muttered the old man through gummy teeth. "So you've come to play have you?"

"Well yes," Sol admitted unsure whether to stand or sit, speak or not, look directly at the blind man or to follow his gaze over the water. It was a moment of confusion.

"With the fiddle or the fish?" Joe asked and his smile opened up as he waited for the answer.

"What?"

"Are you here to play fiddle or play with the fish?"

"Well..." Sol hadn't even thought of the fish. His mission up here had been a different one.

"Let's start with fish shall we?" the old man suggested and left Sol little chance to answer.

"If you say so," Sol agreed. "But..."

"Smell the air," said Joe and Sol sniffed deeply twitching his nose rabbit-like and aware he would be appearing foolish if the man could see him. "Not like that," Joe scolded. "Sniff but stop using your eyes. They're distracting you. Close them. Aye that's better."

Sol looked at Joe with half open slits.

How did he know?

Joe's eyes were closed. "Now sniff. That's better isn't it?"

How could the blind man know it was better?

But Sol succumbed and did what he was told. Closing his eyes, he drew in slowly.

"What can you smell?"

Sol paused and thought. *What could he smell?* He wasn't sure. "The air?" he offered meekly.

"Oh, bless me. What's on the air?" There was a sense of urgency spoken.

Sol searched the next in-gasp for any information and squeezed his eyes tight with the olfactory concentration it took to analyse what he rarely took the time to acknowledge. "The moors?" he added. "I can smell a honey flavour. I think it's the moors. Maybe the heathers or something?"

"Anything else?"

He pictured the plants that rocked in the sun and the wind that came over them to greet him. "Yes. It's smells of that pink-purple colour of the heather."

"Good... ...but what's beyond it? Is it wet or dry?"

"Moist..."

"Incoming storm. I expect it'll be here by sundown. That gives us a few hours fishing and then we can play fiddle after when the weathers less important. The storm'll bring flies off the moors as it comes – large midges which we can replicate if we're careful." Joe nodded and Sol sneaked a quick glance to see what he was doing.

"Now," Joe announced making Sol jump. "Now, look at the water... ...what do you see?"

Sol looked. He couldn't see anything really. A level billiard table flatness of loch occasionally undulating under the downdrafts of a slight breeze and with ripples where flies touched its surface.

"Water?"

"No. Look again. What's on the water? I know as I can hear them. But you can see and so you'll find it harder."

Sol looked again. "Well, there are small flies and things. They keep touching the surface and making rings in it."

"That's better. What colour?"

"...black?"

"Mostly, aye. But there's a few brown 'uns too. Aren't there?"

Sol looked more closely and then he picked them out. Black with an occasional brown fly dancing amongst them. "Oh, I see them now."

"Ever cast a fly before?"

"What?" Sol asked looking out to the flies on the water.

"A fishing fly. Have you ever cast one before?"

"No," Sol answered honestly.

"Okay, hold this and watch then," and he reached behind him to get an old-looking wooden rod which looked more like it was fashioned from bamboo canes than anything devised by man. A black reel loaded with brown line was attached to the corked handle end that was wrapped in bike bar fashion in strips of leather and hide. Sol took it gently, not keen to break what appeared to be an ancient relic from the annals of fishing history.

Joe reached down a second time and drew out a similar rod, slightly longer.

"The fish are there, there and there," he pointed out as ripples broke the mirror still surface revealing the presence of piscine life below.

"But... ...how blind are you Joe?" Sol asked marvelling at what the old man had seen through other senses. "How bad are your eyes?"

"Oh who needs these old things?" he laughed pointing at his eyes. "They were always getting in the way. I see in shadows of what you do, that's all. But I listen and I can hear the fish. They give themselves away. You just need to stop looking for them. Unless you can see in x-ray and spot the blighters under the water? Sadly, I've never met someone who can."

Joe stepped cautiously forward as if he was creeping up on an enemy or playing a highly competitive form of '*hide and seek*'. Then, he flicked his rod back and forward twice before allowing the line to shoot ahead in a straight line and to rest, feather-like on the surface, leaving a small black sedge fly, a fake, floating at the end of the invisible leader. It was positioned to the left of where the last fish had broken the surface as flies pirouetted about it.

"And then we'll leave it," he whispered.

Sol looked at the fly thinking Joe has misplaced it too far to the left. But it was caught by a gentle breeze and slowly drifted over the position the fish had revealed itself to be laying in, and then '*splash*' the trout had hooked itself and Joe played it for a moment before asking Sol for the net. He landed it, dispatched it and then placed it reverently next to Sol on the grass.

"A brownie. Beautiful, look at it. It's come up the river fresh this morning. There's still sea lice on it. I can feel them here and here." His hands moved nimbly over the creature as he pointed out the segmented, jelly-bodies of the long-tailed lice which he deftly flicked off into the undergrowth.

"But…"

"I can feel them," Joe explained reading Sol's inquisitive mind before he had chance to formulate the question. "Just because I'm blind doesn't mean I can't see you know?"

"A brownie," Sol repeated.

"Yes, a brown trout. Not one of those rainbows that you would buy from the shops all wrapped in cling film and plastic bags. This is the native fish, together with salmon and grayling. It grows slowly, feeds less harmfully to the environment and tastes far superior on the table. But they don't make as much money for the supermarkets and the get-rich-quick fish farmers and so they don't grow 'em."

"But how do you know it's a brownie. Well. Firstly, I might be blind but I am not stupid. Secondly, it rose, caught and then felt like a brownie. Thirdly, the only natural rainbow trout round here should be a few thousand miles away in America or else stuck in some fishery or loch. Sometimes you get them in the supermarket fish aisle too. It would be very lost if it was swimming up here wouldn't it?"

Sol started to say something but stopped himself again. Joe had more words to voice, and there was no doubt that he had sensed the fish in some way, had caught it and could tell him something about it.

"I think being able to see can be a handicap at times. It's just that most people have to live with it and therefore don't realise that they have been blinded with sight. I used to be like that too, but then I got old. They were never that good though. Ever since my eyes failed me I feel I've been able to see much clearer. Funny isn't it. Besides, since *she* went away I've not wanted to see much else anyway."

He was suddenly humble and sombre, far off yet near. "Never could see anything more beautiful… …and never will. God gave me the chance to use my eyes properly just the once and that was when I found her…" and he trailed off leaving Sol devoid of a name even though he knew full well of whom Joe spoke about.

He snapped out of his malaise. "Right, your turn."

He instructed Sol how to cast and where to point the rod, indicated a spot on the loch where a fish had been moments before and let go of Sol's arms and stood back with only the instruction to '*cast*' to lead him.

'*Swish-swish*' the line sailed the air in a sinuous curve and then '*tuck*' it snagged a grass tuft behind and the hook tightened well.

Joe untied it quickly with nimble, dextrous movements of his fingers and then showed Sol what to do again, moving him to a different spot where the fish were less disturbed by his movements and the anger he had displayed on catching the grass. "We all catch the plant life sometimes. Even the best of us."

'*Swish-swish*' the line moved easily and fluidly through the air, high above Sol's head. It felt good and it felt natural, but Joe wasn't satisfied with something in his action. "Stop trying to see where the fish are and trust what you feel," Joe encouraged.

'*Swish-swish*' and then '*slosh*' the tip of the rod hit the water and broke the evenness of its surface in ripples that spread quickly away.

"Well, that's one way, but you won't catch fish. It's much easier to use the hook than to try and harpoon them." Sol apologised.

They moved further around the loch and tried and tried again until the line left the end of the rod, shot forward and landed gently amongst the rising flies struggling to break free from the water's pull, trapped underneath by that polar force between molecules that maintained surface tension. Sol knew it was a good cast, not by the straightness of the line before him but because it felt good and had a '*jizz*' all of its own.

The line drifted and a fish did rise but Sol was too quick and keen as he recoiled the rod and the submarine trout missed despite giving chase to the fly on the end. Something about his action spooked it, was unnatural or gave away his position.

"Aye, I bet you're like that with the women too." Joe chuntered. "All pull and no action, thrashing about wildly but getting no joy." "Well, not..."

"Fishing is a bit like..." and he checked over his shoulder and looked furtively around before continuing in a secretive whisper. "Fishing is a bit like sex. You don't have to be any good at it to enjoy it and to get some success from it and an awful lot of joy. But in the same way, there are some of us who are better than others. We know it, but don't always let on. That would be unfair." He paused. "I am talking about fishing now you understand?"

Sol couldn't help but smile

Again they moved, and the ever-patient gillie directed as swish after swish the line was cast and then redrawn until the cottage was quite a way off and Sol's arm ached with the effort. But he wanted to succeed, a seer in a blind man's element, who had previously assumed that this made him more able.

"Not all that have eyes can see," said Joe again, sitting behind on a rock reading Sol's thoughts, "and not all who are blind can't see. It just depends what you are looking for. Take those pipits in the background and the lark. Can you hear them? They no longer even notice us but before they avoided our every move. Cast again, and this time cast to the left to ten o'clock and...   ...close your eyes."

Sol looked at the smiling old man whose toothless grin and unseeing, unfocused, shadow eyes stared off over the hill somewhere with their dazzling, grey-blue irises and dopey wide pupils. He could now hear the larks and pipits as they defended and wooed amongst the rocks and heather or up where they clung on to the sky.

"Try it," Said Joe. "Trust me."

Trust is a word that few can comply with, that many find difficult, and Sol was not accustomed to it. But trust he did and he closed his eyes and swept the rod back and forth so that the line curved in the air. He could sense the line stretch out to its full extent as the false cast was fed more and more line to nourish it.

Swish.

The fine linear cable formed a sigmoid past his head and then straightened out forward before he drew back again. His wrist informed him.

Swish.

The rod took it back and it aligned with the line, an extension of his arm, before it was cast forwards again and over the water.

Swish.

And the leader shot frontward to silently lay on the surface, its fly proffered to the fish god below, with little ripple to show for its presence. Now it was just a slight down-pulled tension that threatened to open the water, breaking the hydrogen bonds between molecules that held it afloat, making any up-looking fish presume it was watching a small aquatic larva'd fly trying to break free. The wind caught the fly and the cleverly tied bunch of black and brown feather, for that was all it was, drifted slightly.

"Leave it there," whispered Joe knowingly, a gillie whose experience and patience had delivered many a visitor their first caught supper.

How he knew, Sol would never be able to tell. His understanding and knowledge of the water far exceeded so many others and stretched back through an entire lifetime of experience, trial and error. But it happened. A fish leapt with full force into the fly and took it from the surface in a thrash of piscine movement and Sol was able to hold it, play it and with Joe's help land it and kill it so that two fish now lay on the bank by the cottage.

They were speckled with myriad dark splotches and golden bellies, and an orange glow to their midlines where the spots took on an iridescent, warm hue. Large predatory mouths, the secret of their downfalls, frowned ahead of goggled eyes and they were finished off with strong fins to drive their motion.

"Unfortunately," said Joe, judging the weight of the two animals, one in each hand, "yours is heavier than mine. Still…
…beginner's luck will mean you'll come back for more."

"That's what all the ladies used to say," laughed Sol.

"I'm sure they did," Joe replied. "But they wouldn't have wanted to hurt your feelings would they?"

Walking through the dusty heather along a decade worn path, they returned to the house where Joe gutted the fish and part-prepared them for Sol to take back with him to the *Bothan*.

"Shall we play?" he later asked. "I'll use my fiddle and you can use your violin and let's see if we can't come up with something to impress the crowd next week when the band plays down in the town again." And they played away an hour, which in their minds lasted only a fraction of that time, both stood by the water as the trout jumped, the flies rose and the storm Joe predicted came up and over the horizon when eventually the rain cut their music short and they retired to the cottage.

Packing their instruments away, Sol leant over to look closely into Joe's case. Sure enough, as in his dream there was a piece of crinkled paper stuck to the inside with flowing writing. On it there were a few indecipherable scrawls, what looked like a name and a possible date made of four numbers.

Quickly, Sol took out his phone and snapped a shot of the paper with an electric flash.

"What was that?" asked Joe more alert than Sol had expected.

"Just checking my phone, sorry," Sol replied. He checked the photograph and made sure that he had the whole note in focus and then took his leave of Joe who returned to his bench under the eaves to watch over the upper loch, just as Sol had found him earlier.

The lake was two fish lighter than it had been before his arrival, and Sol, feeling superior in having caught his own fish, even if it had taken much of the day, had supper enough for the evening. It was later than he had suspected as Addie descended from the gillie house and he had the chance to pull over to watch a large brown short-eared owl quarter the rain-misted moors as the sun started to set and drain the life away from the day into greyness.

On the lower slopes he saw a barn owl flit as a ghostly illuminated form off the post of a wall and into the space only a few feet above the grasses, screeching to entice the hunkered rodents to move and give themselves away. Its technique was different to the short-eared. Where the latter glided and drifted out in the open head down and trigger-ready, the former hovered and then moved on, hovered and then moved, a white spirit quartering the grassland.

Approaching the *Bothan*, with the light now faded fully, the tawny scooped the road before his full-beamed headlights and he counted himself lucky enough to be able to claim three owl species in just one journey in that way that collectors and list tickers do. There is something primal in that need to count things off and to accumulate, even if it has no survival advantage.

Some might collect train numbers or like to see types of plane, lorry, car or bike. Yet others accumulate first editions of every one of an author's books or must have a gathering of records, tapes or CDs.

Like the blood-lusted fox in a chicken run, who cannot help itself but to kill everything and take as many hens as it can, the collector becomes obsessed and obsessive, will spend time, part with money and even ruin a friendship simply to get the last tick, the final book and the one missing piece. A *'twitcher'* is a danger to have driving a car if they lurch with the spot of every bird that passes them just on the off chance it is something special.

Sol knew that G was one such a man but was aware that it was embryonically developing in him, almost cancerously; a steady growth followed by a mushrooming outburst.

Back in through the porch and into the kitchen, he had the knife out on the board and was already beheading the fish, de-finning them and dressing them for tea, making sure that the cast offs, now undressed from the flesh, were ready to present to the wildcat this evening. Into the re-stoked oven went the bodies, baked quickly in a simple butter sauce and fired by the smoke of two damp oak chops. The rest was in the bucket and ready at the porch door, and he was thrilled to know that he would be out there tonight, weather willing, hoping to catch sight of that illusive creature that seemed house-tamed to the *Bothan*.

Then, whilst supper cooked itself, he firstly inspected the photograph he had taken of the note in Joe's battered old violin case, and once convinced it was genuine, he sent it on to Al, the man who could find a price for and sell anything, and he waited.

Money is a strange concept, not least as it is in reality worthless and only has value because we all trust its arbitrary worth as given it by the bank that governs our country. The only reason we don't deal in shells and pebbles, like we probably did at our inception as the selfish species we have turned out to be, is to allow someone to control it for us. Once harnessed by the first to express the '*banker's*' gene, we were all captured and money had its value.

Money is an incredibly good invention allowing us to trade, amass, lose and squander as we want, but it does also make us do regrettable things in its pursuit. Rarely satisfied, we often want more. And when someone puts money in our way or suggests we might get it, that green eyed monster so often raises its wicked head and encourages us to step away from the right path.

Al loved money.

He could make it, but he also knew that he was falling ever short of the best he could do. There was always one more deal to be had, one more commission to seek and one more bid to push. Its pursuit no longer brought him happiness, but his desire for it suggested that it still could.

His reply to Sol was quick, objective and very calculated.

'*Sol,*

The signature is Michel Angelo Bergonzi. Dated 1720. Made in Cremona Lianno. If genuine then worth about half a million at auction in London. Can you get your hands on it? Want to see next week.

Al'

Sol closed his eyes and thought hard. His heart sank in that spiral he got when he sensed that he had done something impulsively foolish, yet again, and hot sweaty prickles radiated across his temples and down his spine as he looked back at his text and the ripples he was setting into motion...   ...again.

'Al,
Instrument not mine. Belongs to a friend.
Am sure you can look at it next week.
Sol'

He waited again, cold and clammy now with the feeling that there was a small tsunami heading his way.

'Sol,
I am sure we can talk this friend of yours around to some agreement. Leave it with me.
Al'

Sol's reply was to the point.

'Al,
No. Or else don't come. He's a friend.
Sol'

But he knew Al would come whatever.

'Sol,
I think I can quote you as once saying that even friends can be bought off for the right amount,
Al'

The rain eased and Sol finished his fish supper before donning the warmest clothes he could muster and setting himself up in his plastic chair with two paraffin lamps set about the yard and the fish entrails spread ready for the night's watch. Obsession often takes us unawares and it is only those outside of our sphere who see it creep up and in to take over our lives. We miss it, being so engrossed in the events that determine our every day in that continuous cinema reel that is our own personal life story.

Sol sweated with the effort of readying himself and preparing his mind for the ordeal of silent observation, something that required little effort but immense concentration and focus.

To watch quietly, observe intently and really see – that takes more out of a human than is often understood.

First, the midges came to entertain, keen to be involved, seeking the exposed bits of skin that Sol left available to them. He could feel them swimming in the salted water that coated his skin and soaked his clothes, and he knew that they would itch when they took their blood samples. But he could not move. He would not allow it.

Cold followed on, finding those same flaws in his ample clothing, and again he fought back the desire to leap up and around, and then the rain tried his patience and dropped his temperature still further such that the feeling in his feet began to wane. A tingle in the spine and numbness of the buttocks irritated him and he tried to draw his attention away from them and back towards that bucket and its spilt remains despite the line of the seat that reduced his sense of feeling. But this is the way of the naturalist, so often misunderstood and written off as a mild mannered, simple pursuit without danger, challenge or trial. Few understand that it is they who sit for hours and concentrate on just that one thing in the hope of a single observation, a photograph or a discovery. They climb cliffs, dive hostile waters, fly at height and even take to the ice caps of the world in search of knowledge and in the name of discovery, even though most of them are more interested in the safe and mundane and too many rely on the television crews to do the hard work for them.

Sol was cracking after an hour and felt he was now spotting the same bat in its repeated flight around the yard, even though he knew he could little identity any individual in the dark and presumed that all bats of a species looked the same. And then it happened, one of those wonders that is difficult to describe but happens if you put yourself in the right place and at the right time long enough to give yourself the right chance.

The cat appeared, satisfying Sol's addictive craving, slinking out of the shadows and across the yard as he had hoped. His fingers, frozen around his phone, were able to take flash free pictures with him using the light of the paraffin lamps only so that he did not shock the creature. But it was behaving oddly, and so he slowly put the mobile down and watched more intently.

The cat turned cautiously to take in the yard and stopped halfway across the open space to the bucket and its trickled contents. It sniffed the air experimentally before turning back to the shadows of the wood and mewing in a gentle calling voice, definitely calling.

Minutes passed with the large cat sat in a pool of paraffin lamp illumination, ignoring the moths that batted passed it and into the glass and the bats that chased them. Then a nervous disruption of the light occurred at the very edge of the circle of light. Just a tiny interruption to the perfection of the circular rim of this well-lit rounded theatre, but Sol knew it was something significant. The mother mewed again and the disturbance at the edge of the pool became a paw, chasing small flies and micromoths, which extended to a leg and into the tiny form of a kitten that the mother was encouraging to the bucket.

Sol was mesmerised and took what he hoped were good enough pictures for Pete and Gerry, and anyone else interested enough. But he hardly dared to move his arm for fear of disturbing the performance before him.

One wild cat had become two.

The kitten wobbled forward on robotic legs and brushed up against the older cat, but she still mewed insistently until two became three and a second kitten marched into the limelight of the stage.

Reunited, the mother ushered the kits to the bucket where she fed and then lay down to allow them access to her teats for milk. All the while, Sol tapped his phone repeatedly in the hope that at least one shot from them all would be worth the effort. But eventually he stopped and allowed them their private moment, unrecorded.

Time, that flexible foe, shifted and became shortened and squashed, and all too quickly this nightly show ended and the wildcats padded towards the light's edge. Sol felt smug that he had remained hidden in plain view all this while, but then the mother turned to him, looked firmly straight at him with her piercing eyes, which she blinked, and she then studied him disdainfully. After a span of a few seconds she slapped a foot to the ground and hissed, showing bared teeth and flaring her nostrils. She was just letting him know that she knew he was there. But maybe this was her way of saying thank you too.

The three slunk away from the yard and Sol was left in a euphoric moment where his heart was unsure what rhythm to play.

He slept soundly that night, falling away whilst listening to the patter of the rain on the leaves. Dreaming of cats, he felt a connection with these creatures and wondered where they sheltered and slept, and what they would be eating if he didn't make feeding so easy for them here at *Bothan Faobhar*.

The river rose high that night and the fish ran well up to the upper loch. Joe knew they would and hoped that he could teach Sol more of the ways of the water world he loved so much. He imagined the water bull climbing up out of the water and when he realised it was just a dream, his mind filled with images of his wife who the bull had already taken at the right time.

Hamish and Euan worried about their sheep, and especially the lambs, as the wildness of the late spring continued unabated. Their seasonal helpers were less affected as shepherding wasn't in their blood. Hamish's dreams were interspersed with music.

Sarah was concerned about baby names and worrying about the final stages of pregnancy and the birth, and she wondered at the life of a shepherd's wife as a mother up here on the moors.

James Nevin thought about Gerry wistfully and considered how best he could mend her roof now that he had inspected it, and Gerry was concerned about James and even more worried about moving in with Sol for the short term. She hardly knew the man, but felt she could trust him. But she also knew that she had made that mistake before.

Sally thought about the wind in the trees and hoped that none would fall before their time. But she knew the direction of the incoming storms was a danger to her woods and as they were plantation trees, established quickly in regular lines, all of equal age and of a foreign imported species, they were not resistant enough to the weather and some may not make it and lose their shallow rooted grasp of the thin soils. Her men slept soundly under beer-hazed fumes.

Mrs Hamish dreamt of songs in the old tongue that she sang as she span yarn at home or knitted with the others of her age in the lonely old shed by the black pool in town where the looms were housed. She visualised those now silent machines '*clicking*' and '*chacking*' again in rhythmical pulses, the way they used to when the wool was kept local and sold global.

In London, Pete got increasingly excited as he downloaded photographs of a cat and her kittens that his friend, probably suffering an early mid-life crisis, had stumbled upon. Another man was dreaming of violins auctioned for millions and a woman across town was missing her ex and felt unsure what to do. She was worried about him, but knew that theirs was not the right relationship. But she still craved his company of some kind.

And somewhere close by a wildcat mother had curled up in the dry shelter of a part dead ash stump that had re-sprouted new growth on its northerly side. It was shrouded in moss, and the ferns grew so that they obscured the entrance to the small cave below. Enclosed within the warmth of her belly fur were two young kittens, well fed with the rich milk that only a mother can give and no artificial substitute can better. They felt safe and secure and the only thing that approximated to love that a wild cat can. It was warm, dry and dark, and their mother had provided well for them and their father's genes were unusually pure and healthy.

The mother dreamt of the hunt and the stalking of a bucket, and in her dream was that strange two legged creature that seemed to haunt her every time she visited the *Bothan*. He didn't bother her much, even though he produced a flash of light just once, and he seemed scared of her when she hissed at him.

The moon broke the clouds and beamed down on the kingdom of *Bothan Faobhar*.

Chapter 16: Deconstructing the Naturalist

(Meditation from Thais, Jules Massenet)

For a few days after Sol explored that land nearest the *Bothan* and feeling the need to establish order in his life, something that he felt had helped him in his business existence, he took time creating a routine for himself. Breakfast and then fill the feeders to then return to them later to see what they had surfaced from the shadows of the wood on his behalf. Record the species, observe their behaviour and consider changes in type, condition and action. Study and exploration was followed by coffee, a snack and a return to study. Lunch, out in the field and an afternoon of more fieldwork. It was either follow on work from the morning or increasingly involved projects that spanned days and would later stretch to weeks. Stoke the fires and prepare supper so that he could read by the lantern or go out again and take on the nightlife and the cat vigil. Bed. Repeat.

It is a common misconception that the naturalist must travel broadly if he or she is to see anything *'of interest'* and it is a common error that many often do, spending too much time, investing too much money and accruing too much kit, much of which will be consigned to a cupboard at best and the bin most probably. Study can begin at home, sometimes even without the need to leave the bed.

A spindly grey spider descends from its finely woven thread, so thin it cannot be seen in the half-light of the evening. You can sense its movement, either due to a natural fear or a fascination which may be macabre as much as curious. You watch it spinning with the dexterity of a years' trained weaver at the loom, but marvel at how it can produce this sticky yarn at such speed, shape it and even, you have read, alter its tackiness, strength, flexibility and tensile spring to suit its objectives. You know that each species of spider produces a different form of web, but that they can all judge the distances between anchor points and determine the most efficient structures possible to trap or support. All this from a spider dangling from one single thread much like an organic, microscopic plumb lead suspended from a super-glued point somewhere up on the ceiling. *And*, all this from a creature that possesses no real brain and hasn't the capacity for memory.

But where the ordinary person sweeps it away and destroys its work, or worse still flattens the creature in disgust, and that is even though it is beings like this that keep the flies in check and control the commensals and parasites that share our houses with us. No. The naturalist is bursting with questions.

What is it?

It's not just spider, what is its species?

Does it even have a common English name, a European descriptor, or is it just some Latinised-Greco-Frankish-Arabian-English mix of words that the scientists pretend is a proper language and which they use to describe and label living things following Linnaeus's ancient instructions?

Is it male or female? Does it have gender or is a hermaphrodite, ever trapped between and betwixt, being both at the same time and neither by definition?

What is it doing? Why is it doing it? Does season affect these behaviours or does it just exist and do?

Will it breed? Has it bred? Can I successfully breed it in captivity? And, do I even want it to?

Is it native or is it alien?

What does it eat? How does it eat?

In short, what is its niche?

The naturalist cannot help this, in the same way that a real geographer, not just one who has a degree to claim it, sees geography on their doorstep. The geologist knows the rocks under their feet, the astronomer can tell you what stars are visible that night and the chemist should naturally want to experiment. Like children, none of these people should ever have grown up and they should be plagued by countless unanswered questions wherever they go, with a passion for what they believe in.

The best known naturalists speak to us from the television screens, often from exotic locations where the large, well-known, '*sexy*' beasts that the fee-paying, nature-loving, armchair naturalist public recognise and sit to watch and take in. But the things that live in the carpet or degrade the biscuits, the weeds that enter the yard and grow between the neat bricks on the driveway, the over-feared mushrooms in the public parks and the escaped wild boar that the media tells us to run away from, that surely is the world of the specialist?

But in the United Kingdom, where there are reported to be more naturalists per square mile than in any other part of the world, even including where the glossy book-publishing famous brands congregate to photograph lions and cheetahs chasing antelopes and the rich go on safari, they are mostly an amateur bunch. They go on unpaid, unrecognised and all too often derided for their interests. An invaded plant introduced by a garden centre along with its fungal and insect parasites plays havoc with the rivers, our buildings and our land, and it is the amateurs that will spot it, report and help control the newly arrived invaders. A species declines, possibly disappears altogether and may need conservation or reintroduction, it will be amateurs that will do it. An organism migrates northward, inch by hard won inch each year, following the creeping front that global warming allows it, and it is only the amateur who will track its incremental progress, sharing news and reports in an amateur press.

Naturalists are a funny bunch, always spotting something others have not, constantly listening for that different sound or suddenly stopping and smelling an interesting presence. But to be really good, to notice change, to spot the rare amongst the mundane and to realise significance, they do not necessarily venture far but instead focus on knowing much about a very small place. In fact, in the same way that old, mature and knowledgeable naturalists start their life-long interests at home at a young age when their minds are malleable enough to accrue the skills, sponge-like enough to gain the knowledge and teachable enough to want to find out more in the first place, most naturalists start making their initial discoveries at home too.

You ask, like so many do, '*how many species are there in Britain?*' It is doubtful that a naturalist would know. But reframe that question to include their county, their town, their garden or their home, and sit back for as long as you want to hear what detail you could desire. They will be expert in the forms of life about them in their particular sphere in the same way as the sports enthusiastic can outline the history of their team and their game.

A childhood of holidays sent away to be in the care of his grandfather had not been the unhappy place that those who thought they knew better could understand. It was presumed he would miss home. But Sol had always been far from doing that with the complexity and raw emotion of life there, even though he knew that it could not for the most part be helped.

In that house he had experienced a knowledge base that in his eyes seemed unsurpassable and he had learnt those skills young enough to be able to make clear and precise observations, not becoming too old to notice or care anymore. It had been an informal but vital education that few come to realise upon.

Now trying to identify the plants growing in the yard Sol was quite surprised by the ease with which he could return to that time. This was even though he was certain that in his later years, competitively trying to demonstrate that he was good enough in other aspects in this world, he had devoted much attention to unlearning the innocent and valueless skills and sentiments of his childhood. Instead he had become skilled at shifting invisible money electronically for faceless customers and convincing them he knew better than they did. This required a much less virtuous approach and one that was all the more worldly.

But here he was book in hand sorting out the common, looking up the unusual and trying to find the different. He wanted names, he wanted descriptions, he wanted habits and he wanted... ...*information.* Give it a name and he gave it a label, a handle to define its character. His relationship with each thing was thus altered with each gleaned and accumulated fact and with it his connection with the *Bothan* and her estate.

To some, to make a naturalist, you just add people to a place branded '*reserve*' and surely out would appear a fully-fledged naturalist at the end of the day. But, as for any good hobby, it takes time to become expert in the field, a lifetime really.

The recipe for naturalist is more subtle and complex, with an infinite number of variations to make it unique or give it your own flavour.

'Recipe for a Naturalist

Firstly take one person, preferably young and open-minded. Older people will require more work and may lack some of the freshness and ability required to achieve their full potential however willing they may be. A perfectly adequate naturalist can of course be brewed from an older person if they have the desire and can remain open to advice.

Add the spirit of enquiry. Very little is needed from then onwards and only a small volume is required as, like yeast, it will grow if given enough nutrient, oxygen and it is continually nurtured.

Take the person and give them a large enough space containing wild things. It is best to start in a relatively interesting environment, one that provides stimulus, such as a pond where there are ducks easily seen and invertebrates to dip for. Animals seem to be more accessible to start with but the inclusion of plants should be an objective as ultimately animals cannot live without them.

Provide equipment such as binoculars, a hand lens, a pencil and a pad, and consider the weather and local conditions. Not all of this is necessary but it certainly adds to the fun of experiment enquiry and adventure to any activity. The only essential thing needed is of course the ability to observe, not just visually, but perhaps sometimes with sight and at others hearing. But a budding naturalist must never ignore smell, touch and even taste.

Reading material will help develop the depth of knowledge, although the Internet can be useful too. It is good to know that a book can work without electricity or a signal whereas the Internet cannot and that wildlife is not always found in a place that can provide either.

Encourage relatives to feed this habit and to purchase appropriate books and reference material or even equipment if well-endowed enough.

Find mentors or network with a wildlife group who can provide local information, continue feeding the interest and give advice. Note: this rarely needs to cost much as real naturalists are so saturated with knowledge and enthusiasm that they will give freely, most notably of their time, for they want to share.

Travel, but only if necessary, starting at home and then moving further afield.

Allow a budget to obtain more expensive equipment as necessary. This element is achieved only when the person has become able to fund his or her own enterprise.

Season to taste with specific interest and specialism if required.

Join in and become a naturalist yourself.

Be constantly surprised in what you find and who you become, the interest you develop and the world you are now able to see.

You have produced a naturalist. But there is a warning. You will never complete the recipe as there is always more to be added however long you work on it.'

From the *Bothan* to the woodland edge Sol cut a straight transect line picking up and bottling insects using glassware he had found in the sheds and the large black insect net left in the back bedroom. These finds he then checked more closely with the hand lens from the front room, attempting to photograph them on his phone or to draw them before they were released back, each to where he found them. G's library of identification books soon became an invaluable resource and the table in the front room quickly piled up with a wreckage of partially explored titles left stranded in his wake.

Next came a study of the birds on the loch and those he could see around the glen. Binoculars slung around his neck he scanned from his precious plastic chair throne and was surprised when the light started to drop and seeing them became more difficult. On days like this, his problem was going to be time, as there simply didn't seem enough of it to take in the diversity of life that he had thrown himself in to being with.

The late afternoon was interrupted by the arrival of Gerry in *Sireadh-thall* skipping the water at the headland and then beckoning around up to the beach and sending the water birds up into the sky in salt-dripping cascades of surprised flight.

She had come with an estimate from Nevin for the repairs on the Boat House and wanted to ask Sol to reconsider. Towing the boat up the shore she returned back to where he watched the returning water fowl and handed him the typed script of information. It was a formally presented list of costly actions and Sol could not help himself but whistle as he read the damage requirements and Nevin's initial report.

'Roof first and fixing of the chimneybreasts, repointing also needed.
Repair to the walls and re-rendering where damp.
Re-roof of the studio shed.
Minor electrical work.
Improved lighting to replace that filled with water.
Re-plaster inside.
Carpets for two rooms.'

"It doesn't matter if you can't afford it," said Gerry, interrupting his reading. She had real concern in her voice, not fully knowing what

Sol was worth. Part of her feared the control that Sol potentially had over her already, even though he had not envisaged this at all. "And," she continued. "The boat's finished. James is sailing here now with it."

Then she paused before emitting a stream of words laced further with more of her guilt-thought. "Listen. I've lived with it for long enough and it's not that bad once you get used to it. There are people out there who don't even have a roof over their heads and so I'm quite lucky really. I'll…"

"No. It's okay," answered Sol taking the list with him in through the *Bothan*'s kitchen. "But I do need to look at how I'm going to finance everything I'll be expected to do over the long term. There are a few jobs up in the other houses as well that I've committed myself to. But this is the largest and most significant."

A moth fluttered by and distracted him. Gerry watched Sol as he stalked it across the ceiling and around the pre-lit lamp.

"Sol?" she asked.

"Hmm?" He was unusually inattentive as his eyes moved with the flapping of the brown dusted wings that caught the flickering of the lamp's light with unexpected iridescence. It was like trying to hold the attention of a small child whilst passing the excitement of a toy or sweet shop. She felt the frustration of the instructive parent whose vital commands had been ignored or only partially received, or the airport control tower officer who knew that their radio signal had broken up and only half of the essential details could be conveyed.

"What are you doing?" she asked watching him croon around the room with a container taken from the surface held aloft in his hand.

"Hmm?" he looked at her and then whipped his head back to see where the moth flew to rest before neatly dropping the green-tint glass jar over it, screwing on the lid and then holding it up to the flare of the paraffin to see better.

"What are you doing?" she repeated. "Sol?"

"Identifying something…" he answered and then wandered off from the kitchen into the living room. "Just a minute, I've seen one like this in this book… …here."

She could hear as he flicked frantically through one of several old tomes he had piled on the front room table.

"But Sol?" she tried again. "Since when have you been interested in moths?"

"Childhood," he muttered squinting at the moth and then back to a picture on a page as the insect continued to batter the smooth glass sides with it wings in an ineffectual escape leaving dust dunes on the jar's base. "I just forgot."

"Forgot what?"

"Hmm?"

"What did you forget?"

"That I was interested," and he turned a page thoughtfully and then scratched his chin. "Isn't it funny what growing up can do?"

"Isn't what funny?" she moved alongside him to see the page he was now running his finger down. Victorian ink-tinted moths were painted with static care into a scene of mixed species on the left hand side of the large leather-bound book, with small type-printed script lining the right to describe form, habitat, niche and distribution. There were black ink and shaded pencil handwritten notes in the margins accompanying that printed. Sol was scanning the text.

Suddenly aware that Gerry was beside him, he looked at her the way that the diabetic does when they realise they must have been low on sugar or the dreamer when they find they have already eaten breakfast but can't remember leaving their bed.

"Sorry?" he questioned. "I don't think I was listening. What did you ask?"

"Isn't what funny?" she repeated patiently. "You said it was funny what growing up can do to someone."

"I just think it's strange. I mean isn't it funny that I forgot this is what I used to do all the time if I had the chance," and he indicated to the books, stray pots and discarded papers. "It's like a *Peter Pan* thing. We grow up and go out into the big bad world and we become serious, infected by commerce and big boy things, and suddenly we forget what it is was that mattered so much when we were children. This," and he pointed again at the moth in the jar. "This was so incredible when I was little. A living thing covered in light-refracting scales that flapped its wings and followed the light. A fat hairy body that I could have hatched out of a caterpillar if I fed it enough in a bottle with a piece of cloth over the top. It was like a toy but not. I needed to feed it, keep it warm, but also cool enough to maintain the right conditions. It had to have the right food plant, the right light and I had to check for parasites and clean them out. I was responsible. Don't you remember doing things like that? It's one of those activities that made childhood and defined it – watching the metamorphosis of an insect from egg to adult. Don't you remember?"

She nodded, but he wasn't finished. With a look of delighted wonderment smeared over his over-stubble'd face, he nodded. "And *then* we let them go in the garden! To be free"

He looked in on the imprisoned lepidopteran, getting ready to allow it freedom now that it had been given its proper name. But then he started to speak again, the words flowing as if pent up behind some barrier of adulthood denied to him since he was young. "Only, some of it does still remain fascinating if we get the chance to rediscover what we got up to before – it feels like a good reason to have children really. Giving us an excuse to go back and do things we wished we hadn't left behind that adults don't let us carry on with."

"There are other reasons to have children," she explained.

"Yes, I know. But I can't believe that I forgot how fascinating all this was. Like this…" and he pushed the jar close to Gerry's face so that her image was distorted and stretched in reflection and the lights of the paraffin flame danced energetically about it in curvaceous lines.

She was unfazed but concerned. "Sol, have you gone mad?"
"No. I've never been saner."
"All mad people say that."
"Do you know what this is?" he asked, ignoring her and indicating the jar.
Gerry looked at it. "No," she replied honestly, sighing at his attitude. "It's just a moth."
"Well look again. There's nothing such as *just* a moth. Like there's nothing such as *just* a bird, *just* a mammal... ...*just* a human. Every one of them is an individual. This is an emperor. I haven't seen one since I was small. It's beautiful. Isn't it?" And he demanded an answer in his poise and expression and so she looked more closely.
It was true. The large grey moth in the jar was half the size of Gerry's palm with clear eyespots marked on its pied-striped fore and hind wings and it had ticks of red that it wore like the epaulets of some elevated military rank.
"Is it rare?"
"No, it's as common as muck. But isn't it great? Who cares about rare when you have this beauty? Only a fool wants to shoot the last rhino. A real safari goer wants to see it all. Even the dung beetle who recycles the poop and without whom we wouldn't have any rhinos anyway."
"Sol, why the sudden interest in moths? And, what are these?" She indicated to cloth bags filled with collecting jars, each containing live insects in various states of dormancy.
"Don't worry," he explained, "they are all being released in a moment. I've identified them."
"But why? It's just like having old G here again."
"Call it a continuation of his work then... ...why is of course an unfair question. The sort of thing that little children ask to annoy their parents. Why do most people do the things they do? Why climb Everest? Why go for a walk? Why collect cars or stamps?"

Gerry answered him dutifully. "Because we can and it makes the person doing it happy?"

"That's good enough reason for me…"

"It's like having an addict in the house. Just look at the mess! You used to smoke didn't you?"

"Yes, why?"

"Is this what you're replacing it with? Putting one addiction in to make up for the other?"

Sol grinned. "I used to do a lot of things. Maybe I'm going to replace them all with just one great big obsession."

It was true that the house looked a state today, with there being a series of messed up clues to his activities around the place laying discarded where he had lost interest in them and flitted on to the next. And so he allowed Gerry to boss him into putting the books back on to the shelves, the coffee mugs through the sink and the insects back out into the garden. She in turn listened to what he had seen that day, being somewhat thankful when she saw Nevin arriving nervously at the door to disturb them.

James coughed as he entered the porch.

"Nevin, please *do* come in," Gerry greeted. "Sol's gone mad. It's the fresh air or the brown water or something. It seems to have sent him completely bonkers."

"I'm not disturbing am I?" James asked hesitantly crossing the threshold. Sol was in the living room recounting bird names to an unseen audience and Gerry was busy cleaning the range top of the scars left from Sol's attempts to cook.

"Disturb us?" she laughed. "Please do." She then indicated towards the living room. "It's too late for Sol. He's already very disturbed."

Sol appeared at the door to the kitchen.

"James. Welcome. I was just telling Gerry about what I've found over the last few days. Are you interested?"

James was about to say that he was, when Gerry butted in to explain that he was in too much of a rush. "Important business to catch up with," was her only genuine attempt at moving them on and out.

"And the quote?" Nevin asked with some trepidation.

Sol quickly agreed to the repair costs with little haggling for price, and together James and he worked out a basic schedule by which the work would be done, with Sol setting the caveat that where possible no bats would be disturbed in the roof if there were any. Instead he wanted photographs taken for identification purposes. Gerry giggled at this sudden concern for the wild world and then went to make a late supper for them all in the kitchen.

"Is this the attention to detail that made you such a good businessman in London?" she asked as she left the room.

"Know thy enemy!" he called through to her. "If you know more than the competition, if you have one more fact to impress a client, if you can act just that second faster in a deal, if you have a better picture of what you are buying or selling, then…"

Gerry interrupted him. "…you'll be a business man my son? Isn't that by Rudyard Kipling?"

They ate a hearty meal of bread, butter and cheese, with some left over trout from Sol's catch of the day before. They enjoyed a glass of '*Gerry red*' which she had brought with her as a thank you gift to Sol. It was a pleasant wine, poured from a recycled, second-hand, green-glass bottle wrapped up in a handmade poorly-glued label, not in the league of the good reds that Sol usually ordered without discretion. But it was a virtuous drink in which he did not get the usual *hints* of berries, because it tasted of berries, nor the *suggestion* of oak, as it had a full-bodied oakiness and tannic nature. It was nothing like his usual high class, expensive wine. It was just good and uncomplicated, and it complimented well the local bread, local cheese and local butter without the need for *swaffing* and a pretentious well-trained nose and palate to appreciate it.

James had made the fire well, with all thoughts of rushing off now far from his mind, and promised to brush the *Bothan's* chimney at the earliest possible opportunity as he did not want Sol smoked out or to die of carbon monoxide poisoning, for which Sol was thankful. James was quick to say that this was not necessarily friendship – he would only get paid if Sol were alive. The air warmed with the emotion of the hearth and the glow of its embers but was further heated by the gentle flow of the conversation.

Sol learnt James' thoughts on the glen and how one man could not own it all. He took no offence that it had been purchased by him and caused no offence in his replies either. But he also found out how Nevin feared for the future of the whole area and the way in which it would have to change if any of them were to survive and continue to enjoy a livelihood.

"What do you need?" asked Sol. "What do you need to carry on?"

"Boats on the water," James answered. "Wooden boats to build or repair and a fishing fleet would be a start, and someone to start using the creels again for the lobster and the crabs. There's hundreds stacked up waiting but no money to entice anyone back out on to the water. The nets are there too. All I want is for the firm to continue for another generation so that I'm not the James Nevin it ends with."

"So you want kids as well then?" asked Sol. "You have two babies to invest your future in. The boatyard and a child."

"Doesn't everyone want kids?" James retorted. "Otherwise what legacy have we left once we've gone? We're here for a short while, borrow our bit of the earth and then what? It rots back down and everything we were is simply forgotten and recycled. Children take something of us on and are the reason to make sure that we look on to what the next generation has left. There's no point just living for the now. That's too finite."

Sol went quiet and stared into the flames. "I've never thought that far ahead before," he replied after a while. "Life's always been in the immediate. You know? Whatever I've been up to at that particular moment, how much I can make, what can I sell. But it's funny, now I have started to...   ...well, I want another generation to have this estate after me. People to enjoy it in the future if I can bring it about. I don't want to let everyone down, nor the wild things."

"So you do want children?" asked Gerry suddenly moved.

"I didn't say that," Sol replied. "I'm not sure what I want. Except I do know that I want my legacy left right here in this house. A few days ago I didn't. Now I do."

Gerry sailed Nevin back to the yard in *The Tern*, quickly floating off into the evening's blackness, and Sol sat and thought about what it was that he wanted in and from life.

What legacy did he really desire? What did he want to leave? What was his mark going to be? Would it be seen as good or bad in hindsight? Would anyone care or remember his brief spell here in the Bothan?

He turned in for the night early after leaving scraps out for the cats in the bucket. Tonight he would give them the privacy of darkness. Unusually he used a bed, packing up his damp dirty sleeping bag from where it lay stranded on the mattress of the back room and finding sheets in the drawers and a patchwork quilt that gave the room a homely look. This would be Gerry's room in the future. It was larger, had good views and was more what he would want her to have whilst under his care. He liked her, already cared for her and was just slightly aware that Nevin was in the way of any relationship that he might want to develop. But Nevin too was a good man and seemed happy to be a friend for now.

Tomorrow he would clear the spare room better, but at this moment, fatigued, he threw his sleeping bag onto the musty single that lay there, hidden behind the cabinets, inched his way in, snuffed the lamp and then fell quickly asleep, but on the wrong side of the depth his body required.

Sounds travel further in the cold air when there aren't the distractions of rising particles to filter and deaden them. Night brings greater clarity still as if the air rarefies in some strange way and gives noise properties that it cannot have during the day when even light appears to disturb and muffle it. Then we ourselves are less side-tracked anyway as we experience so little that can take our attention away from hearing the sound and our senses are more aware.

In darkness, in an unfamiliar place, such as a change of room, we become alert to so much more.

With his eyes closed, Sol could hear the night noises of the *Bothan*. The ticking of her walls as they lost their temperature to the evening's sky and the scratching of the rodents who probed it for succour. Even slugs make sound as they glisten their way across a cold wall and scratch it with their arc-sweeping radula teeth.

A housefly buzzes louder than a wasp and walls, no matter their thickness, still allow through the call of the owl, the pipe of the curlew, the barking of deer and the unearthly screech of a mating fox. The roof tiles creaked and pulsated with the wind's massage and above he could sense that bats were on the prowl by that pressurised sensation of the temples that cannot be placed as a sound but instead is felt and absorbed into the centre of the brain.

However, he lay content. Only days before he would have been in fear of the ghost-calls of the night. But now he was able to give each sound a label and to produce a mind's picture of the creature that bore it, and with informed knowledge he had lost his fear. After all, the greatest terror is ignorance and not knowing.

With the wind and weather more settled, Sol spent Sunday out on the headland either watching the sea or looking through the plants that grew thick and dry up there. He followed the river for a while along its snaking course where it opened out and then contracted again and again to form shallow pools that slid over and then between rocks or dropped into steep narrow gullies. At times pebble beaches had been laid up on the bends and it seemed to meander in an unrushed lazy fashion and yet at others the same river took to rushing and crashing, descending down riffled banks, singing the sweetest notes, or simply dropped several feet into deep darkness from which it gurgled and coughed.

Flies haunted its surface. Some, rising in magnificent swarms, broke the surface from below and learnt to fly innately in the few seconds it took them to crack out of their back-split cases, struggle against the tension and then dry their wings. Others needed time to hang limply from the stems of emergent vegetation as they pumped their tubular wing veins to un-crimp and extend the satin-finished membranes that would give them flight. Yet others came from the moor itself, gathering in spinning clouds to dip into the wider tarns and puddles, mating in their nuptial throngs, dropping eggs in dashed sorties of the water and fighting for the best and most likely spaces within their mobs.

Blue damselflies, dragon-faced and bright with side-flung eyes and biting jaws, defended territory from the grasses that rocked over the water where it drifted slowest along in peat-tainted brownness. Sol presumed they were males as they flew in to attack or impress any insect that passed within their set boundaries and they courted the drabber green-brown females, linked with them and then continued to fly in their duet dance until her eggs were laid on the surface and the genetics of their next generation secured.

Water drained from the higher peat hags in random burns cut deep into the moor. They babbled and chuckled as they bounded and fled the high ground. Logs of fallen timber had been driven down into the soft earth until they hit the iron rich layer of the podsol and held fast against the stones and shingles transported and polished by the glaciers of the last ice-age. Some shepherd before him had fashioned a network of sheep tracks and shooter ways, creating these bridges to take the wary on a safe route through the moor.

There were cairns placed along the way which marked the paths from above, stood as if they were carved cobbled sentry guards to an ancient civilisation. Piles of stones built up to be seen in the worst of weathers or when the snows were drifting the upper lands, they were watchmen in the clag and mist and would appear as magical guiding characters when the clouds hemmed in. They were decorated in Pictish fashion by the lichens that clung to their weather-etched surfaces.

Here, where the rain's attention left few days unnoticed, the sphagnum developed huge flat masses, and, where the waters gathered in boggy sink pits, it grew to form a continuous sheet that made the traveller feel secure enough to walk across it, but also concealed a deep dangerous quagmire below. Placing his already wet foot experimentally on the edge of a morass, Sol tested the strength of this floating pitfall and watched the land ahead of him rock in synchrony with the waves he had set up. It was anything but innocent and pleaded with him to join it and be enveloped in a mire grave that would preserve his body for the future in its tannic depths.

Grouse '*cocked*' and spluttered, and red-leg partridge '*chuk-chuck-chakked*' as he passed too close, they suddenly breaking cover and revealing a flock of at least ten of them, desperate and edgy. There were deer on the horizon but they knew he was there and matched his speed and kept their distance as if programmed to always retain the same equidistant space between them at all times.

When the track split Sol decided he would heed Gerry's advice for now and not take the higher road that chased on and upwards towards the mountain's top. It was mostly visible and exciting in its scale. Sweeping scree slopes dropped rapidly from a sheer horseshoe and ice had formed rock solid waterfalls that crept down the hillside and flung themselves into the dips in its structure, giving a sense of harmony that was pleasing to the eye. In its beauty Sol knew that, like in the sea, danger lay there, and without experience and preparation what appeared striking and majestic could quickly lead to injury or death, and for once he understood the term '*limitation*'. '*Better to be fearful and live than be too brave and die,*' his grandfather's gentle voice chimed in his mind's memory voice.

Gerry would have been proud!
Instead, he unwrapped thick-crusted sandwiches, spread out his coat on the ground, sat down in the hot May sun and drank soiled water scooped in the cup of his hand direct from the burn. It was chocolate in tint, thinly-soiled in texture and coppered with the hint of whisky to the taste; a sharp relief of ice-coldness.

The second spur of the path led across the moor and took an ambling route that more or less kept with the wide and shallow basin of the river, rising and falling with the gullies that fed it. Sol could trace it further up to the hills where a small cottage sat in the distance that he immediately recognised as Joe's and the Gillie House. A flat, sun-reflecting body of water expanded beyond under the care of the mountain, and he wondered at what distance the trout must have fought and migrated to get up that far, where they had come from and why. Yet more questions for the enquiring naturalist's mind busied themselves around his brain burgeoning into the need for research and the potential for a myriad projects and field studies.

He placed his chin on a rock and looked down on the river, moving gravity-powered in its strained-tea, frothed edged way. A dipper skipped up against it *'peeping'*, before it settled on the exposed head of a water-lapped boulder, dipped its legs and then dived again under the water and into the splash-side of a plunging rapid. It emerged in seconds with a beak filled with invertebrates, shuddering at the knee on its short legs, living up to its name and flashing its white brown bib synchronously with the water's rippling.

Linnets, larks and pipits sang and peeped from the heather and wagtails dallied around the waters giving their positions away by their loud *'chiset'* calling. Above were the hirundines, hawking and cycling in bundles of flocking bodies for the flies that abounded and there was a small predatory bird that launched itself out of the dwarf trees that crept into the gullies and sheltered places. It was too quick for Sol to put a name to it, lithely skipping the tufts of vegetation.

Once, a small striped lizard sinuously crossed the sand of the dry section of path he sat on. It stopped, mid slope, and tried to make sense of him. Head on its side, it looked intently as if trying to determine if he was friend or foe. The two engaged, the diminutive and the gargantuan. The lizard lost interest first and skidded off with a side-rocking body on alternately placed feet to be lost again in the overgrown jungle of the heathland stems.

Sol took out a notepad and scribbled enough detail to be able to recall it later and made a sketch map of his location, attempting a simple drawing of his position in case he were to stop here again. He then decided that he would walk up to Joe's the next day, whatever the weather, and surprise him, taking a gift just out of kindness. Sol was missing people in some sense and he wondered if Joe felt the same way, especially after so many years of married life before him. He seemed quite content to sit by his loch and watch it blindly, waiting for the end. But then Sol speculated that there might also be a very lonely man up there by the upper waters, hiding behind the façade of contentment that he displayed to everyone who asked him. He might have been blind but it would be nice for him to be seen.

The moors seemed as if they were an empty place between winter and summer, different from the way they were now. Surely there was desolation in those months, when it was hemmed in by snow and when the wind, the wet and the hail hampered ordinary living. Then Joe's existence must be tested.

The multi-horned head of a Jacob sheep raised its profile above the heather and gorse. Only Hamish could own a sheep like this one, traditional, hardy and ancient-styled. A remnant of the old ways and a survivor of the moors, who despite every pressure to conform, adapt and change to the commercialised method of today had resisted. They were just like Hamish, and, of course, Joe.

Sol returned to the rock on the headland via the fly-strewn path and sat to make another sketch and record further notes.

'*Gannets are diving the water close to the shore. Terns there too. I can see sand eels and expect there will be mackerel shoals feeding on them. Shags flying up the loch, look full up and heading towards rocks by the Bothan to dry. Ugly, sinister things, but quite spectacular stood on their rocky outcrops hanging their feathers out to dry. Lend a real sense of mysterious ambience to the scene and look like dinosaurs with their beaks upright and backward glances.*

Geese have goslings with them and I've seen speckled chicks that I suspect are waders. There are a large number of golden plover gathered on the shore and I can see a heron fishing the shallows on the river where it opens into the loch.

Sea eagle flew over again today – what a bird! Wings stretched to the size of a small car. Am certain it is the same one I saw fishing the other day but it doesn't behave as if it has seen me even.

The Bothan needs a good whitewash this summer as it looks quite yellow-green from up here.'

That night, Sol prepared food for the wildcats as normal and then searched the drawers for a white sheet. He remembered an experiment as a boy that he wanted to repeat and he spread the cloth evenly over the flattest section of the yard, close to the wood edge but also with a clear view up the woodland ride, up the glen and out to the loch. He made sure that the near white wall of the *Bothan* was also within the sphere of the sheet and a light source placed on it to offer a further site of entrapment.

Then he placed a paraffin lamp in the middle of the area and lit it as the light fell away and the dusk became master of the cottage's scenery.

The evening was damp but warm with a thick insulating layer of cloud to hem the heat of the Earth back down and to prevent it from radiating wastefully out into space. It was an evening designed for mothing, where all that could, as determined by their speed of growth according to the theory of '*day-degrees*', would hatch early, metamorphose quickly and fly out on the wing as fully developed as they could be for this time of the year.

He used his laptop to place an order for food to be delivered in the week and a camera with flash to arrive on the same day, both to the end of the drive. Then he foolishly checked his messages and the state of his steadily declining shareholdings. Neither made him feel more upbeat, but he ran a thought process in his head, so different to his previous mind-set that he was startled; but he was heartened by it too.

If the share prices drop and I am bankrupt, the sun will still rise tomorrow.

If the sun still rises tomorrow then there is hope for the wild things here.

If there is hope, then the shares may improve.

Let's remain hopeful.

So much in life seemed to rely on this sort of confidence and he saw some evidence of the effect that wild things can have on even the most urbane of lifestyles.

He read through the messages that his phone retained.

Sue had written just to tell him how she was getting on... ...going out with some friends... ...they had found someone they wanted her to meet... ...another man... ...did that bother him?

He wrote back slightly downbeat but as positive as he could. Of course he did not mind. She had her own life and he had his, and they should both move on. As it was, he was meeting plenty of new people. He wished her luck in meeting the new person and asked some basic questions to feign interest.

It was definitely at an end, then.

But he knew that already, and was at least enjoying closure, and had to move on.

She replied quickly and thanked him, also congratulating him on the photographs that Pete was circulating of the wildcat and her kittens. He was causing quite a stir.

Office finalising his accounts with them and making allowances for his continued commissions to be paid...   ...however small they predicted them to be in the current financial markets.

There was no message from the therapist that strangely had the greatest impact on Sol's stress levels of anything she had done for him in the last few, somewhat expensive, years. He sensed relief and a total lack of guilt – he actually felt quite free.

Brother writing a brief message in the hope that he was well... ...glad he had moved out of the city...   ...maybe he could see more sense in the world and find a heart worthy of a thus far wasted life.

Sol wrote back his thanks, stating that he felt he was a changing man. He asked how life was up on their grandfather's old farm and sought information as to his nephew and how he was growing up. Was there anything they needed?

As a first proper text exchange between them for eleven years, Sol felt it went quite well.

Pete asking what kit he might need and what habitats were available to work in...   ...huge excitement mounting as a result of Sol's photographs taken on his phone of all things...   ...quite a queue of people wanting to come up and see the wildcats...   ...they could talk next week...   ...could he have a selfie for the blog?

Sol declined to send a portrait for now and outlined the different biomes on the estate. He also enquired as to when Al and he proposed to visit and for how long.

Al seeking information on the accommodation and the nearest hotel if necessary...   ...had Sol sussed out the local hostelries yet? There was not much to go on the net and his guides were drawing up a blank...   ...he was keen to connect with the wild if in a clean, warm way and preferably one that was augmented by the application of television or IT...   ...he would leave any rough stuff to Pete... ...how far was he off the beaten track? Was there any news on obtaining the violin?

The reply simply suggested that Al might need to stay in New Town and commute up to *Bothan Faobhar* if he was going to be satisfied with anything less than a few cushions on the floor or a tent. Sol ignored the violin comment. He copied his reply to Pete who seemed only too eager to bring a tent and stay out in the wilds if he could – with the landowner's permission of course, which he hoped Sol would agree to.

Sol laughed as he sent back another message. He knew Pete would love it up here and would need little encouragement to get the most out of it. Al was a different animal who kept nature at bay and lived within very strict limits as to how much of the natural world he was to be exposed to at any time.

True he had put himself in harm's way on an everyday basis with his predilection for alcohol, wild living and food, and herbal experimentation, but it was restricted to that which he felt he had control over, that had been tested through its normalisation in his upper echelon of society and what was considered fashionable within the circles he moved within. However, that did not mean that someone like him could live happily if he was deprived of fine food, well-presented wine, clean sheets and staff to wait on him. That sort of thing never happened to him, even when he travelled on safari or tour in developing nations where, despite experiencing local poverty from the safety and security of his air-conditioned wagon, and understanding the hardships of those he was allowed to see from the window of his sumptuous hotel room, he was never quite exposed to the reality. From his position he could buy the carefully selected favours of the equally well-chosen natives he was allowed to meet, harvest and waste the hard won resources needed by the starving, poorly treated and sanitised populous, and reek environmental havoc, without ever once having to get his own hands dirty. No, his sheets were to be clean or they would be changed, his food perfect or it would be returned, his wine the right temperature or it would be tipped away, and his entertainment lavish or fashionable, or else it would be ignored at best and shunned or criticised publicly at worst. The Internet was the friend of a man like Al, both for the power of good and the potential for publicity and success, and for what it could do to deliver the worst in society to his own benefit.

He paid for things and often owned them, and thus he expected something beyond the sustainable and Sol began to worry about his imminent arrival and decided to broach the problem with Gerry in the morning.

Phone away and placed on charge he headed out to the garden, spreading himself out by the white sheet and wall where he started to collect moths and to try and identify them in the close slung humidity of the evening. There were many of just a few species, but the light trap produced a widening diversity the longer he sat, as frantic shapes buzzed in and fluttered his face. Midges started to discover the exposed salt-water'd skin on his sweating forehead and arms, finding the gaps where his socks did not fit tight to his trouser legs. Scratching was futile but unavoidable.

He reeled off the descriptive names of his lepidoteran finds, scribbling notes in his book to add to G's record and keeping those he found more difficult in jars to identify later. But the sky was alive with them as a result of the pollution free air and land the estate provided.

Some sat in groups, '*carpets; the garden, common and water*', the overbearing '*drabs*' and '*quakers*', and the '*prominents*'. Others' names described their patterns, '*yellow-barred brindle, beautiful hooktip and brimstone*' and texture '*muslin moth*', or their food plant, '*scalloped hazel*', and even their seasonal timing '*early thorn*'. But there was one moth of them all, flying in its tens that lived up to its name to perfection. The '*Hebrew character*' each with their own white Hebrew scroll written on every forewing; descriptive in name and nature.

It was enough to send an entomologist into raving cycles and when satiated with more than a hundred moths on the sheet and the wall Sol silenced the lamp, overwhelmed at those little things that fly and were so often and so easily ignored; the night-fliers, the moths. The cats came and went, the mother with her two kits in tow who were chastised as they played at the edge of the white cotton spread around the lamp, hooking at shadow moths and snatching at real ones. The largest pounced successfully to bring down a fat brown-bodied moon chaser with white highlights to its wings and padded it soundly to the ground. There it de-winged and devoured it, chewing stickily on the side as cats do as they cut tooth against tooth, scissor-like carnassial teeth chopping cleanly. Proud of its kill, it sneezed at the wing-scale dust before backing off into the shadows to follow the security of its bucket-stalking mamma.

Nights are not always like this for the naturalist, following on from days as before, but when they do occur they stick in the mind and encourage the seeker through the drought times when nothing sought is seen, smelt, sensed or heard. Very few places yield something unusual every calendar day. But that again brings into question what a naturalist actually is.

Are they people looking for the unusual or working in exotic places?

No, the real naturalists are those who find questions in nature to ask wherever they are and whatever they are watching. Because they are in fact the only person seeing that one thing they are actually sighting, at that very time in that very place, making every observation unique; even the mundane and even the everyday and even the common.

The naturalist is an ordinary person.

What makes them different is just that they are the ones who stop to look at what others miss and who openly and wantonly ask the questions that cross their minds in the first place.

Chapter 17: The Tenacity of Heather

(The Lark Ascending, Ralph Vaughan Williams)

The desire for company is a natural one even though we each have differing requirements for it with some just needing the occasional letter or posting and others requiring continual affirmation and contact. The former would be no good if working in a busy boarding house where they are likely to be with people all of the time and disturbed throughout their sleeping hours, and the latter would have been unable to carry out roles such as that of a lonely lighthouse keeper in a bygone age. But few could cope with such conditions, some even having gone mad after a period of time, and others, either out of choice or desperation, turned to study of the wildlife and seas around them instead, or took up art, writing, poetry or music.

But company we do all need in some way and without it some smaller, or possibly greater, part of us withers and then dies. Like a tree separated from its roots, the fresh leafy canopy will rapidly fade and dry, crinkle up and then drop, leaving just the bare structures that were once nutrient and succour-transporting supports. Now they are left as internally parched and dead crisps that will soon rot and join the other dead leaves in their perpetual return to the humus of the future soil.

The tree's own protective bark will peel away and insects, fungi and other saprotrophs will move in, take their share, and eventually reduce it to dust or liquid. What had been a magnificent crown, capable of having future beauty, potential flowers and fruit, or to persistently grow outwards in its continual strive for the sky's light in up-praising branched arms, will be no more, much reduced and then gone.

It is possible that the roots are still alive, connecting, anchoring, supplying and giving life. They may re-shoot given the right conditions, and one single standard tree produces a replacement, never the same as before but a near replica in basic form. Or else, with careful pruning the stool stump could throw up poles to become an increasingly complex character of many stems, coppiced just the once or many times, creating a tree that can last many more times than its former singular-stemmed self could. Few of us think that such brutal damage can be good for us in the long term, and certainly it is impossible to realise it at the time of suffering or hardship. But there it is in the analogy of a tree where the cut back growth re-shoots and takes on a new path – but it is the old roots that retain it and allow it to flourish or fail.

But then, any ecologist knows full well that it is far deeper white mushroom roots and cycles that sustain real growth. A tree can only succeed if that plethora of fungal fingers, the hyphal mycelia, allows it to, tapping into the carbon richness of the grandest trees, interconnecting it with others, the stragglers and the runts, the young and the infirm, the locally dispersed and the alien invader alike. One tree, like one man, is no island, and instead only lives on to a fulfilled life if in some very small way it remains part of an integrated community and union. Then it can utilise the full resource of the woodland and the hidden roots and networks that often go undetected below ground, until we lose them, when we, like trees, wither and we die. That is what it is like to be totally alone.

Sol woke from a deep slumber with a start, but he didn't know why.

He was slotted into the single bed of the spare room where the light struggled to fully filter the chamber and touch was a greater asset than sight. Organisms floated in bottles of formaldehyde and alcohol on the flat tops of insect drawers and the herbarium, and it took him a while to focus and dispel sleep from his eyes. He wondered if something had moved amongst them or if his mind was just playing tricks after a night obsessing over moths, those fluttering tenants of the dark that had followed him to sleep mentally and physically. Certainly he had felt them crawling through his hair and clothes during the night as they had refused to leave him after the moth trap had been silenced, and he had been forced to brush more than a few away now in the dim-light seen as smears of darkness pressed flat against the inconsistency of the paint covering on the walls.

Nothing moved, but the air wasn't still either.

He lay in the sinking bed considering if it was a good enough place of sleep for Al to use later this week. Realistically he knew not but then tried to justify it in his thoughts for a few minutes longer.

It was too lumpy and poorly sprung, smaller than he would have been used to, and like much of the building and its contents it held a musty odour about it, something that would not go unless it was deeply cleaned or replaced. The ends of the bed were brass but the close proximity of the cabinets left little room for anyone to appreciate their intertwined cast metal floral designs, showing sinuous copper stems and thorny branches ending cleverly in stylised brass lacquered flowers. They would polish well and he could make the place more comfortable with little effort. But he doubted it would be enough for Al.

There was space about the room into which he could push the collection cabinets, and with he could make the place more habitable. But the walls would always be dark and the room never fully lit. Sol decided this was probably a good thing so that Al could not be too critical of it, and hoped that he would become used to the surroundings quickly or else take up residence in one of the inns in the two towns.

Scratch, scratch, scratch.

A scrabbling and scraping rushed itself to the fore of Sol's attention and he slowly rose in the bed, joints creaking and complaining as much as the springs as they held almost taught in the frame below him. Something *was* there.

He steadily vacated his sleeping bag – Al would need proper sheets and a blanket – and followed the noises coming from the kitchen.

Crash!
Something large enough to move plates was here and Sol started to list the bigger creatures he could think of that would be capable of doing this. Most, he recalled with sincere gratitude, were extinct in Britain, and an initial fear was replaced by curious excitement; very different to the Sol who arrived at the *Bothan* previously, who always aired on the side of the fantastical, movie-bred or imaginative. Now he was inquisitive and exhilarated.
Lap, lap, lap.
The creature was obviously taking advantage of his poor housekeeping, the unwashed dishes in the porch and, as judged by the steady passage of fresh, dawn-moistened air, the open door. Sol was on his feet and had slipped through the bedroom and hall and then across the groaning floor-boarded living room, between the fire and the easy chairs, without being detected. Then gripping the solid wall of the kitchen, he inched his way into the room.
Just visible from the doorway was a red-orange bristletail, flecked with black and brown and tipped with its overall undercoat of cream-white. Soft flanks were supporting a well-formed waist and the rear paws were each painted black with clawed pads. Sol positioned himself so as to get a clearer view, but knew that much closer, or less cautious movement, and the creature would be gone.
It was the smell that stood out most, and even though he understood that this highly scented canid was an unpopular animal for many in the countryside, he was quite touched by the presence of the usually 'oh-so-cautious' red fox in his own porch. However, he also knew this was not a relationship to be encouraged as this commensal of man and advantage taker of the farmer and pheasant breeder, the wily Reynard himself, would soon be in the kitchen every day, pinching the scraps or beating the wildcats to their food, or worse still injuring the kittens. Despite this, he could not help but be warmed by the rich colours, lit by a low draped morning sun that tinted the world; a burning red to complement the fox's own.

The musked animal lapped noisily at the fragment of a plate now spread over the stone flags and was enjoying the refined sugar taste of jam and the richness of salted, yellow-fatty butter.

Sol moved a chair so that he could sit and watch, wishing that coffee could be made silently so that it felt more like breakfast TV and he could sit in comfort whilst the wild played out their carefully co-ordinated theatre. His phone was on the table and so he thought, '*why not?*' and he stretched out, leant forwards and reeled off several snaps.

The fox looked up, aware of disturbance close by, licked its lips with a black-pink sandpaper tongue, and then the rear flanks disappeared, Sol presumed through the door. But he held his breath and waited just in case, holding the mobile up in hope that there would be a second and better chance of some visible display that would remunerate his unusual patience and stealth. Rewarded, an intelligent white-cheeked face peered around the doorframe, with sharp, some would say devious, auburn eyes. Black-fringed ears were pricked up in their hunt for detail and information, and a coal-coloured nose, mat yet wet, was a quiver in search of the source of that change in the atmosphere that had caused its distraction. Clean upper teeth, just visible, were suspended from a jaw that jutted out straight and dog like, drawn into a muzzle that reflected its domestic cousin's origins, and a black-gummed lower palate protected a deep pink, panting tongue, that was still stippled with crumbs of bread, and was lined neatly with the ivory pegs of its teeth. It heaved a puffed up chest, downy and white.

The picture was perfect and Sol only hoped that his phone's camera was good enough.

The photograph was taken.

The animal was recorded.

The moment in time was captured for as long as the digital existed.

He then lowered the mobile and gave the wild animal before him the proper respect it demanded, and they watched each other from across the kitchen table, both acutely aware of the other, until the fox decided the risks were too great. It slipped away, melting backwards through the open porch doorway and slinking into the yard.

"Not what I expected before breakfast," Sol muttered, and then he set to clearing the mess the fox had left and hoping its rank smell would soon clear from his kitchen. "At least, " he thought, "that's one less plate to clean."

And then, after he had re-stoked the fire for coffee, he laughed at how Al was going to respond to a fox on the kitchen tiles, a wildcat in the yard, mice that pinched the bread crumbs and birds that given half the chance would be in through the door taking what was left. This was not to mention the spiders in every room and the snails and slugs that were living by, and probably in, the beds, the birds in the roof space that scratched all night, the sounds of the woodland animals and the screams of the owl. He began to pity the visit of Al and so he sent his photograph on to Pete with a message that sustained his laughter throughout his forcibly early breakfast.

Dropping his mobile phone clumsily on to the kitchen table he made himself ready for the day. But when he left through the open porch door this time he checked it was firmly closed. It seemed that at *Bothan Faobhar* you never quite knew who, or what, would pop in uninvited if you gave them half a chance.

The air was refined bright and clear with the distant horizon appearing closer that it was in reality giving the mountains steeper gradients, the sea loch greater depth and a more intense green and blue, and the sky a formidable stretch that seemed to span wider than it usually was. The scenes were broad and the joy of being alive far-reaching.

Sol headed on up the crag face behind the wood where every new blossom claimed his attention victim as he steadily made the headland path and beat a track through the heather that itself was showing the bright green buds of new growth and preparedness to flower in July. Tracks of land were enclosed in its blanket, except where a finely winnowed birch or haggard scot's pine broke the monotony, and it was also bisected by the burn-ridden track that would eventually lead on to Joe's.

In his shoulder-slung holdall Sol carried biscuits and a half bottle of whisky together with the wisdom of a raincoat and an extra layer to wear should the rains come, which up here they could do rapidly and unbidden. He was hastily learning that the weather cycled and recycled rain on a daily basis and that although the advantage of living so close to the sea was greenery and life, this was only possible because of the continuity of supply of water. Over his other shoulder he carried his violin case, and as he walked he added a new riff to the symphony of his mind to play to Joe.

To him it was the music that floated over the heathland heather, that most tenacious of plants that beat back the inclemency of the elements to eek out a crowded existence up here on the moor and stretched high up in glen-hugging spits on to the mountain itself. There were ash-fired sections where the shepherds had burnt the deadwood of old stems back to the precious olive rootstocks that were already regenerating and shooting, sprouting and greening. They would provide nutritious relief to the sheep and the grouse, another onslaught set against it. But no matter what hit it, the heather returned.

Above, the ubiquitous lark trilled and hovered, and now it could not help itself but marry its soft accompaniment into the counter melody captured in his head, light and airy over the brooding mass of purpling shrub. The lapwing leapt in flop-winged ecstasy screaming its ancient name of '*pee-wit*' as it flew in and slumped to the ground to feign injury and to draw the unwary away from its camouflage-hidden eggs or chicks.

A diamond-backed adder uncoiled its fat grey roundness from its sunning rock and melted across the dusty crack-dried peat and into the heather stems of an un-burnt patch. Here Carex grasses and cotton tufts, which blew like miniature flags, revealed where a boggy hag had snuffed the flames. Alert, it had felt his footfall vibrations from a distance and had waited until the last minute before making its hasty departure and taking its leave. Funny how the poison-fanged predator, one feared by so many humans, is, like any bully, the first to run away from the unknown or a potential threat.

A snake! Initial heart-speeding fear gave way to morbid fascination and immediate revulsion was smothered as Sol chased it into the undergrowth tracing its winding, flowing shadow-route into a shaded unknown, the rodent-predator in waiting. Then it was gone, silent and invisible, a cryptic ambush setting a future trap.

The Gillie House came into view as a distant stone edifice speck that wandered in and out of sight as it stood stock still against the hazed ripple and shimmer of the upper loch and the movements of the traveller as they approached. Stopping in the heat of the sky's mid-morning clarity, when the sun had started to have longer each day to heat the land of Scotland than those areas of Britain at lower latitude, Sol caught sight of a tall standing stone, perched at an angle atop a raised peat-smoothed outcrop set above the track way. Inquisitive, he climbed up to join it, cutting a wave through the heather and casting an ever-widening halo of flies that formed an eruption before him.

It was a member of a gathered circle of rocks, huge at about fifty feet across. Sol was surprised by the scale of the stones themselves, each rough cut but stood on end, part buried into the ground and requiring ingenuity to transport, position and erect in a time that Sol assumed pre-dated wheels but obviously also pre-dated health and safety protocols too. Within the outer ring of the twelve largest apostle-like stones was a smaller, concentric one of just two that stood either side of a round pit containing a flattened altar stone. The lichens and mosses here were blacker and more cushioned showing how the water had accumulated in the pits on its surface and allowed the growth of more frondose and thicker leaves.

Sol wondered what these depressions meant to the past race who etched them, and he shuddered convulsively at some of the possibilities that flashed through his mind.

Following the line of view from the centre out to sea, there was a haphazard promenade made of similar large uprights that extended off into the distance and he quickly located the stone on the headland where he had sat so often at a ninety degree angle to the right of this and another up on the hillside to the left. A distant stone lording it above the river's dell marked the position immediately behind and in line with the colonnade ahead. They were man-placed rock beacons, like the ultraviolet reflecting honey guides on flowers painted there by nature to attract the bees, drawing the follower into this circle. But he could only ask why they were here as no one would be left that knew. But it was clearly marked from four different angles, lining up with features on each horizon; a stack of crag-edged stone that emerged out of the white-capped estuary where the gannets wheeled, the cloud-mobbed mountain and her snowfields, the distant peaks across the sea loch where the future storms plotted their next insertion and behind the *Bothan* lain peaceful and at rest in the glen with the track to the main road leading off and beyond.

The spiritual significance of this area of land stretched too far back for memory to recall and beyond that which aural stories retained. When the Christian tradition arrived they too built their church, as Sol well knew, in the bay in the valley at the end of the lines of stones that pointed out to the sea like landing lights lining the sides of an ancient runway. *Strange theories will have been suggested if anyone had the time or inclination to visit this lonely spot. Someone may have an idea, but no one could be certain.*

Sol wondered where the people who left this mark on the landscape had lived and if the very spot where the *Bothan* now lay hid the relics of that age. He would keep this sacred sight secret from Al in case on a whim he came up here to find treasures to sell and make his fortune in recompense for Sol not obtaining him his priceless violin. There were mounded humps in the land around that suggested burial had taken place here and Sol, feeling a sombre and hallowed edge to his intrusion, silently bowed and closed his eyes, then left. Even the plant life on these suspected barrows was different to that around, shorter in stature, darker in shade and more bruised in colour. This was a place he did not want to return to in the dark or even the mist or fog. He felt it held too many ghosts and the coldness of a forgotten lost religion whose gods remained unsure where their followers had gone and now left them, and they therefore no longer had power and yet loitered to see if they could return some day.

Only the heather knew their secrets, and Sol felt that their roots will have penetrated many a dead man and woman, and with a shiver down his spine wondered why he was so affected. Even the grouse called '*go-back, go-back*' which was advice enough for him to follow.

The Gillie House was quickly achieved at a brisk walk with Sol counting the fish that jumped on his way up to the upper loch, staggered at the ordeals they must overcome if they were to migrate up to here in the spring to breed. Although there were pools and refreshing shallows, there were also waterfalls and riffles, white waters and rocks, not to mention the overall distance of some miles inland and up.

Joe was sat on the bench as usual watching the waters blankly.

"Hello, Sol," he called, giving away his usual overly informed knowledge of who was coming up the track. "I thought it was you but was only really sure when I heard your feet on the scree. You have an uneven walk and it has different timbre to the others."

"Joe," Sol greeted, "I came to keep you company."

"Or to get some for yourself," laughed the old man.

"Yes, maybe."

"I've some fish keen to meet you and the fiddle has been idle all day long so far. I'd gladly be your company and it's very pleasant you walked up to see me. Thank you."

They fished, they talked, they fished some more and Joe spoke of legends and bulls of the water, but he also told Sol of the thousand mile journeys of the fish, the food they ate, then about their enemies and the sea. Sol was surprised that the old man had never been to London, and had hardly left this area, but gave him a potted history of his life there and what he did and what he wished he hadn't done. It was as if Joe were some priest and here by this baptismal pool of the upper loch he could be freer having completed his confession.

Back to the rod, they both caught trout but then released any they did not need or which were too small for the table. Joe talked Sol through their shapes, their sexes, their ages and was able to determine something of their life histories each time. He showed care and connection with the animal as he held them under the water, stood waste deep next to them, gently ensuring their safety and health before he let them escape to hide by the reeds to recover.

"So," asked Joe, "when did you last see your father?"

The silence that followed interested him but he moved on not wanting to pry on any one topic.

"…and your brother?"

There was a pause before which Sol muttered, "eleven years ago." He swallowed as he spoke which affected his clarity and so he repeated it again. "But I have written to him. Texts."

"He'll write back, just you see," the old man said confidently and he felt the need to move on in the subject of discussion. "Shall we play?"

Thankful for the change of conversational direction, Sol collected his violin from its case. As he lifted it he heard the tinkle of glass breaking in shards, the music of icicles fragmented at the tip. There was a small, brass lined oval photograph in one of the cases' pockets. It pictured in minute scale a happy moment between Sue and he in that photo booth dressed up as if for dinner. He pushed the picture and the blades of glass back down into the flap and pretended not to have seen it. Somethings would always remain broken.

Joe sensed a change and wondered at the noise, at the charge of emotion and at the silence that followed before the two struck their strings together.

Joe taught Sol three new melodies that they could play as fiddle duets at the next meeting on Thursday and then asked Sol to describe his walk up to the Gillie House in music, which he did. The old man sat throughout with his eyes closed, smiling in response to Sol's working of the river and frowning at the angst felt in the stone circle and responding to the relief of the retreat and then the final walk up to the loch.

"That's good," he muttered. "I could remember the walk up from the *Bothan* through that music and...   ...did you visit the stone circle on the way too?" Sol nodded. "Yes, it spooks me as well... ...write that music down, it has to go in your symphony." And then he thought carefully before speaking again. "G would have loved it."

They shared biscuits and demonstrated a mutual interest in whisky with Joe bringing his own half bottle out to accompany Sol's and for them to compare.

The company of the old is something the young so often fail to appreciate, even forgetting that one day, when youth has passed them by and in a future they cannot envisage, as in their minds they will be forever young and age will never catch them up, they too will join the ranks of the old. There is much to learn from those who have lived life at our age before us, and much to give. But, more importantly, there is always so much more to gain and the investment is so vital to the wellbeing of the older person and our selves.

Just because technology has marched on in ever increasing stride lengths, so that it is no longer recognisable between single generations let alone when we skip two or more, it is important to recall that humans have not. We still have the same desires and ambitions they did even if we have moved on from sepia, through black and white, and, no longer satisfied with mere natural colour and believable texture, we have enhanced it into the realms of the virtual. But we still love and we still hate, we still laugh and we still cry, we still feed and we still get sick, we live and we die, we have our memories, our current lives and hope for our futures, however short the past is or long it has become.

Becoming old is the destination of the majority and being older is the future of us all.

"He took me in, you know?" said Joe in answer to a question that Sol had not asked, and they both sipped whisky from glass tumblers that refracted the light in crystalline patterns, stars trapped in their cut.

"G?"

"Aye. Soon after the war when he left the old house and cut them off from the estate. *'You can't choose your relatives'* he used to say, *'but you can choose your friends'.*" They looked over the loch, neither needing to take the other in visually.

"Were you friends then?" Sol asked.

"Not before I moved in. Born on other sides of the street we were. Him at the big house, and me? Well, let's say I was from a different sort of place." Joe smiled to himself, fond memories sifting through his facial features. "He left to fight in the war as a brave young officer of a thing. I lived down in the town at the time and my mother used to be in service at the big house for the family. It's just a ruin of what it was then. The war didn't seem to affect us much up here, although we did see big ships pass the end of the loch and the soldiers were keen to guard the water but we never found out what from. When he came back he decided he didn't much like people anymore and he wanted nothing but to be left alone. So he took up in *Bothan Faobhar* and cut the family off. He left them stranded in the big house and came and lived in that little house all on his own even though it needed a lot of work on it to make it habitable." Joe indicated roughly in the direction of *Bothan Faobhar*, a buzzard drifting lazily overhead marking the glen. "Something happened that he didn't want to talk about... ...he watched me fishing in his river one day, liked what he saw in me and asked if I wanted the job of looking after the loch."

"So you were a fisherman?" asked Sol attentively.

"In a way... ...and I jumped at the chance, as he should really have had me arrested for poaching. I'd been in the jail before for that you see?"

"What? In jail for poaching? For pinching a few fish?" Sol found this hard to follow. Jail to him was for major crimes involving millions or fraud.

"Aye, and borrowing things that weren't mine to borrow. We didn't have much and well... ...sometimes if you needed it, well... ...maybe I was a bit feral."

"But surely that doesn't lead to jail? Taking food to feed yourself?"

"Times have changed boy. People didn't look for reasonable explanation in those days. A thief was a thief. A poacher was a poacher. There was never a suitable explanation to satisfy the local policeman who'd sooner cuff you or clout you than listen. But that man, G. He changed me and gave me a second chance... ...even housed and employed me... ...bought my loyalty with it... ...and here I am. Same goes for most of the people living on the estate. G was always their second chance."

"And then I came along when G left?"

"Aye and nobody thought he could choose a decent successor, especially one coming straight from the city. Mind you, he did his research before he let you near the place. A lot of people owed him a lot of favours and he knew about you all right. Came up here and talked to me just like you're doing now and in the last few weeks before you arrived you were the only thing he discussed. You see, where others thought you'd be a lost cause, he believed in you..."

"Well that's good. But what did he see?" asked Sol. "What can I do to keep the estate going? I don't know how I'm going to do it Joe. I mean this estate will cost…"

"…money isn't everything Sol." Joe hawked round on Sol with the look of the eagle in his now chiselled features. He held his index finger pointed at Sol's temple, crooked and gnarled with decades of use in the cold and the rain. This was a hand that knew hardship and understood the effects of the iced waters of the rivers, the loch and the tarns. "You've been hooked by the wild things like him. We can also sense that. G netted you because he felt your potential and then the *Bothan* has simply cast the final spell. You'll find a way."

"But money is all I can do and without it…   …well, what am I?"

"Well you are a bigger man than you were when you arrived in your silly little sports car…   …aye, I've heard about it."

"How am I different? How?"

"Well, let's consider that." Joe relaxed back into the character he had been before and closed his dim eyes to focus. "Have you started taking a note of the wild things about you?"

"Yes."

"Had you before?"

"Not since childhood," he admitted.

"Have you taken care of your tenants and kept the rents low and promised to fix their houses if and when you can?"

"Well, yes. But who wouldn't?"

"Anybody else I reckon. Especially if they couldn't see how to afford it."

"I was just trying to do the right thing."

"At your own expense? And, when did you last do that?"

"Ah…"

"Have you paid for Gerry's boat to be repaired and offered to house her whilst you have her roof fixed?"

"Yes."

"And, you've got Gerry talking to Nevin again and given him hope for his yard…"

"Yes, but…"

"You've contacted that long lost brother of yours too?"

"Yes, but Joe…"

"What made you want to do that? Have you become human or something? We wouldn't want a city boy banker becoming one of them would we?"

"But…"

"And, aren't you up here talking to me?"

"Well, yes."

"Aye. Why? Why are you up here?"

"Because, it's the right thing to do and I wanted to, and I enjoy your conversation and we fish and play fiddle…"

"And when did you last play to an audience or even practice with others? You've even learnt to fish…   …well, sort of…   …and you've taken on a new style of playing…   …fiddling not that violin'ing nonsense!" Joe was laughing with tears streaking down his brown skin from the corner of each eye.

"Well…"

But Joe was not about to let him finish.

"G experienced a bad life in the army as an officer. Something changed him. But for the better. There's no reason why your past wrongs have to catch up with you here. Stop running away and instead focus on what you're going to do with your future. Look at that heather," and he blindly pointed beyond the loch. "Every few years it's burnt back until it looks dead and there's nothing but ash. But up it sprouts better than before. Without that drive and determination of the heather to keep fighting back, in no time at all these moors would be lifeless and empty. They wouldn't feed the insects and the birds, they wouldn't have their heady, lovely honey scent in the high summer and bring in the bees, and they wouldn't turn purple and…"

"Okay," said Sol quietly. "So, I've changed... ...a bit. But I still need to pay for the estate and I'm worrying about the taxes I'll face on it let alone any other costs. I just don't want to let everybody down."

"What?"

"They're all relying on me to get it right. What if I let them down and G was wrong?"

"Oh G wasn't wrong. We thought he was and trust me expected nothing from you at all. That we've got all the things, and more, from you that I've already listed, is infinitely better than anything we expected. Even you really do have to work hard if you're going to let us down from such a low point of expectation as we had about you. Where's that money man confidence? You've changed, but not everything has to go."

"Okay."

"So, if you've changed and now want something for the good of everyone else, and not just yourself, even though you will benefit too if and when you succeed, then put that financial planning mind to the task. Find us a solution to protect the *Bothan's* estate."

"But..."

"No buts allowed. We haven't time?"

"Haven't we?"

"No. There's a storm on the way. It will take you at least two hours to walk back and the next front will be here in two and a half."

"How do you...?" Sol questioned keen to learn something of this man's natural skills of weather forecasting.

"I can smell it..."

Sol sniffed the air experimentally trying to elicit the information Joe was taking from the moisture in the air. Joe grinned and then added, "Oh, and I listened to the radio forecast earlier. Clever things those forecasters."

They packed up the fish in neatly folded bags and Joe stood with Sol at the head of the path into the heather that followed the river down on her gravity-abandoned route to the loch. He looked up into the younger man's face. "Think of all the wild things reliant on that heather's tenacity to grow. Imagine the surprises it hides under its shade and cover. List the birds you see, the animals you can track and the insects you could catch. Amazing stuff isn't it? But remember, you're a member of the only species amongst them all capable of doing just that, the thinking, the imagining and the listing. And, what's more is that you're the only one of your species who can make the difference to maintain that heather on your estate and to find the right solution to keep it going." And with this, he pushed Sol on his way down the track towards *Bothan Faobhar* in the distance.

"Joe?" Sol called as the dust about his feet jostled with his legs and then settled. The old man looked up from where he was settling back on the bench by the cottage and already looking out across the placid loch, now blackening under the shadow of the mountain. "Where did G go to?"

"Away," said Joe.

"To where?"

"*Tir na nÒg.*"

"Where's that?"

"Ask someone else. It's another island. I'm too blind to see that far."

Sol trooped on down the track and into the heather along by the sparkling river who was so glad he was joining her on his route over the moor and down the glen almost as far as the sea that she sang her tinkling charm song to accompany the melody in his head. He smiled as Joe closed his eyes, spinally took the shape of the bench and listened to the loch.

'Maybe tonight,' thought Joe.

The rain arrived as predicted as the sky turned charcoal and Sol sat at the piano to recall his tune and to write it down. He wrote notes into the manuscript to remind him of where he was and what he felt. As the day ended he also completed G's journal as fish poached in *Bothan* brown water, mixed with herbs, stock, vegetables and butter.

Gerry had been into the house in his absence and left a few items in the living room for Sol to store until Nevin started his work on the Boat House. There was a fine loaf of bread, which he suspected she had made, waiting on the kitchen table for him to have as a gift. This he used to soak up the juices from around the trout and for making a simple pudding of thick buttered bread and jam.

Tomorrow would be Tuesday, a day about which he had mixed emotions. He would be out with Hamish and Mrs Hamish in the evening and was unsure how it would go. In the morning he would take Addie to the town and find a present for them. *But what was a good enough gift for a man like Hamish and his wife?*

He moved Gerry's belongings through to the larger bedroom and then started to clear the back room so that it would be presentable enough for his guests, whenever they proposed to arrive. When satisfied that there was a route to the bed and space to store possessions, he stepped back. The room still looked like some fanatic's laboratory with a bed placed in the corner, but it was better than it had been and he had discovered an old fire grate built into the wall whose chimney flue must connect to the main fireplace. He could even make it warm if needed.

Texts off to Al and Pete asking when they would arrive, he sat by the front room fire and worried about the future. A quick check of the laptop revealed shares had continued to plummet and interest rates were low.

He had money, but little income.

He felt that he was rich in a humble man's world and that he was surrounded by a natural wealth but remained poor.

He knew that there was some fix somewhere, but that he couldn't yet see it.

G had believed in him, Joe seemed to believe in him too. But there was an uncalled for, usually deeply hidden, lack of confidence that tugged at his natural self-assuredness.

'*Be like heather,*' he thought, something he had never considered before.

The lark soared up and above.

It was a bird alone in a wide blue sky that stretched as far as the eye could focus and up into the heavens. Below, a carpet of pungent pink purple blossoms wafted honey-scented perfume in warm waves that whipped as unseen spindrift of scent with the caress of the light winds off the sea; that body of flat grey-blue that existed beyond the realm and interest of the lark.

Fluting a tune that wavered and fell, rose and excited, all the bird knew what to do was to sing; for territory, for mates and for pleasure. If it could, it would warble its resonant notes for simple joy, but it did not know why it sang. It just responded to the urge brought about by an accumulation of spring hormones that had responded to the lengthening days, timed by eons of evolution and a need to breed and pass on the same desires and adaptations to its offspring.

Confident, the little bird worried off a peat-headed gull that trespassed too closely in its heathland wanderings, a giant in comparison. It rounded in on the neighbouring larks if they too encroached or showed interest in his part of the monotonous, contiguous land below. It wooed a female who stopped to assess his singing and to admire his patch from the top of a lichened rock that floated in the waves of heather. Impressed, she stayed and his urges grew stronger.

He knew his space, he knew his song and he would sing it. He had no need for money and possessions, just his patch of heather moorland and a song.

The faceless G stood next to Sol within the shrubbery and they watched the diminutive lark.

"He sings well," said G as they strode closer to inspect a hidden cup-shaped nest of dry grass and straw cleverly woven to produce a smooth inner lining. Inside five tan-brown speckled eggs awaited the brood patch of an adult. But the two humans were not seen as they were just dream folk. "It is funny how he uses just his song to choose a territory, defend it, call a mate, bring her into season and then watch over the nest site and the chicks until they fledge. No money between them at all poor things. But does he care? No. He doesn't even notice anything beyond his little sphere. He is not interfering with the lives of others or bothered by possessions. Interesting that isn't it? He's as committed as the heather."

And Sol woke up sat in the easy chair by the fire, notes spread about him and the dawn screaming through the windows to wake him up.

There was a lark singing on the wind.

After breakfast Gerry arrived in *The Tern* and brought with her another load of luggage.

"It's only for two weeks whilst James gets the roof fixed," she explained. "There's not much more."

Sol smiled as the bags slowly filled what had appeared to be a large bedroom.

"What are these?" he asked wading through padded items she had bagged up.

"Cushions," she replied.

"Why? What for?"

"Women always bring cushions," she explained. "It's just a given."

"Oh. Why?"

"No idea, but I presume you have seen the state of your chairs?"

Sol described his plans for the day and they arranged for Gerry to move in during the morning. The sooner she was ensconced then the sooner she could lay claim to the large bedroom and prevent Al or Pete from taking it. One of them would sleep in the back room and Sol was happy to use G's chair to sleep in and to offer the other easy chair to another, so long as his feet didn't go too numb. The idea of rotating beds and chairs seemed a non-starter.

"What would you buy Hamish and Mrs Hamish as a gift for having me to supper?" he asked.

"Nothing," said Gerry quite basically.

"I can't do that."

"Why not?"

"I have to take something."

"But why?"

"I just do." He sighed. "It's what I've always done."

"Well, think of it like this," said Gerry. "Even if you were going to get them something, then what would they want? So why bother?"

"But wouldn't that be impolite?"

"Not to Hamish. Take something if you want, but he doesn't want possessions. He wants security of the estate. He cares so much about it that the only thing he is worried about is if you can run it properly and look after the land and the people in it."

Sol grimaced. This worried him.

"I've decided something," Gerry announced from the bedroom door. "I've decided I'm going to pay you rent for living in your house."

"What? But you haven't got any money."

"There you go again. Money, money, money… I'm not talking about money."

"Oh. It's just that where I come from everything *is* about money. Nothing's free."

"But the free things are worth far more than the ones you can buy."

"Such as what?"

"Well, let's be honest. You are living in a pit."

Sol had to agree looking around at the state of disrepair and uncleanliness of his house.

"Well," she continued. "I'll clean it up starting this morning so that you aren't too embarrassed when your friends arrive. And, while I'm here, I'll cook. I can teach you to sail too if you want?"

"Deal," he exclaimed with rapidity. "You'd better teach me to cook as well then."
"And the cost of the rent?" she enquired. "The rent would be how much?"
"If you are willing… …free."
"Deal," she replied with a smug expression. "Not everything can be paid for in money you see?"
They parted, Gerry back around the choppy waters of the headland to the Boat House in *The Tern* for more belongings, and Sol along the slippery driveway in Addie to collect his shopping, check the post and to find suitable presents for Hamish and Mrs Hamish. For these he would have to scour both Old Town and New Town. He took recycling with him as directed by Gerry and promised to return as much packaging as he could to the supermarket delivery van, from which she hoped he had selected more carefully than last time.
"I'm sorry to bully you," she said, "but as soon-to-be resident sister, someone has to!"
Whilst out he had a hair cut in New Town and had them trim his roughened beard that had sprouted un-cleanly from his chin and crept over his marked cheek bones to meet his descending sideburns. After all, he was going out tonight and did not want to disappoint with his appearance, not that it was on show.

On his later than intended return, he was shocked. The house exterior lay there waiting in its normal end glen, hidden manner. But the layer of dust he had become accustomed to and accepted inside was gone from the house. He knew there was a change from his arrival when he saw the front step, washed and clean and the porch windows at the back shining and not dulled by grime.
The pans were stacked in the kitchen and the wood of the table smelt of vegetable oil with which it glistened as it had nearly dried. The stone flags were still wet but smelt of soap and so he left his

boots at the back door before entering to pass the gleaming range cooker.

In the living room the easy chairs were plumped up and the hearth emptied, cleaned and a fire ready set in anticipation of being lit again, just as on his arrival. The wood timbers of the floors were dusted and the books on the clean table returned to their proper shelves. Even the writing desk was rearranged with G's bounded notes stacked in order and the lidded ink pen ready with a blank sheet for Sol's next use.

His piano shone and the grimy keys were bright ivory white and pitched boxwood black, with his part-written manuscript neatly presented on the music stand. It stood before a window bright with washing that allowed a clearer view of the beach and the loch, and even the curtains stood more to attention than he recalled.

Freshly cut wild flowers were bunched in a vase on the table.

The little back room had taken on the visage of somewhere that Al could potentially sleep, although still cluttered and lab like, and Sol found that Gerry had completed cleaning of the hallway down to her room where he found she was still at work.

"You've been busy," he said.

"A woman's touch," she replied.

"Thank you. And, in this gender-neutral, non-sexist age, what do you mean by that?"

"That in common with a number of men I know, you are a mucky and untidy creature. It's not sexist. It's an observation based on a well-known fact."

"So how will you cope when there are three men living under the same roof?"

There was a pause.

"Badly," she said.

Gerry left for the Boat House for the night and wished Sol luck at Hamish's, asking him not to take anything said too personally. He unpacked the shopping, thrown baglessly into the boot of Addie to reduce packaging, and placed his new camera in the centre of the living room table to unwrap in the morning.

The post had been sparse, but he saw that there was an interesting handwritten letter amongst the offers of holidays and the chance for nought percent finance on a car. The writing was familiar, floral and old-fashioned, written in ink, but Sol wondered whom it was from.

But the horn outside on the drive told him Hamish was here and waiting, and so he distractedly put the letter down next to the camera box and ran for the drive. Sol picked up his presents for the Hamish's on the way and securely closed the porch door behind him. The letter would have to wait until later.

"Greetings city boy," Hamish called through the open cab window of his Land Rover from where the dog panted heavily into Sol's face. "Where's your fiddle?"

"What?" asked Sol pushing the dog's face back so that he could see around it to where Hamish sat high up on the well-sprung seat.

"Well, it'll be a boring evening if we have to talk all night. You'll end up asking difficult questions and Mrs Hamish will start talking about your family and what kids you want to have. I think its better you brought the fiddle with you for both our sake's. Besides, I want you to practise a duet for Thursday if you can. Got some good ideas I need to try with you."

Sol returned to collect his violin. It's case, although still battered and chipped, had been polished over and was cleaned to a state of being almost dust-free and he noticed that Gerry had taken the broken picture of Sue and him out of the pocket inside and left it on the desk together with its glass pieces.

"Aye that's better," said Hamish in the waggon. "I've a tune I want Mrs Hamish to sing and I want you to accompany her, you know, make it up as you go along. If you like the tune, maybe you could write it into that...   ...that symphony of yours?"

"Well..."

"Only if you like it though?"

"I'd be honoured... ...if I like it."

"So would I."

"What's it called, the song?"

"Call it '*Mrs Hamish*'... ...if you like it." And later he did.

The evening was somehow not what Sol had expected.

The cluttered little cottage up on the hillside, surrounded by its chickens, Jacob sheep, antediluvian goats and a herd of wild roaming dwarf mountain ponies was tumbledown but warm and cosy. It had clear views all around except for a small copse of wind-lashed trees that protected it from the worst of the weather, and washing flapped merrily away to itself on the line.

A spinning wheel dominated the living room where a happy fire crackled and spat and instruments lined the shelves including harps, flutes and bagpipes of varying styles and sizes, and Hamish proudly showed off his collection of handmade crooks and sticks that he had made for himself over the years. All other wall spaces were crammed with pictures and photographs with a history of the cottage and the life of the Hamish's on display in this private gallery. There they were, a couple and then a family, their children, all four of them, their grandchildren, just six for now, their sheep and their charges; all staring back from behind bubbled and imperfect glass.

The dimly lit building was permeated with the smell of pipe tobacco and gave Sol a relaxed feel, one that he had least presumed.

They ate a fine lamb dish, talked and laughed, with Hamish on best behaviour under instruction from his wife. Then they played and sang and finally Hamish asked Sol to accompany his wife in the melody '*Mrs Hamish*' that he had written. And there was the enchantment of life amongst the moors in the air as the Gaelic words flowed forth and Sol's fiddle caught the counter. For a while he was the lark floating above it and he returned to his dream of the night before.

"And?" asked Hamish in the fire-crackle disturbed silence that followed. "What do you think?"

"Beautiful," Sol replied, mystified as to how this man could be so different at home to the one he saw out and about.

"Can you use it?" the man asked in earnest.

"Yes, so long as you are happy for me to."

"Will you play it on Thursday?"

"Of course. I'd love to."

"I think I was wrong about you," said Hamish eventually, muttering quietly as his eyes danced alive in the light of the hearth. "I might've judged you a bit quickly."

"Good."

"Aye you say that. But then you don't actually know what I think of you now." Sol turned to catch that sparkle in Hamish's eye; wicked, funny but full of humour.

As they left to descend the hill in Hamish's truck, he asked Sol to pick a walking staff from the umbrella stand by the creaking old kitchen door.

"Go on, choose," he urged. "Which is your favourite?"

Sol looked carefully, worried about making the right choice.

"It's not like you are choosing your magic wand at wizard school," Hamish laughed. "Just choose."

Sol placed his hand on a cherry wood stem that stood out from the rest and somehow seemed to call him. It was beautifully carved with Celtic patterns entwined with the natural knots and grain of the branch. It was a long straight staff that stretched to a height just below Sol's shoulder with a highly polished forked deer antler to the end between which the hand could easily rest in the palm and on which the owner could lean.

"Good choice," Hamish drawled lighting his pipe in a puff of blue, scented smog. "Practical and poetic all in one. And, it's yours."

"What?" Sol asked.

"Yours. A gift. A home warming present."

"Thank you." And then Sol remembered his presents for them back. "I didn't know what to get you for having me up here for supper."

"You've done enough by accompanying Mrs Hamish," said Hamish.

"Well I brought *you* these," he said and delved down into his coat pockets, resting the stick on the wall. "Coffee for the morning to wash out the whisky...   ...tobacco for your pipe to replace the toxins from the whisky...   ...and a small dram of whisky to treat the tobacco...   ...made locally I believe."

Hamish smiled drawing deeply on his pipe stem. "Don't show Mrs Hamish though," and he chuckled whilst looking at his wife.

"And for Mrs Hamish, well I didn't know, so I got her this." In his hand was a pot of honey made it said from the pollen of 'Heather blossom'. Both laughed heartily at Sol.

"Thank you," said Mrs Hamish in her glowing voice that warmed Sol's heart as she spoke. "That's made very locally too," she explained.

"Yes. It said so on the label. But I've got this thing about heather at present. How local is it?"

"Oh, I'd say about two hundred yards from here. That's from the beehives we keep up on the moor. This is *our* honey. But thanks for supporting the local business."

They left snickering as Mrs Hamish pressed a paper-wrapped block of cheese into Sol's hand.

"It's goat's cheese from our milk, but someone else's factory," she explained. "It's about as local as it comes."

The journey back was quiet as if two old friends travelled together, satisfied with their company and without the need to speak and fill in the gaps. Sol held his staff close and was happy. That is until he saw a yellow sports car crashed in the dyke on a corner at the side of the drive with the solid form behind of a large shiny black Land Rover attempting to winch it out of the ditch. The two men stood arguing by the roadside, illuminated in car headlights, could not have been more different from each other.

One, Pete, was scruffily garbed and happily involved in the carnage by the track. He was dressed for the outdoors and pleased to be up to his neck in mud already. The other, Al, wore a flannel shirt and cleanly pressed jeans over thin shabby-chic shoes, a suede jacket and sunglasses, worn despite the darkness.

"Bloody hell," said Hamish. "Friends of yours I presume?"

"Sadly, yes," said Sol.

Chapter 18: The Species Human

(Toccata, Gaston Bélier)

The description of any species is a very important thing. It gives details of not just its form and structure, colour and size, but it also provides an account of its habitat, where possible ensuring that the reader is aware of the recognised range and distribution of the species, its behaviour if known, and even migratory pathways and seasonal alterations. Well understood species are fully described with more recently discovered ones, those that are difficult to observe, the restricted, or the very rare and threatened put under special measures, protected and conserved, however limited our knowledge base to help defend them and clumsy our efforts may be. Above all, they are then studied, so long as the resources are available.

An alien invader trying to describe the human species would struggle. Not because of diversity of race and culture, as these differences are so insignificantly small that they account for nothing on the grand scale of things. Humans vary widely even within a single country, county or principality. So divided is the human species' total pool of variation that each small, closely inbred population has invented class and caste systems to further subdivide themselves so that what would not even be considered a sub-species becomes even more intensely inward looking as a result of rules of dress, sexual dimorphism, behaviour and the codes of conduct that limit their interests and pastimes, religious beliefs, friendships and breeding relationships.

Those crossing these boundaries, or through an ignorance or lack of local, sub-population education not even realising those rules are there, are judged badly, condemned for their behaviour, and if not quickly rectified are split from the group and denied the opportunities that allow others to flourish or the dominant ones to determine the new rules of exclusion or inclusion. Some are able to hold these positions through the media, constantly informing their population of the right thing to do or buy, the correct attire to wear and the best events to attend or foods and drinks to be had.

In short, the human being is a complex species, incapable of proper description due to its constantly changing, fluid behaviour and the inability of any single species, however intelligent, to describe itself.

Sol stepped out of the Land Rover cab into the cooling of the night where his breath hung misted in front of him, silver-lined as dragon smoke by the headlights ahead, and the dog immediately took to his vacated warm seat. Al and Pete stared into the lights like frightened rabbits hypnotised on a shoot, unable to gain sight from beyond the beams' brightness and yet fixated in their attempt to get more information from the surrounding dark.

"I say," said Al, not able to see Sol through the glare, holding his hands up as protection, as Hamish stepped down and left the cab as well. He slammed the door shut heavily, it creaking on its rusting hinges. "We seem to have struck a spot of bother."

"Nay bother," said Hamish abruptly. "I'd say you've hit a rock." He stated this in a terse manner and then turned back to Sol, still hidden in the lights. "Do all Londoners drive like this then?"

"Yes," Al chided. "All very funny but I need to shift my car and I can't get anyone on the mobile, least of all our friend Sol who lives..."

Sol stepped forward and spoke, "...just up here. Yes, I know."

"Sol? Is that you?" asked the surprised Al. But he was relieved. With nothing but the sound of a voice he was quieted for the moment.

"My man," Pete greeted dropping the winch hook and walking over and slipping in the muds that followed Al's car in streaks down into the trickling drainage brook that lined the track.

"You could have phoned and let me know you were coming," said Sol exchanging weak embraces with the London boys each in their turn. He didn't feel great affection seeing them out here in the wild.
"We did," Al explained huffily. "We left you several messages until we lost signal about twenty minutes ago."
"Oh," laughed Sol, "then I suppose I should carry my phone more often then. I left it back at the *Bothan*." He pronounced this in the Gaelic.
"The where?" Al asked struggling with the strange pronunciation, so very alien to the language of the city.
"*Bothan Faobhar*. My home."
"No," Al corrected angered at Sol's sentiment. "This is your holiday home where you will take vacations. Home is in London where any sensible person should be." He talked as if Sol was stupid and looked around him, searching for something in the dark beyond the beams of the headlights and the shafts of light they cut into the moorland and plant life now attracting moths and attendant bats in from miles around.
"These *are* good people?" asked Hamish. "I mean friends?"
"Yes they are," Sol stated turning back to take him in. "I should have introduced you. Sorry."
"So I shouldn't have them shot yet then?" laughed the old man with a voice that to the uninitiated rumbled with menace.
"No. Boys. This is my good friend Hamish..." and he pointed off ineffectively into the dark. "...Hamish this is Al...   ...and back there is Pete." Again, it didn't matter where he pointed, but he did as he walked around the front of the Land Rover. "Boys, pay little attention to any of what Hamish says. He means none of it."
They all exchanged greetings and formal handshakes before Sol added, "and *this* is home...   ...although I may take occasional vacations in London sometimes in the future."
Pete looked mournfully at the sports car. "I can't shift this until the morning when I can see well." He shook his head. "I told you not to race up the track, but no..."

Al mimicked at Pete who continued. "Get your stuff into my Landie Al, and I'll take you the rest of the way. We can shift the car in the morning."

"No need," said Hamish. "You'll find it at the end of the drive in the morning... ..by seven? Is that early enough?"

Pete looked at the old man and then at his tattered old Land Rover. It was a battered old square type series III from the nineteen seventies. It had dents running along most of its panels and was a high percentage of rust. It did have good tyres, but was still leaf sprung underneath. There was also a pied border collie sat in the front seat acting as driver. The vehicle was painted with mud and even in the dark moss could be seen growing along the window seals in hummocks that gave the impression of the car having developed boils.

"In that?" he asked in disbelief.

"Aye," chuckled Hamish looking wryly at Sol. "I may have done it before. Just leave it to me." Then he turned to Sol quietly and muttered. "They are friends of yours, aye?"

"Yes," whispered Sol. "Don't kill them yet. They need time to acclimatise. It's not like the city and they might find it hard to adjust."

Hamish turned back to the London boys. "Much use for a Land Rover of that size in London then?" He indicated to Pete's large, polished wagon. "Funny, I don't remember there being that much off road when I last visited. Was there some that I missed?" he was much amused. "Mind you it was a long time since I last ventured down there..." and he trailed off to add effect to his words.

"Not really," Pete defended. "I use it for expedition work mostly. Well more for travelling around taking wildlife photographs really."

"So you've come for his cat then have you?" Hamish was interested in this answer and waited for the reply with some curiosity.

"The wildcat? Well yes...   ...amazing what photos Sol's taken already on just his phone."

"So I've heard," Hamish shook his head more to himself than anyone else and then he rounded on Al who was unloading kit to put into the back of Pete's waggon. "So what have *you* come for?" Hamish asked of Al aggressively.

"Interest," answered Al steadily slipping in the mud as he emptied the under bonnet storage compartment of his sports car. "How did you get your car along this road, Sol?"

"I didn't," Sol replied. "Hamish did. Or rather, he pulled it out of the same ditch as you've landed yours up in. It's going to recycling or something."

"It was the white car I saw back at the scrap yard then?" asked Pete as Sol nodded and helped Al with his bags. "I knew it looked familiar and out of place."

"You should get the council to mend this," moaned Al looking at the state of the track, its pockmarks and the plant life growing from the deep water-filled puddles that leaked up and out of it. "You know, fill in the holes and add some better lighting. It's terrible. You shouldn't have to put up with this. That's what they charge their tax for. It's a disgrace!"

"The council won't touch it, silly," joked Sol as Hamish joined him.

"Of course they will. Public highway. What kind of backwater is this?"

"Well excuse me," said Sol, "but the council have no jurisdiction on this land. They wouldn't pay for any repairs."

"Well who does?"

"Me."

There was silence as the two London boys stood and took in what Sol had just said.

"What?" Pete asked.

"I'd have to pay for any repairs," explained Sol. "And anyway, I quite like it this way...   ...gives a sense of privacy. Prevents unwanted tourists straying too far off the beaten track."

"Why wouldn't they pay?" It was Al this time with an adamant tone to his voice.

"Because it's mine. Welcome to my driveway. If anyone's got to pay for it, then it will be me. And right now, I've got other more important jobs to focus on first."

"Aye," chuckled Hamish with that wicked twinkle in his eye nodding emphatically. "Show some respect boys. You are after all speaking to the laird of the estate."

"Laird?" quizzed Al looking around. "Of what?"

"Well," said Sol in as straight away as he could muster. "I accidentally bought more than I intended to when I purchased my *little* retreat...   ...*Bothan Faobhar*...   ...with land."

"What did you buy?" Pete questioned.

"Oh, a mountain, a loch...

"...a moor," added Hamish thoughtfully.

"...thank you, yes...   ...a moor, actually quite a lot of moor, a few hundred sheep, and deer, a church..."

"...a river..."

"...and fish, and half a loch, and woodlands, lots of them."

"What?" the London boys asked together.

"There was a bit more land than I thought? You know? That came with the house."

"How much?" It was Al, as ever interested in value, possession and extent.

"Fourteen and half thousand acres," said Sol in as matter-of-fact manner as he could.

Pete considered this as Al whistled through his teeth. "Shall we go?" Sol offered.

"Just say the word, my Laird," said Hamish climbing up into the Land Rover cab with Sol. "Just say the word, and I can have them shot. It would look like an accident too!"

"Not today Hamish," said Sol getting in next to him and shoving the dog across. "Not today."

"But, just say the word."

And then Sol paused for a moment. "Hamish?"

"Yes?" the old man asked.

"What is the name of this dog?"

"Cù."

The dog pricked her ears up, directing them towards her master, ready to do Hamish's bidding in the way that well-trained obedient dogs do.

"Oh, that's nice. As in Highland Coo?"

The dog looked back at Sol.

"No you great sausage! Cù. It's Gaelic...   ...for dog. I couldn't think of anything better at the time."

The dog lay down between them with its head on Sol's lap and moaned a most forlorn sigh. Obviously there were no sheep to herd, no walks to tread and no runs to be had.

They left the upended sports car in the ditch and the two London boys followed on in headlight convoy along the driveway to the *Bothan* in Pete's Land Rover.

Whatever they were expecting at the end of the track the *Bothan* was not it. Al imagined a castle and Pete at least a large house. But there she was tucked away under the wood in the glen by the sea loch shore. The sight of her gladdened Sol's heart with pride, the views around in the crisp moonlight of a clearing sky sent Pete into an ecstasy of a natural history photographer's heaven, but it all made Al's stomach lurch.

There was a flickering light on the living room window and an obvious fire smoked up into the chimney as Hamish's Land Rover traversed its way back along the track leaving Sol to his guests and trailing the red glow of rearward lights. He was leaning on his new engraved cherry wood staff, already falling into the stance of a farmer's hand, and holding his goat's cheese block in his hand like some talisman.

He shovelled the two up the garden path where the fallen sign failed to welcome them, trying to remember his own first dark evening discovering the cottage. Then they spilled in through the front door with Pete at the head, automatically seeking a light switch that he could not find.

"Where's the...?" he called back.

"Just go in," Sol encouraged, pushing past from the rear. "It's easier if I explain later."

Sol led them into the front room and settled the perplexed Al into the ring of spluttering light that the paraffin lamp threw out from the middle of the table, sending up dancing images around it. He was pleased with its ambience and looked longingly at his favourite chair next to the ember-smouldered fire whose rays penetrated deep into the room and filled it with the scent of oak wood ash. Pete and Al's faces were painted with the shadows of the warming light and Sol felt that there was no way that they could feel any different to himself at that moment.

But then Al spoke.

"Sol, what is this place? Please tell me this is not the great house you've told me about? Its freezing and my god...   ...it needs a makeover. And what's this lighting?"

Pete burst in. "Shut up, Al. I like it, Sol. It has character."

Al again, "character yes, and lice, and...   ...where's the... ...well, where's anything?"

"Well," started Sol somewhat disheartened but not really surprised, "the kitchen is through there...   ...and your bedroom Al is through the other way, and there's another room beyond, but that's occupied. There are sheds out the back and a shower room... ...sort of. The toilet is a way up in the wood."

"The wood?"

"Yes. It means it's a safe distance from the house and stops the waters cross contaminating each other. The drinking water is off the hill and the waste goes into the river."

"Occupied?" Pete asked. Sol and he looked at each other across the room and held gazes. "You said that the other room was occupied."

"Yes," replied Sol, "occupied. By another guest."

"Who? What other guest?"

"Me," answered Gerry coming out of the double bedroom at the back of the *Bothan* in floral pyjamas and a plain woollen dressing gown that looked overly knitted and warm.

"Bloody hell," said Al sitting down at the dining room table, "you move fast Sol. Does Sue know?"

"It's not like that. We're just friends." Sol sighed a prolonged outlet of air; the sound of a disappointed teacher. "Hello Gerry, I thought you were coming back tomorrow."

"I thought I'd come early to surprise you and warm the place up in case your guests arrived, which I see that they did." She walked in. "I'm Gerry, the temporary lodger. You must be Pete and Al." She took command of the situation and stepped deeper into the lamplight. "Anyone for a drink?"

Sol offered the boys water, but when it ran peat brown they declined and asked for anything that contained alcohol to kill off the bacteria despite Gerry and Sol's protestations that the water was safe. "From the hill?" Al questioned. Then they settled down with oatcake biscuits, butter and the goat's cheese made out of the milk of Hamish's animals.

It wasn't long until the fire encouraged them into open conversation about business and London life, whilst Sol talked through the wildlife and people he had met, and Gerry listed flowers in season and the currents in the water. It was late when they had finished eating and drinking and after experiencing the distant toilet and primitive cleaning facilities, Al retreated to the room that was his in a hysteric mood. He went complaining about light, and space, décor and everything that a man of his type could, and obviously should, expect. Pete sat long into the night talking to Sol with Gerry; she sat on the floor and he in G's easy chair. Conversation like that, by firelight and in the reduced glow of a low-pressured paraffin lamp, amply warmed over with whisky, has a magic of its own. Pete was keen to learn more about the animals, the plants and the way of life, especially that of the wildcats.

"I've started a blog about them," he announced eventually and quite suddenly. "Got quite a following already."

"But you've not seen them yet," answered Sol looking deep into the scarlet-ember'd fire.

"I know, but I've used your pictures and the followers know that I'm coming up to visit you at some point soon."

"They don't know where I live do they?"

"No," Pete answered truthfully.

"Well, please don't tell them. I'm not sure why, but I feel I need to keep the location secret. You know, to protect the cats?"

Gerry agreed. "They are rare enough without everyone coming along to see them and scaring them away."

"Okay. I do understand. We can use the blog to illustrate them but give nothing away in the process."

Sol felt better then.

"Can I take a picture of you both now?" asked Pete, suddenly aware of the moment, the mood and the possibilities of a snap.

"What for?" Gerry asked.

"The blog. It sets up a scene for the story to unfold. The two of you, the fireplace, the atmosphere, even that woolly jumper you have on Sol."

They agreed and then sipped fiery whisky from metallic mugs whilst waiting for Pete to reclaim his equipment from out in the car. They were rosy faced, heated by the scorch of the malt and the strength of the red-hot wood cinders. His hair was wind-snagged and unkempt, and his beard, although trimmed earlier, was less cared for as it gripped his chin over his thick Arran cable-knit sweater. She was snuggled up inside her dressing gown, with her unruly ginger-flamed hair awash over her shoulders, framing a natural beauty.

Pete fired off several shots and added them to those he had just taken outside from the garden of the moonlit cottage and he rattled off a story to accompany them on his laptop.

He read it aloud describing the journey up as far as the towns and the loss of their all-important phone signal. He carried the reader on the road trail up to the crash on the drive and the mysterious appearance of Sol and Hamish out of the dark and the threat of being shot, which he kept humorous. Then there was that fairy-tale cottage at the end of the track, pooled in moonlight, with the loch beach behind, the river besides, the woods around and the mountain beyond the moor. This was in spite of the limitations and technological restrictions of the *Bothan*. The blog ended with the perfect hosts entertaining him in fireside chat until the early hours of the morning and the hopeful three-word statement of '*maybe cats tomorrow*'.

Pete sent the posting on using Sol's dish connection and instantaneously it was received by distant devices around the world, was logged on a server for others to find, connected with search engines and alerted the two hundred and seventy seven followers it already had. Some, notified by the '*ping*' of their phones had read the story and seen the pictures within two minutes of it being sent and most '*liked*' it and a few sent it on. By the morning it would have been read, re-read or scanned by three hundred and fourteen people.

Gerry made her excuses and went to bed leaving Sol in one chair and Pete in the other.

"She's nice," said Pete.

"I know," answered Sol. "She's a good friend... ...just a friend."

"What happened to the old Sol then? He never had *just* friends. Not that were women anyway."

"I changed," he answered thoughtfully.

"People can't change."

"Unless you give them a clean break and the chance to change, no. I know people who are becoming very close to me who had their second chance and changed. It seems to be a common feature of *Bothan Faobhar.*"

There was a natural break in the conversation disturbed only by the owl outside.

"Sue is missing you too you know?" Pete added.

"I know."

They slept either side of the fireplace, feet stretched out to try and glean the last warmth of the embers, tucked under blankets as they took the shape of their chairs underneath.

It was good to have Pete back, although Sol worried about Al and how he would find his short time here. He was not keen to re-visit his past and have it stay here in the form of his own house guests, but he knew that at some time he would have to face up to it, and them too.

He did not remember his dreams that night, but they were troubled such that the charm of *Bothan Faobhar* could not easily dispel them. But then, such are the effects and costs of a previously high life based on money, power and corruption.

In the morning Sol sloped off out of the house early and went to fill the bird feeders before breakfast. He wanted a quick walk before touring the boys around the estate and showing them the towns and, suddenly more importantly than ever, the habitats. Whilst he was out Gerry also woke and for a while the two of them sat barefoot on the beach drinking coffee as the geese busied themselves about their feeding and the waders hassled each other in between.

There were gannets out on the water, drifting effortlessly against the wind in swirling circles. Their narrow white wings stretched lengthily into blackened tips and even from this distance their chisel-beaks and focused eyes were obvious as they scanned the loch below for fish and good eating. Porpoises skipped the waves as unreal cut-out tessellations, schooling in a shiny grey pod that exposed only their backs and fins to the air as they leapt their way across the bay in butterfly crawl. And there were cormorants and shags loitering in the choppier waters where the spume brought up nutrient from below and with it fish to feed and to be fed on.

Nevin and two hired hands waved from a long wooden boat part way into the loch, heading towards the Boat House with timbers, ladders and tools to start the roof repairs. He was glad to be at work again and to be able to employ a small crew. It was good for morale and good for the business, and he felt they all had a chance if this could continue. These highly skilled craftsmen had waited on in the town finding other work for the last few months in the hope that jobs would come up again, and somehow they had been, re-sourced by Sol of all people.

James felt the twang of jealousy as he gestured across the chopping water to Sol and Gerry on the shore at *Bothan Faobhar*. But he also felt the affection of friendship towards them both, and in his heart he wished Sol luck.

A porpoise was now escorting the ship at its bow, skipping as if to impress what it presumed was some strange, large creature, as Pete appeared at the cottage side and took photographs.

"More for the blog," he replied when the others became aware in a narrative that was already becoming familiar.

"Who reads it?" Gerry enquired as they walked back to the *Bothan* to prepare a breakfast for them all. "Who looks at your blog? Does it just go out into the ether and nobody reads it or what?"

"No idea," Pete answered. "Somebodies, nobodies, interested people...   ...I don't know and I don't really care. It's just like writing and taking pictures and somebody out there keeps reading it. But they're growing in number."

There was a startled man's scream from the kitchen and the three looked at each other in horror.

"Al?" Sol asked more of the others than himself.

"Is Al squeamish?" Gerry asked.

"Yes, very," Pete answered.

"Only I left a brace of pheasant and a roe deer hanging up in the larder. In case we got peckish through the week. He may be looking for breakfast and found them."

"That'll be it then," laughed Sol. He suddenly loved the country life more than ever before.

Breakfast made up for much of Al's bad feeling about the cottage and his lack of sleep. Locally cured bacon made from pigs across the loch, local eggs rich and yolky, homemade bread formed from local ingredients, local sausage and butter all washed down with tea from India and coffee from Kenya. The air miles of the drinks increased the carbon footprint of their meal hundreds fold alone, but the milk they added was from a local farm.

Al asked about the origin of the food, interested in its source and flavour, and then he probed for more information on costs and suppliers.

"Why?" Sol quizzed.

"Why what?" Innocence emitted from every one of Al's pores.

"Why do you want to know? There's always a reason with you? When do you ask questions without there being something for you to gain from them?"

"Just a thought. Let me mull on it. Do these people want to trade? That'll be my next question."

"Someone has replied to the blog asking where the beach is," shouted Pete from behind his laptop screen, where an air of excitement was growing. "Excellent."

"Tell them it's a secret," Sol called back gruffly. "It *must* remain a secret. Or else you won't get to see cats tonight."

His answer had the sentiment of a spoilt child about it, as if ready to cry and stamp his foot. *This was his valley.*

This was his beach.

These were his cats.

All of it was his responsibility and he had to keep it as much to himself as he could – possession was as important as protection.

Pete replied to the interested reader that he would not reveal the location of the beach and checked through his previous postings to ensure that he had not given too much away before. There was mention of the area, a picture of the drive, a photograph from the front of the *Bothan* at night, but no direct name or address and a search on various online sites showed that the area remained invisible to the Internet and street maps. They would have to work very hard to find the place as there did not appear to be enough detail to give away the cottage's location; not yet anyway, but he would need to be careful.

Gerry left to find out how Nevin and his crew were getting on with the Boat House and Sol took Pete and Al up to the crossroads on the moor from which he could show them the estate and a few of the cottages. They travelled in Addie who coped easily with the muds, ruts and runnels along the way and noted that Al's car had already gone from its injured position on the driveway. Hamish had once again been proven good to his word and he and his battered old Land Rover had somehow taken control and replaced another sports car back to the roadside where it belonged; a lost migrant replaced to its proper place. Like the American passerine that had flown too far as directed by the overzealous nature of the trade winds and was now found stranded on a different European continent and in an unsuitable habitat, the car had been very much misplaced and poorly evolved for where it had driven. It needed tarmac below the tires, little resistance and a continuous, monotonous smooth surface that allowed their meagre tread to grip; a plane'd land that did not leave much for use by wild things except offering a quick and unrealised death.

The weather stayed fine, that flash of blue-sunned brightness that the sky can produce in May, if the clouds allow it, convincing us all that a good summer is on its way before the maritime temperate climate that is Britain once again succumbs to the jet stream and we suffer a damp squib of a season. The black and red grouse displayed, a merlin scooped the heather tops, and a flock of curlew, long billed and heavy-chested, beat their mottled wings in synchrony as they flew in a loose skein over the road calling their own names out loud.

The mountain, blue-rocked and snow-frosted, towered above, scooping the scene as its shoulder curved gracefully around and enclosed the moorlands. Sol pointed out towards the individual houses that lay hidden by the loch at the head of the river, within the forest, in the next glen, or up and keep on going until it felt that it was impossibly high for a human to live in the barrenness of the rock-strewn land. The skylark accompanied them where it was pinned to the horizon in a full fluted song, and the pipits walked alongside eyes always sideways to gain the best view of these potential threats to their livelihoods.

"I should be able to get the car up here," said Pete looking intently at a copy of the world through his camera lens from a position lying in the gorse beside the road. "You don't mind do you, Sol?"

"I'll not be driving my car up here," muttered Al. "Desolate and devoid of beauty though it is, these are not features that I look for in a holiday destination! There's only so much heather a person can appreciate." He sat on Addie's bonnet idly flicking at the flies that swarmed his head in their nuptial throng. "Sol, what do you do for company? It's more populated on safari holidays than it is out here. Just what do you do?"

"Well there are plenty of people round here." Sol felt unusually defensive of the area. He knew where Al was coming from as he too had been that man only a matter of days ago, and it was surprising even to himself that he was so quickly affected.

"Yes, but where are they? You're a London boy, used to being surrounded on every level. I actually can't see a single house…" He looked around him in dismay at the moorland that spread in all directions like a poorly-laid undulating carpet spread over an uneven floor that retained both its water-warped character and the blemishes in the wood it was manufactured from. "…and god it was dark last night... ...and quiet. What do you do for company? Go on, where are they?"

"They are there if I need them and they are only a short distance walk away. They are good people and they are fiercely protective of their way of living. We are as alien to them as they are to us."

"Think of the money you could make if you broke all this up and sold..." Al was always on the lookout for profit. He saw the world overlaid with financial blueprints that revealed themselves to him more clearly the deeper he delved. He could see land. He could see potential. He could see development opportunity.

"...but, that won't happen." Sol was adamant and kicked a stone off the track and up into the dry-barked twigs of a creeping willow that entwined through the heather in a unique pattern that would not repeated anywhere else on Earth.

"You are not seriously going to stay up here?" Al goaded.

"That's the plan." Sol's voice was readably firm. "It's changed a bit... ...the plan. Besides, this land isn't suitable for building. And who would want to destroy it? Look at it."

Al looked around, taking the view in with a single scan that missed the birds, the plants, the terrain and the soul of the scene. All he could see was the envy-inducing profit bird that helped him to soar financially on a liquidity sea of asset waves. "But you could sell that *Bothan* and the properties to any number of developers, and that's even if the land was protected with the highest level conservation order. Anyone can be bought if you offer the right incentives. It would add to the value having all this wildlife on the doorstep. Wherever it is."

"Yes, and the wildlife would move away and be lost."

"So what?"

"Where would it go?"

"Another moorland wilderness."

"What if there are none left?"

"I'm sure there are?"

"Where then?"

"Listen, you are potentially talking a lot of money here. You'd be turning your back on all that if you just kept it so you could be the wild laird and all that. Can you do that? I'm not sure the old Sol, the one you were last month, could. Can you?"

"Yes."

"Then how are you going to afford it?"

"I don't know. That's where I need your help."

"Mine?" Al was incredulous. "I've given you my advice already."

"I want people to visit the area. You own hotels and things?"

"Yes, and I sell off anything that loses me money...   ...for profit too! I'd start with that *Bothan*. It's a pit!"

"Yes. But it's my pit."

After a moment's thought Al asked where Joe lived and turned his questioning of Sol around to more specific things such as Joe's violin and if he'd found out if it was genuine or not. Sol cut the conversation short and climbed back up into Addie's cab.

"Just remember," murmured Al, "you may be glad of the money that would bring at auction one day. Especially if you keep this place the way it is."

Pete returned to the Land Rover ecstatic. "Look at these," he said and shoved the long-lensed camera through the open window, held just tight by the moss-ridden seals that pooled water in the channel that gripped the glass. They reminded Sol of the seaweed at the top end of the shore. The photographs on the bright liquid crystal screen were stunningly clear and something well beyond that which Sol had been capturing and then sending on via his phone. Pictured flies buzzed over burgeoning heather bells where only the one fly, bulbous-eyed, hairy and metallic-coloured, was fully in focus. A lapwing's head poked up proud of the shrubs, a meadow pipit stood on a rock, chest puffed up and piping, a lark in the sky hung motionless in a photo, and another feigning injury hoped to lead potential predators away from the nest, and there was a female hen harrier gliding in frozen v-pose over the moor. There was a stag taken in a stance both prominent and dominant in his herd of red-brown hinds, and a wild looking sheep stared vacantly into the digital world of the camera's body, looking directly along the axis of the lens. He had captured the emotion of a lone standing stone, the mountain shimmering behind and Nevin's boat bobbing back along the sea loch in the distance where clouds were hesitant on the horizon trying to decide whether to ruin a perfectly good day.

"I could live here," Pete laughed.

"Have my room," announced Al. "I will find a hostelry by the end of the day, in a town with fewer flies and more alcohol to pickle and purify me. Sol, my friend, please take me to my car."

"Could you?" Sol addressed Pete, and he pressed on. "Why could you live here? I mean how?"

Pete climbed up next to Al pushing him into the middle seat, where he slid over the gearbox and bounced on the cracking grey hide covers. The springs complained and Al drew himself up fearing for his skin as the sharpened coil ends threatened to break free and punctuate his body.

"I'd take photographs all day... ...give up the studio job and just return to London as a guest photographer. I'd still own the firm and be able to invest the profits up here in a small place to base myself." There was an excitement in his voice that cheered Sol immensely. Pete had seen something of what he felt.

"But," reminded Al, "as the voice of reason, may I remind you that it's not like being on holiday. Everyone leaves a holiday home and wished they lived in that place forever. It always looks better when you've only been there a few hours or days. It's simply a case of the grass is always greener on the other side. Besides where would you live? There aren't any houses!"

"Well," Pete replied. "Sol took a punt on it and seems to have moved up here quite happily." He looked dejectedly at Al.

"Yes, and with all due respect, look at him. He needs a decent clean, as we all do, a brush has not offended his hair for some time, and what's going on with the beard and the clothes? He's dressed like a twenties sea fisherman, not a modern day laird. In fact, in only a few weeks, he seems to have turned completely native!"

Sol was crying through laughter. He knew Al was right in so many ways, but the irony was that he was also simply wrong, as at the fundamental level he could not have been further from the truth. He had missed something important, and that was the indescribable part, the factor that made it work regardless of the sense and the odds being so stacked against it – Sol had actually fallen in love with the estate and its people in the very short time he had been here, in whatever condition he found them; second chances and all.

"I quite like the look," giggled Pete snapping a shot of the hearty-looking Sol for the blog as he draped himself giddily over the well-worn steering wheel.

"Will you stop taking pictures of him?" snapped Al. "It should be more about me!" And he rolled his eyes. "That's all I need, two men having their midlife crises in some synchronous breakdown whilst here I am stuck in the middle. What the bloody hell am I doing all the way up here? I miss my city! I just hope it's not catching and that I at least remain sane."

They ambled their way down the hillside passed Euan and Sarah's little house towards the garage, Addie trundling with apparent ease over the steep sections of lose earth and slippery muddied rocks, with some work from Sol at the helm. Deep in thought he mulled as a blackbird noisily crossed the road low in a terrified flight from its hidden position in a many-leafed rowan tree. If it had not flown it would have remained safe, but such was its programming that its terror gave it away – something the thankful sparrowhawk has been adapted to take advantage of.

Al was correct when it came to holidays.

So many of us take a cottage, stay in a hotel, camp or otherwise in somewhere different to our own, without the pressures of work and our everyday lives, and we assume that life in that place must be better. It would of course be better wherever we are without the busyness and mundaneness of ordinary life.

But the sun seems brighter, the scenery more pleasant, the houses homelier, the food different, and even the water tastes unusual, unless you are one of those who refuses to drink it and instead sips the carefully controlled overpriced uniformity that is bottled. That is what our minds do to a holiday location and what makes it an enjoyable time away.

The art of the real holiday firm is to ensure that those staying with you or in your properties envy your lifestyle and want to return, will talk about it to their friends or give the right recommendations on the Internet or in the media. It does not matter the real state of things as just the perceived counts. No one will stop long enough to dig under the surface and find out the real story and that crime, poverty and depravity lurk in every neighbourhood however 'nice' it appears whilst we are on holiday.

Sol considered the thought.

Was it possible that people could be lulled in to visiting any part of the estate to experience a holiday? Could he convince them that it was all just perfect and that the life was good, and the wildlife easily seen without disturbing it? Could conservation be married with economy?

"Can we stop?" asked Pete, not waiting and throwing himself out of the sauntering vehicle as Sol struggled with it down a travelling morass of wet muds and running pebbles. He cut the engine and followed Pete's journey with a track of an eye towards the solid stone of the garage barns before dismounting himself and following him through the marsh.

"What have you seen?" he called catching up.

Taking his chance, Al slipped out of the waggon and lit a cigar up behind, revealed by a plume of yellow-brown tobacco smoke like the sniper's curse, and then inched his way around the Land Rover avoiding the wet slurry-like silts that Sol had seemed to park in. He was trapped, stranded in a pool of iron-rich mud water, leaving Sol and Pete to talk. It worried him. Pete had a wild dazzled look about him, Sol had turned mad and only he, Al, had remained cogent throughout. They needed his city sense. The photographer couldn't see beyond his lens and the trader had sold up. The potential for disaster was immense.

"What's my favourite bird?" Pete asked Sol by the garage.

"What?"

"What bird won the competition and got me all the business in the first place? The one that gave me the break I needed? You know...

...*Pete, you'll never make money from photography without the lucky break...* ...that one."

"Short eared owl."

"Exactly. There was one here up on the eaves a moment ago..." He pointed up at the roof where the tiles had slipped leaving holes from within which the whistle of the starling and the '*chip*' of the sparrow could be heard. There were lichen-daubed coving stones capping the ridge that ended in a hand-carved stone ball mounted on the gable.

"...stop right there," called Al from the Land Rover's side. "It's not a sign! Wait for me."

Pete and Sol walked on and Al struggled to venture beyond the Land Rover, stay clean and keep his cigar lit and well puffed.

"You'll regret it!" Al shouted loudly, swearing as he slipped and swayed.

The others entered the barn complex. It made up an arc of well-constructed stone workshops and a two-storey dwelling with open barns on either of the side arms from which the birds called noisily, cheered on by the lengthening days of the approaching summer. The staircases up to the haylofts and the housetop were external and hewn from solid sedimentary rock that stretched the width of the steps and still held the fossils they were originally made from. Each descended to connect with a weedy cobbled courtyard that undulated with age and was split in the centre by an old oak tree that had somehow found its way as an acorn into the soil-filled gaps between cobblestones. The leaves, not yet open, had started to cast a surreal green light onto the courtyard, and although the tree's girth was large, there was still enough room to turn a tractor or a car around it.

The windows were small, but they were numerous and when Pete pushed the house door open he and Sol found that by the ethereal dust-light that penetrated the glass, there was a dwelling not much changed from when the last owner had vacated. A table and chairs still set, greyed with a powdery web layer, and a large range with pantries either side.

Unlike at the *Bothan* there was a light switch on the wall with enough thumb and finger grease to suggest that it had had recent use. Pete flicked it, more in hope than anything else, and was surprised that a single bulb lit up from its colourfully wired fitting with a whiz sound that took Sol back to early *Flash Gordon* spaceships. The wire inside glowed bright orange and both illuminated and frenzied the air around it, burning off the dust, with the hum of the science class transformer.

Each human left a trail of footprints in the ground covering, but underneath its veil it was all still there; a sink, a surface, cupboards and, curiously, a rusted mangle that had once been red and green. There were rooms beyond, one large living room and the luxury of a toilet off of it and a further study, and when they ventured up the external stairs there were two interconnected bedrooms roofed in bare tiles and each still furnished with a hard sprung bed and mattress.

Exploring the barns and byres, they put up bats from the hay loft and sent rodents scurrying into the age-old straw bales that sagged where they were still stacked waiting for the owner to return and to put them to use. Meanwhile, Al had found signal and had wandered off the track into the moors, shouting aggressively into his phone. He may have been away a day, but he did not expect those left back in the city to relax as a result.

"Do you think you could use it for photography?" Sol asked naively as he stood in the dusty sunbeams that a roof light allowed to fall all the way to the floor.

"I was thinking more than that," Pete replied opening drawers and rubbing his fingers through window dust to get a better view. His voice sounded far away with the distance being mental not physical. "How much do you want for it?"

"What?"

"You heard me, how much?"

"But..."

"It's perfect. Just imagine it. My house here in the centre," and he walked out into the courtyard indicating the original central farmhouse. "On this side I could have a studio and gallery with workshops here...   ...and here. We could fill these arches in with timber framed windows and...   ...on the outer side too...   ...to get views over the moorland and over to the loch. Maybe add a line of telescopes and have drawing classes."

Sol followed him into the barns and agreed with Pete that it was feasible to have this large space converted into a studio if there was the capital to complete such a job.

"The gallery would be upstairs." They looked up to the hayloft above them from where a barn owl hissed. "I'd even fit a box for *you* somewhere nearby so that we can film you twenty-four seven and put a link of it on to the website."

He strode across the yard skipping the unevenly cobbled stones.

"In here," he broadcast from the opposite barn, "we could have three self-catering cottages to attract in the trendy visitors. There's room for a classroom and a building for a resident to stay so that we could have a tour guide or someone on hand if needed. And, so long as it didn't rain we would have room for tables and chairs out on the courtyard outside."

He then walked around the property to the back with Sol in tow. "...and these sheds could house the Land Rovers and the

equipment needed to take the people out. It would be like a Scottish safari."
He wheeled round on Sol.
"What do you think?" he asked seriously. "Could it work?"
"Well, yes it could. But you do need to think about it first."
"Why? You didn't and look what you got?"
"But I was lucky. You need to think about it first. For a start, where are you going to get your punters from?"
"Here," answered Pete and pointed desperately at his phone. "Today I have just over five hundred and fifty visitors on my blog. Five want to know how they can visit you at the *Bothan* and six want to learn photography from me and visit to photograph the wildlife here. It can only grow!"
"Possibly yes. But you are counting your eggs before they've hatched. This needs a business plan first."
"So, how much do you want for it? Where is the old Sol? He'd have been bursting to sell things to me at a profit even if it was a non-starter. Think of all the times you've ripped me off for fun over the years. How much?"
"Well, I don't know," mused Sol, for once unsure in a deal. "I promised the locals not to break up the estate if I could help it. Maybe I could rent it to you with the caveat that I get a percentage of your profits to put back into the estate."
"Fine by me. How much?"
Sol bid low out of kindness and in the knowledge of what the other tenants paid him for their cottages. Pete aimed high and offered a London price for the same accommodation with a down payment as refundable security in case his business went bust. They compromised with Sol worrying that he had settled for too much and Pete concerned that he had offended his new landlord by agreeing to too little and then losing him money instead. It felt like an unusual lose-lose scenario for both of them.
Al walked into the barn, flustered and trying to clean red-brown splattered mud marks out of his jeans. "Have I missed anything?"

he asked. "Tell me no one has agreed to anything stupid and that Pete has not been through his midlife crisis too whilst I've been away."

"Too late," said Pete and he shook Sol's hand firmly. "I need to find a good solicitor and an even better builder."

"Bollocks," said Al and pretended to weep and then asked about the water in case it contained an infectious waterborne disease that made people turn loopy. He next requested to be taken to his car at the end of the drive immediately so that he could make some enquiries and find a good doctor.

"Don't expect me back this evening," he added as they dropped him off by his rear-dinted, but still glossy vehicle stranded at the end of the driveway like some shiny aerodynamic predator. "I need to conduct some business and that will require time in a hotel, a good one, some fine wine and a better night's sleep. I also need Wi-Fi."

Sol directed him towards New Town and hoped that good enough accommodation could be found at the end of the road before watching him career off into the distance leaving just Pete and him and the dust Al's wheels had kicked up.

"We humans are all very different, aren't we?" joked Sol, and Pete agreed. "But we wouldn't be half as much fun if we were all the same."

Pete talked about his ambitions for the garage plot and Sol discouraged his proposals until he had thought them through and made sure that Pete knew that the deal was only complete and conditional when he had a coherent business plan drawn up. They enjoyed a good lunch at the Old Town Inn and then meandered back to *Bothan Faobhar* where Gerry had started preparations for the evening's meal - rabbit stew made up to full flavour with hand-collected mushrooms, herbs and vegetables.

Once it was in the oven, Gerry and Sol took Pete out in *Sireadh-thall* and they rode the waves into the incoming tide with Gerry teaching them to handle the sails and the tiller to best utilise the boat. She responded well and they cut into the centre of the loch to take in the seabirds on the cragged rock that jutted up through the waters and the swell that the fetch had allowed the loch to unleash against it. The gannets performed for the camera, along with terns, eider and puffins, with the shags and cormorants drifting in and out of the scene.

They returned to a hearty supper and drank the wine brewed by Gerry and later whisky, over which Pete outlined his plan for the garage to Gerry.

"Do you think the locals will like the idea?" asked Sol. "Two Londoners moving in and needing help setting up, managing and running the places we own?"

"Well it will bring money. But what about when the winter comes? It's not so easy then," she replied thoughtfully.

Pete interjected. "I'd move back to London for the winter and use the studio there. Although the snow would bring a whole new set of features to photograph as well."

"Maybe you could announce it tomorrow at the next gig in the inn at Old Town? If you get half the audience Sol did last week you'll get to know what the locals want very quickly."

And so they agreed and made a pact. *They would see what the people thought. If they could think local then maybe this would work local.*

Pete published his latest blog and pictures on the web, commenting that he now had seven hundred and thirteen readers, twelve wanting to meet Sol or visit the *Bothan*, and nearly twenty demanding photography lessons. The business plan looked increasingly viable and Sol cursed himself for being so easily talked into agreeing to Pete's embryonic thought.

Later Sol showed Pete how he had enticed the wildcats in using the bones of the rabbits, cut out and kept raw by the skilful Gerry. He set up a paraffin lamp so that the bucket was illumined and found a second chair so that the two men could sit out in vigil for the night's visitor and her kittens.

Pete grappled with more photographic equipment extracted from his plush Land Rover, including alternative lenses and lighting for a series of cameras, and he set up as indicated by Sol. Then, as Gerry retired to her bedroom, the two city friends sat together and they waited amongst the looping moths and the fluttering bats, out where the owls called and the woodcock still croaked.

The clouds remained peripheral for the early part of the night and the northern lights gave their last flickers of the season before the light of the later setting sun engulfed and banished them until the next winter. The show they portrayed in folding and outstretching leaf greens and flower reds was still spectacular but held nothing of the previous visitations of this astral skylight. The stars held crisp in the thin air and the moon was kind enough to smile, her fixed expression bringing joy to the *Bothan* and her glen.

Sol's phone connected and bleeped. He had not managed to stop the automatic retrieval and pick up reflex he had developed over the years that still meant he always grabbed and pocketed his phone whenever he saw it. He cursed and looked at the most recent message that had just arrived. It was from Sue.

"*Sol,*

Who's the woman? The one in the photographs on Pete's bog? I'm fine about it but you didn't let me know there was another woman!

Sue'

He laughed and then replied.

"*Sue,*

It's not like that. She's just a friend. Don't worry. How did your date go? The other chap?

Sol"

He silenced the phone, throwing it deep into his borrowed coat's pocket, sat back in his squeaky plastic chair and waited.

More than an hour passed, Sol counting the moths whose markings he recognised and trying to judge the size and sound of bats that cut

the air's darkness and caught the flaring light of the lamp in an attempt to identify their species. Pete stared at the bucket in anticipation, it growing in increasing increments as the minutes passed. It was filling him like a helium balloon where the cylinder's valve had broken and it was then endangered by bursting. But he was always like this on a wildlife stakeout.
Ignore the pains in the legs and the desire to stretch.
Ignore the itching sensations and the need to scratch.
Ignore the thoughts that threatened to distract.
Instead just hold position, camera ready and focus.
And then, there was that sloping movement along the shadows, outside of the lighted circle edge, that could only rightly be called feline. It was bushy and large, low to the ground and walling the light in an attempt to judge the contents of the bucket better. Eyes lit up from the darkness and a nose twitched. Pete captured each movement in digital memory-sapping high definition. And then, it stepped into the glare and stalked the bones in their static, lifeless state, aware of the presence of humans at the far side of the lit pool. The wildcat considered them, now twice more in number than before. Then in that disdainful manner of cats, she walked on and plunged her head into the rabbit's carcass and fed. The two playful kits ambled on behind and into the scene, mewing and moth chasing, prancing in false attack of each other's tails and attempting to kill shadows that danced with the paraffin lamp's wick light.
They were only there for just a few minutes; those ghost forms visiting from the dark and then vanishing back into it. But they left a sense of their presence behind them and both men were humbled and electrified.
"Well," said Sol quietly, respectfully. "Do you believe me now?"
"Yes. You've got wildcats. I believe you," replied the other, trembling as he scanned the pictures he had caught. They were images of reality that were expertly taken but they were still only wraiths of the actual animals that had been there before them, contact close. And Pete, in the true spirit of art, knew it. He would

never be truly satisfied and it was that continual search for perfection that would forever keep him at his hobby and profession in pursuit of the one faultless image he could never attain. In actual fact, that was why he was so good and why he would always be improving too.

"Well, what do you think?" asked Sol after a few minutes' pause.

There was silence from Pete as he enjoyed the air, the moment, even the hoot of the tawny owl and the lap of the water on the shore. He watched the clouds grow and the shadows of a goose skein crossing the star spangled sky. He felt the enormity of what Sol had taken on, and was partly jealous but partly humbled. Finally he spoke.

"I think you're the luckiest man alive, Jake Solomon. I don't know how you managed it or how you got here, but some god somewhere has blessed you tremendously and I will do whatever I can to help you keep this the way it is...   ...so long as you sell me that damned farm!"

And then he looked at the photographs again '*tutting*' under his breath, a click of the tongue over the teeth, planning his next blog entry and wondering how many more people would be asking for the location after he posted it.

"The luckiest man alive," he repeated. "How on earth can anyone buy moments like this?"

"You can't buy them," Sol answered. "You can't sell them either. They find you and you feel like you've found them. How could we simple humans buy and sell things like that and sill have the satisfaction of knowing that they are wild and free?"

The quiet of contentment hung between them and for the briefest period Pete allowed his dream the space it needed to expand fully into a possibility, a reality and a business.

All Sol could think of was pebbles and that he had met someone who not only wanted to be near those pebbles himself, but who was quite keen to sell images and views of pebbles to other people too.

Pebbles.
He would discuss pebbles with Gerry again in the morning.

Chapter 19: Picturing a New Future

(Violin Concerto, Second Movement, Edward Elgar)

The flush of sunshine matured into Thursday bringing with it a balmy air that quickened the pulse as the loch's haze lifted in the morning to expand into a wide mountainous view of sheer clarity that once again fooled the observer into believing that everything was much closer than it really was. Sol stole out of the house to watch gulls and listen to the river as she burst out towards the sea in gambolling gaiety.

Each seaweed strand, left straggled downward by the descending tide, was dotted with the sun's reflection so that it glistened as the wind embraced it, and out on the water the fat back of a fish-hunting seal was breaking the surface, a dark blubbered sea monster of a thing that played with Sol's fascination and imagination. The undulating shape of the dog otter left his peripheral vision too late for him to get a proper image of this timid beast, but he knew that it was there as it left enough vision for his mind to fill in the blanks.

Sol joined the river as she became a broad, shallow estuary that fought with the tides and catching sight of shaded movements in a deeper pool, he jumped stones to get a better view, moving cautiously and with care. There was a large trout, black in the light of daybreak and twitching sinuously, head up in the swell that formed behind a fast-rolling cascade of peat flow.

Sol sat, moving with extreme concentration and trying to imagine what his silhouette on the rocks looked like to the fish. *How did the heron do this without being observed? What did the fish see as the fly, natural or imitation, floated or fell on the surface? How did the fisherman convince the fish that the feather was real?* Questions remained posed but unanswered and experiments to prove this or that crowded his mind.

The fish trembled and rose up to the surface, and sucking in a small black organism that fought with the surface tension it pulled it back down with it to the stone-covered bottom of the pool where it became cryptic with the cobbled bed. Sol caught the shimmer of golden sides as the sun streaked brown through the water and revealed a speckled flank of spots all cast the over-colour of the soiled water, as if as it passed through the liquid it somehow washed everything in a peaty glaze.

And then the fish flushed up through the pool's water and leapt. Driven by some internal innate desire to be further upstream, it quivered from its tail forward, building a drive of pent-up force that zipped up through its spine and then onwards to head on to the rocks and up the tumbling river, against her desire to be gravity fed down. The silvery, metallic form of fish, in a medium not its own, flew through the sky over the boulders by which Sol sat. Water, dripping in large round globs, fell backwards and the animal was free of gravity and free of the water, now for a brief moment uninhibited by both until eventually the laws that determine everything caught up with it and it dropped back down with a hollow splash. But now the fish lay one pool higher in the river, swimming forward to meet the next rock in its way, just one of a million hurdles.

Sol looked up the river. He certainly had to admire the persistence of a migratory trout and the lengths it would go to spawn. Size for size, this journey was immense and treacherous. But the fish seemed undeterred as it glimmered from the brown further up the water's flow and twitched in preparation for the next leap into the unknown.

Sitting and watching for a while, the drama was re-enacted several times with other fish, more or less successful than the first, following the same pilgrimage up to the upper loch. The usual human twelve 'stations of the cross' were replaced with hundreds of obstacles and challenges, but they pressed on whatever and it gave Sol some kind of hope to understand that if a fish could do this seemingly impossible thing then maybe he could keep the estate going too. As is usual for our kind when seeking some hidden message or guidance, his human anthropomorphism of the natural world was leading him to conclusions and philosophies that simply were never intended. But we often look for tendencies, even when they don't really exist.

It is a human thing to search for patterns wherever we go, even if the trend we think we have discovered is not a real one. To us everything must have reason and method, be predictable and mathematical. There are even some convinced that there is an algorithm that can describe the whole universe if only we had the time to work it out, the brains to cope with it and the ability to simplify everything to a basic formula. It is considered that this is what Einstein sought as he pondered his formulae of relativity; the mathematical fingerprints of God.

If something happens twice then we have a suspicion and start to believe. Rumours are spread and people begin to talk and there is a murmur of something significant. Three time occurrences see us start to make inferences and conclusion, making links between the variables that hearsay predicts must be responsible. We go with our gut reaction and only spot those who were lucky enough to be right, giving them the prized position of being chief guru of the hour. Again, and now everyone thinks that there is a genuine phenomenon and articles begin to spring up claiming prior knowledge or forecasting, usually with a catch requiring the parting of cash. At this point, there must be a reason. Five times, and it has become incontrovertible, surely? If only the world were that simple.

Humans are restricted in their sight. At maximum we deal easily in what occurs over a lifetime, but are better in watching the passing of years or even seasons, better still at considering a monthly observation, a daily trend or a short term repeated incidence of just a few minutes. Tortoises mark time in decades and trees in centuries; countries count in millennia and continents eons. A subatomic particle may last fractions of a second and what happens to an electron that means it responds to excitation instantaneously is anyone's guess - especially as it is so small, it cannot be seen, we cannot actually find them, and they are only mathematically deduced any way.

Of course the chances of anything to happen more than once is simply halved each time it occurs and there is potentially nothing necessarily linking an effect with a perceived cause. Three children born to a couple are just as likely to be three boys, three girls or any other combination in between. But if we see a family with three of just one gender, what is the trend we see if restricting our observations to just that one generation? Take it back one step and now find out how many boys and how many girls there were? And eventually, in this case, when enough of a family has been sampled to be representative we end up with only one trend in gender, and that is that there are roughly the same number of boys born as girls; and there is no trend at all.

Scale is significant and given enough time to judge it by we can be surprised by the patterns we see. Short-term fluctuations iron out to produce flat lines or a completely contrary tendency to the one we thought we saw before. We see it in Biology, its there in the market prices and shares; it follows us in education and every part of every day life.

Tune out the picture on a television screen until it gives you that diffuse snowstorm of pixelated confusion and the speakers hiss and turn up the volume and switch off the lights so that your mind can be lost in it for a moment. You are hearing and seeing an electronic interpretation of the background radiation of the universe, the footprint of the single entity we call the 'Big Bang' that extends back to a time when our universe began. You cannot go back any further than this stamp of the beginning. And yet within minutes of focus your brain will try to make patterns and spot the trends - white dots that surely make a line, a pulse in the fizz and even

shapes and faces if imaginative or drunk enough to see them or just plain tired.
We look for it even in a disarray of dots and flashes and hissing. Annoyingly, for a species hooked on observable trends and things we like to pretend are fact, our world has a frustratingly large component of randomness and chaos, which we just don't seem to be able to get used to.
And what about those who are lucky and play the markets well, get the good deals, find the right people and bargain their way to the top, surely they were destined for it and chaos did not play its part? Perhaps some will have been lucky and had the right chance, serendipity working at its best for the few who position well.
But, you may ask, if we all just gave in to destiny and presumed a predetermined path for our lives, then why try at all and why bother? Then you must have been cast before you could mould yourself and will ever be limited and frustrated by your own ability to take advantage of what chaos has on offer for you.
Don't just accept a trend or a pattern.
With attention, some day, when you are given the opportunity, you too could take advantage of chaos and chance, or even help create it.

A fish timed its jump badly and landed with a slap on a flat rock near to where Sol sat and watched it, a flimsy thing now that it had lost the support of its watery medium and the buoyancy of its swim bladder. It gasped and fluttered exposing deep pink-red gills under their covers as it lay defenceless in a mire of its own mucus and wretched its body to no effect. It was damaged down its ventral side where it had hit the sharp rock and slipped back down the mosses that covered it, stuck now in a depression where past waters had etched their fluid shapes.

Chaos had played its hand both for this fish and Sol, and only he could decide the finish and its destiny.

From one angle it was lucky for the fish that Sol was sat there to see it and possibly to rescue it. After all, in this world, in this place and in this time, what were the chances of him being there to observe the moment? He could reach down now, scoop that twitching silver-scaled body up, fight its retching slippery form and drop it gently back into the water, keeping it afloat just below the unstoppable ripple-textured surface until the passing oxygen revived it. But it was injured and if he did that then the chances were high that it would bleed, be unable to complete its journey and be swept back out to sea, unable to fulfil its calling and with its genes removed from the gene pool; a waste of a fish, a waste of a life and the nutrients that built and sustained it.

On the other side the fish had been delivered to him and to avoid the waste he could kill it, put it out of its misery, the humane thing, and take it back with him. It was just lucky for him that he came across it here on the river at this moment. *What were the chances of that?*

But what to do?

Was it even possible for there to be a right or a wrong decision made at this strange juxtaposition in both of their times?

He looked down at the pathetic stranded creature, unable to save itself, and he dispatched it before taking it home for breakfast. Like the native Indian of North America he was thankful for its life and this simple provision of nature. He wondered if it could be smoked over the fire in the way that a kipper could be and how it would taste. But on his return, Gerry said it would taste better fresh and not salted.

They stripped the bones and gutted it before filleting it and making it ready as Pete finally rose from slumber and joined them, drawn in by the smell of melting butter crisping orange-fried porridge oats, and announcing that his blog now had over nine hundred followers.

"You see?" he called. "There is a market for it."

Sol sighed and then agreed to a walk up to the headland to show Pete the moorland after which they would split whilst Pete went to town to discuss some financial options and to arrange a little longer away from the London studio. Al was neither seen nor heard from and so they sent him a message to say when they could all meet at the inn in Old Town for the weekly band concert if he was keen enough. There was no reply.

Mute swans played out a ballet scene on the loch as Gerry struck out into the returning currents in the *The Tern*, the water picking the seaweeds back up from their stranded lines of abandon, and once they were reunited it buoyantly lifted them to form complex underwater thalloid jungles of brown-green fucoid macro-algae. She was intending to work in the studio at the Boat House today and wanted to see how James and his team were proceeding with the roof repairs. They had seen Nevin pass by in his ship again and knew that he would be there already. The sea eagle had meandered across the bay and dragged Pete out to snap shots of it as quickly as he could, an organic photographer magnet that had the power of uncontrolled attraction as its greatest gift. It had passed by unaware of its pull on Pete, simply scanning the waters in its daily passage, adrift of everything including the attention of the man below.

Although Sol enjoyed his morning, walking the wood, following the river, climbing the cliff and taking the foot-beaten track to the stone on the headland, it was the solitude of the afternoon that most took him. He was able to relax and be himself, expand into his own space, play at the piano and just '*be*' without the pretence required for entertaining others. He took the boat out on the water for an hour, practising the techniques taught him by Gerry, and managed to circle her around the beach and out again, steering well clear of the home of the *Blue Men* and thus avoiding any costly sacrifices. He had packed a richly tessellated slice of fruit cake, moist and black with the berries and currants it was packed with, just in case he was tempted to pass too far into the loch or felt obliged to visit the ladies across the lake, even unintentionally like last time. It lay by his hand on the cross bar, neatly folded into a napkin. As a cake he rated highly, it was a greatly prized sacrifice indeed and should be acceptable to even the most discernible of the *Blue Men* of the loch.

Eventually he lay back in the hull and listened to the sea sounds through the thin clinkered timbers that kept him from drowning and he imagined the drifts of the water and the plethora of life that it contained just beyond his sight but not beyond his hearing. The wood yawed slightly as the water lifted and caressed it in wave after gentle wave and he knew that their rhythm was being felt by his relaxing soul but memorised in his body, something it would replay later tonight when he finally settled down to rest.

Eating the cake, he identified gulls, waders, ducks and geese by their calls and surprised himself by the internal vision he was able to draw to mind of each species. In so short a time he had learnt so much.

He returned to the *Bothan* sea sticky and emotionally high having taken *Sireadh-thall* out into a flock of terns who had continued to plummet around him like a shower of living meteorites raining in storms that only attacked sand eels. The water boiled with their pitted craters as each fell bullet-like, forming circular explosions and then erupted back up in a beak-filled escape of the liquid that seemed sure to grapple on and drown them. Sol had taken his own new camera and rattled off shots randomly in the hope of having something to be proud of. But so many bodies falling at such great speed and the pictures were a melee of motion and white against the deep blue of water and the refracted brightness of the sky. The clarity he had secured in first-hand vision was lost to photographs so abstract that they could never have graced a gallery's walls.

Readying to wash in the shower room he placed the bucket out in the yard in early preparation for the cats' supper and then walked naked across the remaining cobbles. He gasped as the water's ice cold covered his body, gurgling as air bubbles shifted along the pipe work and took spiders and their webs down the plughole with them. He had lost his initial fear of these unseen monsters, the ones who left their legs only exposed on the white of the bath base, hiding the rest of them on the other side of the plug grate in a space that seemed impossibly small for such large, hairy spiders. *Tegenaria domestica* the books told him; the common house spider. Once named, they somehow took on a less terrifying persona and became acceptable to live with and around. *After all, scale for scale, who was the scariest to the other?*

Like Robert the Bruce's spider every time the web was broken in the plug it was rebuilt by the next day and Sol was taken again by the tenacity of Mother Nature if it felt it was doing the right thing. Organisms seemed programmed to repeat what should be successful, even in the face of disaster and failure, because that had proven right in the evolutionary past. It lacked the flexibility required to change those genetically programmed instructions that had previously served it so well, some being destined to destruction as a result of recent human changes and developments. We were the one thing that wildlife had failed to accommodate for and adaptation could not predict.

He shut off the water that clunked noisily before it was reduced to a spurting drip and then stopped, and he dried himself on the rough towel whilst eyeing up songbirds on the feeders through the grubby window. Next he entered the yard, waiting for a moment and straining as his eyes were forced from the darkness of the shower room out into the brightness of the sun's unfriendly glare across the plot.

It was a Mediterranean scene that reminded Sol of holidays abroad. There was the pretty white painted cottage, slightly weatherworn and undoubtedly with its corners knocked off of it over its many years of use. It had age, surrounded by its attendant sheds and cobbled yard where the weeds sprang up merrily and the flies buzzed. Beyond were the cove-enclosing headlands, rocky and sun-struck with their dry-headed sea pinks rocking from the ledges and gulls perched up high. Topped with fading gorse and sprouting heather, they stuck out in loch-piercing fashion in parallel arrangement to encircle a coral sand beach that reflected the sun and hemmed in the water to the bowl of the sea. His boat lay up here, traditional wooden and with a charm of her own, skipped by gulls, herring, common, lesser-black backed and black-headed, and the swans still strutted backwards and forwards in their dance routine with the waders and the geese.

In the distance a mountainous unpopulated shoreline sprung up from the flat surface of the loch where clouds hid ready for the rain of a future day and behind were the woods and his own montane environ that stretched upwards beyond where he could see. It was a panoramic postcard view and he was inclined to agree with Pete that he was the luckiest man alive, and he breathed deeply of the fresh, bright, sun-warmed air.

He would need to picture this scene and remind himself of it whenever he was challenged in the future, when the winds and snows came of a winter and he was stuck here alone, when money seemed too precious for him to retain or gather, if food ran short or his plans failed, even if the roof caved in and he was left destitute. This was to be his mental encouragement, to remind him that it was all worth it and that life was still good and all of this was beyond price; no one could purchase it and it would never be for sale whilst he lived.

It was mid afternoon and the day's length now exceeding that of England in its southerly position below. The shadows were elongating, but the warmth of the air was increasing daily with the flowers of the valley pushing on speedily in preparation for bursting open and revealing their coloured-glories.

His goose-bumped skin lost its pimpled covering and loosened as the sun thawed him with its breezy touch, and he closed his eyes to connect with it more easily without the distraction of sight, as old Joe might say. He sensed the Earth deep beneath him and the souls of his feet tingled with the essence of volcanic age, a sensation that prickled up through his legs to his exposed naked body and the towel flung over his shoulder. His scalp bristled with the caress of light and air.

This was a good place and he knew it.

He breathed deep again to take in something extra from the scent of the yard, the pine freshness of the plantation trees and the heady scent of the already sprung flowers, and sweetly rich honey smell of the moors, all blending and accumulating at the mouth of the glen and the location of *Bothan Faobhar*. His chest rose and fell slowly, but sincerely, and exhilaration sent his mind into whirls as he focused on the individual call of birds that joined together musically to create choirs of mixed flocks. Then, added in to the edge of his conscience were the rustle of each leaf, the whisper of every branch, the rattle of the driest grass blades, and the singular laps of the water that made up the constant motion of the sea.

Here, nothing was alone and he basked in the sunlight, the soundscape and the refreshing air.

And then he heard it, a noise intended to be silent but not managing to muffle itself quite. He came to his senses and was immediately aware that he was stood stripped in the yard by the shower room with his eyes closed, his towel now dropped to the floor, and all of his city based sentiments, and modesty and worries were flooding back to him. *He was naked after all!*

Again the unnatural sound of a footfall, this time pressing too clumsily on leaves that had baked to cracking.

Sol dared to open his eyes a fraction and scanned the yard trying to locate any movement or more noise. Whoever it was, they were not keen to be seen and had approached the yard from the right. If they were to continue they would be forced to come between the buildings along the path from the toilet track hidden in the shade of the trees.

Another footfall, this time with more care and deliberation, but it was heavy despite a steadiness that tried to hide it within the other sounds of the yard.

Sol's heart beat. He had the advantage of knowing the place well, the local knowledge required to run away, hide or stand and fight. He also knew that whoever it was would not yet know that Sol was aware. He had the element of surprise over this creeping being. *Was it Pete, Gerry, Hamish, Al...?*
However, he also had the distinct disadvantage of being totally naked and stood at a distance from the shower shed that would mean he was completely observable and unable to escape easily, nor protect himself should the need arise. Sol was all too aware of this last, and most important point, although he presumed that whoever it was would be equally shocked to find him in this state.
A controlled press into the ground and another leaf was crushed to reveal the intruder's position.
Sol craned his neck slowly and there was the wildcat in the plain light of day, nose twitching wildly and neck craning forward as the smell of trout bones reeled her in and out of the shadows by the wall and into the exposure of the yard.
He knew she was aware of him and that she had chosen to be near only in her pursuit of food. She told him so. Mewing to her kittens who fell from the grasses behind and lacked the fear or the skill to join their mother in the hunt of the bucket and safe passage across the yard, she looked straight at Sol, closed her eyes in alert acknowledgement and then walked on to the slops to feed.
Sol felt aware of his nakedness but no longer cared. She had not judged him, only he had. The feeling was that something that humans do all too easily of themselves or other people they share this world with. Judgement was not invented for nature, it is a uniquely anthropoid disposition designed to form divides, protect us within our little flocks and to give us something over other people where we can make ourselves feel better at their expense. Wildlife doesn't have time for that, it needing to focus on survival and reproduction instead.
The cat relaxed too. She now had her watchman, the strange two-legged form that tracked her when she visited the *Bothan*, to keep a

look out over the kittens whilst she fed. She side-chewed through the bones on offer, eyes closed in response to her taste buds' stimulation and the pleasure of a stomach filling with more than the putrid meat on the deer carcass along the river and the elytra of beetles and the wings of flies that refused to digest satisfactorily.

The kittens rolled and leapt, warming themselves in the sunshine and chasing the butterflies that flitted across the yard or foolishly landed to lick salt from the cobbles. Every rocking stem shadow was a motion to be explored, hunted and learnt about.

When she had finished the mother cat lay down and invited the kittens to suckle, leaving Sol now unaware of his dress and instead honoured by what the wildcat was allowing him into. He was conscious of noises in the background and tugs on his senses, but for now that could wait. This needed to be recorded in his mind's memory. It was another thing to return to whenever he needed the inspiration to go beyond the doldrums and worries of his life, and unlike any of his fantasies or dreams for the *Bothan*, or for life, this was real and not just a creation of his own wishes.

The wildcat, laid back in the sun in false sleep with its pale belly fur and teats uppermost and the two kittens tiring under the weight of their milk meal, suddenly looked up. Her ears pricked and the markings over her forehead drew together as she sought information on what noise she had heard, perceived or detected. Minutes passed and she relaxed again, tail flicking and left ear twitching in that way that shows a cat never truly switches off.

And then something told her that they were not alone. But whatever it was, Sol never heard or saw it. She mewed loudly, shrilly and with a sense of emotion and fear, one that immediately woke her slumbering kits and brought them up out of their milk-induced slumber. The three fell up to their feet and then slunk with grace and speed, but without noise, into the shadows and they were gone.

Sol turned to watch them and exchanged a knowing look with the mother cat from the shade of the canopy, irises caught by dappled rays of green-filtered leaf light, before her eyes closed and she became invisible again and just another one of the shadows.

"That was amazing," called Pete lowering his camera. He was stood at the corner of the *Bothan* a way behind Sol.

"Hmm," agreed Sol as he grabbed his cobble-dusted towel from the yard floor and wrapped it around his midline in an immediate moment of concern.

"Don't worry. I've protected your modesty," Pete bantered. "But she really does trust you doesn't she? I'm sorry though, to disturb that moment like that. She heard me back here somewhere. But... ...just look at these pictures!"

Sol felt strangely as if his privacy had been invaded and was initially angered and fiery. But when he saw the photographs, their drama and the way that Pete had framed them, he understood something of what the man was saying.

"Naked enthusiasm for the wildcats. That's what I'll call the blog." Sol smiled. "Just make sure you put age-appropriate warnings on it, okay? I don't want any of your followers fainting or writing in to complain."

They had a light supper and then headed down into the old town for the gig, taking the track steadily in Addie.

Pete was excited, not only for the event but also because he wanted to pitch his ideas to anyone who would listen, to see if he got the local vote or not. They arrived at the inn in good time, but there was already a crowd milling around in holiday fashion to greet them. Some had beer glasses raised to their lips, draining the cool dregs of a first or second pulled pint, whilst many were deep in conversation enjoying the balmy feel of a warm day's humid end and extending the life of the drinks they cupped or held.

There was the air of the carnival about the place as Sol pressed through the throng to take up his place amongst the musicians and Pete quickly got to talking to a local crowd, trying to judge local feeling and assess the local people. The proprietor placed a thick black beer in front of Sol with a thud, announcing that it was "*on the house*".

"Thank you," said Sol, "why?"

"Aye, why?" asked Hamish. "*You* never give stuff away Tom."

"This boy's good for business," the rotund, rosy faced man replied. "I've had folk coming in looking for him all day *and* they've bought drinks *and* they've eaten food. Not only that, but look at the crowds for a second week on the trot. People want to see and hear 'im." Tom patted Sol on the back heartily. "So, it's on the house."

"Who?" quizzed Sol suddenly alert. "Who's been looking for me?"

"Lots of folk. Asking where you live and about a wildcat."

Sol went stone cold and the colour drained from his face leaving his skim a pallid ash. His heart pounded so that he could sense it in his ears and his temples felt pressured and tight. "Did you tell them anything?" he asked anxiously.

"No, of course not. I told them you were playing tonight though and if they were that keen to see you then they could come and speak to you personally. I know your type. You must be running away from something, otherwise you'd never have moved up here in the first place. But a man deserves his privacy whoever asks after him." Tom mopped his sweaty brow with a beer towel advertising a brand of ale that had probably never been sold in the inn and leaned back against a dark-wood pillar.

"Privacy?" laughed a second man producing his phone and showing a picture of a naked Sol watching wildcat kittens suckle on their mother's exposed belly. "Not the most private person are we Mr Solomon. However, I too owe you one."

"Why?" asked Sol. "What have I done for you?"

"Tim Fosse, pleased to meet you." The man was small and wiry, with a friendly expression hidden under a mop of brown hair that had been ironed into a ring by the over-use of some form of hat. "I own the Fosse Stores on the main Street. Never sold so much. I've even had to stay in my shop all day in case people popped in and spent money. Shocking effect on my fishing, but much better for the pocket. Thanks."

"Oh, okay." Sol was unsure whether to be happy or not, but he was still wanting his estate kept private where he could as his underlying desire. *He had to protect the wildness of his cats.*

"Never mind that for now," said Hamish feeling Sol's concerns. "We've a gig to play." And he cleverly distracted Sol by asking if he would be happy to play the piece he had written to accompany Mrs Hamish. Old Joe was next in seeing if Sol would perform one of the duets they had practised together too. He might have been blind but he could sense the tension and fear in Sol and knew how defensive he was likely to feel about the *Bothan*. After all, this was G's choice of proprietor. *What else would he feel?*

Then before Sol could descend into any depressed state, with a tap of his foot and a light jig on the fiddle, Joe started the concert and the music was off for another evening's sublime playing. It met the sponge-like ears of those gathered, which absorbed it and transferred it down the cabling of their nerves to stimulate brains into thought, taking them on a tour of the islands and highlands, the shores and the land, the past and the present, and with a little of the future mixed in. The duets were met with appreciative applause and cheers as the horde in the pub built up, their shuffling bodies pressing inwards raising the moisture and closeness of the atmosphere. By the interval Sol had all but forgotten what the innkeeper had said.

He sat in a corner enjoying the company of a few old timers and loosening his fingers for further violin fiddling. He did not want to drink much alcohol as he intended to drive home along the track tonight and now that he was not playing for a few minutes he had become aware again of what the landlord had told him. It was an insidious thought that like so many that we do not want to entertain sat there just beyond his periphery of controllable mind where he was unable to fully acknowledge it. But it was there, nagging from the side and draining his potential to process and think.

People had been asking after him?
What people?
He looked around at the gathered crowd, all appreciating the time themselves and jostling in humorous attitude. There were those few faces he knew, James and Gerry, Pete and the band, but oh so many whom he did not know and of whom he had suddenly found himself mindful. To some he would be the faceless newcomer who only had a name or a reason now that they knew he could play in the band. They knew nothing else nor did most of them want to. But somewhere in that crowd it felt as though someone or some people were hunting him, watching and waiting for their chance.

A man stepped forward and offered him a drink.

"Just lemonade, thank you," said Sol expecting more conversation in return. Lemonade appeared, but there were no follow up questions, just thanks for his playing, hoping he was enjoying life in the area; welcome.

Whilst the band retuned at the end of the interval, seeing his chance, Pete called for order, shouting that he had an announcement to make and wanted the local opinion on an idea of his. There was a hushed expectation, except for Hamish who whispered to Sol. "Had I better put him out of his misery now or let him make a fool of himself first? What's he after?"

"Hear him out," Sol replied. "The idea is mad, but no madder than me buying *Bothan Faobhar*."

"Thank you," called Pete as the people hushed. "I just wanted to thank you all for your welcome here this evening as a friend of Sol's." There was a mutter of approval around the pub. "I've only been in the area for a few days, taking photographs and writing, but there is no doubt that this is a very special place and I, like my good friend Sol here, want to do something to preserve it."

"Forget it," shouted a voice from the back. "What you see here's history and as soon as the money runs out that's where our old way of life'll end. We should have changed years ago, but..."

Hamish stood up to regain the control that had instantly started to slip away. "Give the man chance to speak. You never know. Even *he* could make sense!"

"There's a turn up for the books," laughed Mrs Hamish. "Normally we're asking you to be quiet."

After the laughter, Pete thanked Hamish and then started to address the shifting-sea crowd again. "It's only a start, but I've been writing a blog and publishing pictures from the area and it's generated a lot of interest." He looked down at his phone screen to check. "One thousand four hundred and seven people are following to be exact."

"Well," came a dissenting voice, "that won't earn us any money." And whilst others agreed Tim Fosse made a joke about Sol's nude photograph. "But don't worry Sol, I didn't recognise you from the picture. Well not with your trousers on."

There was mirth again, raucous this time.

"Stop," shouted Pete angrily. "I think I can start to bring some money into the area *and* begin to convert some of this Internet following into hard cash to be reinvested into the local economy. *Your* local economy."

Pete was surprised at the lack of support he was receiving until James Nevin took to the floor. "He's right. We cannot carry on as if nothing is going wrong." He held a pint of slopping black ale to his chest as he addressed them. "The farmers are making nothing and are destitute, we can't sell our goods and nobody wants out houses or our boats. I am a proud man, born and bred here, but until Sol arrived I was thinking of packing up the boat yard. Nobody wants wooden boats. Since Sol came, I've had work and even reemployed the men I laid off before." Nevin looked around. "I hate to say it, but I think we need some help, or else we all fail, and the way of life we all want is as good as gone."

His speech was met with silence as he put his face furiously to the floor unable to fix another's gaze. "I say we hear him out!" And he returned quietly to a stool in the corner where Gerry greeted him affectionately. Aware of the tension in the air, Joe lent forward and tapped Sol's violin.

"Play them the melody of the river like you did for me that time," he said audibly enough for the crowd to hear, and Sol stood awkwardly to address the brooding number that paced uneasily; a shape-shifting mass of people.

"I," he began, "have fallen in love with this place as you know, and I want to do anything I can to preserve it. My friend Pete here has seen that and understood it too. Those who have met my other friend will already know that he sees life in a slightly different way." Mutters and giggles around the floor meant that at least a few had made contact with Al. "Pete is an award winning photographer with a huge following and, in London, his is a famous name. He takes amazing pictures. Can Tom get them up on the screens?"

Tom squeezed forwards, larger than life and wheezing under the pressure of working so hard for the night. He spoke to Pete and the two of them disappeared towards the bar to see if they could get any of Pete's wildlife images up on to the four large television screens that were positioned unobtrusively around the pub.

"Whilst they work on that, I have written a new section for my symphony which I hope you will recognise as a description of my walk up the river to visit old Joe. It starts by the cottage, *Bothan Faobhar* and then meanders up with the river."

The screens flickered on and there was a gasp of appreciation as the face of the wildcat appeared, crystal focused and clear, lapping at fish bones in the yard at *Bothan Faobhar*. Every few seconds another and then another shot was displayed in over-enlarged clarity. The fish eagle haunting the waters, the dipper on the river, butterflies and moths, heady blooms in full flush and vast scenes of mountains and moorland.

Sol, eyes sealed shut, took himself to the estuary where that bundling water of the river mixed with salt and became the loch and then the sea. In his mind he transformed into a fish, powerful and energetic and, metaphorically turning, he slowly faced the flow and force of the descending water and with a flick of his bow he was running the river and the music played.

It drove on up through the churning waters, over the rocks and through deep pools and dark recesses where a fish could rest. It ascended the waterfalls and skipped with the flies and the insectivorous birds, even the scooping dipper who vibrated on the current-smoothed boulders as if to dry. To the side it cut up the crags and encompassed the loneliness of moorland and was distracted by the dark mystery of the standing stones. It widened into sweeping corners and ran wild through gullies and burns until finally he and his tune were free in the open flat expanse of the upper loch under the mountain's sweeping escarpment, and the playing ended.

Stillness reigned, and then came the steady trickle of applause as if the river had taken the fish and started to send it back down the river accompanied by the ripple and splash of hand claps. The power of pictures and the emotion of music had taken the crowd where Joe knew it would, into a land of receptivity. He too had been on that fish's viewed journey with them.

"Now speak," said Sol pushing Pete forward as the pictures continued to change in their sequence.

"I am a photographer as you can see. I work in London but have been looking for a country site for a studio for a while now, and well I think I may have found one..." The crowd listened and considered his speech. "...I am proposing to regenerate the garage on Sol's drive...   ...the barn complex...   ...to turn it into a house and studio for wildlife study and photography classes." Still they listened. "I know I've only just arrived and I've hardly got to know about the place but...   ...I'd need local roofers and builders, and hopefully you're here in this room right now? I'd be keen to employ local people to run the place and take punters out on to the moors or to the woods and to stop them wandering off the beaten track..."

"...or frightening the livestock!" muttered Hamish who was quickly silenced by Mrs Hamish.

"Would you need boats?" asked Nevin.

"Can you provide them?"

"Given time. But you'd need crews too then and I'd have to employ a few more of the old hands to make them and maintain them as loch-worthy. Presuming you want traditional wooden craft?"

"Yes, I would," agreed Pete. "I'd need cleaners as well and some way of feeding and housing the punters if there were too many to keep up at the garage. Of course, there could be spin offs too. Tourists need things to buy, trinkets, local produce; you know the stuff? The plans are still embryonic but I wanted to get the local opinion first...   ...before I got too carried away. So...   ...what do you think?"

There followed a moment of confused politics.

A desire to preserve the world as it was is strong in all people, who will defend even the most illogical of stances and traditions regardless of their use or any pleasure derived from them, simply because it is what has always happened. But add into that the opposite call for finance to maintain anything and that pull on the purse strings then works antagonistically against the one already tugging at the heart strings. It leaves a confusion and emotional tension which is only ever going to be quashed through compromise. There is one thing humans seem very poor at accepting though, and that is of course compromise.

Pete and Sol became conscious that no one wanted to be the first to state their view or make their point and instead there was natural collective looking for leadership and someone to make it for them. The crowd's eyes turned to the nearest they had to an accepted decision-maker in their community and they all slowly turned and looked at Hamish.

Unfazed, Hamish sat and mulled the thought over in his mind and then, looking deep into her eyes as if reading her thoughts in a way that years of love and marriage had trained him to, his wife pushed him to his feet. And the crowd waited expectantly, almost reverently.

He cleared his throat before he spoke. "I am just a lowly shepherd." He waited whilst the thoughts he had crystallised into communicable words. "I lead dumb flocks of animals, helping them to breed successfully, keeping them alive even when they seem dead set against it themselves, and then selling their fleeces, if worth it, and their meat which is beyond comparison the world over. You each have your own thoughts and unlike sheep are capable of deciding what is right for yourselves. However, there is nothing such as the wisdom of sheep. They just follow and they are just pushed. Therefore, I am not going to make a decision for you tonight. Pete might be bloody mad for all I know... ...I'm still not sure if I shouldn't just euthanize him now and save the whole flock of us a lot of trouble, but... ...I was wrong about Sol and I'm probably wrong about Pete. I only understand sheep you see. But I'll vote with him if it helps preserve my life and the one I have up there on that hill, so long as any wild tourists are kept away from the sheep and the rarest of living things." And he stood by Pete and raised his hand. "Those in favour of the second idiot from London moving in, say 'aye'."

To Pete and Sol's amazement, there was a chorus of '*ayes*' and hands and glasses were upstretched.

"Fabulous," said Hamish slapping Pete on the back. "Now we can finish this bloody concert?"

Music over, Sol was carefully putting his violin away as the crowd slowly departed. Pete was talking to Tom, the landlord, and his wife about how they could improve facilities in the town and a few interested locals were working out if there would be finance to recover and redevelop some of the abandoned properties on the shorefront.

Sol was pleased for Pete, but equally worried. He would have to make sure that there was a restriction zone around the *Bothan* where only visits with official guides were allowed near the cats. *How quickly they had become his primary concern, as if he had replaced all hope of working, relationships and a family with a wild animal's welfare. Even his vices for tobacco and alcohol seemed quashed in comparison.*

"Excuse me," asked a lady's voice from behind him. She had an English accent of southern origin and he was startled not only by its intrusion into his thoughts, but by how unusual the sound was now that he had been surrounded by stronger-accents for a while.

He turned to find a man and a woman. He was bearded and dressed in an attempt to look scruffy but with all new clothes that were designed to be that way, only too cleanly, and she similarly attired, trendily and expensively downtrodden; shabby-chic. Sol judged them quickly and applied his business sense to gauge what they wanted and who they were.

They had probably travelled up from the southern counties given the accent.

Well-dressed, but trying too desperately not to be so, suggested they had plenty of money – maybe used to getting their way but wanting to appear to be roughing it.

Clean nails meant that they didn't get their hands dirty.

Shoes were impractical and would struggle up the tracks round here. However, they too screamed of wealth and cleanliness – nothing off the beaten track.

Hair was made to look scuffed up and required regular styling to maintain this impression. Would the mousse attract flies and the wind cause havoc? He could smell powerful sweet-scented perfume as well – this would scare off most animals, even if upwind.

They were keen and enthusiastic, young and energetic – good qualities to have.

The conclusion: *they've read Pete's blog and have probably come to find the Bothan or to see wildcats.*

He stopped himself mid thought.

"Yes?" he answered without a hint of this mental stream showing.

"You must be Jake Solomon?" she said again and smiled warmly. An extended hand was thrust almost up his nose and he stood to shake it.

"I must, yes," he replied, gingerly taking the limp hand and rocking it. "And you are?"

"Kim and John," she said. "We were just wondering if..."

"...I'm actually quite tired tonight and..."

"...we've read Pete's blog and..."

"...I do need to get going..."

"...but we just want to see..."

"...I..."

"The man needs to go," Hamish interrupted pushing in and giving Sol the space to pack his instrument carefully away; something he unusually rushed tonight, clumsily slowing himself down.

The girl smiled and then made one more attempt. "We just wanted to come and see the *Bothan* and maybe the wildcats too, but it isn't listed on any map."

"And hopefully it won't be," said Sol. "I don't mean to sound rude, but the only reason I have wildcats is because no one can find the place. The *Bothan* is my home and I would prefer it if the only window into it was via the blog. When Pete opens up his studio, I am sure he will be keen to sort out a site for photographing wildcats. Just not my home. I really do need to go now?"

He shouted for Pete, but he had decided to stay in the inn for the night and so Sol left alone, making his apologies to the young couple and anyone else he felt he had offended. They took instead to talking to Pete, seeking information, location, detail, and Sol's fears grew even stronger.

He did not want visitors to the Bothan.

He did not want eco-tourists on his drive.

He did not want people traipsing around his yard.

And he did not want the wildcats scaring away.

The cats had trusted him, he had let their secret out in that silly text to Pete and he had broadcast it to the world.

Now he had to defend the estate and keep the location secret.
Bustling through the bar door, he found Addie and checked suspiciously that no one was watching him in the dark or was in a position to follow him, and then he climbed up into the cab and started her engine up. Hamish walked up and tapped on the glass which Sol slid back so that it overlapped the fixed sheet joined to the door. It scraped over the fixings like chalk on a blackboard.
"It'll be alright, Sol. I'm not convinced it'll be perfect, but this might be one of the answers the estate needs. You admit yourself you aren't sure how to fund it. But without something, the cats are as good as gone any way. Think about the opportunities as well as the risk."
"But…" Sol started his complaint; his defence.
"Do you think the fish out there in the loch," Hamish pointed out to where the moon-reflected back off the water, "begin their day worrying about the chance of being eaten? If they did, they'd never feed, never grow, never mate and never amount to anything. No. They don't think about every possible danger. Instead they weigh up the pros and the cons, and without taking unnecessary risks they get on with it."
Sol agreed miserably, thanked Hamish, closed the window miserably and then rumbled off up the road leaving Hamish illuminated red by the rear lights. Mrs Hamish joined him and they stood watching Addie take her master around the harbour road and off towards his home whilst gulls floated silently, ghost-like, in the opaque night air, as surreal white-winged forms; Valkyries.
"He's as good as G was," said Hamish. "Already cares more about the wildlife than people. I don't know how G found him. But he's found a good 'un."
"Aye," she agreed and moved closer to her old man.

Sol was surprised with himself, slowing only when he hit the *Bothan* track and passed the unwelcome sign that stood there proclaiming nothing to anyone but barring obvious entry. Huge relief flooded him and emotions rose up, plumbed from depths he did not know about nor understand, and he started to cry in floods that he would not have believed possible.

He left Addie ticking over as he jumped down from the cab and removed the rotting remains of the house sign from the base of the post, checked there was no mail to give anything away, and then tossed the name plate into the back of the truck.

Addie's headlights beamed across the track as he crawled up the miles into the hills and down into the glen. Two deer bounded alongside his passage and the brown owl scooted the path ahead as he entered his hidden world, and the secrecy, security and sanctity of the *Bothan*. It was his home and his family, the cats and the other wild things.

He wished for so many things different, with regret being that constant nag that he would have changed the world to avoid, and he decided that he would be more guarded and shun people more often if he could and still had the chance. *After all, why did he need other humans anyway? Those that knew him had all suggested he needed a retreat and some time out.*

And then he was there, pulling in to the end of the drive and silencing Addie's engine. The cottage waited invitingly and once clear of the odours of diesel and oil, Sol could experience and relish the scents of the sea, the night, the mountain, and the woods and of home. An oystercatcher heralded his return.

The fire lit, a lamp alight and the porch door closed, Sol walked in to the living room to settle into the easy chair with a glass of whisky in his hand. It was then that he noticed the hand addressed letter still lying on the table, patiently waiting inanimately to be opened from several days ago.

It called to him and told him that now was not a good time to ignore it.

He picked it up, thumbed it over and looked at the address. Sweeping floral letters written in ink graced the white of the stiff-papered envelope.

Then, slipping the bone handled knife on the writing desk along the uppermost fold of the envelope, he sliced it cleanly open and withdrew the parchment from inside.

Sol scanned down the paper, taking in the beautiful hand-inked script, with perfect angled lines and exacting margins, to see an instantly recognisable single letter signature at the bottom of the page.

It was, as he had come to suspect, a letter from G.

Chapter 20: Mothering Nature

(Pavane for a Dead Princess, Maurice Ravel)

Sol held the letter fast in his hand as he discarded the envelope on the table and found his way, fumbling in the glow-light of the fire, back to that comfortable warm spot sunk amongst the upholstery of G's chair. He poked the fire distractedly and then began to read the letter in full, carefully sucking the marrow and meaning from any word he could. He knew from an indeterminable part of his central core that his mentor had written this and, as all good tutors do, he had chosen his moment to communicate to perfection.

"Dear Sol,

Can I apologise for the time that it will have taken for this letter to arrive, but it should more or less coincide with the month's anniversary of you taking over at Bothan Faobhar. I trust she has made you feel welcome and that you have become aware of how special she is. She will be proud of you by now.

I expect that the fox will have greeted you. Beware as both the dog and the bitch fox will be in through your kitchen door given half the chance. They will leave their musk scent and take what they can. You'll know if they've been.

All of the migrants should be in by now and if you are lucky enough to be in the high fields at night you may hear the gentle 'swipe-swipe' call of the quail or even the croak of the corncrake. However, both of these species have become difficult to find of late. Migration through Europe is a dangerous form of Russian roulette for wildlife these days. What damage one man can do with a gun and a spare hour is anyone's guess and no amount of international protection seems to be good enough to deter them.

I hope that my journals are providing you with enough information about the seasons and that I have left enough reading material to support your studies, in addition to the birdseed required to keep the feeders filled until the New Year. The cats should have blessed you with their presence if you have fed them and the female looked as if she were expecting kittens soon when I left. Beware of the Tom, he is aggressive and the only animal in the woods I think that might attack you. He will only appear round the Bothan around Christmas time when other food is scarce. Remember that the wildcat is exactly that – a 'wild' cat. You'll never be able to tame one and even if you did you would have ruined one of the most feral creatures in the world. It is better just to watch them from a distance and let them come to you. Anything else and you will probably scare them off.

I left clothes and sheets and other things for you. I have no use for them now that I have left and so you should feel free to use what you like. Someone should have given you my Land Rover Addie by now too. She was a great asset for me until I grew too old to get out over the estate.

You will have found the locals friendly enough even though most of them are struggling financially. I wish you good luck in maintaining the estate and its wild life in the hope that you are able to bring some of your economic wisdom to protect its future; something I have been struggling to do for some time now. My research suggests that you have the skills the estate needs now.

I hope that you do not feel that you have been trapped into buying the Faobhar Estate. It chose you above all others who applied for it and I am certain that it will have chosen you well. The costs are high but the benefits far greater – you will understand this more on a cold day, when the snow prevents anyone getting in or out and you are sat amongst ten thousand geese and ducks and the loon is singing. Poetry cannot express how it feels to know that you are the only one witnessing such a spectacle and that it only exists because you have protected it.

It is mid-May now, and so to know that you have truly bought somewhere special, wake up early (before sunrise), climb into the woods behind the Bothan and head up to the crags; there was a

fallen deer in the river there when I last looked. Hug the rocks, travelling inland, until you are at the interface between the open woodland and the plantation trees. The cliffs will be behind you if you face back towards the Bothan, the plantation will be on your right and the ancient wood on your left. You'll know the spot is right because the manmade wood is all of one species, tall and straight spruces imported from Europe, and the wild wood is mixed and more diverse with more gnarled trees in it. There is a wide ride between them which you should now be looking down. Sit and watch what happens as the sun rises. If you are the man I thought you were, you will understand and you will continue to protect the estate, but most especially the glen.
Yours with very best wishes,
G"

Sol read and re-read the letter.

There was no hint of an address or any other way of contacting G, but just that instruction to wake up early and head off into the woods, and so after considering everything else in the letter, Sol put it aside and tried to search for sleep.

The fox; oh yes he had been.

The quail and the corncrake; he would have to travel to the top meadow to see or hear them.

The other migrants; even Sol was noticing the changes in bird species out on the loch – the gradual seasonal cline of song, behaviour, colour and form.

The cats; Sol's emblematic animals.

The clothes; freedom to wear what he had already borrowed and taken on as his own.

The choice; once again the Bothan chooses him and not he the Bothan.

And a call to look down the ride early on a morning; this he must do.

He was aware that today he was alone in the house and that Pete was staying away and Gerry had obviously chosen not to return.

However he was happy with his own company tonight and decided to use the opportunity to discover what G had asked him to look for; understanding. Setting an alarm on his mobile for three the next day, he battled in the way that anyone needing to sleep has to if they intend to switch off, constantly turning and rechecking the time just in case. It is a human thing that only those who do not need it or who are dead are able to sleep well.

But sleep did come eventually. It was a troubled slumber that lacked the comfort of knowing what was right to do, how he could contact G and ask his advice, or where to turn if this wasn't possible, and when the alarm finally sprung to life, before even the sun had shown itself clearly, he was tired, agitated and weary. But rise he did, cramming his camera into his holdall and grabbing whatever over clothes he felt he would need on a day that had not yet decided what weather it would wear.

The sky was dark blue, inky and oppressive as he entered the wood and headed for the track that accompanied the river, ever eager as it descended to find the loch. He smelt the stag well in advance of finding it in a misted dawn-view across the cascading waters. But he pushed on to the crags, not having the time to stop as the blue lightened and took on a pinkish tinge at the horizon.

Along the edge of the rocks he pressed, tugged back by blaeberry, the first shoots of bramble and the clutching stems of thorns and spines. The rock face was cold and bright, being painted crimson at its head in a light that was slowly descending as the sun itself rose, hot and fiery, portending later rain. Rough to the touch, he felt the crisp-dried cups of lichens and allowed his fingers to drift through pendulous fern fronds where the tacky threads of dew-enchanted spider silk attempted to impede his passage.

A roe deer buck lifted its head proud of the underwood scrub, surprised that the 'human' was awake at this hour, a presence not normally seen unless the hunt was on. It sampled the air, distrustful and attentive, steam clinging to its wet muzzle as it chewed in round circular motion a fermenting grass bolus which it turned with its thick tongue. Then, something in Sol's movement finally spooked it and it turned to bound into the wood, noiseless and agile with a white bob-tail prominently stotting at its rear. Its bark echoed back from the half-light, unearthly and haunting, and other deer replied to acknowledge the threat in the woods.

And then he was at the ride as instructed by G, the darkness of the light-absorbing pinewood to his right, the rocks to his back and the open shrub-leafed understory of the mixed wood to his left. There birch mingled with oak and Scot's pine, rowan and yew to create a canopy of changing height and species, here a glade and there a hollow, flat and deep soiled, moss'd and rocky. One wood was diverse and natural, the other a past ecological mistake planted in the hope of money that would never be realised.

Was this what G wanted him to see? Was there some hidden metaphor between the world of the natural and the world of the controlled, one diverse in ecology and the other devoid of it but worth potential financial reward? Did G want Sol to see that money wasn't everything and that what was once intended for profit could mean ruin of the natural?

The light caught up with him and broke into a dawn whose vision exploded over the horizon and spilled its visual chorus down into the woodland ride casting long shadows as it tipped each flower head and grass stalk, every tuft and mound, all with a halo of sun. As if the ride were cut just for this moment, Sol watched as the dawn carried on its relentless mission to light all the way down to the *Bothan* far below.

Surely, this Monet painted scene was what G had wanted for him to see? He needed Sol to take in the beauty of the glen, the position of the Bothan and the wonder of the dawn. Did G want Sol to simply understand the splendour of the emergent light?

But then a noise from the undergrowth clutched him by the gut. It was a rolling sound as if drumsticks had been dropped and fallen all about on a hard surface and continued to be pushed into each other and shaken. This was followed by clicks and knocks, with an almost unmistakeable *'plop'* sound and an altogether unnatural yet still organic sound of scratching and squealing; a percussion ensemble of avian origin.

A large black grouse head, housing a thunderously clopping beak and scuffed up, fluffed out throat wattle, rose up clumsily from within the shrubs and strutted towards another head that responded in like aggressive manner. Huge fanned tails were dragged behind these turkey-like creatures and they flashed white patches under the oil-blue of their wings, and large red combs, highlighted with the grey flecks of maturity, exaggerated their eye lines and the cold, anger of their backward glare.

Sol took pictures as the two sized each other up and then went in for the attack with talon'd feet and clopping bills. They ignored him.

'Capercaillie' he thought as they lekked aggressively in drunken fashion as smaller, browner, pheasant like females congregated around to witness the spectacle and to choose the best beast to father their young.

This, one of the most enigmatic, but also threatened, of all of Scotland's birds, was what G had wanted Sol to witness! And yes, Sol would understand. These creatures were only left here, in this fragment of the wild, because of the Bothan and the estate, and the protection that G had given it all. He understood.

And watch he did until the lek was over and the fight moved on to further stamping grounds, and the midges, hatched and matured to biting strength, drove him back down to the *Bothan* for breakfast.

Gerry returned later that morning, guiltily entering the kitchen with a timidity via the porch, and Pete phoned in to say he would be absent for the day whilst he discussed plans with a builder he had found in the pub last night.

Oddly Sol exuded a contented satisfaction that Gerry found difficult to pinpoint and her guilt at leaving him alone the night before was soon lost, evaporating with his good mood and genuine glow. He seemed only keen to take his violin up to talk to Joe on the hill. With the encroachment of the clouds that broiled over the loch-scape, something in it agitated the dabbling geese who looked over their shoulders more frequently than usual as they felt the storm's oppression build. He decided taking Addie was the wisest approach of the Gillie House that day.

Gerry made bread, kneading it on a well-floured wooden board where she left it to rise and prove, and insisted on weeding the garden and carrying out menial tasks around *Bothan Faobhar*, and so Sol excused himself and then drove on up to Joe's with a few gifts of food. He wanted to mull thoughts over with him and try for the corncrakes and the quails on the top fields. This visitation became a routine Sol would repeat on an ever-increasing basis for the weeks to come as May passed by into June and then erupted into the flowers of July. He marked the seasons' passage with the dynamic temporal period each species and community occupied as its place and allotted slot on the hedge bank stage. Here was a time when suddenly every border was filled with blossoms, the fields took on a painter's palette of expression and the heathers purpled and pinked. Like the changing of the guard, one cropped colour gave way to another as he reiterated the same physical journey along the tracks, a voyage which despite being along the identical route was never really the same with each repetition. There was a different bird here, another insect there, a mammal crossing then but a buzzard descending now; always varied.

The stags grew restless as the flies bothered them more and the lambs put on enough weight to be safe and give their shepherds pride and security enough to spend their weekends away from the moors and fields trialling their dogs in the summer displays. The deciduous trees burst out to fill every gap their fingers could extend to, depriving light from the floor below and adding a dappled effect to help camouflage the chicks and babies that clucked and mewed below them. And bluebells allowed for the later entrance of orchids, which then gave way to the firework explosion of the foxgloves and the woods eventually took on a carpet of dog's mercury, bright silver-green leaved with fluoresces of tiny pastel flowers, each an explosion held in a vertical brush of many. From nowhere the dainty humble heads of the harebell appeared and swayed recklessly in the wind despite the flimsy construction suggested by their feminine form that, as it so often did, hid their true mechanical strength. Sea pinks lived up to their names as faded straw stems and dried maraca heads that rattled in the wind were replaced and reconstructed as deep blushing petal pompoms.

The machair grasses on the foreshore became unrecognisable in their tint and shade as the waders, ducks and geese picked their way through the florist's exhibit that had emerged there as if arranged by a champion of the '*Institute*'. Goslings and chicks pecked their precocial paths amongst the towering plants, mothers in attendance at a distance. Parenthood had arrived at the glen of the *Bothan* and everywhere was the evidence of fledging young and concerned relations, the cries of the lost and the hunger-panged despair of the starving.

Even the top most slopes of the mountain took on hues that suggested a new floral expression. The distant angle was coloured differently in that high summer, and it became increasingly that place which continually drew Sol upwards to explore, ever higher, its crags and tops. Then one day, following a white-backed bundle of feathers that he hoped would be a snow bunting as it flitted upwards from rock to rock, he fell upon the trig point unkindly blemishing the mountain's wilderness top, where no walker seemed ever to have strayed. The stark concrete lump stood monolith like the white head of a mountainous spot and Sol wanted to knock it down and remove this human built monstrosity secured here by helicopter in a bid just to give the mountain an accurate measure of its height, a number that gave nothing more than exactly that; a height and a number.

Scanning the panorama of the land descending around, everything leading up to this one sharp point, he considered his mountain was far too beautiful to be described in that way, as a simple statistic. How could it be limited in such a manner, probably placed in a list in its order of rank or difficulty of climb? So offended was he, that on his first visit Sol collected a few stones from around the flat top to start the construction of a more naturally-shaped and sympathetic cairn to cover the trig point. Initially he just wanted to make an impact on the hard-edged surface of the concrete pyramid and to break up the shock of its grey-whiteness that contrasted so formally with the alpines amongst the gravels and rocks way up here beyond the timberline and treeline. Then he brought stone from the lower slopes up with him each time he visited, to sketch, write or play his violin, in an attempt to hide it still further. It became something of a pilgrimage for him in the hope that one day he would have covered the whole block of concrete and in the process would have finished his mountain off and probably made it just slightly bigger than it was when it had been measured and its height recorded in the official charts of the ordnance office.

It was a curious preoccupation, but if he asked himself why he played music, Sol would have struggled to give a reason; he was just musical and wanted to express himself through the violin. The artist and the writer can give no purpose to their calling any better than the poet or singer, or even the sports person, knitter or any other hobbyist. These religions of our minds are somehow programmed within us from birth and even though only few will ever gain notable success from our ventures, we feel compelled to do them all the same.

Did the painter of the animals on the burning torch-lit walls of the caves in Lascaux know they were creating a daubed image that would last the millennia and still be recognised as archetypal primitive cave artwork even today? What made them do it? Maybe it was a simple expression of a hunt they had been involved with, a tutorial for others or even a moment of religious connection with a spiritual world, the first recorded moment of our present sacred programming and the need we all have for 'something' beyond, whatever that might be. Or, was it a desire to record and express, to alter or to influence, something that humans had to do, making it just that, '*human*'.

Sol's creation became artistic in the way the rocks tessellated with each other and suggested a fit, a circular pyramid pointing to the sky, and it morphed into a bulbous outline. Yet in detail it was cragged and ragged if the observer took the time to look closely enough. Like anything that looks smooth, the further in you explore then the less perfect it becomes. Even paper which is bleached pure white and is smooth and plain to the finger, within a few turns of the magnification becomes a mess of fibres and strings, each frayed and complex like the ruined ropes of a snarled fisherman's net discarded in the yard. Our rugged coastline, with its rocks and bays, sands and cliffs, intrusions and extrusions, once spanned backwards and out into space quickly softens to produce that image of Britain we all recognise as our small collection of islands on this vast planet. The Earth itself is a mere space-haunting slight-squashed sphere if we look past the bowls of the oceans and the spikes of the mountain ranges, each a very shallow scoop or mound if studied from a distance. *Everything depended on scale and perspective.*

Up close, and Sol connected with the hundreds of hand-fitted rocks, their shapes and imperfections and the elements they were made of, and he felt aware of the immediacy of the crust that had produced the land form he climbed. Stepping back he could take in the mountain and its range, and the cairn became a small thing, a folly, and Sol just a parasitic blemish that moved about over something much mightier than he was.

Rubbing his fingers over a wind-smoothed stone, etched with weather, he became aware of the high-pitched ultrasounds of chicks somewhere deep within the rocks' sponge-like build. Some pair of birds, hopefully the buntings, had taken advantage of this small, man-made protection way up here on the most exposed ridge on the estate. Sol marvelled at nature's obstinacy, and then took his leave so as not to disturb the nest site and the efforts this couple would be investing in feeding such a high altitude brood.

Pete's plans for the garage were passed by the council and accepted by the locals, and from an embryonic start where little seemed to happen and the internal, hidden parts of the build were completed, it suddenly took on a new appearance. Still an old building hewn from rock and topped with flat stones, the windows were repaired, the walls plastered and the barn doors filled with glass and wood. Retaining a rustic ambience, it kept a charm that allowed it to complement its moorland surround, and it hummed with the sound of workmen and flies, tools and the bees that took succour from the heather and returned it to the hives on the hill at Hamish's.

It was still the same old recognisable barn complex, but like the familiar room where a subtle change has taken place it took on an altered look.

Pete visited often having left a manager both in London and here at the garage. The garage was due to be finished by the autumn and he had started taking bookings for the first visitors in November when the winter started its prolonged arrival, the days shortened even when compared to that which England enjoyed, and the wind and the snow swept in from the far north. He had been warned about the weather, but also encouraged that only Sol, Gerry, Joe and the shepherds would ever truly get cut off, with Sol and Joe's habitats being equal worst.

Al left for London as soon as he could but on the promise that he would return, after what he had described as 'his information gathering trip to the area'. He had a plan that he would not share, and this worried Sol as it felt to him as if Al had a different vision to his own for almost everything and he wondered just how they had remained such good friends for all this time. When Sol asked what Al had been up to after he disappeared from the *Bothan*, all he would answer was, "eating and drinking and testing the potential."

Sol paid for repairs on some of the houses and set aside a decreasingly impressive budget to make sure money would remain available for emergencies if it was required. He was not helped by the crashing of the markets or the bills that flooded in for the upkeep of the estate.

The roof on Gerry's house was removed and returned to the town, towed by James Nevin's long wooden ship, and was stripped, cleaned and made sound again in his yard. Whilst her house was covered with wind-cracking plastic to keep the worst of the rain out, Gerry stayed with Sol, although she spent increasingly long hours away in her workshop painting or wandering the hills managing the game animals and removing enough to keep the stock healthy and to produce sufficient meat to sell.

Sol had grown to love her, as the sister they had both intended she should be, and although everyone about suspected the relationship would grow to be more than that of siblings, neither of them was surprised that it did not. They felt no pressure for it to be anything more, being quite satisfied each with the other or without. She taught Sol to manage the boat properly and to handle the sail and tiller together, and the way to impress the *Blue Men* most effectively so that they gave him free passage to visit the ladies across the loch on his own, and one day she even suggested that he should take old Joe with him.

The loch's character could change in the matter of a minute, and what one day could be a dangerous battle with the riptides the next could be a placid calm when Sol could drop the sail and drift safely, even falling asleep to the lullaby of the seabirds.

The cats came back every night and became the closest thing Sol had to constant companions and allies. They never trusted him fully, but did enough to give him a feeling of specialness and for him to know that he was set apart by them as the kittens took on size and filled out but still relied on their mother's sustenance, training and care. He learnt from the notes G had left him and was surprised that every mid-month a new hand written letter arrived, written in G's flowing font, outlining the wild things that Sol should ensure he took in and experienced; a flower here, a bird there or a behaviour beyond, and even a view to collect in his mind's eye gallery. There were gentle instructions and reminders to prepare for the winter, be aware of local custom, and suggestions of what might be thoughtful for one of the estate tenants, such as birthday dates and anniversaries.

A baby was born, at home as suspected, to Sarah and Euan, and he was named simply Gee, with his cries and adamant screaming being heard clearly from well beyond the door of their cottage on the track. But they were a delighted family and pleased when the laird appeared with a child's flat woollen cap, a toy sheep and a wooden crook as gifts. Sol wanted to encourage a future generation of shepherds if he could.

London became just a past memory to Sol, a place he only wantonly returned to in dreams, although he was forcibly reminded of it at times when messages came through on his phone, where the troubles of the Tokyo deal kept rumbling along in the background and his share prices continued to drop. But it descended into another world, almost forgotten but always there on the periphery of his mental vision.

Visitors still arrived at the town where James was constructing a glass-bottomed boat for eco-tourists, a string of houses on the front were being redecorated for accommodation and an old shop was being worked on, but nobody really knew who by. They often asked for Sol, his house, or a number to call, and used any number of ways to try and find out where the reclusive man of the virtual blog-sphere lived. But the locals were in a pact now and were sworn to as much secrecy as they could afford. And like all country folk, they were very good at guarding secrets and not saying those things that should not be said in the open; and sadly like in any society this could be for good and for bad in equal measure. However, information always manages to seep out in some small way, like water held in cupped hands when the tighter it is squeezed then the more inadvertently drips out, and details did began to emerge and patterns were created that might lead somewhere if the right mind was applied to it.

Life was not idyllic, the weather still broke and the Atlantic threw its worst at them as often as maybe, people were ill and injured, and sheep died without reason, and even the river, ever desperate to be noticed, flooded twice. But it was as close to an idyll as that summer could be and Sol was happy and content. Indeed he was at first jealous of the stories he heard of others' lives but not when he reminded himself of what he now had. His was not a rich existence but it was a wealthy one, and with each investment he felt his roots deepen and his heart soften. It was what one could call the boy changed to man, or the man aged to maturity.

Each Thursday the band met and played either side of a short meeting when the community took the opportunity of their assemblies to discuss plans and ideas, needs and issues. Inadvertently, the gigs had become the central chance for the people to work together and form a true cooperative in the area, one that had existed for centuries but which needed reinvention for its value to be realised afresh. The wisdom of the old mixed freely with the rashness and energy of the young, but for a common goal. Pete joined in when he was there.

"The shed next to Black Pool?" asked Sol at one meeting. "What's it for?"

"The wool used to be taken there for knitting," explained Mrs Hamish. "The water's only any good for dying wool as it's poisonous to anything else. Something about the old quarry and the minerals they accidentally dug up. But there are still looms in the shed there that can be used for making fabric and tweed."

"Let me guess," Sol said. "There's no market for it?"

They chuntered in agreement and there was much dismal head nodding.

"Well," Sol suddenly announced, silencing the meeting. "I think the markets have changed and there might be one out there again. It's a bit of a punt but I'd like to reopen the wool shed and have tweed made in it if possible. I used to wear a three piece in green in London. Is it still possible for anyone to make a fabric for city use like that? Someone that I can employ for a few months?"

Hands were hesitantly raised, cautious at first and then with greater certainty once the owners of the arms could see that theirs was not alone.

"Do we have local wool?" *There were nods, mainly from shepherds and workers on the land who started to show more of an interest in Sol's plan.*

"What about natural dyes?" *They could be sourced from the hills said the beaters and the shooters.*

"What size workforce could we bring together?" *There was a team of six formed quickly. Two would work the looms, one would make the suits and three agreed to use wool to knit jumpers, this latter being an operation that would also continue back in the houses around about the town.*

"Pete?"

"Yes, boss."

"Don't call me boss."

"Yes, comrade."

"Call me boss then." They both laughed. "How many people are following your blog now?"

"Just shy of eleven thousand."

"Excellent. There's our market. As soon as the suit is made and I have a new Arran sweater to wear I need to be photographed alongside the wild cats or about the *Bothan*, maybe even out on the boat wearing them. Whatever, the image must be saleable. If we can get enough interest in the life we lead, maybe people would want to come. You did say you could photograph even the worst-looking model and make her look attractive. Could you do it with me?"

"It'd be hard, but I could give it a go..."

"Excellent. Now, how quickly can we..."

Hamish watched from a distance, amused as Sol created plans and dissected them down to the smallest detail. The city boy could do deals well and was obviously in his element working at the lead of his force. He had an idea to use wool and skills from the area and market it to London. It was a pleasing mix of the two and reminded Hamish of a conversation he had enjoyed with Sol about pebbles and how to sell them.

"Pebbles," he laughed to himself.

"Yes," grinned Sol back over his shoulder. "If we have enough pebbles, then there's bound to be one type of pebble that will interest someone out there. We're going to start exporting pebbles."

"Pebbles," Hamish chuckled again.

After the concert a middle-aged man appeared at Sol's arm.

He materialised without introduction. One minute there was just a friendly hubbub of sound and the milling about of unfocused people beyond Sol's sphere of concentration, and then the next there was this man, too close for comfortable greeting.

"I've come to see the wildcats," he announced in a curt southern accent without any courtesies.

"Excellent," answered Sol, focused on his violin and its case. "If you talk to Pete here, he is making bookings for..."

"...I want to see them today."

The man was adamant and although Sol had become quite used to people asking for him, trying to visit and even being rude when he denied the opportunity to them, this person made him feel decidedly uncomfortable. Something about his gaze, his attention and his demeanour gave him an unreadable adamant purpose.

"Well," he began and Sol was aware that Hamish and Pete had both moved in closer to listen in too. "I'm afraid that they live on private property and you can't see them tonight."

"I'll just follow along behind then," said the man leaving no room for Sol's manoeuvre. "You'd never know I was there. Just like a shadow. That's all I'd be."

"I'd rather you didn't as that would be trespassing and that would be illegal."

"No such thing in Scottish law. It's my right to wander, enshrined in law. I'll go where I please, thank you very much."

"But you can't trespass in my garden."

"But the cats might wander out of it."

"I don't like the way you are sounding."

"Tough."

"Well you can't follow me."

"Why?"

It was a good question. One to which Sol did not have a sufficiently good answer.

"They aren't your cats," the man stated quite bluntly. "You're just lucky enough to have them on your doorstep in a house you were fortunate to be able to buy. Well done. Now, I want pictures of them and, as I always do, I *will* get them. It's what I do you see?"

Hamish stepped forward. "You won't track the laird."

"Says who?" The man stood tall over the undeterred Hamish and seemed little bothered by the number of people who were taking an interest in their escalating conversation. There was an aggressive atmosphere broiling in the sweaty air of this section of the pub.

"This is my fault," said Pete. "I should never have published the pictures. Let me deal with this."

"Rubbish," said the man. "They're public property. Wild things. That's what the blog calls them...   ...*wild* cats." He leant on the word 'wild' giving it intended malevolency.

"But," explained Sol, "it is only the lack of the site being public that keeps the cats safe. I want them protected, not scared away."

"You just want them for yourself."

The man had hit a raw nerve in Sol as he knew full well that there was more than a grain of truth in what he had said. To avoid incident, he span round, wished everyone good night as he headed for the door and, once free of the room, he ran for Addie parked obediently out on the road.

The man gave pursuit despite the best efforts of Hamish and the few others who had moved in to prevent his exit.

"You can't touch me," argued the man avoiding a swipe at him, "I have the law on my side." They knew he was right, whatever they thought of the legal freedom he could enjoy, but it did not make watching him slide out between the people milling the street to give their friend chase any easier. It was one thing having individuals wanting to revel in the life they led for a holiday period, to want to photograph it or enjoy the wilds, it was another having the tourist interfere and affect it, removing the very privacy and isolation that such wilderness living demanded.

Sol in the meantime forced Addie on and along the main road from Old Town, taking the shore-side lane too quickly to be safe, and only when he was beyond the black pool and its loom shed did he take his foot off the accelerator and relax somewhat in his driving style. This track had claimed its lives before and his was not to be added to the roster.

He knew his rear lights would give away his location to any pursuer and so he thought through how he could hide them as he rose up into the hills and they became even more obvious from below. He did not want anyone unwanted up his drive.

When he was certain that he was not being followed, he turned off the road and up the rutted track driveway towards the *Bothan*, pulled over where the fork led up to the bealach crossroad and the garage, and the trees provided enough shelter to hide a car from the main road below. He switched off Addie's lights, silencing her tick-cooling engine.

Sitting for a while, he then left the vehicle, picking up Hamish's walking staff as he slammed the door, and walling the trees that lined the drive as any scared lost animal would do, he then stood in silence and listened intently trying to read sounds in the cool noise of the night.

Nothing but the owl, the sheep, the distant gulls and an unidentifiable screech.

His phone buzzed to life in his pocket and on retrieving it from its depths he looked at the over-bright, blue-lit screen. It was Pete.

'*Sol,*

We couldn't stop him. He's heading towards you up the main road quite quickly in pursuit in a black off roader, Japanese make. It has roof bars on top and four shooting lamps arranged along the front bar. Hide if possible and don't try to outrun him, his engine and tyres are better than Addie's, or else drive on to New Town and confuse him. The locals are sworn to secrecy but who knows if any will give in for enough money?

Sorry, mate.

Pete'

Sol looked at the screen. Its cerulean intensity shone strongly illuminating the tree leaves above him sapphire shades. He had forgotten what an intrusion the device was in his life. The phone pocketed, and the pocket sealed to try and limit the light's escape, he switched it to silent, hunched in the steadily undulating undergrowth and then listened.

There *was* the approaching roar of an over-revved vehicle hugging the dangerous corners of the main road feet from where Sol crouched in hidden refuge. Starting as a distant invasion of the soundscape, it grew until it rapidly became a vehicle that took the bends too quickly and bounded past at a speed unwise on such a road.

Sol breathed a sigh of relief. *It had passed on by.*

He was about to stand up and mock the passage when he heard the car skid to a halt, and there was a clunk from within as the gears were forced against each other and it reversed backwards slowly towards the track's entrance - that delta of tread marks that spread into a junction - before the brakes squeaked to contain it. He could clearly see the man he had argued with earlier through the electric window as it whirred down into the space within the door that no one but an engineer ever thinks about.

The man leant out, a face at the void of the cab, and looked with focus at tyre tracks on the ground leading into and out of the unguarded but un-announced driveway that led up towards *Bothan Faobhar*. He sniffed the air like a dog as if he could smell the fumes of the last vehicle to have passed through, Addie, and Sol knew the fear of the hunted and the exhilaration of the fox in its final moments before discovery. Sweat trickled down his back and he felt that cold clamminess that starts in the skin and churns the pit of the stomach giving it the desire to wretch and vomit.

Sol gripped the staff closely to his chest as he squatted lower into the trackside dyke, its waters filtering into his boots and staining his brown trousers a darker shade, something he knew even in the darkness. He could sense the Celtic designs that interweaved up and around the staff and found himself in prayer to whatever god or God could hear him, sense him or want to communicate with him; he desperately needed to connect to some deity of any kind that would let this one thing go his way.

But of course, prayer does not work that way and gods forgotten can rarely be conjured up just when we want or need them.

The man scratched his chin and looked up into the hills thoughtfully, watching for signs or symbols that would confirm that maybe this was the track that Sol had taken a few minutes before. The door swung open noiselessly on heavy well-greased hinges, and climbing down the man stooped smoothly to the ground to look at the mud from the lower angle and at the tyre treads that crisscrossed the entrance.

It was too dark and he should have seen the lights up in the hills giving Sol's position away if this had been the way. But these tracks were fresh and they were the right sort of distance apart for an older Land Rover. He could have driven this direction earlier or it could have been someone else.

Then he spotted the letterbox under the sign suggesting that the road was not suitable for vehicles and he decided to check it for mail to see whose house actually lay beyond and up there. Sol prayed harder, his fingers tracing and retracing the movement of the patterns in the wood and thumbing the knots and grain that took on strange significance at this moment. As the unknown man walked forward, Sol made up his mind to stand up, surprise him, and even knock him to the ground with the staff. But they were both stopped in their thoughts' flows as they heard the approaching rumble of another Land Rover up the road.

Hamish rounded the corner with Pete in the passenger seat and Joe in the middle, and they pulled up next to the parked vehicle stranded in the way blocking their passage up the drive. It wasn't the usual appearance for a team of heroes, but for Sol it would do. A battered old waggon that had seen much better days, shuddering and coughing in the muds, shivering under the efforts of its stuttering diesel engine, containing a city-bred photographer, a withered old blind man and an angry-looking shepherd and his dog.

"Can I help you?" asked Hamish leaning out of the driver's window.

"I was just..." started the man.

"...stealing my mail by the looks of it. Aye, I can see. For a man well versed in the law you seem to be unaware that stealing mail is a crime. Oh, and that's even in Scotland."

"I was not trying to..."

"Then if you please, step away from my mail box." And Hamish pointed over to the tumbledown sign with its dejected tin box slung poorly to it.

"Do you live up here?"

"Aye, I do, and so do they," Hamish indicated to Pete and Joe, "and I see you've already met our joint mail box."

"Who else lives up there?"

"Now what's that to you?" asked Hamish sloping calmly back in to the window ledge of the cab. "Folks like their privacy round here. It wouldn't do to go poking your nose in to too many people's business would it?"

"I want to find Mr Solomon."

"We know you do," called Pete, "and if you remember he wasn't keen to be found."

"Just tell me where he lives and I'll be gone."

"Have you asked in town?" asked Joe with a wily smile across his face. He craned across the seats so that he could be heard.

"Yes," the man grumbled. "Everyone seems to have forgotten where he lives or tells me they don't know."

"Funny that," shouted Joe. "I can't remember either. What about you two?" They shook their heads. "Maybe try in New Town, they are not as old as Old Town and their memories might be better."

The man cursed and kicked the ground.

"He can hide but I'll find him eventually. I don't see how he gets to buy an area of land like this and to see and photograph all he wants to, when he wants and choose who he wants to share it with. All I want is a photograph of a wildcat. It's my right!"

"There we go again," chided Hamish, "rights and laws. I think you've got it wrong. Legal permission may not give you ethical right. Now get off my drive and let me go home!"

The man strode to his car, clambered up and slammed the door shut, fired up the engine and sped away towards New Town after fanning up a huge arc of mud from his deep-treaded tyres. He left the three men laughing and Cu the dog barking in the back. After a few minutes they quietened down and then Hamish leant further out of the window and shouted.

"Okay Sol, you can stand up now. It's safe."

Sol sprung up and out of the ditch. "How...?"

"Well let's just hope that he's blinder than old Joe here as if he had turned just a little that way he'd have seen you for sure."

"Shit," said Sol.

"Tomorrow we fit a gate over the end of your drive where our drives split off from yours and hang some chain over it and an unfriendly notice about privacy and sheep. Then we can lay enough fencing up either side far enough into the wood to make it look like the whole area is fenced off. That way animals get in and out by going round and humans give up before they've had chance to think it through. You can sail now I hear, so sail whenever you can for the now and avoid using Addie unless you have to. Park her at the garage and walk down from the *Bothan* if you need to drive. It won't stop strangers rifling through your mail but it's a start."

"Hamish?"

"Yes?"

"Did you just think of all that just now?"

"Aye?"

"Thank you. You're a genius... ...and a friend."

Hamish smiled.

He enjoyed the word, relished it and span it around his head. This was a funny moment for him as a thought cycled itself around his mind. The last thing he had expected with Sol was for them to become friends, and yet it had all happened so very quickly; he hadn't realised, but they were.

"Nice walking stick," he laughed breaking the chance for the mental process to develop any further. "Looks well made too."

Sol returned to Addie, cautiously hugging to the margins so as not to leave marks in the gripping mud that annoyingly desired reciprocal contact with his boots, and he drove her back to *Bothan Faobhar* where he found an agitated Gerry, who had sailed back, waiting for him and news of the chase. She was glad he was back and the two sat up late into the night talking over whisky and glowing in the warmth of fire and friendship.

Early into the morning, she stood quickly and kissed him good night on the forehead. He was glad she was here tonight, that the Boat House was not ready, that James Nevin was not as near to her as Sol now was. His heart raced with a torrent of emotions including jealously and possession, friendship and more, but care and moderation too.

"I'm glad you came here Jake Solomon," she whispered. "That you came and joined us and we all became friends – comrades."

"And," he replied, "I'm glad too." In the past this would have been excuse for so much, but he hesitated and looked deeply back into her eyes. She was one of the best friends he had and enjoyed, and that is what he wanted more than anything, having denied it for himself for so long by pursuing the carnal extreme of relationships and forgetting the one part that really counted.

"But," he added thoughtfully considering the wider grouping of friends he enjoyed, "you still love James too... ...don't you?"

She nodded, wet-eyed.

"Good," Sol answered, his mind whinnying madly. It was like a horse racing in wild abandoned freedom in its paddock after weeks in the stable, being both difficult to control but full of energy to harness. Creatively it leapt onwards.

Gerry stared at him in disbelief and then tears dropped down her cheeks. She was not one for crying, especially where others could see her. This was an emotion to be hidden deep within and only revealed when she and her shadow were the only ones around to share it.

"He loves you too," explained Sol drawing Gerry on to the arm of the easy chair where he sat. "He'll give you time this time around too, and I believe he'll be a good man to you. Nothing could be greater for him than to be the man responsible for rebuilding your house. He's even allowed his workmen to construct Pete's new boat whilst he carries on with your place, because it's *your* place. And do you know what?"

She shook her head.

"That roof will last longer than anything that was there before it. He's used an ancient old boat of his to re-make it from that he's been saving for something special at the back of the boatyard. I've been down at the sheds to see. He has completely restored it in the last few months and turned it upside down. He could have sold it to some rich millionaire, if we ever get to attract one in. He could have kept it for himself and still have been doing a decent job of your house. He used that boat even though he still resents me for having you here to stay and wishes I was a thousand miles away somewhere else. He's being my friend because of you. And above all, he's investing love in the Boat House that he cannot invest in you directly. But the most delicious part of it all is that he thinks that none of us has noticed."

Gerry looked at Sol, talking quietly and drifting his gaze from her to the irregular hypnotic lick of the fire and back again.

"So," she asked, "what are you saying?"

"That I, just your inherited brother of course, who loves you madly too, as a friend, want you to ask James out for a meal or something."

"You're giving me date advice?"

"I suppose so, yes."

"Okay. But, what about you?"

"Three would be a crowd..."

"No, what happens to you? You're hardly going to meet someone out here and I think everyone half suspects we're supposed to get together at some point."

"I've done some silly things in the past and lived more of my life than I should have. I am happier now than I've ever remembered being and have learnt more..."

"All very noble, but what? What are you going to do?"

"I don't know. Something will happen. Talk to James today whilst he works on your house will you?"

"Okay," she agreed. "Okay."

As Sol fell asleep he fought back the mounting anxieties of running his estate and protecting its wild relatives, replacing these fears with thankfulness for friends and an inaudible prayer to whichever of the usually-silent deities had helped him tonight. He was content that out there in the dark his cats were safe.

Had they become his family, with him feeding them every night and sitting watching for them whenever he could?

Who could tell?

The rains came through the night, breaking a recent monoculture of weather that had dominated the summer. It brought its own preferable wind with it that lashed in from the sea and whipped up the loch like ice-cream in ivory peaks that held for a while as if they had been licked up by the lips of a greedy child and left there, stationary. The gulls huddled the shore for security and the geese were flocked on the easterly edge of the bay as the sands were thrown up and the weeds ripped from their holdfast rocks and beaten against the cliffs.

Sol came through to this world with the rattling of the windows banging in his mind, as if being shaken from slumber by a mad man, maybe the man last night, and shouted at as the wind hurtled train-fashion down the chimney.

Gerry joined him in the kitchen as he prepared breakfast and she looked at him closely to see what his emotional state was. It seemed buoyant and good, almost satisfied, and she suspected he was true to his word when he said that he was well. Here was a man who could have taken advantage of his position, the element of control he had and the way she now felt about him, but who had chosen not to. Here was a very rare man in her poor experience of the species human.

Both of them regretted the position of the toilet on days like this, but eventually each had to make a run for it, wet to the skin on either journey. Still, it often meant that Sol spied deer and red squirrels as he left the door open and watched. He had finally overcome his London modesty enough to understand that no one was really likely to walk on past. And if they did, it would be they that would be more likely shocked than him. *After all, who expects to find an occupied toilet in the middle of the woods?*

A text arrived from Pete. Hamish and a few others had started work on the gate already but there was a concern about Sol's post.

'Had you left anything in the box last night? Only it's hanging open now? It could have been the wind of course, but we were just wondering.

Pete'

Sol replied to say he did not know as he so often forgot the post anyway and agreed to meet them at the new entrance to the *Bothan* as soon as he could.

Gerry and he dressed and took Addie along the track. Although the wind had died and the rain subsided, parched ground had quickly built up a head of runoff that spilled over the hard surfaces and broke out into the road bringing down gravels and soils, like bleeds in the Earth. The Land Rover needed careful control.

They talked merrily, both excited to see how Hamish was going to create his deception at the *Bothan* end of the drive. But Sol's talk suddenly turned furtive when still several miles off the junction up to the bealach. Gerry picked up on the change of emotion, like the sensing of the steady turn of milk in thundery weather where there is a time when you are unsure if it is still potable or not.

"Sol?"

"Fresh tracks in the muds coming down the hill," he pointed out as he pulled Addie up and left her cab with purpose with his staff at hand, the engine chucking happily and inconsistently. Gerry joined him wrapping her coat around her for warmth as both doors swung limply on their hinges.

There they were plain to see, the parallel imprints of a large vehicle with tread far greater than anyone's they knew, the forensic evidence of trespass. Sol's heart sank and the colour drained from his exposed face as he traced their passage over the brow and down towards the loch side.

Whoever it was had driven too fast. The vehicle has slipped left and right, riding the rocks at the edge for a bit and filling the dyke with soil so that it flooded, before breaking and skidding to a halt in the far ditch. They had lost traction for a while and obviously revved their way out before turning clumsily, catching shrubs and trees in their haste and racing up the hill and away. There were shiny black paint flecks lodged under a pine's age-toughened bark and scraped onto the craggy tips of a glacial strewn boulder, one that any local would have known to avoid.

"He's been here already," he muttered as anger welled up inside. "He, that man. He knows where we live!"

"Who has?" she asked, perplexed and struggling to follow his train of thought.

"The man from the pub, the photographer," and he painstakingly showed her the paint flecks and described the abortive journey he must have taken. It was all there for the careful observer to see; an invasion of the wild by the poorly-controlled mechanised. "Call Hamish, please," he uttered in a monosyllabic voice trudging with shoulders down to the site where the vehicle had obviously left the road and then accelerated excessively to be released.

There was a curdled iron-red stain darkening in the mud mounded at the loch side of the ditch which Sol bent down to look at more closely. It was a stark dark contrast to the otherwise bright-red-brown pebble and sand that trickled with water, freely dribbling to the ground rock. Tacky to the touch, it was wet but drying despite the rain that had only managed to make it run in just a few places. This ran thicker than water.

He knew it was blood and that something had been caught on the high fender of the vehicle and rammed at speed into the embankment. That would have explained the swerving of the tracks behind and the eventual loss of control and leaving of the road. The man, probably intent on his finding the *Bothan* or any sign of Sol and Addie, and in his desperate bid to see the cats, had hit some poor animal.

But, what?

Sol leapt up the bank side, nimble and angular, following a thin scarlet trail of clotting blood pocks that blemished the green of the plant foliage and held to the muds where they were exposed.

'*Let it be a rabbit,*' he thought unkindly, his staff gripped in manically rubbing hands. '*Too much blood.*'

'*Let it be a deer then.*'

But he knew there wasn't enough blood and there were no hoof prints.

This was the last stand of a medium sized creature, a summer lamb maybe, a gimmer.

He pushed back vegetation and grass stems a few feet from the road, and there, with no fight left in her, he came face to face with the mother wildcat, before collapsing next to her, as his legs lost strength and his knees unlocked, him now crying convulsively out loud.

It was *his* wildcat.

And then he knew for sure that she had really become a member of his family.

Chapter 21: In the Shadow

(Siegfried's Death and Funeral March from Götterdämmerung,
Richard Wagner)

Emotions are things that we have little control over. They are the
way we feel at the time and spring up with little warning from that
primitive brain deep within our skulls, the amygdale. They can
make us do surprising things and find depths of strength and
courage we could never find if we allowed ourselves the time to
think consciously and sensibly about it. They help us to stand up
and fight, give us the adrenaline needed to run away and even the
anger to take up a cause.
When programmed so many millions of years ago, the blindness of
evolution could never have foreseen the direction of human
development and the stresses and strains we would put on our
caveman minds and the subsequent confusion our repressed
emotions would be under. But when emotions do break free, like the
bull from the war, they rise up, take over and no sensible thought
can pass or be given the resources to regain control. The emotions
are raw.

Sol's anger was complete as he lifted the despoiled body of the cat
up and wept openly. She hung limp in his arms, congealed black
blood clotting her beautiful tiger stripes and her tail swung
flaccidly with each laboured breath he animated it with. Her eyes
had lost their fire and barely opened, anger-drained and passionless,
devoid of these elements that made her wild, as she greeted his with
a low rumble that came from somewhere in her spirit, so little life
was left in her.
She knew he cared. He had no idea how she was able to understand
or whether this was simply his human interpretation or a personal
need, but his brain kept telling him that she knew. She understood.

Otherwise this wild beast, this untameable cat, would have taken her claws to his face however little she had left to draw on.

Gerry stood at a distance, the emotion retching her face too so that it contorted, on the edge of full expression but on an interface with another. They say that a good friend is the one that can celebrate your success as well as their own. They should also add that the true friend is the one who can weep with you and feel your pain. But she held her nerve for Sol.

Hamish appeared at the brow of the hill, pulling up with a group of men in the back of his Land Rover. Pete fell from the cab before stopping dead in his tracks so that only the noise of the dying engine could be heard, cooling behind an exaggerated fan, and then silence, save for the morbidity of the ravens who gambolled on the hill; they had an uncanny ability to appear at times like this. He stared down to where Sol staggered into the roadside ditch, where only the water seemed to have the potential to move, with the failing animal in his arms, cheeks running.

Just the corvids' '*crarck*'. Black shadow birds that hung on the sky and stooped on the dreariest of lichen-clad branches within the gloom of the dew-dripped forest. They were waiting for something. Maybe the exit of a life, the sacrifice of a body or the movement of a soul.

Pete felt the swoon of irresolution, guilt and panic.

What had he done?

Why had he published that blog?

What was he doing here in this world? Sol's world.

Then Hamish woke him up abruptly from his self-pitied thoughts and dragged his mental scope into the realm of community. "For God's sake man," he murmured, barely audible for fear of some curse of nature casting its twisted spell in the valley. "Get down there and help him." And Hamish watched the younger man's steady approach of his friend as he slipped down through the crisp-topped muds where the particles had begun to dry hard at their heads leaving mired valleys where feet and tyres had passed.

The large crow-shapes still loitered and brought with them an oppression to the land such that the light felt lifeless, the land more drained of its blush, the clouds of the sky more malevolent and angry, and there was an electric sense of something about to happen. It was as if nature expected it, demanded it.

Sol laid the cat down on the edge of the road as her head lolled back. He stroked her forehead and softened her ears, tufts that were now relaxed and not held erect and alert as they normally were. He placed the staff that Hamish had given him on the road beside him, where it sank into the surface mud, and then scooped the cat's head and shoulders into his lap to caress it fondly in a way that only near-death allowed.

Her golden green eyes opened one last time, crystals that refracted the sun's vagrant rays, and she stared to somewhere deep inside his being, searching as a spiritual cat about to be returned to the nether world to which we all one day go. He felt she was trying to speak to him and looked back, receiving whatever message he could. And then, he thought of her kittens, either by chance, from her message or by a logical deduction. They were still reliant on her for their food and protection and without her they would be lost, along with their valuable wild genes. One vanished wildcat was significant enough, but to lose three would be a disaster, not only ecologically, but for the next generation and the family of this, one of the last wildcats; one of the last of its kind.

Message received, he understood.

"I'll find them," he whispered through the mist of tears in his eyes. "I'll find them, and I'll raise them and they will live on in this glen under my protection. I promise."

And then she died.

He knew she had gone as her body continued to breathe out for far too long and she became heavier and limper than he had felt before, sinking down into the cup of his leg-locked lap. Her feline spirit left her body and, Sol felt, somehow joined with his own. But he waited a moment longer to be sure before he turned to face the onlookers who were nearly with him now.

Death, despite its natural requirement, seems such an alien concept. The indescribable loss of something once living is beyond comprehension, where despite all the chemicals of life remaining, all the physical attributes possessed whilst alive and the very structures needed to function still being present, they no longer work. It is easier to imagine it in trees and the relatively inanimate kingdoms of life. But the closer we get to our own species or the more they become part of our family, then the harder it is. The pet's death has a huge impact, the wild animal befriended too, but a human, a friend or a lover are some way beyond even this. Their humanity is lost with them. All existence is then reduced to just the body and that will soon go as life recycles it. The body of a loved one is recognisable as to whom it once contained, but like a recently vacated building they are now empty – the human has gone.

Trapped in just this one life we are incapable of understanding what happens next even though we are so often searching for answers about what it entails. But we do recognise when something or someone has gone, realise we are finite in our time here and see something of our own limitations in the death of those close to us.

Death, the returning and recovering of the chemicals and the space we borrowed and occupied whilst we were here, pips all.

The ravens circled, '*crackawl*' calling in their gambolled figure of eights, and then they dispersed.

Pete was the first to Sol's side, pushing past Gerry in his sudden race to get to him. But he stopped short when he saw the cat's limp form and the blood running down Sol's trousers, drying there and clinging where it had fallen and then ceased as the heart removed its pulsed pressure.

Then Sol looked up as Hamish, his own face angst-contorted and brow furrowed, joined the others in their witness of solace.

"I want them found," said Sol in an overly peaceful tone, one that worried the others greatly. It had the sense of malice that only the calm have; a truly terrifying nuance and clip and something that a human expresses when the primitive has taken over.

"We'll get on it," said Pete. "I'll call the others. Someone will have seen the man leave or clocked the state of his car at some garage or something. People round here notice things."

"No," Sol replied. "I meant the kittens. There were two of them and they need to be found. I'll take them in and look after them."

"With all due respect Sol," Hamish began. "These are *wild* cats and they aren't exactly fluffy little kittens. They'll have your arm off."

"Be as it may. But I have made a promise to her and I need to find them."

The small gathering of friends stood bleakly for a moment. Only the wind wicked between them, tousled their hair and playfully flicked the fur of the dead cat. After a while Hamish felt the desire to do or say the right thing, and fighting against the urge to throw his hands up in the air and curse everything he looked around for inspiration. Light hit the waters of the loch so that they shimmered at distance, an internal halo on an otherwise deep donkey-flank brown-grey. The rays cut the heavens; beaming search lights from the sky. The mountains glowered under turbid cloud paintings and the course vegetation rippled in the breeze, waves that swelled in patterns up and across every slope. Unusually it was the intense smell of heather and juniper that combined in the nostrils – a wild, yet today oppressive concoction that held the air heavy, nature's perfumery.

This land like this was desolate, but something would be missing from it if the knowledge of the cats' presence was lost for ever. Sol was right. If they could, they should. And so Hamish wrestled the turmoil inside and eventually spoke, his words breaking into the seemingly unsurpassable silence that had brewed between them.

"You heard the man," said Hamish and he shook his head in despair, looking at the gaunt and drawn features of the fallen city boy, out of his element and yet now very much the centre of it. He knew full well that this was a significant turning point in that life and could not see clearly what the right thing to do in his continued education would be. Take on the kittens and suffer the pain of trying to raise them, their possible death and then the almost impossible task of releasing them back into the wild, or leave them to die defenceless and hungry. He knew why Sol wanted to find them but was worried. It was hard enough looking after motherless lambs. But two wildcat kits were different beasts entirely.

The workers split up to conduct a thorough search as Sol placed the mother's body carefully in the back of Addie on a bed of tarpaulin and covered her over loosely and cautiously. He had only really met death once, being still young enough to consider himself immortal and not having been old enough when his own parents had died to fully understand what had happened, how quickly it had visited and what was being hidden from him; either sensibly or not. But here he was, stricken with grief for an animal he had wantonly befriended, but at a distance, one maintained by the cat itself.

It felt odd that he had only ever touched this animal, made contact and felt the luxuriant nature of its underlain fur and the fading warmth of its body, now that she was dead. But on consideration, this was the way it should have been with a creature like that.

He cut in on his own inward thoughts, noting detail of the glen around him in emphasised feature. The sweep of the glacier-cut valley sides, the life that clung to it as far up as it could, each species dropping off in zonal succession until only those that could hang on grimly to survival against the elements could make their living amongst the highest rocks, eventually only leaving exposed stone extant. The burning gold light that pirouetted across the shrub layer and lit up even the densest forest trees hugging the lowest slopes, so that its green became more verdant and alive, animated the insects into mechanical flight and stimulated the photosynthesis in the plant life that would eventually succour everything in every food chain. The trace of the land-bound wind off the sea and the turmoil she endured as she caressed the land, divided amongst the stems and reformed in maddening eddies behind each solid body, picking up chemical traces as she left the purity of the water and steadily dropped her innocence to become a tainted air, polluted with whatever she had experienced. The gentle lap of the water out on the loch, draining from the land, even turning the rocks that rumbled in a sound felt by the souls of the feet, those appendages we bound up in cotton, wool and then rubber and leather to prevent us ever really relating with the ground, keeping ourselves sacrosanct and disconnected. And then there was the Earth itself, red-grained and vital, humic and rich in places, barren and thin in others, but right here by his observant position it was marked, stained with the blood of an animal now gone – *his* animal missing, bringing with it an ecological incompleteness to the glen; *his* glen.

"There's been a crime committed," he said to Pete. "Call the police and have a description made of the man that did it. I'll give a statement too. The wildcat is a protected species and the man must be found." He spoke calmly and in an organised manner. "Can you do that for me?"

"Yes," said Pete and left to find a signal up the track behind lifting his mobile to his ear.

"Gerry?"

"Sol?"

"I need food for the kittens when they are found. Something fresh would be best. They're used to fish bones, rabbit, venison scraps and pheasant." The list seemed well planned as if it were something he had thought about before. "Can you get me anything? I'll need one of the sheds setting up as a cage too. Can you and Nevin get on to that as well?"

"I'll get him," she answered and swept away to cadge a lift back to the *Bothan*. "The food'll be easy too."

"Hamish?"

"Sol?"

"This is all my fault isn't it?" Sol looked blankly out to where bees were swarming on a branch of a tuft-headed Scots pine, one that had grown the proper way the glen and its genes had intended, without any pruning or anthropomorphic disturbance. It was a series of flattened needle masses that reached skyward on branches that stretched away from the search of the wind. Although there seemed no order in any one part of its apparently random growth, it had an overall naturally pleasing design that when taken in as a whole comforted the eye and gave it the impression of direction, as if the branches were examining the sky's texture for some landward relief. Its scabbed bark twisted around and back across itself, scarred and gnarled with an expression not dissimilar to cracked rain-parched soil in a crop-deserted field.

"No," Hamish answered following Sol's gaze. "That isn't right. How could it be?"

The bees bundled in their jostling horde and the hum of a thousand wing muscles carried the short distance to the humans' ears resonating in a harmonic of swells and dissipation. Sometimes it was tuneful and then it would become chaotic as the notes of each small bee diverged and recoalesced so that the swarm's pitch teased upwards before settling back down again.

"I let the world know about them, the cats, and thought I could sell the idea." Sol's eyes were scared and furtive, bright and alert.

"Or else," the older man interrupted, not allowing Sol's remorse to run away and placing a rough yet caring hand on Sol's shoulder, "you would have ignored us all and our way of life, and watched the place run out of money and the cats would then have been lost anyway. You didn't have much of a choice did you?"

"But there could have been a better way if I'd thought about it longer."

"And that's the disease they call hindsight, the one we all suffer in the land of 'if only'."

The swarm dropped from the branch leaving just a few hormonally-drunk workers rolling on the bark and dizzying around it. The rest followed some unseen urge, the pheromone trail of the queen within, an entomological football that bounced the air before entering the deeps of the wood from which their buzz hummed back to the colony in echo. A few trailed, happily straggling in discordant flight.

"When the time comes, will you help me bury her?" Sol asked still tracking the progress of the bees until they were gone, both visually and audibly.

"It would be my honour," muttered Hamish.

"Those bees?" Sol asked.

"Honey bees," Hamish answered. *"Apis melifera.* What about them?"

"How do they know what to do?"

"They trust the new queen and they follow her instincts."

"Then they're very lucky aren't they?"

Both men nodded.

They searched for over an hour to no avail and Gerry returned with warm food and steaming white-painted metal mugs of drink poured from a series of battered vacuum flasks. She had left Nevin at the closest shed behind *Bothan Faobhar* converting it into a safe cage in case they found the kittens. She had brought a cock pheasant from the larder, fully feathered but limply inglorious, should it help in the hunt. But nothing was seen or heard.

Most of the help left after sustenance and went to complete the gate and line the fences as decoy to avoid any further trespass on to the estate and Sol thanked them for their help.

By mid-afternoon only Gerry, Joe, Pete and Hamish were left behind, Sol's closest friends to whom he was not afraid to admit he felt the chances were slim that he would find the kits at all. A loan policeman arrived in a white painted Land Rover, striped along the side in florescent and reflective mimicry of a large wasp, dangerous and foreboding. The man, resolute and sturdy, took statements and inspected the body, patiently taking photographs of blood, paint and tyre marks whilst the increasingly furtive search for the kittens continued in the shrubs and grasses around. Descriptions were made of the vehicle and the driver, paint flecks were scraped into transparent plastic bags as evidence, and radio information was then sent on to neighbouring police who were on the roads that day. Sol thanked him for his time and asked what he would need to do if they found the kittens.

"Look after them I suppose and…"

"I'll contact the wildlife groups for more detail as to what to do," Sol muttered, answering his own question, and the policeman left, all with diminishing hopes for a criminal's capture and a successful rehousing.

Sol backed away and then walked onwards alone, sentinel, to stand up in the grasses well away from the road's side leaning his chin on his hands now scooped in the forked tip of the staff's antler handle thinking, scanning the hills. *They could be anywhere.*

He sat down on an abandoned anthill, capped with moss and sprouting tall tubular stems of sap green. Staining browns caught his eye in their contrast of colouring.

The land slipped away into a wet runnel dominated by ferns and moss that hugged the damp protection of the miniature valley formed. A fallen tree was copiously finished off in leafy viridian with the yellow of wind-shaken buttercups and the scarlet of the wild strawberry dotted within. Under its fallen carcass, where the rot was decaying the wood back to soil detritus, was a dark hole in the fern and grass, just enough to be an entrance to something secret. *But what was the chance?*

But then, what was the chance of anything being the way it was? Almost zero. But it had all happened, all played out the way it had and he found himself where he was and at this time. That was in spite of the chances being near zero.

Sol made an experimental '*mew*' with the expectation of nothing. As his grandfather always said '*expect nothing, gain everything*'. *And there was nothing.*

Nothing, but then, what could he expect? The chances were still almost zero.

But he wasn't giving up now and something tugged at his consciousness.

He '*mewed*' again, the nearest noise he could muster to that which he had heard the mother cat do on numerous occasions in the yard as the cats came to feed and frolic, and that is when he heard the reply. Faint and scared, hidden and overwhelmed, a kitten called back to him from under the tree, somewhere down within those shadows that filled the damp void below the log.

Intuition, or something like it, had played its trump card.

Sol stood and walked steadily over to the mouth of the moss-lined cavity and peered in from above seeing distantly the movement of something within. He continued to '*mew*' and '*maw*' encouragingly and the kittens called back but pushed themselves further into the cave, a space that expanded further than Sol had expected into the banks and under the fallen wood skeleton. He cursed.

Of course they were frightened and would not want to come out without encouragement and help.

On his knees, he reached his right hand in through the ferns and, turning his head away to allow him greatest stretch, he forced his arm as deep as he could, feeling blindly with his groping exposed hand. The kittens hissed and spat in reply, padding their forepaws in terror and defensive anger, and so he withdrew and returned his face to the hole and peered in a second time, now allowing his eyes to become accustomed to the gloom beyond the greenery.

How?

In his pocket were cuts of the pheasant carcass.

He pulled them out, wet with perspiration and with feathers matted, and wondered at how two such small animals could be lured out with the parts of it he had. String laces held the heavy boots he wore secure on his feet and so he removed both pairs and tied them together to produce a fair length twine that would easily stretch back and into the cave all the way to the rear. He looked carefully again at the pheasant wings, scuffing them up roughly, and tied one to the end of the lace rope and tossed it into the darkness as far as he could and then slowly teased it back along the floor, retrieving it in the hope that one of the kits might run for it or attack it. He found himself fishing for cats.

Nothing happened and instead the kittens both hissed and cried.

He repeated the procedure and held his breath in that prayerful attitude he had suddenly become reliant on, but this time he withdrew it with greater care, moving the wing slowly and stealthily, changing its speed and occasionally jerking it. He wanted natural movement where he could produce it, something that might stimulate the hunting instinct in any of the cats, and he tried to imagine the wing as viewed by one of the kits themselves.

Blind to what was happening at the far end of the cave, he just hoped and continued pulling on the string.

Nothing occurred for a second time.

An image of Bruce's spider, trying and trying again to make her web, suffering failure after failure until eventual success was gained, flickered through Sol's mind and he cast the string yet again, more in desperate hope than expectation of success. On hearing the muffled thud as the wing landed on the moss at the end of the cave, he tugged and teased.

Tension formed in the line.

Assuming that it had snagged, Sol pulled again, hard this time. But to his excitement and joy, the string was yanked backwards. This was no catch on a root or twig, this was an attack and the kitten on the other end of it was pulling to retrieve the food.

Sol pulled, but was aware that there was still another two and a half foot of string still to come and he worried that he might lose the kitten in that distance. Deftly he drew his staff forwards and pushed the antler'd crook into the hole pressing his face up close to see better.

The kitten was there, pouncing and biting at the pheasant wing, illuminated in rays by what light could find its way through the root-infested roof. It must have been hungry as it remained distracted by the wing and did not see the descent of the crook until it was pinned to the ground with '*squeals*', thrashes of its teeth and claws, and much hissing.

Sol fought to keep the crook in place and then pulled to draw it in, calling for help as the thrashing beast was dragged, raking spongey moss up with its talons to the entrance of the den.

Gerry appeared at his shoulder as Sol forced his hands in to grab the kitten in a regrettable moment when human meets wildcat and discovers just how well armed and ferocious they can be, regardless of how much that human wishes to help them. Despite the pain and the blood that his scratched hands and arms quickly produced, he refused to let go, instead investing what he could into grim determination.

"I've got one," he called back and Gerry threw off her coat and used it to remove the whirling dervish of an animal held tightly in Sol's grip. She bundled it up and held the suddenly silent package close to prevent any escape.

"Well," laughed Sol. "That's one. Just the second to go... ...I will pay for a new coat if that one gets trounced."

Gerry laughed as the sweating Sol got back down on his knees and started the process again, aiming for the second kitten.

"Hamish," Gerry called over, "one down and another to go but we need your coat or something to wrap it in."

Hamish appeared moments later with two heavy sacks from the back of his Land Rover. They were lambing sacks used in the hills, made of a hessian that was soft enough not to harm the animals inside but thick enough to withstand damage whilst working in the wet and wild. He unfolded Gerry's coat so that the kitten fell into the first bag, knotting it quickly and then, placing the writhing mass safely on the ground, he stepped down to join Sol in the ditch.

"You know," he said, "I still hold out that you are completely mad, Jake Solomon, and that you do not behave like any of the folk round here. But it's obviously catching as what the heck am I doing here with you?"

Sol smiled at him, taking the briefest of moments to exchange a mutual disbelief, and then peered back into the hole. His heart raced with an exhilaration that far exceeded anything he could have achieved even when a deal was struck before. But then he saw the second of the kittens, cornered and pressed up against the crumbling soils of the end wall and he knew that now there was a war of attrition to be fought. No cornered wild animal comes easily whatever the motivation behind its capture. Ask any animal rescuer or well-meaning farmer and they will attest to this without hesitation.

"It won't budge," he muttered through clenched teeth. "It's scared stiff and backed right up."

"I'll go and stamp at the other end and see if the noise forces its hand," Hamish offered and he trudged up and over the fallen log crawling through a fern jungle and sinking into airy wood with too much give and bounce in it. The two of them made a judgement as to how deep under the kitten would be and then Hamish stamped hard forcing earth to drop around the kit and causing it to flare its teeth in fear. He did it again, but the cat just backed up even further into a space that seemed impossible for such a creature.

"We could dig it out but that might frighten it even more, or we might hurt it." Hamish suggested this as a last resort. He'd been there with sheep but they rarely fought back and never offered teeth or talons. He was also unsure how helpful he was being.

"You got your stick?" mused Sol.

"Aye," answered Hamish looking at his own lengthy staff with the crooked end. It had been carved for him by his father and bent slowly in the steam of an open pot kettle suspended over the fireplace for a good number of hours.

"Can you push it down into the ground and between the rotten bits of wood?"

"Aye," said Hamish pushing it experimentally into the rotten wood and easing it slowly down. It kept on going through bubbles of air and pools of sodden wood until it hit hard sound timber, banging like the resound of a hollow drum.

The kitten looked up, alert, silent and trying hard to focus on the sudden and unexpected noise and find its source. It lost interest in the staff ahead of it and instead watched the ceiling intently and twitched.

"Again," called the muffled reply of Sol from under the ground.

Hamish drummed a second time, this time harder, and the wood gave just a little so that Sol could see it waver and splinter at the back of the cave where the kitten curled and snarled. And then a third time as the stick passed into the void below and the kitten, seeing the end of the staff rushed for the hole where Sol's face was stationed.

Withdrawing for safety, Sol slipped the second lambing bag over the entrance and the kit sped into it, thrashing into the end with all its strength and attacking the hessian with its claws, polished black needles that pocked through the material. Sol scooped up the bag and tied it off.

"Success!" shouted Hamish clambering back to Sol and Gerry, and the rotten log he was walking on dropped a foot into the ditch to a level that would have surely crushed the kittens underneath if they had still been there. He looked guiltily at Sol and both understood the relief the other felt.

Picking up both of the steadily morphing bags, one in each arm, and holding them away from his body to avoid scratching and injury, Sol, accompanied by Gerry and Hamish, strolled happily back to the vehicles where Joe sat whistling. Next the party convoyed their way back towards *Bothan Faobhar* to see how Nevin had progressed with the conversion of the shed into a house suitable for the kits. Sol sat in the back with the bags holding them in place between the tarps as the vehicle rolled under Gerry's careful leadership.

When they arrived the shed had a new door fitted securely over it, framed in strong wood and lined with chicken wire so that the kittens could not escape. All the wire ends were bent over so that they, at least in theory, should not injure anything. Inside old wool fleeces had been arranged as makeshift beds under the shelf that ran along one side and further sheets had been nailed to the edge of the surface so that they hung down and provided a natural cave behind. James had found several bowls that were now on the floor, one filled with water, another diluted cow's milk and a few more left for food once prepared.

An old litter tray had been scrounged and it was piled with lose soil in the far corner.

Two logs had been secured to the wall so that they made good climbing trees for the animals and two more were suspended from the rafters on thick ropes, regularly knotted to aid ascending and descending. Further riggings dropped to the ground to give even more opportunity to the cats as they developed.

The rest of the shed had been cleared of firewood and tools.

Sol was almost overwhelmed by the efforts of Nevin and thanked him profusely before he returned to Addie and took secure hold of the two sacks, still in the back of the waggon. He carried them carefully over to the fortified door where latches and a large padlock were now being fitted.

Nevin pushed the door inwards, creaking on the frame, and let Sol inside. It was hinged so that the original wooden outer door could still be closed tightly shut over it with a reassuring thud. James then let the door gently swing too on the tight-sprung spring that he had screwed in place.

"I'll wire up a heating lamp once we can draw some power off the turbine," he explained. "It's all a bit rustic, but it should do for now though. Are you happy?"

"It's perfect," Sol replied from inside where the light had faded leaving growing shadows. "Thank you. Thanks for getting it finished so quickly."

One of Nevin's crew rounded the corner of the sheds with bracken, aromatic and offensive, and moss, viridian green and snarled up into finger-scraped bundles, and a bale of dried grasses in his arms to add to the bedroom cave under the shelving. Once they were satisfied and Sol had added pheasant remains to two of the remaining bowls everyone vacated the cage except for him so that the kittens could be released under only his watchful eye.

The bags writhed and rustled as he eased the knots open, loosened first and then pushed to bursting. And then, he pointed their ends away from him and towards the covered nest area and carefully raised the mouth of the two bags open.

Silence as the kittens studied what they could see, analysing it in the way that a wild predator, ever aware and wary does.

Then, one after another as if life had burst from the bags, they rushed rapidly out of their hessian sack prisons and into the darkness and security of the shelf-cave at the back, from which they growled and hissed until Sol left them, the cage door was closed and bolted, and the outer door was secured. They settled into the glooms and were not seen again that evening.

Tonight they would be left alone, even though Sol felt an almost overwhelming temptation to stay in with them, to try and offer them comfort and to interfere. With some release from his guilt at the death of the mother, he retired with the others back to the house to eat a cold supper and drink a well-earned bottle of wine; good wine of the type that they drank in London.

"We'll help you bury her Sol," said Hamish swirling a glass of malt round and around his glass tumbler later. They sat around the front room, images frozen in flame-licked light. "Where do you want her to go?"

Sol closed his eyes and considered that thought. *Where?*

The yard was her patch but he did not want that reminder here, so close and immediate. He, the living, needed distance. In life she had haunted the woods and the moors, the fields and the glen down to the water, but he wanted her away from the destructive forces of the loch, the invasion of the roots of the trees and the intrusion of the heathers. And then, in his wandering mind, he came to that curious flat area in front of the standing stone on the headland. Here her spirit could wander and watch over, and he had that curious superstition that this would be a good resting place for an animal whose life had been stolen so abruptly.

"I won't need help," he said after a while, the fire snapping and cracking and sending up sparks that chased exit via the chimney. "I'll take her up tomorrow to the place I want her to be." And they all nodded in judgement, knowing that he wanted to do this one last thing for this untameable creature, the one he had come to so nearly tame that she visited him nightly and had entrusted her kits with him.

"So be it," Joe agreed nodding his head, "but now that you're mother and have babies... ...just call if you need help."

Hamish took Pete up to the garage, now named the *Bothan Garage Studio.* It contained an office for a newly founded *Faobhar Estate Conservation Trust* that would record the wildlife present and help manage the observations of incoming eco-tourists who were expected to visit the area and stay.

Hamish also had Joe in the car. Before leaving, Joe asked if Sol would visit again with his violin when possible. Joe felt they needed to talk sooner rather than later.

Gerry and James also left but voyaging in *The Tern* once they were sure that the exhausted Sol was all right on his own. They sailed down to the harbour and intended to eat out at the inn in Old Town.

Sol sat on his own by the fire, which popped as entertainment better than TV for him. He watched the flames flicker and leap up in rampant tongues that chased the rising air they warmed in their ascent of the chimney, that void in the wall in to which so much disappeared.

There was a brief text chime and the phone screen lit the room an unnatural blue. It was from Al.

'*Sol,*

Am sorry to hear about the cat but am pleased to read that the kits are now with you – even a heartless bastard like me has feelings. I know I haven't been in touch for a while but if you change your mind I have people interested in bits of the estate. I've also confirmed the value of the violin. From the photographs you sent it appears genuine and could be an estate saving sale if you could get it off the old man.

Spoken to my head chef. He is keen to buy in some of that local produce you've been eating and using it down here. Could you speak to your friends and make me up a list of what they produce? I might have found you a new niche market but I need to cost it.

I've done a silly thing too. Speak when I'm next up.

Al'

Sol replied to say that the violin was a friend's and that no amount of money would tempt him to take it or to try and get it off Joe, even legitimately. It was always about value for Al, but Sol was forgiving because he too had been there as well only a few months ago. Life has a funny way of reflecting back our actions and feelings from different angles if only we take the time to look up and utilise what views it has on offer. And humans are unique in being the only ones capable of choosing to look, choosing to change or choosing to ignore what we can see.

He played his own violin for an hour, creating a lament for the cat and a yet more hopeful tune for the kittens, liking to imagine that they were listening from the confines of the shed where they were probably still lurking under the shelf. When sleep finally caught him it allowed him to trail the escaping spirit of the wildcat as she circled the glen and rested in the place he intended to bury her. He followed her restless soul and he listened to its instruction in the care of her young. But his sleep was disturbed by images of more photographers and more tourists closing in on the wilderness of the *Bothan* and he could only scream silently in his slumber, unable to keep them at bay.

He woke up in a panic and a sweat as a camera flash blew up in his face in the dream world and flung him immediately back into the light of the real.

Photographers bring us the natural world in crisp focus and wonderful supra-natural colour. They allow us entry into a realm we could only dream of discovering or seeing for ourselves and make the natural world look easy to observe and capture if only we had the time and the expensive equipment required.

Anyone can carry a camera these days as part of his or her baggage or just on the phone as an added extra. Their size and weight, cost and required skills has all dropped away leaving us with a tool we can take anywhere and use at any time. And therein lies the temptation.

Most take snapshots that adorn a family album or can extend to a good picture here and there. Some, interested in the wilds, grab scenes and wildlife and are able to capture something of the world they observe. There are also the professionals who act appropriately and spend the time making their work look easy and perfect, but hiding the real commitment and investment needed to produce each and every spellbinding shot that the mere mortal can only wish to achieve.

But there is one unforgiveable element in the wildlife photography fraternity who will go just that bit closer, prune the shot that bit more or adapt it to suit their needs and improve their clarity of view. They will be prepared to intrude on the territory, the nest or the personal space of anything, however rare or timid, if it will gain them that shot they desire or for which they can earn capital, either financial or prestigious. These are the ones who destroy, frighten or kill to achieve their ends and by whom the rest are often judged or condemned, as it is always the selfish few who tarnish the harmless majority - it is a law of behaviour and the desire of the critical media to point a finger at the small number who bring the hobby in to disrepute.

One such man was Arthur Peterson, and he may have killed a cat, but he had photographs to die for, and so to him it was justified and justifiable.

He sat in his hotel room in New Town and felt clever, able, skilled and noble as he flicked through image after image of wildcat shots he had taken, fooling those locals and that London boy, Sol. It was the same feeling had by the egg collector who cannot show their trophies for fear of the law but who has managed to gain that extra rarest of species' egg. He shared the satisfaction felt by the rogue gamekeeper who had burnt the nest site of the hen harrier to save just five or six pheasant chicks but by whose actions another species edged towards extinction from the United Kingdom.

Arthur was a happy man in those few minutes as he sat back and enjoyed his success and the spoils of being the alpha male. But he was an empty man who needed more to continue to gratify his soul, that which sought for so much extra. He was unaware that he was now also a hunted man with a marked vehicle about to drive through a watching town in a very alert region where strangers were observed, noted and reported on through the network of phones and the Internet, a far more effective weapon than any police force could hope to wield for itself. Yet something of the chase also excited him. It added to the intrinsic danger of what he did and somehow it qualified him and gave him internal kudos.

Running through Pete's blog he looked for more information and detail.

What else might live there in that estate where the cats were?

There must have been something else; he knew it, as the place had that feel about it, that sense of isolation, one unmolested by people and their disruption. It was an awkward irony that he, Arthur Peterson, was causing the very disturbance that would prevent others from appreciating what he had already recognised as pristine. But like so many, even in the face of overwhelming evidence against them, he was blind to that and had justified his own actions easily, remaining critical of others for what they did instead.

The pictures looked good and easily compensated for any action he took.

Sol went to look in on the kittens, just to see.

The morning was early-lit and grey-sepia, the black and white of old television, and the air remained cool with an eerie mist that formed over the loch during the night that would steadily roll back out to sea as the sun eventually had the energy about it to warm it thoroughly enough. There was a shallow pool of fog that stretched its lapping tendrils up the glen and rippled softly like an extra sea somehow suspended ethereally over the loch water, each crest catching the breaking dawn's orange light. It was an icy, mobile heat-seeking thing that was sensed as much as seen, drawing out the body heat downwards and away, but from high enough up into the mountains it created a different, illusionary vision, than that of reality.

Pigeons cooed tonelessly and monotonously, and from within the mist the geese could be heard in garbled conversation, with the occasional head raised in alarm so that these bodiless creatures could scope above broiling whiteness as if submarine birds were dabbling there. The swifts, swallows and martins were up early, scouring the skies and screaming in their delight, and they were joined by the boozy braying of the stags' echoes from the woodland as the young males came in to shelter from a night on the moors, like the beer-charged youth in a suburb; antlered and over-confident.

Forcing the little wooden door open as it repealed against his strength, Sol peered into the shadows and felt the warmth from within. The shed had remained protected.

The pheasant was gone and feathers around the bowls showed that the two occupants had plucked bits of the body. The milk was spilt but mostly drunk, lapped outwards to form a drying spreading pool as evidence of their feeding, and the water bowl was upset, its contents staining the floor a dark shade that reminded Sol of their mother's blood.

But there was no sign of the kittens themselves. It was the zookeeper's paradox. There was a cage obviously well designed for the health and welfare of the occupant with all the indications required that the animals inside had eaten, drunk, played and slept. However, it was so well devised with the creature's requirements in mind that the paying public would never be able to see the occupants. They could hide too easily, shelter amongst the caves and scenery, and sleep unseen. Any zoo curator knows that the fickle public expects more, demands a show and wants to see into the life of the inmate regardless of the difficulty of convincing the animal inside that they are not being observed or acclimatising them so much that they ignore their human spectators.

Sol unlocked and unlatched the caged inner door and entered, his greeting being the hiss of angry and scared kittens from somewhere in the darkness where the shadows offered the greatest cover. Sitting by the dangling sheets and fleeces that made the cage wall, Sol focused his mind's eye on that of his appearance from the kitten's perspective and then made reassuring '*mew*' sounds and emitted a gentle '*purr*'.

Anywhere else and he would had felt foolish, a child's game of animal noises emitted by an adult. But the kittens quietened for time enough for him to know that they had heard him, were responding. But they remained resolutely hidden before breaking their thought silence and hissing louder when urged to and growling deep tiger snarls when he attempted to look in on their den.

He placed more raw meat in the bowls after cleaning them. Re-filled the milk and re-set the water. Taking out scats from the litter tray before '*mewing*' one last time, he turned and left in a quiet manner. He took a final glance back as he closed the outer door expecting to see just one last movement. But if they had ventured from the den, they were invisible and he was not treated to the site of a kitten running to stop him leaving and demanding his company. *These were just not that sort of cat; they were wildcats, the untameable, real cats.*

He breakfasted alone and then selected a large bag from a further shed into which he placed the well-wrapped body of the wildcat mother over which he lay his violin case, and he picked up a spade in one hand and his trusted staff in the other. As he left the house he struck the staff into the ground in a determined thrust. This would be no easy journey but instead would take on the massed-importance of a ceremonial voyage, one carrying an object of huge importance to its final resting place. The pace was brisk and the dead weight that he carried pulled back at him throughout, digging into his shoulders and marring them.

They passed the rotting stag, whose grey skin now hung tightly between bones that were chewed back to the white. It was losing that shape that said '*stag*' in the mind and was becoming just an internal structure of one, still recognisable for what it had been but not the wonderful, toned and muscular creature it had proudly stood to be. Its teeth were scarred with the tartar of use and lined in metamorphic layers of enamel and calcium that folded inwards and outwards to give them their herbivorous grinding surfaces. Sockets had sunk within and become simple spaces that once housed those important sense organs that had saved it from past danger, now just pits that gazed uselessly out and down a long white nasal ridge that itself had grown holes where the nostrils once were. Gum-less, its skeletal face grinned forever down into the river; now it was just a spectre stag.

Maggots still crawled below to make flies in their time. Beetles were deep under doing their work. Birds fed on the insects and predators took the birds. Death was final and death was changing, but death was just the beginning of the recycling processes investing well in the next generation of life.

Sol sensed the heat generated from within; respiration's waste.

The river, entertained as always, bounced by without concern. Unlike us she had millions of years left to run her course even though through summer drought she was on lower ebb than the winter. She still had enough in her to house the trout in her deeper pools and to give succour to the cushions of the mosses, the mats of the liverworts and the fronds of the ferns. All relied on her and the minerals she carried and gladly she gave as she wildly splashed and fell.

Sol fought his way up the crag path to the headland, struggling with the pulling weight of the bag and the unforgiving nature of the heavy iron-worked spade he had selected for the burial job. But he pushed on and up with the calling of a missionary in the face of rebellion until he was there and cresting the headland heather that was in all of its full purple glory, warmed by the sun that worked to evaporate the churning mists below, skimming them off like the fat from good stock.

He took the winding heather-smothered path to the standing stone and held that sacred rock in his fingers and palms, gripping their lichens and rubbing their sandy texture, making the contact of oneness with the land. The waters were still mist clagged but now it was vaporous and thin, and beyond the flat area in front of the stone the cliffs fell down as the prow of a mystical boat that cut through a choppy sun-illumined cloud sea.

'*Here she will rest,*' Sol thought and stepping ahead of the trodden rectangle, he picked up the spade and started to dig, easily at first, until metal clanged against stone throwing up sparks and he had to pick his way with more care. He dug until his hands ached and his skin ruptured in blisters across his hankered digits. But he scrabbled on taking stones out and tossing them aside using the digging action of his fingertips until they bled freely and the dirt clagged up black under his nails mixing to form a dark paste with his body's fluids. But he was prepared to pay this pain and blood price, something to alleviate the guilt fee his mind had convinced him he owed.

After an hour a shallow grave was achieved and Sol returned to the body, picking its sagging heaviness up, earth-pulled as if it knew that this was where it now belonged and sought for. He placed her uncovered from the tarpaulin sheets into the superficial scrape and caressed her lidded face, inflexible with death, arranging her body into a rigamortis-stiffened pose of sleep, half-curled and half natural.

He then took flowers as an offering of some natural beauty and placed them in pagan ritual over her. He did not understand why he did this, but it felt right to do. He next added pheasant feathers that had accumulated in his pockets to symbolise food and feeding and nodded. Again it seemed the correct thing to do although there was no credible, sensible, city-bred explanation as to why.

Then he took a handful of earth and stone and tossed it in from the crumbled pile that had accumulated to his side. The first felt an offence and the second was easier, and finally he was able to shovel it over with less worry as he gained closure and the body was hidden from view. Theirs had been a short relationship but a far deeper and important one than even he had realised, and he knew then that he had missed something fundamental in his human interactions and spiritual life if he had given and received more from a wild animal in such a short time than he had from anywhere else.

Quickly a mound formed. One that he knew would sink with time as she returned to sustain the plants. He created a low barrow of rocks that would protect the grave and one day be engulfed by the encroachment of moor plants, and then he turned to look out at the view he had left her with. There was another huge knoll off to his right, now earthed over and mossy with tufts of heather sprouting inconsistently over it.

It was strange how this unnatural form had never called his attention before, part-hidden by the texture of the undergrowth and yet distinct and human-made.

"That was *his* stag," came the voice of Joe from where he had been watching blindly a way off behind in the heather. Sol was surprised. In his grimy work he had sweated and toiled without any thought as to who else would be around him.

"Whose?" asked Sol looking back to where Joe was struggling to get to the standing stone carrying his old violin over his shoulder. Sol shuddered to think of its value and the potential there was for such an expensive instrument to have been destroyed on Joe's torturous travels down from the upper loch.

"G's. Someone shot it as G was watching it up here and so he chased the perpetrator off the estate and returned to bury that stag up here, right where it fell. He refused to let anyone help him. That's why I knew you'd be up here. You're just like him in so many ways."

Sol smiled. Of all the people he could want to be compared to, G seemed to the best option, even though they had never met.

"How did you get here?" he asked of the old man.

"With difficulty."

They laughed at the thought.

"Oh, I know the way all right," said Joe. "The old eyes aren't the best anyone could have in their head, but I could sense enough, and for the rest of the detail I used memories and that music of yours to describe it to me... ...you know, the tune you wrote about the path? It got me here in the end. I can see shadows and blurred images of the world. That's enough really. I suspect if I could see clearly I'd never have got down here."

"Joe, you really are amazing," Sol commented.

"I know that, but thanks anyway." There was a wry chuckle in the reply.

"Do you miss your sight?"

"Sometimes. But I've seen enough for a lifetime and that's good because I won't get any more."

They sat for a while and talked, leaning on the rock and with closed eyes feeling the summer peak in their faces and across their wind-hardened skins. They stood and played duet out there on the headland, knowing how to accompany each other in some strange way. And then Joe talked, telling tales of G, and then about the sea, and then the many years ago that he had last sailed and fished out there on the loch.

"So let's go out now then," announced Sol.

"What?" Joe asked.

"Let's go out on the water now. I have a boat and am nearly safe enough to take you. There are nets in the sheds and a few rods. If you think they're any good we can take them out with us to fish with. We could listen to the birds and take on the waves and then you could teach me where to fish and how. We could even take the fiddles out!"

The old man's face lit up, "You'd do that?"

"Joe, you're as good as a father to me these days. It would be my pleasure."

They packed up quickly with the gentle wind's assistance, and with Sol's help Joe descended the crag path, which was appreciably much harder than he considered it would be for the old man in his blindness. They travelled by the river back to the *Bothan*, a house Joe had not visited for many years.

Sol left Joe in the cottage exploring for a while and then making them a drink, feeling his ways around the unfamiliar arrangement of items in a very familiar place where the fabric had not changed but the placings had. Meanwhile, nets collected and rods, lines, feathers, lures and weights bagged, Sol placed each in front of Joe to check that they were suitable. Next he put them carefully in the bottom of *Sireadh-thall* and then returned to the house to ask Joe what else they needed.

"Lunch," Joe answered holding up a bag filled with food from the larder, "and these." He handed Sol worms he had gathered from the compost heaps. "They aren't lunch though!"

"And we'll need a sacrifice each in case we meet the *Blue Men*," said Sol. "We don't want to go upsetting *them* today. I want us both back safely. I have family to look after these days. So have you got something to offer to the *Blue Men*?"

"Oh, they've taught you well haven't they?" Joe replied with that guilty twinkle of the naughty schoolboy in his glazed and unfocussed eyes. He took up his fiddle case, gave Sol the food bag and pocketed the worms. "I've already got my sacrifice ready," he said, looking around the house as if for the last time.

Joe considered what he sensed about him. "Money's still going to be tight isn't it?" he asked.

"Aye," said Sol, "but we'll manage somehow. Money isn't everything."

Joe agreed and enjoyed the sense of change in the younger man.

After checking on the kittens, still hidden and secretive, they set out to sea and fished, the old man directing the vessel from memory, using his hazy sight for the final details. The two cast rods out to those places where Joe knew the edible denizens of the deeps would still live, choosing them for their productivity and the upwellings through which they delivered the most nutrients. He even described the fishing birds to look out for that might indicate the greatest potential.

He was confident that tonight they would eat richly of the fruits of the sea, and the old man relished the thought of it.

Chapter 22: Wood and Glue

(Piano Concerto II, Adagio, Edvard Grieg)

Memories are such curious things, impossible to pinpoint in the brain and often difficult to recall when we most need or want them. At other times they are pulled back into reality when we least expect them, retrieved by a reminiscent sound, or an archived voice, a similar experience or ambience, and bizarrely more times than we would expect resulting from a smell or taste that takes us straight back there to the point of that memory's making and its subsequent storage.

As *Sireadh-thall* took the current, bobbing and excitable with the wash of the water, Joe was instantaneously back there in a time many years before when he had last taken to the water. The reality of an age-past formed itself around his blinded sight and he could for that second see again and smell the sticky saltiness of the sea air, even feel its tender breeze as the sail flapped to life and tugged the boat's hull deep to starboard so that she listed, strained and then righted and flew. He leant on the tiller, hearing the birds and being drawn out to waters thought forgotten but not. Instead they were instantly rediscovered having been disturbed from their latent slumber of many years ago. In the same way that a heavy anchor dredged through deep sediment can unearth a prehistoric reef-grown wreck, filled with holes of marine worms and half buried so that it avoids decay, becoming instead a glistening black and oily representation of what it was, memories surfaced.

The terns squealed in delight as they hit the deeper waters out by the headland's rocks and Joe instructed Sol where to cast following their direction.

"Sand eels below the surface," he said. "The terns are flocking around them trying to catch the mackerel. You just need a few feathers and hooks on the end of your line." And he asked for a small weight, some line and a few hook-tied chicken feathers. "In the water, they'll follow the motion of your line if you jerk it up and down and spin it. Mackerel attack first and think later, like most group living predators...   ...like bankers too if you aren't careful. If they thought first then they would miss out on feeding opportunities as others will have taken it from them. It's like a number of people I once knew. They act first, impulsively and without thought, and only later think through what they've just done."

He attached a line and reel to a rod, deftly feeling the twine and tying flies in with an action that seemed impossible for someone with so little sight, and he then handed it on to Sol. "Aim there," he said, pointing. "Into the middle of the flock of terns. They sound like they know what they're doing and have the advantage of better sight than either of us, and as they can see the water from above they're looking straight down on their prey too."

Sol did as he was told whilst Joe set up a second rod and then cast himself.

His instructions were basic and clear.

"Cast...
...let it drop...
...then jerk it up and down and...
...reel in a few seconds...
...let it drop...
...wait a few seconds more...
...and then repeat the draw...
...again and again."

The line trembled in Sol's hand.

"Are you in?" asked Joe. "I can hear your line singing."

There it was, the note of the fish in the tension of the wire that began a rhythmic pulsing that bent the rod's very tip.

"Yes," laughed Sol sensing the urgent wobble in the pole. "I'll reel it in."

"No," Joe snapped holding a steadying hand out to emphasise the point. "Be steady and keep repeating the draw and drop technique. If you've got one you'll get another, and… …I'm in too."
Sol pulled in four fresh mackerel, green and shimmering, wide-eyed and striped, which he dispatched and bagged, and Joe produced another three. They caught for a few more minutes before the school moved on. But they were happy with their trawl and the fresh-oiled dinner it would cook up for them.
"There's no use doing what some do," explained Joe sitting back with a satisfied gummy smile. "They find a shoal and they keep on fishing it and fishing it. Eventually they've taken so much they won't be able to eat them all and half the fish end up wasted. It's an offence to mother nature if you ask me." It was a very human tale.
Joe led them from memory to the stack rocks out in the loch where the gannets plummeted offshore and the puffins waddled in bright-bibbed uniform. There were kittiwake pure white and angelic, razorbills the penguin of the shore, and little auks diminutive and squat, each perched in their position on the rocks above the crash of the sea and the thunder of the waves that air-filled etched caves at the cliff's feet, compressed it and then exploded with a spume that filled the air. Birds wheeled the sky as they allowed the boat to drift and bob to the moaned singing of the seals hauled up on the lowest rocks, velvety when dry but speckled dark grey and smooth when wet.
Joe sang back to them in Gaelic, words he claimed they would understand. Tradition told him that they were the spirits of lost fisherman forever trapped on the weed-cropped stones from where they communicated with the living about the dangers that lay ahead. Certainly the seals and he held quite a conversation. After ten minutes of exchange, Joe stood up, rocking the boat, and asked Sol to accompany him, and, once ready and steady enough on his feet, Sol joined him on the violin and they performed harmoniously together, creating variations of a sea lament that Joe taught, until

Sireadh-thall met the current change. Here the banging of the *Blue Men* started to rattle and clang from underneath the hull.

"Well," shouted Sol, turning *Sireadh-thall* against her will so that she cut the interface of the currents how Gerry had taught him to during lessons. The banging grew louder and the feeling of men trying to scratch and hammer their way in through the hull became increasingly indisputable as the boat jerked and rallied. "I hope you've bought a good sacrifice."

"Aye, that I have," answered the old man with that glint of the school boy in his eye. "You offer first though. Age before beauty."

Sol took a fish from the pile they had accumulated. It was the first that they had caught, kept aside and special for this very purpose. As the boat shook and the raking from below grew in amplitude, he withdrew a knife from his cloth satchel bag and cut the last feather and its tied in hook off his line with one clean flash. These were they that had taken this first life from the sea, conned into the belief that it was alive, snared it and plucked it up and out of its watery medium, and he placed it in the mouth of the fish which he closed shut. It was an odd ritual, with no purpose other than to recognise that he had killed something only gasping water for its oxygen moments before, but it gave termination and closure to his thoughts and felt right. A thankful moment of the native Indian.

"This is for you *Blue Men* of the loch," Sol called into the spindrift and wind, dropping the fish over the side. It caught the current and its nose rose in a false impression of swim-induced life before dropping and worming its way down and out of the extent of the light. "May you feed well on it, use the hook to catch your own and thank you for allowing us both safe passage, and for providing us with food from your water for tonight to feed ourselves."

Joe nodded to himself, his eyes half closed. Then he picked up his fiddle case, stored with him at the prow of the boat where he sat enjoying the passing of the air and the spray of the prow-cut water. He had not played the fiddle on this journey and he sat in the bowl of the stern and considered this as a musical sacrifice to those demanding *Blue Men* below; the ones who had claimed past friends of his as they crossed these very waters.

"Are you going to play them a tune?" laughed Sol. "You'd better be quick. They seem to be getting quite angry!"

The banging amplified until Sol felt quite sure that the timbers lining *Sireadh-thall*'s hull were about to burst as he used the sail to drag her back towards the *Bothan* and into the churn and strop of the confused currents and agitated white horses. The tiller shook and the mast wobbled as the pressure pent up and built, rocking them all in what would have been frightening lists if they had still believed in the gods of the sea and were not modern men of science living in an age where the inquisitive had explored the ocean's floor and many understood the movement of the tides.

Joe held the case close to his chest, almost prayerfully with his blind eyes shut, remembering something.

"And?" shouted Sol over the rattling and scraping. "What tune will it be Joe? Make it a good one…   …something to stir even the soul of the *Blue Men*."

Joe lifted the fiddle case and stooping first, he stood in the stern and leaned against the finely seamed timbers that made *Sireadh-thall*'s rounded end. Then he looked over the edge and in one swift and easy movement he dropped the case over the side.

"Joe? Your violin?" screamed Sol racing to the back of the boat to try and rescue the case as it fell down through the deep green waters and away from sight and rescue. "Joe?"

"Yes," he replied calmly as the banging from below ceased and they passed through the last of the realm of the *Blue Men*.

"Your fiddle!"

"I know. But they liked it didn't they?"

"But Joe?"

"Yes. My Fiddle."

"But Joe? What have you done?"

"I've got another one."

"But, that one was worth hundreds of thousands of pounds!" Sol was almost crying with disbelief as he stared down into the choppy green abyss where only his own fragmented reflection greeted him. "Yes. I know. It's been in the family for years. A gift from someone I believe."

"You know its value?"

"Yes. A friend had it valued some years ago now. But it's not really worth that much is it?"

"What?"

"Well it's just a bit of old wood and glue."

"But it's a very valuable bit of wood and glue!"

"But it is still just a fiddle and plays a nice tune. As I said, I've got another one and it'll do the same too."

"But Joe... ...it was worth so much."

"And, the sacrifice? Surely it should be a valuable one if the *Blue Men* are going to accept it. It's in the rules."

"But?"

"I saw your friend... ...Al... ...he was looking at it the other day. It was probably the only reason he came to the pub that night. I couldn't see his expression or read his eyes, but I could feel what he was thinking." Sol sat down on the beam his head in his hands. "He came up to visit me before he left to go back to London – told me not to mention it to you as you would've been cross. A proper little Golum he was becoming. Wanted to see the fiddle again and ask me questions as if I were too stupid to see through him. He was right that I couldn't see, but not about anything else... ...you get that a lot when you lose your sight. People assume that you lose everything else at the same time. But to compensate, sometimes your other senses get better; they sort of take over. You end up getting more information from other avenues than anyone presumes possible and I could sense his urgency and growing frustrations. Before long Al would have been trying to get that fiddle off of me so that he could sell it and make lots of money from it. Greed has a funny way of doing that sort of thing to people. It eats them up from inside. First they're jealous and then they resent you for what you have. If it's unchecked then it carries on until they convert thoughts into words and words into actions – it wasn't going to end well for any of us. And then...   ...and then, if he had done anything you would've been the one left feeling guilty wouldn't you?" Sol nodded, a disbelieving movement of shock. "And you're my friend. I don't want that for you. And so, you see, I think the fiddle is better off with the *Blue Men* and then no one feels tempted. They can play it, probably much better than me. After all, it was valuable enough for them to stop their banging and so I think they like it."

"But," Sol muttered to no one person in particular as he stared out and down into the water seeing nothing of the highly prized case which by now would have been lower than the algae could bloom and further behind than he could swim. He sighed. "I suppose you're right. I told Al to leave you alone. But he would've tried to take it off you eventually. Although he claimed that we could've sold it to repair the houses on the estate but...   ...you're right... ...its only money isn't it? And it wasn't even his, ours, or even mine, to sell. "

"And if you had sold it? What then? The money would have gone soon enough and you would still have needed more. If you'd never realised its value you would've been none the wiser and still been facing the same financial problems as you are now. That you've seen it taken away changes nothing except that you now know it's beyond you; untouchable. Unless that is, you want to swim after it? Then you can ask the *Blue Men* for its return? Sol, the estate has to pay for itself sustainably, not be cash-injected with money that isn't rightfully yours and carry along with some financial limp for all time. If it fails it should fail with you trying. If it succeeds, it will be your efforts that sustained and nurtured it."

"Do you ever get the feeling that you're responsible for much but in control of very little?"

"All the time." Joe was sombre and thoughtful. "That's been the commonest feature of my life."

"What do you do about it then?"

"Some of us turn to God but so often run the risk of the ceremonial taking over and us missing the whole point of what we do in an attempt to justify it, to the point that we ruin that concept and humanise the divine. Others choose the lesser gods and follow a more Earth-based, pagan or humanist route to salvation and edification. In our bid to become modern, though, the human race seems to have forgotten our mortality, departed from the spiritual and left vacuous gaps in our souls. Money can be your god if you want it to be, or you can pursue the path of self-gratification. Each of us has our choice. But it's often too late that we humans realise that we *are* spiritual creatures, however you define that word, and the emptier our routes of passage in this life. Then the further we get from being truly satisfied and happy with our lot and, more importantly, ourselves. They say you only live once. What happens if *they* are wrong?"

Sol began to formulate an answer but then stopped as they departed from the centre of the water and headed back towards that other land of the glen, the antithesis of everything out here.

The rest of the journey was a quiet affair with Sol looking longingly back to the middle of the loch and Joe smiling to no one but himself in the prow as if some wicked lesson for Sol had been executed and completed. Sol felt tested and judged, but remained calm, knowing that Joe was right in the end as he was about so many things he spoke of; the philosopher who lived by the lake and the oracle on the hill. Joe was the owner of the instrument after all and could choose its fate however useful it would have been for Sol or Al to obtain to sell.

Sireadh-thall ran aground on the beach with the swish of the sand taking up her weight, grinding smoothly like the paper along a desk, and Sol jumped ashore and pulled her up to security using the painter. He helped Joe on to the beach and they divided the fish between them in silence until Joe gripped his hand tightly with his sinewy but strong bony fingers.

"There are bigger things in this world than the money we feel we need to buy the things we so often do not require." He spoke closely to Sol's face. "There is the wealth of Mother Nature and the richness of friendship, there is the tapestry of life and the depth of the soul. Remember this will you even when you are tested to the absolute brink?"

Sol looked at him earnestly searching his blank pupils, trying to put away that image of the valuable violin case sinking into the water of the loch and from sight. "I will," he said.

"Good. Are we still friends then?"

"Of course," laughed Sol. "It would take more than wood and glue to break that!"

"Excellent... ...can I cadge a lift home then?"

The two chuckled as they bagged their fish and cleared the boat of kit and lines and Sol's lonely violin case.

"It was only wood and glue," Sol repeated as if to convince himself. "I'll tell Al that in person when he next appears so long as you promise to get the ambulance here as quickly as you can."

"You can only quote me," Joe sniggered, "if I'm allowed to be there when you do it. I'll pre-order both of the ambulances required."

"Deal. In fact you can tell him. I think he might struggle with your logic though. To him the only thing that matters is the worth of something, the bottom dollar and all that. I bet he'd sell relatives and friends if there were a market for it."

"Then watch your back. You've been losing value since you arrived here and he might need to act quickly if he wants to make a profit."

Sol laughed at the beautiful irony of this.

They checked on the kittens, still invisible but having left evidence that they had fed well and enjoyed the milk, leaving white inverse footprints along the shed floor where they had explored. One of the fleeces was ragged where claws had been tested and the litter tray held testimony to meals appreciated.

Sol drove Joe along the drive until they met the new gate constructed by Hamish's team. It was a strong five barred affair made with mortised joints, which had been built from old timber to give it an especially aged appearance of the type that suggested it had been stood there, locked, for a long while. Anyone arriving on the far side would have seen the drive to *Bothan Faobhar* as an old abandoned forestry track left locked and unused as the wood had degenerated to the moulded and gnarled conifers that could be seen on either side of the rutted overgrown lane. The natural route now appeared to lead up off the driveway to take the traveller to the garage complex, Euan's and the bealach crossroads on the moor. With the change of an entrance the dominant direction had been altered and the eye was naturally drawn away from the path to Sol's house.

Similarly the fences that extended up on either side and under the trees stretched far enough that they gave the impression of a fenced in plantation left to fall back to an unprofitable ruin. They had been fashioned from recycled posts from the shepherds' homes and what was found on the moor tops and Hamish had hand selected the oldest most corroded wires to complete the camouflage.

If they did not know to look, no one would, and Addie's tracks would soon be ignored, leaving just the one photographer out there on the loose who knew the real secret of the driveway. But he, the hunter of pictures of the unwary animal, was now the unwary hunted himself. Hopefully time would deliver him to them and the law complete its due process.

"What happened to the man who shot the stag? G's stag?" Sol asked as he uncoiled the heavy discoloured chain that was looped around the gate fastening it, but not as it looked locking it. The large metal padlock was simply there for show and could be moved easily if anyone made an attempt.

He swung the gate open. Even the rusting of the squeaky hinges that were tormented by the action of being forced to open, screaming their disgust, demonstrated the attention to detail to finish off the subterfuge by those that had worked on the gate.

Joe leant on Addie's chugging bonnet.

"Typical G story really. He forgave him and gave him a house and a job."

"What?" Sol stood stock-still. "Does he still live here?"

"Oh yes."

"Who?"

"Now that of course would be telling. But beware who you ask."

Sol drove Addie through the gate and went to shut it and re-wrap the chain around it. An old, paint-flecked sign hung on the gate reading, *'PRIVATE WOODLAND, WARNING Forestry Operations'* with an indecipherable number below it. The gate suggested anything but welcome, and strangely Sol was gladdened by its dismal appearance and message.

They drove on up to the crossroads and then over the moor to Joe's where the short-eared owl was patrolling the heathers as the light faded.

"When I'm dead," Joe laughed, "do tell the story of the mad old sod on the hill who threw away half a millions pounds worth of wood and glue. And, if anyone hears the fiddle out at sea, tell them it's the *Blue Men* playing or my ghost come back to haunt them. Make up some myth please – something to scare the tourists with."

"Oh, I will," replied Sol.

"Thank you Sol."

"What for?"

"Understanding that it was just wood and glue."

"Joe, you're worth more as a friend than just wood and glue." Sol paused, "but only just okay?"

Sol steered Addie down the hillside and Joe took his fish inside to prepare for supper before sitting himself out in vigil for the water bull in case tonight was the night it came for him.

"Wood and glue," sniggered Sol as Addie's tyres gripped the mud and clawed her up to the crossroads. "*Just* wood and glue."
But what he would have given to be holding that wood and glue right now.

Value, that unpredictable thing we each place on our own possessions, those of others and on the things which we perceive as being more than just the norm. The same house in one town, where there is one good school and a pleasing view can be worth so much more than the same in the next place of residence. And yet it cost the same to build and provides the same comforts and resources. We simply value one over the next. It's part of the infamous postcode lottery that's all part of being British.
We have a product that people like with a label they recognise and they will pay for it. Make it less numerous or limit the numbers produced and the price can be manipulated upwards even though it might be identical in all respects, bar emblem, to that worn by the next man or woman. It may even have been produced in the same factory using the same loom and possibly bagged by the same robot. Flood the market and the price will drop.
An old violin may have ripened and become less pleasing to the ear when played. But if it has the right maker and a story, for example if it is named and considered lost then is found, then a less precisely constructed instrument, more difficult to control and possibly even inferior in quality to its modern counterparts can fetch considerable price at the right auction, marketed in the best way. Value is a pretext of mind, reliant on word of mouth, gambling and here say, and is not a measure of anything real.
But then this immeasurable value is nothing compared to that which any object picks up when it is given sentimental significance as well. Then an item worth pence to the auctioneer becomes impossible to buy or sell, enjoying that strange juxtaposition of price, it being worth nothing but also worth everything at the same time.

Joe was right. The violin was just wood and glue and in the end worth the same as any other violin made of the same materials. It would still have been nice to have kept it and sold it.

On his way back Sol drove to the post box at the end of the drive that now had what appeared to be a lock on it but was in fact just another disguised latch. There was a brown envelope in it, which gave it an official visage, and a second scruffier one with a handwritten address label.

He parked Addie up in the pull-in close to the end of the drive and then walked back towards the *Bothan* taking the letters with him. Passing through the gate and re-fastening it behind him he made sure that it looked as unused as possible and then swept the Land Rover's tyre tracks over using a death-stiffened larch branch. He would sail this section of the estate when he could from now on to ensure he left as little disturbance here at the gate as possible.

The walk was a cold one and he worried that the kittens might be chilled with the shed door open to allow them to air behind the caging and he pushed on, feeling the responsibility of the curator-keeper put in charge of the rarest creatures in the zoo. When he reached *Bothan Faobhar* she greeted him with the colour of the setting sun reflecting off her painted walls where through the months he had slowly whitewashed her to give her a few more years' protection from the winters.

The moths were beginning to play their shadow puppetry against the cottage backdrop as he crept around to the back to spy on the kittens.

Two noses were pressed up against the dull grey zinc coating of the chicken wire. One extended to paws that scratched at the caging to find a weakness in it and the other kept a watchful glare on its sibling. The kittens were at least out and therefore easier to assess. They seemed fit and healthy in the way they paced about the cage and pounced on the insects that dared to approach.

There was an alertness about them and they were larger than Sol had appreciated when he last saw them tugging along behind their mother, under her guidance and instruction. He wondered at their independence so soon after the sudden loss of the wildcat parent feeling that they had been forced into growing up too quickly. There were parallels between him and they and he sensed a form of poetic justice in that it was he who was now their guide after their loss. He wanted to look after them, mother them for her, but his real ambition was to see these creatures released back into the wild and developing beyond a reliance on him.

He walked across the yard stealthily, pausing when the kittens retreated back into the lengthening shadows of the evening. But as if there was something in him that they remembered, each time he waited, they returned within a few moments back to the patch of setting sun that lit their doorway.

When he was only feet away the more dominant of the two hissed and snarled, stamping its forepaw at him as it bared its pin sharp canines.

"I'm afraid you don't scare me," Sol chuntered. "I know you'd draw blood given the chance. But I promised your mother I'd see to you. And so, I'm sorry but you can't scare me."

The second cat purred loudly and brushed up against the caging and Sol sat down for a few minutes to watch them, edging along the door front as the shade pushed the sun further around until it was snubbed out and lost.

"Good night," he called as the first hoot of the owl marked the beginning of the night shift, and he closed the wooden door sending the kittens to the cover of their den.

He took the two letters into the living room where he sat, fireless for the evening, under the fizzing glow of a paraffin lamp.

The brown envelope was a summons to London for the findings of a future enquiry into the Tokyo deal. It would not be until next year but it was the intention of his previous employers to give Sol the chance to mount his own case and to engage sufficient legal representatives to defend him in court. He felt his heart gain weight and sink within his chest, plummeting like a lead dropped into a chasm to a depth where light could not penetrate.

There was currently little paper work and they hoped that he would be able to fill them in on information that was missing. They had entrusted large sums of money with him and although they were confident that he would be able to explain where it was eventually sent, evidence was needed or else he would face a criminal prosecution. The letter listed embezzlement of funds, theft of company assets, and several minor cases of deception and misuse of his professional position as an investor on their behalf. He would hear from their solicitors in due course but was advised to gather his legal team ready for a date to be set in April of the next year.

He sat in disbelief as he scanned through the notes that had been sent in order to start the law proceedings against him. *Surely they were not serious?*

But there it was written in the over-charged official black and white of the company's own legal department, and they were filing to sue him for upwards of five hundred thousand pounds. If the Tokyo deal had been pulled off, even though it looked increasingly unlikely, it would have eclipsed that figure manifold. *Surely they must know that?*

He sat and cold-sweated.

He was little concerned about his own fortunes but was wondering how he could ensure that the estate remained as a whole, protected, and how he was going to guarantee that his wildcat reserve would continue and the *Bothan* enjoy its wilderness isolation. The obsession had grown and taken over what sentient thoughts he could muster; a positive mental cancer.

He picked up the second envelope and turned it slowly in his hand. *Did it too contain some misfortune or bad news like everything else seemed to?* A letter can change so much of our emotional state, bringing us down on to our knees with its news or creating elative moments when read. *What would this one hold?*

He replaced it on the table to read another time, fearful of the effect it could have.

Each day Sol went out to feed and clean the wildcat kittens and would sit nearer and nearer the cage for longer and longer periods, steadily turning recluse in his actions. His absence was noted from the town in only a few days and he had to be reminded of the Thursday night musical meet as his preoccupation with the cats and money overtook his rational mind.

He wrote back to the company that had once employed him and agreed to the dates they suggested and made sure that nothing would get in the way of the final reckoning by writing the date down on a piece of paper on which he listed all the days to come between now and then. He let them know that he would represent himself.

That week's concert was good, but not his best. The inn held less appeal to Sol than it had done before and the music found itself less naturally, more confused and the tunes difficult to find and draw out. Joe played an inferior instrument to usual, the crowd were less attentive, the air was more strained and something pulled Sol's attention towards absence from the sounds and melodies that normally took his mind away from every thought and worry. Although they played on, Hamish and Joe were very aware of it and they pressed him at the interval.

"Come on Sol," chided Hamish. "Your heart isn't in it today."

"It's just…" he wanted to tell them about the summons and the proceedings against him, but he had no words to describe how he felt, no wisdom to let them know how he would fix things and he could only see a broad gulf before him with respect to the finances of the estate.

"…a bad week," Joe helped out. "I know."

"A meeting," called a furtive man in the crowd. "I'd like us to call a meeting."

It had become usual for Sol to call meetings with the backing of Hamish. For someone else to shout for one was unusual and there were mutterings of dissent from the people, but a meeting gathered nevertheless, even if it were lacklustre.

"You," said the man rounding on the defenceless Sol. He was small and square, fiery eyed and with the logic of beer in his thinking he was prepared to speak freely. "You. Is it true the cat is dead like it said on the blog?"

Hamish stepped in to defend the weakened Sol. "You know it is."

"It's just the start then isn't it? Once those tourists start flooding in, what then? It'll be the end of our way. They'll bring in their money and expect the world and they'll change it, you see. First the cat'll die and then we will."

"That's nonsense," said Hamish. "A lot of work has been undertaken to protect the estate and will be put in to protect the town and the whole area."

The man looked shrewdly at Sol. "Look at him. As you once said yourself, his heart isn't even in it. Give him a few months and he'll be off. He'll turn his back and sell out. Everyone knows the estate is losing him money or will be soon, and he won't be able to run it for much longer."

Hamish dived in for the defence, but Sol spoke first, quietly and consistently, with manners and almost a touch of malice. "Thank you my friend. Yes, today I am suffering a little it is true, but I can assure you that my heart is truly in this venture and I know that there is more than my welfare at stake. There are the wildcat kittens, there is the glen and the entire estate, there are all those who depend on the success of the estate and its continued future, and of course, there are the people in the surrounding towns and villages. Do you really think I'm so self-centred that I hadn't thought of all that? And then there are the riches that we cannot count or value." He stood as Hamish pushed the angered man back on to a stool, and in the background Joe's face lit up with a curious smile as he realised that the spirit of G was well and truly awoken within Sol. The more he spoke, then the more Joe knew that G's choice was correct, however much everyone else had at one time or another questioned it.

"There are the trees and flowers, some rare and special, still others common but without which the land would be poorer and less diverse and colourful. There are even the jewels of the mosses and ferns – have you seen the way they look in the early morning sunshine when the dew hangs from them in bulbous drops, flawlessly formed, and the sunlight breaks the horizon? No? They sparkle better than any diamond and are more perfect - without any fault.

And then, there are the spider webs designed to capture insect life but which take on the mist of the mornings as if sprayed with precious stones, and even the mist itself that hangs like a living, churning shroud in the glen early of a morning. It's beautiful. Have you seen it?" He stared straight at the man piercingly as he paced towards him, but the man had nowhere left to look. He listened and he heard and he saw the heart of Sol, bared and exposed, and he too knew that something had happened to this city man of the past. Madness had brought him here but only death could take someone like this away.

"Then you look up and there you see the mountains. Proud and majestic, towering above and making this land what it is, and protecting it from the invasion of commerce and technology. Today they are purple and through the winter they will be burnt brown by the scourge of the wind and the rain, and later they will be white as the snows cap them. But even then they are beautiful, if deadly. They give succour to the sheep and a home to our deer, honey to our bellies and they are all to the larks and the pipits. Without them the ptarmigan would have nowhere to cluck, stamp and breed, the harrier would be extinct and the short-eared owl would be gone. But without them we would also be a flat land and uninteresting, our more productive fields would be prairies, sprayed to a monoculture where the insects fear to roam, devoid of diversity and without our songbirds and the migrants that come here for the summer or for the winter. Everything we recognise as special to here would have gone, and they have nowhere else to belong. And that includes you and now it includes me."

It was if some poet of the past, a mage, was orating an ancient story of the aural tradition. Hypnotised, the bawdy crowd silenced and pressed in to hear what the man enacted, gesturing with his hands and imploring to the seated fool before him. Here was passion and here was rawness that none suspected the city man, a man now dead but very much alive, to be capable of.

At that moment everyone saw the similarity between all the peoples there of every diverse extreme as one, and everyone in that room with only the simple goal, the estate, the wildlife, the people.

"And then there is the river. She gurgles and runs all the time, but brings life of her own. In the water, along the water, up the water and down, until she splashes into that great loch that so quickly becomes the mighty sea. There are the fish that visit the lake, migrants from afar. Like me, some have chosen to stay where they now share the upper loch with Joe. Others will descend back down to the bigger sea, but that's not me. They come for the peaty pureness of the water and its insect food. Some internal compass and a desire to be part of it drew them there. I too have that urge. I have been drawn in here, and here I will stay.

True, I bought this estate with little knowledge of what I had done. I thought I had everything back in my London life and that remains enough for some people. But when I left it, I found myself and saw the emptiness of what I had before. That life was a false me.

I have done some questionable things in life. I will have to pay for some of those actions one day as all events have a consequence of some kind. But I will make sure that this estate is safe and the wildlife protected and the people looked out for.

And then, there is the loch and the birds she draws in too. Every day there is a different emotion painted in the colour and shape of her water. One day she is bright, inviting and blue, on others she is chopped up and squalled, and the *Blue Men* challenge anyone to come in to join them. She can take life like that and yet she is productive and gives us fish. The birds feed in her and nest by her and some come to enjoy her shelter year round or just for a season. And the sound she makes? Sometimes a gentle lap that rocks me to sleep through the open window, and yet she can be a crashing storm throwing her weight at the rocks and flinging the broken seaweed up the shore. She shapes the land.

My friend Pete has captured much of that in his images, something I cannot do. I can only play this viol...   ...this fiddle. No one is more heart-broken about the death of the wildcat than me. I want nothing more than the man who did it found and look forward to the day I get to meet him face to face. I am not sure how best to raise two wildcat kittens and there is little help available from zoos who don't want them because they are wild and are not bred in captivity, nor the rescue centres that can't afford to keep two more motherless kittens. But I *will* do it. Not because I must, because anyone can be forced to do something against their will. No, I do it because I can and most importantly because I want to.

This way of life, this estate and the wild things we enjoy are under threat. There *is* the threat of extinction as we run out of money and fade away back into poverty. Everything will be sold or else will be left to ruin. There is also the threat of development that will homogenise everything we enjoy into the way of living as it seems to be everywhere else. That is just as unattractive as the first extreme.

I can only propose one thing. We have to merge the two together, keeping the old way safe where we can and losing what we do not need. This is the only way the estate will survive. It's like my fiddle. It is a beautiful thing and if played properly it can sound amazing. But it itself isn't worth much preserved in a case in a museum or kept hidden away in someone's home. To be beautiful it needs to be heard. It needs to be a fiddle.

As someone once told me, a fiddle is just wood and glue. I think we here have the wood, we just need to attract in some glue to keep it all together.

But I promise you this, I am not going anywhere but home tonight and that is where I intend to stay for as long as I can."

Sol stopped, turned and sat back down on his stool where his violin sat and waited patiently for him. It might just have been wood and glue, but it was *his* wood and glue. He was unaware of anything other than the expression of his soul and how he felt. He was tired and felt the fatigue of responsibility with no clear idea of how to win the battle that he had started, the combat for the estate. But he knew that he could not afford to lose it.

The little man, the one who had challenged Sol earlier, clambered and staggered over towards Sol where he stood swaying slightly as if some unseen wind was making it difficult for him to stand. His breathing was heavy and fumed with the scent of beer.

"Do you mean it?"

"What?"

"What you just said?"

"Yes."

"Then if I can...   ...I for one will help you. I'll find your photographer for you and I'll bring him to your door. That'll be the day I find out what kind of man you really are."

Sol watched the man as he slowly left the room following a confused course and became one with the silent crowd of onlookers beyond, merging fluidly into their heaving mass and then exiting into the warmth of the outside air.

"He's called John Roberts," said Hamish. "He's a good man and he'll find your man if he can. You watch and see if he doesn't."

Sol sighed loudly. He had no idea how he was going to do it but he knew he had a limited time frame within which to work – April loomed closer than ever in the fore of his mind and his brain was washed with that thought such that he could not focus on much else. The concert never really took off that night. Sol wanted to be

elsewhere with the cats, the river or the mountains, watching and hoping, not because of apathy but in search of inspiration from the very thing he wanted to save. He returned to the *Bothan* and found that the dominant kitten was climbing a branch in the cage and that the other slept out on the shelf, curled up but with a tail that twitched as if to suggest it was never quite relaxed.
Sol was happiest when he knew they were safe.

The summer passed through to the beginning of autumn and the flowers melted into the ground and the green became more of a brown, joining even the colour of the sand particles as their pigments were reabsorbed back into nature. The mornings grew steadily longer in coming and whatever sun there was found it had less time to heat the Earth each subsequent twenty-four hours such that every day's break was incrementally colder than the last.
Flowers passed through in series, breaking and then fading into decay ready to be replaced by the next most promising bloom, until eventually frost etchings were the final flower of the season.
The broadleaf trees felt it most and allowed their canopies to turn russet and then a rich citrus orange to paint the landscape in the rich tapestry of the deciduous, surrounded and dotted by their viridian coniferous cousins who held their leaves, pin-cushioned, even though their shade did darken just slightly. The martins, swallows and swifts who had gathered on the roof tops were gone one morning and their absence, although not easy to pinpoint in time, was obvious as their screaming frenzies ended and they instead chased insects on the way to Africa, some for the first time and yet more for the last. Urges primal had welled up inside of them, heated by the passion of hormone, and they had succumbed to the desire to travel and to find wintering habits elsewhere.
Geese and waders started to descend from the high arctic as the winter took its grip following the shift in the Earth's axis as it tilted north away from our sun in its annual orbital wobble, like the astral spinning top it really was. Suddenly the glen was awash with birds,

gabbling their accounts of their luscious summer breeding grounds in accents unrecognisable at first to Sol as he took in their tens of thousands.

The feeders, filled every day, swarmed with flocking life as if the food in the wood was running out and only Sol could sustain the songbirds and their lust for survival.

Each morning he looked for the big white whooper swans in the glen, but they did not come.

Each morning he would feed the growing kittens, clean them out and check their behaviour. He could by now sit inside the cage and they would brush up against him and talk to him about their own desires to leave the pen, to do more than walk about and climb and to eat food that had been put there on a plate. Sol started playing games with them, attaching pieces of meat to strings for them to chase and kill, and only when defended, in the thick-padded protection of a pair of red welding gloves he had found in another one of the sheds, he used his fingers as bait for them to foil.

Pete's studio was finished and open for business and a steady chain of visitors had started to arrive to learn about the wildlife, take photographs and use the facilities. Money had begun to come into Old Town as the accommodation was finished and readers of the blog and seekers of the wild started to respond to the pictures that were published on the new trust's sight. The locals were benefiting directly and Sol was pleased for them.

Al had come up trumps too and as promised had spent time talking to the producers of food in the area. Lamb, venison, beef, chicken, goose, duck, fresh and smoked fish, they were all being supplied to his distant restaurants and a gastro-pub he had opened in New Town. He himself rarely visited Sol or Old Town. It was not his scene and the place afforded few of the luxuries he enjoyed. But in New Town he now had the coffee, accommodation and what he described as the proper food he expected. He was always away on business and expected his rare appearances to attract both Pete and

Sol at an instant's notice. The farmers and producers were also beginning to benefit directly and Sol was pleased for them too.

Pete photographed Sol in the sweaters and the tweed suit produced by the knitters on the looms in the shed by the black pool that now rattled like a continuous train track between the hours of nine and five most days. The pictures were trendily posed and Gerry was brought in to model the ladies' equivalent. Stylish and retro, well taken and knowledgeably marketed through the right sort of website and magazines, sales of jumpers picked up and the orders for suits and jackets grew in length. The shepherds and the knitters had now begun to benefit too and again Sol was pleased.

Nevin's yard also featured in Pete's work and began to receive orders and he had set up a gallery at the back of the workshop where any visiting customer could see and purchase works by local artists including his very own Gerry. Sol saw little of them now as Nevin had completed the roofing work on the Boat House, Gerry had moved out, and the two spent much of their time together. She still tended his garden and delivered him food, but Sol appreciated that she was busy painting and drawing, collecting and hunting. Nevin, Gerry and others were all benefitting as well, and suddenly, although everyone was still in real terms poor, in local terms they were above the poverty line and had money in their pockets, and Sol was pleased.

The only part of the enterprise not to benefit as yet was the estate itself. Sol judged he had enough of his diminishing capital left to fund the operation until at least April, but if he should fail in the court case then he would have less than nothing. Even the free food the locals provided would not be enough to maintain him if the estate fell into debt because of him, and still the share prices dropped in line with the world's financial turmoil as if to taunt him further.

He stood by the kitten cage door with a head full of worry.

The occupants both stared up at him expectantly when he felt the sudden urge to let them go. The first snows were forecast to arrive in the next few days as storms hit from the west, and he knew they needed to get used to life in the wild if they were ever to survive on their own.

He had named one Quicksilver for the colour that ran through her mane and the fluidity of her movement that reminded him of the motion of the mercury they illegally played with in science when they purposefully broke the thermometers. They had flicked the blobs of liquid metal around the desks until they merged or split, which Sol felt described well the way that this Quicksilver could fuse with the shadows or break up her image when she wanted to, becoming just an extension of the background gloom.

The other was larger and fiercer, always ready for the fight, and so Sol presumed that it was a male. With teeth armed and quick to be used this forceful animal would defend any morsel of food and was always the first to condemn a moth or chase a toy to the death. He had received the name Felix because he was sly and surprising, and the name somehow suited his personality.

Sol stepped to the cage door and the two flitted backwards to the rear of the shed as they normally did. Felix thrashed and spat, Quicksilver purred but flowed away into the darkness.

Unbolted and unlatched Sol pushed the door in on its repellent hinges, against the power of the too-tight spring, and he blocked the door open with a piece of wood from the yard.

Felix studied this new action with mistrust and climbed the highest suspended log to get a better view of the outer world without caging to hold it out or hold him in. He lay on the wood and flexed his claws, in and out, scratching. His tail dangled low and swished in every direction at its very tip and his ears listened to see what would happen next.

Quicksilver was invisible.

Sol walked slowly in, 'mewing', and removed the bowls and the water and placed them in the centre of the yard where he used to feed their mother. Next he went to the kitchen and collected the carcass of a rabbit that he cut up and placed in the bowl, before he retreated to the porch to sit and watch.

Every parent fears the leaving of their child, its eventual '*growing up*' and moving out of the family home. It may be a natural part of life as a human, but it does not make it any easier for the caring parent. Sol felt a strange pang of this emotion as Felix's nose cornered the wooden frame of the shed door and sniffed.

'Well,' he whispered in the hope that the wildcat mother could hear him, "this is it. I hope that you're pleased for them." And, Felix, belly to the floor and head outstretched, as alert as ever, but excited and fast, left the shed, walled along the edge of the yard and was gone into the shade of the fall coloured trees.

Quicksilver followed shortly after, but remained in the doorway long enough to stop and consider Sol first before she found the grasses in the wood and became one with the shadows underneath.

Whatever the future held for them, they were both free now and Sol could do little to protect or harness them. They were no longer his captive wild cats. For the second time in their lives, they were true wild cats.

Chapter 23: The Future of Hope

(Gnossienne No 4 & 5, Erik Satie)

All loss needs closure and in his mind's reflection of the kittens' leaving moment Sol saw a closure on his relationship with the wildcats; a final reckoning that gave them release. He would feed them until they needed him no more but then they would be gone, having left his care to be out there and 'free' for as long as the environment would allow them, but no longer his. There was a sense of imminent completion and success, if tinged with a deep fear of loneliness in the light of him losing these two obsessions in his life, and he watched where their shadows had left him to become one with the woodland's shade for longer than he thought he would.

Sleep brought with it eccentric imaginings of the cats in that sorting process that dreams must be, where he ordered his thoughts and the experiences of the day into what his brain could process and use later in life or discard, unless pulled forward in a request from his central data banks.

He was in one moment allowing Quicksilver and Felix out of the cage door at the *Bothan,* and the next up on the headland by the mother cat's barrow, now grown over and all but lost. G was sat there pondering the sea in his faceless way and his stag stood by him ever defendant and present. It was funny how the loss of facial feature made initial contact and communication so very difficult between them, but once they began to speak how little it then mattered.

The spirit mother cat was waiting for Sol up there and allowed him to scratch her behind the ear in greeting as she purred and mewed. She was pleased with what he had done and had chosen to wait here for him by the standing stone.

Sol sat down by G and they both watched the passage of birds coming in from their migrant journeys finding an end to their travels and safety within the estate as the two men had provided in their time. The wildcat nestled down by his side and curled up, ever sentry and tiger-alert despite the first appearance of calm and sleep. "Just remember," said G. "None of us needs much, not to really live. But if we really live we gain so much more. The difficulty is knowing how to live and understanding how little it costs."
Sol recalled little else on returning to the world of wakening.

Checking the sheds in the morning Sol found the kittens still gone but their food had been eaten from the yard, and so he replenished it knowing he could just be feeding the foxes and supplementing their diets as much as his intended. But he had hope and there was little evidence of the musk that the foxes would have behind.
Staff in hand and shoulder bag loaded he walked broadly that day, visiting the grave and adding a stone to his cairn on the mountain top where the snows had left a shallow covering. He descended by a different path, taking in the whole ridge, and there he sat to watch the hares, turning their blue-white for the winter, and the patchy coloured ptarmigans who were once again undecided whether to be brown or white and instead wore an ungainly mix of the two outfits.
He then walked into Gerry's valley to see the completed roof and to cadge a cup of coffee. She was away and Nevin was at the boat yard and so he used the kitchen, boiled water, drank a brew, washed up and left a note. Tempted to break the golden rule of looking in on the picture she was painting for him in the studio at the back Sol came across a scribbled sign on the door that made him laugh out loud.
'Dear Sol,
If you are reading this note then you are already where you should not be.
Do not enter.

Love Gerry'
She knew him so much better than he thought.
Taking the steep route up and over the headland he found his way into the next glen and in front of the little chapel on the shore. It was little different, hardly changed from his last time here. Even the Jackdaws still picked at the moss on the roof and eked out the grubs amongst the soil accumulations that cemented the slates together. The sea may have ebbed away as the tides dictated leaving the crystal beach of shell-ground sand and the chapel stranded well above its current flow, but otherwise the picture was as he remembered.
He entered the building for a few minutes of solace thinking through the wise words of Joe, that the contemporary human had forgotten the spiritual pre-modernity that gave us all sustenance in some way and that a reconnection with this did not require religion, even if for some it helped. He had not been in there since his first visit in May.
Inside little had altered. It still felt clean and cool, but someone had changed the flowers on the altar cloth. There was still that sense of calm in the building and the mustiness of recently burnt candle wax suspended in air that held clarity in its coolness and age in its humidity.
Not a naturally prayerful man he felt more connected this time around and wondered which of the gods, or even God, was in fact in control of his destiny and which he had or could connect with. The building felt static and unchanging, a rock upon which he could anchor his thoughts in the same way as the standing stone on the headland above and the disturbing stone circle behind. He understood the need for something, even if it were just a link between him and the Earth itself.
He closed his eyes and attempted to find unity with something, anything, hearing the '*crack*' of the jackdaws and crows outside and the '*chisick*' of the wagtails on the shore. The sparrows '*chipped*' and '*cheeped*' in their buoyant flock as they picked

through the gable and argued about their precious finds. There was the lap of the water on the shifting coral of sands and the solidity of the ground below it all through which he could feel the shudder of the waves as they collided with the headland. There was so much more to the world than the simple present and his own mind, his thoughts and his problems, and he felt supported and understood, humble and strong, nothing but something. It was a strange paradox and a sensation of faith in something he could not put his finger on. An innate spiritual need and yearning churned inside of him forming thoughts and questions.

How am I going to stop the estate from folding?

How am I going to win the case?

No amount of money is going to pay for it and keep it together, is it?

The bible was left open, the marked pages different to what he had seen there before, and so drawn to words as usual, with a need to read anything printed, he stood, found himself by the lectern and read.

'*Fear ye not.*'

Oh the irony of reading that as the opening sentence. Fear did not come close to the anxiety he now felt.

'*...sparrows...*'

Sol looked up to where he could hear the incessant noise of the sparrows made above him. Through his focus on them, they were the only sound now that could be heard. *What did the sparrows have to do with anything?*

'*...ye are of more worth...*'

There was that word '*worth*' again, that flexible term that gave value to all things. He was soon to be worth very little if commerce and law took their natural courses.

He left perplexed at why someone had left that passage for him to read, if intended for him at all, and he returned home via the headland following the river down to the shore from which he gained the cottage. He needed to play the violin and work though in his mind a route out of the financial mess the future seemed to hold.

Nothing was clear and once again he considered the natural messages the planet offered to him. The spider that built and rebuilt its wiry web until it was complete and perfect for the abyssal space it spanned. The draw that kept the migrating birds leaving and returning to find succour and mates at the appropriate times. Even the faith of the bees that swarmed and followed their newly-hatched queen. They all found ways despite the worst attempts of humans to stop them.

The cats were still absent for the rest of that day which Sol took to be a good sign.

He sauntered amongst the geese for a while listening to their continual '*gandering*' and then went back to the front room of the *Bothan* to work on his symphony score, recording the approach of winter in musical notes that he felt described best the wealth of wildlife but the lingering frosts and the advance of the storm fronts. In those notes was the loitering mystery of the evergreen and the woodland understory where the deep viridians of yew, holly and the pagan-celebrated ivy remained as emerging denizens, which of the forest alone kept green and seasonally unaffected. Instead they were revealed in the same way that rubbing off the silver coating from a scratch card leaves a startlingly different image as their deciduous overlords fell back to their bare-leafed autumnal skeletons.

He picked up his violin, tucking it fluidly under his chin, and rested the bow smoothly on the strings, and with tight shut eyes he thought of the skeins of geese and the exhilaration of their arrival as they flew in from the sea and saw their journey's end in his little cliff-shrouded valley. Their final flight line was here, down and between the pillars of static rock, those which defined the open waters as bounded from the loch, where the waves had the power of their distant fetch taken from them, standing like the gate posts of an ancient castle hewn from the land itself.

They would pass the central stack where the seabirds milled and toiled, skimming lower as they sensed the anticipation of rested wings and good feeding in the protected shallows and out in the ending crops of the drying machair and grasses. And then, with feet spread wide, they would end their descent and skid down into the water forcing breasts forward and necks back to stall their progress and find their winter's target.

They would have re-made the *Glen of Faobhar* and be welcomed back into its glad company yet another time.

Sol held that thought, felt that undertaking and struck his first chord across the strings, picking up the melody of flight and final assembled joy as a new movement wrote itself in his mind and was played out aloud to be later translated into the hand writing of the manuscript. A week of composer's block was over, the months of wildcat obsession was passed, and now he was a re-focused man with a mission to finish this symphony and to explore how to save this estate before the hearing in April.

Laying his violin gently, tenderly, on the piano top, he started to daub the notes on to the parallel lines printed on the manuscript paper on the piano's music stand. His pencil snapped with an audible crack and he cursed his speed and the pressure he was exerting on the soft lead where the layers of elemental carbon were forced into alignment and then gave. He went over the room to retrieve the sharpener from the dining room table. There in the middle, island-stranded, he found the scrubby white enveloped letter with the handwritten address on the front, delivered weeks before. He had presumed it would be more bad news and had left it here unopened, a momentary fear arising as he thumbed it all over for clue of what might lay within.

Ripping open the seal he removed the square card from inside and tossed the envelope into the fire where it was welcomed and engulfed, uncurling as the heat seared and then caught it.

There was a drawing of a farmhouse on the front. It was quaint and rustic in construction, made of irregular stone walling that sat neatly under a slated roof, with regular windows and a two-pieced wooden barn-type door. It was symmetric enough to have been raised from children's bricks. The byre on the side had a blackface sheep's head poking out from the darkness inside and a large red antiquarian tractor hid the barns he knew would be beyond.

The picture took him back to his grandfather's days and he knew before he had opened the card that it was from his brother, the remaining shepherd out on the farm, who like the prodigal son's brother had kept his inheritance to work the fields whilst Sol had sold up and left for the bright lights of the city. From a young age he had been enticed to leave, following the others who swarmed like the moths in the dark to the lantern or the window chasing their false hopes of a counterfeit navigational aid; they hadn't found a far off moon to anchor their movements by, but instead had been taken in by something far inferior that would lead them astray and possible kill them in the end.

The writing was clumsy and untidy, and Sol was aware that to write any word was a challenge for someone who throughout school had struggled with the demands of the curriculum through no fault of his own. He cursed the expectations of qualifications and a tear came to his eyes as he thought of how he had treated this boy, and his needs, before he had left and they eventually split ties.

No examination had ever helped this man even though it had handed financial benefit after benefit to Sol on a plate. *But who was the greater as a result? Who lived the most satisfied life until now? Who knew the strength of resilience and independence?*
He looked down with a sense of shame and read the carefully crafted words inside.

'Dear Jake,
Wishing you luck in your new home. I hope you are happy there. If I can help, I will. The farm is going well and you would be proud of

your nephew and niece. Family send their love and Angie wants us to make up.
Sorry for being slow at writing. I never would have been fast would I?
Can we visit you as we have never been to Scotland?
Martin'
There was a ten-pound note secured to the back of the card with a paperclip and a postscript that went with it.
'PS. It is not much, but the money is to buy a house warming gift for your new place. We hope it's nicer than London.'
Sol stood still, rocking uncomfortably on the balls of his feet as he re-read the card. Then he placed it on the mantelpiece above the crackling fire, ashamed that it had taken him so long to open and appreciate what had been within that simple white envelope. It is amazing that one envelope can change a life in such different ways simply depending on its contents. A bill or bad news can reduce us to tears, an announcement or money send us into reels of joy, and still more affective is the handwritten letter giving news and views and a variety of crafted emotions.
A *'quanking'* noise brought him around to himself, and then there was the whistling hoop of large wing downdrafts through the wind, and Sol rushed to the front window to see the long sleek-necked saintly forms of the Whooper Swans returning to the shore.
'The peace of the swans' he thought and chuckled before sitting down to write a letter in return to his brother with an invitation for him and his family to visit when they could so long as they were prepared to rough it. Moved to make peace with others, he then phoned Sue, unsure as to how she would receive his first call to her in several months. Today, he decided, was a day to make friends and to break down boundaries. After all, he had been freely offered the peace of the swans for yet another year and it seemed only right that he should pass it on.

Winter came quickly to the glen with snow falling with increasing depth and deadening the sounds of the wild so that all calls were muffled and the end of the red deer's rut became less of a bellowing match and more a muted outcry that no longer echoed amongst the trees. The concentrated sounds of the birds on the loch were instead reverberated to an extreme between them and could be heard from the high end of the valley as they passed through the increased clarity of the air with greater ease as so little remained in it to interfere even with sound.

With snow came a new pursuit and the tracking of the wild where footprints gave Sol traceable indications as to who had passed and when. The fox had pounced here and the weasel scurried there, and the tunnels of rodents, that now hid them from aerial predation, were easily discovered in the ditches and where the drifts swept and were stacked most. He knew that one of the cats was also around the yard at times as they left their marks and scratches, and were obviously exploring the sheds when they were left open. He kept the doors ajar so that they always had access.

The *Bothan* was far from lonely and visitors came regularly through November to make sure that he was provided with food and was coping with the cold. Sally delivered wood and the cat shed was returned to its original function in an attempt to dry the timber fast enough to burn and she taught Sol to sharpen a saw, to cut wood efficiently and to '*man up*', as she kept telling him, when the blisters hurt most. The ladies visited from across the loch bringing fish, eggs, chicken and beef to store in the coldest shed. They were thankful that Sol had secured a market for their rare breed produce and were planning to increase the scale of their salmon production in the New Year, and wanted his opinion in the form of a consultant. He refused to accept payment. In return they unfroze his water supply and showed him why it was important to empty the header tank and to remove the dead leaves and rotting accumulations that gathered there at least every so often. If he wouldn't take money then he would take their advice and together they would keep him healthy.

It seemed that money was a million miles away during this time and that it could not affect *Bothan Faobhar* when Sol took in the beauty of what he had and whom he shared it with. The sun still came up, although later every morning, and fell, sooner each night, and the wild things came back to the feeders and something took the meat he left out for the wildcats. The symphony slowly headed towards completion and he still played exerts of it at the Thursday meetings where the locals still discussed the goings on of Old Town and the estate. But by December the curse of finance hung over Sol like the sword of Damocles, ever present and increasingly dangerous.

He sat by the bucket in the yard, haw-frost clinging to the deadened plants that lined the denuded wood, with the sound of the woodpecker drilling a stump at a distance, and the geese, ducks and swans warbling and gaggling behind. He added another piece of venison to the pile he had made, in case of the cats' return, and then sat back in his white plastic chair, huddled up in layers of woollen clothing and thick gloves.

He had thought it too cold to sleep that afternoon, but fell away anyway into a listless dream of worries, gently softened by the calls and sounds of nature.

Snow makes a particular sound when stepped on. It crunches and compresses, but stifles its own noise so that a step into deep snow is easily heard and recognised once experienced, however carefully the move is performed.

Scrunch.

He tried not to smile as he brought himself back into wakening, not wanting to move despite the desire to stretch out of sleep and welcome oxygen deep into his tissues.

Scrunch.

Sol opened his yes, slit-fashion; the comedy spy pose from childish slapstick movies.

Scrunch.

There was Quicksilver, larger than before and fluffed up in full grey winter coat in readiness for what would be a much colder season yet when January arrived. She was beautifully striped like her mother had been before her stalking the bucket and the remains of the deer he had put there. She had sleekness about her, a gloss to each agouti hair that allowed the wind to rustle them individually so that they reflected and refracted the bright winter light, touched by cold sky blue. Her fur shimmered in waves with every movement that progressed and expanded with the breeze forming field patterns the way the wind does in a drying crop at the beginning of its harvest season.

Scrunch.

He laughed inwardly to see her.

In good condition she was obviously faring well in the wild and even though he had been supplementing her food in the yard, she was obviously hunting for herself too. Feeling clever, he had thought she was unaware of his presence. But she turned to take up his watch, '*mewed*', hissed and then walked on to the bucket and fed, disdainful of the human; truly cat-like. She had only deigned to let him see her and he felt that humility one should if they ever assumed an animal less intelligent than it actually was.

Sol found his phone deep in his pocket and unhurriedly took three photographs that he sent on to Pete.

'*Pete,*

Blog these please. She's back! Quicksilver has returned!

Sol'

Like an old friend seen in the distance and instantly recognised, Quicksilver spurred Sol's heart and picked up his mood as if a malaise was withdrawn from his weary soul. If she was okay then there was every possibility that Felix, the stronger of the two as a kitten, was too. She ate well in his company and took her time licking her paws clean and wiping over her ears before she sauntered away in that aloof way that the feline justly do. And then, as speed picked up and the urge to run took over, she leapt and bounded the last run to the trees and was gone.

A shadow cat again.

And then just a shadow, one of many that hassled the underwood.

A text arrived almost immediately.

'*Sol,*

You lucky bugger. Is she still with you? I can get down in twenty.

Pete'

Sol replied with a grin spread widely across his tight lips.

'*Twenty minutes too late then,*' he replied. '*She's gone. But she'll be back through the winter I'm sure. I think I could cry.*

Sol.'

Quicksilver visited most days but although Sol found the footprints of a larger cat he never caught sight of Felix. The photographs that Sol had taken caused a stir when they went up on the blog and website, and they were added to by Pete who braved the drive to get pictures even though the depth and smoothening of the scene by the snow made it difficult and dangerous at times. Hazards are often only what we perceive them to be and fear is the real enemy, along with unpreparedness and too great a confidence in our own abilities and immortality.

Until then, the foil at the gate had worked, and Sol found himself in blissful isolation - just him and the wild things with which he shared his valley. He had bought presents for those whom he was closest to, and come early December he had sent small gifts off to his brother, his wife and children, to Al and to Sue. None of them was expensive but he had tried to select things that would mean something about *Bothan Faobhar* making a resolution for the New Year – one that his brother should visit.

He walked the drive, which had cleared enough to trudge along, took Addie to New Town and mailed the gifts at the post office. He then visited Al's gastro-pub for a rare '*quality*' coffee, which he was given '*on the house*' as usual, with the compliments of Al who too had left a Christmas present for Sol in his absence. The label told him he could open it when he liked.

Sol sat in a sumptuous tanned-black leather-cushioned chair built into the alcove of a bay window. The business was doing well and he was pleased for Al who had an eye for such opportunities. No diner recognised him, but a number were talking about wildcats and bird life and were there because of him. He even heard his own name more than once. It was what could be described as hiding in full view. Before that first text not one of these people would have known about the estate, the area or the wildlife, and the pub that he was sat in would not have been re-designed and thriving the way it was. It had still been there, all of it, just not for them, and they were instantly recognisable by their foreignness of dress, of accent, of language and of general blueprint.

Sol did not really consider this as he processed his usual order, although those in the know did.

A large black off road vehicle passed slowly along the main street. Sol's eye was drawn to it not only because of its brand, shape and colour, but because it still had a damaged front bumper where the plastic had once impacted with something. The windows were reflective and dark, but as it passed by, the driver's window glass dropped with the silkiness of electric control and Sol found that he was looking directly into the hard cut face of Arthur Peterson, man, photographer, and murderer.

Blood boiled somewhere deep within Sol, and a tension raged inside that made his ears ring and somehow his sight fade slightly so that he had to blink to bring himself back round to full focus and return the colour to what he saw.

"Are you okay?" asked a young waitress seeing the strange scruffy man in the window swoon. He was very different to the rest of the diners. He only ever had coffee, always used the same seat when he came appearing from nowhere, and he was always treated to free service and waited on as if he were someone important.

"Yes," he replied recovering and looking up at her momentarily so as to make sure he acknowledge her even though he felt the pressure thudding with his heart beat within his ears. "Thank you."

She loitered for a moment and then pried further. "Who are you?"

"Now that would be telling." Sol looked back to the window but the vehicle had gone. *Had madness caught up with him? And the car, was it real or just a vision?* Scan as he might, there was nothing on the road but a gull that had landed to inspect something driven over and tyre-trod into the cracks of the patchwork tarmac.

"It's just that you're always treated so very well when you come here. Are you a celebrity in hiding? I won't tell anyone if you are. I'd lose my job if I did."

The waitress fiddled in her pocket and brought out a pen and a small pad.

"I tell you what," she said. "You could write it down for me… …who you are I mean…   …and then you wouldn't have had to tell me. It'd be our secret."

"You want my autograph?" Sol laughed. "Young lady you *are* forward." He looked back at the road with a desire to be in two places, here in the warmth of a pub with conversation for a few minutes and a good steaming brew, or out there on the road trying to determine if that was *him*, that man, in the car.

She apologised.

"No need to say sorry," he grinned. "I'm nobody of significance except to the people to whom I'm important, just like any man. I have to eat and drink and use the toilet, just like any man. I have my moments and most of my life is fairly mundane, just like any man."

"But," she muttered. "If you're just an ordinary man, then why do you get free coffee and the window seat every time you appear and whenever you appear?"

Sol looked out of the window again scanning for *that* car. He was glad of the girl's interest, as it had distracted him and calmed him. *He was just an ordinary man and always would be. He had once confused himself with being someone greater. But that had just been the illusion of money and false power, and that was all. Soon that would be a year ago and he felt almost forgotten by a majority with whom he shared that past life and called friends.*
A short stocky man ran into the car park from the road. He was sweating and looked agitated with his collars turned up and his coat worn tight to keep in the warmth that was checked at his neck by a thick woollen muffler. It was John Roberts, the man from the inn at Old Town who had challenged Sol's motivation. Seeing Sol in the window seat, he waved and then came into the pub, first having a short altercation with the maître de on the door before pushing through the tables and diners to join Sol on the seat.
"Will he be having coffee too?" asked the waitress considering the commotion created by John's entrance.
"No," said John between breaths. "Not time. Thank you." He turned to Sol. "Sol."
"Sol? Jake Solomon?" asked the woman.
"Yes," he smiled. "I hope that's okay?"
"The reclusive laird of *Bothan Faobhar*?"
"This is him, yes," explained John. "Most people recognise him only with his clothes off from a photograph on the web. The famous '*bottom of Sol*'? But, yes this is him."
"Pleased to meet you, Sol," she whispered.
"And you," he replied smiling thinly his subterfuge ruined.
"Sol," John spoke with urgency. "He's in the town...   ...the photographer. I knew I'd find you here as my spies are out. There always out. The locals. But that man. He's back."
Sol nodded.
"Who *is* back?" asked the waitress.
"It's not really your business," said John.

"The man who killed my wildcat," Sol answered with growing malice. "I suppose he thinks we've forgotten or something similar, or dropped our guard."
They left soon afterwards.

Peterson had been observed driving through both New Town and Old Town, obviously looking for a place to stay. He had been surprised to find that all accommodation was taken and disappointed that he was going to have to rough it in his waggon for the night. Frustrated, he now drove the short snowy road over the hill to Sol's drive where he knew the entrance lay on the left just above the shore line of a pebble beach.

Turning off onto the drive he followed the well-marked runnels of tyre marks which then cut off up the hill to the garage and beyond to the crossroads that split off at the top of the bealach on the moor to allow communication between the different dwellings on the estate. But now there was a gate in front of him that he did not remember, and yet it looked old and had an inherent age about the wood and metal it was constructed of, with wired fences running off and upwards into the wood on either side.

Curious, he stepped down from the cab and went to investigate as his vehicle continued to tick over, burning precious fuel and releasing its excessively conditioned and warmed air into the snow scape around through the open door. The gate was chained shut with a large padlock on it, and there was sign that suggested the track led to nothing more than an old forestry plantation. There were no wheel ruts or tyre tracks along the road ahead, just virgin snow slightly melted in places and blue where ice had thawed and refrozen. He was confused, as the lie of the valley was exactly how he remembered it with venerable pine trees extending up the hills both left and right, smothering the landscape with a blanket of dark frost-silver green.

A raven chuckled ominously from what looked like a well-rooted post's top and its eerie sound echoed through the plantation and back to Peterson.

He could turn back?

So often the drive for something we want takes us further along a route than we intend to travel. We go to that place beyond reason where the acceptable is surpassed and a madness that only the human can suffer makes us, even the most ordinary of people, willingly do the unforgiveable or indescribable.

Peterson placed his hand on the chain and tugged. It fell away and he saw through the disguise and the foil of the gate and the fence and the unused drive. As he pushed the access open he recalled the scene and the cat in the dark, a chase and capture of a kitten and the cornering of a mother in the lights of his waggon. He now even saw the tracks of humans walking along the side of the road, not something usually observed on an abandoned forestry track that led to nowhere. The footsteps had quickly left the drive and headed to a well beaten path a few feet into the canopy shade where they would be difficult to spot from the gateway.

Who were they to try and fool him?

The gate flung wide, he returned to the vehicle and drove on to the forbidden lane, making the first tracks in the snow that it had felt for a long time. It greeted him in, and his pride along with it, treating him to that view that can only be attained by trespass as acknowledged by the poet John Clare as he too dared to take the path beyond the forbidden gate in his own time. Somehow now, from the far side of the gate, the glen took on a less foreboding appeal and the light felt bluer, the snow crisper, the trees more gnarled and twisted with their decorations of moss, all lending a sense of the comforting and not the weary.

He stretched out to the seat next to him and retrieved one of his cameras and took a photograph to record his progress. He leant out of the open window far enough to improve his view and assess the prints of animals that relayed information to him about their species, direction, size and behaviour. Despite his blinkered perception of the conservation of wild things he was a knowledgeable and well-informed tracker who in another age would have stared down the barrel of a gun and made a success as a hunter, a gamekeeper or a poacher.

He noticed the footprints' size and saw the tell-tale spread that told him their speed and type. He saw the fur where it had snatched under a branch and the discarded pool of feathers that marked the end of a pigeon where the sparrowhawk had dispatched and plucked it. This was an observant man, a cautious man and an arrogant man, now wrapped up into one obsessed stalker, keen for a second shot of a wildcat.

The car scrunched through the frosted land with him, an oblivious robot inside, not taking in the grandeur of scale of the world around him and into which he trespassed. The loch was missed and the hills beyond, the boiling of a future snowstorm rising up and churning out to sea was a mystery that simply provided backdrop to his photo board story of an animal hunt, as if all detail were lost save the single focused one.

He eventually made the *Bothan*, further than he had ventured before, and switching the engine to dead he parked up, wrapped an extra layer around him and approached the building with caution. He knew the structure well from photographs on Pete's website, the secret location hidden in very plain sight of the millions that had access to it. Like so much, it was something that should never have been aired, but once it was out, electronically or otherwise, it was too late; someone would find it.

Although the chimney smoked, *Bothan Faobhar* felt empty and the vacancy of the house was confirmed when no one came to question the presence of an uninvited vehicle in this car-less idyll. The geese complained, but they soon forgot and returned to their grazing of the algae, and seven whooper swans craned necks to get a better view of the intruder. He picked up two cameras and then after a considered pause took hold of the rifle he kept lying in the back, in case there was trouble. He knew the adage that only those who carry a gun can fire it, but chose to ignore it this time.

He stumbled through the snow, crisply patterned by his well-rutted boots, following a pathway, cut deep with a spade and swept with a twig-built brush, that arced around to the rear of the property to a glass-framed porch, and a yard, and...   ...there it was, a metal bucket on the brushed clear cobbles; *the bucket that had drawn in that first wildcat to the overly-fortunate Sol who had accidentally bought this place, fool that he was!*

Caution to the wind, he crept to the little metal shrine and seeing that it contained bright red meat remains, furred skin of rabbit and the striking whiteness of bone, he stepped back again to where he found a white plastic chair, grey-stained with algae and with lichens attached to its legs. It had been positioned with care in a place that provided a clear view, an unobstructed view and, above all, a photographer's view.

It struck him that there was no cover between the chair and the bucket. No hide to prevent the animals from seeing the observer or to break up their outline. Whoever had placed it there had no knowledge or care of the need for secrecy. Instead they had sat themselves in the most open and exposed place possible where only a wild animal that did not worry would visit and feed.

This was alien to him as he sat on the edge of the chair, feeling its cold hardness bite through his trouser legs. He would wait for a while, taking the opportunity that had arisen. His cameras hung on their lanyards around his neck and his rifle lay loaded but harmless across his lap.

"It takes trust," retorted the surprisingly calm male voice from the side of the *Bothan*. It came from the path cut through the snow by the porch door.

He turned to look across to the sad face of Sol who leant there. He looked old and worn. Primed and ready to run if required, his right hand naturally moved to the trigger of the gun.

"Only an animal that trusts you will feed in the open. Especially if it is as cautious as a wildcat."

Peterson continued to watch Sol who did not flinch nor go to move either towards or away from the stranger sat in his chair, in his yard, in his glen, in his estate. Sol could not have missed the rifle, ready for use within grasp. It was wooden butted and a silenced black-metal barrel ended in a dangerous hole that seemed to slip back down in darkness to the mechanism where Sol knew the bullets lay in wait of their powerful release.

"I saw you wondering why the chair was where it was. Unlike you, I'm not a photographer. I prefer to watch, but on the animals' terms. You want to capture, but on your terms, and you don't ask what the animal wants. You simply want to steal its image. In some cultures photography is still banned as the locals feel each picture takes something of their soul away with it. Did you know that?"

Peterson swallowed. "No," he replied.

"Trust," Sol repeated. "My house is left unlocked and you could have taken anything you wanted from it. I don't have much. Not that *you* would want anyway. But, you see, it's all precious to me. But what is value? My gate, as you have found, is also unlocked and anyone can come in and out of it. But we know you've been before. We found the paint from your car on the trees and the rocks, the tracks from your tyres on the drive and the wildcat mother you..." He too swallowed. "You killed."

"But..."

"I hope your pictures were good?"

The other nodded; wordless and stunned.

"Do you want a cup of tea or coffee?" asked Sol out of the blue.

He looked confused at him, at the very nature of the question and the absurdity of the moment. *Was he offering him a drink?*

"They're drinks. It's what we offer to guests around here. Ah... ...let me guess, you're from the city."

"Coffee," said Peterson.

"Good. I think we could both do with a strong coffee couldn't we? You can sit out there getting cold or leave it until later when the cat will return. She won't be here for a few hours yet. In the meantime, I think we'd better talk. Don't you? You are after all sat in my chair in my garden with a gun, and that's got to be wrong in everybody's book."

Peterson sat and stared. "You're offering me a coffee and a chat?"

"You really aren't from around here are you? You won't need your gun though. You can unload that and leave it just there...   ...if you don't mind? Unless you've come to kill me?"

"No," said Peterson, simply. "I've not come to kill you."

"Then you don't need it."

He un-cocked the rifle and put it by the chair and then followed Sol through the porch into the kitchen. It was dark but pleasantly warm with the wood-fired cooker glowing gently away to itself through its well-soot'd glass-fronted door. He worried about a trap of some kind but went anyway.

"I'm afraid the locals will be after your blood and by now they'll all know you're in the area. Word of mouth travels very quickly in these hills. I don't think we'd better waste any time."

He filled a black metal kettle with brown water from the tap and placed it on the hob top to boil. Then Sol pulled out a chair for Peterson to sit on. "Sorry the water's a funny colour. You get used to it after a while."

He gestured for him to sit.

"Of course, we have met before, but I haven't had the pleasure of a proper introduction. Jake Solomon. But my friends call me Sol," and he extended his hand to Arthur.

"Arthur Peterson."

They shook hands and the intruder sat, cautiously at first before he relaxed.

"Now, to see this cat...   ...she has a name, Quicksilver...   ...and the best way to see her ironically is not to go looking for her. Let her come to you..."

Peterson warmed to Sol rapidly. He had a manner about him that put him at ease, even though he was aware that he had wronged the man terribly, trespassed on his land and killed his pet. He did not understand why Sol should behave the way he did towards him. It didn't make sense and he felt it was more than he actually deserved. They talked for a long time about wildcats. Sol had a lot to say.

Peterson was curious and was about to ask why Sol was doing this, when Sol announced it was time for them to go outside.

Sol placed him in the plastic chair.

"I usually find I see the most if I start to fall asleep. You'll hear her first."

"But where are you going?" he asked.

"To make supper. We are going to have to eat and I am presuming that even city folk still have to do that? They used to when I lived there."

And Sol left the undeserving Peterson in the plastic chair whilst he went to prepare the evening's dinner. He expected a number of guests would arrive now that the killer of his cat was here and so needed to make a good stew large enough that it would feed many mouths.

Hamish was the first on the scene, parking up behind Addie, further blocking Peterson's off road vehicle in so that even if he wanted to escape he would have been unable to. He entered formally by the front door as it had been left ajar as an indication to the most observant.

"Hello," he called and then followed the smell of cooking through to the kitchen. "Where's the bugger? Have you caught him?"

"Sh," Sol held his finger up to his lips. "I've left him in the yard photographing Quicksilver."

"But?"

"Education is better than retribution."

"But he killed..." Hamish trailed off. "You know about the stag don't you?"

Sol nodded before he spoke. "*Bothan Faobhar* has always given second chances hasn't it? I can't forget what he has done, but I can forgive it and hope that one day some good will come of it. He will still need to face up to the responsibility of his past actions. But what happens if his skills can be used on the estate?"

Hamish nodded thoughtfully. The estate had been there before, closer to home than he liked to admit. It had given many second chances which he knew only too well.

"Are you expecting a crowd then?" he asked looking at the peelings and the cuts of meat being sealed in a pan, and the large copper stew pot already bubbling.

"There'll be a few more yet I expect," said Sol from the business of the work surface.

Gerry and Nevin arrived by sea and John Roberts came along with Euan and Pete in another car - yet more crowding of the drive digging up the pristine snow into muddy tracks that melted through to the ground below. Finally a police Land Rover joined the queue of vehicles giving the *Bothan* the appearance of a country off-roader's meet.

Sol held them all in the front room until Peterson came back in, eyes tearful and red, with the strain of a condemned man about them. He looked deeply into Sol's face.

"So she visited then?" Sol asked.

He nodded.

"You've got your photographs?"

Again he nodded.

"You have your memories?"

Another nod.

"Good. We'll discuss the future after some supper. I hope stew is enough for everyone?"

Peterson found himself floating in some nether world he could not understand. He had committed an injustice to all of these gathered people and yet they carried on welcoming him as if nothing had happened. Only the policeman seemed at all aware of his crime, issuing him with a caution, taking address details and informing him that he would be charged in court and given the fine he was due once the case was processed. Then the officer removed his hat, stated that he was off duty for a few minutes and joined the others in eating the stew. It was good, flavoured with the spice conversation.

They all asked to see the pictures and Pete then took Peterson aside to talk about lighting, angles and equipment in the way only a true professional or committed amateur, usually male, can.

He was eventually taken away by the police officer, tailing him to the station in his own car, for further questioning and to make sure a full report of the wildlife crime was completed and lodged.

"So, what are you going to do?" Hamish quizzed afterwards as they sat huddled around the fire. "Is he to get that second chance?"

The embers crackled, spat and fumed from within the sanctity of the hearth.

"It isn't just up to me," Sol replied. "What about the people?"

"You, may I remind you, are the laird. The decision rests with you."

"I know. In the New Year, once the police have brought the charges against him, I'll take it to one of the gigs in Old Town and hold a meeting. I have a plan, but it will require a lot of trust all round. I think we could use a man like that if he can be trusted."

The next day Sol trudged up to see Joe, tramping along the snow-driven river track, to discuss his ideas. A plan for Arthur Peterson, a plan for finance of the estate separate to his own money so that the old company could not claim it for themselves in April, and a plan to sell his violin to keep his private funds going a little longer. The two sat for a while by the upper loch and talked of a future estate and life, and Sol revealed for the first time the depths of his anxieties about its moneys, the work still required to be carried out and the approaching date in April.

"Hope," muttered Joe, pausing to breathe through a chesty cold that rattled in his lungs. "You enjoyed a good full life in the past I presume?"

"Too full, yes," Sol agreed tasting the clarity of the air in an intake of frozen air.

"But that's all it is...   ...or was. It's been and it has gone and it's now in the past and can't be returned to. If we live back there in the past, then where do we go from here? We always see happiness as something we can no longer return to and folks become depressed and anxious and can't enjoy things the way they used to. That it wasn't always happy back then is lost to them, and they've edited out the bits they found hard or challenging – all the unhappiness. It just seemed better back then...   ...rubbish. It will have been just as good as now, they just can't see it. Did you enjoy a happy past?"

"Some of it yes."

"Exactly. Some was good and some was bad. How you choose to remember it? Well that's up to you and your state of mind. Importantly, it wasn't *all* good in the past."

Sol agreed, enjoying as normal the old man's wisdom.

"The present might be good, and too many of us simply live for the now with no thought of the future or responsibility. That Peterson man was like that. He wanted things now, to experience them for himself. Well current happiness will be history by tomorrow and will soon enough join all that stuff in the past. It is gone before you know it and then you want to fill the void with more and better things. Now is full of the anxieties of tomorrow too, cramming in and making vision difficult."

Joe trailed off and stared listlessly over the loch.

"What do you hope for Sol?" he asked.

"To be able to run the estate, conserve the wildlife and help the local people."

"Aren't you already doing that? And without money?"

"Well…"

"You need a focus admittedly – a distant horizon to aim for so that you can steer the good ship *Faobhar* in the right direction. Hope is always in the future with an aim in mind. Without hopes and dreams we are nothing. So happiness always lies in the future and we should look forward to it – not worry about it."

They sat in silence.

"What do you hope for Joe?"

"The return of the water bull," he replied without delay and then he produced a small paper parcel for Sol. "For Christmas," he announced.

"Thank you. But I've not brought your presents up yet," laughed Sol.

"I don't need your presents, your presence is worth far more," Joe chortled. "I won't see you for a while. There are storms afoot and I may go travelling soon."

Sol looked up and sure enough there were clouds gathering on the horizon behind the mountaintop and its curvaceous scree-draped horseshoe now decorated with snow like the icing on a cake.

"Where will you go?"

"Oh, I don't know. I'd like to see G again."

"Does he live far away?"

"*Tir na nÓg*? It's just quite difficult to get there if you're not properly prepared for the journey. I'll need to get the transport sorted."

"If I can take you there…" But Sol never finished as Joe got up, coughing laboriously and went inside for a little while leaving Sol looking out across the stillness of the lake, serene before the breaking of the incoming storm Joe predicted would come; probably just by the smell of it. He understood why Joe sat here admiring this tranquillity, listening to its gentle sounds and the calls of the birds on the moor and down in the trees. The feel of breeze on the face bringing news of the sea on its breath and the state of the heather in its scent met with him and entwined itself within his nasal channels. He understood.

Joe hobbled around the corner from the kitchen.

"If you'll be selling your fiddle then you'll need another."

He handed over an exceedingly battered old case dusty and threadbare in places. In it was Joe's second fiddle, the replacement to the one he had thrown over the side to the *Blue Men*. "It's not worth the same as the other one, but…"

"…it's worth far more as it's *yours* even if it is just wood and glue. But don't *you* need it?"

"No. I have another one stored away for a rainy day. It would bring me greater pleasure if when you sell that other one of yours you consider this one worthy enough to play."

"That would be my honour."

"But it is just wood and glue."

"But it's your wood and glue, Joe."

The stride back was pleasant as Sol traipsed along by the river with the small gift from Joe tumbling in his pocket and the fiddle case under his arm. A dram of whisky in his belly kept him warm against the wind as he descended; listening for the river when she passed under snow caves or was overcome by ice and attacked by plummeting icicles that shone brighter than any diadem. Her bubbling, gurgling and buffeting was always there, constant and encouraging, drawing him away and then back to the warmth of the awaiting *Bothan* in the glen below.

A mixture of grouse coughed from the dieback of the moorland's heather, now colourless and just a dried up extension of the peat hags, topped with flowers of ice and snow crystal. The short-eared owl, tossed by the air, quartered in hopeful hunt and a blue-rinsed hare lolloped from one drift to the cover of the next in its pursuit of vegetation and a safe scrape to shelter in.

The low sun had dropped to leave an inky blue sky by the time he broke out of the wood and into the yard, with a reversal of the norm as the ground emitted more light than the heavens above. The first attempts of the northern lights to brighten the arctic hemisphere spun and stretched over the distant shores of the far side of the loch, but they were beaten back by the engulfing darkness of a sea blown storm. It felt dangerous and thick, heavy and ever growing in its strength as it picked up moisture from the water in its haste and desire to attack the rising land.

The geese sensed it and edged in their flock to the shelter of the headland. The swans too came up to the house and in slow motion the waters cleared of their surface life to make way for that against which they could not defend themselves; the climate.

A small black bird dropped on to the yard close to Sol's feet and limped in its exhaustion, fluttering on the ice in an attempt to take flight again. It was a seabird, like a miniature gull dipped in coal dust, but with a tubular growth at the base of its hooked bill. Its brown-black eyes stared into his with little obvious effort left to fight. A chalked rump and feinted whiteness under the wings was all that gave this sparrow-sized creature definitive colour.

Sol held it cupped in his hands, feeling its life ebb away from it as the first patter of rain and wetted snow started to fall, and the bird went limp.

"What are you?" he asked of himself. "A tiny gull brought in from the sea by an approaching storm." And then he guessed. "A storm petrel. You are the harbinger of the storm to come aren't you? Nature's storm barometer. G writes about you."

Sol lay the tiny body by the porch door and then walked around the *Bothan* securing the shutters to protect the windows as the wind rose and the glass began to rattle and the trees started to shake and bend. By the time he had finished and the cottage was locked down, the smoke from the chimneys had leant over to the horizontal as it escaped, taking most of its vital heat with it.

He closed the porch door on the storm and then unusually the door to the porch from the kitchen. He stoked the fires up to full burning and then settled down to cook and then to play his violin, compose and read, placing the small gift from Joe on the mantelpiece next to the card from his brother. The noise of the wind rose from that of a charming attention to a raging force that rent the solidity of *Bothan Faobhar* with all that it could muster, angry that this long-standing building had the audacity to maintain itself and hold on to its roof. It threw leaves and then branches in its demand for submission, as it did to every cottage it could find, and every cliff and peak, moor and tree.

This was a maddened storm, pent up for hundreds of miles across the ocean, in need of blowing itself out and incensed that the land could stand up to it and force it up and over the mountains. It cascaded rain, then hail, sleet and then snow as it bellowed like an endlessly passing train.

But the *Bothan* stood still, as she always had done.

Sol found sleep difficult to come by that night. Something in the storm disturbed him beyond its noise and the relentless beating of the shutters and the walls and the destruction of ancient trees that he could hear crack. He knew they would either die and rot back to the Earth or recover and grow stronger with their staghorn tops held high as dead trophies of their past survival and resilience.

In his dreams, every so often he could hear the noise of the wind pick up a haunting sound. Not a ghostly noise or a wailing of the type a banshee or ghoul would call to frighten us prior to our last moment with it. Instead it was a bellow, as if a red deer stag were defending its harem to the death, or a whale was moaning in the deeps. And then, in his dream he became aware of what it was. It was the braying of a large wide-horned Highland bull, shaggy and wind swept, but muscular and strong.

Its breath hung moistly at its nostrils as it stepped up and out of the water, strangely dry and unaffected by the billow of the storm. The eyes when shaken free of thick ginger-orange hairs were more human than cow, loving than angry, and it raised its head one more time and thundered, approaching slowly yet with purpose up and out of the lake towards a house.

In his dreamscape the moonlit pool became the upper loch, the darkness behind developed into the mountain, and the cottage took on the form of the Gillie House.

The bull roared one last time and Sol woke up to the dead silence of the calm after the storm, the blackness of a cottage shuttered closed and the dulling effects of deep snow piled up behind the building.

"Joe," he said. "The bull has been for Joe."

Chapter 24: The Purity of Snow

(Det är en Ros Utsprungen, Jan Sandtröm)

Powdery snow had piled by the side and back of the house, thick and somehow internally lit blue, so that Sol could only leave the *Bothan* via the porch door. Its texture was one that was easily whipped up to form drifts and ice-cream cone peaks and would have made wonderful sculpting clay for any child if it could be kept at the right temperature. Roughly following the lines of whatever lay beneath it, it gave a distorted view of the landscape where it was both familiar with its larger identifiable features and general shape, but also twisted, altered, smoothed and re-contoured such that even its light fell differently to that of the day before.

It is claimed that it rarely snows by the sea and yet now the little cottage seemed buried in what looked like a drift that rose up from the coral beach where the geese dabbled, up and over the wall, then sweeping down into the garden itself before climbing up to meet the roof like a series of enlarged sand dunes made of crystalline white. It was as if huge breakers of spuming sea had been frozen in tsunami up through the valley until it met the trees who had shaken free of the weighted white. The tiles of the roof broke through as flattened rock edges that jutted at obtuse mossed angles in the way that the harder stones resisted the seizure of a cracking glacier as it barged and scoured its way in passing to savage and erode the softer material around it.

Jackdaws perched about the smoking chimney stacks, willing the heat into their frosted feet and fluffing their feathers up against the piercing air that was so cold that everything felt close and clear, bright and sparkling, an offence to the eye and a biting pain to the exposed skin. The birds sat and waited for an organic thaw in their legs, thankful without being aware of it of the heat exchange that took place within them to prevent too much of their bodily warmth being sucked down and into the crystalline snow. Where the loch lapped the drift was melted to form a cavernous edge, smoothed where the chemistry and physics of salt expected the temperature to be lower to allow it to remain solidified. The geese stood proud and scattered alongside the ducks and the waders who chased the dying tide and receded back with it to lower grounds where the loch had been searching at high tide minutes before.

Weeds were left discarded in the wake of the storm and trees, felled or broken by its might, lay where they were slain or injured, cast aside by the renting of the wind. The snow was littered with branches, leaves, lichen and moss, forensic littered evidence to its night of wild carnage, an abiotic midden.

Sol cut a track to the yard and thankfully found the path up through the wood passable. He called through to Hamish to let him know he was on his way up to Joe's, worried for some reason, and promised he would phone again if he needed help getting up to the lonely little Gillie House out in the hills. Returning to the path with Joe's violin slung over his shoulder, Sol headed to the river, that non-living feature of the valley that always seemed so full of life, and she received his presence gladly as ever as she fell downwards to the sea, bursting with the icy excitement of fresh melt water. Cutting up through the crags he made a precarious ascent on slippery surfaces freshly polished by frozen run off and solid algae that held pear-shaped as it clung to the rock like deep green permafrost.

Gulls called him to look back and the geese willed him to stay, but this man was on a mission now from which he could not be deterred. The headland made, he was met by the wind from the sea, the loch's air cold and unwilling, unkind to the lungs that wheezed and stung as he drew in deeply. Sweat built up under his layered clothing and so he stripped his outer garments and headed up into mist that clung to the moor as a swirling morass of white, a distortion of reality that was both unwelcoming and eerie as it passed and recycled around him. The grouse and the black cock called their negative refrain, '*go-back, go-back*' and a mourning redshank piped him a grief stricken medley reminding him that there were happier places to be other than up here on this moor, today.

The river was his friend, guiding him through sound when all vision was lost in the white out of snow at the feet and the swirl of fog to the face. There was a sun trying hard to burn it away, but it was weakened by winter, low and too wan to have effect. Instead it loitered a faded yellow-white, a burning disc dim enough to be stared at without danger to sight and only visible if the clag thinned as it sometimes did in its anarchic eddies.

When he stumbled in to the stone circle he understood that in this mist the druid pagan's past still held power and he left trembling as the ancient spirits of the moor were disturbed and the looming shadows of the tall hewn stones leaned in as if animated to life as the gods themselves. Sol knew this was fancy and only his mind's fear that gave those stones life, but he was afraid to be there in that circle as if it really did still hold some powerful magic of antiquity.

Even their encrusted lichens took on imagery and power. Unnatural sulphurous yellow bloomed alongside the risen blemishes of black moss and the white guano stains of a top-roosted bird marked a regularly chosen perch. Colours competed with snow to create impressions of hair and facial characteristics.

The stones took on strange importance.

Skirting out of the rocks Sol returned to blindly follow the trickle sound of water in the river again and then chased her up through the deepening drift-piles and the hidden dangers of an invisible footpath in a dead flat moorland smoothed over by snow. He used the staff, the one given by Hamish, to feel his way to safety, prodding to find the surest path and to search out the holes and snares under.

Every so often the cruel conditions cleared enough for Sol to spy snippets of scenes he knew well, drifting away quickly to again vanish in the mist. Closer or further away than expected, a mind game started to play out in his brain and he felt the urge to leave the moors and return home grow stronger. At times it looked as if the land were shifting and not the mist and a dizziness of panic churned on the edge of his sanity. But determination is a great strength and the human is able to overcome far more than they suspect if they have a will to succeed, explaining the endeavours of people and the success of our species, and Sol dug deep as the frost bit his fingers and the elements bid him to return back to the *Bothan*. He walked on with the attendant '*truch-truch*' of every step as his boot was welcomed in by compacting ice. It solidified on impact becoming brittle yet malleable such that as his foot rose up his passage was recorded in cerulean complement, a winding interpretation of the track.

Splayed geometric line shapes picked out where the grouse had walked, barely engraving the crystalline surface. They looked like maths problems where regular angles between the three forward-pronged toes were to be measured, anchored by the stirrup-positioned talon at the back. The bounding leap of the hare had scooped the snow where it had passed at speed, long hind legs leaving splayed grooves and dainty forepaws paired indentations, each four clawed. The bisected pear-drop hoof prints of deer were everywhere, digging knee-deep into the drifts where they had passed less impeded than he found he was himself.

And then there it was, the upper loch and the Gillie House, as static and idyllic as it ever was, illuminated in the clarity of a light that descended in rays down from the blistering torrid sky as if painted by an early master. Sol could see old Joe sat there on his bench as always, staring in his unfocused way across the loch, leaning forward with his chin on an old stick.

Sol smiled. *He* was always watching that loch.

Sol called and picked up his stride, but the old man did not respond, just continuing to stare out blindly across his beloved water waiting for his blessed bull and willing the inactive fish to rise and to disturb the surface even on this bitter-cold day. Closer still and he was sure that Joe would have heard, but there was no response. Maybe that cough was getting to him and he couldn't hear.

When not far off Sol called once again, not wanting to frighten Joe if he woke him up or arrived unheralded. But Joe remained unusually still watching the water intently, and by the time he made the cottage Sol realised that the bull had indeed come for him during the night and that the Joe he knew had gone to join his wife in *Tir na nÓg* and only his body remained.

And if Joe was dead and now that was how to get to *Tir na nÓg*, then G who was already there must also be dead too.

His mind whirled at the thoughts and the way they took him to a desperate but obvious conclusion. His ears rang but seemed dulled to sound as if an explosion had damaged his inner chambers and he was feeling that deadly dumbstruck aftershock, the wave that left each healthy man dead in their war time trench yet to all appearances unharmed.

But, the letters he wrote once a month?

Could it be possible that they had been written before he died and be posted each month for Sol's benefit and tuition?

Was one of the locals in on this scam to help him?

Was there even more to his taking over the Bothan than even he suspected?

He was not cross at the deception nor was he sad for Joe or for G. There were wiser people at work here than him and bigger processes in action. He was happy for the life of old Joe, the blind man with greater vision than most who could see. He was pleased that he had lived a happy life here at the Gillie House by the water and enjoyed his second chance to lead a full span, wealthy in his poverty. He knew the joy the man had received through the love of his wife and could only imagine how great the moment was when he re-joined her and when he met the god bull of the water, real or imagined.

And he thought of G and how he would have wanted to meet him, the man behind the glen. And yet in some strange way, he felt he knew him better in death than he would have in life – and maybe meeting in the flesh would have been a disappointment with him never being able to live up to the impression of the man he had built up in his thoughts. He had G's notes and memories, his house, clothes and equipment, and he even had his estate and its wildlife. There was every probability that he would continue to write to him from beyond the grave for a few more months to come, expecting the secret of his new life in *Tir na nÓg* not to have been revealed quite yet.

Sol sat down on the bench next to Joe put his staff down by his side and laid the fiddle case across his lap. He undid the two straps that held it shut purposefully and slowly, and then took the instrument out and tightened the strings on the bow tuning it precisely for this most important performance. Then after standing alone on the water's edge he played for Joe, describing his journey up to find him through the snow and the discovery of this old man where he sat now in his final pose. It was part lament and part description of the tranquillity of the spot, with a sudden crescendo to a climax when the great bull left the water and took the soul of the man who called for him.

Sol ended his piece and stood as still as his breathing allowed, breath hanging limply ahead of his sweating red face staring over the waters for one moment longer.

A wagtail dabbed the muddied margin and skipped along to meet its mate and a fish broke the surface to produce an enlarging elegant ripple circle that spread away and outwards. There was peace here.

Turning to look at Joe he became aware of the outline of Hamish standing at a distance where the upper loch ended and the river started her gentle fall down to the sea loch below. He was watching away out into the swirling mists that were clearing away to reveal the beauty of the landscape and the broad sweep of the home glen that fell away from where he stood. The moor dropped and then scooped around until it became a tessellation of a million different trees separated by the dissipating whiteness of fogs that were rolling away and out to sea. Then the mountain showed itself above, rocky and dangerous and magnificent in its scale, dipped in snow and swept by cloud, and the sea loch came in to full all-encompassing view, and the vista was now complete, the stage set for the next ceremonial performance.

He had been listening to Sol's memorial tune and taking his own time to compose himself.

Dressed in highland garb a tartan Glengarry astride his head flashing a silver broach that caught the winning sun, he waited a further minute and then lifted the full pipes he carried under his arm to his mouth, filled them with air, struck up the drones and then played his own lament, the '*Going Home*' he later explained.

Sol closed his eyes and listened as the sound vibrated his soul and stirred something guttural within him, a feeling that only the pipes played in this kind of land can. Instruments have often evolved with their culture, in turn them too becoming an end product of the land's geography. Here on a mountain side, amongst the misted peaks and above the cascading river and her loch below, where the sea extended into distances unseen, the pipes were the right sound and the spirit was moved, deeply.

He liked to think that a golden eagle courted the air above them and that the stag deer were stood alert in salute, that the wildcats stopped in their tracks and even the fish paused in their restless swimming. The pipes called for it, demanded it.

And then there was silence and Sol opened his eyes and looked at the ground. He knew they were just the cloven-hoofed sheep tracks of those that had visited to drink the water, melted out of all proportion to their real shape and size. But he imagined he saw bull's hoof marks indented into the snow and the tracery of a route up to the house where old Joe still sat staring blindly out into the water.

Sheep or not, there was the passage of the great bull himself.

Hamish had joined him.

"I knew when you called what it meant," he said holding his pipes under his arm against his green tartan'd flanks, the drones sagging but still attached to the unpressurised skin bag that gave them resonant voice like some half dead multi-legged animal, perhaps a dry form of octopus. They had lost their turgid forces and failed to retain shape.

"We'll need to contact someone official but they'll not get up here for weeks in a car and getting some unfit doctor to walk up will be an impossibility," he said in a matter of fact manner. "It seems a shame to move him though...   ...he loved that scene so much, sat there by the loch. But we'd better lay him inside where the birds won't scavenge. At least he died with his favourite view in his mind. Blind he might've been, but his picture of this world would have been clearer than yours or mine."

"I know," chuckled Sol. "He'd have smelt the view as well."

The two carried the stiff body, still belonging to the Joe they knew but no longer occupied by him, into the Gillie House and lay it on the kitchen table placing his cap and stick next to him. As it wasn't Joe anymore, he was dead, it was easy enough for them to do with Sol taking the arms and Hamish the legs. Dead-weighted, he dragged them downwards and was difficult to move respectfully. It is curious how the departed do.

Then they snubbed the glow-smouldering peat on the kitchen fire to reduce the temperature, secured the windows open to keep it cool and closed the doors to make sure his body would be left secure and then they went out, walking almost backwards through the final exit. They left the upper loch walking as a moorland wader piped its own dirge from the shore.

Hamish contacted the local funeral directors who said that they would be up as soon as the weather allowed but Sol interjected and asked if he couldn't be buried up at the Gillie House by the water there as soon as the ground thawed enough to allow them to dig. It was arranged and a young doctor was eventually found and sent on from the towns up on foot to confirm the death up at the Gillie House. It took them days to arrive.

Sol walked along with him, trudging through the snow as if charged with a mission of the state. The medic was a sprightly well-shaved man, only recently qualified by all accounts, and felt that he had drawn the short straw being selected for this case. He struggled on the slopes having come dressed inadequately for the role, expecting a Land Rover to drive him the whole way. Addie was capable and Sol was able to handle the track up to the crossroads, but the last few miles were a simple trudge and the doctor found the slopes hard and was left bewildered by the poorly attired, scruffy older man who was Sol. He marvelled at the energy and zeal, the breadth of conversation and diversity of wild knowledge this dishevelled being was able to maintain, and realised he was in the presence of the nearest he would ever be again to a polymath.

"It's the country air," laughed Sol as the doctor wheezed humidly through dragon smoke clouds from within his doubled coat and layers of fleece, artificially spun from recycled plastic bags and sent from all parts of the globe. Sol wore an open shirt of cotton and a thick wool jumper spun from the wool of sheep grazed within the estate. This was the fabric of the land and suited its climate well.

"Now don't give up yet, there's only a few more miles to go," he reassured as the younger man flagged further behind again. "I don't suppose you get many calls like this then?"

"No, not many," came the feeble reply.

And Sol turned and paced on dragging the man up with him.

Christmas day came quietly.

Sol had not felt lonely up until this day. The night before he had that childhood expectancy about something special being about to happen. A fire that burnt bright against the cold and darkness of the night, shutters that kept out the snow and the brunt of the wind on the glass, and the glow of the little *Bothan* stranded at the end of its driveway. But when that something special did not arrive in the morning, it *was* just another day; alone but never alone.

He sat with Quicksilver for a while, watching her creep into the yard and feed, and he added more fat and seed to the feeders enjoying the thrill of the siskins and yellowhammers coming in with the bramblings, the chaffinch, the green and the goldfinch too. A male capercaillie provided the exotic as it stumbled below the feeder and strutted about until it had cleared room big enough for it to peck with the personal space it desired, clucking like some over-filled chicken that had been dipped in pitch.

Then moving on to the beach he gazed at shore birds and fowl, engrossing his preoccupation with self in the milling assemblage of birds gathered in the marshes and shallows of his protected basin. They fed as spirit birds turned shades of grey, brown and white by a clammy mist that rose from the water in a mythic steam, catching the muted rays of the sun. It was just visible above the distant mountains where snow clouds hung like light grey pompoms that looked impossibly heavy as if they could fall from the sky.

Waders skitted the shallows and gulls caught the breeze in the air so that movement sandwiched the sea loch, between the layers of which shags hung their wings out to dry as greasy-green gargoyles atop black-slickened rocks.

Geese, the brant, Canada, greylag, white fronted and bean, they all gaggled here and mixed in their cosmopolitan parades of black, grey and white, orange-legged, pink-legged and grey-legged. Three swan types drifted between, mute the bulbous nosed, the whooper huge and wedge-billed, and the Bewick's lesser and more gentile, all variations upon the shape that is swan and colour that is white. None the same, but none that different either.

He listed the ducks too. Shelduck and shoveler were showy with chestnut brown bars and fine black-green heads that took the little light and used it so efficiently that they glowed with their own phosphorescence in unreal shades of metallic and chiffon. The mallard were recognisable but obviously ready for winter, outclassed by the perfection of the chocolate-headed pintails, and there were wigeon, pochard and teal by the thousand. He found gadwall by searching and the white-striped eye of the garganey showed itself as he scanned more closely with the help of binoculars and a telescope discovered in the back sheds. And then there were the little ducks, the tufted and the scaup, the sea ducks further out, the eider with their straightened bills and questioning calls, and the scoters, velvet bodied but bizarrely shaped and brightly coloured in the bill. The highly painted clowns of the water were the long-tailed ducks with their surprised expressions and elongated tail feathers that doubled the body's proportions. Goldeneye, dark heads pinpricked with the allusion of precious metal for an eye, swam with the brightened whiteness of the smew, highlighted in black fine brush-stroked lines to finish off their artistic images.

Sol's vision was drawn up and outwards reaching beyond the weed-strewn shoreline and into the loch, further still to where mergansers hunted. There too were the wintering divers, heads slung back as they cruised, and the grebes in their range of shapes and sizes, little, great-crested, and both black-necked and red-necked.

All this was here in the glen of the *Bothan* and so how could he claim to be alone, solitary or isolated? Instead, he listened to their sounds, wove them together and created another melody in his mind, one for a full orchestra and part of the symphony. It was a celebratory carolling in its own natural right, proclaiming the freedom of the life natural and the diversity of the avian class.

Returning to *Bothan Faobhar* Sol prepared a plucked goose for the oven, given as a present from the ladies over the loch, Iona and

Skye, and arranged the trophy bird on a tray with potatoes and vegetables enough for a few days. There were other presents on the dining table left through the week too.

First he retrieved the small paper-wrapped gift given by Joe before he died. Peeling it of its wrappings he found a brown crinkled handmade newspaper bag inside, one that he carefully opened up to find, like the Russian doll, a scrawled note wrapped over something within. It unravelled to become attached to a large feathered fishing fly. He flattened the note and read the spidery scrappy writing aloud.

'*Sol,*

Happy Christmas. I think you're ready for this now. It's a salmon fly. The rest of the present is on the table in my living room. There is my best rod, my favourite reel and a line. The metal case is for flies. I think you'll soon have more use for it than me as Tir na nÓg calls.

Tight lines and catch me a good one in the New Year.

Joe'

Sol looked judiciously at this gaudy imitation turning it over between his fingers and then licking it so that the moisture of his tongue changed its form and it took on something of the fish it was supposed to impersonate. He then replaced the mimic fly on the mantelpiece above the busy fire and next opened the other gifts that were waiting on the table.

"One day," he muttered to the fly, "you and I will go out together on the boat and catch us a salmon. How's about that then?"

There was a whistle whittled by Hamish from the end of an antler with a leather thong to attach it to a belt and a new Arran sweater from Mrs Hamish with a pound jar of honey from their summer hive. The attached card read that three pips on the whistle would indicate trouble and at least somebody on the hillside would try to come and rescue him unless he was too far away or simply too stupid and placed himself in irretrievable danger.

Al had bought him a wind-up radio *'as used in developing nations where they struggle to get sufficient power'* and Pete had framed a series of photographs of the wildcats as they had developed, including a shot of Sol's naked rear as he watched them. They were produced in black and white to give it a stylised artistic finish and Sol was pleased with this nostalgic record of some of his earliest encounters with the felines in the garden.

The owners of the inn had sent up a keg of beer to keep him going through the winter, and local producers had donated cheese, bread, oatcakes, butter, wine, beer, whisky, bacon, fish and eggs. He would never go hungry or sober.

His brother had sent him on a hard-spine'd book of the family farm. It was made of photographs and short quotes, obviously being produced by an Internet-based company, finished off in a satin sheen coating to each page. He recognised the buildings and out houses, and the breeds of the sheep who were numerous as they flocked over familiar hills. But the people were changed. As an illustration of the length of time since they'd last met, everyone was older, children now existed that had not before and Sol felt sad that he had allowed so long to drift by without his attention; it had slipped by whilst he was in some money-filled haze, a malaise and blight from which he was now fully recovered. *How easy it was to become preoccupied with the single life, the one that dominated the cinema screen and thought story of only his one world? How basic a need had he ignored in not considering the world beyond this singular mind's view? How much had he missed that he should not have done? And, how much could he still catch up on?*

How curious the thoughts of the lonely are at times like Christmas when so many others are enjoying festivities, feasting and party, or are too drunk to think.

He sat by the fire to enjoy a lump of cheese with a creamy butter-carpeted cob of fresh bread, seeded and gritty as he had come to enjoy. Beside him was a lonely tumbler of amber whisky in a glass sent down by Euan, Sally and little Gee sat on the hearth, gently warming and glowing in reflection of the fire's ritual sky searching dance. It was the first time in months that he had missed his roll up cigarettes and he was thankful of the impassable distance between him and any shop that might have been open thus preventing him from seeking the cure for his previously forgotten addictive craving.

He *was* alone.

Slurping noisily, he relished the mix of whisky anger and peaty flavour as it burned his mouth and throat and passed downwards to be understood internally.

He was unaccompanied and wished for a companion to be there with him, right now, supping whisky and eating cheese in the second chair opposite him by the fireplace.

His phone bleeped from within his pocket where it lay forgotten. Such was the irony that the intrusion was from Sue.

'*She was wishing him happy Christmas...   ...hoping he was happy...   ...she missed him...   ...was he alone?*

Love,

Sue'

The timing of the message could not have been more apt, and not for the first time he wondered why the gods of chronology seemed to have so much fun at his expense.

He replied briefly but sincerely.

'*Hi Sue, Happy Christmas to you too. Thanks for the socks, very seasonal and warm. I've got them on now and will probably have the mittens on later – nobody can see me right now and so I should get away with it – I don't really have proper heating in the Bothan. Happy, but on my own today. Maybe see friends later but the snow is a bit deep outside.*

I miss you too.

Love,

Sol'

He wondered what he missed from their torrid relationship of a past life. Was it really '*love*', that term so easily bandied around and flippantly added to the end of a text or a message, often with kisses and a symbol, an emoticon at worst? Did his old self have the capacity for love or was it simply addicted to the empty carnal pleasures that replaced it when love was not available nor easily bought for money? In an attempt to fulfil his desires and to satisfy cravings evolutionarily imprinted within, he had *enjoyed* a full life. But it was one that, lacking a true depth of relationship and mutual commitment, had needed to seek for more and more, the experience and the show counting far greater than the reality. Like a valuable vintage car in a salesroom that had had several careful owners before, it could always be made to look good for the public, rebuilt in places for the right amount of money, and it could be cleaned and polished. Of course, it could sound impressive if treated well, roar when required and be adapted and updated as needed. But the owner should be aware that it would always be an old car, previously owned, and even driving it in reverse could not re-set it.

What did he miss?

What did he want?

What would he look for should the need arise again?

He missed constant companionship, that thing that so often had been the source of his conflict with Sue. He was lacking the interplay between two people and a need for someone near, one who understood him and was available as that ear to listen, even though it was in contradiction to his constant requirement for space and freedom. Without the basal understanding of each other's needs that was an impossible thing to achieve. If a relationship started on friendship and respect then it would work. But theirs had not. It had been doomed from its foundation and he had known that, even if at the time he had denied it quite successfully.

Could it be started again?

Could it be worked on like that old vintage car?

A stoat bounded through the snowdrifts that stretched out from the front of the cottage. It left deep tracks in complement to its warm-padded feet, but they were fine enough to be lost in the apparent smoothness of the snow. Everything depended on scale. Close up, things were imperfect. Tracks in the snow marking an animal's passage, the haggard branches of a winter-dead tree and the choppiness of the loch's waters. And yet scan away and the snow became faultless, the forest homogenous and the loch as flat as a billiard table.

Were relationships just the same?

The smell of hot goose fat permeated the damp air and although the shutters were now thrown open, the cottage felt close and small, dark and humid. Sol thumbed through a dusted book on waterfowl, taken from the shelves, to identify the geese he had been watching as he tried to flick through mentally captured images of them in his mind.

Distantly he thought he heard the singing of people over the sounds of the birds gathered on the shore. Dismissing it he carried on reading, dropping rich crumbly cheese into his lap and sucking from the tumbler whilst the fire entertained his spirit and accompanied his thoughts.

But then he heard it again.

He could perceive it properly now, more distinctly and clear. It *was* the voices of human singers coming in off the water, and not just one. Replacing the glass on the hearth slates and the plate on the table, Sol went to the front window to investigate but could see nothing.

Leaving the house he returned to the beach to look out to where a boat was driving cleanly across the fresh waves and approaching through the mist covered water, parting it as the geese and ducks upped and flew, leaving an avian wake in the sky. The sail dropped and *The Tern*, decked in holly and tinsel, brought Nevin and Gerry into the crystal shallows where she hissed up on to the sand to greet him.

"Happy Christmas," they yelled, bottles in hands and bags over shoulders.

"We thought you'd be lonely," called Nevin pulling the painter and carefully retrieving a large wrapped up flat object from the hull of the boat.

"And, well we've not got much food in," laughed Gerry. "I'm broke and he's too disorganised to have thought of anything. And I knew how big that bird was you'd got in, and, well...   ...you know..." She kissed Sol on the cheek.

"Truth be told," called James, "she's missed you and she's worried about you out here on your own. Don't let her pretend it's just the food she's after." He sniffed the air. "That smells good though. What is it?"

"Don't tell the water birds," said Sol, so very pleased to see them both. "It's...   ...well, goose." He looked cautiously around as if to check that the birds outside hadn't overheard. "Probably the cousin of one of these guys. If I didn't like it so much I would be tempted to consider turning vegetarian."

The three went in to the cottage, sat by the fire and talked over cheese and drinks, and the *Bothan* felt suddenly and miraculously like a home again. Not just a lonely empty shell that he struggled to fill on Christmas Day alone, Sol sensed the elation that the building itself enjoyed as people at peace with each other and with genuine happiness between them gathered. Friends brought warmth that added to the strength of the fire and he felt he partially understood the communal life of the birds outside.

James and Gerry thanked Sol for his gifts to them.

'We've tried to be creative in what we've bought you," announced James and he withdrew a wooden box from his shoulder bag now discarded on the kitchen table. It was approximately the length of three hands and the height and width of one, painted black and without any kind of labelling. "It took me quite a while to make."

Gerry gave Nevin a stern look.

"Okay," he admitted. "It took me a while to modify. But I've had to fashion quite a few of the parts from raw materials. Gerry doesn't believe I'm creative enough to build something from scratch."

"Thank you," said Sol sitting back down in the easy chair and turning the box around in his hand. It was light but the thin wood sheets of it obviously contained something that fitted quite snuggly inside. He raised the nailed down lid, which came away easily to reveal a lining of bubble wrapped packaging. Inside, resting on wood shavings and sponge, was the painted hull of a small boat complete with tiller, benches and a flat lain mast with rolled up sails. All the ropes and rigging that should have been there on the real thing were in their place, with a painter at the front. Even a little black anchor like the one *he* carried on board.

Sol gently lifted her out of her box. He knew who it was immediately, but there was the writing on the front, either side of the prow, as if to confirm it. It was a miniature *Sireadh-thall.*

"And," asked James pleadingly as if looking for confirmation, "do you like it?"

"Of course, it's incredible," Sol replied. "But, you've spent so long on it."

"Aye, but firstly I'm a ship builder and I build boats anyway. And secondly, my father used to make these for the showroom so that potential customers could see what he could make in small-scale before they committed to buying the real thing."

"Marketing?"

"Aye. We've got hundreds of them in the workshop. They go back to the days when no one wanted a catalogue. Thirdly, this model is simply an old model adapted. It's a *Birlinn* just like *Sireadh-thall.* And lastly, well you've saved my business for the now and seem to have brought Gerry and me back together too...   ...and so I just thought, why not? You should have one of these, my most prized of possessions."

"Well..." said Sol stuck for words and taking a neatly folded wooden boat stand out of the box and placing it on the mantelpiece above the fire. He set the sail in the mast hole so that the diminutive *Sireadh-thall* looked ready to navigate, her passage along the mantelpiece, blocked only by the salmon fly and a series of propped up cards and letters ahead.

"I just hope that this next year I can keep it all together," Nevin sighed. "The business that is."

"But you won't be on your own," Gerry said and she pulled Sol over to the table where a large flat object lay waiting. "Not this year. I'll do the yard's accounts as there are too many orders currently on your books. You just need to build the boats. That's the bit you're good at."

She pointed to her gift to Sol, lying on the table.

"For you," she announced.

It was obviously a canvass inside and Sol knew that it would be the picture he had asked Gerry to paint for him. It was smaller than the stag that hung on the wall but was still three feet tall and four wide. As all canvasses are, it was lighter to lift than he had expected, picking it up and feeling the wooden frame that stretched it and maintained a forced tension along the underside.

Slowly he peeled away the paper that hid the picture below, where mountains leapt up against a sky in turmoil obscured by the wrappings he had yet to remove. Placing the picture upright on the writing desk to complete the action in a steady tear, he then stepped back to admire what Gerry had produced.

The centrepiece was a wildcat, Quicksilver. She looked out of the canvass through clear, bright oiled eyes and held an intelligent pose, crouched and sleek, alert and stalking. Her ears were raised to scan the sounds ahead out there in the room and she was ready to leap to attack or kill something in its middle if required, like some highly sprung machine. Her banded tail swished down and around her legs and if she weren't made of oil-knifed paint she would have been amongst them by now fighting and cursing or she would have escaped into the lengthening shadows of the cottage's garden.

Behind was *Bothan Faobhar*, bright and white with her wooded glen rising up, the river tumbling down and the great mountain towering and glowering above. But the landscaped image extended out to the bay, encompassing the headland where the standing stone was and the sea loch advanced. And there was *Sireadh-thall* beached on the coral sands surrounded by the geese, the ducks and the waders, exceeding which were the gulls riding the tumultuous firmament waves of the wind against a cloud-blossoming sky.

Out on the water was the loon; a simple blackened shape poised expressively, ready to dive.

Above the *Bothan* coming in from the sea, seven angel-white swans flew in a small v-shaped skein and Sol went back in his mind to that first day he met Gerry out on the headland.

"The peace of swans," he said stepping back into the room and Gerry joined him at his side as he continued his ambling commentary. "The mustering of geese, the diving sea herdsman out on the water, the beauty of the glen, my boat, my little *Bothan Faobhar*, the house on the edge, the headland behind, and my last wildcat. It's all here."

"You missed the bucket," she said.

"What?"

"I painted your bucket here, see?" And Gerry pointed to a small metal bucket painted a way behind Quicksilver's image. "Without that you'd never have seen your first wildcat would you? And so I thought I'd add that precious bucket in too."

"It's incredible," he said quietly and genuinely. "I don't know how you've got it all in. Thank you."

In the picture was a metaphor for his future; Sol felt it. He had come to the *Bothan* a self-obsessed, technologically-dependant city man who appreciated little in his fortunate life. But now *Bothan Faobhar*, its land and wild community, and its people and their rural existence, had captured him.

After much eating and drinking, singing and merriment, the two guests left in *The Tern* and sailed their way back to that happy home, the *Boat House*. The weak sun returned to warm another land where it spent more time at this stage of the year beyond the last of the equinox. The geese settled to huddle amongst the grasses and the waders hid their heads under wings that they felt would protect them from whatever elements came by, backs to the airstream and feathers fluffed up and wind-licked. Sol sat and he looked.

He had placed the picture above the fire on the mantelpiece, now overloaded with the things that showed others cared for him, both the living and those passed on to *Tir na nÓg*. He laughed to see a posthumous Christmas card from G delivered in secret by someone who had kept a promise from beyond the grave. In the flicker of the lamplight and the writhing glow of the fire the cat took on life, watching him as some feline Mona Lisa would, always checking and ever alert. She guided him through the picture and the lessons that could so easily be learnt from the wild things present if only we took the time to do as our forebears had and used the examples Mother Nature provided.

The whooper swans, magnificent and elegant, bringing a peace to all. Travelling far, they always returned to the same place to winter having enjoyed the unexpected balm of the Arctic Circle for the summer breed. *He could use that idea well, needing peace and the ability to return no matter what hardships he faced. He would come back to Bothan Faobhar after the hearing in April, returning to a land of shelter and protection where he hoped he would find a little-disturbed peace again.*

The diversity of geese, different shapes and sizes, species and ages; they too had gathered in the security of his bay drawn in by its shelter and the provision it gave them. *It did not matter if they were vagrant travellers or year round guests, they were all welcome for as long as the valley was protected, which he would fight for if he could. They enjoyed a happiness that he needed to ensure he recognised for himself too, counting his blessings and taking advantage of his good fortune in finding this land or of it finding him through G. He should continue to share its wealth with others and conserve it.*

The mystical diver sang to the moon his eerie cry at night, suggesting mystery and the chance of the rare. *This glen needed its isolation and even though money would be required and it would always be dependent on the help of others, its purity needed guarding and the wild things their space and protection, their fish to feed on, the insects to breed. Visitors could take away their photographs and memories but would always need to leave only their footprints.*

Sireadh-thall waited by the shore, that free provision of the sea filled with life and fed by the ever-tinkling river who brought its joy down from the upper loch. *Nature cannot be canned and limited, being destroyed if we attempt to do it. It needs freedom enough to fulfil the niches of the organisms that dwell in it. The eagle needs land to soar over, the puffin the mud capped rocks to nest within and the salmon an entire ocean before its river. To package it into the small spaces between our developments will never work and we will slowly see the decline of diversity through our obsessive desires to fragment. The Bothan estate needed to stay as a whole.*

Quicksilver the wildcat was ever vigilant to change and ready for action. *She was so great a metaphor for what was required in this place and how he needed to be the watchman over the land. That she passed unnoticed by most showed how in tune with the land she really had been. She had been a hidden keystone species that loitered in the shadows and moved in the dark and hunted in the night. And, she was still there.*

Then there was the house itself and the second chance he had been given to find himself, ironically so very far away from any place he expected to find anything in. The house on the edge was not a boundary but an interface. *It isn't always where we think of looking in which we find what we search for. He thought about this for a while and wondered how he had ended up here, so very lucky.*

Even that bucket was important. Old and dented, the metal had once been filled with the waste of a dinner, the bones he could not use. *By serendipity he had found his first wildcat. Life had thrown up one of its chance surprises. And by mistake, he had taken advantage of it. How often had he missed such opportunities before? It was not true that some people were born lucky and others not, that only the chosen few got all the breaks and chances in life. No, it was simply that some took advantage of what cards they were drawn, focusing on what they could make with their dealt pack. If all we ever see is what went wrong for ourselves, trapped in our own self-pity, then of course we end up convinced it all goes well for everyone else, we resent and we presume.*

The headland stood dominantly projecting into the loch above it all with its little standing stone bringing ancient sanctity to the glen and it was here that Sol found G waiting for him in the dark, but this time he was not alone. Next to him sat old Joe. A stag deer reared prominent looking out to sea, proud and large, G's emblem animal and accomplice in Sol's dreams. A bull, shaggy and heavily horned, now joined it. This was Joe's trophy creature.

Sol drew up to them and leant on the stone, knowing that one day, when he passed the baton of the estate over to the next person to look after, that he too would remain up here as a memory trace of the past if anyone could find him in their dreams, and that he would probably be accompanied by his own animal. Obviously that would be a Scottish wildcat, wild and free, alert and agile. He could feel her now hunting down in the mixed woods somewhere behind the *Bothan* leaving ghost prints in the snow.

The filled clouds continued to drop their silent flurries throughout the night, deadening sound and resting over the valley to fill its indentations and marks in a smooth white purity, every imperfection covered. It was as if snow itself gave the land a second chance every time it fell.

Chapter 25: When Migrants Return

(Five Bagatelles, Op 23, II, Gerald Finzi)

Time ticks away unstoppable, the fourth dimension that refuses to be contained, whose proportions cannot be altered and whose stride walked before us and will continue well beyond when we are gone until the end of the universe. It was there at the creation and will be there at the end, and although it spans all things we cannot go back in it to see what it has seen before. *Could time be our god as each of us are so relentlessly involved with it?*
In life we squander time, waste it and tread water within in it, and all of us need to sleep for a too large a part of it to recover from the other things we have done in life. Sometimes we try to use it well and capture it, making each second of it count more than ever before. Focused, we can lose track of it and watch it slip away, and all too often we run short of it, the one thing we cannot afford to run out of. In the end it will always win and we will lose out to it, and possibly we will have done enough to be prepared for whatever deadline has approached and despite anxiety, restlessness and disturbed sleep we will be ready. Revision for an examination, preparation for a deal, the completion of a masterwork of art, the composition of a yet to be completed musical work or even the production of a good enough lunch. Then there are those bigger things in life, the marriage of two people and the birth of a child, the buying of a house and the ends of things we that we would prefer not to dwell on.
Time ticks on unstoppable, but even though we might wish for more we would find eternity less desirable as the very competition we endure against time is what makes life more vital; the knowledge that we will never have enough.

That Boxing Day Sol changed his approach to time, now counting the days down to April with a greater certainty than ever before, with a life goal and a vigour for preparation. He sensed that he had been given the greatest chance of reinvention and this fortunate choice to move to the *Bothan* was key, and he had gained a sense of an even greater significance than his own short life's span. Call it an obsession or call it a madness, but he began to write letters, texts and emails to make arrangements for that day coming when time would run out as predictably as the tide came in and up or went out and down according to the motions of the sun and the moon as we all waltzed around the solar system and as prescribed by the tables published on the Internet.

He arranged to stay with Sue in London, as a good friend, intending to restart their relationship, as just a friendship, after the year that they had been apart. She, still alone herself, agreed to this. Friendship was after all something they both desired of the other and missed.

Next he legally settled for all commissions made in past deals to be channelled into the estate's trust, based in an office in the garage, Pete's studio. He also organised transfer of all but his basic accounts across to the estate. This way the land would remain preserved and the money would endure secure in the light of it being donated freely as a gift in trust and on the proviso that he would never try to obtain the money back again. The old company he had slavishly worked for could sue him for millions for his past deals and he remain in poverty, but the estate would have sufficient capital to continue as a managed reserve preserving both the wildlife and its rural way of existence. It was his hope that tourism would still flourish; that people would come to look at those metaphorical pebbles and enjoy what they saw enough to tell others, pass on those comments required and encourage the next generation to connect with nature, join with the past, look forward to the future, and ultimately give each of them chance to find themselves.

He invited a choice band of friends and locals to consider governing the estate from now on and all seemed pleased enough with the way the estate had continued to evolve that they agreed to this commission.

The shoots of spring appeared ripe in the buds of the trees and the new growth gave a natural hope for the prospects of the land as it entered its period of development and the early mating heralds of bird song met the ears in the lengthening of the mornings. It was a joy to be up early, to synchronise with the seasons and to feel the relative warmth of the days as they extended enough to allow sap to flow, buds to fill and ripen, catkins to drop and the snow to join the merriment of the river who beckoned for the fish to return. The first flies swarmed in nuptial throngs and the pioneer warblers found land and plenty as they ended their hormonally charged journeying from countries further south.

The geese thinned in number, and where the greys remained, the blacks diminished, left and were lost, or would be until the winter's icy return when its fingers of bitter chill would extend once again as tendrils from the north and welcome the magic light of the Arctic Circle to illuminate the furthest skies. Frosts lingered less and the snowdrops dotted the valley in a floating pile of dangling trumpets, heads down as if embarrassed or abashed by their stain-finished green-marked beauty.

Soon there would be bluebells and then foxgloves, fighting back the swarms of dog's mercury and ransoms, plants that would be smelt as much as felt and seen as they smothered the riversides and cloaked the swampier edges in first a leaf green then flowering white cloak, each with a head of tessellating blossom explosions. It made a bright green bed for the clean-picked stag skeleton, with nettles and thistles utilising the recycled nutrients, phosphorus and nitrogen, it had relinquished back to the Earth; life from death. Sol took the skull and mounted it over a shed door, a macabre display but it giving the grinning dead new life and display with its seven pronged antlers branching outwards in sky pursuit for a second time.

He still met with the cat as often as he could, but with spring her behaviour changed and for a while she had become more cautious and wilder, visiting less frequently and darting in to feed as if hunted or possessed. It was then that Sol noticed the bloating of the body, the tan colouring of the belly and the satisfaction of her licking of swollen teats, and he met with approval in his mind the thought that a new generation of wildcats was due. Nature, however rare or threatened, had taken its course and some hidden father had donated his genes to help with the efforts of the species, whatever his drive.

There was a hope for the wildcats of the *Bothan* glen.

And then, before it seemed possible, it was March's end, and with a heavy heart Sol joined the band on the Thursday night before he left for London and they played their gig, a concert, he felt, for a condemned man about to face his deserved destiny, full of poignancy and emotion. By the end of the month he would be bankrupt and seeking employment elsewhere. If he could, he would keep the house, but it was under threat. At least now the land belonged to the trust and not to him. He was laird of everything but owner of nothing; both responsible and not.

The music was a stunning mix of the traditional and the contemporary and there was a pleasing fusion of local and visitor to enjoy it, with the beer flowing freely and Sol relishing what could be his last few hours amongst friends and besides strangers sharing a mutual love for the Gael culture and of the music they made. There was singing and one man leapt forward during a break in proceedings and gave an oration in the old tongue, which was translated on the quiet by Hamish to make sure Sol understood. Wisdom and irony spoke from the past and instructed him, encouraged him and cheered him up. And yet, comprehension was not absolutely necessary, as just to hear the words, in the knowledge that just beyond the misted windows were the hills and the sea from which the language was born was enough.

And then Sol himself found he was the centre of a meeting as he officially appointed the trustees of the estate who had accepted their posts, to meet annually, or as the land and loch or they saw fit, to maintain the past and conserve the future of the *Faobhar Old Estate* and all that lived within it and made up its way of life. There was a cheer when at last Hamish was elected as Head of Trustees and Sol signed the calligraphic charter that would seal it.

"But what about you?" asked Hamish as the congratulations quelled. He had noted Sol's absence from any list, or council or on any paper concerning the future. "As laird, what's your role to be?"

"To lead from the back and be a part of it all for as long as I can afford. I have left enough money in the account for the estate to remain stable but it will need to draw in tourist money and trade in the homemade produce and locally reared animals if it's to stay afloat."

"That doesn't answer the question," Hamish pushed. "I'm not asking you to be a politician. The only thing left to you is *Bothan Faobhar* house and a bit of land around it."

"That's all I need," Sol replied. "Nature starts on the doorstep and if I don't look after the *Bothan* it'll start inside too. So long as I can wander, I'll be quite happy. Freedom is a great gift."

"But, what's your part to be in the estate? It'll always be your estate."

"I'm now just another tenant, happy to be in *Bothan Faobhar* for as long as I can be. Let's just see where life takes me over the next few days. What do you say to that?"

"Are you going away somewhere?" asked Gerry.

"What?" Sol asked with little enthusiasm to talk.

"You're talking like G did before he died, and Joe."

"I'm not dying though," Sol laughed, uncomfortable and evasive.

"And, you're talking as if you aren't coming back." It was James this time with a sense of urgency in his voice, and a murmur had broken out in the mass. "You are coming back?"

"Well, it's my past," explained Sol. "You see, it's... ...well, I fear it has caught up with me."

"Is this the woman," questioned Mrs Hamish. "Sue was it? We can talk to her."

"Well it is her... ...a bit, but not totally. It's more to do with the deals I made in business. Unlike the arrangements for the estate, they weren't as watertight as they could have been, and well I may have lost them... ...the old company... ...a lot of money. I'm being called back to London to face a hearing about it and they want their money back."

"We'll pay from the trust fund," said Hamish to general agreement.

"I'm afraid there won't be enough."

"Then I'll pay. I've savings."

"Not to the tune of hundreds of thousands or maybe even millions you haven't Hamish. Although I wish you had." There was silence after which Hamish joked. "We'll have a whip around then. I'll put the first fiver in and the rest will..." He tailed off. People laughed but it was an awkward sound, one underlain by shock.

"You see you were right Hamish, when you first met me. I was a bit of an idiot." Hamish started to deny what he had said. "The deal," Sol interjected, "it should have worked. It could still work. But, well... ...so much of business is gambling isn't it? But you don't need to worry, I've diverted all my commissions on past deals into the trust fund. This should help maintain the houses and allow you to develop or conserve aspects of the estate that need it most. That money's safe. But it does mean that if I do lose, and I tell you now I will not be able to pay, well... ...well, I'll be going away for a while."

"But we'll keep the house ready for your return," said Gerry, and there were nods. "It doesn't matter how long you're away for."

"What about years?" Sol asked glumly.

"Years," agreed Gerry, disheartened but keen to sound hopeful.

"Well, I go tomorrow in Addie. She's slower than what I used to have and so it'll take me a few days to get down to London. My hearing is at the end of the month. I've arranged to auction my violin to raise funds enough for a while and I'm going to make up with Sue after being away for a year. I'm sure it will be all right, but I have just one request. I'm still waiting for the next letter from G from *Tir na nÓg*. Can you keep it safe for me until I return, however long it will be?"

Sol turned around to sit down and then faced the crowd again. "I am sorry. Initially, when I first got to the *Bothan*...   ...well, I never wanted to stay there, and now that I am being forced to leave I don't want to go. You see there's just no satisfying some people."

He sat down and Gerry looked across at him, distant yet wishing that in some way her feelings could pass over the room sending some form of comfort.

A lull had fallen on the pub. No one really knew what to say or do. They all liked Sol for what he had done for them.

Then James Nevin stood up with a pint in his hand. "To Sol," he said taking in the crowded room with a swooping, beer swashing hand. "When he arrived I wanted him gone, when he stayed he gave me work, now he goes I'll miss him. I say to Jake Solomon, the greatest laird G could have chosen for the *Bothan* - to Jake Solomon; an unexpected asset."

And glasses were raised to Sol and men and women stood tall, "Jake Solomon," they incanted, "an unexpected asset."

"Thank you," Sol muttered, but he meant it.

"A last melody from the symphony," came a voice from the crowd. "A finale perhaps? Or is it going to be an unfinished symphony?"

There was laughter and Sol was pushed up to his feet with Joe's old fiddle thrust in his hand. He had no choice, he had to play.

"Well, I may have plenty of time to finish it if I end up locked up somewhere as a debtor and criminal, but I suppose it would start from this pub here in Old Town, the friends I have made and the future we will once again share...   ...one day. I'll call it '*Parting Friends: to the migrant that will return*', and it will be in G again for obvious reasons."

There was quickly quieted laughter.

Sol flicked his neck and closed his eyes, thought of the people gathered in, the friends that they all were, and he rested the bow on the strings. His mind followed swans as they re-found their destination hundreds of miles north and swallows who came from Africa.

There was joy in those thoughts. They had each been fed by the desire to leave then return but had been maintained throughout their travels by the memory of places loved, much like he may need in the weeks to come.

He breathed in deeply and struck up a joyful jig that carried him into the hills and amongst the geese that were leaving him for another year, and when he finally came back to the road in his mind he was ready for that trip and the long path to London.

Up early the next day, Sol threw his few belongings into the cab at the front of Addie, closed the *Bothan's* doors tight and made sure that her shutters were secure. They needed repair, grouting and filling, but that would happen in its time and for now it would have to wait. A spider, striped-toed legs exposed, attempted to hide its swollen abdomen in a rotted out knot within the grain. She was beautiful in her precious-stone patterned colours of amber brown, yellow, black and diamond white. *Araneus diadematus*, the crowned orb weaver – just a commonly overlooked creature that rid the house and garden of pests. Yet a year ago he would not have even known its name and would probably have killed it had he seen it.

He left it where it was, thankful that he had changed.

The spider relaxed soon after and used the warmth of the early sun to speed up the digestion processes taking place within it.

Sol knew Gerry, James, Hamish, Pete or others would keep an eye on the cottage, but it felt right to leave her shut down. Electricity wasn't a problem and would not need switching off. The fires had been swept out and all was in better condition than he had found it a year ago.

He was satisfied that the *Bothan* was ready to see him off and he turned to grin at her one last time, connecting with both hands' palms against the wall and willing her to understand that he would be back, one day. He felt her turn a colder shade, knowing she was left behind for now. But she would stand and she would wait. She returned his promise.

He started Addie up with her typical churn of the old engine lying under her shuddering bonnet. It was a heartening and encouraging sound and she felt like a friend who had accompanied him through much over the year. Putting the car in gear, he forced her on along the track, retracing his first meeting with the *Bothan* and the corner where he lost control of his sports car on that initial night. He saw the site where the wildcat had died and passed through the clunky gate that Hamish had set up with his band of helpers to disguise the entrance to *Bothan Faobhar*. Except for Arthur Peterson, it had fooled most people, and even he was a changed man since travelling down this drive, and it was now arranged for him to be ensconced on the estate after a short prison sentence taking up residence in the Gillie House. From there he could watch the lake for Sol and help Pete in the studio. His was a second chance given and a fully pardoned forgiveness expressed in actions that counted far greater than words.

Together they passed through New Town and chugged beside the shop on the side of the road in the middle of nowhere where a scruffy man once again waved from the garden. How like him Sol had become he wondered, waving happily back and checking that he had packed a decent suit, shoes and the shaving gear he would need to give himself a normal appearance for the London meeting.

In an hour he made a main road and after several more a motorway appeared as an extension of continuous grey that expanded into two and later three lanes, all roads being interconnected in some way like the venous network of a great concrete beast whose towns and cities collected into organs and systems. He was able to round Glasgow and stop for a coffee, a brew he no longer recognised for its purity of construction and simple taste. The traffic had raced past him for most of the way as Addie was limited in terms of speed, and he shook his head when thinking about how he would have responded to this smoking, crawling and rust-enclosed agricultural bucket just a year ago. He would have been there, up behind, cursing, maybe flashing and roaring under the influence of caffeine and nicotine. Now the coffee drug percolated his blood and made him alert to the red kites that scarred the air, the kestrels that hung and the sparrows in every car park, nervously picking the litter, the scourge of the plastic packaged human race; that which he had never really noticed on previous journeys but which offended him now.

Addie's responses were unaffected by the caffeine, unlike the old sports cars.

He had chosen to drive her all the way as if she were the only old friend who was prepared to travel with him. He knew that ecologically she was more wasteful than say the train, the bus or other public transport, but the cost of any of these was now so great and his finances so fragile that he knew he no longer enjoyed the luxury of simply choosing to be driven, towed or carried by another. It was a catch twenty two which annoyed him and kept poking its way into his wandering thoughts. In order to reduce our emissions public transport should have been the obvious choice for the majority but it was simply beyond the price which the ordinary person could pay and was limited to just the very rich, the upper echelon of society. Not for the first time he speculated what he would be able to do if in government, but realistically knew he would have little effect even if he did have the inclination and popularity required to be electable or elected.

England announced itself as he passed the large white metal sign with the St. George's flag emblazoned over it. But Sol was curious which country he had been in once he left the saltire behind and before he passed this noticeboard. It was a no man's land between names that he felt described the difference between the two countries well; they appeared just the same, separated only by a label, as he crossed the Eden and took the M6 south. He knew that over this river and idyllic pastures blood had been spilled in battle over territory. How different it was now and how homogenous one nation to the next.

Stopping in the Lakes, where the hills were tall enough to give him the security of knowing the Earth was near and that he could connect with the ground, Sol pulled over on a grassy verge and camped rough under the stars, lying within the hedgerow wrapped in a ratted woollen blanket. A barn owl flitted the misted air for an hour before he slept, and he was taken back to the brown owls of his own yard. There he prayed that somewhere miles north his hunting cat and her unborn kits were safe. It was all that he could do to just think of them. And like any migrant, he thought of home; the *Bothan* in the glen, in the hills, by the loch, surrounded by the sea in a different country.

One day he would return.

He looked up at the same constellations in a sky he had shared with anyone down here that had noticed it before, but he knew them from a slightly altered angle, one from hundreds of miles north of where he lay, itching as the hawthorn scratched and the flies rose. Each pinprick of light, millions of years in age, gave him a security that the universe still ticked on and gave an insight into its history if only he could read it.

There was a fox walling the field for a while. Although a familiar animal, he felt that he did not know this scrawny relative of its northern cousin who haunted the *Bothan,* and a strange homesickness pitted itself in his stomach.

He slept fitfully and then woke as an early morning mist started to lift and the chill from his bones went with it. Once again in Addie, he gained some miles before stopping at a 70s Moto that he had visited a season before.

Needing breakfast coffee upon which to drive his spirit on to the city that called for him, Sol joined a short queue for a drink and ordered an '*Americano*'. It felt silly giving black coffee this fake Italian name and he laughed his thoughts out loud as a joke to the lady who served him.

She giggled back nervously as she prepared his drink and sealed it hermetically in its plasticised card cup. Both of them shared recognition of the other. They had met before, a year ago.

"Thank you," he said.

"My pleasure, enjoy your day," she thanked with the same greeting she had probably said to every single customer she had served at this black imitation stone bar worktop for the last twelve months.

"What's your name," he asked, suddenly full of questions.

"Grace," she replied pointing to her obvious badge that stated her name in white on black, and he smiled inwardly to know that grace was what he needed more than anything else, today of all days.

"Thank you, Grace," he said and handed her a tip of twice the value of the over-priced coffee.

"What's this?" she replied.

"A tip."

"What for?"

"We met, a year ago, almost to the day. I was rude to you and you didn't deserve it. I was a different man then. Sorry."

"But…   …lots of people are rude to me. It comes with the job. I'm just a barista."

"Just?" asked Sol.

"Well really that's just a posh way of saying waitress."

"Waitress?" he asked. "What do you want to be?" and he looked around suspiciously. There was no queue. "I'll stop talking if this is at all awkward. But there's no one waiting as it's still quite early."

"No," she said wiping the surface, now a clean wet black, but still artificial. "Not awkward. Just…"

"Well, answer the question then. No strings attached…   …not trying to be weird…   …I'm just interested that's all."

"I want to be a chef," she answered nervously. "But making coffee was the closest I could get to it. I've no qualifications really. Everyone wants certificates and grades now."
"What sort of food?"
"Italian mostly."
He thought for a moment and slurped his coffee, wincing at the heat and flavour. "And what do you think to this coffee?" he asked.
"Honestly?"
"Well it's not that nice. I'd use different beans. An Italian roast of course. They say these are Italian roast but it's not true. I've read the labels on the boxes. But if you charge enough everyone thinks they've been given good coffee and no one complains. Choose a price and double it... ...that's what the boss says."
They both smiled.
"So, how do you intend to become a chef then?"
"I just need a lucky break."
"Well, do you have the Internet?" She nodded. "Good. To check that I'm not just some weirdo you can learn about who I am first of all. You can find out all about me on this blog." He wrote down details on the serviette she had given him to wrap his disposable coffee cup up in. It was an unnecessary nicety and just added to the waste that flitted the wind out in the car park like air riding jellyfish. It directed her to Pete's blog. "If you want to train as a chef, I have friends looking to take someone on in these restaurants, and one friend, called Al, well, he's in the blog... ...well, he could be more than a lucky break for you." Sol scribbled a list of names of hotels and restaurants down on another clean serviette. "They've all got websites and you can check that they're safe and okay."
"But what's the catch?"
"Catch?"
"Yes. There's got to be a catch."
"The catch is that you'd have to live in a very small community, you'll see that on the blog too. It's quite isolated and everybody

will learn your business in no time if you don't keep it a secret. But, the biggest catch is that you'll be living in the most wonderful area of northwest Scotland. I've been away from there for just one day and I'm missing it, its wildlife, its music and its people already."

"That's the catch?"

"Aye," he said with a slight Scottish lilt to his accent. "There's no pressure. I'll be passing through this way soon I hope and I'll see if you've thought about it when I do. And... ...well, it was nice meeting you Grace. I'm just sorry it's taken me a year to apologise to you in person."

"And your name?" she asked offering her hand for him to shake. She was confused by this strange man and his offer.

"Jake Solomon," he said. "But you can call me Sol."

"Solomon the wise?"

"If only."

And he left with his overheated, overpriced coffee in hand with a feeling of freedom in his gait and step, enjoying that chance to hopefully provide a serendipitous moment to another who needed their moment to change their life. Grace stood for a moment at the bar, wiped it with a cloth again and then pocketed the serviettes after folding them neatly.

She would look these places up and check out this blog, she would follow up his recommendations and she would meet Sol again, however soon he passed by in the future.

Hers was a life due to change.

Sol returned to Addie, padding the black alien asphalt that had become tacky under a heightening sun that was already hot. The cars were picking up in their numbers, powering their way left and right behind the hedgerow where he had parked. Sparrows *'cheeped'* from within its badly trimmed structure. It still displayed the brutal scars of an overzealous trim and a poorly-trained gardener who lacked the care or the understanding to want to complete a good job that would extend the life of the hedge, improve its appearance or have any positive impact on its wildlife. Biology felt threatened here, and it put Sol on edge.

Beyond was the roar of car after car. Mechanical monsters which chased each other in caterpillars of motion, leaching from them a developing haze of pollution that was beginning to rise as a mouldy citrus-orange cloud already despite the early time.

In a few hours he would make that metropolis of London where the smog would be fully matured. But even now he was affected and he could perceive the amassing of grit and dirt in his nostrils and roll it over his tongue. It tasted brown.

There was part excitement and exhilaration as the migrant returned after a twelve-month exile. But he also knew he was travelling to a land flattened and then built back up by that ant-like constructor, human. Wild places removed, we had then replaced it with what we considered as enough with parks and manicured spaces of garden where only those forgotten and undergoing succession back towards a climax community of woodland showed any real potential. Sure there would be wildlife there but only where people allowed it, placed it or contained it. And beyond this were the ubiquitous town pigeons, sewer rats, grey squirrels and above all the domestic cats, free to add their controlling element on the smaller things whenever they were allowed to roam, especially at night.

He could see the city from a long way off. Towers that attacked and scarred the horizon, instantly recognisable the world over as that power base of UK commerce stretching its powerful reach ever towards the sun as if one day it could eclipse and control even that great burning fireball star. Modern Towers of Babel, they threatened the heavens. But Sol knew that these buildings, the nesting site of the pigeon and the peregrine, had become essential places of business, worshipped in their own way like enormous stone circles erected of glass and steel in the praise of the money god; modern paradigms of his own monoliths erected in the estate moorland and the standing stone still looking over the sea from the headland. Everything he could see in the distance was built on the promise of worth and value, and how much each person placed on bars of gold stored in vaults, strips of metal sewn in to paper, discs of metal that could be kept in a pocket, the transfer of promises made in emails and the costs of bricks once they had been joined together by mortar. A loss of this faith in the money god and all of it would be gone and surprisingly quickly. The sun would still rise and the moon still wane, the wildlife would return, but the humans would end.

He shivered convulsively. Although he had begun to dislike what he approached, he knew that others would not see that, nor comprehend it, and he understood the requirement for this place for everything he still held dear.

But, here there was coffee that could be purchased from across the world available on every street corner, or if you needed to fill your time to the maximum with every other business, it could be delivered by hand to your place of work. Here was the place where washing the pots was a distant memory only retained in the museum of life, where a machine replaced the human and if a robot could be employed by some then it would be. Here was that sphere which allowed you to eat as much as you desired, seek calories and decadent delights such that eating too much was fully possible, diets necessary and the lack of natural exercise meant an unnatural replacement in the form of a gym or a trainer where needed. Electricity flowed without question and the state would hold up those who most needed it or who could twist their story such that they could demand and claim it, unquestioned. This was the land where community was an artificial construct of your own dwelling and what you chose to surround it with, where *communication virtual* was becoming the preferred norm; relationship at a distance. It had once been his world.

He had somehow evolved, adapting for a new, ironically old, environment and felt somehow outclassed and unprepared for the demanding, competition, red-clawed world he headed back towards as if he had been asleep for the last twelve months. He was concerned and did not look forward to his reinsertion back.

He knew he was being unfair. This was a city that until a year ago had been his home. One he had understood and relished.

It was a cosmopolitan urban mix of all peoples of all thoughts, and its purpose extended well beyond the commercial districts. He remembered that home was what the person made of it and each had a different place to rest their heart, even if he had left his hundreds of miles north of where he now was, driving away from it with a feeling of deep gloom about him.

Before a migrant leaves us, it often exhibits preparatory behaviours. The gathering in numbers on wires, the collection of more food than before and then the wider and wider ventures away from the home site to ensure all land marks are learnt for return journeys. Ordinary life takes on a nostalgic air as the traveller looks back on what it has achieved. A clutch of eggs may have been successful and a nesting location stored for future use, feeding may have better here and worse there, and only during these weeks or those others, or it may recall where the predators tried to get them. All this information and more is stored and logged logically in tiny brains that will be carried maybe just a short distance, but often for thousands of miles, on diminutive wings that seem barely able to go the distance.

And then there are the seasons that bring their species out of torpor or encourage them on to hatch and emerge at the end of which they are gone, having left their germ lines for another year to repeat the process for all time. They can be seen, preparing and making way for the end of a life and the passing of the baton on to another generation or creating a den that will sustain them, even one in which to hibernate or aestivate and emerge from on the other side.

If you had been observant, you would have sensed the changes, seen the performances and predicted the moves and their subsequent loss from the wild scenery; they can all be read about, especially in countries where the written accounts of our wild relatives are so well kept and published. But slowly, anyone who is aware of the sounds of nature and the species that accompany us will notice, however hard it might be to pinpoint the actual date or time, that something has gone and left a void.

Sometimes, whilst they are away we prepare nest boxes and put up feeders to make their return easier. We check things, maintain them, clean them and wonder what we can do to make life with us easier, more attractive and more observable from the comfort of our human circles. And then we have little choice but to wait to see the effects of our improvements, something we are ill designed to do well. But wait me must and wait some of us do, until they come back.

Gerry visited the *Bothan* coming in from the sea loch with Nevin at the tiller. They rode the waves up the hissing beach, she feeling that even the taunt of *The Tern*'s hull over the coral sands was lonelier and emptier than had been before. Something was missing, and although she knew it was her thought that changed the tone of every sound and each sight that greeted her arrival, she knew that the element that made the *Bothan*'s three-dimensional jigsaw complete was Sol.

The cottage was shuttered up and had lost something of its soul without him.

There was his ridiculous plastic chair where it always was out in the yard, black stained by lichen and *Aspergillus* growth, and the battered metal bucket, salt-encrusted and dented, stacked high with blood-reddened bones. They stood remotely in the cobbled yard where the grasses and round leaves of the plantains poked up and dotted the interstitial soils green. Here were the feeders swinging freely on the branches, rocked backwards and forwards by the constant traffic of birds, from the wood to the wood. Colourful motions of feather on wings that beat and flitted around, blurs of delight. There was a deer browsing the edge of the forest, a young olive roe buck. He hadn't heard Gerry's arrival and chewed noisily with head upright on a sinuous neck finished off with a grey tufted line that ran like a tie down its front, bulging where the cartilage of its larynx projected through the skin. Flies buzzed his ears, which twitched in irritation as they searched the glen's soundscape.

But the place was empty now. Joyless and sombre it felt like only a partially complete habitat from which the keystone species had gone, become extinct.

Nevin saw to *The Tern* and then joined Gerry in the garden where she intended for them to hoe the soil and free the vegetables of the weeds that spring had donated to them.

"It's dead without him," she commented, taking in the full vista framed by the frost-capped mountain behind. "Blind without its windows showing through the shutters. I'll have to open them. I can't look at it like this."

The two of them busied themselves opening the *Bothan* back up to life and then stood back to admire what they had done. It still was not whole but James nodded thoughtfully. "She can see again now." He looked up at the chimneystack where a jackdaw had nested, creating a cluttered bowl of twiggy branches, and along the roofline he clocked where mosses were filling the gutter and the tiles had slipped loose. "That needs some work up there," he commented and he pointed out the slates' dropped position and an irregular crack that had burst through the mortar of the wall and rent it apart to reveal slabs of stone under and the internal fluff of horse hair insulation and daub cement; infrastructure that should have remained hidden. In addition he soon picked out those places where biology had successfully overtaken humanity in its eternal battle for succession of the plot.

"I'll get on to that," he said, and he started to draw up the mental list required to complete the repairs in Sol's absence. He then left to search the sheds, returning later with ladders, mortar and tools, placing a call through to some of his workmen to see if they could lend a hand for the day.

Hamish arrived next, unable to help himself and to keep away. He and his wife ambled down the drive in their Land Rover as it tackled the unkempt nature of the red mud and rock, and they joined Nevin and Gerry in front of the little white cottage. He had a letter from G in his hand, due to be delivered on the anniversary of Sol's arrival at the end of the month in just a few days' time. Left with the task of delivering each month's posthumous mail he knew that this last one would be the most poignant, being received on Sol's return to the *Bothan*. He also had an official looking brown envelope that had been placed by the postman in the box at the end of the drive. It caused him concern and he wondered whether to open it.

Across his back was slung a black leather bag, soft and strangely shaped in a feminine fashion. These he put carefully on the dining table in the front room before going out to start chopping wood in the back yard and piling it along the shaded rear wall of the *Bothan* where the algae grew shiny and the mosses formed their miniature thickets of deep emerald. Ferns fanned their unfurled canopies over in diminutive jungles, tropical green and moist. Meanwhile Mrs Hamish started work on deep cleaning what Sol had neglected that year.

Soon Euan appeared with Sarah and their growing baby Gee. Sarah helped Mrs Hamish in the house, as she had promised she would do once able, and Euan joined Nevin on the roof. The whitewash on the walls had been started by Sol but never finished, and when Pete arrived with a team from the studio they set to painting the walls, chipping out rotten wood from the window frames and then filling and touching up the damage they had intentionally incurred.

Sally brought a team down from the plantation, bringing logs for preparation with them on the back of a high-walled low loader that seemed to travel the land in impossible fashion, twisting like a Komodo Dragon at joints all along its structure, sinuous-spine'd and torturous. They brought noise and grease with them, with the heady smell of fresh cut pine. But they worked hard and soon the ready to fire, chopped timbers were being stacked in their species in pyramids to dry as they helped with the hardest work of sawing, splitting and chopping.

Hamish made a good fire in the kitchen range and prepared coffee and tea for everyone in large billycans that he hoped he had cleaned enough. Quite a crowd had appeared - none called upon. There were people from the towns who had never been up to *Bothan Faobhar* before, all the tenants had drifted down and milled in, and even paying tourists who were normally forbidden from this driveway had joined the melee of crawling humans in and around the ordinarily quiet little cottage. Hiving like bees their collective operations would have pleased even the most judgemental of termites.

From a distance, maybe up on the headland, where if they could Joe and G would have been watching over the *Bothan* to make sure all remained well, it looked like there really were insects at work crawling on and around some little colony. It wasn't just to be a day's job, but when struck up to action it is amazing what a community can do.

Over drinks they all looked inwards at their steaming brews as they sat gathered in their sweaty forms in the yard, contemplating many personal thoughts on a group theme.

"How long will he be?" asked one woman, taking shade by the forest where the leaves dappled the high sun's light hues of branch and leaf as a natural camouflage.

"Two days down," someone else added, "two days back, a day for the auction and two days for the hearing. I'd say he'd be a week at least."

"Is it long enough? To finish the cottage for him?"

"Too long," mused Hamish staring down into his *Bothan* brown mug through which he failed to see the permanent stains on the base. "But maybe we *can* finish this old nest box off for his return? Have it ready, waiting and welcoming."

A man became visible at the furthest end of the drive that could be seen, where it swept around the corner of the hill and ran down to the cottage. He was shabbily dressed and as he approached from the shadow of the herbage a murmur spread amongst the people resting in the yard, lasting until the man stood at the edge of the crowd and loitered. He gave the impression of the desire to be included. But he just stood there, not quite close enough to join, requiring invitation first; like the awkward child in the school yard who doesn't know how to be a part of it. He was Arthur Peterson.

Hamish turned to him and under that gaze Peterson felt uncomfortable in the knowledge that Sol's choice to give him a second chance would not necessarily have been a popular one.

"Hello," he said nervously. There were mutters from amongst the people followed by an oppressive silence. And then a prong-tailed silhouette of a bird scooped up and over the crowns of the natural pinewood and everyone looked up.

The bird panned left and directly over Peterson, fanning its tail actively and catching the drifts of the wind on long angular wings daubed red-brown, black and patched with white. With yellow beak down-faced its piercing scavenger's eyes focused on the people by the house giving them a curious sense of being scanned and judged. *Who were they?*

"Welcome," called Hamish coming to and suddenly standing up from Sol's plastic chair and giving his place to Peterson. "Join the group. Coffee or tea?"

"Are you sure?" he asked as the kite drifted around lazily and called a gripping '*keeyar*'.

"If you're a friend of Sol's and he has offered you his protection, then you're a friend of mine, and I offer you my protection too. Believe it or not, we have far more in common with each other than you may yet believe. Sit. Coffee of tea? They both look the same and because of the water they taste the same as well. But it's nice to think you have a choice."

There was laughter and the mass relaxed as the kite moved on. A species once almost lost from Britain, hunted to the very brink of extinction as an unwanted threat to livestock and game, it had returned, was welcomed and was a pleasure to see. The irony was not lost on Hamish.

They worked for a week and the *Bothan,* although she retained her rustic charm and her battered appeal, was whitened and made sound, cleaned and prepared for a return. But Sol did not come back as predicted. Like the anxious wait of the birder for the migrants, who must pass through the unselective shellfire of the Mediterranean and other countries where unregulated shooting is rife, the locals missed him and waited for news of his reappearance or any signs.

There had been a text to say that Sol had arrived safely in London and his violin was due to be auctioned, but like that signal from a tracking device that suddenly dies, nothing was heard from then onwards, and a week had gone rapidly by. The people began to worry, talk and make up facts that had '*probably*' occurred, as they naturally do when short of actual information.

Day by day as the house was completed and repaired, fewer and fewer visited the *Bothan* until it was left alone, clean bright and ready, with regular-changed flowers in the vases, a pantry full of often checked and changed food, and fires prepared for action.

Pete fed Quicksilver. He sat nightly in Sol's chair and captured images of this heavily pregnant female that he posted on the blog as an almost religious act and daily service to his missing friend.

It was just under two weeks when Sol did reappear at the end of the drive in Addie, when nobody was watching and the wildlife had turned a blind eye. They chugged up to the gate, where the box had been re-hung and painted, although there was now no name to identify what house lay beyond the apparently locked gate. It was nearing dark and it was Thursday and so he knew that a gig would be starting down at the inn in an hour or two. Now, without an instrument, he would be unable to play, but he could listen, maybe just slip in at the back and enjoy some music over a beer.

He passed through the gate and eavesdropped on the steady drips of water rolling from the water-saturated cloud that stayed low to the ground to cover his passage along the drive. A deer barked and the hoot of an early evening owl echoed through the mists that hung and moped along the rain-flushed ground and then, once grounded, tinkled in rivulets through the dells and between the moss-daubed rocks.

He had once been scared by those noises, had almost run along the track in macabre, fictional fear, one instilled in him by a dependence on light and control from the city. But now he welcomed them.

He was home and those night noises were the best welcome this hour could provide.

He drove Addie steadily along the track until he knew the moment would come when the cottage would open its vista out to him, and then there she was, in the clarity of the fog-lifted valley. Whiter than he remembered, and cleaner of window, with the black-painted shutters thrust back, cobweb free and gloss shiny. The garden was neat, and flowers blossomed in the beds that ran along the wall, the yard clear, save for a bucket of rabbit bones, had been tidied and even the roof looked squarer and more weed free than before.

Alighting from Addie's cab he leapt down to the ground and walked the last few yards with real spring to his step feeling the comfort of mud under his shoes and stones that poked up into the souls of his feet. It was a strange comparison to the flat homogeny of city tarmac. He entered by the garden gate, re-hung on its hinges, painted and with a sign on a post clearly stating that he had returned to *Bothan Faobhar*. It was like home but different, as if seeing a familiar view of a room where the pictures had been straightened from the crooked angle you've become used to seeing them, feeling fresher and yet the same. And then he heard the geese on the water and the lap of the shore, the pipe of the redshank and the call of a crying loon out there in some indefinable position in the mist, herding the water spirits and kelpies. No sirens, no lights, no voices, no music, just calm.

He stood for a moment and listened, filling his ears with the sounds, his nostrils with the scents and sensing the electric excitement of the air across his skin. His shivers were of the thrill to be right here right now.

Inside he paced the dark-lit passageway knowingly seeking the doorway to the front room filled with the dusk shadows of the window frame, shapes that spilled over the floor in a comfortable way. He lit a paraffin lamp and pumped it up to full pressure so that it glowed that spitting welder white that burnt the retina if you looked too intently into it, the mantle inside spluttering as the liquid vaporised and caught. He placed it on the dining room table as the orb of illumination spread out from the centre of the room and sent shadows in radial patterns away to show him his missed front room. Even inside, even in this inadequate light, so pale in contrast to the diffused and controlled rooms he had spent the last few weeks in, where power was no concern and on immediate wired supply, he could see that the place was cleaner than he had left it.

There were two letters there waiting and a large leather item, black and coffin-shaped that for all intents and purposes looked like a violin case. *How he missed having a quality instrument. Now would have been an ideal time to play it and reconnect, to express and create.*

The first of the envelopes was brown and unexciting, computer printed and formal. He slid his fingers under the fold and slit it open, leaving the gummed vee stuck down. Withdrawing the bright white-papered perfect-typed letter it contained he read it and then sat down at the table to laugh at the details inside. It was all past news to him, confirming what he had already found out whilst down in London at the hearings. Timing was everything and this was received simply days too late.

The second envelope interested him more. It was formed from firm white paper, thick and fibrous. It contained the handwritten letter he was expecting from G, announcing that this would be his last and admitting to Sol what he already knew about G's destination, *Tir na nÓg*. And then it went on to tell him more, something he had not expected at all.

He laughed loudly to himself, seeing a wonderful irony in the old man's posthumous words. He, Sol, sat there and contemplated that he had been well tested by a dead man and he now knew it.

Then Sol placed his hand on the soft and supple leather bag left in the middle of the table and felt it carefully. He ran his fingers up and down the soft casing, worn dry in places where the etching of much use had aged and fatigued it. There was a wooden stem and a curvaceous body underneath, and it certainly felt very much like a violin, and so he untied its fixings and parted the supple hide material to see what it actually was. Then he closed his eyes and staggered backwards with a sense of disbelief.

Now he knew that he *had* to make the inn in Old Town, whatever the costs in time, and join in the gig before it was over. Anything else was inconceivable.

It took him a while to conduct Addie along the track safely, guided by her inadequate lights set in the middle of the bonnet either side of the grate. Little crossed in front but it was too slow. He then drove her down the meandering road, passed the knitting shed by the black pool into New Town with time slipping backwards and away. But he made it in time for the interval, hearing the magical notes of a Scottish small pipe solo played by Hamish, the notes each hanging there in the stillness of the air. It was hypnotic and mythical, the notes drifting out on to the street as he strode along. Some essence from the inn passed clean over the road carrying out to the sea where the seals wailed their appreciation in return and the bells at the mast tops clanged and their ropes jabbered in a lose wind.

Walking into the pub Sol was met by surprised faces that parted and gave way, their bodies falling back into the crowd in wonder, like Moses separating the seas to lead the Israelites to safety. Sol stepped in and through in their protection as the crowd pressed in behind, re-closing in. The notes drew him onwards until he was there at the front, eyes fixed on Hamish's as he played his final lingering note.

They smiled at each other and Hamish dropped the pipes from his mouth letting their bag sink flaccidly under gravity. He stood to address his long gone friend.

"Took your bloody time," he greeted and stretched out his arms in natural embrace.

"Sorry, yes," answered Sol returning the gesture. "I forgot I had a phone whilst I was in London and then as things moved faster than I thought they would I went up to visit my brother and he's got the same reception as I used to have. Then I was a bit embarrassed and came straight back. But I thought no one would've missed me anyway. Sorry."

"Missed you?" chided Hamish to the agreement of others around. "Of course we have. You see you're one of us lad, part of the community here; a native – or else you've just turned feral. We've been worried sick. What happened? And, are you going to jail or not?"

A froth-glassed drink appeared on the table, the black and tarry beer locally brewed and now nationally enjoyed, which was then thrust into Sol's hand. A chair was drawn up and a crowd drew in to hear. There was a story to be told and ears to listen, there were histories to be understood and pathways to be assessed.

"I believe a meeting has been called," Hamish added as people continued to gather around, interested and thirsty for answers. "What happened?"

"Well," started Sol addressing the muffled silence. "I got down to London and met up with Sue, but on the way I met Grace."

"Grace?" shouted the Landlord. "Wants to be a chef? She's called me. Tells me she's a friend of yours? She comes up next month for a trial and Al has agreed to give her some time at his place too. Lovely girl by the sounds of it."

"That'll be her. But anyway, that's another story…"

He had sold his violin at auction and made quite a profit and enough to keep him at *Bothan Faobhar* for now. Then he had gone to the hearing at the old company as requested but couldn't find anyone there to greet him. As he never answered texts these days, they had written to him instead informing him of news that affected the case. But he had not received that letter in time and so he had gone to the hearing they had called him to anyway. A few weeks ahead of the year's anniversary of the Tokyo deal it had finally gone through and made good, producing such a profit that the company were more interested in having him back as an employee than suing him and sending him to jail. They had offered him large financial incentives, because *"people with that tenacity and nerve were what made Britain great!"*

"Or broke," shouted Hamish.

So he had naturally turned them down and asked instead for the commission he was due. This of course was paid straight to the estate trust fund and so guaranteed the future of the *Faobhar* estate, its houses and wildlife for quite some time after he had left.

There was a cheer.

He had secured the estate and he had made up with Sue enough to be friends at least. But, Sol explained, he knew he was still as good as bankrupt in the very near future without an income and with no prospect of employment, especially now that he had turned down work with the old company. Keen to leave the city he had headed north and on a whim had been to visit his old music teacher, now an old and decrepit man long retired. Ever an encouragement they played through the symphony together and he had given Sol the confidence to approach a music publisher and they had shown remarkable and unusual interest in his symphony in memory of G if he were to finish it. Such was the power of the personal introduction and the networking capacity of his old teacher and mentor. He had potentially found a new career that would keep him employed and the bailiffs away from the door, if only for now.

On his journey back he had then visited his brother and made his peace there and then returned to the inn via the *Bothan* where he found the letter from G. It ended thus,

'And so Sol, if I have chosen wisely you remain still at the Bothan on the edge, the estate remains intact and the people well cared for, the wildlife still thrives and the locals have taken you in as one of their own.'

Sol looked around for confirmation and then thanked them for what they had done to tidy and repair *Bothan Faobhar* in his absence. He read on.

'Which leaves me one last thing to write before I pass on to Tir na nÒg.

I have asked my solicitors to transfer the money you paid for the estate back into your account on the year's anniversary of your purchasing the property I love, in the full knowledge that I chose the right man to succeed me. Use this investment wisely.

Look after her until we meet on another shore at Tir na nÒg. I am certain we shall once you have discovered the appropriate route to get here.

Yours sincerely,

G'

"And so," announced Sol standing with his beer held aloft, "I can finally afford to stay!"

And there was a resounding cheer around the inn and glasses chinked and ale flowed and a tune was demanded of Sol on his violin.

"Which," he shouted in great mirth, "brings me to this." And he drew up the simple leather case that he had found on the dining room table next to his two letters.

There was silence as the crowd drew in witness what he did. Carefully and with utmost tenderness he unlatched the straps and parted the black leather and withdrew a dark wood violin from inside. Around its neck hung a handwritten label card label dangling on a twisted string loop, which stated in spidery but clear writing '*To Sol, this is not for sale however much Al offers you, Joe*'.

"That old Joe always had the last laugh," called Sol. "He never threw this beautiful old fiddle over the side to the *Blue Men* of the loch at all." He stroked its precious, sonorous wood reverently as he thought back to that moment when the old hard case had dropped over the edge of the boat out on the loch and recalled that wicked glint in old Joe's eye. "No. He left it for me with one of you." And he caught that same mischievous look in Hamish's face, the friend to so many here even after death.

"Then, let's hear you play it," goaded the older man, more satisfied to his wrinkled old heart than he could express in words, with crease lines of pleasure radiating his eyes and cheeks.

And play Sol did.

He chose a Scottish themed tune that to him described the moorland and hills, and the expanse of the scenery they all shared, that land which had accepted him as one of its own and welcomed him back as a flying migrant returning from foreign shores.

It was his finale for the symphony in G.

Chapter 26: Finale

(Casta Diva from Norma, Vincenzo Bellini)

He sat on the headland and watched the sea.

It rocked and bobbed in eccentric activity, sometimes blue and at other times green with coral sand reflection. There were white tops further out and the light wind licked it up into swirling patterns that stained the surface as cream in strong coffee, stirred but not mixed. He could see the gannets, sleek bullets of birds, twisting in their flight to dive bomb the fish and return in glistening droplets of spume and water to capture food from heavenly heights, fish-filled and satisfied. Their beady bandit-ringed eyes were suspended above and beyond chisel beaks that spoke of power and grip.

Sol had enjoyed a good day's hunting. Not at the cost of lives, but at the cost of his time. He had listed birds and beetles, fungi and plants, some of which he had never seen before. Now he was ready to return home exhausted but happy to be on the estate where he was laird of nothing but everything at the same time. His symphony manuscript was posted away, hidden in an ordinary brown envelope that was chasing his creative dreams across Britain in the back of a red van, and he awaited news of his melodious description of the *Bothan's* biosphere, the one he kept hidden in plain sight of the rest of the world. Physically it was trapped behind a camouflaged gate and approached mostly by sea, and yet electronically and emotionally it was reported on through the blog and the endless photographs and memories that the tourists staying at the garage took with them as they learnt the best ways to capture the wilds on digital screens and film. Art had become its medium and even painters had started to visit.

He stood and played his priceless violin to the seabirds and the heathers, the grasses and the rocks themselves, bare foot so as to bond more readily with the essence of the land and to distil it directly into a voice through his melodies. Call it a fiddle or a violin; it really had no value as an instrument despite being a much sort after contraption by quirk of its rarity and age and the name its builder had left upon it – it was just a violin, just a fiddle, and just wood and glue. But to Sol it was beyond the value that could be obtained through auction alone as it was now an heirloom of *Bothan Faobhar* and her estate where it would remain for as long as it could be tuned or recognised as the instrument it was.

It was made for playing and it would be played.

It was made for hearing and it would be heard.

It was made to create music and together they would create it.

When he had finished, sweating a skin of moisture that clung to his shirt, and was finally fatigued, he dropped the instrument and bow to either side of his panting chest and acknowledged his invisible audience in a moment of madness, and then looked directly up into the face of the sun. A swiping sound, regular and metronomic had plucked his attention. There, angelic and huge, the whooper swans took their wide circle of him and then set off in a straight line out to the sea, taking their annual leave of the glen and its winter protection. For a second year they had come to give him their peace for another summer and he waved to see them go, wild friends lost for another season.

Sol could not help but sigh to watch their departure and to recognise the coincidental timing of yet another natural scene for which he had been witness when no one else had or could have. He was blessed.

Leaving the headland he found the crag path down to where the woodland's flora had engulfed the deer carcass so that even its skull-less bones were lost from sight and the flies had forgotten its existence. The river gloried in a fine day when the water was full within her and the power surged down and along, drawing the trout upwards to the loch where the body of old Joe lay sleeping. That empty shell, lacking the real spirit of what made it that great, blind, old man, was now buried deep under a cairn marked with a memorial rock and a finely carved Celtic salmon in mid leap. The river continuously accompanied his final resting place with a steady trickling tune that descended as she dropped from the loch and cascaded the algae-entombed rocks of the first waterfall. She met the fish as they rose upstream, and she encouraged them to jump the torrents of weirs and rocks she had left ready for their ascent of the impossible, leaping the air when the water would not allow them onwards in her life-giving medium.

Sol took the wood quickly and enjoyed their dappled shade of greens and of hues he felt he had never seen before, and he envied the artist who could capture them. Tempted by a stray thought, he wondered if he could learn to daub the canvass with oil or splash pigments over paper well enough to record these moments graphically, which until now in his head played as an uninterrupted musical score. The birds sang, a choir of singers who naturally found melody and counter tune, harmonising without effort and a buzzard called 'kee-arr' as it drifted the canopy top and announced its territory.

And then he was there in the yard by the bucket.

Home.

He filled the small and innocuous metal container, that secret to his success at finding his first wildcat, placing in it a pheasant head, some feathers and bones that he had saved from the bird he had prepared for supper. Then as religious tradition demanded he settled down in the plastic chair as he so often did and quickly fell into his reverential watch, half sleeping and half sentry.

It didn't take long for Quicksilver to visit, she knew his pattern of life so well, read him and sensed him. Before then Sol was kept entertained by the clown-like behaviour of the long-tails as they bounded and ambled as cleverly trained acrobats might, along the shrub tops and through the leaves of trees on the edge of the forest. The waders called to each other and gathered their speckled broods from across the machair grasses that were pushing up fly-drenched flowers from within their shallow sea-salted soils.

He considered himself a lucky man to have been given this grandest of second chances, and to have been put in a position where at times he could give others theirs too. It was not the feeling of power that he enjoyed, but the opportunity it allowed for redemption both for himself and the others he met on the way. Here there was a healing by nature that he could not have achieved anywhere else; a result of that time for reflection that meant he could consider the right and the wrong, when before he would have rushed and flitted blindly from one thing on to the next. True, he was drawn strangely by the pagan relic rocks on the hillside and the little chapel beyond the headland having discovered a connection to something far greater than the immediate and what he could fully understand. But he was both gladdened and humbled by the lack of concern that the natural things had for his past, his present and his future. And it extended this to all people, even the killer of his cat.

The sun still came up and the sun still went down.

The seasons still came and the seasons still went.

The only judges and ones that could afford to dwell on past mistakes and futures worries were the humans, ironically the last to come to occupy this isolated bit of land, water, air and sea and the ones with the greatest impact.

Quicksilver appeared as if from nowhere as she always did, creeping in towards the bucket before he had really registered her presence. She was sleek and beautiful with that grey tiger striping that made her so distinctive and that ever-mobile tail that twitched at the end. Looking straight through him she then continued to the bucket and lapped at the dry scarlet that had crusted to the bones turning brown at its edges.

Sol looked her up and down. She was thinner than she had been, more feline and less round. His brain wondered and whirled. *Could it be? Can she have?*

Then she turned and '*mewed*' several times as two wobble-legged kittens staggered into the yard from out of the shadow of the wood, crying and '*mawing*'.

They chased butterflies at the interface between that of the wild forest and the cleared and tamed world of the enclosure between the *Bothan* and the sheds. Quicksilver left Sol as nursery attendant as she fed, trusting him to be her ears and eyes in defence of her young. When she was ready, she '*mewed*' again, calling them in, and then flopped so that they could suckle then sleep in disturbed growling feline dreamlands and playful slumber.

After several minutes Quicksilver caught wind of something beyond the house and leapt up, ears forward and whiskers twitching. The kits innately rounded behind her, curious from between the protection of well-furred legs and hidden behind a high hackled black-striped back and irate tail. The mother hissed in warning, turning and leaping, and left with her kittens close behind, herding them instinctively until they were all but shadows and nothing more to the untrained eye than leaves that moved oddly or that parted the bushes in an unusual manner.

Sol sat and wondered what it was that had caused the alarm. His ears too were alert, his pupils tight and keen, his nostrils flared and his hairs erect – he was on edge, like a protective father cat himself. Then, from a distance at first, footsteps could be heard from around the side of the house. They were human, but unusually careful and cautious, each taken with difficulty as if something inappropriate was being worn and the owner was now finding the going tough. The boots sounded harsh and solid as they caught stones and slipped into hardened pits and ruts. They must have been high-heeled shoes as he could hear the clicking as they caught rock.

There was the sighing of a woman and an occasional cry of anger and possible of fear or hurt.

Then a lady appeared at the side of *Bothan Faobhar*. She seemed out of place and was lost, facing away for the moment. Looking around she had an element of anxiety about her actions, as if this were all new to her and she was not comfortable with what she was experiencing.

She was well dressed, removing lengthy expensive-looking brown leather boots from her feet as she leant against the wall, still facing away, face hidden by a crop of straightened hair. Everything about her suggested wealth and a highly manicured finish except for now bared feet that were muddied with the trace of a bruise on the left. A tight tweed skirt restricted her leg movements; being designed more for glamour than country use despite its tartan finish attempting to give it an air of rural Scotland.

She had obviously made an effort to blend in with what she thought was local custom as she wore a white green-checked blouse, open at the collar, and a jacket over, which matched her skirt. Her long blonde hair was free flowing, but the wind had attacked its intended style, giving it what Sol thought was a more attractive look than what she had probably intended.

In her hands she now carried the pair of long-heeled leather boots and Sol laughed quietly, but not unkindly, to think of how she had managed the drive in them.

Here was a tourist who had taken the wrong track and stumbled into the yard at the *Bothan*. He would no doubt have to walk down the drive and collect Addie to then take her back up to the garage from where she had obviously strayed. But that was fine and it happened often enough. He had the rest of the day to waste and the paperwork for the estate could wait for another, as it so often had to when there were so many distractions to fill a man's time, both natural and human.

"Hello," he called across to her, making her jump and turn to face him. "Can I help you?"

"I'm sorry," she said nervously. "I seem to have got a bit lost. I'm looking for…"

She moved around to look directly at him, recognition turning both of their faces into confused smiles.

"Sue?" he questioned. "What are you doing here?"

"I thought I'd come and find you. I mean I wanted to come and find you."

She hobbled towards him revealing a possible twist to the ankle.

"Well," he replied getting up from the chair, brushing himself down, running an ineffective hand through his hair and crossing the yard to support her. "Well, here I am. This is it. You've found me." He helped her to his white plastic chair, suddenly embarrassed at how dirty it looked and aware of his dishevelled appearance, even his stubble'd chin. "This is it," he repeated. "I mean, I haven't much money, and what you see is all I really own, and who you see is all I really am. I hope that's okay?"

"Yes I know all that," she replied curtly. "I've read all about it on the blog of course, and you've told me too."

Sol swallowed in an awkward moment then spoke again. "And, I'm not the man you used to know either. I mean, I don't think I'm the city boy you used to hang around with."

"Yes, I am aware."

"Oh... ...then why did you want to come all the way out here to find me then?"

He scanned around to take in the glen and *Bothan* in one sweeping action. It was beautiful, tranquil, wild and isolated. He could not help but marvel at it, even now as his heart beat wildly on finding Sue so very far from her home and the usual securities of her city life.

"You..." The word was left hanging, powerful and shocking.

"Me?" he asked in reply. "What about me?"

She thought for a few seconds, stretching her bare feet out and testing her ankle in a swirling motion.

"You talked about second chances," she said, feeling strangely happy that she had made it all the way here to Sol's *Bothan,* the cottage that she had heard so much contradictory news about.

"Yes, I know I did."

"Then, I've come to give one," she stated simply.

They both smiled and Sol knew that as friends then perhaps they could start over again after all as the different people they had now become.

And later the sun set, and the moon waxed and waned, before the sun rose again the next morning, as it always had, always does and always will do. The loon cried all night long, and somewhere seven whooper swans landed in an arctic playground to breed for another year.

Postscript

(A Gaelic Blessing, John Rutter)

Extract from a letter:

Mr Jake Solomon,
Bothan Faobhar,
Faobhar Estate,
Nr Old Town,
Etc..

Dear Mr Solomon,

Thank you for the final manuscript for 'Symphony in G' that I am pleased to announce will be published as printed copy by the end of the month, and, as requested, all profits, royalties and proceeds arising from its sale or performance will be transferred into the Faobhar Estate Conservation Trust Fund. Its inaugural performance is being arranged as discussed and we look forward to sending complementary tickets on as soon as the venue is finalised and I am pleased to inform you that we have one studio interested in recording and broadcasting the event already.

Can I congratulate you on completing the work and thank you for the insight your handwritten notes have given to the conductor of the orchestra and his musicians so that they can further capture the scenes you pictured whilst writing it. It is truly a remarkable piece and we are only too pleased that we have finally found a solo violinist (fiddler you write) worthy of the melodies you have devised.

I will be in contact again in due course, but thank you again for using our publishing services.

Yours sincerely,

Gordon Buck

The Scottish Wild Cat (*Felis silvestris*)

(The Lamb, John Tavener)

Although the story of Sol's journey into the wilds of Scotland is intended to be one about the philosophy of people, the harmony of music that we all carry with us as we travel our life's paths, and most importantly the relationship we should all have with wildlife, I chose North West Scotland for one purpose only. The reason could have been the beauty and majesty of the Scottish scenery, the close proximity and importance of the mountains and the sea, the lochs and the birds of the air, the barrenness and isolation that can only really be gained in a place like that, or even the history and pride of the Scottish people, so accepting of an Englishman like me. But, even though these are all important, the reason for the location was to introduce readers to that untameable spirit of the woods that once frequented much of Britain but which is now only restricted to the north and west of the Scottish wild country; the wild cat.

Despite a lifetime of searching for wild things, I have never seen a wild cat in the flesh outside of a reserve or breeding sanctuary. Even the picture painted on the cover of this book is of a captive specimen at the Scottish Deer Centre, Fife, close to where I live, which is part of a British-wide programme to try and breed these wonderful felines, Britain's only native cats, ready for re-introduction.

There is one reason for the plight of this striped, tiger-like creature and that is man.

As we have encroached and our conurbations grown, and as we have demanded more from the land, replacing natural woodland with alien plantations of monoculture trees and planting well-lineated, fertiliser demanding crops, we have reduced the seclusion required by this quiet, private hunter. Next we have mercilessly hunted, shot, poisoned and trapped the wild cat as a potential threat to domestic and game animals. Then we have removed much of its prey by reducing the pests in our fields and the diversity of life around us. But worse still we have introduced an insidious competitor, the domestic cat, which has accidentally become a feral part of our un-natural world and reduced the numbers of many of our small mammals and song birds, especially when owners have mistakenly assumed it is all right to leave their pets out for the night when all cats do their worst. But the moggie cat has gone one threat further and interbred with many of our wild cats such that a number of crossbreeds of less purity and with less of the tenacity and fight have been produced and now only a handful of true wild cats hold on where they are protected.

The domestic cat has been in Europe since 1200BC where wild cat bones place *them* as arriving at least 2 million years ago. It would be a shame if we could lose this important, endangered and ill-understood species from our natural world in our generation.

Part of the inspiration for writing this book is to awaken an interest in the wild cats of Britain, now called the Scottish Wild Cat. If it has had any effect, then please do consider looking at the '*Save the Scottish Wildcat*' website (www.scottishwildcats.co.uk) and supporting their '*Wildcat Haven*' project (www.wildcathaven.com).

Leslie A Kent

L - #0199 - 261118 - C0 - 210/148/37 - PB - DID2371816